Tales of

HOFFMANN

Tales of

HOFFMANN

EDITED BY

Christopher Lazare

GROVE PRESS INC.   NEW YORK

JOHN CALDER LTD.   LONDON

Tales of Hoffmann is published in two editions:

An Evergreen Book (E-147)
A cloth bound edition

Grove Press Books and Evergreen Books
are published by Barney Rosset at Grove Press Inc.
795 Broadway   New York 3, N. Y.

Foreign Distributors

In U.K.: John Calder Ltd., 17 Sackville St., London, W. 1
In Canada: McClelland & Stewart Ltd., 25 Hollinger Road, Toronto 16

CONTENTS

Tales of

HOFFMANN

INTRODUCTION

The prodigiousness of Hoffmann's influence is, quite naturally, comparable only to his talent. Derivation has neither sapped his writing of its vitality nor his imagination of originality. It would be a profound mistake to emphasize only his historic importance or his value to the work of others, although such an emphasis would have the advantage of immediately defining Hoffmann's literary position and his worth. Hoffmann himself knew the value of entertainment too well to neglect the timeless qualities of suspense and good storytelling.

This is the first publication in modern translation of Hoffmann's famous tales. Hoffmann's name has long been synonymous with the fabulous, the supernatural, and the grotesque and, with the possible exception of Heine, the author is the best known of the German Romanticists. His creative energy, so typical of the early nineteenth century with its genius for art and its lack of talent for living—it was the era of striving after spiritual absolutes, of poverty and debauchery, of the cult of beauty and death for the artist—shaped the interests of his contemporaries and provided a fecund source for future talent in a variety of mediums and countries.

In European literature, Hoffmann's unmistakable mark can be seen in the work of Hauff, Hans Christian Andersen, and Gottfried Keller; in Hugo, Alexandre Dumas (who adapted one of his tales), Gautier, and in the mystical novels and Contes Philosophiques of Balzac. Hoffmann's is the theme of dual identity (The Double) which inspired Robert Louis Stevenson in Doctor Jekyll and Mr. Hyde and Markheim; his signature is the Gothic melancholy and Teutonic Romanticism which charged the work of the Brontës and Mrs. Hemans. He was serialized in English in Blackwood's as early as 1824. In America, Hawthorne's preoccupation with the ancestral curse can be traced to Hoffmann's The Legacy. Longfellow literally borrowed whole passages of fantastic description from the same source for his prose romance, *Hyperion*, and the inestimable indebtedness of Poe's "horror" stories to Hoffmann's *Tales* has motivated the admirable detective work and incontrovertible evidence of a dozen monographs and Ph.D. theses.

BIOGRAPHICAL NOTE
ON E. T. A. HOFFMANN

Artists often publish, in their self-portraits, secrets which they with-hold from their diaries and keep from themselves. There is a drawing of Hoffmann by himself, reproduced in the Ellinger edition of the *Gesammelte Werke*, which speaks out of the page with the subjectivity of a voice in a hallucination, and even the reader, who has opened the book prepared for some bizarre flourish, will realize that he is confronted instead by a privileged revelation: a nude face, with all the internal tics and throbs, the very privacy of the personality exposed. Yet the directness of the revelation results in mystification and ambiguity, like those photo-graphs, taken in a scientifically candid light, which (people insist) bear no resemblance to the sitter, or the once popular *trompe l'oeil* lithos of *Vanity* in which Beauty at the dressing table turns into a death's head under the eyes of the observer. The self-portrait seems to take on a double meaning, to throw its own distorted shadow across the frontispiece with all the implications of another, less visible, and more fatal reality.

The head, as the reader sees it, is drawn in full-face, topped, one might almost say surrounded, by a shock of wild, "creative" hair which becomes more careful in the side whiskers and outlines the cheeks, curling up on each side to the corners of the mouth. The lips are tight, narrow, but curved in a rigid sensual line like a *tilde*, curiously stubborn and un-weaned in their expression. The eyes, ringed by shadows, are large and wide, with a deep, receding look that somehow suggests those Pieter de Hooch interiors whose doors only open on further interiors that lead in turn to other doors and into the vanishing point. After the eyes, the nose is conspicuously anonymous, subordinated to the baleful, psychic quality of the rest of the face; as a feature it belongs more naturally to another

11

perspective, to the profile which, one senses, must be sharp and aggressive, the outline of an exaggerated contradiction in character.

A practical joke completes the description of the picture. Hoffmann decided one afternoon, while his wife was out visiting, to give her "a little jolt" (einen kleinen Schreck), and hastily drew a life-sized replica of the self-portrait. He then propped this double at a vertiginous angle between some flowerpots on the window ledge of their fourth-story apartment in Berlin's Taubenstrasse, and settled himself comfortably behind a curtain to wait. On her return, Frau Hoffmann, who had learned nothing from life but a few false cues for disaster, glanced mechanically up and discovered her "husband" fatally dangling between heaven and earth.

The butt of the joke, of course, is material reality, not Frau Hoffmann; the pun upon identity, the contradiction between the internal and external man, the moral symbolism of the gesture, offer an accurate synthesis of Hoffmann's personality. And the personality of this German romanticist, it almost goes without saying, was the dangling simulacrum, the split counterpart of his work; the two must be viewed together, doubled up, as it were, for the picture of the complete man.

He was born Ernst Theodor Wilhelm Hoffmann (the Amadeus, later substituted for Wilhelm, was a Mozartean afterthought), in Königsberg, Prussia, on the 24th of January, 1776. Both his parents belonged to the "old" bourgeoisie of the town, whose families, dedicated to respectability, had supplied generations of functionaries to the Church and the law. The elder Hoffmann, himself, was a lawyer and jurist, and his wife, who also happened to be his cousin, was the daughter of the locally influential Konsistorialrat, Doerffer. The marriage from its outset was ill-advised and worse-matched, the result of the perverse sort of clannishness which deems it wiser to keep imbecility in the family than turn it loose upon the world.

Frau Doerffer-Hoffmann was nineteen, vacant-eyed, maladive, frigid. Her husband was thirty-one, a conspicuous Bohemian in the narrow, regimented circle of relatives that constituted the Doerffer social life. He was fond of the bottle, and rather more eager than courtly with the ladies. At home, he was brash, unpredictable, easily exasperated by his wife's nervous resignation and by her lack of responsiveness. She bore him three sons in the mood of a woman who was serving her country and dying for her vows; the first scarcely survived infancy, the second, Karl Wilhelm, vanished into obscurity as soon as he was old enough to be missed, and the youngest, Ernst Theodor, eventually enjoyed the satisfaction of being described as a genius by his contemporaries.

When Ernst Theodor was two years old, his father was appointed judge of the criminal court at Insterburg, a forsaken Prussian town close to the Russian border, and the Hoffmanns, realizing, no doubt, that neither could tolerate the other and the monotony of Insterburg as well, agreed upon a divorce. Karl Wilhelm was given into the custody of his father and the future oblivion of a vague reputation for "evil ways," evidently based on an unfinished letter, dated 10 July, 1817, found among Hoffmann's papers after his death, a reply, in the negative, to his elder brother's request for money.

Ernst Theodor returned with his mother to the Doerffer household. He never saw his father again nor gave any direct indication of missing him. A rare reference to the Judge in Hoffmann's later correspondence seems to strike the proper morbid and sensitive note for the son but reveals the father in a slightly ridiculous aspect:

"I remember that one day Papa played the *viola da gamba*—I was (*sic!*) three or four years old—I dissolved into tears. Nothing could calm me, they had to give me a great chunk of gingerbread. But Papa did not play in tempo and some mischievous tongues even asserted that once he had danced a minuet to the tune of a polonaise which the prankish councillor of justice played on the piano, the red-lacquered piano that I recall so well."

The tears had already begun, those uncontrollable outbursts of emotion on the part of this child who sensed in the presence of music some mystic equivalent of the affection he had been denied. The little hysterical seizures continued in the Doerffer household; he wept whenever his Aunt Sophie played the harp, and even in maturity could produce tears at the mere recollection of her performance. She was the only sympathetic member of the family, a tiny, good-natured spinster who had never quite put aside her dolls, and who humored and coddled her nephew whenever she remembered his existence.

The others were all senile or sickly. Old Frau Doerffer, the grand-

mother, a woman of Amazonian proportions who had spawned a race of
pygmies, had secluded herself in her apartment at the death of her husband, and now spent her days aloof and apart from her children, muttering her prayers, reading the Bible and rehearsing for Heaven. Ernst
Theodor's mother, after her disappointment in marriage and "love," had
retired from the world to the bedroom she had once occupied as a girl,
and on those few occasions when she emerged would sit for hours without
speaking or moving, staring into unfocused space with unnaturally bright
eyes or contemplating her son with an expression of desperate pity and
misgiving. The fourth member of the household was Uncle Otto Wilhelm
(his mother still pinched his cheeks and called him Ottchen), a middle-
aged bachelor who shared his sitting room and bed with Ernst Theodor.
He had been trained for the law, but his very first case had turned into
such a fiasco that he had been compelled to withdraw from practice to
spare his family further embarrassment. Uncle Otto was a short, heavy-
bellied man, as precise as an insect in his habits and untroubled by any
of the responsibilities or experiences of maturity. The Doerffers considered
him in every sense the most natural companion for the child—Aunt
Sophie had to look after her mother and the house—and he was soon
tyrannizing over little Hoffmann, winding up both their lives for the
relentless routine that had become the purpose of his vegetative existence.
In his simple, delusional way and during the moments of self-importance
that followed his moods of blank introspection, little Otto fancied himself
a disciple of Immanuel Kant, the venerable celibate of Königsberg, by
whose undeviating living schedule the townspeople had been setting their
clocks for the last thirty years. And it should be said for Otto Wilhelm
that his insistence on rule and rote was responsible for his nephew's
thorough grounding in music and for the regularity, once Hoffmann had
turned night into day, of his later working habits.

The Doerffers were scarcely on speaking terms among themselves
and naturally led a withdrawn and antisocial life. Ernst Theodor's contact
with the outside world was limited to the infrequent but carefully fixed
visits of a few doddering family acquaintances (an acquaintanceship of
decades, to be sure!) who called to participate in the little concerts given
from time to time by the Doerffers by way of entertainment. Gathered
around their instruments in the drafty salon, their features distorted by

the sputtering candlelight and the galling effort of their incompetence, as awkward and unconvincing as figures in a conversation piece by some itinerant artist, Aunt Sophie, Uncle Ottchen, and their guests would grind away at some uninspired piece by Stamitz or Johann Hiller or Georg Benda while their nephew, standing unnoticed in some darkened corner of the room, sharpened his eyes on the spectacle.

More recently another visitor had begun to enliven the scene. Frau Hoffmann, with the instinctive talent which morbidity brings to seeking its own level, had found a friend. Frau Werner lived on the floor above the Doerffers, enthralled by the belief that she was a latter-day Virgin; the halos around her son's head convinced her utterly that she had brought a new Messiah into the world, and she would sing hymns to little Zacharias Werner on her knees or rise from her bed in the middle of the night to heap blue flowers on his coverlet and to announce his existence, with prophetic wails and cries, to the sleeping town below her windows. Her company seemed to sustain rather than disturb Frau Hoffmann's solitude; and the two women, each profoundly unbalanced by the shock of fleshly experience, became inseparable companions, gliding up and down the stairs toward each other to share their visions and their sometimes far from metaphysical complaints.

This, then, was the child's growing acquaintance with reality: the dark corners of the house and the strange sights; the grandmother and mother, locked in their separate lives and wasting away, like some parable of the death of the body and the death of the spirit; the maiden aunt blowing hot and the epicene uncle blowing cold; the stale atmosphere of morbidity; the absence of a master and the haunting pursuit of discipline; and, on every side, folly and derangement building up the evidence against love.

"I am a Sunday's child," Hoffmann once said, "with the power to see things invisible to other men." The pattern was already taking form. Escape into the abstract was inevitable; visible human values were too narrow, too remote; the community of the spirit was vast and hospitable and the boy could find comfort in those self-induced states, half brooding and half clairvoyance, in which the object turned into the metaphor and the metaphor into the myth.

But poetry is not the only revenge of loneliness. Ernst Theodor was

also becoming acute and devious in having his own way, capable of sarcasm and malice. Otto Wilhelm now rejoiced in the nickname, Uncle
O Weh! (a pun on the German pronunciation of the initials), and Grandmother Doerffer's Bible had a habit of disappearing periodically from her
side to be returned with the drawings of satyrs and demons and precocious
versions of the torments of Hell decorating its margins. By the time Hoffmann was twelve he had studied his uncle's weaknesses and gullibilities
shrewdly enough to have him completely under his control and rarely
spoke to him "except for the purposes of mystification."

His more subjective and melancholy side produced other accomplish-
ments: sensitive and even brilliant performances on the harpsichord and
violin, a talent for composition and improvisation—he could transpose a
piece from one key to another on sight when he was eight—and a frighteningly bitter facility, in a child, for the drawing of caricatures. He was slow
and unco-operative in his studies at the local Lutheran school, out of
tune with the apparent normality of other children's lives, and remained
friendless until he met Theodor Hippel on a summer vacation from
Königsberg in Arnau. Both boys were eleven years old, both had been
brought up in the exclusive and disinterested company of adults; and
both of them, suffering with imagination and precocity, yearned for some
signal from the Unknown, some spiritual resolution of their nameless
worldly ills.

In the fall, Hippel was registered at Hoffmann's school and the
friendship continued—it was to last until Hoffmann's death. The Doerffers
approved of the little stranger. He was a bright student, the nephew and
heir of the Privy Councillor, Theodor Gottlieb Hippel (later von Hippel),
and it was devoutly hoped he would be a sobering influence on young
Hoffmann. At first he called at the Doerffer house on Wednesday after-
noons, ostensibly to help Ernst Theodor with his school work while Uncle
O Weh was out on one of his weekly rounds. Then Otto Wilhelm,
determined upon benefiting his nephew even at the expense of his own
Kantian routine, took to leaving the house on Saturdays as well and the
boys were provided with another afternoon together. With their school
texts of Xenophon and Cicero spread out open before them like a barrier
against intrusion, the young friends pored feverishly through the *Sorrows
of Young Werther*, the tales of Jean Paul Richter, Laurence Sterne's

Sentimental Journey, the works of Shakespeare, Smollett, Swift, and Schiller, and of course that handbook of adolescents, Rousseau's *Confessions*. They copied reproductions out of Winckelmann's sad treatises on art (which had already damaged the taste of an era), played Bach and Mozart on the piano and, for recreation, invented picturesque games that were inevitably based on rescue and escape, dug tunnels and canals in the back garden and on one occasion devised a balloon out of Aunt Sophie's discarded taffeta, which unfortunately collapsed before it could carry them off into the empyrean.

During this hypnotic period of literary stimulation and vicarious experience, Hoffmann suffered his first disappointment in love. The episode is only noteworthy because its theme, repeated and varied in Hoffmann's life, will appear, rephrased and reformulated, in his writing. He had conceived a passion for Amelia Neumann, a girl in his class at school. She was as sublime as a goddess and he loved her with the pure heart of a poet—he had been feeding on *Werther* and the literature of sentiment—but she was unaware of his existence. He drew dozens of sketches of her face, dedicated sonnets and songs to her, endured agonies of embarrassment and confusion in her presence, but Amelia still noticed nothing, remained inaccessible and rare.

He was fifteen now, with the stunted figure, the tiny feet and hands, characteristic of the Doerffers; his head was disproportionately large, and, although it did not lack distinction or even a recognizable kind of uniqueness (the eighteenth century seems to have produced an entire *genre* of genius-face), the extreme mobility of its features, the nervous shifting and play of its expression, as if motivated by a conscious desire for self-distortion, and the beaked irregularity of the profile created an impression close to ugliness.

"Since I can't please her by being handsome," he sobbed to Hippel in a rage, "I wish I were a monster of ugliness—then she would be compelled to take notice of me!"

He was learning his own form of orientation.

The next year Hoffmann entered the University of Königsberg to prepare for the traditional profession of his family. He had resigned himself to law, no doubt with some persuasion from Hippel, as the most expeditious means of achieving the independence to devote himself to art and freeing himself from the oppressive dominance of the Doerffers. His career at the University was inconspicuous, sober, and uneventful. Whatever time was found from prescribed work was given to music and painting and to the literature of mysticism, magic, and the occult. Quite characteristically, he avoided Dr. Kant's seminars in logic and metaphysics, thronged by the devout; he was avenging himself now on his uncle's idolatry.

He passed his preliminary legal examinations at nineteen and, according to the rather pointless custom of the period, was obliged to serve a probationary term at the court of Königsberg without salary, fixed employment, or appointment. He spent this interval of impatient leisure painting landscapes in the wild, obsessive style of Salvator Rosa; writing voluminous, overwrought letters to Hippel who had, in the meantime, received an appointment in Marienwerder; and earning small sums of money by giving lessons in music and drawing around Königsberg, where he enjoyed some reputation for talent.

Among his piano pupils there was a young woman of his own age, Johanna Dorothea Hatt, the wife of a prosperous businessman well over sixty. Frau Hatt was attractive, sentimental, and bored; her husband was the conventional "brute" of a businessman, ignorant of the trivial attentions that gratify a young woman and incapable of the more significant ones. It was inevitable that Frau Hatt should turn for release to this *enfant terrible* of a music master with his clairvoyant eyes and feverish manner, his devastating hatred of the commonplace and his astonishing pronouncements on poetry and life (delivered with a deprecatory twitch of the lips while his childlike, evocative hands sparkled through Mozart on the keys).

Hoffmann's reaction at first was cautious and self-conscious. "I am more than doubtful that I love her," he wrote Hippel, "with the depth of feeling of which my heart is capable and there is nothing I desire less than to encounter an object that arouses these dormant emotions. Each time I feel myself drawn to Cora I think up some bit of buffoonery as a *sourdine*—it stifles the chords of sentiment so well one no longer hears them vibrate." But he was already calling her Cora after the heroine of Kotzebue's *Sun Priestess* who, for the sake of love, violates her vestal vows. In another few weeks Cora had become his "radiant" ideal, the composite of everything he had ever loved.

The progress of the affair may be followed in the letters to Hippel which range from shyness to exaltation and from exaltation to frustration and despair. Hoffmann was rarely discreet, never respectful of public opinion, and not devoid of a pleasurably vulgar streak of exhibitionism. His attentions to Cora Hatt at balls and parties, his conspicuous pangs and ecstasies, became a matter of gossip in Königsberg, and soon enough reached her husband's ears. A month after Hoffmann had confessed his love to Hippel, he wrote him to tell him he would probably never see Cora again. "If my life is threatened, if I must finally die, mourn for me —you will find my last will and testament among my papers . . . my hand-writing, itself, should prove to you how calm I am as I write this." (One must remember this was the era of exaggerated sensibility when all the world was *souffrant de l'amour;* women swooned into the tufted brocade of their carriages at the pressure of a handclasp, and love was like a disease that attacked sleep, a kind of passionate insomnia that devoured the vic-tim's tranquillity and filled his waking hours with somnambulism and tor-menting dreams.)

The relationship was broken off. Hoffmann attempted to distract him-self in a fury of creative activity. Under the influence of Karl Grosse's *Der Genius,* a period piece of the *Sturm und Drang,* he finished a novel, *Cornaro,* which never succeeded in finding a publisher, but did not dis-courage him from a second attempt, *Der Geheimnisvolle (The Mysteri-ous One),* which survives only as a fragment, or from two other literary experiments of which only the titles are known: *Aphorismenbändchen (A Little Book of Aphorisms)* and *Gedanken über Vieles (Thoughts on a Variety of Things).* He also composed a motet to the *"judes ille cum sedibit"* scene in Goethe's *Faust,* in which Marguerite listens to the threats of Mephisto and the singing of the *Dies Irae.*

But his situation was goading and unendurable. The victim of a tragic love affair does not continue to share his bedroom with an officious and obscenely inquisitive old man, nor does he return to his childhood rôle with his family as though nothing had intervened. He longed des-perately to get away and experienced hypochondriacal attacks of anxiety, daily nosebleeds and splintering seizures of vertigo. "My body," he wrote

Hippel, "is too weak not to suffer along with my spirit." He finally appeased both by resuming his friendship with Cora Hatt. But after the interval of separation, his sense of exaltation could not be revived. "My mighty plans are finished forever . . . My music—my painting—my writing —everything has gone to the devil . . . Let me stay here and eat my heart out . . . I cannot go away—I don't want to leave her although she, for her part, would weep for me for twenty-four hours and then forget me." Shortly thereafter he packed his bags and quit Königsberg for Great Glogau in Silesia.

The compulsive, contradictory reaction was becoming a principle of his personality. His life would continue to be an exhausting ambivalence between extremes, the self would split and divide against itself; the conflict and its symbols may be found on almost any page of Hoffmann's writings.

The flight to Glogau was not without its characteristic folly; he had escaped, not into freedom, but from one branch of the family to another. His mother, it is true, was now dead, but she had always been the most negative element in the Königsberg household. The enemy was Uncle Otto and the whole poking, ineffectual world of supervision and duty which Otto represented. This had been exchanged for the authority of Otto's brother, Johann Ludwig Doerffer, a court official under whom Hoffmann was to serve a vague apprenticeship while waiting to take his second or "referendary" examination.

The overwhelming boredom of his next two years in the midst of Uncle Johann's family may be followed in his letters, heaped with bitterness and derision even for his cousin Mina Doerffer to whom he had become engaged shortly after his arrival and whose affectionate fiancé he remained for the next four years. She was a "blabbering idiot" with whom he would rather share a coffin than a bed. He had quit Hell, he was prepared to admit, for the desert.

In the summer of 1798 Hoffmann passed his referendary, and at about the same time his Uncle Johann was transferred to Berlin. The Glogau Doerffers removed to the capital en masse. The President of the court to which Hoffmann was attached for his next probation, Freiherr von Schleinitz, was one of Hippel's friends. He encouraged Ernst Theodor in his studies; if the young man would co-operate, things could be arranged. For the first time since his vague plans in Königsberg, independence was in sight; Hoffmann gave himself over to his work with excitement and enthusiasm. The following year he passed his third and final examination, the *examen rigorosum*, with honors, and was qualified to serve as a councillor in any provincial Supreme Court. But first there was another period of probation, this time as assessor at Posen, in the newly acquired Polish territory. Hippel came to Berlin to celebrate this triumph of postponement, and the friends spent two months together. They parted company at Dresden, and Hoffmann continued alone to Poland and the dubious rewards of an existence that he could finally call his own.

Events in Posen took a natural and predictable course. For the first time in his experience, Hoffmann was free from constraint and supervision; he could purge himself now of the accumulated horrors of his childhood and youth, the memories of Cora Hatt, the resentment of authority, and even of the inadmissible longing he was feeling for "home." Sentiment and the life of the heart had been explored during the Königsberg captivity. Now it was the body's turn. He gave himself over to physical sensation and to what his contemporaries have described as "coarse and riotous living" in an attempt to refer euphemistically to the bottle and the hired, anonymous bed.

Posen had little more to offer. It was the typical provincial town of Prussian occupation, with a cowed native population, a military governor and a mixed foreign society of civil servants, soldiers, and camp followers. Its diversions, other than debauchery, were limited to the little dramas of precedence and rank, the displays of rivalry and malice, which constitute the livery and stays, if not the body, of bureaucracy. Hoffmann's talent for satire quickly found its uses and admirers in this *milieu*. His caricatures and lampoons of various unpopular officials were circulated in local salons, smuggled into the pages of dossiers, passed from hand to hand in the cafés. One evening, two of Hoffmann's colleagues, disguised as Italian street vendors, distributed a new series of these burlesques at the gates of the season's opening ball to which the Governor had failed to invite any officials below the rank of Councillor. His Excellency had not been spared; he was represented in half-a-dozen drawings in the uniform of a drummer boy, beating a teapot with two spoons and crying: "To tea!"

This little joke cost Hoffmann his appointment as Councillor in Posen which was waiting to be signed in Berlin. When his patent came through it was to the same rank but for the tiny Polish town of Plock— a promotion into exile. Plock, with its dreary wooden huts, its population of 2,578 (nearly all of whom were farmers and none of whom spoke a word of German), its eight months of rain and snow, was more than Hoffmann could face alone. Before he left Posen he married a girl toward whom he had never indicated any particular affection, Michaelina Rorer, the sister of one of the men who had hawked his unfortunate cartoons at the ball. Hoffmann's own description of his new bride lacks the customary note of enchantment: ". . . daughter of the former town councillor T. of Posen, twenty-two years old, of medium stature and good figure, with dark brown hair and dark blue eyes." Michaelina had the advantage, however, of having been born in Poland of a Germanized family, and, unlike her husband, she could speak the Polish language. It was the only accomplishment she ever revealed.

A quotation from almost any page of Hoffmann's Plock journal will serve as a summary of the entire sojourn:

" 9 October (1802): Black day. Worked until midnight.
"10 October   : *Ditto*. Black day.
"17 October   : Worked all day. Misery. I am turning more and more into the councillor of justice . . . The Muse is in flight . . . This journal is becoming remarkable—it is the evidence of the pathetic mediocrity which is engulfing me here.
"18, 19, 20, 21, 22, 23, 24, 25 October: *Dies tristes et miserables.*"

Yet in the two years Hoffmann spent in Plock before he was transferred to Warsaw, thanks to Hippel's intervention, he had turned out his first published work, *Schreiben eines Klostergeistlichen an seinen Freund in der Hauptstadt* (*Letter from a Monk to his Friend in the Capital*); *Der Preis* (*The Prize*), a comedy; a *Mass in D Major* (for one of the local convents) and a *Sonata for Piano in A Flat Major*. With the assistance of large and regular dosages of liquor, he had succeeded in creating a complete separation between his career as an assessor and his activities as an artist, but this contradictory existence was beginning to produce strange manifestations:

> "6 January (1803): From four to ten o'clock at the *Nouvelle Ressource*, drinking *l'Evêque* . . . State of dreadful tension in the evening. All my nerves excited by the spiced wine. Obsessed by premonitions of death, by Doubles . . ."

After the misery of Plock, life in the Polish capital had its obvious attractions and rewards. Warsaw, at the beginning of the nineteenth century, was an exotic and perverse city, a mixture of Asiatic sumptuousness and filth, with its Italianate palaces, sprawling parks, and herds of swine rooting through the streets; its bazaarlike squares with their shifting crowds of Turks and Greeks, Italians and Russians; its Janizary bands and Punch-and-Judy shows, mountebanks, dancing bears, and hawkers; its theatres in Polish, French, and German; and finally, its Italian Opera where Hoffmann's *Lustige Musikanten* (*Merry Musicians*) would soon be presented. For the Councillor was at peace with his surroundings now, and had turned seriously to the composing of music in a variety of forms. His court work was light and rendered more sympathetic by the company of two unusual colleagues: Eduard Hitzig and Zacharias Werner. Hitzig had recently been transferred to Warsaw from Berlin, where he had studied with Schlegel and become an intimate of the new Romantic Movement. He introduced Hoffmann to the writings of Brentano, Tieck, and Novalis; generally filled the place left vacant by Hippel's continued absence, and eventually became Hoffmann's biographer. Zacharias Werner, the "new Messiah" of the Doerffer house in Königsberg, had just finished the *Kreuz an der Ostsee* (*The Cross on the Baltic*), an enormous poetic drama concerning the conversion of the first Prussians to Christianity, which Hoffmann was setting to music. Werner was an assessor at the moment, but his brief, obsessed existence (not untouched by genius) would embrace a dozen careers from poetry and the founding of a new mystic order to Catholic conversion and the performance of miracles in Rome; from orgies with adolescent girls to ordained priesthood; from starvation and near-madness to a suite in the Archbishop's palace in

Vienna and the adulation of the ladies of the Hapsburg court; long before his death, the blue flowers his mother had tossed on his coverlet would come back jewel-encrusted snuffboxes and doting, public acclaim.

Hoffmann's intellectual interests were given further encouragment by a group of wealthy Polish dilettanti who had just conceived the project of founding a Warsaw Academy of Music and now enlisted the Councillor's services as their musical director. When they bought the old Mniszek Palace, which had been damaged by fire, for their headquarters, Hoffmann assumed other duties as well: he supervised the reconstruction of the dilapidated building from his own architectural designs and began a series of murals in its public halls and corridors. The Academy now absorbed almost all of his time; litigants, instead of waiting endless hours for him at his chambers, had grown accustomed to coming to him in the Mniszek Palace, where they would find him perched on his scaffold with a bottle of Hungarian wine at his side and paintbrush in hand, adding the features of some recognizable local personage to the painting of some mythological Egyptian god, and prepared, in another moment, to leap to the ground and dispatch his legal business with efficiency and expert knowledge.

The Academy prospered. Hoffmann's concerts were a public and aesthetic success as well as an excellent stimulus to his creative musical writing. He had, in fact, just finished a *Missa Solemne* for large orchestra, in honor of the birth of his daughter, Cäcilia, when news of the disastrous battle of Jena reached Warsaw. Napoleon's soldiers were already occupying Berlin, and the royal family had fled to Königsberg. On November 28, 1806, the main body of Murat's forces entered Warsaw, and the next day Napoleon had appointed a provisional Polish government to supersede the Prussian one. Hoffmann's independence, through no folly that could possibly be described as his own, had come to an end.

Hitzig returned to Berlin, where he opened a bookshop, and Zacharias Werner attached himself to the court of the Grand Duke of Dalberg. Hoffmann remained in Warsaw. His mechanical response (accompanied by an equally mechanical but terrifying grimace) to anyone who introduced the subject of politics in his presence had always been, "Have you nothing more interesting to talk about?" Now he was proving his political disinterest.

He moved into one of the attics of the Mniszek Palace; the Academy's deserted but well-equipped library and music room were still at his disposal, and "that was all he wanted to make him forget the French and the future." The future, however, reminded him of itself in terms of poverty, and he was obliged to send off his wife and daughter to be fed by their relatives in Posen. Shortly thereafter his funds gave out, nonetheless, and he suffered a complete collapse, raging attacks of fever which, according to his own account, turned his body phosphorescent at night.

On his recovery, he managed to hang on in Warsaw long enough to compose an opera, *Liebe und Eifersucht* (*Love and Jealousy*), based on a comedy by Calderón. He had planned to move on to Vienna where, Hitzig's letters cautiously assured him, the musical scene offered more hope than Berlin, but his letters to Uncle Otto were either lost or ignored and he was unable to raise the money for the trip. In June, 1807, with nowhere else to turn, he finally left Poland for Berlin.

Hitzig had not exaggerated conditions in the capital. Hoffmann struggled along miserably, living whole days on bread. He earned occasional fees for his caricatures or drawings of soldiers' uniforms. In August, the news from Posen of the death of his daughter and the serious illness of his wife reduced him to a state of hysterical morbidity and persecution. He attempted to propitiate what by this time he was convinced was his evil destiny with an act of public mortification. The former Councillor of the Crown and Director of the Warsaw Music Academy (who had never renounced his middle-class Prussian notions of rank) advertised his services as an orchestra conductor in any provincial theatre at a most moderate salary. In response he was hired by the managers of the theatre in Bamberg. He gratefully accepted his new employment—but the engagement was not to begin until October, 1808. Hoffmann was obliged to wait and want, and he survived the intervening months, familiarizing himself with the merciless barter which society imposes upon the hungry, the exchange of large humiliations for small favors. In September, 1808, he finally fetched his wife at Posen and left for Bamberg.

The Bamberg venture turned into a series of disasters. After two months of friction with the singers and argument with the management, Hoffmann resigned as conductor but agreed to stay on, at a reduced salary (thirty crowns a month), to compose the incidental music, ballets, and prologues for the theatre's productions. This income was augmented by the expedient of his student days, music lessons and occasional portrait commissions, a sufficiently goading routine to give him the impression he was expiating his follies and working out his salvation. Then, in February, 1809, the theatre, which had been tottering for months, failed entirely. And to make matters worse the families of his best-paying pupils had hastily removed themselves from Bamberg at the threat of another Napoleonic crisis.

Berlin had cured Hoffmann of his belief in miracles, and his taste for bread. He immediately sent off a letter to Rochlitz, the editor of the *Allgemeine Musikalische Zeitung* in Leipzig, stating his case wittily and ingratiatingly but nevertheless with desperate urgency, and soliciting work as a writer—he had been reduced to his last talent now. Rochlitz, not without irony, suggested a story or character sketch on the theme of a mad musician (Wilhelm Friedemann Bach might be taken as an example, he tactfully added) who suffers increasing delusions of grandeur and ends by identifying himself entirely with some such genius as Mozart or Händel. Hoffmann replied with the first installment of his *Kreisleriana*, and he continued to contribute to the Leipzig publication for the remainder of his five years in Bamberg. These pieces, collected and enlarged, were later issued as Hoffmann's first book (1814) under the title *Fantasiestücke in Callot's Manier* (*Fantasy Pieces in the Style of Callot*).

In the summer of 1810, one of Hoffmann's old Glogau acquaintances, Franz von Holbein, came to Bamberg and reopened the theatre. He engaged Hoffmann in a variety of capacities, from scenic designer and stage manager to repertory supervisor and composer; and pay was to be fifty florins a month, scarcely a generous sum but one which promised some regularity of income. Hoffmann finally relaxed.

He was thirty-six now, thwarted and eccentric, with a liverish complexion and a habit for the bottle. Reality had shut the doors, one by one, on the plans and evocations of his childhood, the feverish revelations he had once shared with Cora Hatt. When he envisioned the future now it only reminded him of the past, the wasted years and the broken promises, or he would suddenly remember his mother and become filled with the fear of going mad.

One day, in the midst of a singing lesson, he noticed, as though for the first time, the face of a child who had been his pupil for over a year: Julia Marc, sixteen, tender and sympathetic, with the eyes and smile of inexperience, and a voice that was like a *reprise* of all the green emotions of Königsberg. Her name is written on every page of Hoffmann's diary for 1811, or rather the name of Kleist's heroine, "Katharina von Heilbronn" —by which Hoffmann designated her—and its various diminutives and abbreviations, "Käthchen," "Ktchn," "Ktch." The early entries have the ring of exultation; the doom has been lifted, the evil spell broken: "Exalted, happy mood . . ."; "Ktch—Ktch—Ktch!!! exalted to the point of insanity . . ."; "Ktch: *plus belle que jamais et moi—amoureux comme quatre-vingts diables.* Exaltation—in the evening drunk at the Kunzes'."

But the tone soon changes and the familiar conflict begins: "Devil take this paradoxical mood (*Stimmung*)—Either I shoot myself down like a dog or I shall go mad!—*quod deus bene vertat!*" Then again: "Sang duets with Ktch . . . *Exaltatione, exaltatione grandissima!!!*" and, "Ktch! Ktch! Ktch! Oh, Satan! Satan! I believe that something of the higher poetry lurks behind this demon, and Julia must be regarded only as a mask —*demasquez vous donc mon petit Monsieur!*" followed in a few days by: "Presentiments of strange events which will either give life some [new] direction or . . . end it all!" (illustrated with the drawing of a fired pistol). The reprieve was over, the conventional pattern resumed.

The relationship was destined for frustration. Julia remained happily unaware of Hoffmann's inner torments, or at best only noticed a somewhat comic intensity on her music master's part which she was at a loss to attribute to any fatal passion. As for Hoffmann, himself, he had finally realized the abstract embodiment of love that he had sought in Amelia Neumann and Cora Hatt, the *Künstlerliebe*, the ideal image, for which the poet must be prepared to immolate himself, and he abandoned himself now to extravagances of self-pity, to fits of alcoholic depression and an obsessive preoccupation with death.

The course of practical events, however, shocked Hoffmann out of this poetic state of self-negation. The Bamberg Theatre failed, and almost at the same time Julia Marc was married off to a prosperous Hamburg merchant. "*Il colpo e fatto! La Donna e diventa la sposa di questo maledetto asino di mercante!*" The episode marks the end of the creative "personality" and its mature transformation in the creative "talent"; the fulfillment which Hoffmann sought in life would be translated, in the future, into a *passion morbide* for art. Don Juan belongs to this period, and it is the first work in which Hoffmann, the jurist, musician, architect, muralist, painter, caricaturist, composer, and civil servant finally reveals writing as his chosen *metier*.

With the loss of his income from the theatre, Hoffmann faced poverty again. The entry in his diary for 26 November, 1812, notes briefly: "Sold my old coat just to be able to get something to eat." This desperate state of affairs was ameliorated at the beginning of the next year by a legacy from Uncle Otto (which can hardly be described as a windfall; Hoffmann had been impatiently, even eagerly, looking forward to a much larger sum for years) and Hoffmann applied himself to the plans for a new opera to be set to La Motte Fouqué's *Undine*. Rochlitz had, in the meantime, arranged for him to join Joseph Seconda's opera company in Dresden as its conductor; in April, 1813, Hoffmann quit Bamberg and enthusiastically set out for his new engagement.

Hoffmann's experiences with Seconda involved the usual disagreements and vicissitudes. The company shuttled back and forth between Dresden and Leipzig, sometimes within earshot, often within range of Napoleonic cannon and gunfire. "What," he exclaimed one day after he had witnessed a shell burst in the Dresden market place, crushing a soldier's head and tearing open the body of a passer-by, "is this the significance of human life? Inferior to a little piece of hot iron?" The proximity of death, the evidence of havoc and destruction, stimulated him to a fever of creative activity. In addition to his far from light duties at the opera (he supervised rehearsals and conducted at all performances from a repertory that included Mozart, Gluck, Méhul, and Paër) he wrote the following works in the interval between April, 1813, and September, 1814: *Beethovens Instrumentalmusik*; *Der Magnetiseur* (*The Mesmerist*); *Der Dichter und der Komponist* (*The Poet and the Composer*); *Der Goldene Topf* (*The Golden Pot*); *Vision auf dem Schlactfelde bei Dresden* (*Vision on the Dresden Battlefield*); *Erscheinungen* (*Apparitions*); *Schreiben des Affen Milo* (*The Writings of Milo, the Ape*); *Die Automate* (*The Automaton*); *Die Elixiere des Teufels*, 1. *Teil* (*The Devil's Elixir, Part 1*); *Ignaz Denner*; *Über alte und neue Kirchenmusik* (*On Sacred Music, Old and New*); as well as a play, *Prinzessin Blandina*, the musical composition, *Die Schlacht bei Leipzig (The Battle of Leipzig)* and the complete score of the opera, *Undine*. This was the first spurt of a fecundity which in less than eight years would produce twenty-five volumes.

In July, 1814, Hippel arrived in Leipzig for a two-day visit and found Hoffmann in the midst of another quarrel with Seconda. Hippel was now President of the Court at Marienwerder where he had begun his career as an assessor; Hoffmann appealed to his old friend to exert his influence to place him with the government in Berlin. Two months later, Hoffmann was informed by the Ministry of Justice that if he served a half-year period of probation (Napoleon's rise and defeat had not altered the system) he would be restored to councillorship and his former rights of seniority (*Anciennität*). He abandoned Bamberg and the life of a strolling player without a qualm.

Curiously enough, Hoffmann's return to civil office established him publicly as a writer. Not too many years before, during one of his worst periods of insecurity, he had dismissed his bureaucratic career with relief: ". . . I shall never again have to write another *Relatio ex Actis* as long as I live, and so the Fountain of all Evil is dried up." Now in Berlin, working at the same table with Hitzig, and meeting Hitzig's friends, Fouqué, Chamisso, Contessa, Koreff (just appointed to the newly created "chair of mesmerism" at the University of Berlin: a postwar wave of mysticism and cabalism was sweeping the city), Tieck, Bernhardi, and Devrient, he discovered himself a figure in the literary life of the capital. Fouqué and the others had followed his work since its first publication in the *Allgemeine Musikalische Zeitung* and *Die Musen;* and the appearance of the first volume of the *Fantasiestücke* in the early part of the year of his arrival in Berlin had won him almost immediate acclaim. Hoffmann scarcely required the encouragement of success. His output continued at the prodigious rate he had established for himself at Bamberg. The next three years saw the publication of seven more volumes and some of his best stories, among them *Die Jesuitkirche in G. (Berthold, the Madman); Rat Krespel (Antonia's Song); Das Majorat (The Legacy); Das Gelübde (The Vow);* and *Das Fräulein von Scudéry (Mademoiselle de Scudéry)* included in the present collection.

In 1817 the performance in Berlin of *Undine* increased his popularity and the legend of his versatility, and though now it is an all but forgotten opera, *Undine* still remains an important connecting link between Mozart, von Weber, and Wagner, foreshadowing the use of the *leit-motiv* developed so successfully by the last-named, who, it should be added parenthetically, readily admitted his obligation to Hoffmann. Von Weber reviewed *Undine* and paid it public tribute, and a few years later (1820) Beethoven committed the uncharacteristic gesture of writing Hoffmann a letter of appreciation and basing a canon on his name (Nohl No. 328).

Every editor in the country clamored for his work now, and Berlin with its cosmopolitan passion for celebrity prepared to lionize him. But Hoffmann had not forgotten his early rebuffs. He attended literary drawing rooms and fashionable receptions merely to witness the enthusiasm of his admirers freeze on their lips. His behavior was deliberately insolent and perverse; he cracked his wit like a whip and never hesitated to flog a dead horse. The praise of his hostess would be rewarded with a sarcastic grimace and the information that she had mistaken him, the Councillor Hoffmann, for the other Hoffmann, the writer, a man of unmistakable genius who would hardly deem her invitation worthy of his notice; or if the lady attempted to guide the conversation along intellectual lines, he would quarrel with her on every matter of opinion and taste—including the admiration of his own work—and defend his point of view with a stream of nonsense uttered in the most pontifical tones; or he would separate himself entirely from the guests and sit glowering in a corner of the salon, punctuating his silence from time to time with the exclamation *"Odióso!"* pronounced in the penetrating, slightly falsetto voice he reserved for expressions of disgust.

This form of diversion, however, soon palled, and Hoffmann withdrew entirely from conventional social life to install himself at the *café* table at Lutter and Wegener's Berlin establishment which was to remain the pulpit and throne of the Romantic Movement in literature and music to the end of his day. His "exaltations" now were entirely alcoholic, produced by his favorite punch (a mixture of cognac, arak, and rum) or wine. But Hoffmann never drank merely to become sodden; ever since Posen and Plock, liquor had been the means of reviving his creative life from bureaucratic inanity, the stimulus of his imagination and fantasy ("I associate *Rhein* wine with church music, Burgundy with tragic opera, champagne with comic opera, and punch is for a highly romantic work

like *Don Juan*," he once observed in a passage doubtless later read by
Huysmans). After hours of drinking and oracular monologue at Lutter
and Wegener's, he would rise from his table at dawn and, leaving his
disciples all but asleep in their cups behind him, repair home to write
until noon; then he would take a walk and go to bed; in the evening the
routine was begun again. On Monday and Thursday mornings he would
go directly to court from his *café*, then write and sleep for the remainder
of the day. These habits affected neither his professional coherence nor his
scrupulous attention to his duties, for he received a succession of promo-
tions in office during a régime which was not accustomed to wink at the
inefficiency of its servants. With the characteristic contradiction of his
personality, he was most lucid when intoxicated; it was only during these
states that the spectres of his childhood were banished, and that aspect
of his consciousness which sometimes assumed the proportions of another
identity obsessed with loneliness and the fear of life was silenced; then
he would hear the angels sing and experience that mystic accord with the
universe which to the Romantic poet is conversation with God. (In another fifty years, the French would coin a phrase for his ills to describe
Baudelaire, Rimbaud, Nerval, and the Symbolists: "*le mal du siècle*.")

Hoffmann's drinking days, in any case, were numbered. In 1819 he
came down with an attack of arthritis which necessitated total abstinence,
and after a "cure" at the Silesian mineral baths, he was restricted, by his
doctor, to light wines.

It was an evil omen in the life of this writer whose fertility, itself, was
instinctive of an early death and who sometimes suffered such overwhelming attacks of anxiety that he would rouse his wife out of sleep to sit with
him at his desk while he worked. An even more specific warning followed
this omen. Between the regular appearances of his tales and the volumes
of *Serapionsbrüder* (*The Serapion Brethren*), Hoffmann had been at
work on a lengthy manuscript which he considered his *chef d'oeuvre*,
Kater Murr. This work purported to be the philosophic and moral reflections of Hoffmann's household pet, the tomcat Murr, who had recently
learned to read and write, and in the process of scribbling out his opinions
had interspersed his manuscript with pages torn from Hoffmann's note-
book containing the *Life of the Kapellmeister Johannes Kreisler* which
had served the cat as blotting paper (actually, "*Makulaturblätter*," or

wastepaper); the volume thus alternates arbitrarily between the narrative of the tomcat and the experiences of the half-mad musician, providing an amusing play on dualism, a dialogue between opposing alter egos. Kater Murr is a kind of literary Biedermeier, blessed by the angels of banality, complacent, *schöngeistig*, supremely trivial, the symbol of adjustment to material existence; Kreisler, at the other extreme, is one of Nature's orphans, inhabiting both his body and the world with frantic dissatisfaction, striving tragically after some inaccessible spiritual absolute. The first volume of *Kater Murr* was written during Hoffmann's illness and finished just before his departure in July, 1819, for the Schlesïen spa; after various postponements, the second volume appeared on November 30, 1821—and precisely on that date its protagonist died. Hoffmann sent out formal announcements of the cat's death, and his friends, aware of the pet's symbolism in its master's life, were inclined to regard the gesture as neither humorous nor whimsical. In another six weeks, Hoffmann was unable to move from his chair.

On January 24, 1822, when Hippel and Hitzig joined the little party that had gathered at Hoffmann's apartment in *Taubenstrasse* to celebrate his forty-sixth birthday, they found him rooted to his chair, morosely clinking his glass with the others but drinking mineral water. Hoffmann's conversation with Hippel, who had just arrived in Berlin, had shifted from sentimental reminiscence to morbidity, and Hitzig, in an awkward attempt to revive the evening from the pall that had overtaken it, observed that "life was not the highest of all goods." Hoffmann's reaction to this remark was almost convulsive: "No, no! Let me live, live," he cried. "Let me only live, no matter in what condition!" His wish was fulfilled with a vengeance that would have gratified Mozart's *Commendatore*: he remained alive for the next five months, but a paralysis crept by inches up his body from his feet, slowly killing off limb after limb. His debts accumulated, and editors and publishers began to dun him for work the advances for which had long been spent. He wrote until the very end, dictating to a secretary or to his wife when he was no longer able to clench a pen between his stiffened fingers. Pain and fever riddled him almost constantly now, and his small body had shriveled so that the maid could pick him up and carry him in her arms like a child. A month before his death, he was subjected to a final torment. His doctor in an effort to "relieve" the agony of *tabes dorsalis* applied red-hot irons to either side of the base of his spine. When Hitzig came to see him half an hour later, Hoffmann called out: "Do you detect the odor of roast meat? The doctor has branded me to keep me from being smuggled into Paradise."

On the evening of June 24th, the pain suddenly came to an end; Hoffmann's body had become numb and lifeless up to his neck. "I think I shall soon be rid of this illness, now," he said to his doctor. "Yes," said the doctor, "soon." The next morning he insisted he was well and asked to continue with the dictation of his story, *Der Feind* (*The Enemy*). His wife encouraged him to rest and he lapsed into silence. Then he asked to be turned to the wall. In another moment, the unwelcome child, the disenchanted, shrunken man, had died, as he had learned to live, with his back turned to the world.

CHRISTOPHER LAZARE

Tales of

HOFFMANN

MADEMOISELLE DE SCUDERY

A Tale of the Times of Louis XIV

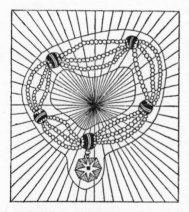

MADELEINE DE SCUDÉRY, WHO WAS well known for her charming verses but perhaps more celebrated for having enjoyed the favor of Louis XIV and the friendship of Madame de Maintenon, lived in a little house on the Rue Saint-Honoré.

One night almost at midnight—it would be about the autumn of the year 1680—there came such a loud and violent knocking at the door of this house that the whole entrance hall reverberated with it, amplifying the noise and making it seem even more fierce and importunate. Baptiste—cook, footman, and porter in the lady's small household—had gone (with his mistress' permission) to the country to attend his sister's wedding; and thus it happened that the only servant in the house was La Martinière, Mademoiselle's lady's-maid, who was still sitting up. She heard the knockings and, when they were repeated insistently, she suddenly realized that Baptiste was away, and she and her mistress were alone and unprotected in the house. Crime was sweeping Paris like a pestilence, and all the burglaries, thefts, and murders that had ever been committed crowded upon her mind. She was sure it was a band of cutthroats who were making all this disturbance outside; they must be well aware how deserted and isolated the house was, and if she admitted them they would perpetrate some wicked deed against her mistress. She remained in her room, trembling and quaking with fear, cursing Baptiste, his sister's wedding, and whatever else came to mind.

Meanwhile the intruders thundered away at the door, and she thought she heard a voice crying out, between the knocks: "Open the door! For Christ's sake, do open!"

At last, out of sheer agitation, La Martinière seized a lighted candle and ran down to the landing. There she could quite plainly hear the voice of the person knocking: "For Christ's sake, do open the door! Please!"

"Surely," thought La Martinière, "that is not the way a robber talks. Who knows whether it is not some poor man in trouble, come to seek the protection of Mademoiselle, who is always ready to do anybody a kindness? But it is better to be cautious."

She opened a window, and called out, asking who was down there making such a noise at the door so late at night, waking everybody out of his sleep; and she tried to make her naturally deep voice sound as much like a man's as possible.

In the glimmering light of the moon, which just then broke through the dark clouds, she could make out a tall figure, wrapped in a light grey mantle, and with a broad-brimmed hat pulled down right over his eyes. Then she called out in a loud voice, so that the man below could hear her:

"Baptiste, Claude, Pierre, get up and see who this good-for-nothing wretch is, who is trying to break down our door!"

But the voice from below called back gently, and almost plaintively, "Ah! La Martinière, I know that it is you, my good woman, however much you try to disguise your voice. I also know that Baptiste has gone to the country, and that you are alone in the house with your mistress. But you have nothing to fear. Open the door for me. I must speak with your mistress, urgently and this very minute."

"I don't know what you can be thinking of!" replied La Martinière. "Do you expect to speak to Mademoiselle in the middle of the night? Don't you know that she has gone to bed long ago, and that nothing on earth would induce me to wake her out of her first sound sleep, which at her time of life she has so much need of?"

"But I know," said the man below, "that your mistress has only just laid aside her new romance *Clélie*, at which she works so tirelessly; and she is still up and at this moment writing certain verses which she intends to read at Madame de Maintenon's tomorrow. I implore you, Madame Martinière, have pity on me and open the door. I tell you it is a matter of saving a miserable wretch from destruction. Honor, freedom, even the life of a man, are dependent upon this moment, and upon my speaking to Mademoiselle. Just consider how hard it will go with you when your mistress finds out that out of the stubbornness of your heart you drove from her door an unfortunate soul who came to beg her help."

"But why do you come to appeal to my mistress' compassion at this unusual hour? Come back again early in the morning," said La Martinière, still leaning from the window.

Whereupon, he replied from below, "Does destiny, then, heed times and hours when it strikes? When there is but a single moment longer in which it is still possible to save a man's life, should assistance be delayed? Open the door! You have nothing to fear from a poor defenseless wretch, who hasn't a friend in the world and is pursued and harrowed by an awful fate, when he comes to beseech Mademoiselle to save him from danger!"

La Martinière heard him moaning and sobbing with anguish as he said these words in a voice that was youthful, gentle, and irresistibly persuasive. She was greatly touched and without further deliberation went to fetch the keys.

But she had hardly unlocked the door when the figure enveloped in the mantle burst tumultuously in, and striding past La Martinière into the passage, cried wildly, "Take me to your mistress!"

La Martinière lifted up her candlestick in terror and let the light fall on his features: it showed the face of a young man, deathly pale and fearfully agitated. What La Martinière saw, next, caused her almost to drop to the floor with fright, for the young man had thrown open his mantle and revealed the bright hilt of a stiletto which he was carrying unsheathed in the open bosom of his doublet. His eyes flashed fire as he fixed them upon her, crying even more desperately than before, "Take me to your mistress, I tell you!"

La Martinière now believed Mademoiselle to be in the most immediate danger. All her affection for her dear mistress, whom she honored, moreover, as though she were her kind and devoted mother, flamed up fiercely in her heart, kindling a courage which she had not conceived herself capable of showing. Hastily pulling shut the door of her room, which she had left standing open, she planted herself before it, and said in a loud, firm voice, "It seems to me your furious behavior in the house, here, is very much at odds with your pathetic performance outside. I obviously have let my pity mislead me. You neither ought to, nor shall you, speak to my mistress now. If you have no evil designs, you need not fear the light of day; so come back again tomorrow and state your business then. Now, get out of the house."

The young man sighed deeply and audibly; then, turning the most menacing look upon La Martinière, he grasped the hilt of his stiletto.

The poor servant silently commended her soul to Heaven, but she stood her ground, boldly returning his glance and at the same time drawing closer to the door through which he would have to pass to get to her mistress' chamber.

"Take me to your mistress, I tell you!" he insisted.

"Do what you will," replied La Martinière, "I shall not stir from this spot. Come, get it over with quickly. But remember that sooner or later, like your other vicious partners in crime, you also will meet your death at the Place Grève."

"You are right, La Martinière," replied the man, "I do look like a robber and cutthroat, and am armed like one, but my partners have not been executed—no, not yet." Thereupon, glaring venomously at the poor woman, who was almost dead with terror, he drew his stiletto.

"O God! O God!" she moaned, expecting her deathblow. But just at that moment the clatter of arms and hoofbeats echoed through the street.

"The *Maréchaussée!* the *Maréchaussée!*" screamed La Martinière. "Help! Help!"

"You abominable hag, you are determined to ruin me!" He snatched the light from La Martinière's hand and extinguished it. "It is too late now—all is lost. But here, here—take this. Give it to your mistress this very night—now if you like." And with these words, he forced a casket into her hands. "As you love your soul, give this casket to Mademoiselle," he hoarsely repeated. And then he rushed out of the house.

For several minutes La Martinière stood, dazed, where he had left her. At length she possessed herself of her senses and groped her way back through the darkness to her own room, where she sank down in an arm-chair completely exhausted, unable to utter a sound. Then she heard the rattling of the keys which she had left in the lock of the street door. She heard the door being closed and locked, and then she heard cautious, uncertain footsteps approaching her room. She sat riveted to her chair, paralyzed with fear, and filled with the most gruesome conjectures. Her relief may be imagined when the door opened, and by the light of the night taper she recognized Baptiste at a glance.

"In the name of all the saints!" he began. "Tell me, Madame Martinière, what has happened? Oh the worry and fear I have had! I don't know what it was, but something drove me away from the wedding last night. I couldn't help myself. I had a feeling something was wrong and I had to come.

"When I reached our street, I thought to myself, Madame Martinière sleeps lightly. She'll be sure to hear me if I tap softly and gently at the door, and will come out and let me in. Then, when I got to the corner, I was stopped by a patrol on horseback, all armed to the teeth, and they wouldn't let me go on. But luckily Desgrais, the lieutenant of the Maréchaussée, was among them, and he knows me quite well. So when they shoved their lanterns under my nose, he says, 'Why, Baptiste, where are you coming from at this time of night? You'd better stay in and look after your house. There's trouble loose tonight, and we're out to put a stop to it. The street is no place for an honest man at this hour.' You wouldn't believe, feeling the way I did, how his words upset me. And then when I get here, and before I can even set foot on the threshold, a man, all muffled up, comes tearing out of the house with a drawn dagger in his hands, runs into me and knocks me head over heels. When I get up I find the door open, and the keys sticking in the lock. Tell me, what is going on? What does it all mean?"

La Martinière required no further coaxing; in an outburst of relief she related all that had taken place. Then she and Baptiste went out into the passage, and there they found the candlestick lying on the floor where the stranger had thrown it as he ran away.

"It is only too clear," said Baptiste, "that our Mademoiselle was about to have been robbed and, possibly, even murdered. The fellow knew, as you say, that you were alone with Mademoiselle—why, he even knew that she was awake and at her writings. No doubt about it, he was one of those sly prowlers who first spy out every bit of information that may be of use to them in carrying out their plans, and then force their way right into a house. As for that little casket, Madame Martinière— I think we'd better throw it into the deepest part of the Seine. Who knows that there's not some evil design on our good lady's life, and that if she opens the box she won't fall down dead like the old Marquis de Tournay did, when he opened a letter that came from somebody he didn't know?"

After a long consultation the two faithful souls made up their minds to tell their mistress everything next morning, and also to place the mysterious casket in her hands, for it could, of course, be opened with proper precautions. After minutely weighing every circumstance connected with the suspicious stranger's appearance, they both came to the same conclusion. There was some special mystery connected with the matter for which they dared not assume responsibility; they must leave it to their good lady to unriddle.

Baptiste's apprehensions were founded on something more than mere intuition. Paris at the time was the scene of the most atrocious crimes, and just then, too, the most diabolical of Satan's inventions came into existence, supplying the readiest means for perpetrating these atrocities.

Glaser, a German apothecary, the best chemist of his age, had busied himself, in the customary fashion of members of his profession, with experiments in alchemy. The discovery of the Philosopher's Stone had become the obsession of his life. His assistant in many experiments was an Italian called Exili. But this man only practiced alchemy as a blind. His real object was to learn the secrets of the mixing, decoction, and sublimating of poisonous compounds, and at last he succeeded in formulating a subtle poison that was tasteless and odorless, that took effect either instantly or gradually, that left no trace in the human body, and that consequently defied all the skill and art of physicians, who, unsuspicious of the presence of poison, inevitably ascribed the victim's death to natural causes.

Circumspectly though Exili worked, he nevertheless fell under suspicion of trafficking in poisons, and was thrown into the Bastille. Soon afterwards Captain Godin de Sainte-Croix was confined in the same dungeon. This man had for a long time been enjoying an illicit relationship with the Marquise de Brinvillier, which brought disgrace on all her family. The Marquis, however, remained indifferent to his wife's shameful conduct, so that finally her father, Dreux d'Aubray, Civil Lieutenant of Paris, was compelled to break up the liaison by ordering a warrant to be executed upon the Captain. Passionate, unprincipled, hypocritically pious, and yet given from his earliest youth to vice and excess of every variety, jealous, revengeful to the point of madness, the Captain could not have happened upon any more welcome information than Exili's diabolical formula which offered him the power to destroy all his enemies. He became Exili's eager disciple and, soon, his master's equal, so that, on being released from the Bastille, he was able to continue his work unaided.

The Marquise de Brinvillier had formerly been merely a loose woman, but now Sainte-Croix proceeded to turn her into a monster. He contrived to induce her to poison first her own father, whom she was nursing with heartless hypocrisy in his declining days; then her two brothers, and finally her sister. Her father was murdered out of revenge, and the others for their share of the rich family inheritance. The history of crime abounds in examples of how the committing of acts of this sort ends by becoming an all-absorbing passion. Often, without any further purpose than the mere depraved pleasure of the thing, poisoners, like chemists who perform experiments for their own enjoyment, have destroyed persons whose life or death must have been a matter of perfect indifference to them.

The sudden death of dozens of paupers at the Hôtel-Dieu aroused the suspicion, some time later, that there had been poison in the bread which the Marquise de Brinvillier, in order to acquire a reputation for piety and benevolence, used to distribute to the inmates every week. At any rate, it is definitely known that the Marquise, at home, was in the habit of serving poisoned pigeon pie to her guests. The Chevalier de Guet and various other victims paid all too dearly for the delicacies they enjoyed at her hellish table. La Brinvillier, Sainte-Croix and his confederate, La Chaussée, were able for a long time to enshroud their deeds within an impenetrable veil of evil genius. But of what avail is the infamous cunning of reprobate man when the Divine Power has decreed that punishment shall overtake the guilty here on earth?

The poisons which Sainte-Croix compounded were of such a potent nature that if the mixer exposed his face during the preparation of the powder (called by the Parisians *Poudre de Succession*) a single inhalation might cause instantaneous death. Sainte-Croix therefore, when engaged in its manufacture, always wore a mask made of fine glass. One day, just as he was pouring a completed formula into a phial, his mask fell off; the fine particles of the poison reached his nostrils, and he instantly fell down dead.

Since the Captain had died without heirs, the officers of the law lost no time in placing his effects under seal. Among them they found a locked box, which contained the whole infernal arsenal of poisons that Sainte-Croix had once had at his command.

They also found the Marquise de Brinvillier's letters, which left no doubt as to her hideous crimes. She fled to Liége, into a convent there. Desgrais, an officer of the *Maréchaussée*, was sent after her. He assumed the disguise of a monk, and followed her to the nunnery, where he contrived to engage the terrible woman in a love affair, and finally, under the pretext of a secret rendezvous, enticed her out to a deserted garden on the outskirts of the town. Directly the Marquise arrived at the appointed place she was surrounded by Desgrais' henchmen, while her monkish lover was suddenly converted into an officer of the *Maréchaussée*, who compelled her to get into the carriage which stood ready near the garden. Thus, surrounded by the police troop, she was driven straight off to Paris. La Chaussée had been already beheaded somewhat earlier; the Marquise de Brinvillier suffered the same death, after which her body was burned and the ashes scattered to the winds.

Now that the monster, who had been able, indiscriminately and unpunished, to direct his secret homicidal powers against both friend and foe, was out of the world, the Parisians breathed freely once more. But it soon became public knowledge that Sainte-Croix's abominable art had been handed down to certain successors. Like a malignant invisible spirit, murder insinuated itself into the most intimate circles, into the closest relationships of blood, love, and friendship, and laid a quick sure hand upon its unfortunate victims. He who was seen one day in the full vigor of health, tottered about on the morrow, weak and ravaged, beyond the skill of any physician or the cure of medicine.

Wealth, a lucrative office, a beautiful and perhaps too youthful wife —any of these was sufficient provocation for this persecution unto death. The most sacred bonds were riddled by doubt and the most appalling mistrust. The husband trembled in fear of his wife, the father of his son, the sister of her brother. Dishes which a friend put before his friends remained untouched on the table, while wine sparkled untasted in the glasses. Where formerly good humor and mirth had prevailed, savage glances now spied about for a secret assassin. Fathers of families were observed shopping for provisions in remote districts with uneasy looks and movements, and preparing the food themselves in the first dirty eating-house they came to, since they feared evil and treachery in their own homes. And yet even the greatest and most thorough precautions were often of no avail.

In order to put a stop to this evil state of things, which continued to gain ground and grow more oppressive each day, the King appointed a special Court of Justice for the exclusive purpose of inquiring into and punishing these secret crimes. This was the so-called *Chambre Ardente*, which held its hearings with the notorious La Reynie presiding, not far from the Bastille. For a considerable time all La Reynie's efforts, however zealously they were put into practice, remained fruitless. It was the crafty Desgrais who was destined to track the criminals to their most secret haunts.

In the Faubourg Saint-Germain there lived an old woman called Voisin, who made a regular business of fortune-telling and raising the spirits of the departed; and with the help of her confederates, Le Sage and Le Vigoureux, she managed to excite fear and astonishment in the minds of persons who could not be accurately called either weak or credulous. But she had other talents, as well. A pupil of Exili, like Sainte-Croix, she, too, knew how to concoct the subtle poison that killed and left no trace. Thus she was of invaluable assistance to profligate sons who found it necessary to come into early possession of their inheritance, or to depraved wives who were equally impatient for another and younger husband. Desgrais, whose methods seem to have been irresistible, found his way into her confidence; she confessed all. The *Chambre Ardente* condemned her to be burned alive, and the sentence was executed in the Place Grève.

Among her effects was found a list of all the persons who had availed themselves of her co-operation; and not only did execution follow upon execution, but grave suspicion fell even upon persons of high position. Thus it was believed that Cardinal Bonzy had obtained from La Voisin the means of bringing to an untimely end all those persons to whom, as Archbishop of Narbonne, he was obliged to pay annuities. So also the Duchess de Bouillon, and the Countess de Soissons, whose names were found on the list, were accused of having had dealings with the devilish woman; and even Francois Henri de Montmorency, Boudebelle, Duke of Luxembourg, peer and marshal of the Kingdom, was not spared. He, too, was prosecuted by the terrible *Chambre Ardente*. He voluntarily gave himself up to be imprisoned in the Bastille, where through Louvois' and La Reynie's hatred he was confined in a cell only six feet long. Months passed before it was satisfactorily proved that the Duke's transgression did not merit any punishment: he had merely once had his horoscope cast by Le Sage.

It is certain that President La Reynie was betrayed by his blind zeal into acts of cruelty and terrorism. The tribunal acquired the character of an Inquisition; the most trifling suspicion was sufficient cause for strict incarceration; and it was left to chance to establish the innocence of a person accused of a capital crime. Moreover, La Reynie was hideous in appearance, and malicious by temperament, so that he aroused the hatred, alike, of those whose avenger or protector he was appointed to be. The Duchess de Bouillon, being asked by him during her trial if she had seen the Devil, replied, "It seems to me, I see him this very moment."

But while the blood of the guilty and the suspected flowed alike in streams along the Place Grève, until after a time the number of secret poisonings had thinned out conspicuously, a new kind of outrage came to light, and again filled the city with alarm. A group of thieves seemed suddenly to have banded together with the apparent intention of getting every piece of jewelry in Paris into their possession.

No sooner was a valuable ornament bought than, no matter how or where it was kept, it would vanish in some incomprehensible way. But what was still worse, anyone who ventured to wear jewelry on his person at night was robbed, and often murdered, either in the public street or in some dark doorway. Those who escaped with their lives declared that they had been struck down by a blow on the head, like a bolt of lightning, and that on awaking from their stupor they had found they had been robbed and were lying in quite a different place from the one where they had originally been attacked. Those who were murdered—corpses were found nearly every morning lying either in the streets or house-entrances—all bore the same fatal wound: a dagger-thrust in the heart, which brought about death, according to the opinion of the doctors, so instantaneously and so surely that the victim would drop without being able to utter a cry.

Was there anyone at the voluptuous court of Louis XIV who was not involved in some clandestine love affair, and did not go stealing off to his mistress at a late hour, often carrying some valuable gift on his person? The thieves, as if in league with the spirit-world, seemed forewarned when anything of this sort was going on. The victim rarely reached his rendezvous or achieved the rewards of his passion; or, often, he fell, covered with blood and still warm, at the very door of his mistress' chamber.

In vain did Argenson, the Minister of Police, order the arrest of every person against whom there was the least suspicion; in vain did La Reynie rage and try to extort confessions; in vain were the watches and patrols doubled. No trace of the criminals could be found.

There was only one precaution that proved at all efficacious. It became necessary for Parisians to go about armed to the teeth and preceded by a torchbearer; and yet instances were not lacking in which the attendant was beaten off by stones while his master, at the same moment, was murdered and robbed. It was especially remarkable that, in spite of the most detailed investigation into every corner where traffic in jewelry was in any way possible, not the smallest specimen of the stolen goods ever came to light, so that even this method of tracing clues could not be followed.

Desgrais was furious, baffled by having the culprits consistently escape his net. Whatever district happened to be his station for the night was spared; while in the other parts of town, where surveillance was for the moment neglected, these robberies and murders claimed their richest victims.

Desgrais hit upon the ruse of producing several Desgraises, so exactly alike in gait, posture, speech, figure, and face, that even the police themselves did not know which was the real one. Meanwhile, alone and at the risk of his life, Desgrais used to go about his spying in the most secret haunts and lairs of crime; or he would follow at a distance first this man and then that, who at his suggestion wore some rich ornament on his person. These people, however, were never attacked. The robbers, evidently, were acquainted with this device, too. Desgrais was at his wit's end.

One morning Desgrais called on President La Reynie in his chambers, pale, agitated, beside himself.

"What's up? Good news? Have you come upon a clue?" the President called out to him.

"Last night, Your Excellency," Desgrais began, and as soon as he spoke his anger became apparent, "last night—not far from the Louvre —the Marquis de la Fare was attacked in my presence."

"Perfect! Then we have them!"

"Perhaps you had best hear me out, first," Desgrais went on, with a bitter smile, "and let me tell you how it all happened. Well, then, I had taken up my stand near the Louvre, waiting for these devils who are determined to make a fool of me, and my heart was burning with fury. Without seeing me, a man passed close beside me, walking with unsteady steps and constantly turning to look behind him. By the faint moonlight I recognized him as the Marquis de la Fare. I might have expected to see him there. I knew where he was stealing to. But he had scarcely gone more than ten or twelve paces beyond me when something that seemed to spring up right out of the earth flung itself upon him and threw him down. In my surprise at this sudden chance, which would otherwise have delivered the criminal into my hands, I was thoughtless enough to cry out; and to make matters worse, just as I burst out of my hiding place with every intention of throwing myself upon him, I became tangled in my mantle and fell down.

"I saw the man making off as if on the wings of the wind. Hastily I picked myself up and ran after him; and as I ran I blew my horn. From the distance came the answering whistles of my men; the streets were suddenly alive; the rattling of arms and trampling of horses came from all directions. 'Here I am! Here! It's Desgrais! Desgrais!' I shouted, till the streets echoed. All the while, by the bright moonlight, I could see the man in front of me, dodging here and there to confuse me. I followed him to the Rue Nicaise, and then his strength seemed to be failing. Now he was only leading me by fifteen paces at the most—"

"You have got him then! You caught him and the patrol came up in time?" asked La Reynie, his eyes flashing, while he seized Desgrais by the arm as though *he* were the escaping murderer.

"Fifteen paces," continued Desgrais in a hollow voice, "he was fifteen paces from me—and then he leaped into the shadows and disappeared through a wall."

"Disappeared? Through a wall? Are you mad?" cried La Reynie.

"From this moment on," continued Desgrais, rubbing his brow like a man tormented by frightening thoughts, "Your Excellency may call me a madman, or accuse me of seeing ghosts, but it happened just as I describe it.

"I stood there, dumfounded, staring at the wall, until several of my men came running up, out of breath; with them was the Marquis de la Fare, happily unharmed, a drawn sword in his hand. We lighted torches and sounded every inch of the wall—not a trace of a door or a window or an opening of any kind! It was the solid stone wall of a courtyard belonging to a house lived in by people who are above suspicion. Today again I carefully went over the whole place. It must be the Devil himself who is duping us."

Desgrais' story became known in Paris. People's heads were full of the sorceries, incantations, and compacts with Satan of Voisin, Le Vigoureux, and the reprobate priest, Le Sage; and perhaps because in the eternal nature of mortal man, the leaning toward the miraculous and the supernatural so often outweighs all the authority of reason, the public soon began to believe wholeheartedly what Desgrais in his mortification had said: Satan himself really did protect the abominable wretches, who must have sold their souls to him. It goes without saying that Desgrais' story benefited by all sorts of embellishments. An account of the adventure, with a woodcut on the title-page representing a grim Satanic form before which the terrified Desgrais was revealed sinking into the earth, was printed and hawked in every corner of Paris. This alone was enough to terrorize the common folk, and even to steal the courage of the police, who now wandered along the streets at night trembling and quaking, hung about with amulets, and soaked in holy water.

Argenson, aware that the exertions of the *Chambre Ardente* were proving ineffectual, appealed to Louis to appoint a tribunal with still more extensive powers to deal with this new epidemic of crime, to hunt down the criminals and mete out their punishment. The King, convinced that he had already vested too much power in the *Chambre Ardente*, and horrified at the innumerable executions which the bloodthirsty La Reynie had decreed, flatly rejected the whole project.

Another means was chosen to stimulate the King's interest in the matter.

Louis was in the habit of spending the afternoon in Madame de Maintenon's apartments, and even of dispatching state business there with his Ministers, sometimes until late into the night. It was here that an occasion was found to present the King with a poem in the name of France's imperiled lovers, complaining that, whenever gallantry required them to honor their mistresses with gifts, their lives were risked in the fulfillment of the injunction. It would be an honor and a pleasure to shed blood for a lady in a knightly encounter; but it was quite another matter when love had to cope with an unseen assailant, against whom one armed oneself in vain. Would not Louis, the very sun of all gallantry and love, turn the resplendent rays of his glory upon this dark night, and so dissipate the black mystery that was concealed within it? The godlike hero, who had broken and shattered his enemies, would surely draw his sword, still gleaming with victory, and, as Hercules destroyed the Lernaean Hydra, or Theseus the Minotaur, would strike down the monster that was feeding on the very rapture of love, and turning all its joy into anguish and pain.

Serious though the matter was, the verses were cleverly and wittily turned. It need only be added that the poem concluded with a grandiloquent panegyric upon Louis XIV, to describe the visible satisfaction with which the King read it. This done, he turned quickly to Madame de Maintenon, without lifting his eyes from the paper, and read the poem through once more (this time aloud); and then he asked her, with an indulgent smile, how she felt about the petition of these persecuted lovers.

Maintenon, who had little bent for the frivolous, and always preserved a certain shade of piety, replied that those who walked along clandestine and forbidden paths did not merit any special protection, but that special measures should be taken to curb the criminals.

The King, dissatisfied with this contradictory answer, folded up the manuscript, and was about to join his Secretary of State, who was working in the next room, when his glance fell upon Mademoiselle de Scudéry, who was in attendance and had just taken her seat in a small easy-chair not far from Maintenon. He now approached her. The pleasant smile which had first played over his features, and then vanished, showed itself again. Stopping immediately in front of Mademoiselle's chair and unfolding the poem once more, he said softly, "Our Marquise refuses to countenance the gallantries of lovelorn beaux, and makes us evasive replies of a kind that are very nearly forbidden. But you, Mademoiselle, what is your opinion of this petition?"

Scudéry rose respectfully from her chair, slowly dropped a curtsey, and then with downcast eyes observed:

> "Un amant qui craint les voleurs
> N'est point digne d'amour."

The King, struck by the romantic spirit of these few words, which encompassed more meaning than the whole of the other poem with its yards and yards of tirades, exclaimed with enthusiasm, "By Saint Denis, you are right, Mademoiselle! Cowardice shall not be protected by any blind measures which would affect the innocent along with the guilty; Argenson and La Reynie must make the best of things as they are."

La Martinière described all the horrors of the time in the most startling colors the next morning, when she told her mistress what she had suffered the previous night, and with damp, trembling hands gave her the mysterious casket. Both she and Baptiste, who stood in the corner pale with anxiety and embarrassment, crumpling his nightcap, and hardly able to speak—both begged Mademoiselle in the most piteous terms, and in the names of all the saints, to use the utmost caution in opening the box.

Scudéry, weighing the locked mystery in her hand, and subjecting it to a careful scrutiny, said with a smile, "You are both of you ghost seers! That I am not rich, that there is no treasure here worth committing murder for, must be known to all these assassins, who, you yourselves tell me, spy out the secrets of every house, just as well as it is known to me and you. Can it be my life they are after? But who could gain anything from the death of an old lady of seventy-three, who never harmed anybody in the world except the villains and meddlers in her own novels; who turns out middling verses which can excite nobody's envy; who will leave nothing behind except the state dresses of an old lady who used sometimes to go to court, and a few dozen books bound with gilt edges! And as for you, Martinière, you may describe the stranger's appearance as frighteningly as you like, I still cannot believe that he had any evil purpose in mind. Now, then, we shall solve this mystery."

La Martinière hurriedly stepped back, and Baptiste almost dropped on his knees with a stifled "Oh!" as Mademoiselle pressed down upon a projecting steel knob. In another moment the lid snapped open with a bang and revealed a sight which dazzled even Mademoiselle's eyes.

A pair of gold bracelets, set with precious stones, and a necklace to match sparkled out of the deep velvet recesses of the box. She took them out; and while she was admiring the exquisite workmanship of the necklace, Martinière, eyeing the valuable bracelets, could not restrain herself from crying out that even the vain Madame de Montespan herself had never had such ornaments as these. "But what is behind all this?" asked Scudéry. And then she noticed at the bottom of the casket a small, folded slip of paper which, no doubt, contained some explanation of the mystery. She picked it up and then, almost without reading it, let it drop from her trembling fingers.

"Oh! This is contemptible!" she exclaimed, her voice half choked with shame. "Must I endure this sort of insult in my old age? Have I acted in folly like some giddy young thing? Are words uttered half in jest capable of being twisted into such an evil interpretation? And am I, who have been virtuous and devoted to God all my life—am I to be involved in crime and a diabolical conspiracy?"

Mademoiselle held her handkerchief to her eyes and began to weep bitterly. Martinière and Baptiste stood by, confused and distracted by their lady's trouble, wanting to help but not knowing what to do. Finally

Martinière picked the ominous slip of paper from the floor. Upon it was written—

> "Un amant qui craint les voleurs
> N'est point digne d'amour."

"Your wisdom and ready wit, honored lady, have saved us from great persecution. We only exercise the right of the strong over the weak and the cowardly in order to possess ourselves of treasures that would otherwise be disgracefully squandered on unworthy objects. Kindly accept these jewels as a token of our gratitude. They are the most brilliant ones we have happened upon in a long time, though indeed you, gracious lady, should be adorned with gems even more rare. We trust we will continue to enjoy your friendship and your favorable regard.

"THE INVISIBLE ONES."

"Is it possible," demanded Mademoiselle de Scudéry, after she had somewhat recovered herself, "is it possible for anyone to carry insolence and sarcasm to greater extremes?"

In the bright sunlight which shone into the room through the maroon silk window curtains, the brilliants, lying on a table beside the open casket, gave out a strange reddish glow. Seeing the ornaments in that light, Scudéry turned her face away in abhorrence, and commanded Martinière to remove the awful jewels at once, for the blood of the murdered victims was still upon them. La Martinière carefully locked up the necklace and bracelets again, and suggested that perhaps the wisest plan would be to hand the casket over to the Minister of Police, and to confide in him everything connected with the terrifying young man and his fantastic gift.

Mademoiselle de Scudéry slowly paced up and down the room in silence, as if she were only now reflecting on what was to be done. She then sent Baptiste to fetch a sedan chair and bade Martinière to prepare her toilet, for she had decided to go straight to Madame de Maintenon with the whole matter.

She had herself carried to the Marquise's apartments at an hour when she knew she would find that lady alone, and she took the casket of jewels with her.

Madame de Maintenon, quite naturally, was astonished to see Mademoiselle, generally a pattern of dignity and grace (notwithstanding her advanced age), come unexpectedly tottering into her salon, pale and disheveled.

"In Heaven's name, what has happened to you?" she called out, hastily pushing a chair towards Scudéry.

Struggling to control herself, Mademoiselle described the nature of the mortification—she would never get over it—which her thoughtless witticism to the King had brought upon her.

The Marquise, after learning the rest of the story bit by bit, arrived at the conclusion that Scudéry took the whole experience far too much to heart, and that the mockery of thieves and cutthroats could never make a target of a mind as pious and noble as Mademoiselle's; and finally Madame de Maintenon asked to see the ornaments.

Mademoiselle de Scudéry handed her the open casket, and the Marquise, on seeing the jewels, could not restrain a cry of admiration. She took out the necklace and the bracelets, and approaching the window with them, first let the sun play upon the stones; then full of admiration she appraised the exquisite workmanship of the gold and the marvelous skill with which every little link in the elaborate chain had been contrived.

"Do you realize," she said at length, returning the casket, and her attention, to Mademoiselle, "that these bracelets and necklace have been turned out by no less an artist than René Cardillac?"

René Cardillac was at that time the most skilful goldsmith in Paris, and also one of the most talented and eccentric men of his day. Built rather on the small side, but broad-shouldered and muscular of frame, Cardillac, although considerably over fifty, still possessed the vitality of a young man. And his strength, which might be said to be exceptional, was further evidenced by his abundant curly reddish hair, and his heavy-set brooding features. In fact, if it were not for Cardillac's reputation, throughout Paris, as one of the most honest and honorable of men, self-effacing, frank, generous, and without guile, the very peculiar quality of his eyes, which were small, deep-set, glittering, and green, might have led one to suspect him of hidden malice and viciousness.

Cardillac, as it has already been observed, was the greatest master of his art, not only in Paris, but probably anywhere at that time. Intimately acquainted with the properties of precious stones, he knew how to treat

them in such a manner that gems which had at first glance been thought
lustreless and slight, came out of his workshop turned into things of
dazzling magnificence. He accepted all commissions with eagerness and
enthusiasm, and would name fees so moderate that they seemed to bear
no proportion whatever to the work to be done. And once a commission
was taken in hand it gave him no rest. Night and day he would be heard
hammering in his workshop, and often when his task was almost finished
he would suddenly conceive a dislike for its design, or begin to question
the elegance of the setting of some of the jewels, or the form of even a
little link. This was quite sufficient reason for him to throw all his work
into the crucible, and begin it entirely over again. Thus every piece of
jewelry that he created was a perfect and matchless masterpiece which excited the wonder of his patrons.

But once the work was done, it was almost impossible to get it out
of his hands. Resorting to a thousand pretexts, he would put the owner
off from week to week, from month to month. It was futile to offer to
pay him double for the work; he would not accept a single louis d'or
more than the price he had originally asked. When at last he had to yield
to the pressure of his customer, he made no effort to conceal the ill-humor,
and even anger, with which the transaction filled him.

If he had to deliver some work of unusual importance and value,
worth perhaps many thousands because of the costliness of its jewels or
the extreme intricacy of its gold-work, he would pace about like a madman,
cursing himself, his work, and everything around him. But then if someone
would run up behind him and call out, "René Cardillac, can you make a
beautiful necklace for my bride—or bracelets for my mistress?" or the
like, he would suddenly stop still, with a bright look in his little eyes, and,
rubbing his hands together, ask: "Well, what have you got?" Thereupon,
the other would perhaps produce a small jewel case, and say, "Oh, just
some stones; really nothing very much; quite ordinary things, but in your
hands. . . ." Cardillac would not let him finish, but snatching the case
away from its owner and taking out the stones (which often were of little
value) he would hold them up to the light and cry out enraptured, "Ho!
Quite ordinary, are they? Not at all! Pretty stones—magnificent stones!
Just let me make them up for you. And if a handful more or less of louis
d'or is of no great concern to you, I will add a few more little gems, that

will sparkle in your eyes like the blinding sun." Then the other would say, "I leave it all to you, Master René, and shall pay whatever you wish."

It made little difference whether his customer was a rich townsman or an important nobleman of the court, Cardillac would throw his arms impetuously round his neck, and hug and kiss him, saying that now he was quite happy again, and that in eight days the work would be finished. Then he would run home, breathless, rush into his workshop and begin to hammer away, and at the end of eight days a masterpiece would be completed.

But the moment the customer came to call for it, more than ready to pay the insignificant fee demanded, and anxious to take the finished ornament away with him, Cardillac would become testy, rude, and obstinate.

"But, Master Cardillac, do you realize that tomorrow is my wedding day?"

"What have I to do with your wedding? Come back again in a fortnight."

"But the jewelry is finished and here is your money. I must have it."

"And I tell you that I've lots of things to change in it, and I can't let you have it today."

"And I tell you that if you won't agree to return my jewelry for which I am ready to pay double the price you ask—I shall come back to fetch it with some of Argenson's very serviceable henchmen."

"Then may Satan torture you with hundreds of red-hot pincers, and hang a ton on the necklace to strangle your bride!" And with that, Cardillac would thrust the jewelry into the bridegroom's breast pocket, seize him by the arm and turn him out of the door so roughly that he would go tumbling down the stairs. Then Cardillac would rush to the window, thrust out his head, and laugh like a demon at the sight of the poor young man limping away from the house, holding his handkerchief to his bleeding nose.

But he was capable of even more inexplicable behavior. Sometimes, after he had enthusiastically begun a piece of work, he would suddenly implore his customer to release him from his obligation and, calling upon the Virgin and all the saints, would evince the deepest agitation, bursting into violent protestations, nay, even into sobs and tears at the mention of continuing. Personages of high rank and with influence at court·had vainly offered him large sums of money to fashion the smallest trinket for them. He threw himself at the King's feet and begged the privilege of rejecting such commissions. In the same way he refused Madame de Maintenon's orders, and it was even with a certain expression of resentment and aversion that he rejected her proposal that he make a little ring with the arts as emblems on it, which she intended to present to Racine.

Accordingly, Madame de Maintenon now said, "I wager that if I sent for him to try to find out, at least, for whom he made these ornaments, Cardillac would refuse to come here, since he would probably fear I had some commission in mind; and he will never, under any circumstances, undertake anything for me. And yet lately he seems to have dropped something of his inflexible obstinacy. I hear that he works more industriously now than ever, and delivers his work on the spot, although he still manages to show his annoyance and disgust."

Mademoiselle de Scudéry, who was greatly concerned that the jewelry be placed in the hands of its proper owner as soon as it could possibly be managed, suggested that word might be sent to Master Whimsicality, asking him to come immediately, and informing him that what was wanted of him was not work but an opinion on some jewels. This suited the Marquise. Cardillac was sent for, and he presented himself at once, almost before the messenger had returned.

On observing Scudéry, he appeared to be embarrassed, and—like someone confronted by something so utterly unexpected that he forgets the conventional rules of behavior—he first bowed deeply and respectfully to that venerable lady, and only after this turned to the Marquise. Pointing to the jewelry, which now lay glittering against the dark green cover of a table, she abruptly asked him if it were of his workmanship.

Cardillac hardly glanced at the necklace and bracelets, but, staring the Marquise in the face, he quickly packed the jewels into the casket, which was standing beside them, and pushed it violently away from him. Then he said with an unpleasant smile:

"If I may say so, Madame la Marquise, one must have a very poor acquaintance with René Cardillac's talents to believe, for a moment, that any other goldsmith in the world is capable of turning out such work. Of course it's mine."

"Tell me then," continued the Marquise, "for whom were these ornaments made?"

"For myself alone," replied Cardillac. "Yes! I dare say your ladyship finds that strange," he continued, since both Maintenon and Scudéry looked at him in astonishment, the former full of mistrust, the latter in uncertain expectation of what turn the affair would take next. "Strange and true. Merely for my own pleasure and my love for the beautiful; I put my finest stones and my best work into it. Then, a short time ago, the jewels disappeared from my workshop in some incomprehensible way."

"Thank Heaven!" exclaimed Mademoiselle de Scudéry, jumping from her chair as quickly and nimbly as a young girl. And going up to Cardillac, she placed both her hands upon his shoulders as she said, "Take back, Master René, the property which these scoundrels stole from you." And then she told him, overlooking no detail, how she had acquired possession of the jewels.

Cardillac heard her out in silence and with downcast eyes. Only now and again he uttered an indistinct, "Hm!—So!—Well, well!" now clasping his hands behind his back, and now gently stroking his chin and cheeks. When Mademoiselle de Scudéry came to the end of her story, Cardillac appeared to be struggling with some strange thought which had occurred to him while she was still speaking, and about which he still seemed undecided. He rubbed his forehead, he sighed, he put his hand over his eyes as if to check a flow of tears. At length he took the casket which Scudéry had offered him, dropped slowly on one knee, and said:

"These jewels have been decreed to you, my noble and respected lady, by destiny. Yes, now I realize that it was you I had in mind when I was working on them, and that it was for you I excelled myself. Do not disdain to accept them, nor refuse to wear them. They are indeed among the best things I have ever made."

"Why, Master René!" replied Scudéry, in obvious good humor. "Would you have me at my age trick myself out with glittering gems? And why should you make me such costly gifts? Come, come, Master René. Now if I were as beautiful and rich as the Marquise de Fontanges, I assure you I would not let these jewels pass out of my hands. But what would these withered arms want with vain display, and how would a glittering necklace look on this throat which I keep muffled and covered up?"

Meanwhile, Cardillac had risen to his feet and, still holding out the casket to Mademoiselle de Scudéry, he said, with a curious, half-mad look in his eyes: "Have pity upon me, Mademoiselle, and take the jewels. You don't know how great a respect for your virtues and your rare qualities I cherish in my heart. Please accept this little gift, then, merely as an effort on my part to express my deep respect and devotion."

But as Mademoiselle de Scudéry still hesitated, the Marquise de Maintenon took the casket out of Cardillac's hands, saying, "Upon my word, Mademoiselle, you are always talking about how old you are! What have we, you and I, to do with the years and their burdens? And aren't you acting just like a shy young thing, who would like only too well to take the sweet forbidden fruit if she could only do so without stretching out hand or finger? Do not refuse to accept from our good Master René a gift that scores of others could never obtain from him, despite all their gold, all their prayers and entreaties!"

As she spoke, Maintenon had forced the casket into Mademoiselle's hands, and now Cardillac dropped to his knees again, kissed Scudéry's gown; kissed her hands; sighed and gasped; wept and sobbed; jumped up; and ran out of the room like a madman, as fast as his legs could carry him, upsetting chairs and tables on his way, and making glass and china rattle.

Mademoiselle de Scudéry was quite alarmed, and cried out: "Good Heavens! What has come over the man?"

But the Marquise, with a gaiety quite foreign to her usual mood, broke into peals of laughter, and said, "Now, I've got it, Mademoiselle. Master René has fallen desperately in love with you, and according to the proper customs and usage of all true love, he is laying siege to your heart with costly gifts." She even pushed her little joke further, and admonished Scudéry not to be too cruel to her despairing lover; while Mademoiselle, taking her cue from Maintenon, gave full play to her own native wit and indulged in even more spirited conceits and fancies. She suggested that if this were really the state of affairs, she would at last yield, and not deprive the world of the unprecedented spectacle of a woman, who, aged seventy-three and of untarnished nobility, had become a goldsmith's bride. Maintenon offered to weave the wedding wreath, and, meanwhile, to instruct her in the duties of a good housewife, since such a young chit of a girl could not of course know much about such things.

But when Scudéry finally rose to take her leave of the Marquise, she became grave again, despite all their jesting, and as she picked up the jewel case she said: "Do you know, Madame la Marquise, I can never wear these ornaments. Whatever their history, they have at one time or another been in the hands of those monsters who commit robbery and murder with the audacity of Satan himself—or even with his unholy assistance. When I look at these glittering stones I see nothing but the blood that still seems to be clinging to them. And then, I must confess, I cannot help feeling that there is something disturbing and uncanny about Cardillac's behavior. I cannot rid myself of the presentiment that there is some terrible secret behind all this. Yet, on the other hand, when I consider the whole matter reasonably, and analyze the circumstances connected with it, I cannot find any basis for a mystery, nor do I understand how an honest, industrious citizen, like our Master René, can play any part in shady or suspicious dealings. But I am quite sure of one thing, and that is that I shall never bring myself to put the jewels on."

The Marquise thought that this was carrying scruples too far. But when Mademoiselle de Scudéry asked her on her conscience what she would really do in her (Scudéry's) place, Maintenon replied seriously and without hesitation: "Far sooner throw the ornaments into the Seine than ever wear them."

The scene with Master René was described by Scudéry in charming verses, which she read to the King on the following evening in Maintenon's salon. And it is not at all unlikely that she overcame her qualms and evil forebodings with certain jests at Master René's expense. It was an amusing version of the episode, drawn in bright lifelike colors, and describing the goldsmith's bride of three-and-seventy who was of such truly ancient nobility. At any rate the King laughed heartily, and swore that Boileau Despréaux had found his master; and Scudéry's poem was therefore popularly adjudged the wittiest ever written.

Several months had passed, when, as chance would have it, Mademoiselle de Scudéry was driving over the Pont-Neuf in the Duchess de Montansier's glass coach. The appearance of this elegant conveyance was still so novel that it never failed to attract the curious, who crowded around it wherever it went. On the present occasion the gaping throng that surrounded Scudéry on the Pont-Neuf had become so large that the horses were almost unable to move.

In the midst of all this confusion, a running outburst of abuse and cursing reached Mademoiselle de Scudéry's ears, and looking up she noticed a man making his way through the thick of the crowd with the help of his fists and carefully directed blows at people's ribs. As he came nearer she saw that his face was pale and suffering, and that his eyes, which were fierce and piercing, were fixed upon her. He energetically worked his way forward with his fists and elbows, until he reached the carriage-door. He pulled it open with violence, threw a folded slip of paper into Scudéry's lap, and then went away as he had come, dealing out and receiving thrusts and blows.

La Martinière was accompanying her mistress, and when she saw the man at the carriage door, she cried out in terror and fell back fainting among the cushions. In vain did Mademoiselle de Scudéry pull at the cord and call out to the driver; he, as if impelled by some evil spirit, whipped up his horses, so that they foamed at the mouth and tossed their heads, and kicked and plunged, and finally thundered over the bridge at a sharp trot. Mademoiselle de Scudéry emptied her scent bottle over the unconscious woman, who at last opened her eyes, and trembling and shaking and clinging convulsively to her mistress, her face blanched with anxiety and fear, painfully gasped out:

"In the name of the Virgin, what did that terrible man want? He is the same one—oh, yes, the very man who brought you the casket on that awful night!"

Mademoiselle calmed the poor woman, assuring her that not the least mischief had been done, and that the thing to do, at the moment, was to see what was written on the slip of paper. She unfolded it and found these words:

"I am being driven to destruction by an evil fate which it is within your power to avert. I implore you, as a son would his mother from whom he cannot part, and for whom he has warmest affection, to send the necklace and bracelets which you have received from me to Master René Cardillac; any pretext will do; have them repaired—or something on them changed. Your welfare, your life, depend on it. If you have not done this by the day after tomorrow, I shall force my way into your house and kill myself before your eyes!"

"Well, now, at any rate, we know," said old Mademoiselle de Scudéry after she had read it, "that this mysterious stranger, even if he does really belong to that band of thieves and cutthroats, has no evil designs against me. Perhaps if he had succeeded in speaking to me that night, I might have learned of some singular incident or mysterious complication that would have made things clear to me about which I now entertain only the vaguest ideas. Be that as it may, I shall certainly do whatever this note requests of me, if for no other reason than to get rid of these unlucky jewels, which seemed to me from the first talismans of evil. And I dare say Cardillac, true to his old habits, won't let them out of his hands again so easily."

Mademoiselle de Scudéry intended to go to the goldsmith's with the jewels the very next day. But somehow it seemed as if all the wits and intellects of Paris had conspired together to descend upon Mademoiselle on just this particular morning with their verses and plays and anecdotes. No sooner had La Chapelle finished reading some scenes from a new tragedy, and had slyly remarked with a certain degree of assurance that he now certainly surpassed Racine, than that very poet himself came in, and routed him with a pathetic speech he had just given a king in one of his plays. Then Boileau sent off some of the rockets of his wit into this black sky of Tragedy, while, in the background, the Louvre and its colonnades were being talked to death by the architect, Claude Perrault, who was present and could not be kept off the subject.

It was now high noon and Scudéry had an engagement with the Duchess de Montansier, so the visit to Master René Cardillac's had to be put off until the next day.

Mademoiselle, however, was tormented by a feeling of extraordinary uneasiness. The young man appeared constantly before her eyes; and buried deep in her mind a dim recollection seemed to be stirring, as though she had seen that face, those features, somewhere before. Her sleep, always light, was now disturbed by fitful dreams. She told herself

that she had acted rashly, and even criminally, in having refused help-
fully to grasp the hand which the unhappy wretch, sinking into the abyss
of ruin, had stretched up to her; and she was haunted by the thought that
she had had it in her power to prevent some fatal event, some hellish crime,
from taking place. As soon as morning had come, she had Martinière
finish her toilet, and drove off to the goldsmith's, taking the casket of
jewels with her.

Crowds of people were pouring into the Rue Nicaise, where Cardillac
lived, and gathering outside his door, shouting, screaming, and creating
a wild tumult of noise; only the presence of the *Maréchaussée*, who had
thrown a cordon around the house, prevented them from forcing their
way in. Angry voices were crying out in the midst of the confusion: "Tear
him to pieces! The murderer! Grind him to dust!"

At last Desgrais appeared on the scene with a strong body of police,
who cleared a passage for him through the heart of the crowd. The house
door flew open, and a man loaded with chains was brought out and
dragged off amidst the most horrible cries and imprecations of the furious
mob.

Just as Mademoiselle de Scudéry, half ill with terror and sleepless
forebodings, witnessed this, a wild shriek of distress pierced her ears.
"Drive on, get through somehow! Up to the house!" she cried to her
coachman, almost out of her mind with misgivings. He scattered the
dense crowd with a dexterous, sudden turn of his horses and pulled up
right in front of Cardillac's door. There Scudéry saw Desgrais, and at his
feet a young girl, as beautiful as the day, only half-dressed and with her
hair hanging down over her shoulders. A look of wild anxiety, of unendurable despair filled her eyes as she clung to Desgrais' knees and cried
aloud in an agonizing voice: "But he is innocent! He is innocent."

Desgrais' efforts to break her grasp, and raise her from the ground,
were futile; so were those of his men. Finally a giant of a brute laid rough
hands upon the poor girl and tore her away from Desgrais by main force,
then stumbled and sent her rolling down the stone steps to the street
where she lay without even a whimper, as though she were dead.

Mademoiselle de Scudéry could restrain herself no longer. "In God's
name, what has happened? What's going on here?" she cried. And she
quickly opened her carriage door and stepped out.

The crowd respectfully made way for the estimable lady. Some kind-hearted old women had, in the meantime, picked the girl up, set her on the steps, and were rubbing her forehead with aromatic spirits. It was a touching scene, and Mademoiselle took it in as she approached Desgrais and repeated her question with some brusqueness.

"Another atrocity has been committed," Desgrais replied. "René Cardillac was found this morning stabbed to death. The murderer is Olivier Brusson, a journeyman in the shop. You have just seen him being taken away to jail."

"And the girl?" asked Scudéry.

"Is Cardillac's daughter, Madelon," Desgrais went on quickly. "The criminal is her lover. Now she's weeping and wailing, and protesting over and over that Olivier is innocent, quite innocent. But the real truth is she has had a hand in it somewhere, herself, and I intend to have her taken to the Conciergerie too."

As he said this, Desgrais directed a look of such malicious triumph at the girl that Scudéry trembled. Madelon was breathing softly now, but her eyes remained closed, and she lay against the steps apparently incapable of either sound or movement. The old women were trying to decide whether to take her into the house or to stay with her longer until she recovered consciousness. Mademoiselle de Scudéry's sympathies were touched; she was convinced of the girl's innocence, and felt nothing but horror for Desgrais and his men. She heard dull measured footsteps descending the stairs. Cardillac's body was being taken away. Mademoiselle de Scudéry made a sudden decision:

"I am taking the girl with me, Desgrais," she said. "You may attend to the rest."

A murmur of approval swept through the crowd. The women bent to lift up the girl, and were immediately surrounded by hundreds of hands, ready to help. She was borne to the carriage as though on air, while blessings showered down upon the noble lady who had snatched innocence from the claws of a blind and bloodthirsty tribunal.

It required the repeated efforts of Seron, the most celebrated doctor in Paris, to bring Madelon back to consciousness after she had lain for hours in a state of dead coma. What the physician began was completed by Scudéry, who attempted to stimulate some mild ray of hope in the girl's mind, until finally the child found some release in a violent outburst of tears and sobbing. Then, slowly, and sometimes interrupted by her own emotion, she began to tell Mademoiselle all that had happened.

About midnight she had been awakened by a light knocking at her bedroom door, and had heard a voice telling her to get up at once, that her father was dying. Startled out of her wits, she had jumped out of bed and opened the door. Olivier confronted her, light in hand, pale, dis- traught, bathed in perspiration. Half-staggering through the corridors, he led the way to her father's workshop, and she followed. They found Cardillac already in the throes of death: his eyes stared blankly into space, incapable of recognition, and in his throat the terrifying rattling had begun. She had flung herself, weeping, upon the body, and then it was that she first saw bloodstains on his shirt. Olivier had gently lifted her away and then occupied himself with a wound in the left side of her father's chest, washing it with balsam and finding its exact location. This operation seemed to restore her father somewhat, for the rattle in his throat ceased, and an expression of affection and tenderness came into his eyes, which he turned first upon her and then upon Olivier. Then taking her hand, he placed it in Olivier's, and fervently pressed them together. She and Olivier had both fallen on their knees beside her father's bed when, with a cry of agony, he raised himself up, but at once sank back again, and sighed his last breath.

For a time neither of them moved, although tears and sobs burst from them. Then, presently, Olivier told her how he had been required by his master to accompany him when he went out that night and how Cardillac had been stabbed in the street in his presence; how, thinking the injury was not mortal, he had exerted all his strength to carry the heavy man home.

At daybreak the other people of the house, who had heard the sounds of bumping and dragging, weeping and lamenting, during the night, had come in and found them still kneeling and disconsolate beside her father's lifeless body. An alarm was raised; the Maréchaussée pushed their way into the house; and Olivier had been dragged off to prison as the murderer of his master.

Madelon added the most touching account of her dear Olivier, describing his virtues, his sense of duty and loyalty. How he had respected his master as though he had been his own father, and how the latter had fully reciprocated this affection. How her father had chosen Brusson, despite his poverty, to be his son-in-law, for his talent was equal to his sincerity and the nobility of his character. All this Madelon revealed to Scudéry, speaking from her inmost heart, and she finished by saying that if Olivier had thrust his dagger into her father's breast in her own presence she would take it for some illusion of Satan, sooner than believe that Olivier could ever be capable of such a gruesome crime.

Mademoiselle de Scudéry, deeply moved by Madelon's anguish, and quite ready, for her own part, to believe in Olivier's innocence, had inquiries made, and found full confirmation of all Madelon had told her of the warm relations between the master and his journeyman. The people in the same house, as well as the neighbors, unanimously extolled Olivier as a model of virtue and industriousness; nobody knew anything against him; and yet when the grisly deed was referred to they merely shrugged their shoulders and remarked that some things were beyond comprehension.

Olivier, brought before the *Chambre Ardente*, denied the accusation made against him, Mademoiselle de Scudéry learned. With the utmost assurance and resoluteness, he maintained that his master had been attacked and struck down in the street in his presence and that he had brought Cardillac back, still alive, to the house where soon afterwards he died. All this agreed with Madelon's account.

Mademoiselle de Scudéry had the girl repeat the most inconsequential details of the story over and over again. She carefully sounded her out on whether there had ever been a quarrel between master and journeyman; whether Olivier were not sometimes given to those violent fits of temper which often possess even the most good-natured of men like a blinding madness, causing them to commit acts which they seem incapable of normally. But the longer Madelon spoke, the more complete became the picture of the quiet domestic happiness in which these three had lived, united by the closest ties of affection, and the less plausible any suspicion against poor Olivier, whose life was now, unfortunately, at stake. Scrupulously weighing every point, and starting with the assumption that Olivier, despite everything that spoke so strongly for his innocence, was nevertheless Cardillac's murderer, Scudéry still could not find any motive within the bounds of possibility for the hideous deed. From any point of view, Olivier had everything to lose and nothing to gain by it. He is poor but clever. He has succeeded in winning the friendship of the most renowned master of his trade; he loves his master's daughter; his master looks upon this love with favor; happiness and prosperity for the rest of his life are within his grasp. But now suppose that, provoked in some way that God alone may know, Olivier had been so overcome by anger that he attempted a murderous assault upon his benefactor, his father, what diabolical hypocrisy he must have practiced to have behaved after the deed in the way he really did behave! Firmly convinced of Olivier's innocence, Mademoiselle made up her mind to save the young man, cost what it might.

Before appealing, however, to the King's mercy, it seemed to her that the most advisable step to take would be to visit La Reynie, and call his attention to all the circumstances that pointed to Olivier's innocence, and so perhaps to awaken in the President's mind a favorable interest in the accused, which might in turn communicate itself to his fellow judges.

La Reynie received Mademoiselle de Scudéry with all the respect which the worthy lady, highly honored as she was by the King himself, might justly claim. He listened quietly to everything she suggested in connection with the terrible crime, Olivier's relations to the victim and his daughter, and his character in general. Nevertheless the only indication he gave that her words were not falling upon totally deaf ears was a faint and almost malicious smile; and in the same way he heard her protestations and tearful admonitions that a judge was not the inevitable enemy of the accused, but must also entertain evidence that spoke in his favor. When at last Mademoiselle was utterly exhausted, dried her tears, and fell silent, La Reynie began:

"It speaks well for your goodness of heart, Mademoiselle, that you are touched by the tears of a young, infatuated girl and believe everything she tells you, and that you are even incapable of conceiving the true nature of such an appalling act. But it is a different matter with a judge, who is accustomed to tear the mask from insolent hypocrisy. I am under no official obligation to explain the various stages of a criminal investigation to anyone who chooses to question me about it. Mademoiselle, I do my duty and trouble myself very little about the opinion of the world. The wicked shall tremble before the *Chambre Ardente*, which knows no punishment but the scaffold and the stake. Yet I do not want you, dear lady, to take me for a monster of intolerance and cruelty. Permit me in a few words to demonstrate to you the guilt of this young criminal, who, thank Heaven, has been overtaken by the avenging arm of justice. Then your own intelligence will prompt you to disown those very feelings of kindness, which do you honor, but would never be proper for anyone in my position, in any case.

"Well then, this is how it goes. One fine day, toward morning, René Cardillac is found stabbed through the heart with a dagger. The only people in the shop are his workman, Olivier Brusson, and his own daughter. Later, a search of Olivier's room uncovers, among other things, a dagger stained with fresh blood, and with a blade that corresponds exactly to the size and shape of the wound.

"Olivier says, 'Cardillac was struck down in the dark under my eyes.'

" 'Was it an attempted robbery?'

" 'I don't know.'

" 'You say he had asked you to accompany him. How is it then you were unable to keep off the murderer, or hold him till the police came, or cry out for help?'

" 'My master was walking fifteen or twenty paces ahead of me. I followed.'

" 'But why in the world at such a distance?'

" 'Those were my instructions.'

" 'And what brought Master Cardillac out at such a late hour?'

" 'That I cannot say.'

" 'But you have never before known him to leave the house after nine o'clock in the evening, have you?'

"This question confused Olivier. He hesitated, stammered, was ready to burst into tears. Cardillac, he protested by all that was holy, really had gone out that night. Gone out and met his death in the manner already described.

"Now please follow me carefully, Mademoiselle. It has been proved to the utmost certainty that Cardillac never left his house on the night in question, and so Olivier's assertion that he went out with him is nothing but a bold lie. The house door is provided with a heavy lock, which makes a shrill piercing noise whenever it is locked or unlocked; moreover, the door squeaks horribly on its hinges, so that, as we have proved by experimenting with it, the noise echoes through the house, even up to the garret. Now on the ground floor, and therefore close to the street door, live old Master Claude Patru and his housekeeper, a woman nearly eighty years old but still quite active and spry for her age. Both these witnesses heard Cardillac come downstairs punctually at nine o'clock that evening, according to his usual custom, lock and bolt the front door with considerable clanking and creaking, and then go upstairs again, where they heard him booming out the evening prayers and then, to judge by the banging of doors, go into his bedroom. Master Claude, like so many old people, suffers from insomnia. That night he had not closed an eye. And so, somewhere about half-past nine, his housekeeper went to the kitchen—which could only be reached through the hall of the house— to get a light for her candle, and then came back and sat down at the table beside Master Claude with an old chronicle, out of which she read aloud while the old man, preoccupied with his own thoughts, either rested in his easy-chair or got up and slowly paced the room in the hope of tiring himself out enough to bring on sleep.

"The house remained peaceful and quiet until after midnight. Then they heard quick steps overhead and a heavy thump as though something of considerable weight had been dropped on the floor. This was followed almost immediately by the sound of muffled groaning. Both of them, without knowing what was happening, experienced a peculiar uneasiness and dread. The horror of the bloody crime had communicated itself to them. When morning came, it brought to light what had been begun in darkness—"

"But," interrupted Mademoiselle de Scudéry, "what motive under the sun can you find for such treachery in anything I have told you about Olivier?"

"Well," replied La Reynie, "Cardillac was far from poor. In fact, he had some valuable gems in his possession."

"But wouldn't his daughter inherit everything?" continued Scudéry. "You forget that Olivier was to be Cardillac's son-in-law."

"It is very likely that he had to share his profits or that he even hired out for murder," said La Reynie.

"Hired out for murder?" asked Scudéry, utterly bewildered.

"I must tell you, Mademoiselle," continued the President, "that Olivier's blood would long since have run in the gutters of the Place Grève, but for his connection with a certain deeply shrouded mystery which until now has terrorized all Paris. It is evident to us that Olivier is a member of that same band which has defied justice, made a mockery of the courts, and still remains free and at large to carry on its work. Through him they all will be—they must be—exposed. Cardillac's wound is precisely like those found on all the other victims of murder and robbery in the dark streets and hallways of Paris. But the most conclusive fact of all is this: since Olivier Brusson's arrest all these murders and robberies have stopped. The streets are now as safe by night as by day—which would seem to indicate that Olivier probably is the leader of this pack of assassins. So far he will admit nothing, but we have ways of making him talk whether he wants to or not."

"And Madelon," demanded Mademoiselle de Scudéry, "and Madelon, that devoted, innocent lamb of a girl?"

"As for Madelon," said La Reynie, with a venomous smile, "what assurance is there that she is not involved in this plot, too? Does she care what has happened to her father? She hasn't shed a tear for anyone but the murderer. You recall, I am sure, similar circumstances in the case of La Brinvillier. I am afraid, Mademoiselle, that very soon I shall have to beg your forgiveness and take your protégée away from you to the cells of the *Conciergerie*."

Mademoiselle de Scudéry shuddered at La Reynie's implacability. It seemed to her that no virtue, no form of integrity, could withstand the suspicious scrutiny of this awful man who seemed capable of prying out the most secret blood lust and murder which may be hidden in the best of us. She rose to go. "Be human!" was all that she could stammer out in her distress.

La Reynie accompanied her with ceremonious courtesy to the head of the stairs. "And may I be allowed to see this unfortunate Brusson?" she suddenly asked, just as she was about to descend the steps, turning round quickly to the President. La Reynie looked at her thoughtfully for a moment, then smiled in his familiar unpleasant way and said: "Certainly, Mademoiselle, since you would rather trust your own instincts concerning Olivier's guilt than the evidence we have before our very eyes. If you are not afraid to visit the dark abodes of crime, if you are not revolted at the sight of depravity in all its stages, you will find the doors of the Conciergerie open to you two hours from now. You shall have the pleasure of meeting this Olivier, whose fate has aroused your interest so much."

Mademoiselle de Scudéry could not, in fact, convince herself of the young man's guilt. Everything spoke against him, and no judge in the world would have acted differently from La Reynie on the basis of the evidence at hand. Yet the picture of domestic happiness, which Madelon had painted with such warm and vital color, discountenanced all suspicion, and Scudéry felt she would rather be taken in by the most implausible explanations than accept, as the truth, something against which her whole being rebelled.

She decided she would get Olivier to go over, with her, all the events of that ill-fated night, and thus see if she could not, herself, uncover some significant evidence which the judges, who relied upon other methods of investigation, had overlooked.

On her arrival at the Conciergerie, Mademoiselle de Scudéry was shown into a large bright reception room. She was not kept waiting long. In a few moments she heard the clanking of chains in the hallway. Then the door was thrown open, and Olivier Brusson stood before her. At the sight of him, she fell into a faint. When she opened her eyes again he was gone. She insisted on being taken to her carriage at once. She would have no more of this place! Not another instant in this asylum of lawlessness and iniquity! At first glance she had recognized Olivier Brusson as the young man who had thrown the note into her carriage on the Pont-Neuf. There was no room for doubt now; La Reynie's horrible theory was fully confirmed. Olivier Brusson belonged to the company of assassins that was terrorizing the city, and undoubtedly he had murdered his master.

And Madelon? Never before had Mademoiselle been so bitterly deceived by the promptings of her own heart. She was ready now to believe that there was some infernal force at work in all this, and she despaired of ever again being able to recognize the truth from the inventions of the devil. Madelon, then, was involved in it, too—perhaps had even assisted in the bloody act. Once this suspicion occurred to her, her mind fixed on the idea of Madelon's culpability, filling in the picture in every hue and tint, finding confirmation in the most trivial detail, the most ambiguous circumstance. Thus many things which she had hitherto considered a proof of the girl's innocence and honesty now presented themselves as the unmistakable evidence of corruption and studied hypocrisy. Those heart-rending lamentations, those bitter floods of tears, might well have been wrung from her, not through any fear of seeing her lover perish on the scaffold, but in mortal terror of herself falling into the hangman's hands. She must rid herself at once of this serpent which she was nourishing in her bosom, Mademoiselle de Scudéry determined, as she got out of her carriage.

When she entered the girl's room, Madelon threw herself at her feet. With her lovely eyes—none of God's angels had truer—directed heavenwards, and with her hands clasped to her bosom, she wept and lamented, begged and pleaded for help. Mademoiselle de Scudéry controlled herself with effort. "Go—go—" she said, "comfort yourself with the thought that righteous punishment will overtake the murderer for his crimes. May God spare you any share in the guilt of this heinous murder."

"Oh! Now all is lost!" cried Madelon, sinking to the floor.

Mademoiselle de Scudéry called La Martinière to look after the girl, and returned to her own apartments. She was shocked and hurt. She felt herself at odds with all that was human and worldly, told herself that she no longer wished to continue in an existence so full of hellish duplicity and deceit. She reproached Destiny, which, in its irony, had encouraged her for so many years to believe in virtue and truth, only now in her old age to destroy the beautiful myth which had lighted her way through life.

She could hear Madelon's whimpering as La Martinière brought her back to consciousness. "Ah! They have won her over, too. Even her. What am I to do? Oh, my poor, unfortunate Olivier!"

There was something utterly convincing in the girl's grief. Once again Scudéry felt an echo stir in the depths of her mind, a vague presentiment of the unknown, that encouraged the return of her belief in Olivier's innocence. She was torn by doubts and contradictions. "What spirit of hell has engulfed me in this terrible affair which will end by killing me!" she cried out.

Almost as though in response, Baptiste appeared at the door, pale and trembling, to announce Monsieur Desgrais. Ever since the unsavory La Voisin trial, the appearance of Desgrais in any household was the unmistakable forerunner of some sort of criminal action. Hence Baptiste's terror.

Mademoiselle turned to him with a faint smile. "What is the matter with you, Baptiste? Are you afraid that the name Scudéry has been found on La Voisin's lists?"

"Oh, in Heaven's name," replied Baptiste, quaking in every limb, "how can you say such a thing? But Desgrais, that terrible man, is behaving so mysteriously, and is being so insistent—he won't be kept waiting a moment to see you."

"Well, then, Baptiste," said Mademoiselle de Scudéry, "bring him up at once, this man who is such a cause of terror to you. He will arouse no anxiety in me."

"President La Reynie has sent me to you, Mademoiselle," said Desgrais when he entered the room, "with a request which he would hardly hope you could grant, if he did not know your integrity and your courage. The last means of throwing light upon a shocking crime lies in your hands. You have already manifested your interest in an investigation which has puzzled the *Chambre Ardente*, and in fact all of us. Olivier Brusson has been half mad since he saw you. He was beginning to show signs of compliance and a readiness to make a confession, but he now swears again, by all the powers of Heaven, that he is perfectly innocent of the murder of Cardillac. Yet he says he is ready to die the death which he deserves. You will observe, Mademoiselle, that this last remark evidently refers to other crimes which weigh upon his conscience. But all our efforts to get him to admit a single word more are useless. Even the threat of torture has had no result. He begs and pleads for an interview with you. To you, to you alone, he says he will confess all. Will you condescend, Mademoiselle, to hear Brusson's confession?"

"What!" exclaimed Scudéry indignantly. "Do you expect me to become the tool of your bloodthirsty justice? Am I to abuse this unhappy man's confidence to bring him to the scaffold? No, Desgrais. However vicious a criminal Brusson may be, I will never, never deceive him in such an unscrupulous way. I don't want to share any of his secrets. And if I did they would be as sacred to me as a holy confession made to a priest."

"Perhaps," suggested Desgrais with an insinuating smile, "perhaps, Mademoiselle, you will change your mind after you have heard Brusson. Did you not yourself exhort the President to be human? And he is being human, in yielding to Brusson's ridiculous request as a last resort before putting him to the rack, for which he was well ripe some time ago."

Scudéry shuddered involuntarily.

"Of course, dear lady," continued Desgrais, "you will not be asked to enter, again, those dismal rooms which filled you with so much horror and aversion. Olivier shall be brought to you here in your own house like a free man, but at night, under the cover of secrecy. Then, without being interfered with in any way, although of course he will be watched, he may break down and confess everything to you. You personally will have nothing to fear from him—I will answer to you for that with my life. He speaks of you with the most intense respect. He swears that it is only the same evil destiny—that prevented him from seeing you before—which has brought him now so close to death. Moreover, it will depend entirely upon yourself how much you divulge to us of what Brusson confesses to you. What more can we do to persuade you?"

Mademoiselle de Scudéry was lost in thought for a moment. It seemed to her that she must obey the dictates of a higher power which had thus marked her for the solution of some terrible mystery and she felt, too, as though she could no longer extricate herself from the extraordinary entanglements in which she had unwittingly become involved. Suddenly she made up her mind, and spoke with dignity, "God will give me firmness and self-command. Bring Brusson here. I will speak with him."

So, just as on that other occasion when Brusson had brought the casket, there was a knocking at Mademoiselle de Scudéry's door at midnight. Baptiste, forewarned of this nocturnal visit, opened at once. Scudéry could tell from the light footsteps and low murmuring voices that echoed through the corridors that the guards who had brought Brusson were taking up their stations along the passages of the house, and the thought made her shudder.

At length the door of the room was softly opened. Desgrais entered, followed by Olivier Brusson, freed from his fetters, and dressed in his own neat clothing.

"Here is Brusson, Mademoiselle," said Desgrais, bowing respectfully; then he left the room.

Brusson fell upon his knees before Scudéry, and raised his clasped hands to her in entreaty, while copious tears ran down his cheeks.

Mademoiselle de Scudéry turned pale and, looking down at him, found herself incapable of uttering a word. Though his features were now gaunt and hollow from trouble and anguish and pain, an expression of the purest sincerity seemed to illuminate them. The longer Mademoiselle allowed her eyes to rest upon his face, the more forcibly there came back to her the memory of someone she had loved. But who it was she could not clearly bring to mind. All feeling of dread and discomfort left her. She forgot that it was Cardillac's murderer who was kneeling before her. She spoke in the calm, reassuring tones that were characteristic of her: "Well, Brusson, what is it you have to tell me?"

Still kneeling, he replied with a sigh of unutterable sadness: "Can it be, most honored lady, that you have no faint recollection of me?"

Mademoiselle scanned his features again, and replied that she had indeed noticed in his face a resemblance to someone she had once loved, and that it was only because of this resemblance that she had been able to overcome her deep repugnance for the murderer, and calmly hear him out.

Brusson, wounded at these words, rose hastily to his feet and stepped back. "Then you have completely forgotten Anne Guiot?" he said darkly. "It is her son Olivier—the child you used to rock on your knee—who now stands before you."

"Heaven help me!" exclaimed Mademoiselle de Scudéry, covering her face with both hands and sinking back upon the cushions. She had good reason to be startled. Anne Guiot, the daughter of an impoverished Parisian, had been taken into Scudéry's house as a little girl, and had been brought up by Mademoiselle with all the care and faithfulness of a mother. When she grew up, Anne was courted by a modest, good-looking, decent young man, named Claude Brusson. And since he was an extremely clever watchmaker, certain to make a very good living in Paris, and since Anne had also fallen very much in love with him, Scudéry had no scruples about giving her consent to her foster-daughter's marriage. The young people soon set up a household of their own, led a modest and happy life, drawn closer to each other than ever by the birth of a remarkably handsome boy, the image of his lovely mother.

Scudéry had made a complete idol of little Olivier. She would take him away from his mother for hours and days at a time, to pet and indulge him. The boy naturally became quite attached to her, and stayed with her as willingly as with his mother. Three years went by in this way when, thanks to the jealous rivalry of Brusson's fellow-craftsmen, his business steadily deteriorated until one day he could hardly eke out a living. At the same time he became more and more homesick for his beautiful native city of Geneva. And so it happened that the little family moved there, despite Scudéry's opposition and her offers of every possible kind of support. After this, Anne wrote two or three times to her foster-mother, and then nothing more was heard from her. Mademoiselle came to the conclusion that Anne's happy life in Brusson's native city was making her forget the memories of her earlier days. It was now just twenty-three years since Claude Brusson had left Paris, and, together with his wife and child, had gone to Geneva.

"This is terrible!" exclaimed Mademoiselle de Scudéry, when she had recovered a little from her surprise. "Terrible! You are Olivier? My Anne's son?"

"Indeed," replied Olivier, calmly and composedly. "And could you ever have imagined, most gracious lady, that the boy whom you used to fondle with all the tenderness of a mother, the child whom you dandled on your knees, stuffing his mouth with sweets and goodies and calling him by the most affectionate names, would one day, when grown up into a young man, stand before you accused of a desperate and ugly crime? I am not free from reproach and the *Chambre Ardente* may justly bring a charge against me; but by my hope of peace after death, though it be by the executioner's hand, I am innocent of this bloody deed. Cardillac did not meet his death at my hands, nor through any guilty connivance on my part.

"I have had time enough to prepare myself for my interview with you," he went on, "which I regard as the last favor granted me by Heaven, and to achieve the calmness and composure it will require for me to tell you the story of my terrible and unheard-of misfortunes. Prove your compassion for me by hearing me calmly to the end, however much you may be surprised or even horrified by the disclosure of a secret which I am sure you have never for a moment suspected. Oh, if only my poor father had never left Paris! As far back as my recollections of Geneva go I remember how I felt the tears of my distraught parents against my cheeks, and how their complaints of misery, which I did not even understand, reduced me to tears, too. Later I fully grasped and really became conscious of the crushing want and poverty in which my parents lived. My father found himself mistaken in all his hopes. He died bowed to the earth with pain, and broken with trouble, immediately after he had succeeded in placing me as an apprentice to a goldsmith.

"My mother spoke of you often. She would have confessed all her troubles to you, but then she was overcome by that kind of despondency which is born of suffering and want. And even more, a false shame, which preys so often on the feelings of those who have already been wounded in every other way, prevented her from making any gesture or step in your direction. A few months after my father died my mother followed him to the grave."

"Poor Anne! My poor Anne!" murmured Mademoiselle de Scudéry.

"All praise and thanks to the eternal powers above that she has gone on, and will not see her beloved son, branded with shame, fall by the executioner's hand!" Olivier cried out, casting a wild unnatural look upwards.

The police grew uneasy outside; footsteps passed to and fro. "Ha!" said Olivier with a scornful smile, "Desgrais is waking up his henchmen, as though I could run away now! But let me get on with my story. I led a hard life with my master, although I soon got to be the best workman in the shop and at last even surpassed the master himself. One day a foreigner happened to come into our shop to buy some jewelry. When he saw a necklace on which I was working he clapped me on the shoulder in a friendly way and without taking his eyes from the ornament, said: 'Well, well, my young friend, that's quite an exceptional piece of work. In fact, I don't know anyone who could improve on it, unless it be René Cardillac, who is assuredly the greatest goldsmith alive today. You ought to go to him. He would be glad to take you into his service, for no other craftsman but you could assist him in his creative work, and on the other hand no other master could still teach you anything!'

"The stranger's words took deep root in my mind. I no longer enjoyed a moment's peace in Geneva. A force too strong to resist was drawing me away. At last I contrived to free myself of my obligations to my master. I came to Paris. René Cardillac gave me a cold and brusque reception. But I refused to give up. He had to give me some work to do no matter how insignificant it might be. Finally he gave me a small ring to finish. When I brought it back, he fixed his glittering eyes upon me as if he wanted to examine the innermost depths of my being. Then he said, 'You are a good clever journeyman. You may come to live with me and help me in my workshop. I shall pay you well and you will be quite satisfied with me.'

"Cardillac kept his word. I had spent several weeks with him before I saw Madelon. She was staying at the time, if I am not mistaken, in the country, with relatives of her father. But at last she came home. Oh, eternal Power of Heaven! What did I not feel when I saw her sweet, angelic face? Did any man ever love as I? And now!—Oh, Madelon!"

Olivier was too distressed to go on. Shielding his face with his hands, he began to sob violently. At last he overcame the outburst of wild anguish that shook him, and he went on with his story:

"Madelon regarded me with friendliness. Her visits to the workshop became and more frequent. I was ecstatic when I realized that she was in love with me. Closely as her father watched us, many a stolen handclasp served to remind us of our secret understanding, and Cardillac never seemed to notice anything. I intended first to win his favor, and then if I became a master goldsmith, to ask his permission to marry Madelon. One morning just as I was about to begin work, Cardillac came up to me, his face lowering with anger and contempt. 'I have no further use for your work,' he began. 'Take yourself out of this house this moment and never let me see your face again. I need not tell you why I will not put up with you here any longer. As for you, you unhappy beggar, the sweet fruit at which you are reaching hangs high out of your grasp.'

"I wanted to explain things to him, but he seized me with all his strength and threw me out of the door, so that I fell down and badly hurt my head and arm. I left the house torn with pain and resentment, and wandered the streets. Finally I looked up a good-natured acquaintance who lived in a remote corner of the Faubourg Saint-Martin, and he shared his garret with me.

"But I could find no peace. Every night I used to prowl about near Cardillac's house, deluding myself with the fancy that Madelon would hear my sighs and complaints and that, perhaps, she would find a way to speak to me from her window without being overheard. All sorts of daring plans were spinning about in my brain and I hoped to persuade her to carry one of them out.

"Now, joining Cardillac's house in the Rue Nicaise, there is a high wall, with niches and old crumbling stone figures standing in them. One night I was standing close beside one of these statues and looking up at those windows of the house which open on a courtyard enclosed in part by the wall. Suddenly I noticed a light in Cardillac's workshop. It was midnight. I had never known him to stay up that late. He was always on his way to bed by the stroke of nine. My heart throbbed with a curious kind of excitement and anticipation. I had the feeling that something was about to happen which would give me the opportunity I had been waiting for. But the next moment the light went out again. I pressed myself close up against the stone figure, into the niche, but I sprang back startled. I had felt another pressure returning mine, as if the statue had come to life. In the dim glimmer of the night I now became aware that the stone figure was slowly revolving, and from behind it a dark form slipped out and crept away down the street with light, furtive foot-steps. I sprang back to the statue. It stood there just as before, fixed to the wall. Without stopping to think, almost as if impelled by some inward force, I stole after the retreating figure. Just beside a statue of the Virgin he turned round. The light of the lamp that burned brightly before the statue fell full upon his face. It was Cardillac! An indescribable feeling of apprehension—an unearthly dread—came over me. Like someone under the power of magic, I felt myself drawn on and on in pursuit of this spectre wanderer of the night.

"Finally Cardillac disappeared into the deep shadow of a side street. By a sort of low involuntary cough, which, however, I knew well, I gathered that he was lurking in the doorway of a house. 'What is the meaning of all this? What can he be up to?' I asked myself in amazement, as I took cover in the entry of a house near by. It was not long before a man with fluttering plumes and jingling spurs came along, singing aloud and trilling away. Like a tiger leaping upon his prey, Cardillac burst out of his hiding place and threw himself upon the man, who fell to the ground almost at once, gasping in the agonies of death. I cried out in horror and rushed up to them. The man was stretched out on the ground and Cardillac was stooping over him.

" 'Master Cardillac, what are you doing?' I shouted. 'Cursed fool!' growled Cardillac and he ran past me with lightning speed. In a moment he had disappeared from sight.

"I went up to the man who had been stabbed. I knelt down beside him. Perhaps, I thought, he may still be saved. But there was no trace of life left.

"In my mortal fright I was hardly aware that the Maréchaussée had surrounded me. 'What? Still another poor soul struck down by those devils! Young man! What are you doing here? Are you one of the band? . . . Take him away!' Then they seized me. I was scarcely able to stammer out that I was incapable of such a hideous crime, and that they might therefore let me go my way in peace. Then one of them turned his lamp upon my face and began to laugh: 'Why, this is Olivier Brusson, the journeyman, who works for our worthy Master René Cardillac. Yes, he would make a fine murderer, indeed! And isn't it just like a murderer to stop and lament over his victim's corpse until someone comes along to arrest him. Well, what happened, young man? Speak up and don't be afraid!' 'A man jumped out of the shadows, struck him down,' I said, 'and then when I called out to him, ran away as quick as lightning. I only wanted to see if there was any chance of saving the wounded man.' 'None, my son,' said one of the gendarmes who had raised the corpse to a sitting position, 'he has been stabbed as usual right through the heart.' 'The Devil!' said another. 'We have come too late again, just as we did yesterday.' And then they went their way, taking the body with them.

"What my feelings were I cannot attempt to describe. I pinched myself to make sure that I was not under the spell of some perverse dream. I fancied I would soon wake up and be amazed at my own mad delusions.

Cardillac, the father of my Madelon, an obsessed murderer! My knees weakened under me. I sank down upon the stone steps leading to a house. It was turning dawn, the light was growing clearer and stronger, and with it reality was returning to the world. I saw the officer's hat with its drooping plumes lying before me on the pavement. Once again I saw Cardillac commit his bloody crime, almost on the spot where I was still sitting. I ran off, horrified.

"I returned to my garret. I would try to make sense out of the confusion and ugly thoughts that filled my mind. But I had hardly sat down when the door opened, and René Cardillac came in. 'What in the name of God do you want?' I cried out on seeing him. He ignored my excitement and came up to me, smiling with a calmness and an air of indulgence which only increased my deep feeling of abhorrence. He pulled up a rickety old stool to the straw mattress where I was resting, unable to rise.

" 'Well, Olivier,' he began, 'how is the world treating you, my poor boy? I admit it was stupid and rash of me to turn you out of my house. I miss you at every step and turn. I have a piece of work on hand just now which I cannot finish without your help. How would it be if you came back to my shop? Have you nothing to say? Yes, I know I have treated you badly. I was angry with you because of your love-making with my daughter—I make no bones about it. But since then I have considered the whole matter more soberly, and come to the conclusion that I could not hope for a better son-in-law than someone with your virtues, your skill and industry. So come back home with me, and see if Madelon will still have you.'

"Cardillac's words shocked me to the heart. I was appalled at his utter shamelessness. I could not bring myself to make a reply. 'I see you hesitate?' he continued in a sharper tone, piercing me through with his glittering eyes. 'Perhaps you can't come right now—perhaps you intend to pay a visit to Desgrais or to get an interview with Argenson or La Reynie. But you'd better take care, my boy, that the claws which you would unsheathe on another's destruction don't seize upon you yourself and tear you to pieces!'

"It was then that I gave way to my indignation. 'Let those who are conscious of having committed crimes'—I cried, 'let them jump at the names you have mentioned. As for me, I have no reason to do so—I have no business with the police.'

" 'Properly spoken,' Cardillac went on. 'Properly spoken, Olivier. And it does you honor to work with me. I am, after all, the most famous master of my time, highly esteemed everywhere for my uprightness and honesty, so that any wicked calumny against me would simply recoil upon the head of its perpetrator. And as far as Madelon is concerned, I must confess that it is she alone to whom you owe this new compliance on my part. She loves you with an intensity that I should not have thought so delicate a child capable of. The moment you had gone she threw herself at my feet, clasped my knees, and, with endless tears and sobs, declared that she could not live without you. At first, I thought it was only the fancy of a young, lovesick girl who imagines she will die of anguish the moment some whey-faced boy gives her a friendly look. But my Madelon did really become ill and begin to pine away, and when I tried to talk her out of it, she would do nothing but repeat your name over and over again. What was a poor father to do to keep his child from dying away in despair? Last night I told her I would consent to everything and would come and fetch you back today. By morning she was blooming like a rose. She is waiting for you this very moment with all the longing and impatience of love.'

"May God in Heaven forgive me! I myself don't know exactly how it came about, but I suddenly found myself in Cardillac's house with Madelon crying aloud with joy, throwing her arms round my neck, pressing me close to her bosom, murmuring over and over again, 'My Olivier! My love! My husband!' till in a perfect delirium of delight I swore by the Virgin and all the saints that I would never, never leave her."

Olivier paused to collect himself after this agitating recollection, and Mademoiselle de Scudéry finally broke in: "It is too incredible! A man whom I have always looked upon as a model of virtue and integrity! So René Cardillac belongs to that band of murderers which has turned our beloved Paris into a charnel house!"

"What do you mean by *band*, Mademoiselle?" asked Olivier. "There never has been a band. It was always Cardillac who, singlehanded and with the energy of a demon, sought out and tracked down his victims all over Paris. And it was because he acted alone that he was able to carry on his operations with so much security. But let me go on with my story.

"The uncomfortable situation in which I now found myself at my master's may be easily imagined. The step was taken; I could not go back. At moments I felt as though I were really Cardillac's accomplice in crime. The only thing that could make me forget my anguish and inner torment was Madelon's love, and it was only in her company that I succeeded in suppressing all external signs of the nameless trouble and anxiety I had in my heart. When I was working with the old man in the shop, I could never look him in the face. I was so filled with repugnance that I was hardly able to utter a word in the presence of this terrible man who, at home, fulfilled all the duties of a faithful and tender father, and passed for a good citizen, while the night veiled his barbarous iniquities. Madelon, dutiful, pure, trusting as an angel, clung to him with idolatrous affection. The thought often struck me like a dagger to the heart that, if justice should one day expose this masquerade, Madelon, taken in by all the hellish art of Satan, would assuredly die in the wildest agonies of despair. This alone was enough to seal my lips, even though it might lead me to the scaffold. Although I had picked up a good deal of information from the Maréchaussée, the motive for Cardillac's atrocities still remained a riddle to me. But I had not long to wait for the solution.

"One day I came down to the shop and found Cardillac sombre and thoroughly preoccupied with his work, instead of in the usual ribald and sardonic humor which so much intensified my horror of him. Suddenly he threw aside the ornament he was working at, so that the pearls and stones rolled across the floor. He got up from the table and said: 'Olivier, things can't go on in this way any longer. I find our relationship more unbearable each day. Chance has played into your hands and brought you the knowledge of a secret which has baffled the imagination and cunning of Desgrais and all his henchmen. You have seen me at my midnight work, to which I am goaded by a destiny so evil that it cannot be opposed. Unfortunately, it was your evil destiny that caused you to follow me, that cloaked you in impenetrability, that lightened your footsteps until you walked as noiselessly as the smallest creature of the woods, so that I, who see through the blackest night with the eyes of a tiger and hear the faintest buzzing of an insect, did not notice you. Your evil destiny has brought you to me, my assistant. You know, of course, that you are in no position to inform on me. And I shall tell you what you have become involved in.'

"I wanted to cry out in protest but the words choked in my throat.

"Cardillac sat down again on his bench, drying the perspiration from his brow. He appeared to be deeply agitated by his recollections of the past, and to have difficulty in preserving his composure. At length he began.

" 'Men who have studied the subject have a great deal to say about the extraordinary effect of certain experiences upon pregnant women, and the strange influence which such involuntary impressions of the outside world have upon the unborn child. I was told a remarkable story about my mother. About eight months before I was born, my mother accompanied several of her friends to a splendid court spectacle in the Trianon. Almost from the moment she got there, she became fascinated by a certain cavalier in a Spanish costume, who wore a flashing jeweled chain round his neck, and she could not keep her eyes off it. Her whole being was concentrated into the desire to possess the glittering stones, which seemed to her to be of almost supernatural beauty and power. The cavalier was none other than a man who had paid marked attention to my mother several years before her marriage, and whom she had repulsed, not without contempt.

" 'My mother recognized him immediately. But now in the reflected light of the brilliant jewels he seemed to her transformed into a member of some superior race—the paragon of all that was beautiful and desirable. He was aware of my mother's glances and intense yearning, and realized that now his advances were more likely to meet with success than with the sort of rebuff he had once received. He contrived to approach her, and to draw her away from her friends to a secluded spot. There he crushed her in embraces to which she yielded willingly enough as long as she could touch the glittering chain. But then, suddenly, the cavalier reeled backwards and, dragging my mother down with him, fell to the ground. Whatever the cause—perhaps he had had a stroke, perhaps it was something else—no matter, the man was dead. All my mother's frantic efforts to release herself from the corpse's stiffened embrace were futile. His glazed eyes, their vision forever extinguished, were fixed upon her, and she lay there, on the ground, clutched in the dance of death by her staring cavalier. Finally her piercing cries for help reached the ears of some merrymakers in the distance. They ran up to her and succeeded in freeing her from the arms of her ghostly lover.

" 'The horror of the whole experience brought on a serious illness. My mother's life and mine were both despaired of. But she recovered, and her *accouchement* was easier than anyone had dared hope. Perhaps because all the terror of that dreadful incident had left its mark upon me. My evil star had risen, and had sent down on me a light that would kindle in me one of the strangest and most devouring of passions. Even in my earliest childhood I would brood and dream of sparkling diamonds and ornaments of gold. It was taken for the usual childish whimsicality. But the desire asserted itself in other ways. When I was a boy I began to steal all the gold and jewelry I could lay my hands on, and like the most experienced connoisseur I could by instinct tell false jewelry from the real. Only the latter attracted me. I would leave anything else lying where I found it. My native talent, however, finally yielded to the gruesome punishment I received at my father's hands.

" 'I set about learning the trade of a goldsmith just to be able constantly to handle gold and precious stones. I worked passionately and relentlessly, until I became the leading master of the craft.

" 'Now began a period when this inborn tendency of mine, so long repressed, burst forth with violence and grew most rapidly, imbibing nourishment from everything about it. As soon as I had completed and delivered a piece of jewelry, I would be seized by a restlessness and discontent that robbed me of sleep and health and even the daily courage to face life. Day and night, the person for whom I had done the work would appear before my eyes like a spectre, decked out in my jewelry, and I would hear a voice whisper in my ear: "It really belongs to you—it's really yours. Take it then! What good are diamonds to the dead?" It was then I began seriously to take up thieving. I had access to the houses of the great, and lost no time in turning every opportunity to good account. No lock could hold out against my touch and skill. Soon every brooch, every necklace I had made was back in my own hands again. But after a time the feeling of unrest returned. That unearthly voice continued to make itself heard, mocking me, ringing in my ears: "Ha! The dead are wearing your jewelry!" And I began to conceive an unspeakable hatred of those for whom I turned out my little masterpieces. Yes, deep in my heart they awakened an impulse to murder, at which I myself trembled with apprehension.

" 'That was about the time I bought this house. I had just struck a bargain with the owner. We were sitting in this very room having a glass of wine together to celebrate settling the deal. Night had come. I got up to go and the former owner said: "Wait a moment, Master René, before you leave, I must show you the secret of the place." He unlocked that cupboard built into the wall there, pushed aside the panels at the back, and stepped into a little compartment where I could see him stooping down to open a trap door. I followed him down a flight of steep, narrow steps until we came to a postern, which he unlocked to let us out into the courtyard. Then the old gentleman stepped up to the wall and pressed an iron knob which projected slightly from it. Immediately a section of the wall swung round, so that a man could easily slip through the opening and out into the street. I will show you the neat little contraption some day, Olivier. No doubt it was installed by the inhabitants of the monastery which formerly stood on this site, in order to provide the sly old rogues with a means of slipping secretly in and out. It is a piece of wood, plastered and whitewashed on the outside only. Set in it, on the street side, is a statue, also of wood, but colored exactly to resemble stone, and the whole affair, statue and all, moves on concealed hinges. Sinister thoughts filled my mind when I saw this contrivance, as though it had been built in anticipation of deeds which as yet remained unknown to myself.

" 'I had just finished making a valuable ornament for a courtier, and knew that he intended it for a certain ballet dancer. The old torture preyed upon me again; the spectre dogged my footsteps; the whispering fiend was at my ear. I moved into my new house. It changed nothing. I tossed sleeplessly on my bed, bathed in perspiration. In my imagination I could see the man creeping through the darkness to his dancer with my jewels. Stung to madness, I leap out of bed, throw on a mantle, go down the secret stairway and out through the wall and into the Rue Nicaise. Eventually he comes along. I throw myself upon him. He screams out, but I have seized him fast from behind, and driven my dagger straight into his heart. The ornament is mine.

" 'Once it was over I experienced a peace, a satisfaction in my soul, which I had never before known. The spectre had vanished; the voice of the fiend was still. Now I knew what my evil destiny required of me. I had the choice of yielding to it or perishing. And now you too understand the secret of my whole existence, Olivier. But do not think, because I am driven on by something beyond help and control, that therefore I have entirely lost all sense of pity and compassion. You know how I struggle against giving up a finished piece of work, and how many people there are for whom I refuse to work at all, in order to avoid bringing about their death. And it has also happened that when I felt my spectre would have to be exorcised on the following day by blood, I have satisfied it with a stout blow of the fist the same day, which stretched on the ground the owner of my jewel, and delivered the jewel itself into my hand.'

"When he finished telling me all this, Cardillac led me into his secret vault and granted me a sight of his jewel-cabinet. The King himself has not one finer. A small tag was attached to each article, stating accurately for whom it was made, when it was recovered, and whether by theft or assault and murder. 'On your wedding-day, Olivier,' Cardillac said in a hollow voice, 'you will have to swear on the crucifix that after I am dead you will reduce all this treasure to dust, through means which I shall at the right time disclose to you. I will not permit any human creature, and least of all Madelon or you, to come into possession of this blood-bought hoard.'

"Entangled in this labyrinth of crime, and with my heart torn by love and abhorrence, by rapture and horror, I was not unlike a man who has been damned, beckoned on one side by a smiling angel while, on the other, Satan holds him fast in his burning talons, until even the angel's smiles of love, in which are reflected the highest bliss of heaven, become transformed into the most agonizing of his miseries. I thought of running away—even of suicide—but there was Madelon! Blame me, reproach me, if you will, Mademoiselle, for my weakness, for not exerting my will to conquer a passion that was fettering me to crime. But am I not about to atone for my errors by a death of shame?

"One day Cardillac came home in uncommonly good spirits. He caressed Madelon and greeted me with the friendliest smile. At dinner he produced a bottle of excellent vintage, usually reserved for high holidays and festivals, and sang and celebrated at the table. When Madelon had left us I rose to return to the workshop. 'Sit still, lad,' said Cardillac; 'we'll not work any more today. Let us drink another glass together to the health of the most worthy and most excellent lady in Paris.' After I had joined glasses with him and had drained mine to the bottom, he went on, 'Tell me, Olivier, how you like these verses:

> " 'Un amant qui craint les voleurs
> N'est point digne d'amour.'

"Then he went on to describe the encounter between you and the King in Madame de Maintenon's salon, adding that he had always honored you above any other human being. You were gifted, he said, with virtues so invincible that they caused his evil star to dim and lose its lustre, and that if you were to wear the handsomest ornament he ever made you could never provoke his sinister and murderous instincts.

" 'This is what I have made my mind up to do, Olivier,' he said. 'A long time ago I received an order and the stones for a necklace and a pair of bracelets for Princess Henrietta of England. The work turned out better than anything I had ever done before. But my heart was torn at the thought of parting with the ornaments, which had become my favorite jewels in the world. You have heard of the Princess' unfortunate death by poisoning. I have kept the jewels ever since, and now I intend to send them to Mademoiselle de Scudéry in the name of the persecuted band as a mark of my respect and gratitude. Not only will Mademoiselle receive a princely trophy for her couplet, but I shall also have the pleasure of making a laughing-stock of Desgrais and his henchmen. I want you to take the jewels to her.'

"The moment Cardillac mentioned your name, Mademoiselle, it was as though a dark veil had been torn from my memory, revealing the fair, bright picture of my early childhood. I felt miraculously comforted, my depression faded, and a ray of new hope entered my soul.

"Cardillac must have noticed the effect his words had upon me and interpreted it in his own way. 'You seem to enjoy my little plan,' he said. 'I am acting, you know, according to the dictates of a deep inner self, utterly different from the voice that cries out for blood like some ravenous beast of prey. Sometimes I get into strange moods. I become filled with anxiety, with the fear of something vague but terrible, and I experience a dread which is like the intimation of some other world. Then I feel as if the crimes I commit as the blind instrument of my ill-starred birth may be charged upon my immortal soul, which has no share in them. It was during one of those moods that I vowed to make a crown of diamonds for the Holy Virgin in Saint Eustache's Church. But every time I thought seriously of beginning the work, I was overwhelmed by that same indescribable sense of anxiety, so that after a time I gave up the idea altogether. Now I feel that in sending Mademoiselle de Scudéry the most beautiful jewelry I have ever made, I am humbly offering a sacrifice at the altar of virtue and piety.'

"Cardillac, who was intimately acquainted with your habits and ways of life, Mademoiselle, gave me instructions regarding the manner and the hour I was to deliver the ornaments into your hands. I was overjoyed, for Heaven itself was now pointing out to me, even through such an infamous tool as Cardillac, a way out of this hell in which I, a sinner and outcast, was slowly wasting away. Those were my thoughts. Entirely contrary to Cardillac's intentions, I resolved to force myself into your presence. I intended to reveal myself as Anne Brusson's son, as your one-time favorite, and to throw myself at your feet and confess all—all. I knew that you would have been so touched by the endless misery with which any disclosure would have threatened poor Madelon that you would have respected my secret. And I knew that your keen intellect would have devised some means of putting a stop to Cardillac's devouring wickedness without making such an exposure. Do not ask me what means you would have found. I do not know. But that you would save Madelon and me, I firmly believed, as firmly as I believe in the comfort and help of the Holy Virgin.

"You know how my plan was frustrated that night, Mademoiselle. I still cherished the hope of being more successful another time. Then, all at once, Cardillac suddenly lost every sign of good humor. He crept about wrapped in gloom, his eyes staring vacantly into space; he muttered unintelligibly to himself, gesticulated with his hands, as if to ward off some invisible enemy, and gave every indication of being tormented by evil thoughts. He had been behaving this way for a whole morning. Finally he sat down to his work-table, jumped up again with annoyance, looked out of the window, and said solemnly and mournfully, 'I wish after all that Henrietta of England had worn my jewels!'

"These words struck terror to my heart. Now I knew that his warped mind was again enthralled by that abominable spirit of murder, and that the voice of the fiend was once more ringing in his ears. I saw your life was threatened by this insatiable demon of murder. If Cardillac only could have his jewels in his hands again, you would be saved.

"The danger increased with every moment. It was then I met you on the Pont-Neuf, forced my way to your carriage, and threw you that note, imploring you at once to restore the ornaments to Cardillac's possession. You did not come. My anxiety turned to desperation when on the following day Cardillac talked about nothing but the magnificent jewels he had seen dangling before his eyes all through the night. I could only interpret this as referring to your jewelry, and it was clear to me that he was brooding over some fresh project for murder which he assuredly intended to carry out that very night. I must save you, even at the cost of Cardillac's own life.

"As soon as he had locked himself up in his room after evening prayers, as was his custom, I climbed out of a window into the courtyard, slipped through the opening in the wall, and took up my station not far off, hidden in the deep shadow. I had not long to wait before Cardillac came out and stole softly up the street. I followed him. He turned in the direction of the Rue Saint-Honoré. My heart quaked. Then, suddenly, I lost sight of him. I decided to post myself at the door of your house. And then just as on that other occasion when chance made me a witness to Cardillac's bloody act, an officer came walking by without seeing me, singing and humming to himself. At almost the same instant a dark figure leapt forward and attacked him. It was Cardillac, of course. This time I would prevent the murder. I reached the spot in two or three bounds. But it was not the officer, it was Cardillac who lay on the ground mortally wounded. The officer dropped his dagger, and drawing his sword prepared himself for me, imagining that I was the murderer's accomplice. But when he saw that I was only concerned with examining the wounded man, and did not trouble myself about him, he hurried away.

"Cardillac was still alive. After taking the officer's dagger for safekeeping, I loaded my master onto my shoulders, with difficulty, and carried him to the house and into the workshop by way of the concealed stairs. The rest you know. You see, my gracious lady, that my only crime consists in the fact that I did not betray Madelon's father to the police, and so put an end to his enormities. I am innocent of any act of violence. No torture shall extort from me a confession of Cardillac's crimes. I will not spite the Eternal Power, which has veiled the father's hideous bloodguiltiness from the eyes of the virtuous daughter, or be instrumental in exposing all the misery of the past, which would now have a far more disastrous effect upon her; nor do I wish to aid worldly vengeance in rooting up the dead man from the earth which covers him, just to enable the hangman to brand already moldering bones with the mark of shame. No, my beloved will weep for me as one who has died innocently, and time will soften her sorrow. But her grief would be endless if she knew that her fond father had performed the work of Hell."

Olivier was silent, but now he yielded to his emotion, sinking to his knees at Mademoiselle de Scudéry's feet. "And now you are convinced of my innocence—oh, surely you must be!" he demanded with tears in his eyes. "Have pity on me and tell me how Madelon is taking it." Mademoiselle summoned La Martinière, and a few moments later Madelon flew into Olivier's arms. "Now I know everything has turned out all right, or you wouldn't be here. I knew it, I knew Mademoiselle would save you!" Madelon repeated the words over and over again, and Olivier forgot his fate and all that threatened him, and for the moment he was free and happy. The two poured out their troubles in the most touching way, each describing a grief that had been felt only over the other's suffering. Then they embraced again, and wept with joy at having met once more.

If Mademoiselle de Scudéry had not already been certain of Olivier's innocence she would assuredly have been convinced of it now, as she sat and watched these two who, in the happiness of the deep love they shared, forgot the world and their misfortunes and all their nameless sufferings.

"No," she said to herself, "it is only a pure heart which is capable of such happy obliviousness."

The bright rays of the dawn were streaming in through the window. Desgrais knocked softly at the door of the room, and reminded them that it was time to take Olivier Brusson away, since this could not be done later without attracting attention. The lovers were obliged to separate.

The gloomy forebodings which had filled Mademoiselle de Scudéry's mind at Olivier's first entrance into the house had now taken on reality and the most frightening shape. She saw the son of her dear Anne innocently involved in such a tangle of circumstances that there seemed no conceivable means of saving him from a death of disgrace. She respected the young man for his heroic spirit in preferring to die falsely accused rather than divulge a secret that would be the death of his Madelon. In the whole realm of possibility she could find no means whatever of snatching this unfortunate young man from the hands of the terrible tribunal. And yet she had definitely made up her mind that she must not hesitate at any sacrifice to avert this injustice which would cry out to Heaven, and which was on the point of being committed. She racked her brain with all kinds of schemes and plans, some of which bordered upon pure fantasy, but she had to reject all of them almost as quickly as they occurred to her. Meanwhile hope grew fainter and fainter, until she was at the point of despair. But Madelon's unquestioning childlike confidence, the radiant assurance with which she spoke of her lover, who soon, absolved of all guilt, would clasp her in his arms as his bride, touched the old lady deeply, and communicated new hope and courage to her.

At length, in order to do something, Mademoiselle de Scudéry wrote a long letter to La Reynie, in which she informed him that Olivier Brusson had proved to her in the most convincing manner his complete innocence of Cardillac's death, and that it was only his heroic resolve to carry with him to the grave a secret, the revelation of which would bring disaster upon the virtuous and innocent, that prevented his making a revelation to the court which would undoubtedly free him, not only from the fearful suspicion of having murdered Cardillac, but also of having belonged to the infamous band of assassins. Scudéry had called upon all the burning zeal, all the spirited eloquence at her command to soften La Reynie's hard heart. La Reynie replied in a few hours that he was heartily pleased to learn that Olivier Brusson had justified himself so completely in the eyes of his noble and worthy protectress. As for Olivier's heroic resolve to carry with him into the grave a secret that had an important bearing upon the case, he was sorry to say that the Chambre Ardente could not respect this kind of heroism, but, on the contrary, would be compelled to adopt the strongest means to break it. At the end of three days he hoped to be in possession of this extraordinary secret, which it might be presumed would bring astounding things to light.

Scudéry knew only too well by what means this awful man intended to break Brusson's spirit. It was clear now that Olivier would be subjected to torture. Scudéry decided, finally, since her personal influence seemed to carry little weight, that the advice of a lawyer might be useful, if only to effect a postponement of the torture. The most famous *avocat* in Paris at that time was Pierre Arnaud d'Andilly; and his profound knowledge and liberal mind were only to be compared to his integrity and his sterling honesty. Scudéry turned, therefore, to him, telling him as much as she could, without violating Brusson's secret. She expected Andilly to take up the cause of the innocent man with enthusiasm but her hopes were bitterly disappointed. Andilly listened calmly to all she had to say, and then replied in Boileau's words, smiling as he did so, *"Le vrai peut quelque fois n'être pas vraisemblable."* He pointed out to Scudéry that there were significant grounds for suspicion against Brusson, that La Reynie's proceedings could neither be called cruel nor impatient, but rather were strictly in accordance with the law, and that he could not act otherwise without betraying his duties as a judge. He (Andilly) did not see any way of saving Brusson from torture, even by the cleverest defense. Brusson alone could avert this, either by an honest confession or, short of that, by a detailed statement of all the circumstances attending Cardillac's murder, which might perhaps furnish grounds for reopening the investigation.

"Then I will throw myself at the King's feet and beg for mercy," said Scudéry, her voice half choked with tears.

"For Heaven's sake!" exclaimed Andilly, "don't do that, Mademoiselle. Don't do it. That is your last resource, for if it fails everything is lost forever. The King will never pardon a criminal of this type. He would bring down upon himself the bitterest reproaches of the people, whose lives have been endangered. Possibly Brusson, either by revealing his secret or by some other means, may find a way of disproving the suspicions against him. Then is the time to appeal to the King for mercy, for he will not inquire what has been proved before the court, but be guided by his own convictions."

Scudéry felt obliged to defer to the superior experience and judgment of a man in Andilly's position.

Late one evening she was sitting in her own room in the deepest despair, wondering what in Heaven's name she could do to save the unlucky Brusson, when La Martinière came in to announce that Count de Miossens, Colonel of the King's Guards, was below and desired most urgently to speak to Mademoiselle.

"Forgive me, Mademoiselle," said Miossens, bowing with soldierly grace, "forgive me for intruding upon you at such a late hour. We soldiers are not always free to come and go, and besides, I know two words that will assure me of a welcome. Olivier Brusson! It is on his account that I have come."

Scudéry became visibly excited. "Olivier Brusson?" she called out. "What connection have you with that most unhappy of mortals?"

"I knew," Miossens went on with a smile, "that your protégé's name would be my password to your house. The whole world is convinced of Brusson's guilt. But you, I know, cling to another opinion, which is based only on the protestations of the accused, as they say. With me, however, it is different. Nobody can have better proof that Brusson is innocent of Cardillac's death than I."

"Please go on. Let me hear everything you have to say!" Scudéry urged, while a new light came into her eyes. Miossens continued, speaking with emphasis:

"It was I," Miossens said emphatically, "I who stabbed the old goldsmith not far from your house here in the Rue Saint-Honoré! And I swear to you, Mademoiselle, that I am proud of it. Cardillac was the most corrupt and hypocritical of criminals, murdering and plundering by night and escaping all traps. Somehow, I can't say how, my suspicions were first aroused against him when he brought me a jewel I had ordered, and appeared so visibly disturbed on giving it to me. Then he tried to find out exactly for whom the gift was intended and questioned my valet, not without cunning, as to when I was in the habit of visiting a certain lady. I had long before noticed that all those who fell victim to this abominable epidemic of murder and robbery bore the same fatal wound. I felt certain that the murderer depended entirely on inflicting death with a single thrust of his dagger. If his first blow failed, he would have to meet his victim on equal terms. This led me to adopt a precaution which is so simple that I cannot understand why it did not occur to others long ago as a means of self-protection. I wore a light shirt of mail under my coat. Cardillac attacked me from behind. He laid hold of me with the strength of a giant, but his dagger thrust glanced off the iron. That same moment I tore myself free from his grasp, and plunged my dagger, which I held in readiness, into his heart."

"And you have remained silent all this time?" asked Mademoiselle de Scudéry. "You did not inform the tribunal of what you had done?"

"Permit me to observe, Mademoiselle, that such a declaration might have ruined my career, and would, in any case, have involved me in a thoroughly disagreeable trial. Would La Reynie, who ferrets out crime everywhere, have believed my unsupported word if I had accused honest Cardillac, the pattern of piety and virtue, of an attempted murder? What if the sword of justice had turned its point against me?"

"That would not be possible," said Scudéry. "Your birth—your rank—"

"Oh," interrupted Miossens, "remember Marshal de Luxembourg, whose whim to have his horoscope cast by Le Sage brought him under the suspicion of being a poisoner, and eventually into the Bastille. No! by Saint Denis! Not an hour of my freedom, not even the tip of my ear, will I put at the mercy of that madman La Reynie, who would like only too well to have his knife at all of our throats."

"But do you know you are bringing innocent Brusson to the scaffold?" Scudéry demanded.

"Innocent?" replied Miossens. "Do you call the accomplice of a man like Cardillac innocent, Mademoiselle? He who helped him in all his deeds? Who has deserved death a hundred times? No, indeed! He will meet his just end on the scaffold. I have only disclosed to you, gracious lady, the details of this affair so that, without involving me with the *Chambre Ardente*, you might find some way of using my secret in your protégé's behalf."

Scudéry was pleased at finding her judgment of Brusson's innocence so decisively confirmed. She did not hesitate to tell the Count the whole story, since he already knew of Cardillac's guilt, and to persuade him to go with her to see Andilly. Everything would be revealed to the latter under seal of professional secrecy, and he would advise them what was to be done.

After Scudéry had told the whole story to Andilly in the most minute detail, he asked seemingly insignificant questions. He particularly asked whether Count de Miossens was perfectly convinced that it was Cardillac who had attacked him, and whether he would be able to identify Olivier Brusson as the man who had carried away the corpse. "Not only did I recognize Cardillac in the bright moonlight," Miossens replied, "but I have also seen in La Reynie's possession the dagger with which Cardillac was stabbed. It is mine, easily recognizable by the decorations on the hilt. I was standing only a few paces away from the young man and could distinctly see his features. His hat had fallen off. I should have no difficulty in recognizing him again."

Andilly sat for some moments staring thoughtfully in silence. Then he said: "Brusson cannot possibly be saved from the hands of justice in any ordinary way. Out of consideration for Madelon he refuses to accuse Cardillac of being a murderer and thief. But even if he should make these accusations, even if he succeeded in proving them by revealing the secret staircase and the hoard of stolen jewelry, he would still be liable to death as a partner in Cardillac's guilt. And the state of the case would not be altered even if Count de Miossens were to admit to the judges the actual truth of his encounter with Cardillac. All we can try to work for is delay. Count de Miossens will go to the *Conciergerie*, have Olivier Brusson brought to him, and identify him as the man who carried Cardillac's body away. Then he will go straight to La Reynie and say: 'I saw a man stabbed in the Rue Saint-Honoré. I had almost reached him when another man sprang out of the darkness near by, bent down over the body, and, apparently, finding some signs of life in it, lifted it up on his shoulders and carried it off. I have recognized this second man as Olivier Brusson.' This evidence will lead to another hearing, for it will be necessary to confront Brusson with the Count de Miossens. Good enough! The torture will be delayed, and further inquiries will be instituted. That will be the proper time to appeal to the King. It will be left to your ingenuity, Mademoiselle, to do this in the most adroit way. In my opinion it would be best to disclose the whole secret to the King. Brusson's confession will be corroborated by the statement of Count de Miossens. And it may, perhaps, be further substantiated by secret investigations of Cardillac's house. All this will not afford grounds for a verdict of acquittal so far as the court is concerned, but it might affect the King's decision, since it is his prerogative to bestow mercy where the judge can only condemn."

Count de Miossens followed Andilly's advice implicitly, and the result was exactly what the latter had foreseen.

But now it was a question of getting at the King. This was the most difficult aspect of the plan, since Louis believed Brusson to be the desperate criminal who had so long kept all of Paris in a state of fear and anxiety, and consequently he had conceived such an animus against him that at the slightest allusion to the notorious case he would burst into a violent fit of passion. Madame de Maintenon, faithful to her principle of never speaking to the King on any subject that was displeasing to him, refused to take any part in the affair, and so Brusson's fate was left entirely in Scudéry's hands. After long consideration she hit upon a plan which she lost no time in carrying out.

She dressed herself in a costume of heavy black silk, adorned herself with Cardillac's valuable necklace and bracelets, covered her head with a black veil, and presented herself in Madame de Maintenon's apartments at an hour when she knew the King would be there. This stately mourning invested the venerable lady with a majesty which could not fail to evoke respect, even in the laughing and frivolous crowd of idlers who customarily collected in the anterooms of the palace. All dutifully made way for her, and when she entered the salon, the King himself, full of surprise, came to meet her. As his eyes caught the glitter of diamonds in her necklace and bracelets, he exclaimed: "By Heaven, that's Cardillac's jewelry!" Then, turning to Maintenon, he added with a playful smile: "See, Madame la Marquise, how our fair bride mourns her lost bridegroom!"

"But, Your Majesty," Scudéry quickly replied, carrying the jest a little further, "would it indeed become a heartbroken bride to adorn herself so splendidly? No, I have altogether given up that goldsmith, and should never think of him at all any more except that the horrid recollection of his being carried past me after he had been murdered keeps returning to my mind."

"Really?" asked the King. "Did you see the poor devil?"

Mademoiselle de Scudéry now related in a few words how she happened to be near Cardillac's house just as the murder was discovered—as yet she made no reference to Brusson's rôle in the affair. She described

Madelon's wild grief and the deep impression this angelic child made upon her, and told how she had rescued the poor girl from Desgrais' hands, amid the cheers of the people. Then came the scenes with La Reynie, with Desgrais, with Brusson—the interest deepening and intensifying from moment to moment. The King, carried away by Scudéry's gift for telling a story and by the realism and power of her narrative, forgot to notice that she was discussing a subject he thoroughly disliked. Before he realized what was happening—he was utterly confused by the astonishing things he had heard—Mademoiselle de Scudéry had thrown herself at his feet, and was imploring mercy for Olivier Brusson.

"What are you doing, Mademoiselle?" the King demanded, taking her by both hands and forcing her into a chair. "What does this mean? You have really taken me completely by surprise. I agree that it is a terrible story. But what confirmation is there of the truth of Brusson's fantastic assertions?"

To which Scudéry replied: "Miossens' evidence—an examination of Cardillac's house—my own deep conviction." The King was on the point of making some reply when he was interrupted by a noise at the door, and turned round. Louvois, who had been at work in the adjoining room, looked in with a worried, harried expression on his face. The King rose and left the room with him.

The two ladies, both Scudéry and Maintenon, regarded this interruption as dangerous, for having once been taken unawares the King might not be so easily trapped a second time. After some minutes the King returned; he paced up and down the room several times, then stopped, with his arms crossed behind him, right in front of Scudéry and without looking her in the face, said almost in an undertone: "I should very much like to see your Madelon."

Mademoiselle replied, "Oh, beloved Sire! What a great—great happiness your condescension will confer upon this poor unhappy child. The little thing is only waiting for the merest sign from you to throw herself at your feet."

She then moved towards the door as briskly as her heavy costume would permit, called out that the King wished Madelon Cardillac to be brought to him, and came back into the room weeping with emotion and delight.

Scudéry had suspected some favor of this sort might be granted and she had brought Madelon along with her. The girl had been sitting with one of the ladies-in-waiting of the Marquise, clutching a petition drawn up by Andilly. In a few moments she had sunk, speechless, at the King's feet. Her anxiety, her bewilderment, her shy reverence, her love, and her grief, had sent the blood throbbing faster and faster through her veins. Her cheeks burned and blushed; her eyes shone with bright pearls of tears, which now and again dropped from her silken lashes to her petal-white bosom. The King seemed struck by the child's unearthly beauty. He gently raised her to her feet and made a movement as if he were going to kiss the hand which he had grasped. But he let it go again, and gazed at the lovely girl with glistening eyes.

Madame de Maintenon whispered softly to Scudéry, "Isn't she exactly like La Vallière? The King is reveling in the sweetest of memories. Your game is won.

Despite the low whisper in which Maintenon spoke, the King appeared to have heard her. His face flushed slightly. He glanced at Maintenon for a moment, and then his eyes shifted to the petition which Madelon had presented to him. He read it and said in a mild, kind voice: "I am quite ready to believe, my dear child, that you are convinced of your lover's innocence, but we must hear what the *Chambre Ardente* has to say about it." Then with a graceful gesture of his hand he dismissed the girl, who was gushing tears like a fountain.

Scudéry observed to her dismay that the recollection of La Vallière, so encouraging at first, had at Maintenon's mere mention of the name caused the King to change his mind. Perhaps His Majesty felt he was being reminded too indelicately, by that, how he was about to sacrifice justice to beauty; or perhaps he was like the dreamer who, suddenly startled out of his revery, sees the visions quickly vanish, which a moment ago seemed almost within his grasp. Perhaps he no longer saw before him *his* La Vallière, but was reminded only of Soeur Louise de la Misericorde (the identity La Vallière had assumed in a Carmelite nunnery) who pained him with her piety and penitence. What else was there now to be done but wait for the King's decision?

Meanwhile Count de Miossens' deposition before the *Chambre Ardente* had become publicly known, and as it frequently happens that public sentiment runs from one extreme to another, so on this occasion the very man who had been denounced as a most abominable murderer, and whom the mob had threatened to tear to pieces, before he could ascend the scaffold, was now pitied on all sides as the innocent victim of bloodthirsty justice. Now his neighbors first began to recall his exemplary conduct, his great love for Madelon, and the faithfulness and respectful affection which he had cherished for the old goldsmith. Whole crowds of people began to appear menacingly before La Reynie's palace, crying out: "Give up Olivier Brusson to us! He is innocent!" And they even stoned the windows, so that La Reynie was obliged to ask the Maréchaussée's protection from the enraged mob.

Several days passed and still Scudéry received no news of the Olivier Brusson case. Almost distracted, she appealed to Madame de Maintenon, who assured her that the King maintained a strict silence on the subject and it would not be advisable to remind him of it. Then when she asked Mademoiselle how the little Vallière was getting on, Scudéry was convinced that in her heart the proud woman had been vexed by a certain aspect of the affair whose blandishments might be apparent to the susceptible King but certainly held little charm for his mistress. Mademoiselle need therefore hope for nothing from the Marquise de Maintenon.

At last, with Andilly's help, Scudéry succeeded in finding out that the King had had a long private interview with the Count de Miossens. Further, she learned that Bontems, His Majesty's confidential valet and agent, had visited the *Conciergerie* and had an interview with Brusson, also that the same Bontems had one night gone with several men to Cardillac's house and spent a considerable time there. Claude Patru, the man who rented the lower floor, maintained that they were knocking about overhead all night long and he was sure Olivier had been with them, for he distinctly heard his voice. So much was, therefore, at any rate certain: the King, himself, was having Olivier's version of the story investigated and checked. But there was still no explanation for His Majesty's long delay in coming to a decision.

Almost a month had gone by when Madame de Maintenon sent word to Scudéry that the King wished to see her that evening in Madame's apartments.

Scudéry's heart beat high. She knew that Brusson's case would now be decided. She told poor Madelon so, and the girl prayed fervently to the Virgin and the saints to awaken in the King's mind a conviction of Brusson's innocence.

Yet it seemed as though the King had completely forgotten the affair, for in his usual way he wittily bandied conversation with the ladies without making even the vaguest reference to Brusson. At last Bontems came in, approached the King, and said a few words so softly that neither Maintenon nor Scudéry could make them out. Mademoiselle's heart quaked. The King rose to his feet, came towards her and said with a smile: "I congratulate you, Mademoiselle. Your protégé, Olivier Brusson, is free. I wish I had you as my advocate in the *Parlement* to plead my cause, for, by Saint Denis, nobody could resist your eloquence! And yet," he continued in a more serious tone, "yet when Virtue herself has taken a man under her protection, is he not safe from all evil accusations, from the *Chambre Ardente*, and all the other tribunals in the world?"

Scudéry poured out her gratitude in a stream of thanks. The King interrupted her by informing her that she would find, awaiting her in her own house, warmer appreciation than he ever had the right to claim from her, for probably at that very moment Olivier was already there, clasping his Madelon in his arms.

"Bontems will turn over to you a thousand louis d'or," the King said in conclusion. "Give them to the little girl in my name as her dowry. Let her marry Brusson, who doesn't deserve such good luck, and then let them both be gone from Paris. That is a command."

La Martinière came running to meet her mistress with Baptiste following close behind. "He is here! He is free!" they both cried out triumphantly. "And what a sweet young couple they make!"

The sweet young couple were at a loss to express their gratitude. "I knew it! I knew it!" cried Madelon. "I knew that you, you alone, would save my darling Olivier!" "My faith in you, my mother," said Olivier, "kept me alive." And they both showered the good lady's hands with kisses and tears. Then they embraced each other again, declaring that the exquisite happiness of that one moment outweighed all the nameless suffering of the days that were past and they vowed never to part from each other until death.

A few days later they were united with the blessings of the priest. Even if the King had not commanded it, Brusson would not have remained in Paris, where everything reminded him of Cardillac's crimes and where some mischance might expose his hateful secret, already known to several persons, and so destroy his hope of a peaceful life. Almost immediately after his marriage he set out with his young wife for Geneva, accompanied by the blessings of Mademoiselle de Scudéry. Madelon's dowry would see him through an excellent beginning and, endowed as he was with unusual skill at his trade, and all the virtues of a good citizen, he might look forward to a happy life, free from care. In time he fulfilled the aspirations which had brought his disappointed father to his grave.

A year after Brusson's departure, a public proclamation was issued, signed by Harloy de Chauvalon, Archbishop of Paris, and by Pierre Arnaud d'Andilly, Advocate of the *Parlement*, to the effect that a repentant sinner had, under the seal of confession, handed over to the Church a large and valuable collection of jewels and gold ornaments which he had stolen. All persons who up to the end of the year 1680 had lost valuables through theft, particularly through assault in the public streets, were to apply to Monsieur d'Andilly, and then, if their descriptions of the stolen articles corresponded exactly to any of the pieces awaiting identification, and if, further, there existed no doubt as to the legitimacy of the claim, the missing property would be restored. Many whose names were down on Cardillac's list as not murdered, but merely stunned by a blow of his fist, came one by one to the Advocate's office and received, to their no small amazement, their stolen valuables back again. What remained unclaimed fell to the coffers of the Church of Saint Eustache.

DON JUAN

or

A Fabulous Adventure that Befell a Music Enthusiast on his Travels

THE SHRILLING OF A BELL AND A LOUD cry of: "The curtain is going up!" roused me from the deep sleep into which I had fallen. Bass notes throbbed in unison, cymbals clashed, trumpets blared. A steady, clear "A" came from the oboe and then the violins joined in. I rubbed my eyes. Could it be that Satan who is never idle when it comes to mischief, had bewitched me in my sleep? But no! I was still in the bedroom of the hotel where I had put up last night aching with fatigue. I pulled firmly on the heavily ornamented bell tassel hanging above my head, and in a moment the valet appeared.

"What on earth is the meaning of this outburst of music next door to me? Is someone giving a concert in the hotel?"

"Your Excellency—" (I had taken champagne with my dinner, the night before!) "Your Excellency is perhaps unaware that this hotel adjoins the theatre. Behind this tapestry there is a concealed door which opens on a short passageway, and that in turn leads directly to Loge Number 23, the visitors' box."

"What? A theatre? A visitors' box?"

"Yes, the small visitors' loge, for two or three persons, no more—and only for gentlemen of quality. All upholstered in green, right off the stage with a screen in front to assure privacy. If it please Your Excellency—today we are giving *Don Juan*, by the famous Maestro Mozart of Vienna. The entrance fee, one thaler and twenty pfennigs, can be charged to Your Excellency's hotel bill."

By the time he had finished speaking, he was already holding open the loge door, for at the first mention of *Don Juan* I had hastily stepped through the concealed door into the passageway.

For a moderate-sized town, the house was spacious, tastefully decorated and brilliantly illuminated. Loges and stalls were filled to capacity. The first chords of the overture convinced me that such an excellent orchestra, even if the singers were not up to the same standard, would in itself assure me the greatest enjoyment of Mozart's masterpiece.

During the *andante*, my spirit was seized with premonitions of horror. I shuddered in awe of the infernal *regno del pianto*. The seventh bar of the *allegro*, with its jubilant fanfare, became the voice of crime itself, exulting. Out of the dark night I saw demons stretch their fiery claws and loom menacingly over the lives of carefree mortals dancing merrily on the thin lid of a bottomless pit. The conflict between human nature and the unknown, the terrible powers that confront man on every side and lie in wait for his ruin, took on a visionary intensity with the music. Then at last the storm subsides and the action begins.

Frigid and gloomy, closely wrapped in his cloak, Leporello strides through the dark night and enters from the pavilion: *Notte e giorno fati-car.* In Italian, then? Italian here, in this German town? Ah, *che piacere!* I shall hear all the recitative, everything just as the great master conceived it in his mind and drew it out of his very soul!

Suddenly Don Juan rushes on, followed by Donna Anna holding fast to the murderer's cloak. Donna Anna, it is true, might be taller, more slender, statelier of carriage. But what a head! Eyes from which love, anger, hate, despair, blaze and commingle in a single flame whose source is an unquenchable phoenix pyramid of fire burning deep in her soul! Loose tresses of dark hair undulate in waves and ringlets down her neck and shoulders. The clinging white nightdress suggests and scarcely conceals provocative charms. Her heart throbs in her bosom with heavy strokes, seized with the horror of the deed. . . . And now—what a voice!

Non sperar se non m'uccidi. Through the storm of instruments the human tones flash like lightning molten of some ethereal metal! Don Juan tries to tear himself away in vain. But does he really want to? Then why not strike the woman one strong blow and escape? Has his crime deprived him of strength, or is it the inner conflict of love and hate that has cheated him of all will and courage?

The senile father has paid with his life for his folly. He should never have attacked his opponent in the dark. Don Juan and Leporello step forward to the proscenium and converse. The Don unwraps his cloak and stands there resplendently clothed in slashed red velvet, embroidered with silver. A powerful, dominant figure. His face is handsome, one might almost call it beautiful in a masculine way, with its proud nose, piercing eyes, and soft curving lips. A peculiar play of the eyebrows gives it, at moments, a Mephistophelean look, that in no way detracts from its beauty but rather inspires involuntary fear. One is ready to believe that the Don has mastered the magic art of the rattlesnake, that he is capable of exercising such secret power over women that one look suffices to enslave and destroy them. Tall and gangling, in a red-and-white striped vest, a short red cloak, and a white hat with a red feather, Leporello minces about his master. His features reveal a curious mixture of kindness, roguery, concupiscence, and impudence; the black eyebrows stand out strangely against the greyish hair and beard. The old rascal obviously merits his position as servant and accomplice to Don Juan. Finally, they succeed in making their escape over the wall.

Torches blaze. Donna Elvira and Don Ottavio enter, the latter an elegant but fatuous young man, no more than twenty-one. As Anna's betrothed, he presumably lives in the house, since he has been fetched so quickly. At the first outcry, which he certainly must have heard, he might easily have come to the old man's assistance, but it is obvious that he had to stop to make himself "presentable," and, in any case, he is most unwilling to risk his health in the night air.

Ma qual mai s'offre, o Dei, spettacolo funesto agli occhi miei! There is more than despair over the Don's shocking crime in the awful, heartbreaking intonations of this dialogue and duet. The murder of Donna Anna's father is only incidental to the doom which Don Juan must bring upon himself, and those notes which wring terror from the heart describe, more than the consequences of the bloody act, the torment of a man who cannot break away from his own evil destiny.

Donna Elvira, tall and slender, with features that still bear the recognizable traces of beauty, was in the midst of inveighing against her betrayer, Don Juan: *Tu nido d'inganni*, and sympathetic Leporello had interjected quite cleverly: *parla come un libro stampato*, when I suddenly had the impression that there was someone next to me in the box. Anyone might easily open the loge door and slip in. The thought depressed me thoroughly. I had been so happy to have the loge to myself, and to be able to absorb with every nervous fibre of my being, as though through tentacles, this perfect version of the masterpiece, that I felt a single spoken word (inevitably a banal one!) would wrench me painfully out of this glorious mood of poetic and musical enchantment! I decided to take no notice whatever of the newcomer, but to remain engrossed in the performance and avoid any exchange of word or glance. With my chin resting on my hand and my back turned to my neighbor, I kept my eyes fixed on the stage.

The performance continued at the excellent level of the beginning. Wanton, infatuated little Zerlina offers clumsy, good-natured Masetto the consolation of her sweet gestures and words. In the wild aria: *Fin ch'han dal vino*, Don Juan (the play of his eyebrows more Mephistophelean than ever) bares his inner wickedness, his contempt for the human puppets who surround him. They have no purpose but his pleasure, and they serve that best by yielding to his capricious destruction of their insipid commonplace lives. The masks appear. Their *terzetto* is a prayer that rises to Heaven in shafts of pure light.

The middle curtain now rises on a scene of gaiety and celebration. Glasses clink, peasants in a variety of masks whirl about, urged on by the Don. The three plotters who have sworn revenge enter, but the gay mood continues as long as the dancing goes on. Then Zerlina is rescued, and to the thundering accompaniment of the finale Don Juan defiantly faces his opponents with drawn sword. He disarms the outraged bridegroom who is carrying a useless dress-sword, and like a redoubtable Roland forces his way out into the open, while the rabble draw back in confusion, stumbling and falling over each other.

Several times during the action on-stage, I thought I had felt a gentle, perfumed breath of air close to me and heard the rustle of a silken garment. This led me to assume the presence of a woman in the loge, but I was engrossed in the poetic world of the opera and took little notice of anything else. Now that the curtain was lowered, I turned round to see who my neighbor was. It is hopeless to try to find words to express my surprise: Donna Anna, in exactly the same costume she had just worn on the stage, was standing behind me, her expressive, unhappy eyes fixed upon me in a piercing stare. I stared back at her, struck dumb. Her lips (or so it seemed to me) formed a gentle, ironical smile in which I saw my own ridiculous appearance reflected. I felt impelled to speak to her, but I was paralyzed by astonishment—I might even say fear—and found myself unable to make my lips move.

Finally (and it seemed an eternity) the words came out almost involuntarily: "How is it possible that I should see you here?" Whereupon she replied in purest Tuscan, that if I did not understand and speak Italian, she would have to forego the pleasure of my conversation, since she could speak no other language.

The sweet words were like music in my ears. When she spoke, the light in her dark blue eyes was intensified, and the lightning flashing from them sent a stream of fire through my veins that pounded in my pulse and vibrated in my every fibre. This was, this could only be, Donna Anna. The possibility of explaining how she could, at one and the same time, be both on the stage and in my loge never occurred to me. Just as a happy dream brings together the strangest events and our instinctive belief freely accepts it, in all its incongruity, as a phenomenon of life, so did I somnambulistically accept the presence of this marvelous creature. More than that, I realized, all at once, that there were secret bonds which tied me so closely to her, that she could not keep away from me even when she appeared on the stage. How I would like to repeat to you, dear Theodore, every word of the remarkable conversation that now began between the Signora and myself. But when I try to write down in German what she said, every word appears stiff and dull to me, every phrase clumsy, incapable of expressing what, in Tuscan, she put so easily and gracefully.

When she spoke about Don Juan, about her part, it seemed as if for the first time the inner workings of the masterpiece were exposed to me and I was permitted to witness and examine the fantastic phenomena of a strange world. She said that music was her only reality, and that she often believed she could understand in song much that was mystically hidden or evaded expression in life.

"Yes, it becomes clear to me when I sing," she continued, with burning eyes and agitation in her voice. "But the world outside of me remains dead and cold, and when a difficult roulade or a successful effect meet with applause, icy hands fasten upon my glowing heart! But you, you understand me. I know that you too are an intimate in the wonderful, romantic realm inhabited by the sublime magic of sound!"

"So you know me, then, miraculous creature?"

"I know the frenzy and yearning of love that were in your heart, when you wrote the part . . . in your last opera. I understood you. Your soul was laid bare to me in song! Yes," (here she called me by my first name) "naturally, I have sung you. I am your melodies."

The intermission bell rang. A strange pallor came over her face. She put her hand to her heart as though in sudden pain, and said in a tired, gentle voice, "Unhappy Anna, now you must face your most terrible moments." Then she disappeared from the box.

The first act had delighted me, but after this remarkable adventure the music affected me in the most extraordinary way. It was as though a long-promised fulfillment of the most unearthly dreams were now actually being realized. As though the most esoteric thoughts of a bewitched soul had become fixed in sound and had taken form and shape, standing out in relief against a remarkable concept. In Donna Anna's scene, a soft, warm breath passed over me. I trembled in passion and intoxication. Unconsciously, I closed my eyes, and a burning caress seemed to linger on my lips: but the kiss was a long note, held as though in an eternal thirst of longing.

The finale began with frivolity and merrymaking: *Gia la mensa è preparata!* Don Juan sat there philandering between two girls and drawing one cork after the other, releasing the fermenting spirits, which had been hermetically imprisoned, and allowing them now to exercise their full freedom. It was a small room with a large Gothic window in the background, through which you could look out into the night. Even while Elvira reminded her faithless lover of all his broken vows, there were several lightning flashes through the window and the deep rumbling of the approaching storm could be heard. At last a mighty, ominous burst of thunder!

Elvira and the girls flee and, to the accompaniment of terrifying chords that invoke the spirits of the damned, the awful marble Colossus enters and towers over Don Juan who seems reduced to the size of a pygmy. The ground quakes under the giant's thundering steps. Through the storm, through the thunder, through the howling of the demons, Don Juan cries his terrifying: "No!" and commits himself to his doom. The hour of destruction is come. The statue disappears, the room is filled with thick smoke out of which rise terrifying spectres. Don Juan, experiencing the torments of Hell, writhes in and out of the crowd of demons. Suddenly there is an explosion, as if a thousand bolts of lightning had all struck the same spot: Don Juan and the demons have disappeared without a trace! Leporello lies unconscious in a corner of the room.

What a relief one feels at the entrance of the other characters, still vainly seeking the Don, snatched, once and for all, beyond the reach of worldly revenge! Donna Anna looks quite different now. A deathly pallor clouds her features, her eyes are dimmed, her voice quivering and uneven; but all this merely enhances the emotional effect of her brief duet with the sweet little bridegroom who is eager to celebrate the nuptials immediately, now that he has been happily relieved by the powers of Heaven of the dangerous duty of avenging the *Commendatore*.

The last fugal strains of the chorus had rounded the masterpiece into a magnificently complete whole, and I hurried back to my room, experiencing an exaltation I had never before known. The servant announced that supper was served and I followed him downstairs mechanically. The fair had brought a brilliant company to town, and this evening's rendition of *Don Juan* was the subject of conversation at the main table. Praise of the Italians and their grasp of the medium was general. But little remarks, dropped quite waggishly here and there, indicated that none of the speakers had any real insight into the inherent significance of this opera of all operas.

Don Ottavio had been very well liked indeed.

Donna Anna had been too passionate for one gentleman. On the stage, he said, one should control oneself and avoid exaggeration. The description of the attack upon her father had definitely disconcerted him. He now took a pinch of snuff and turned his indescribably stupid, sly eyes on his neighbor.

The neighbor declared that the Signora was, to be sure, quite a beautiful woman, but too careless in her dress and appearance. Why, in the very scene just mentioned, a strand of hair had come loose and thrown a shadow on her profile!

Then someone else began to hum quite softly the *Fin ch'han dal vino*, whereupon a lady remarked that Don Juan seemed to her the least satisfactory of the whole cast. The Italian had been too sinister, much too serious. Altogether he had not played the frivolous, carefree character lightly enough. But the effect of the final explosion was extolled on all sides. Weary of this idle talk, I hastened back to my room.

IN LOGE NUMBER 23

I felt so stifled, in that narrow, damp room! At midnight I thought I heard your voice, dear Theodore! You spoke my name quite clearly and there was a rustling behind the tapestried door that leads to the theatre. What is there to prevent me from revisiting the scene of my wonderful adventure? Perhaps I shall see you and see her, the lovely creature who fills all my thoughts and occupies my whole being! How easy it would be to carry in the small table, two lamps, writing materials!

The servant brings the bowl of punch I have ordered and finds the room empty. The concealed door is open: he follows me into the loge and stands there regarding me with confusion. I signal him to leave the drink on the table and he goes away hardly able to restrain his curiosity and still glancing back at me. I turn away from him, lean over the edge of the loge, and look round the deserted house. The darkened interior, brought magically to life by my two lamps, quivers and glimmers fantastically in the reflected light. The curtain sways gently in the draft. What if it were suddenly to billow up and reveal Donna Anna, terrified at the presence of spectres? Donna Anna! I call her name involuntarily.

My cry is lost in the empty house; but it has aroused the spirits of the instruments in the orchestra pit and they respond in vibration, with a wonderful note that seems to carry away and repeat the beloved name in a whisper! I cannot help shuddering, but at the same time, I also experience a curious exhilaration.

But I am no longer dreaming, and I must confess at least to you, my dear Theodore, that I have come only now to understand properly the inner meaning of the divine master's work. Only the poet can understand the poet; only a romantic soul can pass through the portals of romanticism; only the poetically exalted spirit that has been initiated in the temple can understand what the initiate pronounces in his exaltation.

If the libretto of *Don Juan* is taken by itself and considered only for its literary merit, it is difficult to understand how Mozart could conceive and compose such music to it. A *bon vivant*, excessively fond of wine and women, defiantly invites a man of stone to his rowdy table, the statue representing the old father whom he has struck down in self-defense. There is, truly, nothing very poetical in this, and honestly speaking, such a person is scarcely worth the distinction of being singled out by the infernal powers as a good specimen for their collection; of being exhorted to repentance in his final hour as a sinner by the stone man who, possessed by the spirit of enlightenment, takes the trouble to dismount from his horse to convert him; and of being transported to Hell under escort by the best henchmen the Devil has available for that purpose.

Believe me, Theodore, Nature equipped Don Juan, as if he were her favorite child, with all that raises man towards divinity, above the common crowd, above the standard product, above the inferior article whose only worth is in number and aggregate; and this destined him to conquer, to dominate. A powerful, handsome body, a personality radiating the spark which kindles the most sublime feelings in the soul; a profound sensibility, a quick, instinctive understanding.

But the terrible consequence of the fall of man is that the Fiend retains the power to beguile man and prepare wicked pitfalls for him, just when he is striving for that perfection which most expresses his godlike nature. This conflict between the divine and demoniac powers begets the notion of life on earth, just as the ensuing victory begets the notion of life above earth. The demands upon life, exacted by his physical and mental qualities, filled Don Juan with unfailing enthusiasm. Insatiable in his desires, fired by a longing which sent the blood boiling through his veins, he was driven to the greedy, restless experience of all the phenomena of this earthly world, hoping in vain to find satisfaction in them.

There is, indeed, nothing here on earth more exalting for the inner nature of man than love. It is love that, so secretly and powerfully effective, disturbs and transfigures the innermost aspects of existence. Small wonder, then, that Don Juan hoped to still, in love, the longing that burned in his heart. And it was here that the Devil slipped the noose around his neck! Through the cunning of man's hereditary enemy, the thought was planted in Don Juan's soul that through love, through the pleasure of the flesh, there could be achieved on earth that which exists in our hearts as a heavenly promise only, and which amounts to just that longing for infinity which weds us to Heaven. Fleeing restlessly from one more beautiful woman to another; drinking his fill of their charms from burning passion to the point of drunken and exhausted satiety; believing himself always deceived in his choice, hoping always to realize the ideal of ultimate satisfaction, the Don was doomed to find all earthly life dull and shallow in the end; more, since he despised humanity anyhow, he revolted against that delusion which at first had spelled the highest of life's ambitions for him, only to betray him so bitterly at last. The enjoyment of woman no longer offered him any satisfaction of his sensuality, but had become an opportunity atrociously to outrage Nature and the Creator.

Don Juan was driven on by deep contempt for the common aspects of life, to which he felt himself superior. He felt bitter mockery for a humanity which hoped to find, in happy love and in the ensuing homely community it created, the merest fulfillment of the higher aspirations that a treacherous nature has inimically planted in our hearts; and he was compelled to revolt primarily against the very thought of such a relationship and to combat boldly, in anticipation of his own ruin, the unknown Being who guides our destiny and who appeared to Don Juan as a monster of malice rejoicing in the unhappiness of others and playing a cruel game with the pitiful creatures created out of his mocking moods. Every betrayal of a loved bride, every joy destroyed by a fierce blow struck at the lovers, every inconsolable grief the Don brings down upon a happy pair, represents an exalted triumph over that hostile monster, and raises the seducer forever above our narrow life, above Nature, above the Creator! He really desires more and more to transcend life, only to sink deeper and more irretrievably into Hell. The seduction of Anna, with the accompanying circumstances, is the very summit of his achievement.

With regard to the highest favors of Nature, Donna Anna is the counterpart of Don Juan. Just as Don Juan was originally a marvelously strong and handsome man, so she is a divine woman, over whose pure spirit the Devil has no power. All the arts of Hell, combined for her undoing, could ruin her only in an earthly fashion. As soon as Satan has accomplished this ruin, according to the dictates of Heaven, the execution of the revenge may no longer be delayed by the powers of Hell.

Don Juan mockingly invites the statue of the murdered old man to his bawdy feast, and the transfigured spirit, seeing Don Juan for the first time as the fallen man (or as Adam expelled from Paradise) and grieving over him, does not disdain to call upon him, in a terrifying guise, in order to bring about his repentance. But the soul of Don Juan is so corrupt, so ridden and anguished, that not even heavenly salvation can throw a ray of hope into his heart and light his way to a better life!

You have surely noticed, my dear Theodore, that I have spoken of Anna's seduction; and I shall do my best, at this hour of the night when thoughts and ideas seem to rise from the depths of my soul and outdistance my words, to tell you briefly how I interpret the conflict of these two natures (Don Juan and Donna Anna) purely in terms of the music and ignoring the text.

I have already mentioned that Anna is the counterpart of the Don. Suppose Anna had been destined by Heaven to let Don Juan recognize, in the love that ruined him through the arts of Satan, the divine nature that dwelled within him, and to tear him away from his own desperate efforts at destruction? But no, it was too late for that! When he first saw her he was already at the height of his crimes, and could only feel the demoniac desire to corrupt her. There was no rescue for her! When he fled the deed was done! The fire of a superhuman sensuality, a glow from Hell, had cast its reflection over her senses and she was powerless to resist. Only he, only Don Juan, could awaken in her the erotic madness which she lavished upon him—he who sinned with the omnipotent rage of Hell.

He wanted to escape, once the deed was done. But for Donna Anna the awareness of her sin was like a dreadful, poisonous, death-spewing monster growing larger and more hideous each moment and coiling itself

about her being in racking torture. She thought of her father's death at
Don Juan's hand. She remembered her betrothal to frigid, effeminate,
prosaic Don Ottavio, whom she had once thought she loved. Even the
raging love that consumed her soul with hellish flames, flaring up at the
moment of highest gratification, was aglow, now, with annihilating hatred.
All this racks her heart now.

She feels that only the destruction of Don Juan can bring peace to
her mortally tortured soul; but this peace demands her own earthly down-
fall. Unceasingly, therefore, she exhorts her indifferent bridegroom to revenge. She pursues the betrayer herself, and she relents only when the
powers of the underworld have dragged Don Juan down into the bottomless pit.

But she will not yield to the bridegroom now eager for marriage.
Lascia, o caro, un anno ancora, allo sfoga del mio cor! She will not outlive
that year; Don Ottavio will never embrace the woman whose devotion has
saved her from becoming Satan's chosen bride.

How vividly I felt all this in the tragic chords of the first recitative
and of the account of the night attack! Even Donna Anna's scene in the
second act: *Crudele* (which, considered superficially, refers only to Don
Ottavio) , expresses in secret harmonies, in the most wonderful inferences,
that inner state of the soul that consumes all earthly happiness. What
other meaning can we find in the passage added and altered by the poet:
forse un giorno il cielo ancora sentirà pieta di me!

Two o'clock strikes! A warm, electric breath floats over me. I recognize the caressing scent of fine Italian perfume that I first noticed yesterday in the presence of my beautiful neighbor; I am seized by an ecstatic
feeling that can be expressed only in music. The air billows more violently
through the house, the strings of the piano in the pit vibrate like a harp.
Heaven! As from a great distance, accompanied by the harmonica of an
aerial orchestra, I seem to hear Anna's voice: *Non mi dir bell'idol mio!*

Open out before me, oh distant, unknown realm of spirits! Open out,
oh land of genii and jinn! Open out, realm of all splendor whence mystic
and celestial pain falls on me like a joy unutterable, fulfilling everything
that was ever promised to the enraptured soul here below! Let me enter
the circle of most loved apparitions! Let the dreams sent to me from this

enchanted kingdom now terrify me as I shudder, now calm me as a benign messenger to earthly men! And in the hour when sleep holds the body captive in its leaden bonds, let these dreams carry my spirit gently into ethereal fields!

MIDDAY CONVERSATION AT THE MAIN TABLE
(Epilogue)

CLEVER MAN

(*Taking out his snuffbox and tapping emphatically on its lid.*)
It is really unfortunate that we shall hear no more good opera for some time. But that is what comes of overacting.

MULATTO-FACE

Yes, yes. I warned her time and time again! The rôle of Donna Anna always affected her oddly. Yesterday, she carried on like one possessed. They say she lay unconscious in her dressing room throughout the intermission. In her scene in the second act she even had nervous fits.

INSIGNIFICANT PERSON

You don't say . . . !

MULATTO-FACE

Absolutely! Nervous fits, and they couldn't get her out of the theatre.

MYSELF

Good Lord, I hope the fits are nothing serious? We shall hear the Signora soon again, and in good health?

CLEVER MAN

(*Taking a pinch of snuff from the box.*)
Hardly. The Signora died this morning, at exactly two o'clock.

ANTONIA'S SONG

COUNCILLOR KRESPEL WAS ONE OF THE strangest, most fantastic men I ever came across in my entire life.

When I went to live in H— with the intention of settling there for some time, the whole town was full of talk about him, for he happened just then to be in the midst of one of his maddest schemes.

Krespel had the reputation of being a clever, learned lawyer and a skilful diplomat. One of the reigning princes of Germany—not, however, one of the most powerful of them— had appealed to him for assistance in drawing up a petition to the Imperial Court in proof of his legitimate claims to a certain strip of territory. The project was carried through with the happiest success, and as Krespel had once complained that he could never find a place to live comfortably enough to suit him, the Prince, to reward him for his services, undertook to defray the costs of building a house which Krespel was free to plan just as he pleased. Moreover, the Prince offered to purchase any site that struck Krespel's fancy. This latter offer, however, the Councillor would not accept. He insisted that the house should be built in his garden, situated in a very beautiful spot outside the town walls.

He then proceeded to have all sorts of building materials brought out to him there. After that he was to be seen day after day, dressed in his curious costume (which he had designed according to very definite rules of his own), slaking the lime, sifting sand, piling up the bricks and stones in regular heaps, and so on. He did all this before he had ever consulted an architect or settled on a plan of any sort. One fine day, however, he went to an experienced builder in the town and requested him to be in his garden at daybreak the next morning, with all his journeymen and apprentices, plenty of laborers, and whatever equipment was necessary to build him a house.

Naturally the builder asked for the architect's plan, and was not a little astonished when Krespel replied that none was needed, and that things would turn out just as he wanted in the end, without any plan of that kind.

Next morning, when the builder and his men came to the place, they found a trench dug in the shape of an exact square, and Krespel said:

"This is where you must lay the foundation of my house. Then I want you to build the four walls up until I say they are high enough."

"Without windows and doors? Without partitions between the rooms?" demanded the builder, somewhat alarmed at Krespel's suggestion.

"Do what I tell you, my good man," replied the Councillor quite calmly. "And leave the rest to me. It will work out all right."

It was only the promise of extra pay that induced the builder to continue with the ridiculous project. But never was a house erected under merrier circumstances. Since there was an abundant supply of food and drink, the workmen never left the spot and, amidst their constant laughter, the four walls were run up with incredible speed, until one day Krespel cried out: "Stop!" Then, laying down their trowels and hammers, the workmen came down from the scaffolding and gathered around Krespel in a circle, while every laughing face plainly asked: "Well, and what now?"

"Make way!" cried Krespel, and he ran to one end of the garden, then strode slowly back towards the square of brickwork. When he came close to the wall he shook his head in a dissatisfied way, ran to the other end of the garden, and again came striding slowly towards the brickwork behaving just as he had done before. He repeated this performance several times, until, at length, he almost ran his sharp nose into the wall. Then he called out:

"Come here, come here, men! Break a doorway for me right here! Here's where I want a door!"

He gave the exact dimensions in feet and inches, and they did as he bade them.

Then he stepped inside the structure, and smiled with satisfaction when the builder remarked that the walls were just the height of a proper two-storied house. Krespel walked thoughtfully up and down the enclosed area of his house, the workmen following him with their hammers and picks, and wherever he stopped and called out, "Make a window here, six feet high, four feet wide!" or, "A small one there, three by two!" a window was immediately cut.

It was when the proceedings were at this stage that I came to H—, and it was highly amusing to see how hundreds of people would stand around the garden and always burst into loud cheers whenever the stones came flying out and a new window appeared where nobody had, a moment before, expected it. Krespel continued in the same way with all the rest of his house, inside and out; everything had to be done on the spot according to his immediate instructions. However, the absurdity of the whole business, the growing conviction that things would in the end turn out better than might have been expected, and above all, Krespel's generosity—which certainly cost him nothing—kept everyone in the best of humor. Thus all the difficulties which necessarily arose out of this adventurous method of building were overcome, and in a short time there was a completely finished house. Its outside, it is true, created a rather bizarre impression, since no two windows had any resemblance to each other. But its interior arrangements suggested a peculiar atmosphere of comfort. All those who ever set foot in the house agreed on this, and I experienced it myself after Krespel and I had become better acquainted and he invited me to visit him.

So far, however, I had not exchanged a word with this eccentric character. His building had kept him so busy that he had neglected even his regular Tuesday dinners at Professor M—'s. In fact, in reply to a special invitation from the Professor he sent word that he would not set foot outside his own door before he had held a housewarming in his new home. All his friends and acquaintances, therefore, confidently looked forward to a great feast and celebration. But Krespel invited nobody except the masters, journeymen, apprentices, and laborers who had built the house. He entertained these people with the choicest dishes: bricklayers' apprentices mercilessly disposed of dozens of partridge pies; young carpenters joyfully polished off the roast pheasants; and hungry laborers glutted themselves for once on the finest morsels of *truffes fricassées*. In the evening their wives and daughters arrived, and a great ball was held. Krespel executed a few turns with the ladies of this select company and then sat down among the village musicians, took a violin in hand, and led the dance music until daybreak.

On the Tuesday after this festival, which revealed Councillor Krespel in the character of a friend of the common folk, I finally had the pleasure of meeting him at Professor M—'s. It would be impossible to find anything more fantastic than Krespel's behavior and manner. He was so stiff and awkward in his movements that he looked as if at any moment, out of sheer lack of control of his limbs, he might run into something and do damage. But he never did, and one seemed to sense, about him, that he never would. The lady of the house showed no signs of uneasiness when, with great clumsy strides, he pushed his way around a table set with beautiful cups, or maneuvered around a mirror that hung almost down to the floor, or even when he seized a flowerpot of exquisitely painted porcelain and whirled it in the air as if he wanted to see the play of light upon it. Before we sat down to dinner he had subjected everything in the Professor's room to the most minute examination and had even taken down a picture from the wall and hung it up again, standing on one of the cushioned chairs.

In addition to all this, he talked a good deal, and vehemently. Sometimes he would jump from one subject to another (this became most apparent at the table); at others, he was unable to have done with an idea and would return to it again and again, giving it all sorts of unexpected twists and turns, becoming lost in the most wonderful elaborations until something else suddenly struck his imagination. Sometimes his voice was harsh and grating, sometimes it was low, drawling, and singsong, but it always seemed out of key with what he was talking about. We were discussing music, and someone had praised the work of a new composer. Krespel smiled and said in his sweetest, most singing voice: "I'd like to see the Devil drag that God-forsaken music-butcher a million miles down to the deepest pit in Hell!" Then he went on ecstatically: "She is an angel of Heaven, with the purest God-given tone and pitch!—the crown and constellation of all singing!" And tears came into his eyes. He was referring to a celebrated *artiste*, who had been the subject of our conversation an hour before.

We had just been served a roast hare, and I noticed that Krespel carefully removed every particle of meat from the bones on his plate, and made the most particular inquiries after the hare's feet; these the Professor's little five-year-old daughter presently brought him with the most friendly smile on her face. The children had in fact been watching Krespel with the friendliest glances all through dinner. Now they stood up and drew near him, but with a certain shyness, keeping their distance by some three paces. "What is all this about?" I asked myself. Dessert was brought in. Then the Councillor took from his pocket a little box, in which he had a miniature steel lathe. This he immediately screwed fast to the table, and then, working with incredible dexterity and speed, turned the hare's bones into all sorts of tiny little boxes and balls, which the children received with cries of delight.

Just as we were rising from table, the Professor's niece asked, "And what is our Antonia doing?"

Krespel looked as though a bitter taste had suddenly come to his lips, but in another moment his face had become a forbidding mask, out of which he was laughing with the most mordant, fierce, and, as it seemed to me, satanic scorn. "Our Antonia—our dear Antonia?" he asked in his drawling, disagreeable, singing way.

The Professor hastened to intervene; I could see, in the reproving glance which he gave his niece, that she had touched a chord which must have aroused a dissonant echo in Krespel's mind. "How are you getting on with your violins?" asked the Professor with a certain gaiety in his voice, as he took the Councillor by both hands.

Then Krespel's face brightened up, and he answered with enthusiasm: "Capitally, Professor. You remember my telling you of the lucky accident that brought me a splendid Amati—well, I've only begun to cut it open today. I hope by this time Antonia will have finished taking it apart."

"Antonia is a good child," said the Professor.

"Yes, indeed. That she is!" exclaimed the Councillor, whisking suddenly around; then, snatching his hat and stick, he rushed to the door. I could see from his reflection in the mirror that there were tears in his eyes.

As soon as the Councillor was gone, I urged the Professor to explain to me what was all this talk of violins, and particularly how it involved Antonia.

"Well," replied the Professor, "the Councillor is a man of extraordinary interests. He likes to make violins, as he does so many other things, according to a mad theory of his own."

"He makes violins!" I exclaimed in astonishment.

"Yes," continued the Professor, "and if competent judges are to be taken at their word, the instruments are the best that have been produced in modern times. Once, when he really turned out a particularly fine violin, he would permit others to play on it—but that's been all over and done with for some time now. As soon as he finishes a violin he plays it himself for an hour or two with the most sublime expression and brilliant technique, but then he hangs it up alongside all the others, and never touches it again or permits anybody else to touch it. If a violin by any of the famous old masters turns up anywhere, the Councillor buys it immediately, no matter what price is asked. But he plays it as he does his own violins, only once. Then he takes it to pieces in order to examine its inner structure, and if he doesn't precisely find whatever it is he imagines he is looking for, he peevishly throws the pieces into a large chest, already heaped full of the remains of dismembered violins."

"But where does Antonia come into it?" I asked with some impatience.

"Well, now, that," continued the Professor, "that is something which might ordinarily fill me with the strongest prejudice against the Councillor, if it weren't for the fact that I am convinced there is some mysterious explanation for it all—for Krespel is kind almost to the point of weakness.

"When the Councillor first came to H—, several years ago, he lived alone with an old housekeeper in — Street, leading the life of a recluse. In a very short time his eccentricities had excited the curiosity of the entire neighborhood, and as soon as he realized what was happening, he very successfully set about making friends. Not only in my own house but everywhere, everyone grew so accustomed to him that he became almost indispensable. Despite his brusque exterior, even the children liked him, without ever making a nuisance of themselves to him, for notwithstanding all their friendly little exchanges, they remained in a certain shy awe of him, which protected him against overfamiliarity. This evening you saw how well he knows how to win children over with his various tricks and games. We all took him at first for an old bachelor, and he never contradicted us. After he had been living here some time, he went away—no one knew where—and came back in a few months. The evening following his return, all his windows were ablaze with light. This was enough to arouse his neighbors' curiosity, and soon they heard the incredibly beautiful voice of a woman singing to the accompaniment of a piano. Then a violin joined in, fiery, intense, competing with the voice. Everyone felt at once that it was the Councillor who was playing.

"I myself was part of the large crowd which had collected in front of Krespel's house to listen to this extraordinary concert, and I must admit that, compared to the voice of this unknown woman, to this song which rang out with a strange quality of its own and penetrated the deepest fibre of my consciousness, the singing of the most celebrated artist I had ever heard seemed dull and lifeless. I had never before even dreamt of such long-sustained notes, of such nightingale trills, of such undulations of sound, swelling out with the strength of organ tones or dying away to the faintest murmuring breath. There was not one of us who did not feel himself enthralled by the sweet witchery of it, and when the singing stopped, a gasp swept the audience and seemed to fill the stillness of the night.

"It was somewhere around midnight when we heard the Councillor talking excitedly. Then another male voice rose in response and, judging from its tone, seemed to be reproaching Krespel, while from time to time the sobs of a young girl punctuated the dialogue. The Councillor's voice continued to grow louder and louder, until suddenly he changed to that drawling singsong you know so well. A shriek from the girl interrupted him, and for a moment all was still as death, then there was a noise of running footsteps on the stairs and a young man rushed sobbing out of the house, threw himself into a post-chaise waiting near by and drove off at full speed.

"The next day the Councillor seemed to be in the most excellent frame of mind, and no one had the courage to question him about the events of the previous night. But we found out from the housekeeper that the Councillor had brought home with him a young, blooming flower of a girl whom he called Antonia, and that it was she who had sung so beautifully. A young man also had come along with them, and the housekeeper concluded from his display of affection for Antonia that he must be her intended. But he had had to go away very suddenly—the Councillor had insisted on it.

"What the relations between Antonia and the Councillor are still remains a secret to all of us, but this much is clear, that he tyrannizes over the poor girl in the most hateful way. He watches her as jealously as Doctor Bartolo ever guarded his Rosina in *The Barber of Seville.* She hardly dares show herself at a window. And if, now and then, he accepts some pressing invitation and takes her out into society, he follows her about with Argus eyes and will under no condition permit a note of music to be struck in her presence. He absolutely forbids her to sing, and she is no longer allowed to do so even in his own house. And so the people of the town have come to regard Antonia's song that night as a sort of local miracle, like some legend that stirs the heart and excites the imagination; and even those who have never heard her sing a note have acquired the habit of saying, whenever any other artist attempts to give a performance in town: 'What is that cackling supposed to pass for? Nobody but Antonia can really sing!' "

Since I have a particular weakness for the fantastic you may readily imagine how forcefully I was impelled to make Antonia's acquaintance. I myself had often enough heard this talk of her singing, from the villagers, but I had never imagined that this exquisite voice was actually living in the place, held captive by the weird Krespel, like the victim of some tyrannic magician. Naturally I heard Antonia's marvelous song in my dreams the next night, and in a glorious *adagio* (which absurdly enough seemed to have been composed by me) she implored me to save her. I therefore resolved, like a second Astolfo, to penetrate into Krespel's house, as if into another Alzina's enchanted castle, and deliver the Queen of Song from her ignominious fetters.

It all came about in a different way than I had expected. I had hardly seen the Councillor more than two or three times, and had, with a good deal of interest, discussed with him the best method of constructing violins, when he invited me to call on him at his house. Naturally, I did; and he showed me his treasures. There were fully thirty violins on the walls of his study. Among them one, bearing the marks of great antiquity (a carved lion's head, and so forth), stood out conspicuously from the rest. It was hung higher than the others, surrounded by a wreath of flowers, and it seemed to reign like a queen over them.

"This violin," said Krespel, after I had asked him about it, "this violin is a very remarkable and splendid specimen of some unknown master, probably of Tartini's time. I am utterly convinced that there is something extremely unusual about its inner structure, and that, if I took it to pieces, a secret would be revealed to me which I have tried to discover for a long time. But—laugh at me if you like—this dead thing, to which only my touch brings life and sound, often speaks to me of its own accord and in a most marvelous way. The very first time I played on it, I felt somehow as if I were only a mesmerist with the power of influencing his subject to express the hidden instincts and potentialities of her inner nature. Don't think for a moment that I am foolish enough to attach even the slightest importance to such fantasies, but even so it is strange that I have never been able to bring myself to cut open that dumb lifeless thing there. I am even pleased, now, that I have never tampered with it, for since Antonia has been here I sometimes play it for her. Antonia enjoys listening to it—enjoys it very much."

The Councillor spoke these words with visible emotion, and I felt encouraged to say to him: "Won't you give me the pleasure of hearing you play, my good sir?"

Krespel looked at me in a slightly kind, slightly wry way and, falling into his familiar drawl, said: "No. I will not, my good sir!" And that put an end to the matter.

Then I had to go over all sorts of curiosities in his collection, some of them nothing more than childish trifles. At last he put his hands into a little box, brought out a folded piece of paper, which he pressed into my palm, and added solemnly: "You are a lover of art. Take this gift as a priceless memento, which you must value at all times above everything else."

With that he took me by the shoulders and gently pushed me towards the door, embracing me at the threshold. That is to say, as far as symbols are concerned, I was thrown out of his house. When I unfolded the paper, I found in it a piece of a violin string about an eighth of an inch long, with the words, "A bit of the treble string with which the deceased Stamitz strung his violin for the last concert he ever played."

My summary dismissal at the mere mention of Antonia's name led me to believe that I should never get to see her. But I was mistaken, for on my second visit to the Councillor's I found Antonia in his room, helping him put a violin together.

At first sight Antonia did not make a strong impression on me. But soon one found it almost impossible to break the spell of her blue eyes, her rose-petal lips, her strangely fragile, lovely presence. She was very pale, but a quip or a bright remark would bring a warm smile to her lips and suffuse her cheeks with a deep burning flush that quickly, however, faded away to the merest tint of rose. I spoke to Antonia without any particular constraint, and yet I saw no signs of the Argus-like watchfulness which the Professor had attributed to Krespel. On the contrary, he seemed quite content to let things take their natural course and even to approve of my conversations with Antonia. And so it happened that I began to visit the Councillor more often, and, as we came to know each other better, a feeling of warmth and friendship possessed our cosy little company, and became a source of gratification to the three of us.

I still continued to be delighted by the Councillor's unpredictable crotchets and oddities. But of course it was Antonia's magic that really attracted me, and led me to put up with a good deal which I should otherwise have impatiently avoided, for I was in a strained state of mind in those days. Only too often there was a quality in the Councillor's bizarrerie that I found dull and irritating. It particularly got on my nerves that whenever I turned the conversation to music, and especially to singing, he would inevitably interrupt me, with that sardonic smile on his face and those repulsive singsong inflections of his voice, to utter a vague generalization on some other, and often banal, subject. I knew from the look of distress which, at such moments, came into Antonia's eyes that Krespel was merely depriving me of any opportunity to ask her to sing. But I did not give up. The hindrances which the Councillor threw in my way only stimulated my resolution to overcome them. I *must* hear Antonia sing, or I would forget the world entirely and lose myself in dreams of her song!

One evening Krespel was in an uncommonly good humor. He had been taking an old Cremona violin apart, and had found that the sound-post was fixed half a line more obliquely than usual. An important discovery and one of incalculable advantage to his violinmaking! I succeeded in getting him into a conversation on the true art of playing the violin. Then he discussed the style which the really great singers had learned from the old masters, and from there the talk led quite naturally to the remark that now tradition was completely ignored, the vocal score erroneously following the affected and abrupt transitions and rapid scaling of the instrumentalists.

"What can be more ridiculous," I cried, getting up from my chair, moving quickly to the piano and suddenly opening it, "what can be more ridiculous than such stilted mannerisms as these—which sound much more like peas rolling across a wooden floor than like music?" And I sang several of the modern *fermate*, which run buzzing up and down the scale, and struck a few wrong chords by way of accompaniment.

Krespel laughed uproariously, and cried out, "Ha! Ha! I thought for a moment I was listening to one of our Italianized Germans or Germanized Italians struggling with an aria from Pucitta, or Portogallo, or some other *Maestro di capella*, or rather *schiavo d'un primo uomo*."

Now, thought I, now's the time. "But Antonia," I remarked, turning to her, "Antonia would know nothing of such singing as that." And I immediately broke into the phrases of a magnificent, profoundly moving old song by Leonardo Leo.

Antonia's cheeks flushed, and a heavenly light, that brought the soul back to them, sparkled in her eyes. She sprang to the piano, but just as she opened her lips, Krespel came up to her and pushed her away. Then he put his hands on my shoulders, and cried out in the shrillest tenor: "My boy—my boy—my boy!"

Then lapsing immediately into his more customary singsong, and grasping my hand with a polite bow, he went on: "It would, indeed, my esteemed and worthy friend, be a violation of the codes of social intercourse, as well as of all good manners, if I were to express heartily and aloud a wish that here, on this very spot, the Devil would appear out of

Hell and gently, with his burning claws, break your neck, and I could get rid of you in this way. But, since that is out of the question, you must admit, my dear, dear fellow, that it is rapidly growing dark, and there are no street lamps lighted tonight, so that, even though I did not throw you bodily out of my house, you might still do your precious limbs some damage. Go home quickly; and cherish a kind memory of your faithful friend, if it should happen that you never—I think you understand me— even if you should never visit him in his own house again."

Then he embraced me, and, still holding me fast by the shoulders, turned with me slowly towards the door, so that I could not get another look at Antonia.

Of course it is obvious that in my position I couldn't thrash the Councillor, though that is what he really deserved. The Professor enjoyed a hearty laugh at my expense, and assured me that I had ruined forever all hope of retaining that eccentric gentleman's friendship. Antonia was too precious to me, I might even say too sacred to me, for me to play the languishing Amoroso under her window or to assume the airs of a lovesick adventurer. Torn and troubled in my heart, I went away from H—. But what has happened before happened again: my fantasy lost its brilliance and intensity, the colors faded; and yet, the recollection of Antonia, even of Antonia's song—which I had never heard—would sometimes creep into my deepest emotions and shed a shimmering, comforting, roseate light.

I had been settled in B— for two years when I set out on a journey to the south of Germany. In the reddish, misty glow of oncoming evening, the towers of H— rose once again before me. The nearer I approached them the more oppressed I became by a sensation of indescribable and agonizing anxiety. It weighed upon my heart like a heavy burden, and I felt I could no longer breathe. I got out of my carriage into the open air. But my discomfort increased until it actually became physical pain. And then it seemed to me I could hear the solemn strains of a chorale floating through the air; the sounds grew clearer, and I could distinguish the voices of men chanting a hymn.

"What is it I am hearing? What is that?" I cried, while a pain stabbed me like a burning dagger.

"Can't you see?" replied the coachman, who was sitting beside me. "Can't you see them? They're burying somebody up yonder in the church-yard."

We were, in fact, approaching a churchyard, and now I could see a group of people dressed in black standing round a grave, which was about to be closed up. Tears started to my eyes. It seemed to me, somehow, as if all the joy, all the happiness in life were being buried there.

The carriage moved on quickly down the hill, and I was no longer able to see the churchyard. The chorale had come to an end, and I noticed, not far from the town gate, some of the mourners returning from the funeral. The Professor, with his niece leaning on his arm, both of them in deepest black, walked close past me without noticing me. The niece held her handkerchief pressed to her eyes, and was weeping bitterly.

I was in no frame of mind to enter the town, so I sent my servant and carriage ahead to the inn where I usually put up, while I took a turn about the familiar countryside, in the hope of ridding myself of a mood that was probably due to nothing more than some physical cause, such as the heat of the journey. I turned down a walk which leads to the public gardens and came upon the most extraordinary spectacle.

Councillor Krespel was being led by the arm by two mourners, from whom he appeared to be trying to escape by all sorts of strange twists and capers. As usual, he was dressed in his own odd-looking homemade grey coat. But from his little cocked-hat, which he wore perched over one ear in military fashion, a long narrow ribbon of black crape dangled and fluttered in the air. Around his waist he had buckled a black sword belt, but instead of a sword he had stuck a long violin bow into it.

An icy shudder ran through my limbs. He's gone completely mad, thought I, as I slowly followed the remarkable procession.

The Councillor's escort brought him as far as his house. At the door, he embraced the two men, laughing aloud all the time. They went their way, and then his glance fell upon me, for I was standing near him. He stared at me for some little time, and then he cried out in a hollow voice, "Welcome, my young student! Ah! I see you understand what I mean!" Whereupon he took me by the arm and pulled me into the house, up the steps, into the room where the violins hung.

They were all draped in black crape. The violin of the old master was gone, and in its place there hung a cypress wreath.

I knew what had happened. "Antonia! Antonia!" I cried out.

The Councillor, with his arms crossed on his breast, stood beside me, as if turned into stone. I pointed to the cypress wreath.

"When she died," he said in a low, solemn voice, "when she died, the soundpost of that violin broke with a resounding crack, and the soundboard split to pieces. It was faithful to her, and could only live with her, in her. It lies beside her in her coffin now. It is buried with her."

Deeply agitated, I sank down upon a chair, but the Councillor began to sing a gay song in a husky voice, and it was truly horrible to see him hopping about on one foot, with the crape band (he was still wearing his hat) flying about the room after him and fluttering over the violins on the wall. Indeed, I could not restrain a cry when the Councillor, executing an abrupt turn, sent the crape ribbon floating out over my head, for it seemed to me he was trying to entangle me in it and drag me down with him into the dark and terrifying abyss of insanity.

Suddenly he stood stock-still and addressed me in his singing way: "My boy, my boy! Why do you cry out? Have you caught a glimpse of the angel of death? That always comes before the ritual!" Stepping into the middle of the room, he took the violin bow out of his sword belt and, holding it over his head with both hands, broke it into a thousand pieces. Then, with a loud laugh, he cried, "Now the staff has been broken over me, and you imagine my sentence is pronounced, don't you, my boy? But it's nothing of the kind! Not at all! Not at all! Now I'm free, free, free! Hurrah! I'm free! Now I shall make no more violins—no more violins! Hurrah! No more violins!"

This the Councillor sang to a horrible, joyous tune, and again went spinning on one foot around the room. Utterly shocked and disgusted, I tried to make my way hastily out of the room, but the Councillor seized hold of me and said quite calmly: "Stay with me, my young friend! Don't conclude from this outburst of grief, which is racking me with the agonies of death, that I am insane. It is all working out this way because some time ago I designed a dressing gown for myself in which I wanted to look like Fate or like God!"

He continued to babble on, saying mad, terrible things, until at last he collapsed, utterly exhausted. I called his old housekeeper, and was considerably relieved when I found myself in the open air again.

I never doubted for a moment that Krespel had gone mad, but the Professor maintained the contrary.

"There are some men," he remarked, "whom Nature or a strange destiny has deprived of the covering behind which most of us hide our madness from ourselves and the rest of the world. These men are like thin-skinned insects, which, as one watches the restless play of their muscles, appear misshapen and yet in another moment settle down again into their proper normal form. What remains thought in us, becomes action in Krespel. His outrageous gestures, his most nimble and frantic antics, are nothing more than the bitterly contemptuous reaction of the spirit to its contact with mundane and earthly things. They are merely his lightning conductor. He returns to the earth what comes from the earth, but that which is divine he keeps. And so I believe that in his inner consciousness, despite the madness that he displays on the surface, he is balanced and sound. Of course, Antonia's unexpected death grieves him deeply, but I wager that tomorrow will see him going through his usual paces in his old familiar way." And the Professor's prediction was almost literally fulfilled. The next day the Councillor appeared to be very much his former self, but he vowed that he would never make another violin again, or ever play one. I later learned that he had kept his word.

Various hints dropped by the Professor confirmed a personal conviction of my own that the carefully guarded circumstances of the Councillor's relations to Antonia, and even of her death, concealed a guilt on Krespel's part that must weigh heavily upon him and that, perhaps, could never be atoned for. I resolved that I would not leave H— without denouncing him for the crime of which I suspected him. I would shake him to his very soul, and compel him to confess the terrible deed. The more I reflected upon the matter, the greater Krespel's culpability became in my eyes, and in the same proportion my intended reproach, which of its own momentum was turning into a masterpiece of rhetoric, grew more fiery and more impressive.

Thus incensed and prepared, I hurried to the Councillor's house. I found him, calm and smiling, tinkering away at some toys.

"How can you enjoy any peace," I burst out, "how can you have an instant's peace in your soul, when the memory of your terrible deed must be feeding like a serpent upon you?"

He stared at me in amazement, and laid his chisel aside. "Tell me what you are referring to, my good friend," he said. "And do sit down."

But I was carried away by my own rhetoric, and went on more and more passionately until I accused him directly of having murdered Antonia, and threatened him with the vengeance of the Almighty. I even went further than that—I was a newly fledged court official, full of pride in my profession—and I assured the Councillor that I would leave no stone unturned until I had discovered every last scrap of evidence against him. and had delivered him into the hands of his earthly judges, here below.

I must confess that I was considerably disconcerted when, at the conclusion of my violent and pompous harangue, the Councillor, without answering a word, calmly fixed his eyes upon me as though he expected me to begin all over again. And this I did, in fact, attempt to do; but my oration sounded false and even stupid to my own ears, and I soon fell silent.

Krespel gloated over my embarrassment and offered me a smile full of malice and irony, but then he became grave. "Young man," he said, with some solemnity, "I don't mind your taking me for an imbecile or a lunatic. After all we are both inmates of the same madhouse; and you only blame me for deluding myself with the idea that I am God the Father because you imagine yourself to be God the Son. But how dare you attempt to insinuate yourself into the secrets, and grasp the most mysterious threads, of a life that remains and must remain foreign to you? She has gone, and that is the end of the mystery!"

He stopped speaking, rose, and walked back and forth across the room a few times. I ventured to ask him for some explanation. He fixed his eyes upon me, took me by the hand, and led me to the window, which he threw wide open. Then he propped himself up on his elbows, leaned out over the sill, and, looking down into the garden, told me the story of his life. When he finished I went away, touched and not unashamed.

This, briefly, is the story of his connection with Antonia. Some twenty years before I met him, the Councillor had been attracted to Italy by a fondness for tracking down and buying up violins by old masters—a fondness that developed into a passion. At that time he had not yet begun to make violins himself nor, for that matter, to take his instruments to pieces. In Venice he went to hear the famous prima donna, Angela ——i, who was then singing dramatic rôles at the Teatro di San Benedetto. His enthusiasm was aroused, not only by her art, to which the Signora brought the most splendid gifts and style, but by her angelic beauty as well. He succeeded in meeting her and, despite all his brusqueness of manner, won her to his heart—his virtuosity on the violin, no doubt, exercising more influence over her than his personal charms. This musical intimacy led in a few weeks to a marriage, which, however, was kept secret, because Angela was unwilling to give up either the theatre or the name she had made famous, for the cacophonous identity of "Madame Krespel."

He went on to describe to me, with the most merciless irony, what a strange life of worry and torture Signora Angela led him as soon as she had become his wife. It seemed to him as if all the stubbornness, all the perversity, that have ever contributed to the professional temperament of a prima donna, were concentrated in Angela's little person. If he now and again presumed to stand up in his own defense, Angela let loose a whole army of *abbés*, maestros, and music students upon him, who, ignorant of his true connection with her, berated him as a most intolerable, ungallant lover for not eagerly submitting to all the Signora's caprices.

It was just after one of these stormy scenes that Krespel fled to Angela's house in the country and there, improvising on his Cremona violin, he tried to forget the troubles of the day. But he had not been occupied in this way long before the Signora, who had followed quickly after him, came into the room. She was in an affectionate mood. She embraced her husband, overwhelmed him with sweet and languishing glances, and rested her little head on his shoulder. But Krespel, carried away by the harmonies of another world, continued to play on until the walls re-echoed, and, thus, he chanced to touch the Signora somewhat ungently with his arm and bow. She sprang back full of fury, shrieking that he was a "*bestia tedesco*," snatched the violin from his hands, and dashed it on the marble table.

The Councillor stood motionless before her, turned to a statue of stone, but then, as if waking from a dream, he seized her with his giant strength and dropped her out of the window of her own house, and, troubling himself no further about anything, fled back to Venice and then returned to Germany.

It was not, however, until some time had elapsed that he had a clear recollection of what he had done. Although he knew that the window was scarcely five feet from the ground, and although he was aware of the provocation he had had before he had lost his temper, he felt troubled and uneasy, and particularly since the Signora had informed him, with a fair degree of certainty, that she was with child. He hardly dared to make any inquiries, and was not a little surprised when about eight months later he received a quite affectionate letter from his wife, in which, without making the slightest reference to what had happened in the country, she acquainted him with the fact that she had been safely delivered of a precious little girl, and added the warmest invitation to the *marito amato e padre felicissimo* to come at once to Venice.

This, however, Krespel did not do. But, through a trusted friend, he learned all the details of the situation, and was informed that the Signora had landed on the soft grass as lightly as a bird, and that the only effect the fall had had upon her was psychological rather than physical. That is to say, after Krespel's heroic deed the Signora had become a different person. There was no trace of her former capriciousness in her behavior— no childish impetuosity or cruelty. In fact, the maestro who had composed the music for the next carnival was the happiest man under the sun because the Signora was ready to sing his arias as he had written them, without demanding hundreds of minute revisions as she usually did. It was the suggestion of Krespel's friend, however, that Angela's cure be kept secret, for he was afraid that, if word got out, the air would become thick with flying divas.

The Councillor reacted to all this with feverish excitement. He ordered horses, took his seat in the carriage, and then commanded the driver to stop before he had started. "Why, there's not a shadow of a doubt," he murmured to himself, "that as soon as Angela sets eyes upon me again the evil spirit will recover his power and once more take possession of her. And since I have already thrown her out of the window, what would I have to do the next time? What would there be left for me to do?" Whereupon he climbed out of the carriage, wrote an affectionate letter to his wife, referring very gracefully to her tenderness in mentioning

to him the fact that his tiny daughter had, like himself, a little mole behind the ear, and—he remained in Germany.

Now a lively correspondence sprang up between them. Assurances
of unchanged affection, invitations, laments over the absence of the loved
one, thwarted wishes, hopes, and all the other sentimental exchanges
crossed each other from Venice to H—, from H— to Venice. At length
Angela came to Germany, and appeared, as we all know, with brilliant
success as prima donna of the great theatre in F—. Although she was no
longer young, her magnificent singing worked an irresistible charm upon
her audiences. Meanwhile, Antonia had been growing up, and her mother
never tired of writing to tell the father how the girl was blossoming into
a singer of the finest talents. In fact, Krespel's friends in F— confirmed this,
and they urged him to come, if just once, to F— to share this rare experience of hearing two such sublime singers. They had not the slightest
inkling of the close relations in which Krespel stood to the pair. Krespel
would have been only too happy to see with his own eyes the daughter
who occupied so much of his heart and imagination, but the moment
he thought of his wife he became depressed, and so he remained at home
in the company of his dismembered violins.

There was a certain promising young composer in F—, called B—,
who caused quite a stir for a time, and now had completely disappeared
from sight. This young man fell so much in love with Antonia—and she
with him—that he begged her mother to consent to an immediate marriage, sanctified as it would further be by art. Angela was in no way opposed to this, and the Councillor all the more readily gave his consent
because the young maestro's compositions had found favor in his rigor-
ously critical judgment.

Krespel was expecting to hear word of the consummation of the
marriage, when instead he received a black-sealed envelope addressed in
a strange hand. Doctor R— regretted to inform the Councillor that Angela had fallen seriously ill as a result of a cold caught at the theatre, and
that she had died the night before what was to have been Antonia's wedding day. Angela had revealed to the doctor that she was Krespel's wife,
and that Antonia was his daughter; he, Krespel, should, therefore, come
as quickly as possible to take charge of the unprotected child. Although
the Councillor was considerably upset by the news of Angela's death, he

soon began to feel that an uncanny, hostile influence had departed out of his life, and that now for the first time he could breathe freely. He set out for F— that very same day.

You cannot imagine how heart-rending was the Councillor's description of the moment when he first saw Antonia. Even in the fantastic oddities of his expression there was such a marvelous power of description that I find myself unable to reproduce the faintest version of it. Antonia had inherited all her mother's amiable qualities, all her charms, but none of her unpleasantness; none of the vacillation or unpredictable spite that could suddenly flare up and strike one when it was least expected.

Antonia's young man turned up while Antonia herself, with a tender desire to touch the deepest sensibilities of her remarkable father, was in the midst of singing one of old Padre Martini's motets, which, she knew, Krespel in the heyday of his courtship had never grown tired of hearing her mother sing. The tears ran in streams down Krespel's cheeks. Even Angela had never sung like that for him. Antonia's voice was possessed of a rare and distinctive timbre: sometimes it became the sighing of an Aeolian harp, sometimes it was like the pealing warble of a nightingale. There seemed no chamber in the human breast from which such tones could issue. Antonia, flushed with excitement and happiness, sang on and on; between whiles, B— played the pieces with all the intoxicating inspiration of genius.

Krespel was at first ecstatic, but he became pensive—still—self-absorbed. Then suddenly he leaped to his feet, drew Antonia to him, and said to her in a low hoarse voice: "Sing no more if you love me! My heart is bursting. It makes me afraid—afraid! Sing no more!"

"I knew," remarked the Councillor the next day to Doctor R—, "when I saw the color gathering into two dark red spots on her pale cheeks as she sang, I knew then that it had nothing to do with any nonsense about family likenesses; I knew it was what I dreaded most."

The doctor, from the very beginning of the conversation, had made no effort to conceal his own distress. "Whether it is the result of taxing too early her powers of song," he replied, "or whether the fault is all Nature's is difficult to say. Antonia suffers from a curious condition in her chest, which, in fact, provides her voice with its power and singular timbre.

But, unfortunately, it is also premonitory of an early death. If she continues to sing, I cannot give her more than six months longer to live."

Krespel's heart was clawed by the sharpest anguish. It seemed to him as if the one sheltering tree he had ever found in a lifetime of glaring light and heat had been ruthlessly uprooted and that now he must see its magnificent foliage wither and its blossoms drop off.

He made up his mind to tell Antonia everything, and let her decide for herself whether she would yield to the attractions of marriage and worldly success, but with the certainty of an early death, or whether she could accept an existence of retirement which would prolong her life and bring her father the peace and comfort he had never known. He then discussed the matter with her betrothed, and, although the latter swore that he would never again permit a note to cross Antonia's lips, the Councillor was only too well aware that even B— would not be able to resist the temptation of hearing Antonia at least sing arias of his own composition. And the world, the musical public, even though acquainted with the nature of the singer's affliction, would certainly not relinquish its claim upon her, for there is nothing about which people are more ruthless than the gratification of their own pleasure.

One day the Councillor disappeared from F—, taking Antonia with him, and came to H—. B— became desperate when he discovered that they were gone. He set out on their track, overtook them, and arrived at H— the same time that they did.

"Let me see him only once, and then die!" begged Antonia.

"Die! die!" cried Krespel, wild with anger. His daughter, the one creature on earth who had had the power to awaken in him joys he had never before known, she who alone had reconciled him to life, now wrenched herself away from his heart, and he—he submitted and permitted the terrible thing to happen.

B— sat down to the piano; Antonia sang; Krespel fiddled merrily away, until the two red spots showed themselves on Antonia's cheeks. Then the Councillor bade her stop; and as B— was taking leave of his beloved, she suddenly fell to the floor with a shriek.

"I thought, then," Krespel afterwards told me, "I thought that what I had anticipated had come to pass, and that she was really dead. I had prepared myself for the worst and now I remained calm and self-possessed.

B— was standing there looking, for all his sorrow, like a bleating sheep; I took him by the shoulders and said (here the Councillor fell into his sing-song) : 'Now, my most worthy music master, now that you have fulfilled your dearest wish and desire and have, in fact, murdered your future bride, you may quietly go your way. At least have the goodness to make yourself scarce before I run this bright, unstained cutlass through your heart and thereby benefit my daughter, who, as you see, is rather pale and could very well do with some of the color of your precious blood. Hurry! In fact, run as fast as you can, for I might even send a knife or two flying after you!' I dare say, I must have looked rather menacing when I spoke these words, for, with a cry of greatest terror, B— tore him-self loose from my grasp, rushed out of the room and down the steps."

The moment B— was gone, the Councillor tried to lift up his daugh-ter in his arms; she sighed faintly and opened her eyes, but soon they fell shut again as if struck by death. Then Krespel's grief burst from him beyond all restraint and consolation.

The doctor, whom the old housekeeper had called in, pronounced Antonia's condition quite serious, but by no means critical. And she did indeed recover more quickly than her father had ever dared to hope.

She now clung to Krespel with the most absorbing, childlike affec-tion, participating in all his hobbies and entering into his maddest schemes and fancies. She helped him take old violins apart and glue new ones together. "I won't sing ever again. I shall live only for you," she often said, sweetly smiling up at him, after she had been asked to sing and had refused. The Councillor, however, was anxious to spare her such refusals, and therefore resolved to shun all music scrupulously and never to take his daughter into society. He understood only too well how painful his Antonia must find it to renounce, entirely, an art which she had brought to such a pitch of perfection.

When the Councillor bought his wonderful violin (the one that he later had buried with Antonia) and prepared to take it to pieces, his daughter turned to him with unutterable sadness in her eyes and merely said: "What! This one, too?" And some unknown force, which the Councillor, himself, was at a loss to explain, seemed to compel him to spare this one instrument, to leave it unbroken and to play on it.

He had scarcely drawn the first few notes from it with his bow when

Antonia cried out joyfully: "Why, that is Antonia! It is I, I! Now I am singing for you again!" And, indeed, there was an extraordinary quality in the silvery, bell-like tones of the violin that made them sound as if they had issued from the human heart. Krespel, profoundly moved, played more magnificently than ever before, and each time he came upon some brilliant run, some bold passage which he executed with inspired virtuosity and expression, Antonia would clap her hands and cry out in delight: "I did that well! I did that well!"

From this time on, great serenity and peace came into her life. She would often say to the Councillor: "I should like to sing something, Father." Then Krespel would take his violin down from the wall and play her most beautiful songs, and she would feel happy and content in her heart.

Shortly before my arrival in H—, the Councillor imagined one night that he heard someone playing the piano in an adjoining room and he soon distinctly made out B—'s familiar touch and style. He wanted to get up, but it seemed to him as if he were being held down by some dead weight, as if he were lying bound in chains, and he found himself utterly unable to move. Now Antonia's voice reached his ears, singing in low, hushed tones which soon, however, began to rise higher and higher until they reached a shattering fortissimo. Then there came to him the impressive strains of a song which B— had once composed for Antonia in the devotional style of the old masters.

Krespel described his condition as incomprehensible, for terrible dread was mingled with a delight he had never before experienced.

All at once he was surrounded by a dazzling light, in which he beheld B— and Antonia locked in an embrace, and gazing at each other in rapture. The music of the song and the accompaniment of the pianoforte continued, and yet there was no visible sign that Antonia was singing or that B— had touched the instrument. Then the Councillor fell into a sort of dead faint and the images vanished.

On awakening he still experienced the terrible dread of his dream. He rushed into Antonia's room. She lay on the sofa, her eyes closed, a seraphic smile on her face, her hands devoutly folded, and looking as if she were asleep and dreaming of the joys and raptures of Heaven. But she was dead.

THE GOLDEN POT

A Fairy Tale

First Vigil

The Mishaps of the Student Anselmus. Dean Paulmann's Tobacco Box, and the Gold-green Snakes.

ON ASCENSION DAY, ABOUT THREE o'clock in the afternoon, a young man came running through the *Schwarzthor,* or Black Gate, out of Dresden, and right into a basket of apples and cakes, which an old and very ugly woman had there set out for sale. The crash was prodigious; everything that escaped being crushed and broken to bits was scattered in all directions; and the street urchins joyfully divided the booty which this quick-moving gentleman had provided them.

At the shriek of "Murder!" which the crone set up, her neighbors, leaving their cake-and-brandy tables, at once surrounded the young man, and with plebeian violence stormily harangued him; so that, for shame and vexation, he uttered no word, but merely held out his small, and by no means particularly well-filled, purse, which the old hag eagerly clutched and stuck into her pocket.

The circle around him now opened, but as the young man started off, the old woman called after him: "Go on! Go your way, you spawn of the Devil! Run straight to the crystal! Yes, to the crystal!" The beldame's squealing, croaking voice had something uncanny about it, so that the promenaders paused in amazement; and the laughter, which at first had been universal, instantly died away.

The Student Anselmus—for that was who the young man was—felt himself, though he did not in the least understand these singular phrases, nevertheless seized with a certain involuntary horror; and he quickened his steps still more, to escape the curious looks which the multitude on all sides turned upon him. As he worked his way through the crowd of well-dressed people, he heard them murmuring on all sides: "Poor young man! Ha! What a nasty old woman!" The mysterious words of the old hag had oddly enough given this ludicrous adventure a sort of tragic turn; and the youth, hitherto ignored, was now stared after with a certain sympathy. The ladies, because of his fine figure and handsome face, which the glow of inward anger was rendering still more expressive, forgave him his clumsiness, as well as the costume he wore, though it was utterly at variance with all fashion. His pike-grey coat was shaped as if the tailor had known the modern form only by hearsay; and his well-kept black satin breeches gave his whole appearance a certain schoolmasterish air, to which the gait and bearing of the wearer in no way corresponded.

The Student had almost reached the end of the little street which leads out to the Linke Baths, but his breath could no longer stand such a pace. From running he took to walking; but he scarcely yet dared lift his eyes from the ground; for he still saw apples and cakes falling on all sides; and every kind look from this or that fair lady seemed to him nothing more than the echo of the mocking laughter at the *Schwarzthor*. In this mood, he finally arrived at the entrance to the Baths, thronged by festive groups of visitors. The playing of a brass band could be heard inside and, above the music, the din of merrymaking, growing louder each moment.

The poor Student Anselmus was almost on the point of tears; for he too had expected—Ascension Day had always been a family celebration at home—to participate in the festivities at Linke's bath-paradise. More, he had even intended to go so far as to indulge in a half portion of coffee with rum, and a whole bottle of double beer; and in order to dissipate really at his ease he had put more money in his purse than was entirely convenient or advisable. Now, by this fatal step into the apple basket, every penny that he had on him had vanished, as one might say, into thin air. There could be no more thought now of coffee, of double or single beer, of music, of looking at bright girls in their holiday best, or, in short, of any of his fancied enjoyments. He slipped slowly past the Baths and at last turned down the Elbe road, which at that hour happened to be quite deserted.

Beneath an elder tree, which had grown out through the wall, he found a welcoming green resting place. Here he sat down, and filled a pipe from the *Sanitatsknäster*, or Health-tobacco box, which his friend, the Dean Paulmann, had recently given him. Close before him rolled and tossed the gold-tinted waves of the fair Elbe River; behind this rose lordly Dresden, stretching, bold and proud, its luminous towers into the misty sky, which again, farther off, dipped down toward flowery fields and fresh spring woods; while in the dim distance a range of azure peaks gave notice of remote Bohemia. But, heedless of all this, the Student Anselmus stared gloomily before him and silently blew forth his clouds of smoke into the air.

Finally, although there was no one near to hear him, he began to complain aloud: "There can be no doubt about it, I am born to losses and crosses for the rest of my life! That in my schooldays I never won a prize, or that at Odds or Evens I could never once guess the right way, that my bread-and-butter always fell on the buttered side—of all these sorrows I will not speak. But is it not a frightful destiny, that now when, in spite of Satan, I have become a student, I must still remain a dunce? Do I ever put on a new coat, without the first day smearing it with tallow, or catching it on some ill-fastened nail or other and tearing a wretched hole in it? Do I ever bow to any Councillor or any lady without pitching the hat out of my hands, or even slipping on the smooth pavement, and disgracefully stumbling? Was I not obliged, every market day, while I was in Halle, to pay out regularly a sum of three or four groschen for broken pottery, the Devil putting it into my head to walk straight forward over everything, like a lemming-rat? Have I ever once got to my college, or any other place where I had an appointment, at the right time? What good did it do that I set out half an hour before, and planted myself at the door promptly, with the knocker in my hand? Just as the clock is about to strike, bang! some Devil empties a washbasin down on me, or I bolt against some fellow coming out, and get myself engaged in endless quarrels till the time is clean gone . . .

"Ah, they are all fled now, my blissful dreams of sure good fortune, when I proudly thought that here I might even reach the height of Privy Secretary! And has not my evil star estranged my best patrons from me? I learn, for instance, that the Councillor, to whom I have a letter, cannot suffer cropped hair; with enormous trouble the barber fastens a little queue to the back of my head; but at first bow his unblessed knot gives way, and a little dog that has been running sniffling about me joyfully frisks off to the Privy Councillor with the queue in his jaws! I leap after it in terror, and stumble against the table, where the great man has been working during breakfast; and cups, plates, inkwell, sandbox, tumble clattering to the floor, while a flood of chocolate and ink overflows the important public argument he has just been writing. 'Is the Devil in the man?' bellows the furious Privy Councillor, and shoves me out of the room.

"What good is it that Dean Paulmann has given me some hope of a secretaryship? Will my evil fate, which pursues me everywhere, allow it? Even today! Just think of it! I was preparing to celebrate my good old Ascension Day in the proper cheerful state of mind; I was ready to stretch a point for once, I would have gone, like any other guest, into Linke's Baths, and called out proudly: 'Waiter! a bottle of double beer; the best, if you please!' I might have sat there till late into the evening; and, moreover, quite close to this or that fine party of well-dressed ladies. I know it, I feel it! Heart would have come into me, I should have been quite another man; nay, I might have carried it so far, that, when one or another of the ladies asked, 'What o'clock may it be?' or 'What is it they are playing?' I should have started up with light grace, and without overturning my glass, or stumbling over the bench, but in a curved posture, moving one step and a half forward, I should have answered, 'Give me leave, Mademoiselle! It is the overture of the *Donauweibchen*,' or, 'It is just going to strike six.' Could any mortal in the world have taken it ill of me? No! I say. The girls would have looked over, smiling so roguishly, as they always do when I pluck my heart to show them that I too understand the light tone of society, and know how ladies should be spoken to. And now the Devil himself leads me into that cursed apple basket, and I must sit here moping in solitude, with nothing but a poor pipe of—"

But at this point the Student Anselmus was interrupted in his soliloquy by a strange rustling and whisking, which rose close by him in the grass, but soon glided up into the branches and leaves of the elder tree that spread out above his head. It was as if the evening wind were shaking the leaves; as if small birds were twittering among the branches, moving their little wings in capricious flutterings to and fro. Then he heard a whispering and lisping; and it seemed as if the blossoms were making the sound of little crystal bells. Anselmus listened and listened. Before long, the whispering, and lisping, and tinkling grew, he himself knew not how, to faint and half-scattered words:

"In and out, up and down, between the branches, 'twixt blossoms, come shooting, twisting, twirling! Sisters, all! Sisters, we! Swing upon the shimmering light: quickly, quickly, on and off! The sun is setting; winds are rising; now the blossoms begin to sing; sing the blossoms, sing the branches! Stars soon glitter and off we go; in and out, up and down, shooting, twisting, twirling sisters, we!"

And so it went on, in confused and confusing speech. The Student Anselmus thought: "Well, it is only the evening wind, which tonight, in reality, is whispering distinctly enough." But at that moment there sounded over his head, as it were, a triple harmony of clear crystal bells; he looked up, and perceived three little Snakes, glittering with green and gold, twisted round the branches, and stretching out their heads to the evening sun. Then, again, a whispering and twittering began in the same words as before, and the little Snakes went gliding and writhing up and down the twigs. And while they moved so rapidly, it was as if the elder tree were scattering a thousand glittering emeralds through the dark leaves.

"It is the light of the evening sun playing on the elder tree," thought the Student Anselmus. But the bells sounded again; and Anselmus observed that one Snake held out its little head to him. Through all his limbs went a shock like electricity; he quivered in his heart; he kept staring up into the leaves, and he saw a pair of unearthly blue eyes looking down at him with unspeakable longing; an unknown feeling of joy and deepest sorrow stirred within him. And as he stared, and continued to stare, full of warm desire, into those tender eyes, the crystal bells sounded louder in harmonious accord, and the glittering emeralds fell down and encircled him, flickering round him in a thousand reflections and threads of gold. The Elder Tree moved and spoke: "Thou layest in my shadow; my perfume flowed round thee, but thou understoodst it not. The perfume is my speech, when Love kindles it."

The Evening Wind came drifting past, and said: "I played round thy brows, but thou understoodst me not. That breath is my speech, when Love kindles it."

The Sun broke through the clouds, and its rays burned as though with the words: "I overflowed thee with glowing gold, but thou understoodst me not. That glow is my speech, when Love kindles it."

And, still deeper and deeper absorbed in gazing into those glorious eyes, his longing grew keener, his desire more intense. And all the strange scene rose and moved around him, as if awakening to glad life. Flowers and blossoms shed their odors upon him; their fragrance seemed even to fall on his ears, like the lovely singing of a thousand soft voices; and what they sang was borne like an echo on the golden evening clouds, floating away with them into far-off lands. But as the last ray of sunlight abruptly sank behind the hill, and the twilight threw its veil over the scene, a hoarse, deep voice seemed to reach Anselmus from a great distance:

"Hey, hey! What chattering and jingling is that up there? Hey, hey! Who catches me the ray behind the hills? Sunned enough, sung enough. Hey, hey! Through bush and grass, through grass and stream. Hey, hey! Come dow-w-n, dow-w-w-n!"

So the voice faded away, as if in the rumble of distant thunder; but the crystal bells broke off in sharp discords. All became mute; and the Student Anselmus observed how the three Snakes, glittering and sparkling, slipped through the grass towards the river; gliding and sliding, they rushed into the Elbe; and over the waves where they vanished there crackled up a green flame, which, gleaming forward obliquely, vanished in the direction of the city.

SECOND VIGIL

How the Student Anselmus was looked upon as drunk and mad. The crossing of the Elbe. Bandmaster Graun's Bravura. Conradi's Cordial, and the bronzed Apple-woman.

"The gentleman is ailing in some way!" said a respectable burgher's wife, who, returning from a walk with her family, had paused near by and, standing with folded arms, was regarding the mad behavior of the Student Anselmus. The young man had clasped the trunk of the elder tree, and was calling incessantly up to the branches and leaves: "O glitter and shine once more, dear golden Snakes; let me hear your little bell-voices again! Look at me once more, oh, tender eyes; once more, or I must die in pain and yearning!" All this was accompanied by the most pitiful sighing and sobbing, while Anselmus, in his eagerness and impatience, shook the elder tree to and fro; the latter, however, instead of making any reply, only rustled quite stupidly and unintelligibly with its leaves; and so rather seemed, as it were, to be making sport of the young student and his sorrows.

"The gentleman is ailing in some way!" repeated the burgher's wife. And Anselmus felt as if someone had shaken him out of a deep dream, or poured ice-cold water on him, to wake him instantly out of sleep. He now first saw clearly where he was, and remembered what a strange apparition had attacked his senses, nay, had so beguiled them as to make him break into loud talk with himself. In astonishment he gazed at the woman; and at last snatching up his hat, which had fallen to the ground in his transport, was for making off with all speed. The burgher himself had come forward in the meanwhile; and, setting down on the grass the child he was carrying, had been leaning on his staff, listening to and regarding the Student with amazement.

He now picked up the pipe and tobacco box which the Student had let fall, and, holding them out to him, said: "Don't take on so dreadfully, my worthy sir, or alarm people in the dark, when nothing is the matter, after all, but a drop or two too much of liquor; go home, like a good lad, and sleep it off."

The Student Anselmus felt exceedingly ashamed; he uttered nothing but a most pitiful "Ah!"

"Now! Now!" said the burgher. "Don't take it to heart! Such a thing will happen to the best; on a good old Ascension Day a man may readily forget himself in his joy, and gulp down a thought too much. A clergyman himself is no worse for it; I presume, my worthy sir, you are a *Candidatus*. But, with your leave, sir, I shall fill my pipe with your tobacco; I finished the last of mine a little while ago."

The burgher spoke this last sentence as the Student Anselmus was about to put away his pipe and box; and now the good citizen slowly and deliberately cleaned his pipe, and began as slowly to fill it. Several neighborhood girls had come up; these were talking, aside, with the burgher's wife and each other, and tittering as they looked at Anselmus. The Student felt as if he were standing on prickly thorns and burning needles. No sooner had he got back his pipe and tobacco box, than he hurried off at the top of his speed.

All the strange things he had seen were blotted from his memory; he recalled nothing but having babbled all manner of foolish stuff beneath the elder tree. This was the more unpleasant to him, since he had long entertained an inward horror of all soliloquists. It is Satan that chatters out of such monologues, said his Rector; and Anselmus had honestly believed him. But to be regarded as a *Candidatus Theologiae* overtaken with drink on Ascension Day! The thought was intolerable.

As his mind ran on with these mad vexations, he was just about to turn up the Poplar Lane, by the Kosel Garden, when a voice behind him called out: "Anselmus! Anselmus! For the love of Heaven, where are you running in such haste?" The Student paused, as if rooted to the spot, for he was convinced that now some new mischance was about to befall him. The voice rose again: "Anselmus, come back! We are waiting for you here by the river!" And now the Student realized that it was his friend Dean Paulmann's voice; he went back to the Elbe, and found the Dean, with his two daughters, as well as Registrar Heerbrand, all on the point of stepping into their boat. Dean Paulmann invited the Student to go with them across the stream, and then to spend the evening at his house in the Pirna suburb. The Student Anselmus very gladly accepted this suggestion, thinking thereby to escape the evil destiny which had pursued him all day.

Now, as they were crossing the river, it chanced that on the farther bank, in the Anton Garden, fireworks were just being set off. Sputtering and hissing, the rockets soared aloft, shattering their blazing stars in the air, scattering a thousand vague sparks and flashes in the sky around them. The Student Anselmus was sitting by the steersman, sunk in deep thought; but when he noticed the reflection of these darting and wavering sparks and flames in the water, it seemed to him as if the little golden Snakes were sporting again in the waves. All the wonders that he had seen at the elder tree once more sprang to life in his heart and mind; and again he was seized by that unspeakable longing, that glowing desire, which he had felt before.

"Ah, is it you again, my little golden Snakes? Sing now, Oh, sing! In your song let the kind, dear, dark blue eyes again appear to me. Ah! Are ye under the waves, then?"

So cried the Student Anselmus, and at the same time made a violent movement, as if about to plunge from the boat into the river.

"Is the Devil in you, sir?" exclaimed the steersman, and clutched him by the front of his coat. The girls, who were sitting by him, shrieked in terror, and pushed to the other side of the boat. Registrar Heerbrand whispered something in Dean Paulmann's ear, to which the latter answered at considerable length, but in so low a tone that Anselmus could distinguish nothing but the words: "Such attacks more than once?—Never heard of it." Directly after this, the Dean also rose; and then sat down, with a certain earnest, grave, official mien, beside the Student Anselmus, taking his hand, and saying: "How are you feeling, Anselmus?" The Student Anselmus was almost out of his wits, for in his mind there was a mad contradiction, which he strove in vain to reconcile. He now saw plainly that what he had taken for the gleaming of the golden Snakes was nothing but the reflection of the fireworks in the Anton Garden. But a feeling unexperienced till now, he himself knew not whether it was rapture or pain, wrenched his heart. And when the steersman struck through the water with his helm, so that the waves, curling as in anger, spluttered and foamed, he heard in their din a soft whispering: "Anselmus! Anselmus! Can you not see how we are still skimming along with you? Sister is watching you again; believe, believe, believe in us!" And he thought he saw in the reflected light three streaks of glowing green. But then, when he gazed, full of fond sadness, into the water, to see whether these gentle eyes would not again look up to him, he perceived too well that the gleam was reflected only from the windows in the neighboring houses. He was sitting mute in his place, and inwardly struggling with himself, when Dean Paulmann repeated with still greater emphasis: "How are you feeling, Anselmus?"

In the most rueful tone, the Student replied: "Ah! Sir, if you knew what strange things I have been dreaming, quite awake, with open eyes, just now under an elder tree near the wall of Linke's Garden, you would not take it amiss of me that I am a little absent-minded."

"Well, now, my good Anselmus!" interrupted the Dean, "I have always taken you for a solid young man; but to dream, to dream with your eyes wide open, and then, all at once, to start up as if you were leaping into the water! That, if you permit me to say so, is what only fools or madmen are capable of."

The Student Anselmus was deeply distressed by his friend's harsh talk. But then Veronica, Paulmann's eldest daughter, a very pretty and blooming girl of sixteen, came to his defense. "But, dear Father, something strange must have happened to Anselmus," she said. "And perhaps he only thinks he was awake, while he may have really been asleep, and so all sorts of wild ideas have come into his head, and still occupy his thoughts."

"And, my dear Mademoiselle! My worthy Dean!" cried Registrar Heerbrand. "May one not, even when awake, sometimes sink into a sort of dreaming state? I myself have had such fits. One afternoon, for instance, during coffee, in a mood like this, in the special hour of corporeal and spiritual digestion, I suddenly recalled where I had left a missing manuscript, as if by inspiration; and no longer ago than last night, there came a glorious large Latin paper tripping out before my open eyes in the very same way."

"Ah! Most honored Registrar," answered the Dean, "you have always had a tendency to the *Poetica*; and thus one falls into fantasies and romantic humors."

The Student Anselmus, however, was particularly gratified that in this most troublous situation, while in danger of being considered drunk or crazy, anyone should have taken his part; and though it was already fairly dark, he thought he noticed, for the first time, that Veronica had really very fine dark blue eyes, and this too without remembering the strange glance which had peered out at him from the elder tree. On the whole, the adventure under the elder tree had once more effectively vanished from the thoughts of the Student Anselmus. He felt himself at ease and light of heart; indeed, he felt so released from his broodings that, without any fear of clumsiness, he offered a helping hand to his fair advocate, Veronica, as she was stepping from the boat. And without more ado, as she put her arm in his, he escorted her home with so much dexterity and good luck, that he missed his footing only once, and—this being the only wet spot in the whole road—only spattered Veronica's white gown a very little by the incident.

Dean Paulmann did not fail to observe this happy change in Anselmus. His fondness for the Student at once returned, and the Dean begged forgiveness for the harsh words he had uttered earlier. "Yes," he admitted, "we have many examples to show that certain fantasms may rise before a man, and prey upon him, and plague him not a little; but this is bodily disease, and leeches are good for it, if applied to the right part, as a certain learned physician, now deceased, has directed."

The Student Anselmus knew not whether he had been drunk, crazy, or sick; but at all events the leeches seemed entirely superfluous, since these supposed fantasms had utterly vanished. And the Student himself became increasingly happier and happier, the more he succeeded in showering the pretty Veronica with a variety of delicate attentions.

As usual, after the Dean's frugal meal, there was music. The Student Anselmus had to take his seat before the harpsichord, and Veronica accompanied his playing with her pure, clear voice. "Dear Mademoiselle," said Registrar Heerbrand, "you have a voice like a crystal bell!"

"That she has not!" ejaculated the Student Anselmus, he scarcely knew why. "Crystal bells in elder trees make a very strange sound!" continued the Student Anselmus, mumbling half to himself.

Veronica laid her hand on his shoulder. "What are you saying now, Anselmus?" she asked.

Instantly Anselmus recovered his normal cheerfulness, and began to play. Dean Paulmann cast a grim look toward him; but Registrar Heerbrand laid a sheet of music on the music rack, and sang with ravishing grace one of Bandmaster Graun's bravura airs. The Student Anselmus accompanied this, and many more that followed. And a fantasy duet, which Veronica and he now fingered, and Dean Paulmann had himself composed, again put all the little company into the best humor.

The time was now rather late, and Registrar Heerbrand was taking up his hat and stick when the Dean approached him with a mysterious air, and said: "Tun! Would you not, honored Registrar, mention to the good Student Anselmus himself—hum!—what we were speaking of before?"

"With all the pleasure in the world," said Registrar Heerbrand. And having placed himself in the midst of the little group, he began, without further preamble, as follows:

"There is in this city a strange and remarkable man; people say he follows all manner of secret sciences, but since there are no such sciences, I rather take him to be an antiquary, and along with this, an experimental chemist. I mean no other than our Privy Archivist, Lindhorst. He lives, as you know, by himself, in his remote and cloistral old house; and when disengaged from his office work he is to be found in his library, or in his chemical laboratory, to which, however, he admits no stranger. Besides many curious books, he possesses a number of manuscripts, partly Arabic and Coptic, and some of them written in strange characters, which do not belong to any known tongue. These he wishes to have properly copied; and for this purpose he requires a man who can draw with the pen, and so transfer these marks to parchment, in India ink, with extreme strictness and fidelity. The work is carried on in a separate room of his house, under his own supervision; and besides free board during working hours, he pays his man a silver dollar daily, and promises a handsome reward when the copying is properly completed. The hours are from twelve to six. From three to four you rest and take dinner.

"Herr Archivist Lindhorst, having vainly tried one or two young people as copyists for these manuscripts, has at last applied to me to find him an expert master of pen-drawing. And so I have been thinking of you, my dear Anselmus, for I know that you not only write neatly, but likewise draw with the pen to great perfection. Now if in these bad times, and until you have established yourself permanently, you would like to earn a dollar each day, and the promised gift over and above that, you can go tomorrow, precisely at noon, and call upon the Archivist, whose house no doubt you know. But be on your guard against so much as a blot! If such a thing falls on your copy, you must begin it again; if it falls on the original, the Archivist will think nothing of throwing you out of the window, for he is a hot-tempered gentleman."

The Student Anselmus was delighted with Registrar Heerbrand's proposal. For not only did the Student write well and draw well with the pen, but this copying with laborious calligraphic pains was a thing he enjoyed enormously. So he thanked his patron in the most grateful terms, and promised not to fail to be at the Archivist's house at noon next day.

All night the Student Anselmus saw nothing but bright silver dollars, and heard nothing but their lovely clink. Who could blame the poor youth, cheated of so many hopes by capricious destiny, obliged to take counsel with his needs about every farthing, and to forego so many joys which a young heart demands! Early in the morning he brought out his black lead pencils, his crow quills, his India ink; for better materials, thought he, the Archivist can find nowhere. Above all, he mustered and arranged his calligraphic masterpieces and his drawings, to show them to the Archivist, as proof of his ability to do what that exacting gentleman wished. All went well from the start; a peculiar and happy star seemed to be presiding over Anselmus; his neckcloth sat right at the very first trial; no button came off; no thread gave way in his black silk stockings and his hat did not once fall into the dust after he had brushed it. In a word, precisely at half past eleven, the Student Anselmus, in his pike-grey coat and black satin breeches, with a roll of calligraphies and pen-drawings in his pocket, was standing in the *Schlossgasse*, or Castle-gate, in Conradi's shop, and drinking one—two—glasses of the best cordial; for here, thought he, slapping his still empty pocket, for here silver dollars will be clinking soon.

Notwithstanding the distance to the lonely street where the Archivist Lindhorst's ancient residence was situated, the Student Anselmus was at the front door before the stroke of twelve. He stood there, and looked at the large, fine bronze knocker; but now when, as the last stroke tingled through the air with a loud clang from the clock in the church steeple, he lifted his hand to grasp this same knocker, the metal visage twisted itself, with a horrid rolling of its blue gleaming eyes, into a grinning smile. Alas, it was the Apple-woman of the *Schwarzthor!* The pointed teeth gnashed together in the loose jaws, and as they chattered between the skinny lips, she seemed to be mumbling: "You fool, fool, fool!—Wait, wait!—Why did you run away!—Fool!" Horror-stricken, the Student Anselmus jumped back; he clutched at the door-post, but his hand caught the bell-rope, and pulled it, and in piercing discords it rang louder and louder, while through the whole empty house the echo repeated, as if in mockery: "To the crystal fall!" An unearthly terror seized the Student Anselmus, and quivered through all his limbs. The bell-rope lengthened downwards, and became a white, transparent, gigantic serpent, which encircled and crushed him, and squeezed him tighter and tighter in its coils, until his brittle, paralyzed limbs went cracking to pieces, and the blood spouted from his veins, penetrating into the transparent body of the serpent, and dyeing it red. "Kill me! Kill me!" he would have cried, in his horrible agony; but the cry was only a stifled groan in his throat. The serpent lifted its head, and laid its long peaked tongue of shining brass on Anselmus' chest; then a fierce pang suddenly cut asunder the artery of life, and thought gushed and fled from him. On returning to his senses, he found himself lying on his own poor trundle bed; Dean Paulmann was standing before him, and saying: "For Heaven's sake, what mad stuff is this, my dear Anselmus?"

Third Vigil

Notices of Archivist Lindhorst's Family. Veronica's Blue Eyes. Registrar Heerbrand.

"The Spirit looked upon the water, and the water moved itself, and churned in foaming billows, and plunged thundering down into the Abysses, which opened their black throats, and greedily swallowed it. Like triumphant conquerors, the granite Rocks lifted their cleft, peaky crowns, protecting the Valley, until the Sun took it into his paternal bosom, and clasping it within his rays as with glowing arms, cherished it and warmed it. Then a thousand seeds, which had been sleeping under the desert sand, awoke from their deep slumber, and stretched out their little leaves and stalks towards the face of the Sun their father. And, like smiling infants in green cradles, the flowers rested in their buds and blossoms, until they too, awakened by their father, decked themselves in light, which their father, to please them, tinted in a thousand varied hues.

"But in the midst of the Valley was a black Hill, which heaved up and down like the breast of man when warm longing swells it. From the Abysses mounted steaming vapors, which rolled themselves together into huge masses, and strove malignantly to hide the father's face. But he called the Storm, which rushed to him, and scattered them away. And when the pure sunbeam rested again on the bleak Hill, there started from it, in the excess of rapture, a glorious Fire-lily, opening its fair leaves like gentle lips to receive its father's kiss.

"And now came a gleaming Splendor into the Valley; it was the youth Phosphorus; the Lily saw him, and pleaded, seized with yearning love: 'Be mine forever, thou fair youth! For I love thee, and must die if thou forsake me!' Then spake the youth Phosphorus: 'I will be thine, thou fair flower; but then wilt thou, like a naughty child, leave father and mother; thou wilt know thy playmates no longer; thou wilt strive to be greater and stronger than all that now rejoices with thee as thy equal. The longing, which now beneficently warms thy whole being, will be scattered into a thousand rays, and will torture and vex thee; for sense will bring forth senses; and the highest rapture, which the Spark I cast into thee kindles, will be the hopeless pain wherein thou shalt perish, to spring up anew in foreign shape. This spark is Thought!'

" 'Ah!' mourned the Lily, 'can I not be thine in this glow, as it now burns in me; not still be thine? Could I love thee more than now; could I look on thee as now, if thou wert to annihilate me?' Then the youth Phosphorus kissed the Lily; and as if penetrated with light, it mounted up in flame, out of which issued a foreign Being, that, hastily flying from the Valley, roved forth into endless Space, no longer heeding its old playmates, or the youth it had loved. This youth mourned for his lost beloved. For he had loved her. It was love for the fair Lily that had brought him to the lone Valley. And the granite Rocks bent down their heads to participate in his grief.

"But one of these Rocks opened its bosom, and there came a black-winged Dragon flying out of it, and said: 'My brethren, the Metals are sleeping in there; but I am brisk and wide awake, and will help thee.' Dashing up and down on its black pinions, the Dragon at last caught the Being which had sprung from the Lily; bore it to the Hill, and encircled it with his wing; then was it the Lily again; but Thought, which continued with it, tore its heart asunder; and its love for the youth Phosphorus was a searing pain, before which, as if breathed on by poisonous vapors, the flowers which had once rejoiced in the fair Lily's presence faded and died.

"The youth Phosphorus put on a glittering coat of mail, reflecting the light in a thousand hues, and did battle with the Dragon, who struck the youth's cuirass with his black wing, until it rang and resounded; and at this loud clang the flowers again came to life, and like variegated birds fluttered round the Dragon, whose force departed from him, and who, thus being vanquished, hid himself in the depths of the Earth. The Lily was freed; the youth Phosphorus clasped her with a heart full of tender yearning, of heavenly love. And, in triumphant chorus, the flowers, the birds, nay even the high granite Rocks, did reverence to her as the Queen of the Valley."

"By your leave, my worthy Archivist, this is Oriental bombast," said Registrar Heerbrand, "and we beg earnestly that you would choose rather, as you often do, to give us something of your own most remarkable life, of your traveling adventures, for instance; above all, something true."

"What the deuce, then?" answered Archivist Lindhorst. "True? This very tale, which I have been telling, is the truest I could serve forth for you, good people; and it belongs to my life too, in a certain sense. For I come from that very Valley; and the Fire-lily, which at last ruled as Queen there, was my great-great-great-great-grandmother; and so, properly speaking, I am a prince myself."

All his listeners, at this, burst into peals of laughter.

"Ay, laugh your fill," continued Archivist Lindhorst. "To you this matter which I have related, certainly in the most brief and meagre way, may seem senseless and mad; yet, notwithstanding this, it is meant to be anything but incoherent, or even allegorical; and it is, in one word, literally true. Had I known, however, that the glorious love story, to which I owe my existence, would have pleased you so ill, I might have given you a little of the news my brother brought me on his visit yesterday."

"How, how is this? Have you a brother, then? Where is he? Where does he live? Is he in His Majesty's service too? Or is he perhaps a private scholar?" cried the company from all sides.

"No!" replied the Archivist, quite cool, and composedly taking a pinch of snuff. "He has joined the bad side; he has gone over to the Dragons."

"What do you mean by that, my dear Archivist?" cried Registrar Heerbrand. "Over to the Dragons?"—"Over to the Dragons?" resounded like an echo from all the bewildered listeners.

"Yes, over to the Dragons," continued Archivist Lindhorst. "It was sheer desperation, I believe. You know, gentlemen, my father died a short while ago: only three hundred and eighty-five years ago at most; and I am still in mourning for him. He had left me, his favorite son, a fine onyx; this onyx, right or wrong, my brother would have; we quarreled about it, over my father's corpse, in such unseemly wise, that the good man started up, out of all patience, from his coffin, and threw my wicked brother downstairs. This insult stuck in my brother's stomach, and so without loss of time he went over to the Dragons. At present, he lives in a cypress wood, not far from Tunis; he has got a famous mystic carbuncle to watch there, which a dog of a necromancer, who has set up a summerhouse in Lapland, has an eye to; so my poor brother only gets away for a quarter of an hour or so, when the necromancer happens to be out looking after the salamander-bed in his garden, and then he tells me in all haste what good news there is about the Springs of the Nile."

For a second time, the company burst out into a peal of laughter; but the Student Anselmus began to feel curiously sick at heart; and he could scarcely look in Archivist Lindhorst's parched countenance, and fixed, earnest eyes, without shuddering within himself in a way which he could not himself understand. Moreover, in the rude and strangely metallic sound of Lindhorst's voice there was something mysteriously affecting to the Student Anselmus, and he felt his very bones and marrow tingling as the Archivist spoke.

The special object for which Registrar Heerbrand had taken him into the coffeehouse seemed at present not to be attainable. After that accident at Archivist Lindhorst's door, the Student Anselmus had withstood all inducements to risk a second visit. For, according to his own heartfelt conviction, it was only chance that had saved him, if not from death, at least from the danger of insanity. Dean Paulmann had happened to be passing through the street at the time when Anselmus was lying almost unconscious at the door, and an old woman, who had laid her cake-and-apple-basket to one side, was busied about him. The Dean had forthwith called a chair, and so got him carried home.

"Think of me what you will," said the Student Anselmus. "Consider me a fool or not. I say, the cursed visage of that witch at the *Schwarzthor* grinned at me from the door-knocker. What happened after, I would rather not speak of; but had I recovered from my spell and seen that infernal Apple-wife beside me (for the old woman whom you talk of was none other), I should that instant have been struck by apoplexy, or have gone stark mad."

All persuasions, all sensible arguments, on the part of Dean Paulmann and Registrar Heerbrand, profited nothing; and even the blue-eyed Veronica herself could not draw him out of the deep moodiness in which he had ever since been immersed. In fact, these friends considered him to be disturbed in mind, and considered expedients for diverting his thoughts; to which end, Registrar Heerbrand believed there could be nothing so serviceable as this employment of copying Archivist Lindhorst's manuscripts.

The business, therefore, was to introduce the Student in some feasible and proper fashion to Archivist Lindhorst. And so Registrar Heerbrand, knowing that the Archivist used to visit a certain coffeehouse almost nightly, had invited the Student Anselmus to come every evening to that same coffeehouse, and drink a glass of beer and smoke a pipe, at his—the Registrar's—expense, until such time as Archivist Lindhorst should in one way or another see him, and the bargain for this copying work be settled; which offer the Student Anselmus had most gratefully accepted.

"God will reward you, worthy Registrar, if you bring the young man to his right mind!" said Dean Paulmann. "God will reward you!" repeated Veronica, piously raising her eyes to Heaven, and vividly thinking that the Student Anselmus was already a most attractive young man, even without any mind at all.

Now accordingly, as Archivist Lindhorst, with hat and walking-stick, was making for the door, Registrar Heerbrand seized the Student Anselmus briskly by the hand, and stepping with him into the path of the old scholar, he said: "Most esteemed Archivist, here is the Student Anselmus, who has an uncommon talent in calligraphy and drawing, and can undertake the copying of your rare manuscripts."

"I am most particularly glad to hear it," answered Archivist Lindhorst sharply. Then he threw his three-cornered military hat on his head and, shoving Registrar Heerbrand and the Student Anselmus aside, he rushed downstairs with great tumult, so that both men were left standing thunderstruck, gaping at the door, which he had slammed in their faces so hard that the bolts and hinges of it still creaked.

"He is a very strange old gentleman," said Registrar Heerbrand.

"Strange old gentleman," echoed the Student Anselmus, with a feeling as if ice were shivering through all his veins, and he were stiffening into a statue.

All the guests, however, laughed, and said: "Our Archivist is on his high horse today. Tomorrow, you shall see, he will be gentle as a lamb again, and not utter a word all evening, but stare into the pyramids of smoke from his pipe, or read the newspapers. You must not mind these freakish moods."

"That is true, too," thought the Student Anselmus. "Who would mind such a thing, after all? Did not the Archivist tell me he was most particularly glad to hear that I could undertake the copying of his manuscripts? And why did Registrar Heerbrand step directly in his way, when he was going home? No, no, he is a good man at bottom, this Privy Archivist Lindhorst, and surprisingly liberal. A little odd, to be sure, in his figures of speech; but what is that to me? Tomorrow by the stroke of twelve I shall go to him, though fifty bronzed Apple-wives should try to hinder me!"

FOURTH VIGIL

Melancholy of the Student Anselmus. The Emerald Mirror.
How Archivist Lindhorst flew off in the shape of a Kite, and the
Student Anselmus met nobody.

To you yourself, gentle reader, I may well venture the question whether you in your time have not had hours, nay, days and weeks, in which all your customary trading and transacting raised a most vexing dissatisfaction in your soul; and all that you were wont to look upon as worthy and important now seemed paltry and unprofitable . . . You did not know, at this season, what to do, or whither to turn; a dim feeling that somewhere, and sometime or other, there must be a higher wish fulfilled, a wish which would overstep the boundaries of all earthly joys, and which the spirit, like a strictly nurtured and timid child, durst not even utter, still filled your heart; and in this longing for the unknown, you were lost to all that surrounded you here below. You wandered to and fro with troubled mind, like a hopeless lover; and all that you saw men attempting or attaining, in the busy tumult of existence, awakened in you no sorrow and no joy, as if you had neither part nor lot in the affairs of this world.

If such, gentle reader, has at any time been your mood, then from your own experience you know the state into which the Student Anselmus had now fallen. On the whole, I should rather wish, courteous reader, that it were in my power to bring the Student Anselmus with proper vividness before your eyes. For in the night watches, which I spend in recording his highly singular history, I have still so much of the marvelous—which like a spectral vision may remove into faint remoteness the work-a-day life of common mortals—to lay before you, that I fear you will come, in the end, to believe neither in the Student Anselmus, nor in Archivist Lindhorst; indeed, will even entertain some unfounded doubts as to Registrar Heerbrand and Dean Paulmann, though the last two estimable persons, at least, are still walking the pavements of Dresden. Make an effort, generous reader—while in the fairy region of glorious Wonders, which evokes, with simultaneous thrills, the highest rapture and the deepest horror; nay, where the Earnest Goddess herself will put aside her veil, so that we may seem to look upon her countenance (but a smile often glimmers behind her earnest glance; and this is that good-natured teasing, which works upon us all manner of perplexing enchantments, as mothers in nursing and dandling their dearest children)—in this region, which the spirit so often, at least in dreams, lays open to us, I beg you to make an effort, gentle reader, again to recognize the well-known shapes which, even in common life, daily hover about you. You will then find that this glorious Kingdom lies much closer at hand than you ever supposed; a conclusion which I very heartily desire, and am striving to prove to you in the singular story of the Student Anselmus.

So, as has been suggested, the Student Anselmus, ever since the evening when he met with Archivist Lindhorst, had been sunk in a dreamy musing, which rendered him insensible to every outward contact with common life. He felt that something unknown was awakening his inmost soul, and calling forth that ecstatic pain which was, in fact, nothing more than the Longing that serves to remind man of the loftier existence for which he was once intended. He was happiest when he could roam alone through meadows and woods, and, as if freed from all that fettered him to his mundane existence, could, so to speak, again find himself in the manifold images which rose before him out of his deepest spirit.

It happened once that, in returning from a long walk, he passed by that famous elder tree under which, as if carried into the world of the supernatural, he had at one time beheld so many marvels. He felt himself strangely attracted by the welcoming greensward; but no sooner had he seated himself on the grass than the whole vision which he had then seen as in a heavenly trance, and which had since as if by foreign influence been driven from his mind, came once more floating before him in the liveliest colors. In truth, it was clearer to him now than before: he knew that the gentle blue eyes belonged to the gold-green Snake, which had wound itself around the central trunk of the elder tree, and that from the turnings of its slender tapering body all those glorious crystal tones, which had filled him with rapture, must needs have broken forth.

As on Ascension Day, Anselmus now again clasped the elder tree to his bosom, and cried into the branches and leaves, "Ah, once more shoot forth, and turn and wind thyself among the twigs, thou little fair green Snake, that I may see thee! Once more look at me with gentle eyes! Ah, I love thee, and must die in pain and grief, if thou return not!"

All, however, remained silent and without motion; and, as before, the elder tree rustled its branches and leaves quite unintelligibly. But the Student Anselmus now felt as if he knew what it was that so moved and worked within him, more, that so tore his bosom with the pain of an infinite longing. "What else is it," said he, "but that I love thee with my whole heart and soul, and even to the death, thou glorious little golden Snake; nay, that without thee I cannot live, and must perish in hopeless woe, unless I find thee again, unless I have thee as the beloved of my heart? But I know it, thou shalt be mine; and then all that splendid dreams have promised me, of another and higher world, shall be fulfilled."

Henceforth, every evening, when the sun was spreading its bright gold over the peaks of the trees, the Student Anselmus was to be seen under the elder tree and could be heard calling from the depths of his heart, in the most piteous tones, into the branches and leaves, as he pleaded for a sight of his beloved, of his little gold-green Snake. Once, when, according to his custom, he was chanting away to the tree, there suddenly appeared before him a tall and lean man, wrapped up in a wide light-grey surtout, who regarded him with large and fiery eyes and exclaimed: "Well, well, what whining and whimpering do I hear? Well,

well, so this is the Student Anselmus, who was to copy my manuscripts."
The Student Anselmus felt not a little terrified on hearing this strong
voice, for it was the very same which on Ascension Day had called: "Hey,
hey! What chattering and jingling is this?" In his fright and astonishment,
he could not utter a word. "What ails you then, Anselmus?" continued
Archivist Lindhorst—the stranger was no other. "What do you want of
the elder tree, and why do you not come to me, and set about your
work?"

In fact, the Student Anselmus had never yet prevailed upon himself
to visit Archivist Lindhorst's house a second time, though that evening
he had firmly resolved to do so. But now, at this moment, when he saw
his sweet dreams torn asunder, and that too by the same hostile voice
which had once before snatched away his beloved, a desperation came
over him, and he broke out fiercely into these words: "You may think me
mad or not, Herr Archivist; it is all one to me; but here in this tree, on
Ascension Day, I saw the gold-green Snake—Ah, the eternally beloved of
my soul. And she spoke to me in glorious crystal tones. And you, you,
Archivist Lindhorst, cried and shouted horribly over the water."

"What is this, my good sir?" interrupted the Archivist, smiling quite
indescribably, and taking snuff.

The Student Anselmus felt a great ease coming over him, now that
he had succeeded in beginning his strange story; and it seemed to him
as if he were quite right in laying the whole blame for his broken dream
upon the Archivist, and that it was he, and no other, who had so thundered from the distance. He courageously proceeded: "Well, then, I will
tell you the whole mysterious adventure that befell me on Ascension
evening; and then you may say and do, and even think of me, whatever
you please."

He accordingly related the whole miraculous incident, from his unhappy upsetting of the apple basket, to the departure of the three gold-
green Snakes across the river; and how, after, he had been thought drunk
or mad.

"All this," so ended the Student Anselmus, "I actually saw with my
eyes; and deep in my heart are those dear voices still echoing. It was in
nowise a dream; and if I am not to die of longing and desire, I must believe in these gold-green Snakes, though I see by your smile, sir, that you

believe these same Snakes to be nothing more than creatures of my fevered and overstrained imagination."

"Not at all," replied the Archivist, speaking with the greatest calmness and composure. "The gold-green Snakes which you saw in the elder tree, Herr Anselmus, were none other than my three daughters; and that you have fallen over head and ears in love with the blue eyes of Serpentina, the youngest, is now clear enough. Indeed, I knew it on Ascension Day myself; and since I, on that occasion, was busied with my writing at home, I began to become annoyed with so much chattering and jingling and called to the idle minxes that it was time to get home, for the sun was setting, and they had sung and basked enough!"

The Student Anselmus felt as if he now merely heard in plain words something he had long dreamed of; and it seemed to him he could see the elder tree, wall, and greensward, and indeed all the objects about him, begin to whirl round. Courage came back to his heart, and he was ready to speak. But the Archivist prevented him; for quickly pulling the glove from his left hand, and holding the stone of a ring, that flamed and sparkled, before the Student's eyes, he said: "Look into this, Anselmus. What you see may do you good."

The Student Anselmus looked in, and, O wonder! the stone threw a beam of rays round it, as from a burning focus; and the rays wove themselves together into a clear, gleaming, crystal mirror; in which, with many windings, now flying asunder, now twisted together, the three gold-green Snakes were dancing and bounding. And when their slender forms, glittering with a thousand lights, touched each other, there issued from them glorious tones, as of crystal bells; and the midmost of the three stretched forth her little head from the mirror, as if full of tenderness and longing; and her dark blue eyes said: "Knowest thou me, then; believest thou in me, Anselmus? In Belief alone is Love; canst thou love?"

"O Serpentina! Serpentina!" cried the Student Anselmus in rapture. But Archivist Lindhorst suddenly breathed on the mirror, and with an electric sputter the rays sank back into their focus; while on his hand there was now nothing but a little emerald, over which the Archivist drew his glove.

"Did you see the golden Snakes, my good Anselmus?" said the Archivist.

"Ah, by Heaven, yes!" replied the Student. "And the fair, dear Serpentina."

"Hush!" continued the Archivist. "Enough for one time. As for the other matter, if you decide to work with me, you may see my daughter often enough, or, rather, I will grant you this real satisfaction, if you apply yourself thoroughly and truly to your task, that is to say, copy every mark with the greatest clearness and exactitude. But you have not come to me at all, Anselmus, though Registrar Heerbrand promised I should see you forthwith, and I have waited several days in vain."

Not until he heard the mention of Registrar Heerbrand's name did the Student Anselmus again feel as if he were really standing with his two feet on the ground, or realize that he was the Student Anselmus, talking to a man who was unmistakably the Archivist Lindhorst. The tone of indifference with which the latter spoke contrasted rudely with the strange sights which, like a genuine necromancer, he had a moment before called forth, and it awakened a certain horror in the Student, which the piercing look of those fiery eyes, beaming from their bony sockets in the lean, puckered visage, as from a leathern case, did nothing to alleviate. And the Student was again compellingly seized with the same sense of uncanny dread which had taken possession of him in the coffee-house, when Archivist Lindhorst had talked so wildly. With a great effort he retained his self-possession, and as the Archivist again asked, "Well, why have you not come to see me?" the Student exerted the whole force of his energy, and related to him all that had happened at the street door.

"My dear Anselmus, said the Archivist, when the narrative was finished, "I know this Apple-wife whom you mention. She is a deadly old slattern who plays all sorts of tricks on me; but that she should have turned herself to bronze, and taken the shape of a door-knocker, to deter pleasant visitors from calling, is indeed very bad, and truly not to be endured. Will you please, however, my worthy Student, if you come tomorrow at noon, and notice anything more of this grinning and growling, just be so good as to drop a driblet or two of this liquid on her nose? It will put everything to rights immediately. And now, au revoir, my good Anselmus! I move rather quickly, therefore I would not advise you to think of returning to town with me. Till we meet—tomorrow at noon!"

The Archivist had given the Student Anselmus a little vial with a gold-colored fluid in it; and he walked rapidly off—so rapidly that in the twilight, which had now come on, he seemed rather to be floating down to the valley than walking along the path. Already he was near the Kosel Garden; the wind blew inside his wide greatcoat, and spread its skirts apart, so that they fluttered behind him in the air like a pair of large wings. And it seemed to the Student Anselmus, who followed the movements of the Archivist with staring, unbelieving eyes, as if a large bird were spreading out its pinions for rapid flight. Then, as the Student kept peering into the dusk, a grey-white kite soared, with a creaking cry, into the air; and the young man now realized that the white flutter which he had taken for the homeward-bound Archivist must have been this very kite, though he still could not understand where the Archivist had vanished so abruptly.

"Perhaps he may have flown away in person, this mysterious Archivist," said the Student Anselmus to himself. "For I realize now that all these strange visitations from a distant and wondrous world, which formerly I never experienced except in my rarest dreams, have entered into my waking life, and are having sport with me. But that matters little for me now! Serpentina lives and glows in my heart! Lovely, gentle Serpentina! She alone can still my infinite longing! Ah, when shall I look into thy tender eyes, my dearest Serpentina?"

So the Student Anselmus cried aloud.

"That is a vile, unchristian name!" murmured a home-going passer-by in a deep voice. The Student Anselmus, reminded in due time where he was, hurried quickly off; and, as he went, he thought to himself: "Would it not be a proper misfortune now if Dean Paulmann or Registrar Heerbrand were to meet me?" But neither of these gentlemen crossed his path.

FIFTH VIGIL

How it feels to be married to the Privy Councillor, Anselmus. Cicero's de Officiis. Monkeys and other strange creatures. The Equinox.

"There is nothing in the world can be made of this Anselmus," said Dean Paulmann. "All my good advice, all my admonitions, are fruitless.

He will apply himself to nothing; though he is a fine classical scholar too, and that is the foundation of all learning."

But Registrar Heerbrand, with a sly, mysterious smile replied: "Give Anselmus time, my worthy Dean! He is a strange subject, this Anselmus, but there is much to him—and when I say much, I mean that he may become a Privy Secretary, or even a Court Councillor, a *Hofrath*."

"A Court—" began Dean Paulmann, in amazement; but the words stuck in his throat.

"Don't bother to contradict me!" continued Registrar Heerbrand, "I know what I am talking about. These two days he has been with Archivist Lindhorst, copying manuscripts. Last night the Archivist meets me at the coffeehouse, and says: 'You have sent me the right man, good neighbor! There is stuff in that lad!' And now think of Archivist Lindhorst's influence . . . Hush, hush! We will talk of it a year from now." And with these words the Registrar, his face still wrinkled into the same sly smile, went out of the room, leaving the Dean speechless with astonishment and curiosity, and fixed, as if by enchantment, in his chair.

But it was Veronica whom this conversation really impressed profoundly. "Have I not known all along," thought she, "that Anselmus was a most clever and attractive young man, capable of great things? If I could only be certain that he is really fond of me! That night when we rowed across the Elbe, did he not twice press my hand? Did he not look at me, during our duet, with such sweet, intimate glances that I was touched to the very heart? Yes, yes! He really likes me; I, of course . . ." and Veronica gave herself up, in this way, to happy dreams of the future.

She was the Privy Councillor's wife; she lived in a fine house in the *Schlossgasse*, or in the *Neumarkt*, or in the *Moritzstrasse*; the fashionable hat, the new Turkish shawl, suited her admirably; or she was breakfasting on the balcony in an elegant *négligé*, giving orders to her cook for the day: "And be careful, if you please, not to spoil that dish; it is the Councillor's favorite." Then passing beaux glanced up, and she heard them distinctly: "She is really a divine creature, the Privy Councillor's wife! How prettily the lace cap sets off her lovely hair!" Madame Ypsilon, the wife of a court official, sends her servant to ask if it would please Madame Privy Councillor to drive as far as the Linke Baths today? "Many thanks and deep regrets: I am extremely sorry I am engaged to tea already with the President of the Chamber . . ." Then the Privy Councillor, himself, comes back from his office; he is dressed in the height of fashion. "Ten, I declare," cries he, taking out his gold watch and giving his young wife a kiss. "How goes it, little woman? Guess what I have for you here," he continues, roguishly teasing her; then he draws from his waistcoat pocket a pair of beautiful earrings, fashioned in the newest mode, and puts them on her in place of the old ones.

"Ah! What charming, what exquisite earrings!" Veronica cried aloud; and she started up from her chair, throwing aside her work, to see these fair earrings with her own eyes in the glass.

"What is going on here?" asked Dean Paulmann, roused by the noise from his deep study of Cicero's *de Officiis*, and almost dropping the book from his hand. "Are we having fits, like Anselmus?"

But at this moment, the Student Anselmus, who, contrary to his custom, had not called upon the Paulmanns for several days, entered the room, to Veronica's astonishment, and indeed her sudden discomfiture. For, in truth, his whole bearing seemed altered. With a certain lucidity, which was far from usual in him, he spoke of new tendencies of life which had become clear to his mind, of glorious prospects which were opening before him, but which few men had the vision to perceive. Dean Paulmann, remembering Registrar Heerbrand's mysterious speech, was still more impressed, and could scarcely utter a syllable, until the Student Anselmus, after dropping various hints of urgent business at the Archivist's, and kissing Veronica's hand with foppish adroitness, was already downstairs, off, and away.

"He is the Privy Councillor already," murmured Veronica to herself; "and he kissed my hand without once slipping, or stepping on my foot, as he used to do! He gave me the softest look too. Yes, he is really fond of me!"

Veronica again yielded to her dreams. Yet now it was as if a hostile shape were somehow pressing forward among these lovely visions of her future domestic life as the Privy Councillor's wife, and as if the shape were laughing out in mockery of her, and saying: "These dreams of yours are all very stupid and trashy stuff, and false to boot. For Anselmus will never, never become a Privy Councillor or your husband. He is not in love with you in the least, though you do have blue eyes, and a fine figure, and a pretty little hand." Then an icy chill filled Veronica's heart; and a deep sadness swept away the delight with which, a little while ago, she had envisioned herself in the lace cap and the exquisite earrings. Tears almost rushed into her eyes, and she said aloud: "Ah! It is too true: he does not love me in the least; and I shall never, never be the wife of a Privy Councillor!"

"Romantic rubbish! Romantic rubbish!" cried the Dean, then he snatched his hat and stick, and rushed indignantly from the house. "Yes, rubbish is all it is," sighed Veronica; and felt vexed at her little sister, a girl of twelve, because the child sat so unconcerned, and kept sewing at her embroidery frame, as if nothing had happened.

Meanwhile, time had passed and it was now almost three o'clock, and the hour to set the apartment in perfect order and arrange the coffee table; for the Misses Oster had announced that they were coming to call. But from behind every workbox which Veronica put away, behind the notebooks which she removed from the harpsichord, behind the coffee-pot which she took from the cupboard, that same malicious form peeped forth—like the poisonous mandrake with its human shape—and mocked her spitefully, and snapped its little spider tendrils, and cried, "He will not be your husband! He will not be your husband!" and then, when she rushed away from everything and fled to the middle of the room, it peered out again, with long nose, in gigantic bulk, from behind the stove, and snarled and growled, "He will not be your husband!"

"Do you hear nothing, sister? Do you see nothing?" cried Veronica, shivering with fright, and not daring to touch anything in the room. Fränzchen rose, gravely and quietly, from her embroidery frame, and said: "What ails you today, sister? You are turning everything topsy-turvy, and jiggling about so, and fidgeting. I see I must help you."

But here the gay, young visitors came laughing into the room; and at the same moment Veronica realized that what she had taken for a malign and weird shape was only the stove handle, and that the creaking, ill-shut stove door had been the voice that had spoken. Yet her feeling of terror still persisted and she could not recover her composure quickly enough to hide the strange excitement—which even her paleness and agitated looks betrayed—from the Misses Oster. As they at once cut short their merry prattle, and pressed her to tell them what, in Heaven's name, had happened, Veronica was obliged to admit that certain strange thoughts had come into her mind, and that suddenly, in broad daylight and for the first time in her life, she had been seized by a fear of spectres. She described in such vivid detail how a little grey mannikin, peeping out of all the corners of the room, had mocked and plagued her, that the Misses Oster began to look about them with timid glances; all manner of unearthly notions were sprouting in their minds. But Fränzchen came in at this moment with the steaming coffeepot; and all three, brought back to earth and common sense, laughed aloud at their folly.

Angelica, the elder of the Oster sisters, was engaged to be married to an officer. The young man had joined the army, but his friends had gone so long without news of him that everyone was sure that he must be dead, or at least seriously wounded. This had plunged Angelica into the deepest grief, but today she was merry, even to extravagance, and in a state of mind which so surprised Veronica that she could not help mentioning it.

"My dear friend," said Angelica, "do you fancy that my Victor is not still in my heart and my thoughts? It is for him I am so gay—Oh, indeed so happy, so blessed in my whole soul! For my Victor is well, in a little while he will be home, promoted to captain, and covered with all the honors which his courage has won him. A deep but by no means dangerous wound, in the right arm, the result of a sword thrust from a French Hussar, has prevented him from writing; and the army's rapid movement—for he will not consent to leave his regiment—still makes it impossible for him to send me tidings. But tonight he is being ordered to return from the front until his wound is healed. Tomorrow he will set out for home. And just as he is stepping into the coach, he will learn of his new promotion."

"But, my dear Angelica," interrupted Veronica, "how do you know all this already?"

"Do not laugh at me, my friend," continued Angelica. "Surely you will not laugh! For might not the little grey mannikin, to punish you, peep forth from behind the mirror there? In a word, I cannot rid myself of a belief in certain mysterious things, whose manifestations I have seen and felt, from time to time in my life. Nor do I find it so strange and incredible as many others do, that there are people gifted with a certain faculty of prophecy, which they can exercise at will. There is an old woman, right in town here, who possesses this gift to a high degree. She does not, like so many others of her tribe, reveal the future to you by means of cards, or melted lead, or coffee grounds; but after certain preparations, in which you yourself take part, she sets before you a polished metallic mirror, and there rises in it the strangest mixture of figures and forms, all intermingled. These she interprets, and so answers your questions. I was with her last night, and got those tidings of my Victor. I have not doubted them for a moment."

Angelica's narrative seemed to light a spark in Veronica's soul, which instantly kindled into flame with the thought of consulting this same old prophetess about Anselmus and her own future. She learned that the ancient crone was called Frau Rauerin, and lived in a remote street near the Seethor; that she was not to be seen except on Tuesdays, Thursdays, and Fridays, after seven o'clock in the evening—but then, indeed, through the whole night till sunrise; and that she preferred to have her customers come alone. It was Thursday evening, now, and Veronica determined, under pretext of accompanying the Oster sisters to their home, to visit this old woman, and lay her uncertainties before her.

Accordingly, no sooner had her friends, who lived in the Neustadt, parted from her at the Elbe bridge than she hastened with winged steps towards the Seethor. When she had reached the remote narrow street which had been described to her, she saw, at the end of it, the little red house in which Frau Rauerin was said to live. She could not rid herself of certain misgivings, even of a certain horror, as she approached the door. But finally she summoned sufficient resolution, in spite of her inner feelings, to pull the bell. The door opened, and she groped through the dark passage (as Angelica had directed) for the stair which led to the upper story.

"Does Frau Rauerin live here?" she called out into the empty hallway, as no one appeared. Instead of answer, she heard a long clear, "Miaow!" and a large black cat, with its back arched, and its tail whisking to and fro, made its way before her, with much gravity, to the door of the apartment, which, on a second miaow, was opened.

"Ah, what do I see now! You have come to me already, daughter! Come in, pet! Come in!" exclaimed the person who advanced toward

her, and whose appearance rooted Veronica to the spot. She was a tall and
bony woman, covered from head to foot in black rags; when she spoke,
her peaked, projecting chin wagged back and forth, her toothless mouth,
overshadowed by the hook of her bony hawk-nose, twisted itself into a
ghastly smile; and gleaming cat's-eyes flickered and sparkled from behind
her large, owllike spectacles. From beneath a multicolored scarf wrapped
around her head, clumps of wiry black hair hung out. But what deformed
her haggard face to the point of absolute horror was the pair of scars,
which ran like the marks of a burn across her left cheek and over her nose.
Veronica's breathing seemed to fail her. But the shriek which had been
about to burst from her choked throat was transformed into a deep sigh
as the witch's skeleton hand took hold of her, and led her into the adjoining room.

Here all was awake and astir; the place was filled with din and tumult, and squealing, and mewing, and croaking, and piping, all at once,
on every hand. The old hag struck the table with her fist, and screamed:
"Peace, you vermin!" And the monkeys, whimpering, clambered to the
top of the high bed; and the little guinea pigs all ran beneath the stove;
and the raven fluttered up to the round mirror; and the black Cat, as if
the rebuke did not apply to him, remained sitting at his ease on the cushioned chair to which he had jumped directly upon entering the room.

When quiet was finally restored, Veronica took heart. She felt less
dreary and frightened than when she had stood outside in the hall. Even
the old witch herself seemed somewhat less hideous. For the first time,
the girl looked about the room. All manner of odious stuffed beasts hung
down from the ceiling; strange, unknown household implements were
lying in confusion on the floor; and in the grate burned a blue and scanty
fire, which only now and then sputtered up into little bursts of yellow
flame. When it did that, there came, at every sputter, a rustling from
above, and monstrous bats, with their almost human little faces distorted
in strange laughter, went flitting to and fro. At times, too, the flame shot
out, and licked the sooty wall, and then there arose piercing cries of woe,
which shook Veronica with fear and horror.

"With your leave, Mamselle!" said the crone, knitting her brows,
and seized a brush, with which, having dipped it in a copper skillet, she
then besprinkled the grate. The fire went out; and, as if filled with thick

smoke, the room grew pitch-dark. But the old woman, who had gone aside into a closet, soon returned with a lighted lamp.

And now Veronica could see no beasts or curious implements in the apartment; it was a common, meanly furnished room. The beldame came up to her, and said in a croaking voice: "I know what you want here, little daughter. Tush, you would like me to tell you whether you will marry Anselmus, when he has become a Privy Councillor."

Veronica drew back in fright and amazement, but the witch continued: "You told me everything at home, in your papa's house when the coffeepot was standing before you. I was the coffeepot; did you not know me? Little daughter, listen to me! Give up, give up this Anselmus! He is a cruel creature: he stepped on my little sons, my dear little sons, the Apples with the red cheeks, that slip away, after people have bought them, whisk! Out of their pockets again, and roll back into my basket. He trades with the Old One. It was but the day before yesterday that he poured that cursed Auripigment on my face, and I had nigh gone blind with it. You may still see the scars of the burns, little daughter. Give him up, give him up! He does not love you, for he loves the gold-green Snake. He will never be a Privy Councillor, for he has joined the Salamanders, and he means to marry the green Snake. Give him up, give him up!"

Veronica, who had a firm and steadfast spirit of her own, and could quickly overcome her girlish terror, now drew herself up and said, in a serious, resolute voice: "Old dame! I heard of your gift of looking into the future and wished, perhaps too curiously and thoughtlessly, to learn from you whether Anselmus, whom I love and esteem, could ever be mine. But if, instead of fulfilling my desire, you keep vexing me with your foolish and unreasonable babble, you will accomplish nothing. For I have asked of you nothing but what, as I well know, you grant to others. Since you would appear to be acquainted with my inmost thoughts, it should perhaps have been very simple for you to disclose to me much that now pains and grieves my mind. But after your pointless slander of my good Anselmus, I do not wish to have any further talk with you. Good night!"

Veronica hurriedly began to leave, but the old woman, with tears and lamentations, fell upon her knees; and clutching the young lady by her dress, exclaimed: "Veronica! Veronica! Have you forgotten old

Liese, the nurse who so often carried you in her arms, and caressed and cared for you?"

Veronica could scarcely believe her ears and eyes; for here, in truth, was her old nurse, defaced only by old age, and by the two scars: Old Liese, herself, who had vanished from Dean Paulmann's house, some years ago, no one knew whither. The crone, too, had quite another look at this moment. Instead of the ugly, much-patched head-scarf, she had on a decent cap; instead of the black rags, a gay-printed wrapper; she was neatly dressed, as of old.

She got up now from the floor, and taking Veronica in her arms, continued to speak: "What I have just told you may seem mad; but, unluckily, it is too true. Anselmus has done much mischief, though against his will. He has fallen into Archivist Lindhorst's hands, and the Old One means to marry him to his daughter. Archivist Lindhorst is my deadliest enemy. I could tell you thousands of things about him—which, however, you would not understand, or, at best, would be too much frightened by hearing. He is the Wise Man, it seems; but I am the Wise Woman: let this stand for that! I see now that you love this Anselmus wholeheartedly; and I will help you with all my powers, so that you may be happy, and may become his charming bride, just as you desire."

"But tell me, for Heaven's sake, Liese—" interrupted Veronica.

"Hush, child, hush!" cried the old woman, interrupting in her turn. "I know what you are about to ask! I have become what I am, because it was to be so; it could not happen otherwise. Well, then! I know the means to cure Anselmus of his fascination for the green Snake, and lead him, the handsomest young Councillor, into your arms. But you, yourself, must help."

"Speak out, Liese. I will do anything and everything, for I love Anselmus dearly!" whispered Veronica, almost inaudibly.

"I know you," continued the old woman, "for a courageous child; I could never frighten you to sleep with the Bogy-man; for the instant I tried, your eyes would be open to what the Bogy-man was like. You would go without a light into the darkest room; and many a time, wearing Papa's powder mantle over your head, you frightened the neighbors' children. Well, now, if you are in earnest about triumphing over Archivist Lindhorst and the green Snake by my art, if you are in earnest about calling Anselmus by the title of Privy Councillor and husband—then, at the next Equinox, about eleven at night, slip out of your father's house, and come here to me. I will go with you to the crossing of the roads which cut the fields hard by this place. We shall make the necessary preparations. And whatever wonders you may see shall do you no whit of harm. And now, pet, good night. Papa is waiting for you to come to supper."

Veronica hurried home. She had reached the firmest determination not to neglect the night of the Equinox. "For," she thought, "old Liese is right. Anselmus has got himself chained by strange fetters. But I will free him from them, and call him mine forever and aye. Mine he is, and mine he shall be, my Privy Councillor Anselmus."

SIXTH VIGIL

Archivist Lindhorst's Garden, with some Mockingbirds.
The Golden Pot. English Script. Pothooks. The Prince
of the Spirits.

"It may be, after all," said the Student Anselmus to himself, "that the superfine and strong cordial, which I drank somewhat freely at Monsieur Conradi's, might really have been the cause of all those shocking fantasms, which so tortured me at Archivist Lindhorst's door. Therefore I must be sure to be quite sober when I arrive at his house today; and so bid defiance to whatever further mischief may assail me."

On this occasion, as before, when equipping himself for his first call on the Archivist, the Student Anselmus put his pen-drawings and calligraphic masterpieces, his jars of India ink, and his well-pointed crow-pens, into his pockets, and he was just turning to go out, when his eye lighted on the vial with the yellow liquid, which he had been given by the Archivist. All the strange adventures he had encountered rose again in his mind in glowing colors, and a nameless emotion of rapture and pain thrilled him through and through.

Involuntarily he exclaimed, in a most piteous voice: "Ah, am not I going to the Archivist's solely for a glimpse of you, O gentle, lovely Serpentina!" At that moment he felt as if Serpentina's love might be the prize of some laborious and perilous task which he had to undertake, and as if this task were no other than the copying of the Lindhorst manuscripts. That at his very entrance into the house, or, more properly, before his entrance, all manner of mysterious things might happen, as of late, was no more than he might have anticipated. He thought no further of Conradi's strong drink, but hastily put the vial of liquid into his waistcoat pocket, so that he might act strictly in accordance with the Archivist's instructions, should the Apple-woman in bronze again take it upon herself to make faces at him.

And did not the hawk-nose actually peak itself, did not the cat's-eyes actually glare from the knocker, as he raised his hand to it, at the stroke of twelve? But now, without further ceremony, he sprinkled the yellow liquor upon the pestilential visage, and it folded and re-molded itself, that very instant, into a shining bowl-round knocker. The door opened. The beautiful bells tinkled over all the house. With a blithe heart Anselmus mounted the fine broad stair. And his senses feasted on the odors of some strange perfumery that was floating through the house.

He paused uncertainly on the landing, for he did not know at which of these many fine doors to knock. But the Archivist, in a flowered damask dressing gown, stepped up to him, and said: "Well, it is a real pleasure to me, Anselmus, that you have kept your word at last. Come this way, if you please. I shall take you straight into the laboratory."

And with this he passed rapidly through the hallway, and opened a little side door, which led into a long passage. Anselmus followed him in high spirits. They went from this corridor into a salon, or rather into a lordly conservatory, heaped up to the ceiling on both sides with all sorts of rare, wondrous flowers, and even great trees with strangely formed leaves and blossoms. A magically dazzling light illuminated the whole room, though it was impossible to discover whence it came, for no window was to be seen. As the Student Anselmus peered among the bushes and trees, long avenues appeared to open toward remote distances. In the deep shade of thick cypress groves stood glittering marble fountains, out of which rose miraculous statues; crystal water jets spouted their pattering spray into gleaming lilies in fountain pools; strange voices cooed and rustled through the foliage of exotic trees; and the air was redolent with sweetest perfumes.

The Archivist had vanished, and Anselmus saw nothing but a huge bush of glowing fire-lilies before him. Intoxicated with the sights and the odors of this enchanted garden, Anselmus stood fixed to the spot. Then on all sides of him a tittering and laughing began and airy little voices railed and mocked him: "Well, my young Student! What has brought you here? Why have you gotten yourself up so smartly, young man? Will you chat with us for a moment? Tell us how Grandmama sat down upon the egg, and young master got a stain on his Sunday waistcoat! Can you play the new tune, now, which you learned from Daddy Cockadoodle, good master Anselmus? You look very fine in your glossy periwig and elegant thin boots."

So cried and chattered and sniggered the little voices, out of every corner, even close to the Student himself. And now he suddenly observed that a multicolored variety of birds was fluttering above him, and jeering at him heartily. Then the bush of fire-lilies advanced towards him; and he realized that, instead of a bush, it was the Archivist Lindhorst, whose flowered dressing gown, glittering in red and yellow, had deceived his eyes.

"I beg your pardon, my worthy Anselmus," said the Archivist, "for neglecting you. I wanted, in passing, to take a peep at my fine cactus, which should blossom tonight. But how do you like my little indoor garden?"

"Ah, heavens! It is immeasurably lovely, most esteemed sir," replied the Student. "But these multicolored birds have been mocking me a little."

"What is all this chattering?" the Archivist called out angrily into the bushes. Then a huge grey Parrot came fluttering out, and perched itself beside Lindhorst on a myrtle bough; and looking at him with an uncommon earnestness and solemnity through a pair of spectacles that stuck on its hooked bill, it croaked: "Don't take it amiss, master. My wild boys have been a little free, maybe; but the Student has himself to blame in the matter, for—"

"Hush! Hush!" interrupted the Archivist. "I know the rascals. But you must keep them in better discipline, my friend! Now, come along, Anselmus."

And the Archivist again led the way for his guest through many a strangely decorated chamber, so that the Student Anselmus, in following him, could scarcely glance at all the strangely glittering and remarkable

The Golden Pot

furniture, and the other bizarre appointments, with which all the rooms were filled. At last they entered a very large apartment, where the Archivist, casting his eyes aloft, came to a pause, and Anselmus had time to feast his eyes on the glorious sight which the simple decoration of this hall afforded. Standing out from the azure-colored walls rose gold-bronze trunks of high palm trees, which wove their colossal leaves, glittering with the green of emeralds, into a ceiling high above; in the middle of the salon, and resting on three Egyptian lions, cast in dark bronze, lay a porphyry plate; and on this stood a simple Golden Pot, from which, as soon as he beheld it, Anselmus could not turn away his eyes. It was as if in a thousand gleaming reflections, all sorts and varieties of shapes played on the bright polished gold surface; in many places he perceived his own form, with arms outstretched in longing—oh! beneath the elder tree—and Serpentina winding and darting up and down, and again looking at him with her tender eyes.

"Serpentina! Serpentina!" he cried out, almost in a frenzy. And Archivist Lindhorst whirled round abruptly, and said: "How now, my good Anselmus? If I am not mistaken, you were pleased to call for my daughter. She is away on the other side of the house at present, and indeed is just taking her lesson on the harpsichord. Let us get on."

Anselmus, scarcely knowing what he was doing, followed his guide. He saw and heard nothing more, till Archivist Lindhorst suddenly grasped his hand, and said, "Here, this is the place!" Then Anselmus awoke as from a dream, and now realized that he was in a high room lined on all sides with books, and differing in no respect from an ordinary library and study. In the center stood a large writing table, with an upholstered armchair before it.

"This," said the Archivist Lindhorst, "is your workroom for the present. Whether you may work, at some later time, in the blue library, where you so suddenly called out my daughter's name, I do not yet know. But now I should like to convince myself of your ability to execute this task, in the way I wish and require to have it done."

The Student now gathered his courage, and, not without experiencing a certain self-satisfaction in anticipation of the effect he would produce upon the Archivist, he pulled out of his pocket his drawings and specimens of penmanship. But no sooner had the Archivist glanced at the first of them, a piece of writing in the finest English style, than he smiled very oddly, and shook his head. These motions he repeated as he took up each successive sheet of paper, so that the Student Anselmus felt the blood mounting to his face. And at last, when the scholar's smile became quite sarcastic and contemptuous, poor Anselmus broke out in utter agitation: "My new employer does not seem pleased with my poor talents."

"My good sir," said the Archivist Lindhorst, "you do indeed enjoy a fine capacity for the art of calligraphy; but, in the meantime, it is evident enough that I must reckon more on your diligence and goodwill than on your attainments in this craft."

The Student Anselmus spoke at length, in reply, of his often-acknowledged perfection in this art, of his fine India ink, and his most select crow quills. But Lindhorst handed him the sheet written in English, and said: "Judge for yourself!"

Anselmus felt as if struck by a thunderbolt when he looked at his handwriting. It was wretched, beyond measure. There was no rounding in the turns, no hair-stroke where it should be, no proportion between the capitals and small letters; and sometimes even villainous schoolboy pot-hooks spoiled the best lines.

"Then again," continued Archivist Lindhorst, "your ink will not stand." He dipped his finger in a glass of water, and the moment he skimmed it over the lines, they vanished without leaving any trace. The Student Anselmus felt as if some monster were throttling him; he could not utter a word. There he stood, with the unlucky sheet in his hand, choking and speechless. But Lindhorst laughed aloud, and said: "Never mind, young man. What you could not do too well before you will per-haps perfect here. At any rate, you shall have better materials than you have been accustomed to. Now let us begin, in Heaven's name!"

From a locked press Archivist Lindhorst now brought out a dense black substance, which diffused a most peculiar odor; also pens, sharply pointed and of strange color, together with paper of quite uncommon whiteness and smoothness; then at last an Arabic manuscript. And as Anselmus sat down to work the Archivist left the room. The Student Anselmus, before this, had often copied Arabic manuscripts; the first problem, therefore, seemed to him not so very difficult to solve. "How those pothooks came into my fine English running-hand, Heaven—and Archivist Lindhorst—best know," said he. "But that they are not from my hand I will swear till I die!"

With each new word that now stood fair and perfect on the parchment, his courage increased, and with it his adroitness. In truth, these pens wrote exquisitely well; and the mysterious ink flowed smoothly, and black as jet, on the white parchment. As Anselmus worked along so diligently, moreover, and with such concentrated attention, he began to feel more and more at home in the remote and lonely room; and he had already quite suited himself to his task, which he now hoped to finish well, when at the stroke of three the Archivist called him into the adjoining room to partake of a most savory dinner. At table, Archivist Lindhorst was in a particularly gay humor. He inquired about the Student's friends, Dean Paulmann and Registrar Heerbrand; and of the latter especially he had a store of merry anecdotes to tell. The good old Rhenish wine was more than welcome to the Student Anselmus, and he became more talkative than was his custom. When four struck, however, he rose to resume his labors, and this punctuality appeared to please the Archivist.

If the copying of these Arabic manuscripts had prospered in his hands before dinner, the task now progressed even better. Indeed, he himself could not comprehend the rapidity and ease with which he succeeded in transcribing the twisted strokes of these foreign characters. But it was as if, in his inner self, a voice were whispering audibly: "Ah! But could you accomplish it, if you were not thinking of *her*, if you did not believe in *her* and in her love?" Then whispers came quivering, in low, undulating tones, through the room: "I am near, near, near! I am helping you; be bold, be steadfast, dear Anselmus! I shall toil with you, so that you may be mine!" And as, in the fullness of secret rapture, he caught these sounds, the unknown characters grew clearer and clearer to him; he scarcely needed to look at the original script at all; actually it was as if the letters were already standing in pale ink on the parchment, and he had nothing more to do but mark them black. So he labored on, encompassed by those dear, inspiring tones, by that soft, sweet breath, until the clock struck six, and Archivist Lindhorst entered the apartment.

He came up to the table with an odd smile. Anselmus rose in silence. The Archivist continued to gaze at him, with that derisive smile still on his face. But no sooner had he glanced over the copy than the smile changed to an expression of deep, solemn earnestness, to which every feature of his face adapted itself. He seemed no longer the same. His eyes, which usually gleamed with sparkling fire, now looked at Anselmus with unutterable gentleness; a gentle flush tinted the pale cheeks; and instead of the irony which at other times compressed the mouth, the softly curved, graceful lips now seemed to be opening for wise and soul-persuading speech. The man's very stature seemed higher and more stately; the wide dressing gown spread itself like a royal mantle in broad folds over his breast and shoulders; and through the white locks, which lay on his high, open brow, seemed to wind a thin band of gold.

"Young man," began the Archivist in solemn tone, "before you dreamed of it, I knew you; and I knew all the secret relations which bind you to the dearest and holiest of my interests! Serpentina loves you. A singular destiny, whose fateful threads were spun by enemies, would thus be fulfilled, should she be yours, and should you obtain, as an essential dowry, the Golden Pot, which of right belongs to her. But only by effort and struggle can your happiness in the higher life reach fruition; hostile elements assail you, and only the inner force with which you can withstand these contradictions can save you from disgrace and ruin. While laboring here, you are passing through your term of instruction. Belief and full knowledge will lead you to the goal, if you only hold to what you have begun well. Bear *her* always and truly in your thoughts, she who loves you; then shall you see the marvels of the Golden Pot, and be happy forever after. Farewell!"

With these words Archivist Lindhorst gently thrust the Student Anselmus out of the door, which he then locked; and Anselmus found himself in the room where he had had dinner, the single door of which led out to the entrance hall.

Altogether stupefied by these strange happenings, the Student Anselmus stood lingering at the street door. Then he heard a window open above him, and looked up. He saw Archivist Lindhorst, quite the old man again, in his light grey gown, as he usually appeared. The Archivist called to him: "Well, Student, what are you pondering over as you loiter about down there? Tush, the Arabic is still in your head! My compliments to Dean Paulmann, if you see him. And come tomorrow precisely at noon. The fee for this day is in the corner of your right waistcoat pocket."

The Student Anselmus immediately found the silver dollar in the pocket indicated; but he took no joy in it. "What is to come of all this," he said to himself, "I know not. But if it be some mad delusion and spell that has laid hold of me, my dear Serpentina will still live and move in my heart; and rather than leave her I will die. For I know that my love and thought are eternal, and no hostile element can take that from me: what else is this thought but Serpentina's love?"

SEVENTH VIGIL

How Dean Paulmann knocked the Ashes out of his Pipe, and went to Bed. Rembrandt and Breughel. The Magic Mirror; and Dr. Eckstein's Prescription for an unknown Disease.

Dean Paulmann finally knocked the ashes out of his pipe, and said: "Now, then, it is time to go to bed."

"Yes, indeed," replied Veronica, frightened by her father's sitting up so late; for the clock had struck ten long ago. No sooner, accordingly, had the Dean withdrawn to his study and bedroom, and Fränzchen's heavy breathing signified that she was asleep, than Veronica, who, for appearances' sake, had also gone to bed, rose softly and lightly out of it again; put on her clothes, threw her mantle round her, and slipped silently out of the house.

Ever since the moment she had left old Liese, Anselmus had continually stood before Veronica's eyes; and it seemed as if a strange voice, unknown to herself, were now and again repeating in her heart that his reluctance was the result of some hostile force that kept him in bonds, which by some secret magical means Veronica might break. Her confidence in old Liese grew stronger every day; and even her first impression of uncanniness and horror had by degrees worn off so that all the mystery and strangeness of her relation to the old witch appeared to her only in the light of something singular and romantic, and, consequently, not entirely unattractive. Accordingly, she had firmly resolved, even at the risk of being missed from home, and encountering a thousand inconveniences, on going through with the adventure of the Equinox. And now, at last, the fateful night, in which old Liese had promised to afford comfort and help, had come; and Veronica, who had long been accustoming herself to the thought of this night wandering, was full of heart and hope. With winged speed she flew through the deserted streets, heedless of the storm which was howling in the air, and already dashing heavy raindrops in her face.

With a dull, droning clang, the Kreuzthurm clock struck eleven, as Veronica, her clothes now rain-soaked, reached old Liese's house. "You've come, dear! Wait, pet, wait," cried a voice from above her; and in a moment the old woman, laden with a basket, and attended by her Cat, was standing at the door.

"We will go, then, and do what is proper, and prospers in the night, which favors our work." So speaking, the beldame with her cold hands seized the shivering Veronica, to whom she gave the heavy basket to carry, while she herself produced a little cauldron, a three-legged iron stand, and a spade. By the time they reached the open fields, the rain had ceased, but the wind had become stronger; it howled all about them in a thousand tones and modulations. A horrible, heart-piercing lamentation seemed to echo from the black clouds, which piled themselves together, in rapid flight, and veiled all the world in thickest darkness.

But the old hag stepped briskly forward, and cried out in a shrill voice: "Light, light, my lad!" Then blue gleams like forked lightning went quivering and spluttering before them; and Veronica saw that it was the Cat emitting sparks, and bounding forward to light the way, while his doleful and ghastly wails punctuated the pauses of the storm. Veronica pressed closer to the old witch, and said, in a firm voice, "It must all be worked now, come what may!"

"Right, right, little daughter!" the crone replied. "Be steady, like a good girl. You shall be prettily rewarded, and have Anselmus to boot."

At last the old hag came to a halt in her onward march, and said, "Here is the place!" She dug a hole in the ground with the spade, shook some lumps of coal into it, put the iron stand over them, and placed the cauldron on the top of the stand. All this she accomplished with strange gestures, while the Cat continued to circle around her. His tail kept giving off sparkles, which fused together into a ring of fire. The coal began to burn, and at last blue flames rose up round the cauldron. Veronica was directed to take off her mantle and veil, and to crouch down beside the old woman, who seized her hands and pressed them hard, glaring at her with fiery eyes. Before long the strange materials (whether flowers, metals, herbs, or the organs of beasts, nobody could have determined) which the witch had taken from her basket, and thrown into the cauldron, began to seethe and bubble. The old hag now left Veronica's side. She picked up an iron ladle, plunged it into the glowing mass, and began to stir, while Veronica, as instructed, continued to look steadfastly into the cauldron, and fix her thoughts on Anselmus. But now the witch threw in fresh ingredients: glittering pieces of metal, a lock of hair which Veronica had cut from her head, and a little ring which she had long worn—these went into the pot. And meanwhile the beldame's dreadful howling chant echoed through the gloom, and the Cat, in quick, incessant motion, whimpered and whined.

I earnestly wish that you, gentle reader, had on this twenty-third of September been yourself traveling towards Dresden. In vain, when late night enveloped the earth, did the people try to detain you at the last post-stage; the inn's friendly host assured you that the storm and the rain were too fierce to contend with, and, moreover, that it was not safe, for frankly supernatural reasons, to rush away in the dark on the night of the Equinox; but you refused to listen to him, thinking to yourself, "I will tip the postilion well, and so, at the latest, by one o'clock I shall reach Dresden—where, in the Golden Angel, or in the Helmet, or in the City of Naumburg, a well-prepared supper and a soft bed await me."

And now, as you are driving toward the city through the dark, you suddenly observe in the distance a strange flickering light. Coming nearer, you make out a ring of fire; and in the midst of it, beside a pot, out of which thick vapor is mounting with quivering red flashes and sparks of light, you can further note two most disparate figures. Your road leads right through the fire, but the horses snort, and stamp, and rear; the postilion curses and prays, and scourges his beasts withal; they do not stir from the spot. Involuntarily you then leap out of your carriage, and hurry a few steps ahead. And now you can clearly see the fragile, gentle child, who, in her thin white dress, is kneeling by the cauldron. The storm has loosened her braids, and the long chestnut-brown hair is flying free in the wind. Straight above the dazzling light of the flame, flickering up under the three-legged iron stand, rises her angelic face; but in the glacial horror which has overwhelmed it, that lovely face is stiff and pale as death; and by the updrawn eyebrows, by the mouth vainly opened for the shriek of anguish, which cannot find its way from the bosom compressed with nameless torture, you realize her fright, her utter terror. Her soft little hands she holds aloft and spasmodically pressed together, as if she were calling with urgent prayers upon her guardian angel, to deliver her from the monsters of the Pit, which in obedience to this potent spell are forthwith to appear! There she kneels, motionless as a figure of marble. Over against her, crouching on the ground, sits a tall, shriveled, copper-hued crone, with peaked hawk-nose, and glittering cat-eyes; from the black cloak, which is gathered round her, stick out her naked skinny arms; stirring the Hell-broth, she laughs and shrieks in a croaking voice, through the raging, bellowing storm. I can well believe that in you too, kindly reader, though otherwise unacquainted with fear and dread, there might have arisen, at the sight of this Rembrandt or Breughel painting come to life, some unearthly feelings—even that, for very horror, the hairs of your head might have stood on end. But your eye could not have turned away from the gentle child, who was entangled in these infernal activities; the electric shock that quivered through all your nerves and fibres would have kindled in you, with the speed of lightning, the courageous thought of defying the mysterious powers of this circle of monstrous fire; and in this thought, your own terror would have disappeared—indeed the thought itself would have been sired by very terror. Your heart would have felt as if you yourself were one of those guardian angels, to whom this young girl, frightened to death, was praying, even as if you must instantly draw your pocket pistol, and without more ceremony blow out the hag's brains. But while you were thinking all this out, most vividly, you would probably have cried out, "Hullo!" or, "What's the matter here?" or, "What's going on there?" Then at a blast from the postilion's horn, the witch would have stirred about in her cauldron once more, and in a trice everything would have vanished in thick smoke. Whether you would then have found the girl, whom, with most heartfelt longing, you were seeking in the darkness, I cannot say. But the spell of the witch would of a certainty have been destroyed, and broken the magic circle into which Veronica had un-knowingly precipitated herself.

Alas! Neither you, gentle reader, nor any other man either drove or walked this way, on the twenty-third of September, in the tempestuous night so favorable to witches; and Veronica must abide by the cauldron, in deadly terror, till the work was near its close. She heard, indeed, what howling and raging there was around her; she heard all sorts of hateful voices bellowing and bleating and yelling and humming. But she did not open her eyes. For she felt that the sight of the abominations and horrors with which she was literally surrounded might drive her to utter and all-consuming madness. The hag had ceased to stir the pot; the smoke be-neath it became fainter and fainter until at last nothing but a light spirit-flame was burning there. Then the beldame cried: "Veronica! My child! My darling! Look into the grounds there! What do you see? What do you see?"

Veronica could not answer, yet it seemed as if all sorts of confused shapes were dancing and whirling in the cauldron; and suddenly, with a friendly glance and outstretched hand, the Student Anselmus rose from the depths of the vessel. She cried aloud: "It is Anselmus! It is Anselmus!"

Instantly the witch turned the cock fixed at the bottom of the caul-dron, and glowing metal rushed forth, hissing and bubbling, into a little mold which she had placed beside it. The hag now jumped up into the air and shrieked, capering about with wild, horrific gestures: "It is done! It is done! Thanks, my darling lad; have you watched?—Pooh, pooh, he is coming! Bite him to death! Bite him to death!" But now a loud, rushing sound filled the air about them; it was as if a huge eagle were pouncing down, striking round him with his pinions. And a tremendous voice shouted: "Hey, hey, vermin!—It is over! It is over!—Home with ye!" The crone sank to the earth with a bitter lamentation, but Veronica's sense and recollection forsook her utterly.

When she returned to consciousness, it was broad daylight. She was lying in her own bed, and Fränzchen was standing beside her with a cup of steaming tea, and saying to her: "But tell me, sister, what in all the world ails you? I have been standing here for an hour, and you have been lying senseless, as if in the heat of a fever, and moaning and whimpering till we are all frightened to death. Father has not gone to his class this morning, because of your condition. He will be here directly with the Doctor."

Veronica took the tea in silence, and as she drank it, the horrid images of the previous night rose vividly before her eyes. "So it was all nothing but a wild dream that tortured me? Yet last night I surely went to that old woman. It surely was the twenty-third of September? Well, I must have been very ill last night, and so have imagined all this; and nothing has made me ill but my perpetual thinking of Anselmus, and the strange old creature who pretended that she was Liese, but was no such thing, has made a fool of me with that story."

Fränzchen, who had left the room, now came back with Veronica's long cloak, all wet, in her hand. "Do but look, sister," said she, "what a sight your coat is! The storm blew the window open during the night and upset the chair where your coat was hanging; and so the rain came in, and got your clothes all wet."

This speech sank heavily into Veronica's heart. For she now realized that it was no dream which had tormented her, but that she had really been with the witch. Anguish and horror took hold of her at the thought; and a fever frost quivered through all her frame. In a spasm of shuddering, she drew the bedclothes close around her; but with this, she felt something hard pressing on her breast, and as she grasped it with her hand, it seemed like a medallion. She drew it out, as soon as Fränzchen went away with the coat; it was a little, round, brightly polished, metallic mirror. "This is a present from the old woman," she cried eagerly. And it was as if fiery beams were shooting from the mirror, and penetrated into her inmost self with benign warmth. The fever frost was gone, and there streamed through her whole being an unutterable feeling of contentment and calm delight. She could not help remembering Anselmus; and as she turned her thoughts more and more intensely on him, behold he smiled at her with a most friendly countenance out of the mirror, as if this were a living miniature portrait in her hands.

But before long she felt it was no longer the image which she saw; no! it was the Student Anselmus himself, alive and in the flesh. He was sitting in a stately, strangely furnished room, and diligently writing. Veronica was about to step forward, to tap his shoulder, and say to him: "Anselmus, look round; it is I!" But she could not; for it was as if a circle of fire surrounded him; and yet, when she looked more closely, this ring of flame was nothing but a collection of large books with gilt edges.

At last Veronica succeeded in catching Anselmus' eye. It seemed as if he needed, in glancing at her, to remind himself who she was; but finally he smiled and said: "Ah! Is it you, dear Mademoiselle Paulmann? But why do you choose, upon occasion, to take the form of a little Snake?" At these strange words, Veronica could not help laughing aloud; and with this she awoke as from a deep dream. She hastily concealed the little mirror, for the door just then opened, and Dean Paulmann came into the room with Doctor Eckstein. Doctor Eckstein stepped forward to the bed, felt Veronica's pulse with long, profound attention, and then said: "Eh! Eh!" Thereupon he wrote out a prescription, again felt the pulse, said: "Eh! Eh!" a second time and then left his patient. It was difficult from these disclosures of Doctor Eckstein's for Dean Paulmann to make out definitely what it was that ailed his daughter Veronica.

EIGHTH VIGIL

The Library of the Palm Trees. Fortunes of an unhappy Sala-mander. How the Black Quill caressed a Parsnip, and Registrar Heerbrand was overtaken with Liquor.

The Student Anselmus had now worked several days with Archivist Lindhorst. These working hours had been and continued to be for him the happiest of his life; still surrounded by lovely music, ever and anon hearing Serpentina's encouraging voice, he was filled to overflowing with a pure delight which often rose to highest rapture. Every strait, every little care of his needy existence, had vanished from his thought; and in the new life which had risen before him, as in serene and sunny splendor, he seemed to apprehend all the wonders of a higher world, which hitherto had filled him with confusion and even with dread. His copying proceeded with rapidity and ease. For he felt more and more as if he were writing characters long known to him, and he scarcely needed to cast his eyes upon the manuscript while copying it all with the greatest exactness.

Except at the hour of dinner, Archivist Lindhorst seldom made an appearance; when he did turn up, however, it was always precisely at the moment that Anselmus had finished copying in the last letter of some manuscript. Then the Archivist would hand him another, and would immediately leave him without uttering a word, having first stirred the ink with a little black rod and changed the old pens for new sharp-pointed ones. One day when Anselmus, at the stroke of twelve, had climbed the stairs as usual, he found the door, through which he commonly entered, standing locked; and then Archivist Lindhorst came forward from the other side of the lobby, dressed in his strange, flower-figured dressing gown. He called out: "Come this way today, Anselmus; for we must go to the room where *Bhogovotgita's* masters are waiting for us."

He walked along the corridor, leading Anselmus through the same chambers and halls the Student had traversed on his first visit. The Student Anselmus was once more astonished by the marvelous beauty of the garden; but he now realized that many of the strange flowers which hung on the dark bushes were in truth insects of splendid color, hovering up and down on their little wings, as they danced and whirled in clusters, caressing one another with their antennae. On the other hand, the rose- and azure-colored birds were seen to be fragrant flowers; and the perfume which they scattered seemed to rise from their cups with low and lovely sounds, which, with the gurgling of distant fountains, and the sighing of the high groves of trees, mingled into the mysterious accords of a deep, unutterable longing. The parrots, which had so jeered and flouted him before, were again fluttering to and fro over his head, and crying incessantly with their sharp small voices: "My fine scholar, don't be in such a hurry! Don't peep into the clouds so! They may fall about your ears. Ha! Ha! Put your powder mantle on. Cousin Screech Owl will curl your wig for you." And so it went on, in a variety of stupid babble, till Anselmus left the garden.

Archivist Lindhorst at last stepped into the azure chamber. The porphyry, with the Golden Pot, was gone. Instead of this, in the middle of the room stood a table covered with violet-colored satin, upon which lay the writing materials already familiar to Anselmus. And a stuffed arm-chair, upholstered in the same kind of cloth, was placed beside it.

"Dear Anselmus," said Archivist Lindhorst, "you have now copied for me a number of manuscripts, rapidly and correctly, to my no small contentment. You have gained my confidence. But the hardest work is yet to be done; and that is the transcribing, or rather painting, of certain works, written in a peculiar character. I keep them in this room, and they can only be copied on the spot. You will, therefore, in future, work here. But I must recommend to you the greatest foresight and attention: a false stroke, or, Heaven forefend, a blot let fall on the original, will plunge you into great misfortune."

Anselmus had noticed that little, emerald-green leaves projected from the golden trunks of the palm trees. The Archivist now took hold of one of these leaves, and Anselmus suddenly realized that the leaf was, in fact, a roll of parchment, which the Archivist unfolded, and spread out before the Student on the table. Anselmus was struck not a little by these strangely intertwisted characters; and as he looked over the many points, strokes, dashes, and twirls in the manuscript, he almost lost hope of ever copying it.

"Courage, young man!" cried the Archivist. "If you have continuing Belief and true Love, Serpentina will help you."

His voice sounded like ringing metal; and as Anselmus looked up in sudden terror, he saw Lindhorst standing before him in the kingly form which, during the first visit, he had assumed in the library. Anselmus felt as if he must sink to his knees in deep reverence, but the Archivist stepped up the trunk of a palm tree and vanished high among the emerald leaves. The Student Anselmus realized that the Prince of the Spirits had been conversing with him, and was now gone up to his own private study, perhaps intending, by the beams which some of the Planets had dispatched to him as envoys, to send back word what was to become of Anselmus and Serpentina. . . .

"It may be, too," he thought further, "that he is expecting news from the Springs of the Nile, or that some magician from Lapland is paying him a visit. In any case it behooves me to set diligently about my book." And with this, he began to study the foreign characters in the roll of parchment.

The strange music from the garden fell upon his ears, and he was lapped about with sweet and lovely odors. He could hear the parrots, too, still jeering and twittering, but he could not distinguish their words, a thing which greatly pleased him. At times also it seemed to him that the leaves of the palm trees were rustling, and as if the clear crystal tones, which Anselmus on that fateful Ascension Day had heard under the elder tree, were flashing and flitting through the room. Wonderfully strengthened by all this sparkling and tinkling, the Student Anselmus directed his eyes and thoughts more and more intensely upon the superscription of the parchment roll; and before long it came to him almost in a vision, that the characters could denote nothing other than these words: "Of the marriage of the Salamander with the green Snake." Then the air resounded with a louder harmony of those clear crystal bells. The words, "Anselmus! Dear Anselmus!" floated to him from the leaves; and—O wonder of wonders!—the green Snake came gliding down the trunk of the palm tree.

"Serpentina! Serpentina!" cried Anselmus, in the madness of overwhelming joy. For he saw that in truth a lovely and glorious maiden was coming to him from the tree; and she was looking at him with those dark blue eyes, full of inexpressible longing, which lived so poignantly in his heart. The leaves seemed to jut out and expand; on every side thorns seemed to be sprouting from the trunk; but Serpentina twisted and turned herself deftly through them and she drew her fluttering robe, in its glancing, changing colors, along with her so skilfully that, flying round the dainty form, it nowhere caught on the projecting points and prickles of the palm tree. She sat down by Anselmus, on the same chair, clasped him with her arms, and pressed him to her, so that he felt the breath which came from her lips, and the electric warmth of her body as it touched his.

"Dear Anselmus!" began Serpentina. "You shall now soon be wholly mine! By your Belief, by your Love, you shall win me as your bride. And I will bring you the Golden Pot, which shall make us both happy forever."

"O kind and lovely Serpentina!" cried Anselmus. "If I have you, what care I for all else! If only you are mine, I will joyfully accept all these inexplicable mysteries that have plagued me ever since the moment I first saw you."

"I know," continued Serpentina, "that the strange and mysterious things, with which my father—often merely in the play of his humor—has surrounded you, have raised distrust and fear in your mind. But now, I hope, it shall be so no more; for I have come at this moment to tell you, dear Anselmus, everything you need to know, in order to understand my father. And so you will see clearly what your relation to him, and to me, really is."

Anselmus felt as if he were so wholly clasped and encircled by the gentle, lovely form that only with her could he move and live, and it seemed to him that it was the beating of her pulse that throbbed through his nerves and his veins. He had put his arm round her; but the mysterious glittering cloth of her robe was so smooth and slippery that it seemed to him as if at any moment she would writhe out of his arms, and—like a snake again—glide away. He trembled at the thought.

"Ah, do not leave me, gentlest Serpentina!" he cried. "You are all my life!"

"I will not leave you now," said Serpentina, "till I have told you all that, in your love of me, you will comprehend:

"Know then, my dearest one, that my father is sprung from the wondrous race of the Salamanders, and that I owe my existence to his love for the green Snake. In primeval times, in the Fairyland Atlantis, the powerful Spirit-prince Phosphorus was sovereign, and to him the Salamanders, and other Spirits of the Elements, were in fief. Once upon a time, the Salamander whom the Prince loved above all others (it was my father) chanced to be walking in the stately garden which Phosphorus' mother had decked in the lordliest fashion with her best gifts; and the Salamander heard a tall Lily singing in low tones: 'Press down thy little eyelids till my Lover, the Morning-wind, awake thee.'

"He moved toward it; touched by his glowing breath, the Lily opened her leaves; and he saw the Lily's daughter, the green Snake, lying asleep in the hollow of the flower. Then the Salamander became inflamed with ardent love for the fair Snake; and he carried her away from the Lily, whose perfumes in nameless lamentations vainly called for her beloved daughter throughout all the garden. For the Salamander had borne her into the palace of Phosphorus, and was there beseeching him: 'Wed me with my beloved, and she shall be mine forevermore.'—'Madman, what askest thou?' said the Prince of the Spirits. 'Know that once the Lily was my mistress, and bore rule with me; but the Spark, which I cast into her, threatened to annihilate the fair Lily; and only my victory over the black Dragon, whom now the Spirits of the Earth hold in fetters, maintains her, that her leaves continue strong enough to enclose this Spark, and preserve it within them. But when thou claspest the green Snake, thy fire will consume her frame, and a new Being, rapidly arising from her dust, will soar away and leave thee.'

"The Salamander heeded not the warning of the Spirit-prince; in passionate fervor he clasped the green Snake in his arms; she crumbled into ashes; a winged Being, born from her dust, soared away through the sky. Then the madness of desperation seized upon the Salamander. He ran through the garden, dashing forth fire and flames, and laid waste to the lovely spot in his wild fury, till its fairest flowers and blossoms hung down, blackened and scorched, and their lamentations filled the air. The indignant Prince of the Spirits, in his wrath, took hold of the Salamander, and said: 'Thy fire has burnt out, thy flames are extinguished, thy rays darkened; sink down to the Spirits of the Earth; let these mock and jeer thee, and keep thee captive, till the Fire-element shall again kindle, and glow from thee as from a new being from the Earth.'

"The poor Salamander sank down, thus, extinguished. But now the testy old Earth-spirit, who was Phosphorus' gardener, came forth and said: 'Master! Who has greater cause to complain of the Salamander than I? Had not all the fair flowers, which he has burned, been decorated with my gayest pigments? Had I not stoutly nursed and tended them, and spent many a fair hue on their leaves? And yet I must pity the poor Salamander; for it was but Love, in which thou, O Master, hast full often been entangled, that drove him to despair, and so to devastation of the garden. Remit his too harsh punishment!'

" 'His fire is for the present extinguished,' replied the Prince of the Spirits; 'but in the hapless time, when the Speech of Nature shall no longer be intelligible to degenerate man; when the Spirits of the Elements, banished into their own regions, shall speak to him only from afar, in faint, spent echoes; when, exiled from the harmonious circle, an infinite longing alone shall give him tidings of the Land of Marvels, which he once was able to inhabit while Belief and Love still dwelt in his soul; in this hapless time, the fire of the Salamander shall kindle again. But only to manhood shall he be permitted to rise: entering wholly into man's necessitous existence, he shall learn to endure its wants and oppressions. Yet not only shall the remembrance of his first state continue with him, but he shall be again lifted into the sacred harmony of all Nature: he shall understand its wonders, and the power of his Fellow-spirits shall stand at his behest. Then, too, in a Lily-plant he shall find the green Snake again. And the fruit of his marriage with her shall be three daughters, which, to men, shall appear in their mother's form. In the spring season these shall disport themselves in the dark elder tree and sing and prattle with their lovely crystal voices. And then if, in that needy and mean age, there shall be found a youth who understands their song; nay, if one of the little Snakes look at him with her kind eyes; if the look awaken in him some foresight vision of the distant, wondrous Land, to which, having cast away the burden of the commonplace, he can courageously soar; if, with love for the Snake, there rise in him belief in the Wonders of Nature, and, further, in his own existence amid these Wonders—if all this takes place, then the Snake shall be his. But not till three youths of this sort have been found, and wedded to the three daughters, may the Salamander cast away his heavy burden, and return to his brothers.'

" 'Permit me, Master,' said the Earth-spirit, 'to make these three daughters a gift, which may glorify their lives with the husbands they shall find. Let each of them receive from me a Pot, of the fairest metal which I have. I will polish each Pot with lights borrowed from the diamond; in its glitter shall our Kingdom of Wonders, as it now exists in the Harmony of universal Nature, be imaged in gloriously dazzling reflection; and from its interior, on the day of marriage, shall spring forth a Fire-lily, whose eternal blossoms shall forever waft sweet perfume upon the youth that is found worthy. Soon, too, shall he learn the Lily's speech, and shall understand the wonders of our kingdom; and he shall dwell with his beloved in Atlantis itself.'

"You understand, dear Anselmus, that the Salamander of whom I speak is indeed no other than my father. In spite of his higher nature, he was forced to subject himself to the paltriest contradictions of common life; and hence, indeed, comes often the wayward humor with which he vexes many. He has told me, now and then, that for the inward quality of mind which the Spirit-prince Phosphorus required as a condition of marriage with me and my sisters, men have a name at present, which, in truth, they frequently enough misapply; they call it a childlike, poetic character. This character, he says, is often found in youths, who, by reason of their high simplicity of manners, and their total want of what is called knowledge of the world, are mocked by the populace. Ah, dear Anselmus, beneath the elder tree, you understood my song, the look in my eyes; you love the green Snake, you believe in me, you will be mine forevermore! The fair Lily will bloom forth from the Golden Pot; and we shall dwell, happy, and united, and blessed, in Atlantis together!

"Yet I must not hide from you the fact that, in its deadly battle with the Salamanders and Spirits of the Earth, the black Dragon burst from their grasp, and ascended swiftly through the air. Phosphorus, indeed, again holds him in fetters; but from his black Quills, which, in the struggle, rained down on the ground, there sprung up hostile Spirits which on all sides set themselves against the Salamanders and Spirits of the Earth. That woman who so hates you, dear Anselmus, and who, as my father knows full well, is striving for possession of the Golden Pot—that woman owes her existence to the love of such a Quill (plucked in battle from the Dragon's wing) for a certain Parsnip beside which it dropped.

"She knows her origin and her power; for, in the moans and convulsions of the captive Dragon, the secrets of many a mysterious constellation have been revealed to her. And she uses every means, and makes every effort, to work from the Outward into the Inward and Unseen, while my father, with the beams which shoot forth from the spirit of the Salamander, withstands and subdues her. All the baneful principles, which lurk in deadly herbs and the venom of poisonous beasts, she collects; and, mixing them under favorable constellations, she raises therewith many a wicked spell, which overwhelms the soul of man with fear and trembling, and subjects him to the power of those Demons which were produced from the Dragon when it was itself vanquished in battle. Beware of that old woman, dear Anselmus! She hates you, because your childlike, pious character has negated many of her wicked charms. Keep true, true to me; soon you will reach the goal!"

"O my Serpentina! My own Serpentina!" cried the Student Anselmus. "How could I leave you, how should I not love you forever!" A kiss fell burning on his lips; he awoke as from a deep dream; Serpentina had vanished. The hour of six was striking, and it fell heavy on his heart that today he had not copied a single stroke.

Full of anxiety, and dreading the Archivist's reproaches, he looked at the sheet of paper before him. O wonder! The copy of the mysterious manuscript was finished, perfectly. And he thought, on examining the characters more closely, that what was written was nothing other than Serpentina's story of her father, the favorite of the Spirit-prince Phosphorus, in Atlantis, the Land of Marvels.

But now Archivist Lindhorst, wearing his light grey surtout and carrying his hat and stick, came into the room. He looked at the parchment on which Anselmus had been writing, took a large pinch of snuff, and said with a smile: "Just as I thought! Well, Herr Anselmus, here is your silver dollar; we will now go to the Linke Baths; do but follow me!" The Archivist walked rapidly through the garden, in which there was such a din of singing, whistling, talking, that the Student Anselmus was quite deafened by it, and thanked Heaven when he found himself on the street.

Scarcely had they gone twenty paces, when they met Registrar Heerbrand, who joined them in companionable fashion. At the Gate, they filled their pipes, which they had brought with them. Registrar Heerbrand complained that he had left his tinder-box behind, and could not strike fire. "Fire!" cried Archivist Lindhorst, scornfully. "Here is fire enough, and to spare!" And with this he snapped his fingers, out of which came streams of sparks, which immediately lighted the pipes.

"Do but observe the chemical knack of some men!" said Registrar Heerbrand. But the Student Anselmus thought, not without inward awe, of the Salamander and his history. . . .

At the Linke Baths, Registrar Heerbrand drank so much strong double beer, that at last, though usually a good-natured, quiet man, he began singing student songs in a squeaking tenor. He asked every one, sharply, whether he was his friend or not. And finally he had to be taken home by the Student Anselmus, long after Archivist Lindhorst had gone his way.

NINTH VIGIL

How the Student Anselmus attained some Sense. The Punch Party. How the Student Anselmus mistook Dean Paulmann for a Screech Owl, and the latter felt much hurt at it. The Ink-blot, and its Consequences.

The strange and mysterious events, which day by day befell the Student Anselmus, had entirely withdrawn him from his customary life.

He no longer visited any of his friends, and he waited every morning with impatience for the hour of noon to unlock the door of his paradise.

And yet, while his whole soul was turned to the gentle Serpentina, and the wonders of Archivist Lindhorst's enchanted kingdom, he could not help now and then thinking of Veronica. Indeed it often seemed as if she appeared before him and blushingly confessed how wholeheartedly she loved him and how fervently she longed to rescue him from the phantoms which were mocking and befuddling him. At times he felt as if some external force, suddenly breaking in on his mind, were drawing him with irresistible power to the forgotten Veronica—as if he must follow her wherever she pleased to lead him, even as if he were bound to her by ties that nothing could break.

The very night after Serpentina had first appeared to him in the form of a lovely maiden, after the wondrous secret of the Salamander's nuptials with the green Snake had been disclosed, the image of Veronica came to him more vividly than ever before. Not till he awoke, in fact, was he clearly aware that he had only been dreaming. For he had felt persuaded that Veronica was actually beside him, lamenting, with face and voice marked by a keen sorrow that pierced to his spirit soul, that he should sacrifice her deep and true love to fantastic visions, which only his distraught mind called into being, and which, moreover, would at last prove his ruin. Veronica was lovelier than he had ever seen her; he could not drive her from his thoughts; and in this perplexed and contradictory mood he hurried out of the house, hoping to restore his composure by a morning walk.

Some secret, magic influence led him on to the Pirna Gate. He was just turning into a cross street, when he saw Dean Paulmann coming after him, and heard him cry out: "Eh! Eh! Dear Anselmus! *Amice! Amice!* Where, in Heaven's name, have you been buried so long? We never see you at all. Do you know, Veronica is very anxious indeed to have another duet with you? So come along. You were just on the road to our house, at any rate."

The Student Anselmus, constrained by this friendly aggressiveness, went along with the Dean. On entering the house, they were met by Veronica, dressed with such elegance and obvious attention that Dean

Paulmann asked in surprise: "Why so decked out, Mamselle? Were you expecting visitors? Well, here I bring you Anselmus."

Veronica was all gaiety and graciousness. And when Paulmann left them to go to his study, she contrived, with various coquetries, to lead the Student Anselmus on, so that he at last quite forgot his bashfulness, and actually danced a merry step around the room with her.

Yet here his old Demon of Awkwardness got hold of him once more. He stumbled against a table, and Veronica's pretty little workbox fell to the floor. Anselmus picked it up; the lid had fallen open; and his attention was caught by a little round metallic mirror, into which he now looked with peculiar delight. Veronica stepped softly up to him, laid her hand on his arm, and pressing close to him, looked over his shoulder with him into the mirror. And suddenly Anselmus felt as if a battle were beginning in his soul: thoughts, images, flashed before his eyes—Archivist Lindhorst, Serpentina, the green Snake. . . .

At last the tumult abated, and all this chaos arranged and shaped itself into distinct consciousness. It now seemed clear to him that he had always thought of no one but Veronica; nay, that the form which had yesterday appeared to him in the blue chamber had actually been Veronica herself and no one else; and that the wild legend of the Salamander's marriage with the green Snake had merely been copied down by him from the manuscript, and not at all related in his hearing. He wondered not a little at all these dreams, and finally ascribed them to the feverish state of mind into which Veronica's love had thrown him, as well as to his work with Archivist Lindhorst, in whose rooms there were, besides, so many strangely intoxicating odors. He could only heartily laugh at the mad whim of falling in love with a little green Snake, and of mistaking a well-fed Privy Archivist for a Salamander.

"Yes, yes! It is Veronica!" he cried aloud. And then, on turning his head, he looked right into Veronica's blue eyes, from which the warmest love was beaming. A faint, soft "Ah!" escaped her lips, as they now pressed, burning, upon his.

"O happy me!" sighed the enraptured Student. "What last night I only dreamed, today is, in very truth, mine!"

"But will you really marry me, then, when you are a Privy Councillor?" asked Veronica.

"'That I will," replied the Student Anselmus. And just then the door creaked open and Dean Paulmann entered. "Now, dear Anselmus, I will not let you go today," he said. "You will have to put up with a bad dinner; then Veronica will make us delightful coffee, which we shall share with Registrar Heerbrand, for he promised to come here."

"Ah, most kind Dean Paulmann!" answered the Student Anselmus. "Are you not aware that I must go to Archivist Lindhorst's, and copy manuscripts?"

"Look at this, *Amice!*" said Dean Paulmann, holding up his watch, which pointed to half past twelve.

The Student Anselmus realized that he was much too late to begin his task at the Archivist's. And he complied with the Dean's wishes the more readily, since he might now hope to look at Veronica the whole day long, to obtain many a fleeting, significant glance and little pressure of the hand, and even to succeed in stealing a kiss. To such lofty heights had the Student Anselmus' desires now climbed; and he felt more and more contented at heart, the more fully he convinced himself that he should soon be delivered from all the fantastic imaginings which really, he now thought, might sooner or later have rendered him a complete idiot.

Registrar Heerbrand came, as he had promised, after dinner; and coffee being over, and the dusk come on, the Registrar, puckering his face together, and gaily rubbing his hands, signified that he had something with him, which, if properly composed and resolved into form—as it were, paged and titled by Veronica's fair hands—might be pleasant to them all, on this October evening.

"Come out, then, with this mysterious substance which you carry on your person, most valued Registrar," cried Dean Paulmann. Then Registrar Heerbrand thrust his hand into his deep pocket and, in three such trips, brought out a bottle of arrack, two lemons, and a quantity of sugar. Before half an hour had passed, a savory bowl of hot punch was steaming on Paulmann's table. Veronica drank their health in a sip of the liquor; and before long there was plenty of gay, good-natured talk among the friends.

But the Student Anselmus, as the spirit of the drink mounted to his head, felt all the images of those wondrous things, which he had been experiencing these past weeks, again surge into his mind. He saw the Archivist in his damask dressing gown, which glowed like phosphorus in the dark. He saw the azure room, the golden palm trees. More, it now seemed to him as if he must still believe in Serpentina; there was a fermentation, a conflicting tumult within him. Veronica handed him a glass of punch; and in taking it, he gently touched her hand. "Serpentina! Veronica!" sighed he to himself. He sank into deep dreams. But he suddenly heard Registrar Heerbrand saying in a loud voice: "A strange old unfathomable gentleman he is and always will be, this Archivist Lindhorst! Well, long life to him! Your glass, Herr Anselmus!"

Then the Student Anselmus awoke from his dreams, and remarked, quietly, as he touched glasses with Registrar Heerbrand: "That proceeds, respected Registrar, from the fact that the Archivist Lindhorst is, in reality, a Salamander, who devastated the Spirit-prince Phosphorus' garden, in his rage and despair because the green Snake had deserted him."

"How? What?" inquired the Dean.

"Yes," continued the Student Anselmus, "and for this reason he is now forced to be a Royal Archivist, and to keep house here in Dresden with his three daughters, who, after all, are nothing more nor less than little gold-green Snakes, that bask in elder trees, and traitorously sing, and seduce young people, like so many sirens."

"Anselmus! Anselmus!" cried Dean Paulmann. "Is there a crack sprung in your brain? In Heaven's name, what imbecilic stuff is this you are babbling?"

"He is right," interrupted Registrar Heerbrand; "that fellow, that Archivist, is a cursed Salamander, and strikes you fiery snips from his fingers, which burn holes in your surtout like red-hot tinder. Yes, yes, you are in the right, little brother Anselmus, and whoever says no is saying no to me!" And at these words Registrar Heerbrand struck the table with his fist, till the glasses rang out.

"Registrar! Are you mad too?" cried the indignant Dean. "What is this you are all talking about?"

"As for you," said the Student, "you are nothing but a bird. You are a screech owl, and you curl the hair of men's *toupées*, Dean Paulmann!"

"What? I a bird? A screech owl? A hair-curler?" cried the Dean in a rage. "Sir, you are mad, utterly mad!"

"But the old witch will get her hands on him," said Registrar Heer-brand.

"Yes, that crone is powerful," interrupted the Student Anselmus, "though she is of low descent. Her father was nothing but a ragged wing feather, and her mother a dirty parsnip, but the most of her power she owes to all sorts of baneful creatures, poisonous vermin that she keeps in her house."

"That is a horrid calumny," cried Veronica, with eyes glowing in anger. "Old Liese is a wise woman; and the black Cat is no baneful creature, but a polished young aristocrat of elegant manners, and her own cousin."

"Can he eat Salamanders without singeing his whiskers, and dying like a snuffed candle?" cried Registrar Heerbrand.

"No! No!" shouted the Student Anselmus. "That he never can in this world do! And the green Snake loves me, and I have looked into Serpentina's eyes!"

"The Cat will scratch them out," cried Veronica.

"Salamander, Salamander beats them all, all," screamed Dean Paulmann. "But am I in a madhouse? Am I mad myself? What twaddle am I chattering? Yes, I am mad too! Mad too!" And with this, the Dean jumped up, tore the peruke from his head, and dashed it against the ceiling of the room, so that the battered locks of his wig waved about, and, tangled into utter disorder, rained down their powder far and wide. Then the Student Anselmus and Registrar Heerbrand seized the punch bowl and the goblets; and, hallooing and huzzahing, pitched them up to hit the ceiling too, and the bits of glass fell jingling and tingling about their ears.

"*Vivat* the Salamander! *Pereat, pereat* the witch!—Break the metal mirror! Dig the Cat's eyes out! Bird, little Bird, in the air—*Eheu—Eheu—Evoe—Evoe*, Salamander!" So the three men shrieked, and shouted, and bellowed, like utter lunatics. Weeping loudly, Fränzchen ran out of the room, but Veronica remained behind sobbing out her pain and grief on the sofa.

At this moment the door opened. All became instantly still. And a little man, in a short grey cloak, stepped in. His nose, on which rested a huge pair of spectacles, seemed quite different from any other nose that ever was seen. He wore a strange peruke too; more like a feather cap than a wig.

"Eh, many good evenings to you!" cackled the comical little manni-kin. "Is the Student Anselmus among you, gentlemen? Best compliments from Archivist Lindhorst; he has waited today in vain for his calligraphist, but tomorrow he begs most respectfully to request the Student Anselmus not to miss the hour."

And with this he went out again; and all of them now clearly realized that the grave little mannikin was in fact a grey Parrot. Dean Paulmann and Registrar Heerbrand burst out into guffaws, which reverberated through the room, punctuated by Veronica's moaning and sobbing. As for the Student Anselmus, the madness of an inner horror was permeating his very soul; and without knowing what he was doing, he rushed out of the door and into the streets. Guided only by instinct, he reached his house, his garret. And here before long Veronica came to see him, in a peaceful and friendly mood, and asked him why, in the midst of the festivity, he had so vexed her. She begged him to be on his guard against fantastic hallucinations while he was working at Archivist Lindhorst's.

"Good night, good night, my beloved friend!" she then whispered, almost inaudibly, and breathed a kiss on his lips. He stretched out his arms to clasp her, but the dreamlike figure had vanished, and he awoke cheerful and refreshed.

He could only laugh at the effects of the punch. But in remembering Veronica, he felt pervaded by a most delightful sense of warm content-ment. "To her alone," said he to himself, "do I owe this recovery from my insane delusions. In fact, I was little better than the man who believed himself to be made of glass; or the one who did not dare leave his room for fear the hens would eat him, because he was a barleycorn! But just as soon as I am a Councillor, I will marry Mademoiselle Paulmann, and be happy, and there's an end of it."

And at noon, as he walked through Archivist Lindhorst's garden, he could not help wondering how all this had once appeared so strange and marvelous. He now saw nothing out of the ordinary: earthen flowerpots, quantities of geraniums, myrtles, and the like. Instead of the glittering, multicolored birds which used to flout him, there were only a few spar-rows, fluttering about and breaking into unpleasant and unintelligible twitterings at the sight of him. The azure room also had quite a different appearance; and he could not understand how that glaring blue, and those unnatural golden trunks of palm-trees, with their shapeless, glistening leaves, should ever have pleased him for a moment. The Archivist looked at him with a most peculiar and ironical smile, and asked: "Well, how did you like the punch last night, good Anselmus?"

"Ah, doubtless you have heard from the grey Parrot how—" answered the Student Anselmus, quite abashed, but he stopped short, remembering that this appearance of the Parrot was all a piece of jugglery.

"I was there myself," said Archivist Lindhorst. "Did you not see me? But, in the midst of the mad pranks you were playing, I almost got lamed. For I was sitting in the punch bowl, at the very moment the Registrar laid hands on it, to dash it against the ceiling; and I had to make a quick retreat into the Dean's pipe-bowl. Now, *au revoir*, Anselmus! Be diligent at your task. You shall also have a silver dollar for your lost day, because you worked so well before."

"How can the Archivist babble such nonsense?" thought the Student Anselmus, sitting down at the table to begin the copying of the manuscript which Archivist Lindhorst had, as usual, spread out before him. But on the parchment roll he noticed so many strange, crabbed strokes and twirls all twisted together in inexplicable confusion, offering no resting place for the eye, that it seemed to him almost impossible to copy all this exactly. Indeed, in glancing over the whole, you might have thought the parchment was nothing but a piece of thickly veined marble, or a stone sprinkled over with lichens. Nevertheless he determined to do his utmost, and boldly dipped his pen in the ink. But the writing fluid would not run, do what he might. Impatiently he snipped the point of his pen against his finger nail and—O Heavens and Earth!—a huge blot fell on the outspread original! Hissing and foaming, a blue flash rose from the blot; and, crackling and wavering, shot through the room to the ceiling. Then a thick vapor rolled from the walls; the leaves began to rustle, as if shaken by a tempest; and down from them darted glaring basilisks in sparkling fire; these set the vapor alight, and the confused masses of flame rolled round Anselmus. The golden trunks of the palm trees became gigantic snakes, which knocked their frightful heads together with piercing, metallic clang, and wound their scaly bodies round the distracted Student.

"Madman! Suffer now the punishment for what, in capricious irreverence, you have done!" So cried the frightful voice of the crowned Salamander, who appeared above the snakes like a glittering beam in the midst of the flame. And now the yawning jaws of the snakes poured forth cataracts of fire on Anselmus; but suddenly it was as if the fire streams were congealing about his body, and changing into a firm icy mass. Then while Anselmus' limbs were more and more pressed together and contracted more and more, stiffening into powerlessness, all consciousness left him. When he came to, he could not move a muscle. It seemed to him that he was surrounded by a glistening brightness, against which he struck if he but tried to lift his hand. Alas! He was sitting in a well-corked crystal bottle, on a shelf, in the library of Archivist Lindhorst.

TENTH VIGIL

Sorrows of the Student Anselmus in the Glass Bottle. Happy Life of the Cross-Church Scholars and Law Clerks. The Battle in the Library of Archivist Lindhorst. Victory of the Salamander, and Deliverance of the Student Anselmus.

Justly may I doubt whether you, gentle reader, were ever sealed up in a glass bottle, or even whether any vivid tormenting dream ever oppressed you with such necromantic punishment. If such were ever the case, you will keenly enough appreciate the poor Student Anselmus' woe; but should you never have even dreamed such things, then may your quick fancy, for Anselmus' sake and mine, still now be obliging enough to enclose itself for a few moments in crystal. You are drowned in dazzling splendor; all objects about you appear illuminated and surrounded with beaming rainbow hues; all you see quivers and wavers, and clangs and hums, in the magic sheen; you float as if swimming, yet motionless and powerless, in a firmly congealed ether, which so presses your limbs together that the spirit gives orders to the numb and stiffened body in vain. Weightier and weightier the mountainous burden lies upon you; more and more does every breath exhaust the little handful of air that still plays up and down in the narrow space; your pulse throbs madly; and cut through with horrid anguish, every nerve is tense and trembling in this deadly agony.

Have pity, gentle reader, on the Student Anselmus! This inexpressible torture had laid hold of him in his glass prison; but he knew too well that death could not rescue him. For did he not awake from the deep unconsciousness into which the excess of pain had cast him, and open his eyes to new wretchedness, when the morning sun shone brightly into the room? He could move no limb; but his thoughts struck against the glass, and stupefied him with their discordant vibrations. And instead of the words which the spirit used to speak from within him, he now heard only the stifled din of madness.

Then he exclaimed in his despair: "O Serpentina! Serpentina! Save me from this agony of Hell!" And it was as if faint sighs breathed around him, which spread like green, transparent elder leaves over the glass; the ringing noises ceased; the dazzling, perplexing glitter was gone; and he was able to breathe more freely.

"Have I not myself alone to blame for my misery? And have I not sinned against you, O most kind and beloved Serpentina? Have I not yielded to vile doubts of you? Have I not lost my Belief; and with it, all, all that was to make me so blessed? Ah! You will now never, never be mine. The Golden Pot is lost to me also, and I shall not behold its wonders any more. Ah! If only once I might see you, only once hear your sweet and tender voice, my lovely Serpentina!"

So wailed the Student Anselmus, pierced through with his deep sorrow; then he heard words spoken close by him: "What the devil ails you, Student? What makes you lament so, out of all compass and measure?" And the Student Anselmus now for the first time noticed that on the same shelf with him were five other bottles, in which he perceived three Cross-Church Scholars, and two Law Clerks.

"Ah, gentlemen, my fellows in misery," cried he, "how is it possible for you to be so calm, even so happy, as I see by your cheerful looks? You, as well as I, are sitting here corked up in glass bottles, and can no more move a finger, any more than I. Like me, you cannot think a reasonable thought, but there rises such a murder tumult of ringing and humming, and in your head itself such a roaring and rumbling as is enough to drive you mad. But doubtless you do not believe in the Salamander, or the green Snake!"

"You are pleased to jest, Student," replied a Cross-Church Scholar. "We have never been better off than at present. For the silver dollars, which the mad Archivist gave us for all manner of pothook copies, are still in our pockets; now we have no Italian choruses to learn by heart; we go each day to Joseph's or some other public house, where the double beer is good enough; and we can look a pretty girl in the face. So we sing like real students, *Gaudeamus igitur*, and are perfectly contented!"

"The Cross-Churchers are quite right," added a Law Clerk. "I, too, am well provided with silver dollars, like my cherished colleague beside me here. And we now diligently walk about on the Weinberg, instead of doing scurvy copying and composing within four walls."

"But, my best, worthiest masters!" said the Student Anselmus. "Do you not observe, then, that you are all and sundry corked up in glass bottles, and cannot for dear life walk a hairsbreadth?"

Here the Cross-Church Scholars and the Law Clerks set up a loud laugh, and cried: "The Student is mad; he thinks that he is sitting hunched up in a glass bottle, and here he is standing on the Elbe bridge and looking right down into the water! Let us leave this zany and go on our way!"

"Ah!" sighed the Student, "they have never seen the tender and lovely Serpentina. They do not know the meaning of Freedom, and living with Love, and Belief. And so, by reason of their folly and lack of imagination, they do not feel oppressed by their imprisonment. But I, unhappy I, must perish in want and woe, if she, whom I so inexpressibly love, does not deliver me!"

Then, coming to him in faint tinkles, Serpentina's voice floated through the room: "Anselmus! Believe, love, hope!" And every sound seemed to shine into Anselmus' prison; and the crystal yielded to his pressure, and expanded, until the captive's heart felt as if it could stir again in the breast.

The torment of his situation became less acute, and he understood that Serpentina still loved him, and that it was she alone who had rendered his confinement tolerable. He disturbed himself no more about his inane companions in misfortune, but concentrated all his thoughts upon the gentle Serpentina. Suddenly, however, there arose on the other side of him a dull, croaking, repulsive murmur. Before long he could observe that it proceeded from an old coffeepot, with a half-broken lid, which was standing over against him on a little shelf. As he scrutinized it more closely, the ugly features of a wrinkled old woman disclosed themselves by degrees, and in a few moments the Apple-wife of the *Schwarzthor* stood before him. She grinned and laughed at him, and screeched out, "Ei, ei, my pretty boy, must you lie in limbo now? You have run to the crystal; did not I tell you so long ago?"

"Mock and jeer at me; do, you cursed witch!" said the Student Anselmus. "You are to blame for it all; but the Salamander will catch you, you hideous Parsnip!"

"Ho, ho!" replied the hag. "Not so proud, my good writer! You have crushed my little sons to pieces. You have burnt my nose; but I must still like you, you knave, for once you were a pretty fellow; and my little daughter likes you too. You will never get out of the crystal unless I help you. I cannot climb up to you; but my cousin-gossip the Rat, that lives close behind you, will eat the shelf in two. Then down you tumble, and I catch you in my apron, so that your nose be not broken, or your fine, sleek face in any wise injured; and off I carry you to Mamselle Veronica, whom you shall marry when you are a Councillor."

"Get away from me, you Devil's brood!" cried the Student Anselmus, full of fury. "It was you alone and your hellish arts that brought me to the sin which I must now expiate. But I bear it all patiently; for only here will I be where the kind Serpentina surrounds me with her love and consolation. Hear it, wretched beldame, and despair! I bid defiance to your power. I love Serpentina and none but her. I will not be a Councillor, I will not look at Veronica, who through your influence and aid entices me to evil. If the green Snake cannot be mine, I will die in sorrow and longing. Take yourself off, you filthy old crow! Get out of my sight!"

The old witch laughed, till the room echoed. "Sit and die then," cried she. "But now it is time for me to set to work. I have other trades to follow here." Then she threw off her black cloak, and stood in hideous nakedness. Next she ran around in circles, and large folios came tumbling down to her. Out of these she tore parchment leaves, and rapidly patching them together in artful combination, and fixing them on her body, in a few instants she was dressed in a strange, multicolored armor. Spitting fire, the black Cat darted out of the inkwell, which was standing on the table, and ran mewing towards the hag, who shrieked in loud triumph and, accompanied by her minion, vanished through the door.

Anselmus observed that she went towards the azure chamber. And immediately he heard a hissing and storming in the distance. The birds in the garden were crying; the Parrot called out, "Help! Help! Thieves! Thieves!" At that moment the dreadful old woman bounded back into the room, carrying the Golden Pot in her arms. And, making hideous gestures the while, she shrieked wildly through the air: "Joy! Joy! Little son! Kill the green Snake! At her, son! At her!"

Anselmus thought he heard a deep moaning, thought he heard Serpentina's voice. Then horror and despair took hold of him; he gathered all his force; he dashed violently, as if nerve and artery were bursting, against the crystal. Then a loud clang echoed through the room, and the Archivist in his bright damask dressing gown appeared in the door.

"Hey, hey! Vermin! Mad spectre! Witch-worker! Hullo! Here!" he shouted. Then the crone's black hair stood straight up in its coarse tufts; her red eyes gleamed with infernal fire; and clenching together the peaked fangs of her abominable jaws, she sputtered, "Hiss, at him! Hiss, at him! Hiss!" She laughed and neighed in scorn and mockery, pressed the Golden Pot firmly against her hideous body, and threw out of it handfuls of glittering earth onto the Archivist. But as the earth touched his dressing gown, its particles changed into flowers, which pelted down on the floor. Then the lilies on the dressing gown flickered and flamed, and the Archivist caught those lilies blazing in spark-strewn fire, and hurled them on the witch. She howled in agony, but still as she leaped in the air and shook her armor of parchment, the lilies' fires went out and they fell away into ashes.

"At her, my lad!" yelled the hag again. Then the black Cat darted through the air, and jumped clear over the Archivist's head on its way toward the door. But the grey Parrot flew quickly out against him, caught him with his crooked bill by the nape of the neck, tore at him until red and fiery blood burst out—and Serpentina's voice cried: "Saved! Saved!"

Upon this the witch, her mouth foaming with rage and desperation, darted at the Archivist. She threw the Golden Pot behind her, and holding up the long talons of her skinny hands, was intent on clutching the Archivist by the throat. But he immediately pulled off his robe, and threw it over her. Then, hissing, and sputtering, and bursting, blue flames shot from the parchment leaves that were the hag's armor, and she rolled on the floor in agony, as she strove to get fresh earth from the Pot and fresh parchment leaves from the books, to stifle the blazing flames. Whenever any earth or leaves came down on her, the flames went out. But now, from inside the Archivist's own body, issued fiery, crackling tongues of fire that lashed out at the crone.

"Hey, hey! At it again! Salamander! Victory!" the Archivist's voice rang through the chamber; and a hundred fiery bolts whirled forth in burning circles round the shrieking hag. Tearing and spitting, Cat and Parrot flew at each other once more in their furious battle. But at last the Parrot, with his strong wings, dashed the Cat to the ground; and as his equally strong claws transfixed and held fast his adversary—which, in deadly agony, uttered horrid mews and howls—he, with his sharp bill, pecked out the Cat's glowing eyes, and the burning froth spouted from them. Then thick vapor streamed up from the spot where the horrible old woman lay, hurled to the ground, under the enchanted dressing gown; her howling, her terrific, piercing cry of defeat and lamentation, died away as if it were in the remote distance. The smoke, which had spread its per-meating stench through the room, cleared away. The Archivist picked up his magic robe. Beneath it lay a wrinkled Parsnip.

"Most honored Archivist, let me offer you the vanquished foe," said the Parrot, holding out a black hair in his beak to Lindhorst.

"Quite so, my worthy friend," replied the Archivist. "Here, also, lies my vanquished foe. Be so good now as to attend to what remains. This very day, as a small *douceur*, you shall have six coconuts—and a new pair of spectacles also, for I see the Cat has villainously broken the lenses of your old ones."

"Yours forever, most honored friend and patron!" answered the Par-rot, delighted. Then he took the Parsnip in his bill, and flew with it out of the window, which Lindhorst had opened for him.

The Archivist now picked up the Golden Pot, and cried, in a strong voice, "Serpentina! Serpentina!" But as the Student Anselmus, rejoicing in the destruction of the old hag who had been responsible for his misfortunes, cast his eyes on the Archivist, he was abashed anew: here stood once more the tall and majestic form of the Spirit-prince, regarding him with an expression of indescribable grace and dignity. "Anselmus," said the Spirit-prince, "not you, but a hostile Principle, which strove destructively to penetrate into your nature, and divide you against yourself, was to blame for your unbelief. You have kept your inherent faithfulness. Be free, and happy." A bright flash quivered through the spirit of Anselmus; the royal triphony of the crystal bells sounded stronger and louder than he had ever heard it; his nerves and senses thrilled. And as, swelling higher and higher, the melodious tones rang through the room, the glass which enclosed Anselmus broke, and he rushed into the arms of his dear and gentle Serpentina.

Eleventh Vigil

Dean Paulmann's anger at the Madness which had broken out in his Family. How Registrar Heerbrand became a Privy Councillor; and, in the sharpest Frost, walked about in Shoes and Stockings. Veronica's Confession. Betrothment over the steaming Soup Plate.

"But, tell me, most honored Registrar, how could the cursed punch last night so go to our heads, and drive us to such fantastic folly!" Dean Paulmann demanded the next morning, as he entered his study. The room was still full of broken glass, while his hapless peruke, divided again into its original elements, floated in punch among the ruins. For after the Student Anselmus had rushed out of the house, the Dean and Registrar had still kept trotting and hobbling up and down the room, shouting like maniacs, and butting their heads together; until Fränzchen, with great effort, had carried her extremely giddy papa off to bed. Then Registrar Heerbrand, thoroughly exhausted, had sunk down upon the sofa, which Veronica had left to take refuge in her bedroom.

Registrar Heerbrand, this morning, had his blue handkerchief tied about his head; he looked quite pale and melancholy, and he groaned, in answer, "Ah, worthy Dean, it was not the punch, which Mamselle Veronica brewed most admirably. No! It is simply that cursed Student who is to blame for all the mischief. Do you not observe that he has long been *mente captus?* And are you not aware that madness is an infectious disease? One fool makes twenty. Pardon me. That is an old proverb. Especially when you have drunk a glass or two, you fall into madness quite readily, and then involuntarily you maneuver, and go through your exercises, just as the crackbrained leader gives the signals. Would you believe it, Dean? I still become dizzy when I think of that grey Parrot!"

"Grey fiddlestick!" interrupted the Dean. "It was nothing but Archivist Lindhorst's little old librarian, who had thrown a grey cloak over him, and was looking for the Student Anselmus."

"That may be," Registrar Heerbrand admitted. "But I must confess I am quite depressed. The whole night through there was such a booming of organ notes around my head."

"That was I," said the Dean. "I snore very loudly."

"Well, that may be," admitted the Registrar again. "But, Dean! O Dean! Ah, not without cause that I tried to spread an atmosphere of good cheer among us last night—and that Anselmus has spoiled everything! You do not know—O Dean, Dean!" And with this, Registrar Heerbrand sprang up, snatched the blue handkerchief from his head, embraced Paulmann, warmly pressed his hand, and again cried out in quite heartbreaking tones, "O Dean, Dean!" and hastily taking up his hat and stick, rushed out of the house.

"This Anselmus shall never cross my threshold again," said Dean Paulmann. "For I see very well that, with this moping madness of his, he robs the best gentlemen of their senses. The Registrar is now stricken with it too. I have hitherto kept safe; but the Devil, who knocked hard last night at the door of our carousal, may get in at last, and play his tricks with me. So *apage, Satanas!* Off with thee, Anselmus!"

Veronica, during this conversation, had grown quite pensive. She did not speak a word; only smiled now and then very oddly. And as time wore on she continued in this surprising mood—a merry, friendly girl who now liked best to be alone. "She too has Anselmus in her head," said the Dean, fuming with indignation. "But it is well that he does not show himself here. I know he is afraid of me, this Anselmus, and that is why he won't come."

These concluding words Dean Paulmann spoke aloud; then the tears rushed into Veronica's eyes, and she said, sobbing: "Ah! how can Anselmus come here? He has long been corked up in the glass bottle."

"How? What?" cried Dean Paulmann. "Ah, Heaven! Ah, Heaven! She has lost her senses too, like the Registrar; the noisy stage will soon be upon her! Ah, you wretched, abominable, thrice-cursed Anselmus!"

He ran quickly out to find Doctor Eckstein. But the physician only smiled, and said again: "Ei! Ei!"

This time, however, the good doctor prescribed nothing; but added, to the few syllables he had uttered, the following words, as he started away: "Nerves! Come round of itself. Take the air; walks; amusements; theatre; playing *Sonntagskind*, *Schwestern von Prag*. Come round of itself."

"I have rarely seen the Doctor so eloquent," thought Dean Paulmann. "Really talkative, I declare!"

And now days and weeks and months went by. Anselmus had vanished. Registrar Heerbrand also failed to make his appearance. Not till the fourth of February did the Registrar, in a fashionable new coat of the finest cloth, in handsome thin shoes and silk stockings notwithstanding the keen frost, and with a large nosegay of fresh flowers in his hand, enter, precisely at noon, the parlor of Dean Paulmann, who was not a little astonished to see his friend so elegantly turned out. With a solemn air, Registrar Heerbrand advanced toward the Dean, embraced him with the most solemn courtesy, and then said: "Now at last, on the Saint's day of your beloved and most honored Mamselle Veronica, I will tell you, straightforwardly, what I long have kept secret in my heart. That evening, that unfortunate evening, when I brought along the ingredients of our noxious punch in my pocket, I intended to impart to you a piece of good news, and to celebrate the happy day in convivial joys. Already I had learned that I was to be made a Privy Councillor; for which promotion I have now the papers, *cum nomine et sigillo Principis*, in my pocket."

"Ah! My dear Registrar—Privy Councillor, I meant to say," stammered the Dean.

"But it is you, most honored Dean," continued the new Privy Councillor, "it is you alone who can complete my happiness. For a long time, I have secretly loved your daughter, Mamselle Veronica. And I can boast of many a kind look which she has given me, an obvious proof that she would not cast my attentions aside. In a word, honored Dean! I, Privy Councillor Heerbrand, do now entreat you for the hand of your most amiable Mamselle Veronica, whom I, if you have nothing against it, propose shortly to take home as my wife."

Dean Paulmann, astonished beyond measure, clapped his hands together, and cried again and again: "Eh! Eh! My good Registrar—Privy Councillor, I mean to say—who would have thought it? Well, if Veronica does really love you, I for my part have no objections. Indeed it may be that her present melancholy is nothing but concealed love for you, Privy Councillor! You know what whims girls have!"

At this moment Veronica entered, pale and agitated, as she now commonly was. At once Privy Councillor Heerbrand rose and approached her, referred in a neat speech to her Saint's day, and handed her the fragrant nosegay, and with it a little package, from which, when she opened it, a pair of brilliant earrings sparkled on her eyes. A swiftly fleeting blush tinted her cheeks; her eyes gleamed with joy, and she cried: "O gracious Heaven! These are the very earrings which I wore all those weeks ago, and was so proud of."

"How can this be, dearest Mamselle," interrupted the Privy Councillor, somewhat alarmed and hurt, "when I bought these jewels not an hour ago, in the *Schlossgasse*, for cash?"

But Veronica paid no attention to his words. Already she was standing before the mirror to see the effect of the trinkets, which she had quickly fixed in her pretty little ears. Dean Paulmann, however, now disclosed to her, with grave countenance and solemn tone, the news of his friend Heerbrand's promotion and his present proposal. And Veronica turned to the Privy Councillor with a look of scrutiny and said:

"I have long known that you wished to marry me. Well, be it so! I promise you my heart and hand. But I must now reveal to you—to both of you, I mean, my father and my promised bridegroom—much that is lying heavy on my heart; yes, even now, though the soup should get cold, which I see Fränzchen is just putting on the table."

Without waiting for the Dean's, or the Privy Councillor's reply, though words were visibly hovering on the lips of both, Veronica continued: "You may believe me, best of fathers. I loved Anselmus from the bottom of my heart; and when Registrar Heerbrand, who is now become a Privy Councillor himself, assured us that Anselmus was likely enough to reach some such height, I resolved that he and no other should be my husband. But then it seemed as if alien, hostile beings were determined to snatch him away from me. I had recourse then to old Liese, who was once my nurse, but is now learned in necromancy, and has become a great enchantress. She promised to help me, and give Anselmus wholly into my hands. We went at midnight on the Equinox to the crossing of the high-roads; she conjured hellish spirits, and with the aid of the black Cat, we manufactured a little metallic mirror, in which I, directing my thoughts on Anselmus, had but to look, in order to dominate him utterly, in heart and mind.

"But now I heartily repent of having done all this," Veronica added, "and I here abjure all Satanic arts. The Salamander has conquered old Liese. I heard her shrieks; but there was no help I could give her. As soon as the Parrot had eaten the Parsnip, my metallic mirror broke in two."

Veronica took both pieces of the mirror, and a lock of hair out of her workbox, and handing them to Councillor Heerbrand, she continued: "Here, take the fragments of the mirror, Privy Councillor. Throw them into the Elbe, tonight at twelve o'clock, from the bridge, at the place where the Cross stands. The stream is not frozen there. That lock of my hair, however, do you keep and wear. I here abjure all magic," she repeated, "and I heartily wish Anselmus all joy and good fortune, since he is now married to the green Snake, who is much prettier and richer than I. You, dear Privy Councillor, I will love and reverence as becomes a true and loyal wife."

"Alack! Alack!" cried Dean Paulmann, full of sorrow. "She is cracked, she is cracked; she can never be the wife of a Privy Councillor, she is cracked!"

"Not in the least," interrupted Hofrath Heerbrand. "I know well that Mamselle Veronica has felt some kindness for the loutish Anselmus; and it may be that in some fit of passion she has had recourse to the old witch who, as I realize, can be no other than the cards-and-coffee fortune-teller of the Seethor; in a word, old Rauerin. Nor can it be denied that there are secret arts, which exert their influence all too balefully on men. We read of them in the most ancient writings, and doubtless there are still such. But as to what Mamselle Veronica is pleased to say about the victory of the Salamander, and the marriage of Anselmus to the green Snake, this, in reality, I take for nothing but a poetic allegory; a sort of song, wherein she sings her last complete farewell to the Student."

"Take it for what you will, most respected Privy Councillor!" said Veronica. "Perhaps for a very stupid dream."

"That I in nowise do," replied Councillor Heerbrand. "For I know well that Anselmus himself is possessed by secret powers, which vex him and drive him on to all the mad freaks that can be thought of."

Dean Paulmann could stand this no longer. He broke loose: "Stop! For the love of Heaven, stop! Have we again drunk too much of that cursed punch, or has Anselmus' madness come over us too? Privy Councillor, what stuff is this you are talking? I will suppose, however, that it is love which haunts your brain. Marriage will soon set all this to rights. Otherwise I should be apprehensive lest you too were falling into some degree of madness, most honored Privy Councillor. Then what would become of the future branches of the family, inheriting the malum of their parents? But now I give my paternal blessing to this happy union, and permit to you as future bride and bridegroom a happy kiss."

So they kissed forthwith; and thus, before the soup had grown cold, the formal betrothal was concluded. In a few weeks, Madame Privy Councillor Heerbrand was in very fact, as she had been in vision, sitting on the balcony of a fine house in the *Neumarkt*, and looking down with a smile upon the beaux, who passing by turned their glasses up to her and said: "She is a divine creature, the wife of the Privy Councillor Heerbrand."

TWELFTH VIGIL

Account of the estate to which Anselmus removed, as Son-in-law of Archivist Lindhorst; and how he lives there with Serpentina. Conclusion.

How deeply within my spirit could I now feel the blessed contentment of the Student Anselmus, who, indissolubly united with his gentle Serpentina, had withdrawn to the mysterious Land of Wonders, recognized by him as the home toward which his bosom, filled with strange foreknowledge, had always yearned. But in vain was all my striving to set before you, gentle reader, those glories with which Anselmus was encompassed, or even in the faintest degree to give you an impression of them in words. Reluctantly I was obliged to acknowledge to myself the feebleness of my every expression. I felt chained and silenced amid the paltrinesses of everyday life; I sickened in the torment of my own futility; I wandered about as in a dream. In short, I fell into the same condition which engulfed the Student Anselmus, as, in the Fourth Vigil, I have endeavored to set before you. It grieved me to the heart, when I glanced over the Eleven Vigils, now happily accomplished, and thought that to add the Twelfth, the keystone of the whole, would never be vouchsafed me. For whensoever, in the night watches, I set myself to complete the work, it was as if mischievous Spirits (they might be relations, perhaps close cousins, of the slain witch) held a polished, glittering piece of metal before me, in which I beheld my own mean Self, pale, overanxious, and melancholy, like Registrar Heerbrand after his bout with the punch. Then I would throw down my pen, and get quickly into bed, so that I might behold the happy Anselmus and the fair Serpentina at least in my dreams. This had gone on for several days and nights, when at last quite unexpectedly I received a note from Archivist Lindhorst, in which he addressed me as follows:

"Respected Sir,—It is well known to me that you have written down, in Eleven Vigils, the singular fortunes of my good son-in-law Anselmus, erstwhile Student, now Poet; and that you are at present cudgelling your brains very sorely in order that in the Twelfth and Last Vigil you may tell something of his happy life in Atlantis, where he now lives with my daughter, on the pleasant estate which I possess in that country. Now, notwithstanding my great regret that my own peculiar nature is hereby unfolded to the reading world (seeing that this may expose me, in my office as Privy Archivist, to a thousand inconveniences, nay, in the Collegium may even give rise to the question, how far a Salamander can justly, and with binding consequences, plight himself by oath, as a Servant of the State, and how far, on the whole, important affairs may be entrusted to him, since, according to Gabalis and Swedenborg, the Spirits of the Elements are not to be trusted at all), notwithstanding my realization that my best friends must now avoid my embrace (fearing lest, in some sudden anger, I dart out a flash or two, and singe their hair-curls and Sunday frocks), notwithstanding all this, I say, it is still my purpose to assist you in the completion of the Work, since much good of me and of my dear married daughter (would the other two were off my hands also!) has therein been said. Would you write your Twelfth Vigil, therefore, then descend your cursed five flights of stairs, leave your garret, and come over to me. In the blue palm tree, which you already know, you will find suitable writing materials; and you can then, in few words, describe to your readers what you have seen—a better plan for you than any long-winded description of a life which you know only by hearsay. With esteem,

> "Your obedient servant,
> "The Salamander Lindhorst,
> "P. T. Royal Archivist."

This truly rather curt, yet on the whole friendly, note from Archivist Lindhorst gave me high pleasure. It seemed clear enough, indeed, that the singular manner in which the fortunes of his son-in-law had been revealed to me—and which I, bound to silence, must conceal even from you, gentle reader—was well known to this peculiar old gentleman. Yet he had not taken it so ill as I might readily have feared. On the contrary, here he was offering me his helpful hand in the completion of my work. And from this I might justly conclude that at bottom he was not averse to having his marvelous existence in the world of spirits thus divulged through the printed word. . . .

"It may be," thought I, "that he himself expects by this means, perhaps, to get his two other daughters the sooner married. For who knows but a spark may fall in this or that young man's breast, and kindle a longing for another green Snake—whom, on Ascension Day, under the elder tree, he will forthwith seek and find? From the woe which befell Anselmus, when enclosed in the glass bottle, he will take warning to be doubly and trebly on his guard against all Doubt and Unbelief."

Precisely at eleven o'clock I extinguished my study lamp; and made my way to Archivist Lindhorst, who was already waiting for me in his hallway.

"Are you there, my worthy friend? Well, it pleases me that you have not mistrusted my good intentions. Do but follow me!"

And with this he led the way through the garden, now filled with dazzling brightness, into the azure chamber where I observed the same violet table at which Anselmus had been writing.

Archivist Lindhorst disappeared. But he soon came back, carrying in his hand a fair golden goblet, out of which a high blue flame sparkled as it rose. "Here," said he, "I bring you the favorite drink of your friend the Bandmaster, Johannes Kreisler. It is burning arrack, into which I have thrown a little sugar. Take a sip or two of it; I will take off my dressing gown, and, to amuse myself, and enjoy your worthy company while you sit watching and writing, I shall just bob up and down a little in the goblet."

"As you please, honored sir," I answered. "But if I am to keep sipping the liquor, you will get none."

"Have no such fear, my good fellow," cried the Archivist. Then hastily throwing off his robe, he climbed, to my no small amazement, into the goblet, and vanished in the flame-touched wine. Without dread, softly blowing back the glancing fire, I partook of the drink: it was truly precious!

Are not the emerald leaves of the palm trees moving gently, in soft sighing and rustling, as if kissed by the breath of the morning wind? Awakened from their sleep, they stir, and mysteriously whisper of the wonders which, from the far distance, approach like tones of melodious harps! The azure hangings seem to leave the walls, and float like airy vapor to and fro; but dazzling beams shoot through them. And whirling and dancing, as in jubilee of childlike sport, the vapor ascends to immeasurable height, and weaves back and forth above the palm trees. But brighter and brighter shoots beam on beam, until in boundless expanse a grove opens before my eyes, and there I behold Anselmus.

Here glowing hyacinths, and tulips, and roses lift their heads; and their perfumes are like the loveliest sound, which calls to the happy youth: "Wander, wander among us, our beloved; for thou understandest us! Our perfume is the Longing of Love; we love thee, and are thine forevermore!" till these golden rays seem to chant in vibrant tones: "We are Fire, kindled by Love. Perfume is Longing; but Fire is Desire; and dwell we not in thy bosom? We are thy own!" The dark bushes, the high trees, rustle and whisper: "Come to us, thou loved, thou happy one! Fire is Desire; but Hope is our cool Shadow. Lovingly we rustle round thy head; for thou understandest us, because Love dwells in thy breast!" The brooks and fountains murmur and patter: "Loved one, walk not so quickly by; look into our crystal! Thy image dwells in us, which we preserve with Love, for thou hast understood us." In the triumphal choir, bright birds are singing: "Hear us! Hear us! We are Joy, we are Delight, the rapture of Love!" But eagerly Anselmus turns his eyes to the magnificent Temple, which rises behind him in the distance. The stately pillars seem to be trees, and the capitals and friezes acanthus leaves, which in wondrous wreaths and figures form splendid decorations. Anselmus walks to the Temple. He views with inward delight the variegated marble, the steps with their strange veins of moss. "Ah, no!" he cries, as if in the excess of rapture. "She is not far from me now; she is near!"

Then Serpentina advances, in the fullness of beauty and grace, from the Temple; she bears the Golden Pot, from which a bright Lily has sprung. The nameless rapture of infinite longing glows in her gentle eyes; she looks at Anselmus, and says: "Ah! Beloved, the Lily has sent forth her fair cupped flower; what we longed for is fulfilled. Is there a happiness to equal ours?"

Anselmus clasps her with all the tenderness of ardent devotion. The Lily glows as if in flame over his head. And louder grows the happy whisper of the trees and bushes; clearer and gladder is the tinkling music of the brooks; the birds, the shining insects, dance in the waves of perfume; a gay, bright, rejoicing tumult, in the air, in the water, on the earth, is holding the festival of Love! Now sparkling gleams play over all the bushes; diamonds peer up from the ground like shining eyes; strange vapors are wafted hither on sounding wings; they are the Spirits of the Elements, who do homage to the Lily, and proclaim the happiness of Anselmus. Now Anselmus raises his head, as if encircled with a glorious aureole. Is it glances? Is it words? Is it song? You hear the sound: "Serpentina! Belief in thee, Love of thee, has unfolded to my soul the inmost spirit of Nature! Thou hast brought me the Lily, which sprang from Gold, from the primeval Force of the world, before Phosphorus had kindled the spark of Thought; this Lily is Knowledge of the sacred Harmony of all

Beings; and in this do I live in highest blessedness forevermore. Yes, I, thrice happy, have perceived what was highest; I must indeed love thee forever, O Serpentina! Never shall the golden blossoms of the Lily grow pale; for, like Belief and Love, this Knowledge is eternal."

For the vision, in which I had now beheld Anselmus bodily, in his domain in Atlantis, I stand indebted to the arts of the Salamander. And most fortunate was it, that, when all had vanished into air, I found a paper lying on the violet table, with the foregoing statement of the matter, written fairly and distinctly by my own hand.

"Ah, happy Anselmus, who has cast away the burden of workaday life, who in the love of thy gentle Serpentina fliest in Atlantis! While I, poor I, must soon, nay, in a few moments, leave even this fair hall—which itself is far from an estate in Atlantis—and again be transplanted to my garret, where, ensnared among the pettinesses of necessitous existence, my heart and my sight are so bedimmed with a thousand mischiefs, as with thick fog, that the fair Lily will never, never be beheld by me!"

Then Archivist Lindhorst patted me gently on the shoulder, and said: "Soft, soft, my honored friend! Lament not so! Were you not even now in Atlantis? And have you not at least cultivated a pretty little Farm of lovely words there, as the poetical possession of your inner self? And is the blessedness of Anselmus anything but a Living in Poesy? Can anything but Poesy reveal itself as the sacred Harmony of all Beings, as the deepest secret of Nature?"

THE DOUBLES

CHAPTER I

THE INNKEEPER OF THE SILVER LAMB TORE his cap from his head, threw : to the floor, stamped on it with both feet and shouted: "So—just so do you trample under foot all lawfulness, every virtue, all neighborly love, you vile creature, you impious landlord of the Golden Goat!

"Did not the fellow, just to spite me, have the wretched Goat over his door regilded at great cost, so that, in comparison, my sweet little Lamb looks pitiful and pale, and all customers pass me by on their way to this resplendent, glittering beast?

"All the rabble, tightrope walkers, comedians, and jugglers are attracted by the rascal, so that his house is always teeming with people, enjoying themselves and drinking his vinegar-sour, sulphurous wine, while my own choice Hochheimer and Niersteiner go untasted if I don't drink them down myself! And no sooner does the troupe of comedians move out than the wise woman and her raven move in, and then they all stream back again to have their fortunes told and ruin their health with food and drink.

"But I can imagine how the scoundrel treats his guests, for the handsome young gentleman who stopped there just a few days ago, and now has come back to our city today, quite rightly has come to my place this time. And he shall be treated like a prince at the Silver Lamb.

"How's that? What do I see? My young man going to the Golden Goat! It must be the wretched wise woman he wants to see. It is noon and the fine gentleman turns to the Golden Goat, spurning the fare at my Silver Lamb! Gracious Sir! Your Honor!"

Thus shouted the outraged innkeeper through the open window; but the young man, whose name was Deodatus Schwendy, was already caught in the crowd that swept him on into the near-by tavern.

A dense mass of people filled the passageway and the courtyard; a hushed, expectant whisper buzzed in the air. Some stayed in the main room, others stepped out with varying expressions, disturbed, pensive, or happy.

"I cannot understand," said a serious old gentleman who had taken refuge in a corner with Deodatus, "why the authorities do not put a stop to this disorder."

"Why so?" asked Deodatus.

"You are a stranger here," continued the old man, "and therefore unaware that an old woman comes here from time to time to make fools of the public with her miraculous prophecies and oracles. She has an enormous raven that acts as soothsayer, or rather untruth-sayer, about everything the people want to know. But for every true prophecy the wise raven miraculously makes, I am convinced that it tells a hundred lies. Just look at their faces as they come out and you will easily see that the woman and her raven take them in completely. That in our, thank Heaven, enlightened times, such pernicious superstitions . . ."

Deodatus heard no more of this lively talk, for just then a very handsome young man who only a few minutes earlier had entered the hall quite cheerfully and with a smile on his lips now came out as white as a sheet and with his eyes glistening with tears.

At that moment it seemed to Deodatus as if a dark secret power were hidden behind those curtains, a power that disclosed the sad future to those who were happy and thus maliciously killed all joy in the present.

And yet he felt a sudden urge to go in there himself and ask the raven what the next days, even the next moments, might hold in store for him. For his old father, Amadeus Schwendy, had sent Deodatus to Hohenflüh under very mysterious circumstances. Here at the climax of his life, his future was to be decided for him through a miraculous experience which his father announced in mysterious words. With his own eyes he was to behold a creature who had so far entwined herself in his life only as a dream. He was to prove now whether this dream that had waxed ever more fresh and shining from a spark buried in his inner being would really emerge into his outer, worldly life. Should this happen he had been instructed how to act.

He was now standing at the threshold of the hall and, just as he saw the curtains being parted, a voice reached his ears in horrible croaking inflections. He felt as though some unknown power were drawing him back; and so, involuntarily, he mounted the stairs and came to the room where the midday meal was being served to the many guests of the house.

The innkeeper approached Deodatus Schwendy with a great show of heartiness: "Ah! Welcome, Master Haberland! This is indeed a pleasure. Although you first went to that low place, the Silver Lamb, you could not get along without the world-renowned fare of the Golden Goat. I have the honor to lay this place for you."

Deodatus realized well enough that the innkeeper had mistaken him for someone else, but he was so completely overcome by the reluctance to speak that accompanies all powerful emotions, that he did nothing to correct the mistake, but seated himself silently at the table. The wise woman was the subject of conversation and the most varied opinions were put forward, some explaining it all as a childish conjuring trick, others, on the contrary, attributing to the old woman the deepest knowledge of life's complexities, and fully recognizing her gift for prophecy.

One old gentleman, short and rather too stout, who was forever taking snuff from a gold *tabatière*, polishing it every time on his coatsleeve and smiling knowingly, offered the opinion that the omniscient Council, of which he had the honor of being the least influential member, would soon put a stop to the wretched witch's goings-on, primarily because she was a charlatan and no true witch at all. For if she had everyone's life-story in her bag of tricks and made pronouncements through the raven, worded in particularly bad style at that, her achievement was no great masterpiece. Had there not been a painter and sculptor at last year's fair, in whose booth anyone could find his exact likeness?

They all burst into laughter. "That is something for you, Master Haberland," said one young man to Deodatus. "You are an excellent portrait-painter yourself, but you have surely not elevated your art to such heights!"

Deodatus, addressed for the second time as Master Haberland, whom he now understood to be a painter, felt the blood turn cold in his veins, for it suddenly seemed to him that his own body and soul were the ghostly simulacrum of another man, an unknown Haberland. And this inner dread increased to horror the next moment, when, before he could even answer the first speaker, another young man, wearing traveling clothes, threw himself upon him and embraced him warmly, crying out:

"Haberland, my dearest George, at last I have found you! Now we can continue happily on our way to beautiful Italy! But you look so pale and distraught!"

Deodatus returned the unknown stranger's embrace as though he were indeed the long-sought-for painter, George Haberland. He knew for certain that he had now stepped into that realm of miraculous experiences so often prophesied for him by his old father. He must now yield to whatever the dark powers had appointed for him. But the unaccountable instinct that makes us battle against strange and arbitrary decisions, the impulse with which we strive to protect and retain our individuality, gripped him powerfully. He held fast to the stranger's arms and said:

"Ah, you unknown brother, how should I not look ill at ease, when my ego has just stepped into another person, as though into a new overcoat that is too tight and yet too loose, which still pinches me? Am I then not really George Haberland, the painter?"

"I cannot tell you," said the stranger, "how you appear to me today, George. Are you once again in the throes of that strange state that comes over you at times like a chronic illness? In any case, I wanted to ask you what you meant by all the incomprehensible nonsense in your last letter."

Whereupon the stranger took a letter out of his pocket and carefully unfolded it. As soon as Deodatus saw the handwriting, he cried out as though in pain, for he had recognized his own script on the paper.

The stranger threw him a quick glance and read quietly:

"My dear Artist-Brother Berthold! You have no idea what dark and painful, yet benign, melancholy seizes me the farther I wander. Would you believe that my art, nay, my whole life and activity, often seem to me dull and shabby? But suddenly sweet dreams arise out of my happy, pleasant youth. I see myself again lying in the old priest's little garden, stretched out in the grass, gazing up at the lovely spring borne in on golden morning clouds. The little flowers, awakened by the glow of the early sun, open their eyes and disperse their fragrance into the air like a beautiful song of praise. Oh, Berthold! My heart wants to burst with love, with longing, with all-consuming desire! Where shall I ever find her again, for she is my whole life, my whole being! I hope to meet you in Hohenflüh, where I am spending a few days. It seems to me that I will experience something unusual in Hohenflüh, but I do not know the reason for this belief."

"Now tell me," said Berthold, the copper-plate engraver, for this was the stranger, "how do you intend to run after such a happy, tender, and youthful infatuation when you are on your contented way to the land of art?"

"Yes, dear brother-artist," answered Deodatus, "that is the really weird thing about it! I certainly composed in the depths of my soul what you have just read to me, yet in spite of that I am not at all the George Haberland whom you . . ."

Just then the first young man to greet Deodatus as George Haberland entered the room, and said that George had acted quite rightly in returning to Hohenflüh for the sake of the wise woman. He should take no heed of all the gossip at the dinner table, for the raven's prophecies might not always mean very much, but it was nevertheless most remarkable that she, the wise woman, seemed to be a second Sybil or Pythia, making mysterious utterances, with the inspiration of the possessed, to the accompaniment of deep, ghostly voices. She was giving such a performance in the spreading boscage of the garden that day and George must in no event miss it.

Berthold went off to settle some business in Hohenflüh, and Deodatus whiled away the time with the other young man, finishing off a few bottles of wine with him.

Just as the company in the dining-room was breaking up and making for the garden, a tall, slim, well-dressed man, apparently newly arrived in town, passed them in the corridor. He paused, undecided, before entering the room, looked back, and then, when his glance fell on Deodatus, stood rooted to the spot, his hand clutching the doorknob. His dark eyes flashed with wild light, his deathly pale face twitched convulsively. He came forward a few steps, then, as though suddenly recalling something, turned round again, ran into the room and slammed the door behind him, muttering under his breath.

Deodatus' companion was more struck by the stranger's appearance than young Schwendy, who paid little attention to him. They moved on out of doors.

The last rays of the setting sun fell on a tall figure wrapped from head to foot in a loose earthen-yellow garment. Her back was turned to the company. Near her on the ground lay a large raven, with lowered wings as though dead. All were struck by this strange and uncanny sight, the whispering ceased, and in a gloomy, oppressive silence the audience waited for what would come next.

A rustling sound, like the splashing of unseen waves, streamed through the thicket, grew into intonations, and then took on the quality of spoken words:

"Phosphorus is conquered! The fire cauldron flares up in the west! Night eagle, soar up to the waking dreams!"

The raven raised his lowered head, flapped his wings, and soared upwards, croaking loudly. The figure spread her arms wide and the garment fell from her. A woman of extraordinary beauty was revealed, wearing a rich white robe and a jeweled girdle. Dark, luxuriant hair was piled high on her head, and what could be seen of her neck, shoulders, and arms appeared youthful and voluptuous.

"This cannot be the old woman," ran the whisper through the audience.

Now a distant muffled voice began:

"Do you hear the howling and the wailing in the evening wind?"

Another voice, even more distant, mumbled on:

"The lament begins when the worm glimmers!"

At that moment a heart-piercing moan tore the air and the woman spoke:

"Oh, you distant tones of lament, have you torn yourselves loose from the heart of man that you may now rise freely in a mighty choir? But you must fade in joy, for the power, enthroned in blissful Heaven, which commands you is the power of yearning!"

The muffled voices rose in a wail:

"Hope has died. The joy of yearning was hope. Yearning without hope is nameless torture."

The woman sighed deeply and cried out as though in despair:

"Hope is death! Like the gruesome game of the dark powers!"

And suddenly, in a voice that seemed to come from deep within him, Deodatus called out: "Nathalie!"

The woman whirled about abruptly, and the horrible, distorted face of an old hag stared at him with eyes that glowed like coals. Angrily, with arms widespread, she rushed at him and shrieked:

"What are you doing here? Away with you! Away! Murder is close behind you! Save Nathalie!"

And the raven swooped down through the trees and echoed: "Murder! Murder!" in a hideous croak.

Seized with terror, and feeling as though he were losing his mind, Deodatus fled to his room in the tavern.

The innkeeper informed him that a strange gentleman had asked for him several times, describing him accurately, but that he had finally left a note without giving his name. Deodatus tore open the note, which was properly addressed to him and read:

"I do not know whether it is unheard-of impertinence on your part, or simply madness that you permit yourself to be seen here. If you are not, as I must now believe, a faithless scoundrel, leave Hohenflüh immediately, or you must expect me to find the means of curing you forever of your madness.

"Count Hector von Zelies."

After reading this note, Deodatus murmured to himself gloomily: "Hope is death, life the gruesome game of dark powers!" He was determined not to allow himself to be driven out of Hohenflüh by the threats of a stranger, based as they were on a mistaken identity, but to encounter with manly fortitude and vigor whatever he was destined by some mysterious power to experience. His whole being was filled with ominous fore-boding, his heart was ready to burst, and he longed to get away from the house, out into the open. Night had already fallen when Deodatus, with the threats of his unknown and dangerous correspondent in mind, pock-eted his loaded pistol and hurried out of the city through the Neudorfer Gate. When he reached the open space outside the gate, he felt himself being seized from behind and drawn back, while a voice murmured in his ear the words: "Hurry, hurry! Save Nathalie! The time is come!"

It was the dreadful old hag, who had gripped him by the arm and pulled him along irresistibly with her. A carriage drew up close at hand; the door was open. The old woman helped him in and climbed in herself. He felt the embrace of soft arms and a sweet voice lisped to him:

"My beloved! At last! At last you have come!"

"Nathalie, my Nathalie!" he cried, and nearly swooned with delight as he took the loved one in his arms.

The carriage drove on quickly now. Suddenly bright torches shone through the trees. "Here they come!" cried the old woman. "One more step and we shall encounter disaster!"

Deodatus, who had regained his composure, called a halt, stepped down from the carriage, and crept forward silently with cocked pistol; the torches suddenly disappeared. He rushed back to the carriage and stood rooted to the spot, numb with horror, for he glimpsed the silhouette of another man who spoke with his own voice and said: "The danger is passed!" and who then stepped into the carriage and sped off.

Deodatus rushed after the rapidly disappearing vehicle, but a shot rang out from the thicket and he was struck down.

CHAPTER II

There is no need to tell the kind reader that the distant place from which old Amadeus Schwendy had sent his son to Hohenflüh was a country estate in the vicinity of Lucerne. The township of Hohenflüh, in the principality of Reitlingen, was about six or seven hours' ride from Sonsitz, the court of Prince Remigius.

However gay and joyful life might be in Hohenflüh, in Sonsitz on the contrary it was keyed to such a pianissimo that it might have been mistaken for some monkish settlement. The entire population tip-toed around on stockinged feet and even when the inevitable argument broke out upon occasion, it was conducted in hushed voices. The usual pleasures of a court—balls, concerts, plays, and the like—were out of the question, and if the poor Sonsitzers, condemned as they were to joylessness, ever wanted to be amused they had to travel as far as Hohenflüh.

The reason for all this was that Prince Remigius, normally a kindly gentleman, full of the joy of living, had suffered for several years now, it might be as many as twenty, from a terrible form of brooding melancholy bordering on insanity. He never left Sonsitz, and his existence there was arranged to resemble complete solitude, dominated by the dark and listless silence of perpetual mourning. He would tolerate no one around him but his closest advisers and an indispensable number of servants, and even these would not dare to speak if the Prince did not first address them. He was in the habit of driving out in a closed, heavily curtained carriage, and his subjects were prohibited from revealing, even by the slightest sign, that they knew whom the carriage contained.

There were only vague rumors as to the true cause of the Prince's melancholy. This much was certain, however, that once, when the royal consort had brought a son and heir into the world, a different mood had reigned over the Duchy. Then, only a few months later, both mother and child had mysteriously disappeared. There were those who thought the Princess and her young son had been sacrificed to some bloody and sinister conspiracy; others maintained, however, that the Prince had banished the pair. In support of their statement they hinted that, at about the same time, Count von Törny, who was the Prince's chief Minister and publicly accepted favorite, was removed from court, and they plainly suggested that the Prince had happened upon the Princess and the Count under the most incriminating circumstances and that he doubted his son's legitimacy.

All those who had known the Princess at all well, however, were convinced that a lapse of this sort, in the face of the purest and most immaculate virtue, was quite inconceivable, quite impossible.

The inhabitants of Sonsitz were forbidden, under pain of severe punishment, from ever referring to this disappearance in any way. Spies lay in wait on all sides; and the periodic arrests of those who had been indiscreet enough to mention these matters outside the privacy of their own walls, gave proof of the efficacy of the Prince's agents. In the same way, all reference to the Prince, his grief, his state of mind or his activities was likewise prohibited and prosecuted. This tyrannous coercion was the saddest affliction of all for the inhabitants of a small *Residenz* who loved nothing better than to spend their waking hours chattering about their Prince and the life at court.

The Prince's favorite seat was a small country house with a spacious, fenced-in park, not far from the gates of Sonsitz. One day the Prince was strolling along the dismal, wildly overgrown avenues of this park, giving himself up entirely to the destructive grief gnawing at his heart, when he became aware of strange noises: inarticulate sounds, a grunting and moaning interspersed with awful squeals and snorts, then half-muffled oaths uttered in choking fury. Outraged at the thought that anyone had dared, against his strict orders, to trespass in the park, the Prince suddenly stepped out from behind a cluster of bushes which shielded him from sight, and was greeted by a spectacle that would have brought a smile to the lips of the mask of Tragedy.

Two men, the one tall and thin as a skeleton, the other a lively little Falstaff in his spruce Sunday best, were locked in fierce combat. The tall fellow swung his long swordlike arms with clenched fists the size of clubs so mercilessly at the little one that any further retaliation on the latter's part seemed useless, and nothing but hasty retreat advisable. Yet, full of courage, the little one seemed intent upon getting in at least a Parthian shot. Whereupon the tall one reached down and clutched his enemy firmly by the hair. This was an unfortunate stratagem, for the wig remained in his hands while the little one exploited the powder screen that enveloped him to duck down swiftly and rush at his opponent with outthrust fists, so quickly and cleverly that the tall one fell over backwards with a shrill cry. Now the little one threw himself on the tall one, using his left hand as a grappling-iron, with fingers purposefully twisted round his enemy's cravat, and set to work so unsparingly with right hand and both knees that the tall one went blue in the face and gave vent to most horrific yells. But now suddenly the tall one seemed to collect his last ounce of strength and struck the little one in the ribs with his sharp knuckles so hard that he was hurled into the air like a ball and landed right at the Prince's feet.

"Idiots!" roared the Prince like an angry lion. "Who in the name of the Devil let you into the park? What are you doing here?"

One can imagine with what feelings the two bloodthirsty athletes picked themselves up and now stood like poor lost sinners, quivering and quaking, incapable of uttering a single word, a single sound, in front of the wrathful Prince.

"Away!" shouted the Prince. "Away before I have you flogged off the premises!"

The tall one then fell on his knees and groaned deep in despair: "Illustrious ruler, kindest of princes, all I ask is justice, blood for blood!"

The word justice was one of the few that still struck a familiar note in the Prince's ear. He stared into the tall one's eyes and spoke more calmly:

"What is it? Speak up, but I want no nonsense. So make it short!"

The gentle reader has perhaps already surmised that the two brave combatants were none other than the well-known innkeepers of the Golden Goat and the Silver Lamb in Hohenflüh. In the ever-increasing hostility between them, they had come to the insane decision, since the omniscient Council gave them no satisfaction, to complain directly to the Prince about the various wrongs each deemed he had suffered from the other, and they met by accident in front of the park gate which a dull-witted gardener's boy had opened for them. Both may hereafter be very appropriately identified by the names of their respective taverns, to which each bore an uncanny resemblance.

Well, then—the Golden Goat, encouraged by the Prince's request, was just about to launch into a recital of his grievance when he was overcome by a violent fit of coughing, a result no doubt of his recent exertions, so that he found it impossible to speak a single word.

The Silver Lamb instantly took advantage of this accident and recounted to the Prince, in no mean rhetoric, all the injustices the Golden Goat had done him by playing host to all the clowns, quacks, fortune-tellers, and rabble in the world. He described the wise woman and her raven, her iniquitous arts, the deceptions she passed off on the public in the name of prophecy. This seemed to interest the Prince particularly, for he asked the Silver Lamb to describe the woman's exact appearance from head to foot, and wanted to know when she had come to Hohenflüh, and where she stayed. The Lamb was of the opinion that the woman was nothing but a deceiving half-witted gypsy whom the omniscient Council would have done well to have arrested on first sight.

The Prince said nothing but fixed his piercing eyes on the poor Lamb, who immediately burst into a fit of violent sneezing as though he had been staring at the sun.

The Golden Goat had meanwhile recovered from his spasm of coughing and had been waiting for just such an opportunity to cut into the Lamb's speech. He reported in sweet and honeyed words that what the Lamb had said about his taking in undesirable rabble was only base calumny. The Goat paid particular praise to the wise woman who was declared by the cleverest and most brilliant gentlemen, the greatest geniuses of Hohenflüh, whom indeed, he had the honor of serving daily in his tavern, to be a supernatural being, and the superior of even the most skilful and erudite crystal gazers. The Silver Lamb had enticed away a fine gentleman, a young man of quality, when he visited Hohenflüh for the second time, and that very night he had been murderously attacked in his room and now lay there mortally wounded by a pistol shot.

Without further thought for the presence of the Prince, forgetful in his rage of the respect due to His Highness, the Silver Lamb broke into loud denunciations: whoever declared that young Master Haberland had been attacked and wounded in his room was the most contemptible swine, the most abandoned wretch ever to wear fetters and sweep the streets. Furthermore, the worthy police of Hohenflüh had discovered that the young man had taken a walk that same night outside the Neudorfer Gate, that a carriage had stopped there from which a woman's voice had called: "Save Nathalie!" and that the young man had jumped into the carriage and driven away.

"Who was the woman in the carriage?" asked the Prince abruptly.

"They say," stammered the Goat, merely for the sake of getting in a word, "that the wise woman . . ."

But the look in the Prince's eyes was too much for him and the words stuck in his throat. And to the Prince's chilling: "What do they say?" the Silver Lamb, who happened to be out of reach of the flashing eyes, put in hastily:

"Yes, the wise woman and the painter George Haberland. It was in the forest he got shot, the whole town knows that. They found him in the forest and brought him to my tavern in the early morning. He is lying there now, but he will recover, for the service at my tavern . . . And the strange nobleman, Count Hector von Zelies . . ."

"What? Who?" demanded the Prince so fiercely that the Silver Lamb recoiled several paces. "Enough! Be off, immediately, the pair of you! Whoever offers his guests the best service will have most customers! If I hear one more word about a quarrel between you, the Council shall order your tavern signs to be torn down and the two of you driven out of Hohenflüh!"

After passing this brief and stern judgment, the Prince left the two innkeepers standing where they were and disappeared behind the bushes.

The Prince's anger had calmed their excited spirits. Now, deeply contrite, the two looked sadly at each other, tears welled up into their darkened eyes, and with a simultaneous outcry of, "Oh! My best friend," Silver Lamb and Golden Goat fell into each other's arms. The tall Goat held the little Lamb in a close embrace, bending over the top of him to shed numerous tears on the grass, while the other, out of bitter remorse, gently wept on his erstwhile opponent's breast. It was indeed a sublime moment!

But not for the two liveried gamekeepers who came hurrying to the spot. They did not seem to appreciate this pathetic scene, for without further ado they grasped the Golden Goat and the Silver Lamb by their pinions, as it were and threw them outside the park gates.

CHAPTER III

I have wandered back and forth
Over pasture, field and meadow.
Many hopes have created me,
Many joys evaded me,
In the bright and noisy world.

What can stifle this dread longing,
What can staunch this bleeding heart?
Bitter torment! Acrid tears!
Vain endeavor!—False belief!
Will every joy fore'er evade me?

May I still presume to hope,
Is my life star gleaming yet?
Must I suffer, bear this longer,
Will my grief not tell me whether
She is near to me or far?

She, who is my very life,
She, who is my only joy,
The object of my sweetest dreams,
Of all my passionate desires,
Of my gaze that's drunk with love.

Yet in darkness soon is hidden
The daydream figure of my love!
Can I nevermore recover?
Friendly solace, balm of heart wounds,
Is that also lost for me?

Berthold, the copper-plate engraver, was softly singing this song to himself. It had been written by his friend Haberland, and he was singing it under a shady tree while he carefully sketched a section of the village that lay before him in the valley.

But the last lines brought sudden tears to his eyes. He was vividly reminded of his friend, whom he had often roused, by means of heated intellectual discussions, out of the dark, inconsolable depressions that came over him from time to time, and who now was separated from him by some inexplicable chance.

"No!" he cried at last, packing away his drawing equipment and jumping up hastily. "Friendly solace is not yet lost for you, dear George! Forward now in search of you, and I shall not leave you again until I see you snuggling safely in the lap of peace and happiness."

He resolved to go at once to Hohenflüh, and, with that intention in mind, hurriedly returned to the village he had left behind him only a few hours before.

It happened to be a Sunday; twilight was coming on, and the country folk were hurrying to the tavern. Along the village street came a weirdly dressed figure playing a shrill march on the bagpipes he carried under his arm and beating time sharply on a drum suspended from his waist. He was followed by an old gypsy woman dutifully tinkling on a triangle. And behind her, slowly and pensively, strode a stately ass burdened with two heavily packed baskets on top of which two comic little monkeys hopped and capered about. Presently the fellow ceased his piping and broke into a curious wailing song in which the gypsy woman joined with piercing cries, straightening up a little from her bent posture. The ass accompanied them with his own natural lament and the monkeys added their squeaks, so that there arose, as may well be imagined, an amusingly odd chorus.

Berthold's whole attention was fixed on the young man, for young he was; so much was apparent despite the fact that he had smeared his face with a mess of odd colors and further disfigured himself with a doctor's wig and a tiny lace hat. In addition, he wore a threadbare red velvet coat with gold-braid embroideries, and open-necked Hamlet collar, black silk hose in the latest fashion, on his shoes big colored bows, and at his side an elegant knight's sword.

He made the most ridiculous faces and executed the maddest capers, so that the peasant folk were highly amused, but Berthold saw all this as a sinister manifestation of insanity, and when the crazy fellow looked him in the eye this awoke in him sensations which he was at a loss to explain to himself.

The little procession came to a halt, finally, in the middle of a grass plot in front of the tavern, and the young man beat out a long roll on his drum. At this signal the country folk gathered round in a wide circle, and the drummer announced that he would now attempt to amuse his worthy audience with a performance that had delighted the greatest potentates and crowned heads of Europe.

The gypsy woman went round the circle and offered with foolish talk and gestures either to sell coral necklaces, ribbons, religious images, and such things, or to tell fortunes, pausing here and there before some country lass whose cheeks would burn red at the old woman's sly reference to swains, marriages, and christenings, while the crowd giggled and laughed.

The drummer had meanwhile unpacked the baskets and rigged up a light framework which he hung with bright rugs. Berthold watched these preparations and the puppet-show, in the usual Italian style, that followed. Punch was particularly active and daring, ingeniously extricating himself from the most dangerous situations and always besting his enemies.

The play seemed to be finished when the puppeteer suddenly stuck his horribly contorted, grimacing face up through the stage and stared fixedly at the audience. Punch on the one side, the Doctor on the other, appeared terrified at this sudden emergence of a giant head, but they soon regained their composure, examined it carefully with spectacles, felt the nose, the mouth, the brow which they could hardly reach, and began an involved and scholarly discussion about the constitution of the head and the trunk it might belong to or whether they could assume that it belonged to any trunk at all. The Doctor put forward the most bizarre arguments. Punch on the contrary showed much common sense and made the funniest suggestions. They agreed at last that, since they could not take for granted the existence of a body attached to the head, no such body existed, but the Doctor was of the opinion that Nature, when it gave expression to this giant, had made use of a figure of speech, a synecdoche, whereby the part signifies the whole. Punch declared, on the other hand, that the head was an unhappy man who had lost the rest of his body through too much thinking and worrying and who, in his present condition, lacking fists, could protect himself against having his ears boxed or his nose tweaked only by resorting to abuse.

Berthold soon realized that this humor was not of a sort intended to amuse a good-natured village audience, but was prompted rather by the grim irony of a spirit split by contradictions and in conflict with itself. His friendly disposition could not tolerate such an exhibition and he turned away to the tavern where he eventually sat down to a lonely frugal meal.

In the distance he could hear the drum, bagpipes, and triangle resume the merry little march tune. The play was ended, and the country folk poured in a stream into the tavern.

Berthold was preparing to leave his table when the crazy puppeteer, with a loud cry of: "Berthold! My dear brother artist!" came running up to him. He tore the wig from his head and quickly wiped the paint from his face.

"What? George! Is it possible?" stammered Berthold, rooted to the spot.

"What is the matter with you? Don't you recognize me?" asked George Haberland in amazement.

Berthold explained that since he refused to believe in ghosts he certainly could not doubt the reality of his friend's presence, but he was quite incapable of unriddling the whole affair.

"Did you not go to Hohenflüh," asked Berthold further, "in accordance with our arrangement? Did I not meet you there? Did you not have a strange experience with a mysterious woman in the Golden Goat tavern? Did not some strangers want to make use of you in abducting a woman whom you yourself called Nathalie? Were you not severely wounded by a pistol shot out there in the forest, and did I not, with grave misgivings, take my leave of you because you lay exhausted, mortally wounded? Did you not speak of some inexplicable happenings and of a certain Count Hector von Zelies?"

"Enough! Enough!" cried George, as though in violent pain.

"Yes, brother Berthold," he continued more calmly, in another moment, "it is only too certain that I have a second self, a double who persecutes me, who wants to swindle me out of my life and rob me of Nathalie!"

Quite disconsolate, George sank down silently onto the grassy bank. Berthold sat next to him and sang gently, as he pressed his friend's hand:

> "Friendly solace, balm of heart wounds,
> Is that also lost for me?"

"For my part," said George, as he wiped the tears from his eyes, "I understand you fully, dear brother Berthold! It was wrong of me not to open my heart to you about my troubles long ago. That I am in love you probably have guessed for yourself. The story of this love is so artless, so trite, that you can read it in every cheap, insipid novel. I am a painter and nothing belongs more to the established order of things than that I should fall head over heels in love with the pretty young woman whose portrait I am painting. And that is what actually happened to me during my stay in Strasbourg where I busily kept to my pot-boiling—you know that is how I think of portrait painting. I acquired the reputation of a quite exceptional portraitist, one who could really steal the likeness from a mirror and reproduce it in beautiful miniature. And so it happened that an elderly lady who keeps a boarding-house asked me to do the portrait of a young lady staying with her who wanted a memento to send to her absent father. I saw and painted Nathalie. Oh! Eternal powers! My fate was decided.

"I know, brother Berthold, so far it is the same old story. But wait. Let me first tell you that ever since my early boyhood the image of a heavenly woman has figured in my dreams and reveries, one particular creature upon whom I expended all my love and yearning. The clumsiest efforts of the art-struck boy reveal this same image, just as clearly as the later and more accomplished paintings of the wandering artist. It was always Nathalie! That is what is so extraordinary about it, Berthold. And let me tell you, too, that the same spark that inflamed me with love, the first moment I saw Nathalie, also burned in her heart; so we were soon meeting clandestinely.

"Oh! The fading ecstasy of love! Nathalie's father, Count Hector von Zelies, came to visit his daughter. The little portrait pleased him so much that I was invited to paint him too. But when the Count set eyes on me, he was filled with a strange excitement, perhaps I might call it consternation. He questioned me intently, and with noticeable anxiety, about all the circumstances of my life, and cried out, rather than said, that he did not wish to have his portrait painted, but I was an excellent artist; I must go to Italy, immediately; he would provide the money if any were needed!

"Was I to go away and be separated from Nathalie? Well, there are such things as ladders, and venal servant girls. We continued to meet clandestinely. She was in my arms when the Count came into the room, one day. 'Ha! Just as I suspected!' and with these words the Count rushed at me with drawn dagger. I evaded his thrust, knocked him down, and managed to escape. The next day he and Nathalie had vanished without leaving a trace behind them!

"By chance I ran into the old gypsy woman in whose company you saw me today. She chattered on to me about the eventfulness of certain prophecies, and made talk which I was not at all inclined to hear, but suddenly she said something that struck me to the heart: 'George, my child, have you forgotten Nathalie?' Whether or not there is anything in witchcraft, that was enough for me. The old woman knew all about my love ties, exactly how everything had come to pass, and she assured me that through her I would succeed in regaining possession of my Nathalie. She told me to be in Hohenflüh at a certain date, that I would find her there though her appearance would be changed.

"I shall be brief, Berthold. I find myself in Hohenflüh. My heart is on fire with anticipation. A carriage draws up. The riders approach. 'Oh, Lord!' cries a voice from the carriage; it seems to be Nathalie's voice. 'Make haste—make haste!' calls another voice. The riders swerve aside. I call out: 'The danger is passed!' and climb into the carriage. The carriage starts off. Just then there is a shot! My instinct has not deceived me: it is Nathalie, with the old gypsy woman who had fulfilled her promise."

"Lucky George!" said Berthold.

"Lucky?" repeated George with a strange laugh. "We were not yet out of the forest when a troop of police caught up with us. I leaped from the carriage, the gypsy woman followed and gripped me by the arm with enormous strength. She dragged me into the deepest thicket. Nathalie was lost. I was boiling over with rage, but the gypsy knew how to calm me; she persuaded me that resistance would have been useless and that all hope was not lost. I entrusted myself blindly to her, and, as you see us now, this is her plan for evading the persecutions of a murderous enemy."

George had just finished his recital when the old gypsy woman came up to them and said in a croaking voice: "George, already the glow-worm glitters. We must away and over the mountains."

It occurred to Berthold that the old witch was making a dupe of George, whom she had put under a spell in order to profit by his buffoonery.

Angrily he turned on the old woman, and informed her that as George's oldest and most intimate friend, he could not allow him to be dragged all around the countryside in such a vile manner, and sacrifice his art to these despicable exhibitions; George must go to Italy with him. Besides, he demanded, what claim did she pretend to have—upon his friend?

In reply the old woman drew herself up; her features seemed to acquire a sudden nobility, her eyes to sparkle with hidden fire; and when she spoke her whole being was transformed with dignity and majesty: "You ask what claim I have upon this young man? I know you well, Berthold, the copper-plate engraver. You are his friend, but I am—his mother!"

And she put her arms round George and gathered him passionately to her breast. But suddenly a convulsive trembling overcame her, she thrust George from her, averted her face, fell exhausted, almost swooning, onto the greensward, and wept as she covered her face with her long cloak: "Do not stare at me like that with his eyes! George, why do you constantly and eternally reproach me for my crime? You must leave me—go away!"

"Mother!" cried George, throwing himself down at her feet. Once again she embraced him and sighed deeply, incapable of further speech. She seemed almost to drop off to sleep, but then she got up with an effort and spoke once again in the whining gypsy voice: "George, already the glowworm glimmers. We must away and over the mountains." And slowly she strode away.

George embraced his friend without uttering a word, and Berthold, too, struck speechless by astonishment and dismay, could find nothing to say.

Soon Berthold could hear the drum and bagpipes, the tinkling, the dreadful singing, the donkey's braying, the squeaking of the monkeys, and the gay cheering of the country folk as they followed after the procession until the whole hubbub and parade gradually disappeared in the distance.

CHAPTER IV

Some gamekeepers patrolling the forest early in the morning had found young Deodatus Schwendy lying unconscious in a pool of blood. The brandy they carried in their hunting flasks helped considerably in reviving him. They dressed the chest wound as well as they could, lifted Deodatus onto a cart, and brought him to Hohenflüh to the Silver Lamb.

The bullet had not penetrated to any vital organ, and the surgeon therefore explained that there was no question of danger to his life although the shock and exposure to the night air had brought on an exhaustion that left Deodatus prostrate. However, efficacious medicines would soon put him on his feet again.

If it were not for the pain Deodatus felt from his wound the whole inexplicable experience would have remained only a dream to him. He was convinced that the strange secret to which his father had referred so mysteriously was about to be disclosed to him when some hostile force had intervened. Who else could be the agent of this force but George Haberland, the painter who resembled him so closely that he was everywhere mistaken for him?

"And what," he asked himself, "if my Nathalie, if the beautiful image that has colored all my dreams for as long as I can remember, were to belong to him, to my unknown double, my second self, if he has robbed me of her, if all my desires and all my hopes are to remain forever unfulfilled?"

Deodatus lost himself in sad thoughts; his future seemed enveloped in veils that became more and more opaque, concealing every clue and token of what was to come; he was compelled to admit to himself that he could rely only on chance to reveal to him those secrets so charged with danger and fatality that his old father had only dared to hint at them.

The surgeon had just left his patient alone in the sick-room when the door opened quietly and a tall man wrapped in a long greatcoat came in. The stranger threw back his coat and Deodatus immediately recognized the man he had passed in the corridor of the Golden Goat. He surmised that this must be the writer of the incomprehensible letter signed "Count Hector von Zelies." And this was indeed the same stranger.

The Count seemed to make an effort to temper his usual harsh and menacing look, and even went so far as to show certain signs of friendliness.

"No doubt you are surprised," he began, "to see me here, Master Haberland, but you will be even more surprised when I explain that I have come to offer you peace and forgiveness; that is, provided, of course, that certain conditions . . ."

Deodatus interrupted the Count, assuring him emphatically that he was not the painter Haberland, and that as the result of an unfortunate mistake which seemed prevalent in the town, he had become entangled in a maze of experiences utterly incomprehensible to himself. The Count fixed him with an immobile stare, and when he spoke there was a suggestion of something sardonic in his tone:

"Master Schwendy, or Master Haberland, or whatever other name you may care to assume, did you not attempt to abduct Nathalie?"

"Nathalie, alas, poor Nathalie!" sighed Deodatus.

"Aha!" exclaimed the Count with sullen rage, "you are very much in love with Nathalie?"

"I love her," replied Deodatus, falling back weakly on his pillows, "I love her more than life itself. She shall be mine, she must, the deepest instincts inside me promise it and demand it!"

"What unspeakable cheek!" exclaimed the Count. "Why ever did the bullet miss?" He paused suddenly, overcoming his rage with difficulty, then spoke again after a few moments with forced calm: "You owe it to your present helpless condition that I spare you; under other circumstances I would exercise certain prerogatives and have you disposed of! But now I demand that you explain immediately how you happened to meet Nathalie here in Hohenflüh!"

The Count's tone and manner filled Deodatus with profound resentment. Taking a firm hold on himself in spite of his weakness, he raised himself up in the bed and spoke out loudly: "It can be only the prerogative of unspeakable effrontery that you claim to exercise in order to intrude on my privacy and molest me with questions I cannot answer. You are a complete stranger to me, I have never had the slightest traffic with you, and this Nathalie whom you mention, do you realize that she is a divine abstraction that lives nowhere but in my heart? Neither in Hohenflüh nor anywhere else have I ever set eyes on her. But it is outrageous that I should have to account to you for secrets that are buried in my deepest being!"

The Count seemed overwhelmed by astonishment and confusion; he muttered half to himself: "You have never seen Nathalie? But when you painted her portrait? When this Haberland, that is this Schwendy . . ."

"Enough!" cried Deodatus. "Enough! Please go! I want to have nothing further to do with the sinister spirit that some insane mistake has set loose in pursuit of me and that has already murderously attacked me! There are laws to protect me against such sneaking assaults. Do you follow me, Count?"

Deodatus reached for the bell and pulled it energetically.

The Count measured Deodatus with a terrifying look.

"Beware!" he said. "Beware, young man. You have an unlucky face. Beware lest it displease someone other than me!"

At just this moment the door swung open, and in walked the little stout old gentleman with the gold snuffbox whom the kind reader has already met as a member of the omniscient Council arguing so ably at the table of the Golden Goat.

The Count left the room after signaling Deodatus with a gesture so threatening that the little Councillor and his retinue seemed quite astonished and disconcerted.

The Councillor was followed by a tiny dwarf of a creature with a huge file of papers under his arm and by two Council attendants who now stood guard at the door.

The Councillor greeted Deodatus with official formality, while the dwarf with great difficulty dragged a heavy table up close to the bed, spread out his papers, took writing materials from his bag, climbed onto the chair he had pulled forward with equal difficulty, and took up a well-rehearsed writing posture. The little Councillor seated himself on a chair close by the bed and stared at Deodatus with wide-open eyes.

Deodatus waited impatiently to see what would come of all this performance. At last, with pathos, the Councillor began: "Master Haberland or Master Schwendy, for you, Sir, who now lie here in bed before us choose to have two names, although that is a luxury which no sound authority would allow. Well then! I hope, in view of the fact that the omniscient Council is fully informed of this case, that you will not draw out your arrest unnecessarily with lies, tricks, and other hoaxes. For you are henceforth under arrest, as you may surmise from the presence of these upright and worthy Council guards at your door."

Completely taken by surprise, Deodatus demanded to be told what crime he was accused of and by what right they could arrest him, a stranger traveling through the city.

The Councillor explained that he had violated the recent decree against dueling, issued by His Highness the Prince, and had done so with undisguised impudence, for the pistols found in his pocket proved definitely that he had engaged in such an encounter in the forest. He would, therefore, without further evasion, name his impudent opponent, also the seconds, and give a thorough account of how everything had happened from the very start.

Deodatus assured the Councillor very quietly and firmly that, on the contrary, there was no question of a duel but of a murderous attack on his person. A circumstance which he was still at a loss to explain and which, no doubt, the omniscient Council would find even more inexplicable, had led him, without any premeditation on his part, into the forest. A threatening letter was the reason for his going armed, and the omniscient Council would do far more toward the proper discharge of their duties and the guarding of peace and order if they directed their attention to the apprehension of the assassin instead of to the arrest and examination of innocent persons on unfounded suspicions.

Deodatus stood by his argument for all that the Councillor questioned him around and about, and he referred exclusively to his passport when asked about further details of his circumstances, arguing that so long as he was under no suspicion of forgery the document must satisfy the Council.

The Councillor wiped the sweat of anxiety from his brow. The dwarf had more than once dipped his impressive quill in the inkwell and wiped it off again, regarding the Councillor all the while with eyes that expressed an impatient eagerness to write something down. But the Councillor seemed at a loss for words. At last the dwarf began boldly to scribble away, croaking out:

"Official Record, Hohenflüh, this —th day of ———. By Order of the Omniscient Council situate in this township, the undersigned Delegate has . . ."

"Quite right!" exclaimed the Councillor, "quite right, my dear Thrushhead, quite right, divine actuary: the undersigned Delegate has —er—yes, that's me—I have—er—"

In the Council of Heaven, however, it had been ordained that the undersigned Delegate would neither complete nor, in fact, sign his work, and that Deodatus would never have to appeal against the unhappy result.

For at that precise moment an officer of the Prince's bodyguard entered the room accompanied by the innkeeper, whom he asked when he saw Deodatus lying there whether this young man was indeed the one who had been wounded in the forest. The innkeeper affirmed that it was, and the officer approached the bed and explained in a very friendly way that he had orders to bring Master Haberland to see the Prince in Sonsitz. He hoped that his condition would create no difficulties; all arrangements had been made to facilitate the journey and to avoid all possible harm, and furthermore the court physician would be in constant attendance.

The Councillor, unexpectedly relieved of the duty that had brought perspiration to his brow, now approached the officer submissively and deferentially to ask whether he should perhaps, for greater security, have irons put on the prisoner. But the officer looked him up and down amazed and asked in return whether his worship the Councillor had taken leave of his senses and whom did he mean by "prisoner." The Prince desired to speak to Master Haberland in person with a view to clearing up certain circumstances which had aroused the Prince's displeasure. He could not understand, for example, how in his own domain, and in the immediate vicinity of Hohenflüh, a vicious murderer was permitted to go unapprehended, and he would visit the most serious consequences upon the heads of those responsible for the safety of the public.

One can imagine what effect these words had on the fat Councillor, while the little actuary tumbled off his chair and whimpered from the floor: he was only an extremely unfortunate actuary and he would have been in dreadful trouble if he had ever voiced the doubts he had long entertained as to the wisdom of the omniscient Council.

Deodatus gave the officer his assurance, to avoid all misunderstandings, that he was not the painter Haberland whom he apparently resembled very closely, that his name was Deodatus Schwendy as he could prove in creditable manner, and that he had come from Switzerland. The officer assured him in turn that the name was of no importance since the Prince had asked only to speak with the young man who had been attacked in the forest. Deodatus then agreed that he certainly was the one, and that since the wound was not at all serious he felt strong enough to accompany the officer to Sonsitz. The Prince's court physician confirmed this,

Deodatus was settled into the Prince's most comfortable traveling coach, and they immediately set off for Sonsitz.

Deodatus drove through the streets of Hohenflüh and created a public commotion. The worthy townsfolk were overwhelmed at the Prince's unprecedented behavior in asking a stranger to Sonsitz. But in a moment another sight contributed even more to the general bewilderment: the two enemies of so many years' standing, the innkeepers of the Golden Goat and the Silver Lamb, were to be seen by everyone on the Broad Stone in the middle of the street, good-naturedly conversing and even whispering intimately to each other.

The kind reader already knows how the Golden Goat and the Silver Lamb were reconciled, but the two hosts now had an even more vital reason for speaking to each other, for they both were devoured by a consuming curiosity as to the identity of the stranger who figured in this most unprecedented event.

CHAPTER V

At the climax of the storm, the tempest raged quickly on and disappeared over the mountains where only the thunder could be heard rumbling angrily in the distance. The setting sun shone fiercely through the dark thicket that seemed to tremble ecstatically in the billowing evening air, shaking off a thousand crystal drops. In the midst of an open space surrounded with hanging, Babylonic gardens, the Prince stood in his park at Sonsitz, as fixed as a statue, his arms folded, his eyes raised to the open blue expanse of cloudless sky as though entreating surcease from frustrated hopes, from lifelong grief and pain. The officer who had been dispatched to Hohenflüh stepped through the bushes. The Prince beckoned him impatiently to his side, received his report on the safe arrival of the wounded young man, and then ordered him to be brought to the spot immediately in a sedan-chair.

The moment Deodatus was carried into the Prince's presence, His Highness became visibly agitated and, in spite of himself, cried out: "Dear God! My suspicions are confirmed! Yes, he is the one!"

Deodatus attempted to rise, to greet the Prince in respectful obeisance, but the Prince asked him to remain as he was, saying:

"You are weak and faint—your wound may be more dangerous than you think. I should not want my curiosity to end by harming you in some way. Let two armchairs be brought out!"

The Prince spoke in an uneven, half-choked voice, and it was evident that he was struggling to control some profoundly disturbing emotion.

After the armchairs had been set down, after Deodatus at the Prince's suggestion had settled himself in one of them, and even after the servants had withdrawn, the Prince paced, and continued to pace, up and down. Finally, he paused before Deodatus' chair; an expression that was like the living reflection of the most devouring torment and melancholy lighted his eyes; then, in another moment, it flickered out and burst into the rising flames of an inner rage. Some invisible force seemed to rear itself in hostility between the two men, and to fill the Prince with dread and even loathing. He drew away and began again to pace back and forth, furtively regarding the young man, whose bewilderment increased with every step until he became incapable of even imagining what this disturbing performance would lead to in the end.

The Prince, it became apparent, was attempting to accustom himself to Deodatus' appearance; finally he drew the other chair into a position diagonally opposite Deodatus, sank down exhausted into it, and addressed him in a lowered, almost gentle, voice:

"You are a stranger here, sir. You have come to my country as a traveler. You may well ask why your past, and other details of your life, should interest a foreign Prince through whose little Duchy you happen to be passing. But perhaps there are certain contingencies, unknown to you, certain mysterious connections—but enough. Take my princely word for it that I am not prompted by any vain or childish curiosity, nor by any unworthy intentions, but—I shall—you must tell me everything!"

The last words were spoken with rising excitement; the Prince paused for a moment, then he resumed more calmly:

"Confide in me fully, young man. Omit none of the particulars of your existence. Tell me where you come from, what brought you to Hohenflüh, and what connection your experiences here in Hohenflüh have with previous events. Above all I want to know exactly what the wise woman . . ." The Prince broke off abruptly. "It is all insane!" he exclaimed. "Crazy nonsense! All this *trompe l'oeil* and hocus-pocus are either the work of the Devil or else . . . Well, speak up, young man! And to the point! No secret, no li—" but the Prince checked the word on his lips.

It was not difficult for Deodatus to conclude, from this strange and agitated exhibition on the Prince's part, that the mysterious events which had recently overshadowed his own life must in some way involve the Prince and have some dangerous significance for him.

But, for his own part, Deodatus saw no reason for withholding the truth, and therefore, in compliance with the Prince's demands, he began to talk about his father, his childhood and boyhood years, his lonely existence in Switzerland. He went on to describe how his father had sent him to Hohenflüh hinting mysteriously that this would be the turning point of his life, since he would find himself compelled to commit an act there which would determine his whole future for him. He then faithfully reported his experiences in Hohenflüh with the wise woman and the Count.

Several times during Deodatus' recital, the Prince revealed the keenest astonishment; at the mention of Nathalie and Count Hector von Zelies, he jumped up from his chair and resumed his pacing back and forth.

When Deodatus reached the end of his story, the Prince was sunk in silent and absorbing thought; then he suddenly turned to Deodatus with a wild gesture, and cried out: "Oh, the despicable creature, the bullet was meant to pierce your heart and destroy you, and with you the last hope, you my . . ."

But a flood of tears stifled his words, and he took Deodatus in his arms and held him firmly to his heart.

Then, all at once, he drew back as though filled with loathing and cried: "Be gone, serpent! Be gone! You shall not insinuate yourself into my heart! Be gone, you tool of Satan! You shall not destroy my last hopes nor poison my life!"

Whereupon, as though in response, a strange, muffled voice called out in the distance: "Hope is death, life the gruesome game of dark powers!" and a cawing black raven flew into the air and disappeared into the thicket.

The Prince reeled, unconscious, to the ground. Deodatus, too weak to assist him, called loudly for help. The court physician found that the Prince had suffered a stroke, and pronounced his condition serious. Deodatus could not account for the strange feeling of pain and compassion that filled his heart. He knelt down beside the litter upon which the Prince had been laid, and kissed the limp hand dangling over its edge. The Prince seemed to regain consciousness for a moment; a look of recognition came back into his eyes; but then his glance fell upon Deodatus and he waved him away, crying out with twitching lips and in a voice that could scarecly be understood, "Away, get away!"

After the Prince had been carried off in his litter, the physician deemed it fit to examine Deodatus. Excitement had done nothing to improve that young man's health, and he was advised to remain in Sonsitz—it would seriously endanger his condition to be moved the distance of Hohenflüh.

Since the Prince had expressed the wish that the young man make himself scarce, the physician saw no reason why Deodatus should not, for a start at any rate, be accommodated in a remote wing of the country house. There would be no fear that the Prince, who would be confined to his own apartments for some time, might find out about this little sojourn. Deodatus was too exhausted to exercise any volition or offer any resistance, and so it came about that he found himself installed in the princely household.

Life in the country house was, under ordinary circumstances, hushed and gloomy, but now that the Prince was confined to his bed with a serious illness, the quiet of a tomb hovered over the establishment; and it was only when some servant came in response to his summons, or the doctor paid him a visit, that Deodatus was aware that other life was going on in the house. This monastic solitude had its advantages for the young man who had been stormed and beleaguered on every side, and he now felt that he had found an asylum from the malevolent destiny that pursued and menaced him.

The pleasant simplicity of the two small rooms he occupied, and, beyond that, the handsome view from his windows, created an atmosphere of comfort and well-being around him that would have eased the most depressed state of mind. He looked out on the most beautiful area of the park: on its outskirts the picturesque ruins of an old castle crowned the summit of a hill, and, beyond, rose the peaks of distant mountains.

He soon learned to relax again, and since the doctor encouraged him to keep himself busy, he filled in his leisure by writing to his father in the greatest detail, describing everything that had happened to him since his arrival in Hohenflüh and imploring him to break his silence and explain these strange occurrences so that his son would be in a position to take in the whole situation and defend himself against the cunning of unknown enemies.

A small section of the main wing of the old ruined castle across the park still seemed to be in a fair state of repair; it came to an end abruptly in a projecting balcony that hung out into the air as free and carelessly as a swallow's nest, because the main wall on the other side had collapsed. And this balcony, as Deodatus discovered through a telescope, was covered with creepers which had forced their way out through crevices in the walls, improvising a very pleasant arbor. It seemed to Deodatus that it would make a delightful little refuge, but he noticed with regret that the stairway had fallen in and that the place was inaccessible. He was therefore all the more astonished, one night, when he saw that a light was burning in the balcony; and he stood in his window and watched it for more than an hour before it disappeared. He saw it again the next night and on successive nights, and he began to imagine—his life of late had been dogged by nothing but mysteries—that the appearance of the light must be of some ominous and secret significance.

He shared his conclusions with the doctor; the latter, however, offered the most natural explanation for the peculiar occurrence: in the undemolished part of the castle, on the ground floor of the main building, several rooms, which commanded a view of the park, had been put at the disposal of the gamekeeper; it was true, the doctor admitted, that access to the balcony was difficult and dangerous, but there was nothing to prevent the young underkeepers, intent upon mischief, from climbing up into the swallow's nest and doing what they pleased, undisturbed and undetected.

Deodatus found this explanation thoroughly unsatisfactory, and he continued to believe that some lively adventure lay hidden in the ruins.

The doctor finally consented to Deodatus' going on a little tour through the park in the evening, but warned him against setting foot on any part of the grounds overlooked by the Prince's apartments. For the Prince had recovered sufficiently now to sit at his windows, and if his sharp eye should light on the young man, he would be sent packing at once without any further opportunity for appeal or protestation. This much, at any rate, the doctor could safely conclude from the manner in which the Prince had first ordered Deodatus away.

As soon as the doctor left him, Deodatus made his way to the ruined castle. He found the gamekeeper in the rooms the doctor had described and presented himself forthwith, much to the latter's surprise. After Deodatus had explained how he had come to Sonsitz and what had happened upon his arrival, the keeper quite candidly volunteered the opinion that the gentlemen who had quartered him in the country house without the Prince's knowledge were playing a risky game. If the Prince were to find out about it, it was more than likely that he would first have the young gentleman cast out of the temple, so to speak, and then his protectors after him.

Deodatus asked to be shown through that part of the castle which was still preserved, but the keeper informed him drily that such a suggestion was scarcely feasible since at any moment a moldy roof or some section of wall might collapse, so that every step one took would be at the risk of breaking one's neck. But when Deodatus mentioned that he had often seen a light burning in the balcony, he was told with brusque and even coarse emphasis that his eyes must be tricking him and he would do well, besides, to concern himself with his own affairs instead of acting on fool inspiration. He could thank his lucky stars that he, the keeper, took pity on him and did not go straight to the Prince and tell him exactly how his strictest orders had been flouted.

Deodatus realized clearly that the keeper was making an effort to conceal a very real embarrassment behind his rudeness. A moment later, as Deodatus was crossing the inner courtyard of the castle, a narrow wooden staircase caught his eye; it had the look of having been newly added to a quite remote corner of the wall, and it seemed to lead to the upper floor of the main wing. Deodatus knew, when he saw it, that his suspicions were not unfounded.

CHAPTER VI

The Prince's condition, which continued to grow worse, occasioned no little dismay and apprehension among the Sonsitzers. The reader has already been informed of the disappearance of the Prince's consort and child.

The Prince was therefore without an heir, and the apparent successor to the throne, his younger brother, had succeeded in estranging both the court and the people by his wanton behavior and unbridled instinct for evil. It was secretly rumored that, because of an act of outrageous treason against the Prince, he had been obliged to flee the country; and what had become of him since was a matter of vague gossip and surmise.

The citizens of Hohenflüh were now making themselves sick with conjecture as to what the future would bring if the Prince were to die. They trembled at the possibility of the brother's return and hoped the rumor of his having been drowned was really true.

These matters were the main topic of conversation at the guests' table in the Golden Goat, where everyone had some favorite theory to put forth. The well-known Councillor delivered himself of the weighty opinion that an omniscient Council, capable of managing the affairs of the township, was well able to take over the government of the state until things were more certain. One old man who until then had seemed preoccupied with his own thoughts and remote from the discussion now spoke up with obvious emotion: "What bitter calamity has overtaken our poor country; the best and kindest of Princes has become the victim of some strange fate that first deprives him of all joy in living, all peace of mind, and then afflicts him with terrible physical pain! We have everything to fear from his successor, and the only man who would make a stand, like a rock in the storm, who would be our hope and our salvation, this unique man is gone from here!"

He was referring, as everyone present knew, to the Count von Törny who had left the court at Sonsitz shortly after the disappearance of the Princess.

Count von Törny was in every respect an excellent man. He combined the keenest understanding, the most spontaneous originality, from which come the knowledge of what is right and the strength to carry it out, with the most noble temperament, the most zealous feeling for the good and the beautiful. He was the defender of the oppressed and the ruthless enemy of the oppressor. And these qualities had won him not only the favor of the Prince but also the heart of the whole people; only a disgruntled few dared to give credence to the rumors, which the Prince's brother had been careful to disseminate, implicating the Count with the Princess.

"Count von Törny! Our noble Count Törny!" the company cried in unison. "If only he were with us now in these troublesome times!"

A toast was drunk to the Count's health. The talk returned to the gravity of the Prince's illness and it was generally agreed that the worst could be expected, and then it was only natural that the conversation turned to the young man in whose presence the Prince had been stricken.

The clever Councillor had long suspected the most awful things. It had been clear to him that this young rascal was a superior sort of swindler who boded no one good. He had been foolish enough to try to deceive the omniscient Council as to his identity by going under two different names. It was not without reason that the Prince had ordered him out to Sonsitz to question him about all sorts of shady practices, and the friendliness exhibited by the officer, the comfortable coach, the attendance of the court physician, were all designed to keep the criminal in a happy frame of mind and in good spirits, the quicker to force a confession from him. The Prince would assuredly have succeeded in arriving at the truth if the cold and damp evening air had not brought on the attack of apoplexy, and created an opportunity, in the ensuing confusion, for the young man to get away. The Councillor only hoped that the good-for-nothing would show his face in Hohenflüh again, for he would not escape the jurisdiction of the omniscient Council a second time.

The Councillor had scarcely finished speaking when the young man who had been the subject of his remarks entered the tavern, silently bowed to the assembled company, and solemnly joined them at the table.

"Welcome, Master Haberland!" said the innkeeper, who in no way shared the Councillor's harsh judgment. "A hearty welcome to you! Well, one cannot say you are afraid of showing yourself in Hohenflüh!" The young man seemed to take offense at the innkeeper's words, and the

Councillor struck his most official pose and began funereally: "Sir, I hereby inform you that . . ."

But the young man stared him so piercingly in the eye that he was struck dumb as if overcome by some secret guilt, and automatically bowed to him, stammering: "Your most obedient servant!" The young man now proceeded with his meal in utter silence, and the whole company seemed to be oppressed with the same unwillingness to talk.

Finally the old man who had been so eloquent before addressed the young man, asking whether his chest wound was now quite healed. The young man replied that there must be some mistake, since he had never been wounded in the chest.

"I understand," continued the old man with an insinuating smile, "I understand, Master Haberland. You are quite well now and unwilling to refer again to the unpleasant incident. But since you were present when our good Prince had his stroke you are in an excellent position to tell us how it all happened and whether we have anything to hope for but the worst from his condition."

Haberland replied that the old man was still in error for he had neither been to Sonsitz nor seen the Prince. He had heard, however, that the Prince was very ill, and would like to have more news about him.

"Perhaps, Master Haberland," said the old man, "you do not wish to, or may not be permitted to, say very much about your visit to Sonsitz, and no doubt rumor has distorted much of what happened there, but this much is certain: the Prince did summon to Sonsitz the young man who was wounded there, the same young man who answered the exact description of George Haberland, and the Prince did suffer a stroke while engaged in private conversation with that young man in the park. Some servants standing in the distance had also heard a strange hoarse voice call out: 'Hope is death, life the gruesome game of dark powers!' "

The young man turned suddenly pale, sighed, and gave every evidence of profound agitation. He gulped down several glasses of wine in succession, ordered another bottle, and left the room before it arrived. The meal ended without his returning. The porter later declared he had seen him hurrying towards the Neudorfer Gate.

The Councillor now became inspired with official zeal; he talked of pursuit and warrants, of infallible methods and quick arrests, but the old man reminded him of a previous occasion when under similar circumstances he had acted somewhat prematurely and had been rewarded for his pains with a harsh rebuke from the state authority. He would do better to dismiss the whole matter from his mind and let things take their natural course. The assembled company concurred in this advice and the Councillor actually resolved to abide by it himself.

Meanwhile young Deodatus Schwendy, Haberland's double, had landed himself in a new tangle of mysterious complications.

From the first moment he had looked out of his windows, he had been drawn, as though by the power of magic, to the picturesque castle ruins. Then, one afternoon towards dusk, he had been loitering under the suspicious, vine-covered balcony, peering up into the curtained windows above and experiencing a curious yearning and foreboding—it had seemed to him that he could make out a white figure up there, and just as he craned forward the better to see, a stone dropped at his feet. He picked it up, unwrapped the paper around it and read the following, scarcely legible penciled words:

"George! My George! Is it possible? Do my troubled senses deceive me? You here! Oh, may Heaven be merciful! My father lurks behind these crumbling walls like some beast of prey! Escape, George, flee, before his fury seeks you out! But no! Stay rather, for I must see you, just one moment of divine respite, then flight! Come back tonight. By way of the courtyard, the wooden stairs. But no, it is impossible. The keeper and his men! And even if they are asleep the dogs will wake them. On the south side there is another staircase leading to the rooms, but it is broken and unsafe. You must not attempt it—I shall come down to you! Oh, George, what can even the Devil's cunning avail against a loving heart! Nathalie is yours—yours forever!"

"It is she!" cried Deodatus, trembling with excitement. "She, beyond all doubt and dreaming! The image of all my youthful yearning! The glowing vision that has persisted through the years like an instinct of my heart! I must go to her at once! Light, full light now, on my father's dark mysteries!

"But am I the right one? Am I George?" The thought seized him like a paroxysm; it was not he, it was his unknown double, whom Nathalie loved and imagined she had found again. "Yet," argued the desire burning within him, "is it not possible that it is my double who is practicing the delusion by passing himself off for me, and that I am the one for whom Nathalie has always been intended, bound to her by the most mystical destiny? In any case," he decided as he made his way back to the country house, "I shall keep our tryst—George Haberland's or mine!"

Soon after nightfall, Deodatus slipped out of his apartment. In the park, not far from the main house, he heard hushed voices approaching along one of the walks that led through the gardens. He crouched down hastily behind some shrubbery, and in another moment two men strode past him, wrapped in heavy cloaks. One of them was saying:

"So the Prince may last for some time yet, according to what his doctor says?"

"Exactly, Your Excellency," replied the other.

"Then we must resort to other means," continued the first voice, as they moved on out of earshot.

Deodatus drew himself stealthily to his feet; in the distance, the full light of the moon fell on the speaker's face. With horror, Deodatus recognized Count Hector von Zelies.

Full of misgivings, and well aware that he had just witnessed the Devil at his work, hatching murder, Deodatus none the less turned in the direction of the ruins, driven on by the irresistible compulsion of his yearning for Nathalie. He found the staircase on the south side quite easily and, aided by the moonlight, succeeded in making his way up the steps until he came to a wide and lofty chamber. And now, suddenly, he was in the presence of the radiant reality, more miraculous than any dream: Nathalie stood before him. "Beloved," he cried. "My George!" she said with infinite gentleness, and took him into her arms. For a time no other word was spoken save in the mute and expressive language of love, in the exchange of tender glances and caresses.

But then Deodatus could no longer control his terrible, devouring anxiety, and he cried out: "You are mine, Nathalie, mine! Believe in me, in my eternal self and in none other. The other meant you harm. He is my double and he tried to kill you; the bullet hit me instead. It wounded me but it has healed; my true self is still alive! Tell me, Nathalie, that you believe in that self, that you love the self who is not called George!"

"My poor George," Nathalie exclaimed. "What has happened to you? But, no, no! You are excited, overwrought! Be calm, be yourself, like the George I have always known."

Nathalie embraced him again; and holding her pressed close to his heart he said: "Yes, Nathalie, it is I: I am the one you love! No one shall attempt, no one shall dare, to tear me away from this heaven of bliss! Nathalie, we must escape—I must put you beyond his reach. Fear nothing, it is I, his true self, who will kill him!"

At that moment footsteps echoed outside, and a voice that rang through the lofty chamber called: "Nathalie! Nathalie!"

"Be off!" whispered Nathalie as she forced her lover toward the staircase. "Go, before it is too late. My father has come home. Return tomorrow at the same hour, and I shall do as you say!"

Scarcely realizing what he was doing, Deodatus groped and stumbled his way down the broken steps. When he reached the bottom, two men leaped out of the darkness, seized him from behind and carried him as far as the gates. There he was lifted into a waiting carriage and driven off at breakneck speed.

Deodatus imagined he had been traveling for about an hour at this rate, when the carriage finally drew up before a charcoal-burner's hut, somewhere deep in the forest, and was immediately surrounded by men carrying flaming torches. Deodatus was told to step down and follow them. The door of the hut opened and a stately old man came forward to meet him. With a cry of "Father!" Deodatus fell into his arms.

"Out of the toils," said Amadeus Schwendy, "out of the toils and snares of intrigue and evil! I have plucked you out of the jaws of death, my dear son. Soon, now, all that is hidden will be revealed to you, and things you never dreamed of will come to pass."

CHAPTER VII

At daybreak the Prince awoke from a deep, untroubled sleep. He seemed refreshed, and even close to recovery, and he called impatiently for his physician. The latter was more than disconcerted when the Prince quietly ordered him to fetch the young man who, as he well knew, had been hidden in the country house.

The physician attempted to excuse his behavior on professional grounds, pleading that the young man's physical condition had demanded complete quiet and careful attention, but the Prince cut him short with the assurance that there was no need to apologize, because he, the physician, had quite unwittingly done him a great kindness. Besides, the presence of the young man had been revealed to him only the day before by the keeper.

But Deodatus had disappeared without leaving a trace, and when the Prince was informed of this he was overcome with emotion. "But why did he run away?" he sorrowfully asked. "Why did he run away? Doesn't he know that all mysteries retreat and vanish at the approach of death?"

Shortly after this the Prince gave orders for the President of the State Council to convene with the President of the High Court of Justice and two State Councillors. The meeting took place behind locked doors, but it was public knowledge, none the less, that the Prince was drawing up his last will and testament.

The following day the mournful pealing of bells in the royal chapel announced the Prince's death to the citizens of Sonsitz; he had suffered a second stroke during the night and had passed away in his sleep.

The members of the State Council and other high officials were summoned to the palace for the reading of the Prince's will, which, in the absence of a direct successor, was assumed to contain certain provisions for the future government of the Duchy.

The ceremony was hardly under way, however, when a mysterious stranger appeared upon the scene, as though in response to some stroke of magic, and interrupted the proceedings. Striding boldly into the chamber, he announced himself as the missing young brother of the House, with the sole right of succession to the throne, despite any restrictions or prohibitions which might be found in the will. He added, further, that there was no necessity for going on with the ceremony now, and that he himself would examine the document at some future time.

The sudden reappearance of Prince Isadore, now considerably older and wearing false hair and a heavy *maquillage*, shocked and thoroughly mystified the court. No one knew that he had been hiding in the castle ruins for the last several days, awaiting the Prince's death. Before entering the Duchy from the Principality of Reitlingen he had assumed the name of Count Hector von Zelies, taking great care to destroy all evidence of his previous whereabouts.

The President of the State Council, a dignified and senior statesman, assured Prince Isadore unflinchingly that he could not accept the younger brother's claim to the throne until the will had been read. He hinted that the document might reveal certain secrets highly important to the question of the succession. These were words spoken gravely, solemnly, almost as though in warning, and Prince Isadore turned visibly pale.

The reading of the will was resumed with full formality, and the contents proved an agreeable surprise to everyone present, except Prince Isadore.

Not until he lay on his deathbed, the Prince's testament declared, had he realized the extent of his injustice to the virtuous Princess; he had suspected her of infidelity on the mere denunciation of a thoroughly unscrupulous character, and had sentenced her and the child she had borne him to imprisonment in a distant frontier castle, from which she had escaped without leaving a trace. Now, thanks to the Almighty Powers of Heaven, their son had been found again; for his deepest instinct told him that the young man known as Deodatus Schwendy, whom he had summoned to Sonsitz, was none other than the son he had driven away in blind fury. Every doubt concerning the true identity of this young man could be dispelled by Count von Törny, who had rescued the boy and brought him up as his own child, and who now lived in the strictest secrecy under the name of Amadeus Schwendy, somewhere near Lucerne. It was self-evident that the evil suspicions he had entertained concerning his son's legitimacy were completely unfounded. The remainder of the will was filled with outbursts of bitter remorse, protestations that all doubt had been expunged from his heart, and sound fatherly advice addressed to his son as future ruler.

Prince Isadore surveyed the room with smiling, contemptuous indulgence, as he asserted that the entire document might be attributed to the hallucinations of the dying Prince and that he, for one, had no intention whatever of sacrificing his inherited rights to insane and senile fantasies. The alleged successor, at any rate, was not present, and it would be Count von Törny's responsibility to confirm the statements of the will so that no possible doubt might arise as to the identity of this young man who had dropped out of Heaven into the throne, and who might be, for all one knew, nothing more than an adventurer.

Even before the Prince had finished speaking, voices could be heard outside in the corridor, and a curious hushed excitement and anticipation filled the room. Now the doors were flung open and old Amadeus Schwendy, or rather Count von Törny, entered, in dignity and state, wearing the glittering Order of the Star on his breast, and leading by the hand the young man who had for so long been known as his son, Deodatus Schwendy. "It is the Prince! The Prince!" voices cried on every side.

But the day had not yet exhausted its wonders, for almost simultaneously with the cries in the chamber, the sounds of jubilation and cheering rose like a chant from the crowds in the streets: "Long live our Princess! Long live the Princess!" and in another moment a tall, stately woman swept into the room, followed by a young man.

"What dream, what miracle is this?" Count von Törny exclaimed. "It is indeed the Princess, she whom we all thought lost forever. Happy day, blissful moment, when mother and son are found and united again."

Now the Princess spoke, addressing the assembly: "My good people, the death of my unhappy husband has brought your Princess back to you. But it has also brought you much more! See the son to whom she gave birth, see your Prince, your ruler!"

And she led to the center of the hall the young man who had followed her in. The one who had accompanied Count von Törny stepped impetuously up to the newcomer, and both of them, alike feature for feature, exactly duplicating each other in gesture and bearing, stood confronting each other with identical expressions of dismay.

At this point it would be only fair to acquaint the indulgent reader with the background for these events at the court of Prince Remigius.

The Prince had been brought up with Count von Törny, and after the intimacy of their childhood, both men found themselves bound to each other by the even more profound accord of their spiritual and moral principles. And so it happened that when the Prince ascended the throne the friend whom he cherished in his heart and whose life seemed inseparable from his own, became his chief Minister and the next most important personage in the land. (The kind reader has already been informed how the Count won the love and confidence of the whole population through the wise exercise of his office.)

Now both the Prince and Count fell in love at the same time, while visiting a neighboring court, and chance dictated that Princess Angela who was the beloved of Remigius, and Countess Pauline whom the Count had chosen, also happened to be bound to each other by ties of the deepest affection and friendship. Both couples were married on the same day, and their happiness—based as it was on the most mystical coincidences—seemed assured. But an ominous circumstance intervened.

The longer the Princess knew the Count von Törny, the more blandishments and charms his personality revealed to her, and the more forcefully and magically she felt herself drawn to this magnificent man. Despite her irreproachable virtue and faithfulness, the Princess realized with increasing alarm that everything within her was yielding to this most destructive of passions. All she thought, all she felt, was only of him; when he was out of her sight, the desolation of death came over her, while at the sound of his voice, at his mere approach, she was restored again to the delights of Heaven. Flight, separation from him, was inconceivable, and yet the situation in which she found herself, full of conflict and self-castigation, was equally intolerable. She could no longer restrain herself in the presence of her lifelong friend, and she would fling herself into the Countess' arms, sobbing fitfully that she was the most wretched woman on earth, and begging for death. And the Countess, far from suspecting the cause of her friend's outbursts, began half imitatively, half sympathetically, to participate more and more in the Princess' grief, until she also sighed and wept and wished herself dead, while the Count found himself hard put to account for the suddenly melancholy transformation of his one-time gay and artless young wife.

It was true, however, that both young women had, from the days of their early childhood, exhibited symptoms of extreme excitability, bordering, at moments, on hysteria, and therefore the court physicians now quite reasonably interpreted their behavior as an exaggerated reaction to the fact that both of them were with child.

By some peculiar chance—or should it be called a miraculous twist of destiny?—both ladies were delivered of sons at exactly the same moment and hour of the same day. Nor was that all, for with every passing week, sometimes even from day to day, the remarkable resemblance between the two boys grew stronger, so that it soon became impossible to distinguish between them. Both little faces already clearly reflected the features of Count von Törny, and as though to contradict the possibility of change or illusion, both had the Count's perfectly formed skull with the small birthmark in the shape of a crescent on the left temple, that duplicated his.

The hostile mistrust, the instinctive insight into evil, which is always alive in a corrupt heart had betrayed the Princess' secret to Prince Isadore. He hastened to instill Prince Remigius with the poison that he himself had tasted, but the Prince dismissed him with contempt. Prince Isadore now launched a direct attack on Count von Törny and the Princess, who represented everything he despised, and stood in the way of all his malefactions.

Prince Remigius was still reluctant to come to any conclusions of his own in the affair, for the fact, itself, of his son's resemblance to Count von Törny would never have prompted the mercilessness of his sentence against the Princess if her own behavior had been less convincing of her guilt. She seemed to live in a constant torment of grief and regret, weeping away the days, sobbing through the nights. Sometimes she would overwhelm the child with affection, showering him with kisses, stifling him with caresses; at others, she would turn away from him with the deepest loathing and at such moments she had been heard to exclaim: "Righteous God, how severely dost Thou punish my transgression!" And this could only point to her culpability and bitter remorse.

Several months passed before the Prince finally came to a decision. Then he ordered the mother and child to be taken away in the dead of night to a deserted castle near the frontier; he dismissed Count von Törny from the court and sent Prince Isadore into exile to savor his triumph.

The spirit alone had sinned, worldly lust was unknown to the Princess who had never faltered in her faithfulness to the Prince, but in her eyes the sin of the spirit was a transgression that demanded the most bitter expiation.

Yet the sojourn in the deserted castle, and the rigid limitations of her existence there, preyed upon her nerves and aggravated her natural excitability almost to the point of insanity.

Then one day a band of gypsies happened to be driving by the castle and encamped under its walls. From her windows, the Princess could hear their music and singing, the sounds of their frolicking and their spontaneous cries of joy, and she was suddenly reminded, as if a blindfold had been torn from her eyes, of a world that still danced in bright colors and gaiety. Boundless yearning filled her heart: "Freedom, freedom!" she cried, leaning from her window. "Oh, take me away—take me away from here!" One of the gypsy women waved encouragingly back as if she had heard, and in another moment a gypsy boy had climbed over the wall. The Princess snatched up her child and made her escape. The castle door was open; the gypsy took the child from her arms and scrambled, with the agility of a monkey, over the wall with him. Then a rope ladder was flung over for the Princess, and an instant later, she was free.

The gypsies welcomed her to their midst with shouts and cheers, for, according to their superstitions, witnessing the escape of a lady of quality held captive in a castle, brought good luck.

The wild, nomadic existence of the little band appealed to the Princess, and her brooding instability soon yielded to a new enjoyment of freedom which slowly reconciled her with life. The child was lodged, with the contrivance of the gypsies, at the home of a discreet and devout old country priest; and there is hardly any need to add that it was the Princess who appeared about the countryside as the wise woman with the raven. In the same way it should now be clear why Prince Isadore mistook young Haberland and young Deodatus Schwendy for one and the same person, that is, for the young Prince, and why he wanted to do away with this person who stood in the way of his succession to the throne.

The miracle is that both Haberland and Schwendy had long dreamed about the loved one whom they later encountered at the climax of their lives; and it was also nothing short of the miraculous that this Nathalie should be the daughter of Prince Isadore, and that both Count von Törny and the Princess had seen in her the chosen agent, in connection with the young Prince, for arresting the tragic destiny that had so far ruled their lives. They both sought by every means they could devise to bring about this union which seemed preordained by the whole fateful pattern of the past.

We know now how these plans were frustrated, how the doubles crossed each other's paths, and we also know in what manner all those whom the Prince had banished came back into his domain while he still lay in state on his deathbed.

CHAPTER VIII

And now the doubles stood, rooted to the spot, confronting each other with identical expressions of dismay. The heavy, threatening atmosphere of an approaching storm seemed to hang over the whole assembly, while each member asked himself. "Which one is the Prince?"

Count von Törny was the first to break the silence by stepping up to the young man who had accompanied the Princess, and exclaiming with the most heartfelt eloquence: "My son!"

"Your son, Count Törny?" the Princess asked with overwhelming dignity. "Who then is he who stands beside you? Has he come to usurp the throne that belongs to the child I have carried at my breast?"

Prince Isadore turned to the assembly and suggested that since there was complete uncertainty as to the identity of the young Prince and heir, there could be no question of the succession of either pretender; the matter to be settled first was the possible legitimacy of each one's birth and claims.

The Count von Törny, however, assured the assembly that such a procedure would be unnecessary, for he was prepared to prove in a moment's time that his ward and pupil was the son of the late Prince Remigius and therefore his lawful heir. The Count then disclosed the following facts:

Although the Prince's most confidential retainers had been entrusted with the task of effecting the Princess' banishment, they were still too devoted to the Count to withhold the information from him, and he was even aware of the exact hour when the Princess and her child would be taken to the borders of the country. The Count foresaw the danger that threatened the succession to the throne and the confusion that might arise in the future from the resemblance between the heir and his own son. He decided to prevent all this.

Late at night, accompanied by two trusted Councillors, the chief of the secret archives, the court physician, the court surgeon and an old chamberlain, the Count entered the Princess' ante-chamber, where, by prearrangement, a nurse brought them the child while the Princess slept. The child was given a narcotic and the surgeon branded a small sign on the Princeling's left breast. Count Törny then took the child and gave his own son over to the nurse. An exact record was made of the whole procedure; to it was attached a reproduction of the brand; the document was duly signed by all those present and then committed to the safe-keeping of the chief archivist.

Thus the Count's son was taken into banishment by the Princess while the royal heir was brought up by the Count as his own child. The Countess, inconsolable over the fate of her childhood friend, died, as much of grief as of any other visible cause, soon after her arrival in Switzerland.

Of the persons who had witnessed the document, there remained, still alive, the physician, the chief archivist, the nurse, and the chamberlain; they were all summoned at the Count's request.

The chief archivist presented the document to the assembly, and it was read aloud by the President of the State Council; the young Prince bared his breast, the sign was recognized and all doubt was dispelled as to his identity. The new ruler's subjects crowded round him with cheers and benedictions, while Prince Isadore, in a rage that was all but unnoticed, strode out of the assembly.

As soon as the Princess was alone with Count von Törny and the two young men, she no longer made any effort to control her pent-up emotions. "Oh, Törny! Your child!" she cried. "You sacrificed your son to save the one I once carried near my heart! But I have brought you back the one you lost! Oh, Törny! We no longer have any part to play in this existence, no new grief can overtake us now! Let us enjoy peace and heavenly respite and know that his appeased spirit is watching over us. Oh, but what have I forgotten? She is waiting, the happy bride is waiting!"

The Princess went into an adjoining room and in a moment returned with Nathalie in her bridal robes. The two young men about whom so much activity had centered and who, singularly enough, had participated in so little of it, now suddenly sprang to life. With a loud cry of "Nathalie!" they both rushed towards the lovely creature. But Nathalie drew back in confusion at the sight of the two young men, the image of her love in double reproduction.

"So, Prince!" cried young Törny wildly, "so it is you, the double risen out of Hell, who have robbed me of my own self and reality, you who are now plotting to rob me of Nathalie, to tear the throbbing life out of my very body! Vain and insane delusion! She is mine, she belongs to me!"

And the young Prince replied: "Why do you force your way into my self? What concern of yours am I that you mock me with my own gestures and features? Away with you! Nathalie loves me!"

"Decide, Nathalie!" cried young Törny. "Speak! Did you not swear eternal faithfulness to me a thousand times during those happy hours when I was painting your portrait?"

"Ha!" interrupted the Prince, "do you remember that hour in the ruined castle when you wanted to run away with me?"

And now they both shouted simultaneously: "Decide, Nathalie, decide!" and then at each other: "Let us see which of us shall succeed in destroying his double—blood shall be the test unless you really are one of the Devil's own infernal illusions!"

"Righteous God!" Nathalie cried out in anguish and consternation. "Who is it, which one of these two do I love? Is this heart of mine split in two and still alive? Righteous God, let me die this very moment!" Tears choked her voice, and she lowered her head, covering her face with her hands as though to turn her vision inward upon herself. When she finally looked up again, there was an other-worldly calm and gentleness in her eyes and she said simply: "The choice is renunciation."

"It is the Angel of Eternal Light Himself who has spoken to you," the Princess said to the doubles.

The two young men still stood glaring at each other, the fire of resentment in their eyes; then suddenly their tension broke, the fire yielded to tears, and they fell into each other's arms.

"Yes, we must be capable of renunciation and forgiveness," said young Törny. "Forgive me, brother."

"For my sake," said the Prince, "your father sacrificed you. You have suffered much on my account. I shall take that as an example for my renunciation!"

"What am I giving up, compared to you?" asked young Törny. "It was for you, the Prince of the realm, that the Princess was destined."

Nathalie cried: "Thanks to the Eternal Powers of Heaven that it has all ended this way!" She pressed a farewell kiss on the cheek of each young man and then retired, leaning heavily on the Princess' arm.

"Must I lose you so soon again?" Count Törny asked when his son came to take his leave.

"Father," said the young man, "give me time or I shall die. Let this wounded heart mend!" Silently he embraced the Prince once more, then his father, and hastened away.

Nathalie entered a distant convent and eventually became its abbess. The Princess, disappointed in her last expectations, had the deserted castle, in which she had been imprisoned, made over into a dower house for her lonely retirement. Count Törny remained with the Prince and when they learned that Prince Isadore had again left the country, they both received the news with an emotion that can scarcely be described as regret.

All of Hohenflüh was in a fever of excitement and preparation. The members of the carpenters' guild, assisted by their estimable colleagues, the joiners, clambered over the face of the triumphal arch, hammering and working away, heedless of all danger, while the painters, eagerly awaiting an opportunity to slap on their paint, impatiently stirred and mixed colors in their pots, and gardeners' boys sat weaving endless wreaths of yew and multi-colored flowers. The boys from the town orphanage, stiff in their Sunday best, were already lined up in the market place; the schoolchildren bawled: "Hail the Conquering Hero," in final desperate rehearsal, interrupted from time to time by a bugle blaring out as though to clear its throat; the flower of Hohenflüh's maidenhood displayed itself in all its freshly laundered glory, while the burgomaster's daughter, Tinchen, unique and radiant in white satin, stood bathed in perspiration, the victim of the exciting attention of the young candidate for Poet Laureate who was coaching her in the delivery of a eulogistic poem dedicated to His Highness, and who refused to countenance the omission of a single declamatory effect.

The reconciled landlords of the Golden Goat and the Silver Lamb paraded up and down, arm in arm, basking in the memory of having entertained the reigning Prince in their respective houses, both of them appreciatively looking back, from time to time, at the enormous welcome, VIVAT PRINCEPS! that had just been painted over their doorways and that would shine out brilliantly in the evening when the illuminations were turned on. The Prince was expected hourly.

In his traveling clothes, with his knapsack and portfolio strapped to his back, George Haberland—for the young Count von Törny still refused to be known by any other name—slipped out through the Neudorfer Gate. "Ha!" cried Berthold, meeting him, "Well met! Good luck, brother George! I know everything. Thank God, you are no reigning Prince! That would have put an end to all our dreams! And I have no use for the 'Count' either, for I know that you are, and will always remain, an artist. And what about the woman you love? She is no earthly creature, intended for the everyday existence of this world. She belongs to the more ideal realm of art; and thus she will live within you, inspiring your work and speaking through it in the language of sublime experience."

"Yes, brother Berthold," said George, his eyes lighting up. "Yes, you are right. She herself is art; she is the very essence my spirit breathes. I have lost nothing of this world. I have been expelled from Paradise, and now I want to experience earthly pain; I want to submit to mortification —But you, you are so carefree, and so—

> 'Friendly solace, balm of heart wounds,
> That is not yet lost to me!' "

The two young men continued their way over the mountains.

THE VOW

 ON MICHAELMAS DAY, JUST AS THE BELLS OF THE Carmelite monastery were announcing the hour for evening prayer, a handsome traveling coach, drawn by four post-horses, came thundering and clattering through the streets of the little Polish border town of L—, and drew up finally before the old German burgomaster's door.

The children in the house leaned out of the window in curiosity, but their mother rose from her chair, irritably threw her sewing aside and called out to her aged husband as he excitedly entered from the next room: "Some more strangers who have mistaken our peaceful home for an inn! That is what you have brought on us with your sign! And why did you ever have the stone dove over the door repainted?"

The old man smiled slyly and significantly without making any reply In another moment, he had thrown off his dressing gown and put on his state dress, which had been hanging over the back of a chair, neat and brushed, in preparation for his walk to church; then before his astonished wife could open her mouth to ask a question, he was already standing, with his velvet cap respectfully tucked under his arm, and his silver hair gleaming in the twilight, before the coach door, which in the meantime had been opened by a servant.

An elderly lady in a grey traveling cloak stepped from the carriage, followed by a tall, youthful figure whose face was heavily veiled, and who leaned on the burgomaster's arm, staggering rather than walking into the house. Once in the room, she sank lifelessly into the armchair which the burgomaster's wife, at a sign from her husband, had quickly pushed toward her. The elderly lady said softly and very sadly to the burgomaster: "Poor child—I must stay with her a few minutes more." And she proceeded to remove her cloak while the burgomaster's eldest daughter jumped to assist her. In another moment, the nun's costume and sparkling cross, which she wore under her traveling clothes, were exposed to view and revealed her as the abbess of a Cistercian cloister.

The young woman in the veil, who had, in the meanwhile, been resting in her chair, murmuring and sighing to herself almost inaudibly, finally asked her hostess for a glass of water. The latter, however, produced a variety of restorative drops and essences, praising their extraordinary efficacy and interrupting herself to suggest that the young lady remove her thick and heavy veil, which must all but impede her breathing. But the young woman rejected this proposal, shielding her face with her arm at the mere approach of her hostess and drawing her head back with every sign of repugnance; and even when she finally brought herself to inhale a powerful restorative, even when she drank the water which she had requested and into which the solicitous old woman had poured a few drops of the precious elixir, she did all this under her veil without raising it at all.

"You have arranged everything, my dear old friend?" said the abbess, turning to the burgomaster. "You have arranged everything just as it has been requested?"

"Indeed!" replied the old man. "Yes, indeed! I hope his most illustrious Highness, my Prince, will be pleased with my efforts—as well as the lady whom I am ready to serve to the utmost of my powers."

"Then leave me for a few minutes," continued the abbess. "I want to be alone with my poor child."

The family was immediately sent from the room. The abbess could be heard earnestly and reassuringly addressing the young woman, who finally replied in the most pathetic and moving tones. Without quite intending to eavesdrop, the burgomaster's wife, none the less, loitered outside the door so that she was able to hear Italian being spoken in the room and this in itself was enough to convince her of the mysterious implications of the whole situation and to overawe her into secrecy. The old burgomaster drove his wife and daughter from the door, sending them away for wine and other refreshments, and then returned, himself, to the room.

The woman in the veil seemed less disconsolate, more composed, as she stood with bowed head and folded arms before the abbess. The latter graciously accepted the refreshments offered her, and then she said: "The time has come!" The young woman sank to her knees; the abbess laid her hands on the veiled head and softly spoke a prayer. When this was finished, tears came into her eyes and she pressed the veiled young woman tightly to her in an excess of pain and emotion. Then, once more dignified and self-possessed, she turned to the others with a benediction and, accompanied by the burgomaster, hurried to her carriage in front of which fresh horses were champing and neighing in their new harnesses. With cries from the postilion, and the blowing of horns, the coach drove through the streets and out of the town gates.

As soon as the burgomaster's wife saw that the veiled visitor had remained behind and that two heavy trunks had been unloaded from the carriage and brought in—which would indicate a long stay—she could not rid herself of a sensation of devouring curiosity and concern. She stepped out into the hall and into the path of her husband, who was about to enter the room.

"In God's name," she whispered hoarsely and anxiously, "what sort of guest have you brought into the house? You've known all along this was going to happen and you've kept it from me!"

"I shall tell you everything I know, in due time," replied the old man very calmly.

"But there may be one or two things you don't know," his wife continued even more anxiously. "If you had only been in the room just now! After the abbess left, the young lady seemed to find the air too oppressive under her thick veils. She took off the long black crape one which hangs down to her knees and then I saw—"

"Well, what did you see?" interrupted the old man, as his wife peered around her, trembling as though her words had summoned up ghosts.

"No," his wife went on, "I could not make out her features under the thin veils she still kept over her face, but I could see the pallor in her cheeks—a horrible corpselike whiteness. And now, my good husband, let me tell you something: it is clear, as clear, in fact, as the noonday sun, that the lady is with child. It can only be a matter of weeks before she'll be ready for a midwife."

"I am well aware of that," replied the old man dryly, "and to spare you from dying of impatience and curiosity, I'll make everything plain to you in the fewest possible words. Be informed then that Prince Z—, our lord and benefactor, wrote to tell me several weeks ago that the abbess of the Cistercian convent at O— would bring to my house a lady whom I was to receive with the greatest discretion and the least possible to-do. She was to be known by no other name than Celestina, and would await her approaching confinement in my house, after which time she and her child would be called for and taken away again. Let me add that the Prince urged me most emphatically to look after the lady with the greatest care and attention, and supplied, for our initial expense and exertions, a purse stuffed with ducats which is lying this very moment in my bureau drawer and which you may feast your eyes on to your heart's content. That, I hope, will satisfy your curiosity."

"And so," said the wife, "we are expected to accept the worst sins in our betters and even to lend them a helping hand!"

Before the old man had an opportunity to answer, their daughter came out of the room and informed him that the lady had expressed a desire to rest and wished to be shown her sleeping quarters. The burgomaster had furnished the two small rooms in the top story of his house as handsomely as circumstances permitted, and now he was more than a little disconcerted when Celestina asked if there might not be some other room she could occupy, with windows that looked out on the back. He replied that there was not, and added, for the sake of thoroughness, that the house did possess a single room with a window giving on the garden, but that this was, indeed, more of a cell than a habitable chamber and scarcely large enough to contain a bed, a table, and a chair. Celestina immediately asked to see this room, and declared at first glance that it suited her requirements admirably; she would live in it, she added, until her condition required the attendance of a nurse, and only then would she exchange it for a larger apartment.

The burgomaster had already compared the room to a cell, and in the next twenty-four hours it became transformed into one, in reality. Celestina had hung an image of the Virgin Mary on the wall, and placed a crucifix on the old wooden table that stood under it. The bed was made up with a straw mattress and a woolen blanket, and, aside from a wooden stool and a second little table, Celestina would tolerate no other comforts. The burgomaster's wife, reconciled to the visitor through the pain and anguish that seemed to be consuming her whole being, thought to cheer and entertain the stranger in the conventional ways, but Celestina begged her to leave undisturbed a solitude, devoted exclusively to the contemplation of the Virgin and the saints, which was her only consolation.

Each morning at daybreak, Celestina went off to the neighboring Carmelite cloister to hear early mass, the rest of the day she appeared to devote, without pause, to religious exercises, for whenever some unexpected circumstance necessitated a visit to her room she was discovered either in prayer or in pious reading. She disdained all food but vegetables, all liquid sustenance but water, and only the most insistent remonstrance on the old burgomaster's part, that her condition, and the condition of the little creature living within her, demanded better nourishment, finally persuaded her occasionally to taste broth and a little wine.

Although this life of abnegation was regarded by everyone in the house as an atonement for past sin, it aroused, none the less, feelings of the deepest sympathy and respect, which were all the more augmented by the lady's nobility of spirit and ineffable grace. Yet this appreciation was accompanied by a shudder and mingled with a sensation of uneasiness, for the saintly stranger had never laid aside her veils and no one had ever been able to see her face. No one came within sight of her except the old burgomaster and his immediate family; and these good people, who had never gone beyond the bounds of their own little town, could hardly be expected to read the secrets that lay hidden behind the visitor's unfamiliar features, even if the face should be revealed to them.

Why then all this heavy veiling? The busy imagination of the women soon concocted a horrible little fantasy. A frightful mark—according to their fanciful explanation—the scar of the Devil's claw had disfigured the stranger's face in the most ghastly way, and consequently the heavy veils were worn to hide this horror.

The old burgomaster did his best to put a stop to such idle chatter so that at least there would be no gossip at his very door about the stranger, whose sojourn at his house had certainly become known in the town. Nor had her journeys to the Carmelite cloister gone unnoticed, and she soon became known as the burgomaster's black lady, a name which immediately invoked spectral and supernatural associations.

Now it so happened that one day, just as the burgomaster's daughter had brought some food into Celestina's room, a gust of air caught the veil and lifted it; the stranger turned her face away as quick as lightning to avert the girl's searching glance, but when the girl returned downstairs, she was white and trembling. Like her mother, she had seen no distortion of feature, only a deathly pallor, a marble white face out of whose sunken eye-sockets a strange light blazed forth. Her father rightly attributed most of this to the girl's imagination, but, none the less, he took the matter as seriously as the others, and could not help wishing that this disturbing presence, for all its devoutness, would remove itself from his house.

One night, not long after he had come to this conclusion, the old burgomaster awoke his wife and told her that he had been hearing a soft whimpering and moaning, a knocking overhead, that seemed to come from Celestina's room. His wife, who had a fairly good notion of what might be going on, hurried upstairs. She found Celestina fully dressed, and wrapped in her veils, lying half conscious on her bed, and was soon convinced that the confinement was imminent. The various articles which, for some time now, had been kept in readiness for this emergency were hastily brought in, and the veiled stranger was delivered of a healthy, bouncing boy.

This event, for all its anticipation, occurred unexpectedly, none the less, when the family was prepared for nothing but resentment; and now it disposed entirely of the oppressive, strained relationship with the veiled stranger that had weighed so heavily on the little household. The boy, like some agent of expiation, seemed to bring Celestina once more within the reach of humanity. Her condition prevented her from indulging in any severe ascetic practices, and her helplessness forced her to accept the tender attentions of those who looked after her, so that she became more and more accustomed to their presence.

The burgomaster's wife, on the other hand, who could now wait on the invalid, cook up nourishing broths and herself serve them to her, soon forgot, in the rush of her domestic duties, every thought of evil she had ever entertained concerning the mysterious stranger. She dismissed the possibility from her mind that her respectable home might be serving as a hiding place for shame. Her husband acted as though he had recovered his youth and the child were his own grandson. Like the others, he had come to accept the fact of Celestina's veils, which she had kept over her face, in fact, even during the hours of labor. She had made the midwife swear that even if she lost consciousness the veils were not to be lifted, unless she were in danger of dying, and in that eventuality they were to be touched by no one but the old crone. It was likely that this ancient beldame had seen Celestina's face, but all she would say was, "The poor young lady has to be wrapped up like that!"

A few days later, a Carmelite monk came to baptize the boy. He remained closeted with Celestina for more than two hours, and from time to time his voice could be heard raised in zealous prayer. After he had gone, the family found Celestina seated in her easy-chair with the boy in her lap; a scapular covered his little shoulders and an Agnus Dei dangled over his heart.

Weeks and months passed and yet, despite the burgomaster's expectations and the promises of Prince Z—, no one came to take Celestina and her child away. She might have entered wholeheartedly into the family life of the peaceful little household, but those fatal veils always checked any final manifestation of friendliness. The old burgomaster took the liberty of informing the stranger of this, but when she replied in a hollow and solemn voice, "These veils shall fall from me only in death," he pursued the matter no further, and longed more than ever for the return of the carriage and the abbess.

Spring had come. The burgomaster's family were returning from a walk, carrying bouquets of flowers, the loveliest of which were intended for their devout guest. Just as they were about to enter the house, a horseman came galloping up, and excitedly asked for the burgomaster. The old man informed him that he himself was the burgomaster, standing, in fact, in front of his own door. Whereupon the horseman sprang to the ground, tied his horse to the post, and rushed into the house and up the stairs, crying out, "She is here, she is here!" They heard a door being forced open and then a shriek of fright from Celestina. The old burgomaster, seized with dread, followed after in all haste. The horseman—it was apparent now that he was an officer of the French Chasseurs, covered with decorations—had snatched the baby from its cradle and taken it up on his left arm, which was still hidden by his cloak. His right hand was clutched by Celestina, who was exerting all her strength to keep him from carrying off her child.

The officer attempted to pull away from her and, in the struggle, tore loose the veils: a face, set in the white rigidity of death, surrounded by masses of black hair as though by shadows, out of the depths of which the eyes blazed in their hollow sockets, confronted him, while lips fixed like a cipher, open and unmoving, sent forth cries of anguish.

The burgomaster suddenly realized that Celestina was wearing a ghastly, tight-fitting mask.

"Horrible woman! Are you trying to drive me out of my mind, too, with your madness?" cried the officer, wrenching himself away from her so violently that Celestina fell to the ground.

Now, however, she threw her arms around his knees, and in a voice of unfathomable pathos pleaded, "Leave me my child! Oh, leave me my child! You cannot deprive me of my eternal salvation. For Christ's sake, for the sake of the Holy Virgin, leave me my child!"

Yet no visible emotion accompanied all this anguish; not a muscle moved, there was no motion of the lips on this lifeless face, so that the burgomaster, his wife, and the others who had followed him, felt the blood turn cold with horror in their veins.

"No!" cried the officer, like one who has come to the end of all endurance. "No, you inhuman, pitiless woman, you have been able to tear the heart out of this bosom, but your fatal madness shall not destroy the creature who this very moment is lying with sweet assuagement over my gaping wound!" And he pressed the child violently to him so that it began to cry—whereupon Celestina shrieked out:

"Vengeance—the vengeance of Heaven upon you—you murderer!"

"Away! Away from me, you spectre of Hell!" shouted the officer. And with a convulsive twist of his foot he thrust Celestina from him and started for the door. There the burgomaster blocked his path, but he quickly drew his pistol, pointed it at the old man and said, "A bullet through the head of anyone who tries to separate the son from his father!" Then he rushed down the stairs, flung himself upon his horse, with the child still on his arm, and rode off at full gallop.

The burgomaster's wife was now so oppressed by anxiety over Celestina's possible reactions to what had happened, and over the eventual outcome of the whole situation, that she overcame her horror of the grim and impassive mask and resolved to return immediately to the stricken mother to offer her help. She was amazed to find Celestina standing in the middle of the room, still and speechless as a statue, her arms hanging listlessly at her sides. The old woman spoke to her; no answer. Unable to endure the sight of the mask, she picked up one of the veils from the floor and draped it about Celestina; no sign of life, not a movement; it was as though she had turned into an automaton. This filled the burgomaster's wife with new anxiety and torment and she began passionately to pray to God to be relieved of this uncanny stranger.

The prayer must have been heard immediately, for at that very moment the carriage which had brought Celestina to the little town of L— drove up to the door. The abbess alighted, accompanied by Prince Z—, the old burgomaster's powerful protector; and both came into the house. When the Prince was informed of what had just happened, he said very gently and calmly, "So we have come too late. We must leave matters to Providence now."

Celestina was brought downstairs; rigid and mute, without any indication of personal desire or volition, she allowed herself to be led out and seated in the carriage, which then rolled speedily away. The burgomaster and his family felt as if they had been suddenly released from the pall of some evil, haunting dream.

Not long after all this took place at the burgomaster's house, a lay sister was buried with unusual pomp in the Cistercian nunnery at O—; and it was whispered about that this sister was, in reality, the Countess Hermengilda von C—, who was supposed to have left the country some time ago to accompany her father's sister, the Princess Z—, on her travels through Italy. Just as this rumor was spreading, the Count Nepomuk von C—, Hermengilda's father, turned up in Warsaw, and legally transferred the bulk of his property to his two nephews, the sons of Prince Z—, retaining for himself only a small estate in the Ukraine. In reply to questions concerning his daughter's future welfare, he would raise his melancholy, glistening eyes to Heaven and simply say, "She is provided for!"

He not only made no effort to deny the gossip regarding Hermengilda's death at the Cistercian convent, but even freely discussed the strange fate that had taken possession of her and had dragged her like a suffering martyr down to an early grave. He no longer seemed the same person. His friends, various Polish patriots, bowed but not crushed by defeat, who still nourished schemes and projects for restoring the Polish state, found a dispirited and broken old man in place of the ardent confederate for whom no enterprise in the name of freedom and the fatherland had once been too bold; an old man torn with anguish, remote from all worldly contact, who longed only to bury himself deeper in solitude.

Yet once, in the days after the first partition of Poland, when insurrection was in the air, the ancestral estate of Count Nepomuk von C— had been the rallying place of all patriots. There, at solemn and impressive gatherings, men had been inspired to battle for their fallen fatherland; there, too, like a guardian angel dedicated to the cause, Hermengilda had circulated among the young zealots. It was the custom of women of her country to participate in political affairs, and Hermengilda took an active part even in discussions of strategy and policy; carefully examining and weighing every aspect of a situation, this young girl, not yet seventeen, would often express an opinion which was opposed to the judgment of the majority, and would defend it with such perspicacity and wisdom that she more than once determined the outcome of some controversial issue.

Second only to Hermengilda in shrewd insight and instinctive judgment, an ardent and gifted young patriot of twenty, the Count Stanislaus von R—, frequently shared her views, participated in her arguments, seconded her suggestions, and in general worked in such eloquent accord with her that even the most able and seasoned statesmen in the conspiratorial company found themselves deferring to the youthful pair. Nothing seemed more natural to the patriots than an eventual union between these two under whose inspiration the salvation of the fatherland seemed to be burgeoning into life. Then again, the union of the two powerful families, who for generations had been of opposing interests, was considered of immediate political importance to the insurrectionist cause. Hermengilda, whose entire being was fired with such considerations, at once accepted her appointed bridegroom as an award of patriotism, and it was decided that the couple's formal betrothal should take place at the next massing of the insurrectionists at her father's estate.

It is of course known that the Poles were overcome, that, with Kosciusko's fall, an attempt based too much on empty confidence and untried loyalties came to grief. Count Stanislaus, whose youth and strength and early army training destined him for a military rôle in the uprising, had fought with the courage of a lion. At the risk of capture and humiliation, he had returned home dangerously wounded. Hermengilda was now his only bond with life, and he hoped, in her arms, to find solace and comfort from disillusionment.

The moment his wound had healed sufficiently to permit him to move, he hurried to Count Nepomuk's estate, only to be dealt the most painful wound of all. Hermengilda received him with almost merciless contempt.

"Is this the hero, come limping home to me, who was ready to walk through fire for his country?" she asked by way of greeting him. She had always imagined him, in the folly of her patriotic zeal, as some paladin out of the legendary age of knighthood, whose mere sword could smite down whole armies. It was useless for him now to protest that no human power could withstand the roaring, devouring horde that had overrun his country, or to appeal to her love for him. Her frigid heart could only be fired now by victory, and she remained resolute in her decision to withhold herself from him until the invader was driven from their land. She had imposed a condition, the Count felt, that was never likely to be fulfilled, and he realized suddenly that Hermengilda had never really loved him. Vowing loyalty until death, he took leave of his beloved, determined to enter the military service of France, which was then engaged in war with Italy.

A peculiar capriciousness of temperament is said to be characteristic of Polish women. Deep feeling, careless self-indulgence, intense asceticism, burning passion, deathlike frigidity, all this picturesque confusion of attributes which they possess in their souls finds expression in the strange, restless surface play of their personalities, like the splashing and frothing, the tireless shifting and settling, of waves when the sea is stirred in its depths. Hermengilda experienced little more than indifference at her lover's leave-taking, and yet before many days had passed she found herself so overwhelmed with longing for him that she was compelled to admit to herself that she was passionately in love.

The storm of war had subsided, the amnesty was proclaimed, and the Polish officers were released from captivity. So it happened that several of Stanislaus' companions in arms, from time to time, visited Count Nepomuk's estate. Often, in discussions of battles, Stanislaus' name would come up, and they would refer with regret, and the greatest respect for his courage, to the unlucky day when he had been struck down. He had led his retreating battalion back into fire when defeat seemed inevitable, and had succeeded in breaking through the enemy ranks with his cavalry; the fate of the day hung in the balance; then he was struck by a bullet and with the cry, "On for Poland!" he fell, covered with blood, from his horse.

These accounts would leave Hermengilda distraught, devoured by anguish and misgivings. "What delusion out of Hell kept me from realizing that I have always loved him," she would ask herself, "and tricked me into thinking I could live without him who is my only life! I have sent him to his death—he will never come back!" Incapable of sleep, tormented by constant unrest, she began to wander at night through the park grounds, crying aloud into the night air as if the wind might carry her words to her distant lover: "Stanislaus, Stanislaus, come back! It is I, your beloved, who is calling you! Won't you hear me—come back, before I die of loneliness and despair!"

Hermengilda's agitated state of mind seemed to be driving her on to a thousand follies, if not to utter madness. Count Nepomuk, troubled and saddened by his daughter's condition, decided that medical aid might prove effective, and he succeeded, in fact, in finding a physician who agreed to stay on at the estate for some time and look after the patient. His methods were psychical rather than physical, and yet, no matter how correct they were or how incontrovertibly Hermengilda's condition seemed to improve, there still appeared little likelihood of any real cure, since after long periods of tranquillity, the strangest seizures and outbursts would unexpectedly begin.

A peculiar little episode put another complexion on the whole affair. In one of her fits of anger, Hermengilda had thrown into the fire a doll, a little Uhland dragoon, which she had often addressed in the most endearing terms and pressed to her heart as if he were her lover; the reason for this act of immolation was that the "dragoon" had definitely refused to sing the words of a patriotic Polish anthem: "*Podrosz twoia nam niemila, milsza przyiaszn w Kraiwbyla*," and so on. She was on her way to her room to brood over this unpleasant occurrence, when she heard a rattling and clanking of spurs coming up the stairs behind her. She turned around and saw an officer in the full uniform of the French Chasseurs, with his arm in a sling, standing below her. She cried out, "Stanislaus, oh, my Stanislaus!" and the next moment threw herself swooning into his arms.

The officer stood, rooted to the spot, gaping with amazement and attempting to support, with the one arm at his disposal, Hermengilda's awkward weight. He clasped her closer and closer to him, and when he felt Hermengilda's heart beat against his own, he congratulated himself on the beginning of a really delightful adventure. Moment after moment passed in this fashion; the officer, inflamed with the love that seemed to emanate electrically from the charming body in his arms, pressed burning kisses on the sweet, yielding lips. It was in this position that Count Nepomuk, emerging from his room, found him. He, too, cried out in joy, "Count Stanislaus!"

Just then, Hermengilda came back to consciousness, and embracing the officer with feverish excitement, she exclaimed again, "Stanislaus! My beloved! My husband!"

The officer, flushed and trembling, utterly disconcerted, drew back a step and gently extricated himself from Hermengilda's passionate embrace. "This is one of the happiest moments of my life," he stammered out, "but I cannot permit myself to—revel—in delights—that are only mine by mistake—in fact, I am not Stanislaus—ah, definitely not!"

Now Hermengilda drew back, appalled, and when a calmer scrutiny of the officer convinced her that she had been misled by an utter stranger's remarkable resemblance to her lover, she fled to her room, moaning and sobbing to herself.

The officer presented himself to Count Nepomuk, as the Count Xaver von R—, a young cousin of Count Stanislaus. He had left the country at the same time as Stanislaus and, like him, had entered the French service and fought against Italy. In spite of his youth, he had proved his merits as a soldier, and now, at twenty, had already risen to a colonelcy. He was at present on sick-leave, necessitated by wounds received at the front. He had come to the Count's estate to convey certain messages from Stanislaus to his beloved.

Hermengilda, however, was utterly overcome by humiliation and pain, and refused to leave her room as long as the officer remained in the house. Both Count Nepomuk and the physician exhausted their ingenuity in attempting to placate her, but it was useless. Xaver became frantic with disappointment at the thought of never seeing her again, and decided finally to write her and plead his case. He was paying too dearly, he said in his note, for a resemblance that had been his innocent misfortune; but it was not he alone who was paying the penalty for that fatal coincidence: her lover Stanislaus was being punished as well, since his younger cousin, the bearer of love's sweet messages, was deprived of the opportunity to deliver into her own hands, as he should, the letter from Stanislaus which he carried on his person, and that, further, there were various postscripts, to be communicated by word of mouth, which Stanislaus had not had the time to add in writing. Xaver managed to win over Hermengilda's chambermaid and, at a propitious moment, the note was given into her young mistress' hands. Thus he succeeded where both father and doctor had failed; Hermengilda consented to see him.

She received him, with downcast eyes and in the gravest silence, seated on a low sofa in her own room. He sat down opposite, but as he continued to lean more and more forward in his chair he ended almost by kneeling rather than sitting before her, while he implored her in the most touching terms and in a voice that admitted all culpability, to forgive him for the error that had given him a momentary glimpse into another's paradise. It was not he, no it was, in truth, Stanislaus himself whom she had embraced in that impulsive moment of recognition.

He handed her the letter, and then went on to tell her how Stanislaus, with true knightly chivalry, had gone down, in the midst of bloody battle, with his lady's name on his lips, how his heart still burned with loyalty to Poland and the cause. He embellished this account in such lively detail and with such a quality of personal excitement, that Hermengilda found herself being carried away by his enthusiasm, and presently, forgetting all shyness, fixed on him a glance of such tender and loving understanding that he was almost prevented, by his emotion, from going on with the narrative. None the less, unconsciously, he struggled against this guilty attraction which might so easily be inflamed to passion, and gave himself over to the most drawn-out descriptions of individual actions in the campaign. He spoke of cavalry attacks, the blowing up of troops, the seizing of batteries, until Hermengilda interrupted him impatiently, crying, "Enough! Enough of this gory enactment of a drama written in Hell! Tell me no more, tell me—only—that he loves me, that Stanislaus loves me!" Whereupon Xaver, sufficiently encouraged, seized Hermengilda's hand and pressed it violently against his breast.

"Hear him yourself, your Stanislaus!" he cried, and now there streamed from his lips the sort of declarations of love that only someone in the excitement of the wildest passion is capable of uttering. He had sunk down at Hermengilda's feet; she had embraced him with both arms, but as he suddenly leaped up and tried to press her against his heart, he felt himself violently thrust off.

Hermengilda stared at him with a strange, fixed look, and said in a hollow voice: "Vain effigy, even if I should warm you to life on my bosom, you still would not be, nor could you ever become, Stanislaus!" And without another word, she left the room with slow, noiseless steps.

Xaver perceived too late the rashness of his behavior. He was all too well aware that he was in love, almost obsessively, with the intended bride of his kinsman and friend, but he realized now that he would have to reproach himself, each time he attempted to advance his own futile cause, with having violated the confidence and loyalty of friendship. Therefore, he determined to depart at once, without seeing Hermengilda again; and he carried out this courageous resolution to the extent of ordering his luggage packed and his carriage made ready.

Count Nepomuk was completely taken by surprise when Xaver came to bid him farewell, and he made every effort to persuade his guest to stay;

but with a determination that was more the result of hysteria than of any actual strength of will, Xaver insisted that special circumstances necessitated his immediate departure.

He was standing, during this brief exchange, in the middle of the room, his sabre buckled, his Chasseur's field cap in hand; in the antechamber, his servant was waiting with his cloak; outside, in the courtyard, the horses were harnessed and neighing with impatience; and then, the door opened and Hermengilda came in.

She walked up to the Count von R— and asked, with a smile that emanated indescribable charm: "But do you mean to leave us, dear Xaver? And I was expecting to hear so much more about my dear Stanislaus! Do you really know how wonderfully your stories about him comfort me?"

Xaver turned crimson and lowered his eyes; Count Nepomuk suggested that they all sit down, and exclaimed over and over again that it had been months since he had seen Hermengilda in such a free and cheerful state of mind. He rang—it had grown late—and ordered that supper be brought in and served to them where they were. The rarest Hungarian wine sparkled in the glasses, and Hermengilda with glowing cheeks sipped a toast to her lover, to freedom and Poland.

"I will go away later tonight," Xaver thought to himself; and, as the tables were being carried out, he actually asked a servant if his carriage were waiting. The servant replied that, in accordance with Count Nepomuk's instructions, his carriage had long since been unloaded and unhitched and put away in the coach-house, and that by this time the horses were feeding in the stable and Woyciech was snoring away on his straw pallet. Xaver let it go at that. Hermengilda's unexpected appearance, at the moment of his departure, convinced him now that it would not only be possible for him to stay, but advisable and pleasant as well. From this conclusion, he went on quite naturally to the next: it was merely necessary for him to control himself, that is, for him to avoid outbursts of the passion he harbored within him, which would only aggravate Hermengilda's mental condition and create trouble for him, in any case. How matters would turn out after that, even if Hermengilda should awake from her dream and prefer the comforting present to the dismal future, all that, he finally concluded, would depend on the development and happy combination of various circumstances and events; and even in thought there was to be no further disloyalty to Stanislaus.

When Xaver saw Hermengilda the next day, he did, in fact, succeed in controlling his passion, by carefully avoiding the slightest gesture or reference that might stimulate his easily excitable, warm-blooded temperament. He remained within the restrictions of the most rigid decorum, observed the most icy formality, and yet brought to his conversation the play of that gallantry which tastes of honey to women and acts like deadly poison. Xaver, a youth of twenty, inexperienced in love affairs, but guided by an unfailing instinct for evil, revealed the accomplishment of a master. He confined his talk to the subject of Stanislaus and his infinite love for his sweet bride, but he knew exactly how to insinuate his own personality, how to let the light of his own image shine through the flaming response aroused by the mention of his cousin, so that Hermengilda, in sorry confusion, found herself incapable of separating the emotion from the image, and the image from the resemblance.

Xaver's company soon became a necessity to Hermengilda in her aroused state, and they began to be seen almost constantly together, often in what appeared to be confidential love talk. Familiarity increasingly overcame Hermengilda's reticence, and to the same extent Xaver began to overstep those bounds of rigid formality to which he had at first shrewdly restricted himself. Together, they would stroll about the park, arm in arm; or seated in her room, she would forgetfully permit her hand to linger in his while he talked to her of his more fortunate kinsman.

Count Nepomuk had little perspicacity in matters that did not deal with politics or the destiny of his country; he was content with what he perceived on the surface of reality; his imagination was dead to all else and could only reflect like a mirror the fleeting images of life as they impinged from moment to moment; then they vanished and left no trace. It was apparent to him now that Hermengilda had exchanged her doll, the "little dragoon" with whom she used to play lover in her madness, for a live and breathing young officer, and without any further insight into his daughter's true nature, he considered the change desirable. More than that, he foresaw, with what he deemed great worldliness on his part, that Xaver, to whom he had no objection as son-in-law, would eventually take Stanislaus' place, entirely.

Xaver shared the Count's sentiments; and after a few months had passed, Hermengilda, for all her intense preoccupation with Stanislaus, was pleased, none the less, to permit Xaver to court her more and more overtly.

One morning a servant brought word that Hermengilda had shut herself and her maid in her apartments and firmly refused to admit anyone. Count Nepomuk assumed that another attack had come over her and that it would soon subside. He was aware, however, of the influence which Count Xaver had gained over his daughter, and he asked him now to exert his powers to facilitate her recovery. He was amazed not only by Xaver's emphatic refusal to approach Hermengilda, but at the alteration in the young man's whole manner and appearance at the mention of her name. Instead of displaying his customary almost overbearing boldness, he started as if he had seen a ghost, his voice was unsteady, his speech dispirited and incoherent. He said that he must definitely go to Warsaw now, that he would never see Hermengilda again, that her strangely disturbed state, the last time he had seen her, had filled him with foreboding and fear, that he was ready to renounce all the joys of love, that Hermengilda's almost mad loyalty to Stanislaus had finally awakened him to the goading shame of his own disloyal intentions, that immediate escape was the only solution.

Count Nepomuk was at first bewildered by all this, but then it became clear to him that the young man had, in some strange way, become infected with Hermengilda's hectic fantasies. He made an effort to point this out to Xaver, but it was to no purpose. The more urgently Count Nepomuk pointed out to him the necessity of curing Hermengilda of all her freaks and tantrums, and, consequently, of remaining to see her again, the more violently he was opposed by Xaver. The argument ended abruptly, for in the midst of it, Xaver, as though possessed by a demon, suddenly ran from the room and out of the house, flung himself into his carriage and drove off.

Count Nepomuk, now thoroughly wearied and angered by his daughter's conduct, decided to trouble himself about her no further, and so it happened that Hermengilda spent the next several days locked up in her rooms, solitary and undisturbed, except for her maid.

One day Nepomuk was sitting in his study, absorbed in thought, reviewing in his mind the heroic deeds of that man whom the Poles of his day worshiped like a false god, when the door opened and Hermengilda came in. Dressed in complete mourning, and trailing a long widow's veil, she walked with slow, processional steps up to her father's side, then knelt and said in a quavering voice: "Oh, my father—Count Stanislaus, my beloved husband, has left this world. He fell like a hero in bloody battle! His widow, the most miserable of all living creatures, kneels before you."

Count Nepomuk had just received news, the day before, of Stanislaus' good health, and he was all the more convinced, now, that his daughter was being victimized by another of her morbid fantasies. He raised Hermengilda gently to her feet and said, "Calm yourself, dear child, Stanislaus is well and soon will be hurrying back to your arms."

When she heard this, Hermengilda uttered a sigh like the gasp of death, and sank down, in an agony of pain, beside her father on the sofa. But in a moment the attack had passed, and she became extraordinarily calm and self-possessed.

"Let me tell you, dear father, how it all happened," she said. "You must know because you shall have to recognize me as the widow of Count Stanislaus von R—. Six days ago, at twilight, I happened to be in the pavilion on the south side of our park. All my thoughts, my whole being, were concentrated on my beloved; I felt my eyes close involuntarily and then I sank, not into a sleep, but into a strange state that I can only describe as a waking dream.

"I was surrounded by a humming and rumbling that grew into a wild tumult, and I could hear the sound of shots going off all around me. I started out of my revery and was amazed to find myself in a soldier's hut. He, himself, my own Stanislaus, was kneeling before me. I threw my arms around him, I pressed him to my heart. 'God be praised!' he cried. 'You are alive, you are still mine!'

"He told me that immediately after our wedding I had fallen into this faint, and I, foolish creature, now first remembered that Father Cyprianus, who was this very moment leaving the hut, had married us half an hour ago in the near-by chapel, under the thunder of artillery and the raging uproar of battle. The golden wedding ring gleamed on my finger.

"Nothing can describe the sublime joy with which I embraced my new-found husband. A rapture I had never felt before, the nameless delight of a woman blessed by love, thrilled the deepest fibres of my being —my sense deserted me—I opened my eyes. It was dreadful! I was in the midst of a raging battle in the distance, the burning soldier's hut from which I must have just been rescued—Stanislaus hard pressed by enemy troopers—friends galloped up to save him—too late; from behind, an enemy hewed him from his horse!"

Hermengilda paused, shaken by her recital; the Count reached hastily for restoratives, but they were not needed; she had gained control of herself again.

"The will of Heaven is fulfilled," she went on, in a hollow and solemn voice, "and it would not befit me to complain, but I will be faithful to my husband unto death, and no earthly tie shall ever come between us. To mourn for him, to pray for him and for our salvation, that is now my mission in life and nothing shall deter me from it."

Count Nepomuk had every justification for believing that Hermengilda's pent-up and brooding folly had found relief in this vision; and since the restrained and nunlike mourning for her husband would permit her no outlandish or disturbing impulses, the Count was quite content to accept this new condition, which would, in any case, be soon ended by Stanislaus' arrival. If Nepomuk, upon occasion, dropped some remark about dreams and visions, Hermengilda would smile sadly and press to her lips the gold ring that she wore on her finger. The Count noticed with some astonishment that the ring was indeed strange to him and that his daughter had never worn it before. However, since there were countless ways she might have come by it, he made no effort to find any explanation for it. What was more important to him was the bad news that Count Stanislaus had been taken prisoner by the enemy. Hermengilda began to be sickly in a peculiar manner and often complained of a curious sensation, which she could not exactly call sickness but which permeated her whole being strangely.

At about this time, Prince and Princess Z— arrived at Count Nepomuk's estate on one of their regular visits. The Princess had, on the early death of Hermengilda's mother, virtually taken the Countess' place and she was now, therefore, received by her "daughter" with childlike devotion. Hermengilda opened her whole heart to this worthy lady, and complained bitterly that, although she had the most convincing proofs of her marriage to Stanislaus and all the circumstances connected with it, she was treated as if she suffered from hallucinations and fantasies. The Princess, who had been acquainted with all the details of Hermengilda's state and was convinced of the girl's mental instability, carefully avoided contradicting her; she contented herself with assuring her that time would reveal everything in its true light, and suggesting that she yield, humbly and devoutly, to the will of Heaven.

The Princess paid marked attention, however, when Hermengilda spoke of her physical condition and described the peculiar attacks which seemed to disturb her inmost being. The older lady began to watch over Hermengilda with the most anxious care, and her concern became even more apparent when Hermengilda seemed to recover entirely. The color returned once more to the deathly pale cheeks and lips; the eyes lost their unnatural, melancholy fire; their glance became soft and calm; the wasted figure rounded out more and more; in short, Hermengilda blossomed into ripe beauty. And yet the Princess seemed to consider her more ailing than ever, for, "How are you? Is anything wrong? Are you sure you are well?" —such were the questions she would ask, with harassing anxiety in her look, the moment Hermengilda merely sighed or paled slightly.

Count Nepomuk, the Prince, the Princess, took counsel together as to what was to be done about Hermengilda's fixed idea that she was Stanislaus' widow.

"I regret to say," said the Prince, "that I consider her madness to be incurable, for she is in excellent physical health and feeds the disorder of her soul with her full strength— Yes," he continued, while the Princess stared uncomfortably into space, "she is in excellent health, despite the fact that, to all excess and to her own obvious detriment, she is pampered and coddled and worried like an invalid."

The Princess, for whom this observation was intended, turned to Count Nepomuk and said quickly and firmly: "No, Hermengilda is not ill, but if it were not utterly beyond the realm of likelihood for her to have done wrong, then I should be convinced that she is with child!" Whereupon she got up from her chair and left the room.

Count Nepomuk and the Prince stared at each other as though lightning had passed between them. The Prince was the first to speak: "It seems," he remarked, "that my wife, too, is at times visited by rather strange visions." But the Count replied in deadly earnest: "The Princess is right to this extent: a transgression of that sort on Hermengilda's part is utterly inconceivable. And yet, if I tell you that yesterday when I saw Hermengilda pass by I was struck by the absurd notion: 'Just look, the young widow is certainly with child'; that such an idea could obviously only have been brought to my mind by something about her appearance—if I tell you all this, you will find it only natural of me to be alarmed over what the Princess has said, yes, painfully disturbed!"

"Then," replied the Prince, "the doctor or the midwife must decide, and either contradict the Princess' possibly hasty judgment or confirm our shame."

For several days both men vacillated between conclusions as to what they ought to do. Both thought there was something suspicious about Hermengilda's figure, both thought the Princess should decide what was to be done next. She objected to the interference of a physician, who might gossip, and volunteered the opinion that within five months other help would be needed.

"What help?" the Count demanded in horror.

"Yes," the Princess went on, her voice rising with excitement, "there can no longer be the slightest doubt about it. As for Hermengilda, she is either the most conscienceless hypocrite in the world, or something very mysterious is going on—in any case, she is with child!"

The Count controlled his agitation with difficulty; finally, he implored the Princess, cost what it may, to find out from Hermengilda, herself, who the scoundrel was who had brought this ineradicable taint upon his house.

"As yet," said the Princess, "Hermengilda has no idea I know about her condition. I intend to take her by surprise. The moment I tell her I know what is going on, she will either be startled into dropping her mask of hypocrisy or compelled to reveal her innocence in some remarkable way . . . although I don't see how she possibly can."

That same evening the Princess, whose air of maternal authority seemed to increase by the hour, followed Hermengilda to her rooms. Once there, she took the girl by both arms, looked her keenly in the eyes, and said: "My dear, you are with child!"

Hermengilda, in response, flushed with joy and exclaimed in an enraptured voice: "Oh, Mother, Mother, of course I am! For a long time now I have known that although my husband was struck down by the enemy he would still bring me infinite happiness. That moment of our most intense earthly joy lives on in me—and I shall have him all to myself again, my darling husband, in the sweet incarnation of our union."

The Princess felt as if the room were spinning around her, as if, at any moment, she might take leave of her senses. The sincerity of Hermengilda's manner, her joy, her actual transfiguration, discouraged any thought of duplicity or falsehood, and yet, raving madness was the only other interpretation that could be attached to her assertion. Seized by this last thought, the Princess drew back from Hermengilda and cried out with emotion: "Mad woman! Is it a dream then, that has put you in this condition which brings shame and disgrace to all of us? Do you think that you can take me in with idiotic fairy tales? Reconsider what you have said —try to remember everything that has happened these last days. If you repent and confide in us, we shall still forgive you."

Losing all control of herself and breaking into sobs of bitter anguish, Hermengilda sank to her knees before the Princess. "So you, too," she wept, "reproach me and think I invent fantasies! You, too, refuse to believe that the Church united me to Stanislaus, that I am his wife! Haven't you seen his ring here on my finger—but what need is there for words? You know the condition I am in, isn't that enough to convince you that I have not been dreaming?"

The Princess realized to her own astonishment that the idea of misconduct had never occurred to Hermengilda, that she had in no way grasped or understood the reference to it. Hermengilda had assumed the posture of a suppliant, with her hands clasped and raised towards the Princess, and she kept imploring, now that her condition was beyond doubt, that she might keep her belief in her husband; the older woman, thunderstruck and utterly confused, no longer knew what tone to take with the poor girl, or what mode of attack to adopt to get to the bottom of the mystery that seemed involved.

The Princess permitted several days to pass before she explained to the Prince and the Count that it was impossible to get anything more out of Hermengilda than that she was with child by her husband, and that the girl was convinced in her soul of this delusion. The men scornfully dismissed this as pure sham, and Count Nepomuk, in particular, swore that if gentle means would not discourage her from the insane notion of palming off a dull fairy tale on him, he would resort to more extreme measures. The Princess, on the contrary, was of the opinion that any act of severity would inflict needless suffering; she was convinced, in other words, that Hermengilda was in no way dissembling but believed with all her soul in what she had said.

"There are many mysteries in this world," the Princess continued, "that are beyond our grasp and understanding. Suppose it is possible to produce a physical effect by some intense interchange of human thought, suppose some spiritual exchange between Hermengilda and Stanislaus is responsible for this condition in her which we find so inexplicable?"

Despite their sense of irritation and depression, both men burst into hilarious laughter at this suggestion, which they referred to as the most sublime idea that had had ever etherealized humanity. The blood rushed into the Princess' face, and she expressed the opinion that the crude masculine mind was incapable of grasping such thoughts; she declared further that she believed wholeheartedly in the poor child's innocence, that she found the whole situation scandalous and abhorrent, and that she was planning to take the girl with her on a journey which would be the best and only means of removing her from the craftiness and contempt that surrounded her on all sides.

Count Nepomuk was entirely satisfied with this suggestion, since Hermengilda herself made no secret of her condition, and it was unquestionably necessary, if her reputation was to be preserved, to separate her from her friends and acquaintances.

With this matter settled, everyone felt more at ease. Count Nepomuk hardly gave another thought to the disquieting and mysterious situation itself, once he saw the possibility of concealing it from the world whose contempt he feared most; while the Prince judged quite rightly that, in view of the strange circumstances involved and of Hermengilda's very real mental condition, one could do nothing but leave it to time to solve the whole strange riddle.

The little conference was about to break up, when Count Xaver von R— suddenly arrived, creating a new dilemma and new anxieties. He rushed frantically into the room, overheated from his hard drive, covered from head to foot with dust, and without any greeting or regard for propriety, cried out: "He is dead! Count Stanislaus! He was never captured by the enemy—no—he was struck down—here are the proofs!" Whereupon he hastily pulled out several letters and thrust them into Count Nepomuk's hands. The latter, completely disconcerted, began mechanically to read them, holding the pages out so the Princess could look on. She had scarcely glanced at the first few lines, when she exclaimed: "Hermengilda! Poor child! What an unfathomable mystery!" There was evidence in the letter that the date of Stanislaus' death agreed exactly with Hermengilda's assertion, and that everything, in fact, had happened just as she had seen it in that fatal vision.

"He is dead," Xaver said brashly, "and Hermengilda is free. Now nothing stands in the way of my love, and I ask to marry her."

Count Nepomuk found himself incapable of replying to the young man, and the Prince took up the conversation, explaining that certain circumstances made it impossible to agree to his proposal at this time, that it was impossible even to see Hermengilda now, and that, consequently, it would be advisable for him to go away in much the same manner as he had come.

Xaver replied, in turn, that he was thoroughly aware of Hermengilda's unbalanced mental state, to which the Princess apparently was referring, but that this was far from a hindrance to their marriage, since it was just that condition which marriage would remedy. The Princess assured him that Hermengilda had made a vow of lifelong faithfulness to Stanislaus, that any other union would therefore be rejected, and that, besides, Hermengilda was no longer at the castle. Xaver laughed at this explanation, and said all he needed was the father's consent; the changing of Hermengilda's heart and mind could be left to him. Thoroughly irked by the young man's stubborn insistence, Count Nepomuk informed him that it was useless at the moment for him to hope for consent, and that he must leave the castle at once. Xaver stared at the Count without making any response, then opened the door to the antechamber and called to Woyciech to bring in his carpetbag, and put the horses in the stable. He returned to the room, flung himself into an easy-chair which stood by the window, and declared coolly and emphatically that nothing but physical force would drive him from the castle before he had seen Hermengilda and spoken to her. Count Nepomuk remarked that if that were the case, he must be planning on a long stay there, and would first have to permit the owner himself to leave. He then walked out of the room accompanied by the Prince and Princess; it had occurred to all three of them that Hermengilda must be dispatched from the house as quickly as possible.

Now it so happened that, at this very hour, quite contrary to her usual habits, Hermengilda had gone into the park. Xaver glanced out of the window by which he was sitting and saw her strolling in the distance. He ran down into the park and finally reached her just as she was about to enter that fatal pavilion on the south side. Her condition was now almost conspicuously apparent. "Almighty God!" exclaimed Xaver as he stood before her. He overwhelmed her with declarations of his love, to which he attested with the most solemn vows, and then he begged her to marry him. Hermengilda was utterly embarrassed and startled at the sight of him. "Some evil destiny has guided you here," she said, "to disturb my peace." Her love belonged eternally to Stanislaus, and she would never, never violate it by becoming the wife of another.

Xaver refused to be discouraged and continued, unheeded, with his pleas and assertions. Finally, exasperated beyond endurance, he accused her of deceiving herself, declaring that she had already granted him love's sweetest favors, and, springing towards her, attempted to embrace her.

With the look of death upon her face, full of loathing and contempt, she thrust him from her, and said: "You pitiful, self-seeking fool! You are as incapable of seducing me into violating my vow of fidelity to Stanislaus, as you would be of destroying the pledge of love with which he has left me! Out of my sight!"

Then Xaver stretched out his clenched fist towards her, laughed aloud wildly and derisively. "Mad woman!" he cried. "Haven't you broken that senseless vow yourself? The child you bear under your heart is my child! It was I, I, whom you embraced here on this very spot! My mistress you were, my mistress you still remain, unless I exalt you to be my wife!"

Hermengilda glared at him with the fire of Hell in her eyes, then she shrieked, "Monster!" and sank lifelessly to the ground.

Xaver ran back to the castle as though pursued by the Furies; there, he encountered the Princess, just coming to look for him, and, seizing her

292 Tales of Hoffmann

frantically by the hand, he drew her back into the room with him. "She has rejected me like something loathsome—me, the father of her child!"

"In the name of all the saints!" the Princess exclaimed. "You? Xaver? My God, but how is it possible?"

"Let whoever will damn me," Xaver went on, more calmly now, "but if the blood glowed in his veins as it did in mine at that moment, he would have sinned, too. I came upon Hermengilda in the pavilion, that day, in a state I cannot describe. She was lying on the sofa as if fast asleep and dreaming. I had scarcely entered when she rose, came to meet me, took me by the hand, and, with solemn steps, led me through the pavilion. Then she knelt down; I did likewise; she began to pray; and I soon realized that she saw, in spirit, a priest standing before us. She now drew a ring from her finger and offered it to the priest. I took it, and in turn removed from my own hand a gold ring which I placed on her finger; then she sank with the most impassioned love into my arms. . . . When I crept away, she was lying there in a deep, comatose sleep."

"Dreadful, dreadful creature! Monstrous crime!" gasped the Princess, utterly beside herself.

Count Nepomuk and the Prince came in. They were briefly told of Xaver's confession, and, to the Princess' profound shock and pain, found Count Xaver's criminal behavior quite pardonable: they felt it could be expiated by his marriage to Hermengilda.

"No," said the Princess, "Hermengilda will never accept a man who has dared, like the evil spirit of Hell, to poison the most poetic moment of her life with the most monstrous sin."

"She will," said Count Xaver with cold, scornful pride, "she will have to marry me to save her honor. I shall stay here until everything is righted."

At this moment, a shuffling and scraping were heard in the corridor; the door was thrown open, and Hermengilda, whom the gardener had found senseless in the pavilion, was brought into the room and laid on the sofa. Before the Princess could prevent it, Xaver stepped up to Hermengilda and seized her hand. Then she leaped up with a horrible cry, not human in sound, no, like the piercing wail of some beast in the jungle, and stared at him with eyes that seemed to blaze out of the depths of some terrible trance.

Xaver reeled away from her as if stricken, and stammered scarcely intelligibly: "Horses!" At a sign from the Princess, he was led downstairs: "Wine—Wine!" he cried, and gulped down glass after glass until his carriage was brought round; then, somewhat refreshed, he strode out of the house and drove off.

Hermengilda's condition, which seemed on the verge of passing from deep delirium to wild insanity, affected the attitude of even Nepomuk and the Prince, who first realized now the terrible, inexpiable aspect of Xaver's behavior. They wanted to send for a physician, but the Princess objected to all medical assistance where spiritual consolation could be the only possible cure. So instead of the physician, a Carmelite monk, Cyprianus, the father-confessor of the house, was brought in. He succeeded marvelously in arousing Hermengilda out of her stark, staring madness. More than that—she soon became calm and self-controlled. She spoke quite coherently to the Princess, to whom she expressed her wish to pass her life, after her confinement, in the Cistercian convent at O—, where she could devote herself to constant penitence and mourning.

Father Cyprianus left the castle to make his own arrangements, and returned in several days. In the meanwhile, Prince Z— had written to the burgomaster at L—; Hermengilda was to be brought there, to await her confinement, by the abbess of the Cistercian convent, a relative of the house, while the Princess was to travel to Italy and ostensibly take Hermengilda with her.

It was midnight; the carriage which was to take Hermengilda to the convent stood waiting at the door. Nepomuk, bowed with grief, the Prince, the Princess, were waiting for the unhappy child to bid her farewell. Wrapped in her veils, leaning on the monk's arm, she came into the brightly candle-lighted room. Cyprianus spoke out solemnly: "The lay sister Celestina sinned grievously while she was still in the world, for the evil of Satan stained her pure soul; but an unalterable vow shall bring her solace—peace and eternal salvation. The world shall never again look upon the face whose beauty lured the Devil to sin. See! It is thus that Celestina begins, and will end, her atonement!" The monk raised Hermengilda's veils and revealed the pale, corpselike mask in which the angelic beauty of Hermengilda's face was forever encased. The parting took place in tragic silence; Hermengilda found herself incapable of uttering a word, while her family struggled to control their grief until they saw the carriage roll off, like a hearse, into the distance.

It is not clear how Count Xaver discovered the place of Hermengilda's retreat, and learned that the child was to be consecrated to the Church. His theft of the infant was of little avail, for when he reached P—, where he intended to place the boy in the care of a trusted old nurse, he found that the child was not, as he assumed, unconscious from the cold, but dead. After that Count Xaver disappeared without a trace, and it was said that he had taken his life.

Several years after all this had taken place, the young Prince Boleslaw von Z—, journeying to Naples, arrived in the vicinity of Posilippo. There, in that most charming landscape, lies a Camaldolite cloister; the Prince climbed uphill to reach it in order to enjoy a view which had been described to him as the handsomest in all Naples. He was about to step out on a projecting crag in the garden which he had been informed was the most advantageous point of outlook, when he noticed a monk who had sat down on a large rock in front of him, and was staring out, over an open prayerbook, into the distance. His face, although youthful in its features, seemed, none the less, aged, as though by great sorrow. As he watched the monk more closely, a vague recollection seemed to stir in the Prince's mind. He softly crept nearer and his eye was immediately caught by the prayerbook which was printed in Polish. He consequently proceeded to address the monk in that language; the monk turned round in fright, but the moment he saw the Prince, he veiled his face and swiftly made off through the bushes as if pursued by an evil spirit. Prince Boleslaw, relating this adventure to Count Nepomuk, assured him that the monk was none other than Count Xaver von R—.

THE FERMATA

On the Significance of an Interrupted Cadence

HUMMEL'S AMUSING AND VIVACIOUS PIC-
ture, "Company in an Italian Inn," won
immediate renown when it was shown in
the autumn of 1814 at the Art Exhibition
in Berlin, where it delighted everyone
who looked at it. Under an arbor almost
hidden in foliage, the painting shows a
table well furbished with wine flasks and
fruit, and seated facing each other on
the opposite sides two Italian ladies, one
singing, the other playing a guitar; standing somewhat in the background between
them, an abbot acts as music director. With baton raised, he is awaiting
the moment when the Signora, with a long trill, shall end the cadence
in the midst of which—as her eyes are directed towards Heaven—the artist
has just caught her; looking at the picture, one knows that the abbot's
hand will then descend sharply, while the guitarist gaily dashes off the
dominant chord. The abbot is filled with admiration—indeed, with exquisite delight; yet his attention, at the same time, is tautly concentrated.
It is plain that not for the world would he miss the proper downward
beat. He hardly dares to breathe. If he could, he would stop every bee's
buzzing, the movement of every fly. So much the more, then, is he irri-
tated by the bustling intrusion of the host, who must needs choose just
this decisive and supreme moment to come in with the wine! Beyond the

arbor, one can see a tree-arched avenue, where a horseman has just pulled up for a refreshing drink, which is at this moment being handed up to him, so that he can enjoy it without dismounting.

"The more I look at this singer," said Edward, "who, it is true, seems a bit old for her gay costume but, none the less, is obviously fired with the true inspiration of her art; the more I am delighted by the grave but truly Roman profile and lovely form of the guitarist, and the more amused I become by the earnest mien of my estimable friend the abbot, the more the whole painting seems to me instinct with the freedom and vitality of actual life. It is plainly a caricature, in the higher sense of that term; but it also suggests a certain charm and joy. I should like to step into that arbor and open one of those little wine bottles that are tempting me on the table. I tell you more—I fancy that I can already catch something of the bouquet of that rare vintage! And I feel—come, now, it would be a sin if this cheerful solicitation were wasted on the cold, insensitive atmosphere that surrounds us here! Let us go and drain a flask of Italian wine in honor of this fine picture, in honor of art, and in honor of merry Italy, where life is exhilarating and pleasure is given its due!"

While Edward was thus running on in lively—if somewhat disconnected—sentences, Theodore stood silent, deeply absorbed in his own sober reflection. "Yes, that is what we will do. Come along," he said at last, starting up as if he were waking from a dream. It was plain, nevertheless, that he had some difficulty in tearing himself away from the picture. And as, almost mechanically, he followed his friend, he had to stop at the door, and turn around for another lingering and longing look at the singer and the guitarist, and the abbot who was directing their performance. . . .

Edward's proposal, however, was very easy to execute! The friends crossed the street diagonally, and very soon they were seated in the little blue room of the Sala Tarone, before a flask of wine which was the very image of those in the painting they had just left.

"It seems to me," said Edward—as Theodore remained thoughtful and silent, even after several glasses of wine—"it seems to me that you are more deeply impressed by that painting than I am; and that your impression is not so agreeable as mine."

Theodore still did not break his silence for a moment. "I assure you that I did not lose anything of the brightness and grace of that animated composition," he said at last. "And yet," he added, slowly, "it is very strange: that picture is a true and accurate representation of a scene out of my own life. The faithful portraits of the individuals concerned are nothing short of startling. And you will agree with me that such swift memories themselves, unexpectedly and extraordinarily brought to life as if by the stroke of a magician's wand, must exert a sudden and remarkable power over the mind. That is how it stands with me at this moment."

"What!" exclaimed Edward, in astonishment. "A scene out of your own life? Do you mean to say that the picture represents an episode which you have actually seen and can actually remember? I saw at once that the two ladies and the priest were eminently successful pieces of portraiture; but I could never for one moment have dreamed that you had met them in the flesh, in the course of your own personal experience! My dear friend, do tell me about it! We are entirely alone here. Nobody else will come into the café at this hour. Tell me what happened, who they are, how it all came about."

"I will gladly do that," Theodore responded. "But I must go a long way back. You must bear with me if I carry you back to my childhood!"

"Never mind that! Go ahead!" rejoined Edward. "As a matter of fact, I don't know as much as I'd like to about your early youth. And if the story lasts a long time, the worst that can happen is that we shall have to empty a bottle more than we'd bargained for. To that, I know, nobody will have any objections: neither ourselves nor Signor Tarone."

Thus encouraged, Theodore embarked upon his recital. "It can surprise nobody," he began, "that in planning my future I threw everything else aside and devoted myself entirely to the noble art of music. For even as a little boy I would rather play the piano than do anything else; and I spent hours and hours strumming upon my uncle's creaking, jarring, tuneless old instrument. The little town where I lived was badly off for music: there was nobody who could teach an aspiring student except one opinionated old organist, who made a religion of tempo and plagued me almost to death with obscure and unmelodious toccatas and fugues. I would not let myself be daunted, however; I held on like grim death. In fact, although the old fellow was crabbed and faultfinding, he was in his own way something of a master: he had only to play a good piece in his own powerful style, to reconcile me to the man and his art.

"It thus happened that I would often be thrown into a curious state of mind. Especially, many pieces by old Johann Sebastian Bach would seem to me almost like harrowing ghost stories, and I would give myself up to that mood of pleasurable awe to which we are so prone in the days of our fantastic youth. But I entered within the gates of a real Eden when, as sometimes happened in winter, the town bandmaster and his colleagues, supported by a few amateurs of moderate ability, would give a concert, and I would be permitted to play the kettledrum in the symphony. It was not until long afterwards that I realized how extravagant—indeed, how ridiculous—these concerts were. My teacher usually played two piano concerti by Wolff or Karl Philipp Emanuel Bach, a member of the town band would be struggling with Stamitz, while the local tax collector worked away at the flute with unbounded energy, and took in such an immense supply of breath that he blew out both the candles on his music stand, and someone always had to relight them for him.

"As for singing, that wasn't given much attention among us. My uncle, who was a friend of the arts and a great patron of music, always disparaged local talent along this line. His mind still dwelt with exuberant delight upon those days, now long gone by, when the four choristers of the town's four churches would join forces in a performance of *Lottchen am Hofe*. Above all, he was wont, in this connection, to extol the mutual tolerance which united the singers in this work of art—for, you understand, not only were the Catholic and the Evangelical bodies separate and hostile, but the Reformed Community was itself split in two sections: those who spoke German and those who spoke French. The French chorister was not daunted by the *Lottchen*, but, my uncle maintained, sang his part, spectacles on nose, in the finest falsetto that ever proceeded from the human throat!

"Now there was among us at this time—I mean in our town—a spinster named Meibel, whose age was about fifty-five years, and whose only means of livelihood was the scanty pension which she received as a former court singer at the Residenz. And my uncle was rightly of the opinion that Miss Meibel might still do something to earn money in the concert hall. She assumed airs of importance when she was approached on this question, and she required a great deal of coaxing; but at last she consented to appear on our stage, and so we came to have *aria di bravura* at our concerts. She was a singular creature, this Miss Meibel. I still retain the lively recollection of her thin little figure, as, dressed in a parti-colored gown, holding her roll of music in her hand, and looking inexpressibly solemn, she was wont to step to the front of the stage and acknowledge the presence of the audience with a slight inclination of the upper part of her body. Her headdress, especially, was remarkable: I remember that it had a bouquet of china flowers fastened in front, and as she sang these would keep up a continual trembling and nodding, distracting to see. At the end of her song, when the audience had greeted her with unstinted applause, she would first hand her music roll, somewhat haughtily, to my uncle, and would then permit him to dip his thumb and finger into a little porcelain snuffbox, fashioned in the shape of a pug dog, out of which she took a pinch herself with obvious pleasure.

"You will better understand my telling you that we did not pay much attention to singing, when I add that this prima donna of our concert stage had a horrible squeaky voice, with which she indulged in all sorts of ludicrous flourishes and roulades. And you can imagine the effect of all this—combined with her ridiculous manners and style of dress—upon a sensitive music-loving lad like myself. My uncle lost no opportunity to shower praise upon Miss Meibel's performance. And I, who could not understand this at all, turned naturally to my organist; he looked with contempt upon vocal efforts in general, and he delighted me down to the ground by parodying the absurd old spinster's antics, with a certain hypochondriac malice which I found irresistibly amusing.

"The more emphatically I came to share my master's scorn for singing, the higher he rated my musical abilities. He took a great and zealous interest in instructing me in counterpoint, so that I was soon composing the most ingenious toccatas and fugues. And it happened that on my nineteenth birthday I was entertaining my uncle with one of these adroit specimens of my skill, when the head porter of our town's leading hotel stepped into the room to announce the visit of two foreign ladies who had just arrived at his establishment.

"Before my uncle could throw off his dressing gown—its material was of a large flower pattern—and don his coat and waistcoat, his callers entered the room. You know what an electrifying effect every unusual event has upon almost any individual brought up in the narrow confines of a small country town; this sudden encounter was, pre-eminently, of a sort to work a complete revolution in my mind. Picture to yourself two tall and slender Italian ladies, dressed in bright-colored costumes which seemed fantastic to me (though as a matter of fact they were of the latest mode), who approached my uncle with the freedom of professional *artistes*, yet with considerable charm of manner, and addressed him in firm and resonant tones. What the deuce, I asked myself, was that strange language they were speaking? Only now and then was there a sound which bore the slightest resemblance to German. And it was plain that my uncle didn't understand a word. Embarrassed, incapable of intelligible human utterance, he stepped back and pointed to the sofa. The two ladies sat down and talked together—and their voices were like music itself. At length they succeeded in making my good uncle understand that they were singers on tour. They wished to give a concert in our town, and so they had come to him, as the proper man with whom to conduct musical negotiations.

"As they were talking together I picked up their Christian names; and soon I was able to distinguish one from the other. In the confusion of their first overwhelming appearance that had been impossible! Now I noticed that Lauretta, apparently the older of the two, looked about her with sparkling eyes, and talked away at my embarrassed old uncle with an effervescent vivacity which had its natural accompaniment in demonstrative gestures. Teresina, taller, more slender, and with a much more serious face, spoke very little; but what she said was intelligible. Now and then a rather peculiar smile flitted across her face. It almost seemed as if she were amused by my respected uncle, who had withdrawn into his gay silk dressing gown like a snail into its shell, and was desperately preoccupied with the vain effort to push a treacherous yellow string out of sight within its folds: it was the cord of his nightshirt, and it kept falling out from under his dressing gown, apparently yards and yards long.

"At length the ladies rose to take their leave. My uncle promised to make all arrangements for their concert to be given on the third day following. Then the sisters (we knew now that they were sisters) gave him, and me, a most courteous invitation to take chocolate with them in the afternoon. My uncle, in the meantime, had introduced me as a young musician, which naturally pleased me very much.

"That afternoon, then, we went to the hotel restaurant—but I must confess that we made our way up the steps with a solemn and awkward gait. We both felt odd and out-of-place, as if we were going to meet some adventure to which we were not equal. As a result of careful preparation for the occasion, my uncle had at his tongue's end a great many fine things to say about art, which nobody understood—neither he himself nor any of the rest of us. When these impressive pronouncements had been made (and when I, smiling through my pain with the stoical fortitude of a Scaevola, had thrice burned my tongue with the scalding hot chocolate), Lauretta said that she would sing for us. Teresina took up her guitar, tuned it, and struck a few full chords. It was the first time I had ever heard that instrument, and the characteristic mysterious sounds of the trembling strings made a deep and remarkable impression upon me.

"Lauretta began to sing very softly; but soon she held a note to *fortissimo*, and then quickly broke into a crisp and complicated run through an octave and a half. I can still remember the words with which her song began: '*Sento l'amica speme.*' My heart was as if gripped—and even oppressed—by wonder. I had never had an idea of anything of this kind! But as Lauretta's voice continued to soar, in bolder and higher flights, and as the musical notes fell upon me like the sun's sparkling rays, I was roused from any sense of oppression to, indeed, its liveliest opposite. I felt that all the music within my own spirit, which had lain mute and sleeping all my life, had now been awakened and enkindled, so that it could burst forth in strong and splendid flame. Ah, I had never before heard music; in all my nineteen years, I had never known what music was. . . .

"After this, the sisters sang one of those great imposing duets of Abbot Steffani, which confine themselves to notes of low register. My whole soul was stirred by Teresina's alto, sonorous and pure as silver bells. I couldn't for the life of me restrain my emotion; tears started to my eyes. My uncle coughed warningly and cast indignant glances in my direction, but it was no use: I was really quite beside myself. This seemed to please the sisters. They began to inquire into the nature and extent of my musical studies. I was ashamed, now, of my labors and performances in that line;

and with the hardihood born of enthusiastic admiration I bluntly declared aloud what I had already said to myself—that I had today heard music for the first time in my life. . . .

" 'The dear, good boy!' lisped Lauretta, so sweetly and bewitchingly that my head was more than ever in a whirl.

"When I reached home, I was seized with a sort of fury. I pounced upon all the clever toccatas and fugues that I had hammered out, and threw them in the fire; and not only my own compositions, but with them a beautiful copy of forty-five variations on a canonical theme which the organist had written and had done me the honor of presenting to me. And as the double counterpoint smoked and crackled in the flames I laughed with spiteful glee. Then I sat down at the piano, and tried first to imitate the tones of the guitar, then to play the sisters' melodies; I climaxed my efforts by attempting to sing them. My uncle put an end to this at last, about midnight, when he came out of his bedroom and called to me, 'My boy, you'd better just stop that screeching and troop off to bed!' Then he put out both candles, and went back to his own room.

"I had no alternative but to obey. But the mysterious power of song came to me in my dreams—at least I thought it did—and I sang 'Sento l'amica speme' in excellent style!

"The next morning my uncle hunted up everybody who could fiddle and blow, and gathered them together for the rehearsal. He was filled with pride over the idea of showing the visiting *artistes* what good musicians our town possessed; but everything seemed, in stubborn perversity, to go wrong. Lauretta set to work on a fine *scena*, but very soon the orchestra was all at sixes and sevens in the recitative: not one of the players had any idea of the accompaniment. Lauretta screamed, raved, wept with impatience and anger. She poured the bitterest reproaches upon the organist, who was presiding at the piano; silent and obdurate, he got up and marched out of the hall. The orchestra leader (our town bandmaster), whom she had just been railing at as an '*assino tedesco*,' tucked his violin under his arm, slammed his hat down on his head with an air of defiance, and likewise made for the door. The members of his company, respectively sticking their bows under the strings of their violins and unscrewing the mouthpieces of their brass instruments, followed him.

"Only the dilettanti were left in the hall; and they gazed about them disconsolately, while the local tax collector expressed the feelings of them all as he exclaimed, with an air of overwhelming tragedy, 'Gracious Heaven! How mortifying I find all this!'

"All my natural diffidence vanished. I could not let our great occasion fail this way! I could not let this promise of real music go unfulfilled! I jumped right in front of the orchestra leader: I begged, I pleaded, in my desperation I promised him six new minuets with double trios for the town's annual ball! And so I succeeded in appeasing him. He went back to his place; his companions followed suit; and soon the orchestra was reconstituted, with the single exception of the organist, who was already outside the building and crossing the market place, and could not be moved, by any shouting or beckoning, to turn back.

"Teresina had looked on at this whole scene with smothered laughter. And Lauretta was now as full of merriment and delight as she had been, a few moments before, of anger. She was lavish in her praise of my efforts; and, since we had now no one at the piano, she asked me if I could play that instrument. Before I knew what I was about, I was sitting in the organist's place, with the music before me. Never in my life had I accompanied a singer, to say nothing of assisting in the direction of an orchestra! But the sisters were kindness itself. Teresina sat down beside me at the piano, and gave me every beat. Lauretta encouraged me with repeated 'Bravos!' The orchestra proved to be co-operative. And things continued to improve. At the second rehearsal everything went off satisfactorily. And when the townspeople crowded the hall for the great concert, the effect of the sisters' singing was something not to be described.

"The Prince's return to the Residenz was soon to be celebrated with a number of festive demonstrations in the capital, and the sisters had been summoned to sing in the theatre and at concerts then. But until the time came for these command performances they decided to remain in our little town, and so it happened that they gave us several more concerts. The admiration of the public reached the point of frenzy. But old Miss Meibel took a pinch of snuff out of her porcelain pug, and gave it as her opinion that 'such impudent caterwauling was not singing; singing,' she added, 'should be low and melodious.' And my old friend the organist never showed himself once, either among the musicians or in the audience.

"But, to tell the truth, I did not miss him! I was the happiest fellow in the world. I spent all of every day with the sisters, copying out the vocal scores of what they were to sing at the capital. Lauretta was my ideal. I endured with patience her unpredictable—not to say outrageous—caprices, her outbursts of passionate violence, the torments she inflicted upon me as her pianist. What did all that matter? She alone had unsealed for me the springs of true music. . . . I began to study Italian, and I tried my hand at a few canzonets. And in what heavenly rapture was I plunged when Lauretta sang one of my compositions, or even praised it! Often it seemed to me that it was not I who had thought out and set to music what she was singing, but that the creative impulse itself only shone forth for the first time as she sang.

"With Teresina, on the other hand, I somehow could not get on familiar terms. She seldom sang. And she did not seem to take much account of all I was doing. Sometimes I even imagined that she was laughing at me behind my back.

"It was indeed different with Lauretta; and when the time came for them to leave the town, I realized for the first time how dear she was to me, and how unendurable it would be to be separated from her. Often, when she was in a mood of tender playfulness, she had touched my cheek, or stroked my head, in a fashion that was none the less caressing because it was also completely artless. And at such times only the realization of her ordinary coolness towards me would restrain my ardent impulse to clasp her in my arms. But now, as I was about to lose her forever, my passion was heightened by despair.

"I possessed a tolerably good tenor voice, which, however, I had never tried to cultivate. Under the spur of my association with the sisters I began to practice assiduously; and frequently Lauretta and I would sing some tender Italian duet (you know them—there are so many!) together. Now it happened that as the hour of departure was drawing near we were singing one of these pieces: *'Senza di te ben mio, vivere non poss' io!'* (Without thee, my own, I cannot live!) And—can you blame me that I could not resist it? In desperation I threw myself at Lauretta's feet. And she gently pulled me up again.

"'But, my friend,' she said, in tones that moved me through and through, 'need we part?'

"And as I stood there, thunderstruck with amazement, she quietly proposed that I should accompany Teresina and herself to the capital. If I intended to devote myself wholly to music, she continued, I must certainly leave this wretched little town sometime or other. What time could be better than now?

"My friend, can you picture to yourself a man struggling in the dark depths of boundless despair, a man who has given up all hope of happiness and fulfillment in this life, and who now—in the very moment when he awaits the blow that is to crush him forever—suddenly finds himself transported to some gloriously bright rose arbor, where unseen but loving spirits whisper to him, 'You are still alive, and we cherish you—you are still alive!'? I repeat—can you imagine this, my good friend? If so, you will know how I felt at this moment. To go along with Lauretta and Teresina to the capital! The dream came to life as an ineradicable resolution. . . .

"But I won't bore you now with the recital of all the details of my procedure: how I set to work to convince my uncle that I ought by all means to go, and now, to the capital—which, as a matter of fact, was not very far away. At length he gave his consent. And, furthermore, he announced his intention of going with me. I did not dare to state my purpose of traveling in company with the two sisters. Again, I was distracted. But at just the right moment my uncle caught a violent cold; he had to stay at home, and I was free!

"I left the town by the stagecoach, but I went only as far as the first stopping place. There I awaited my divinity. My purse, happily, was well-lined. I had thus been able to make all proper preparations for my journey. And I had been seized with the romantic notion of accompanying the ladies in the character of a protecting paladin, and as such a knight should —on horseback. I procured a horse, which its owner assured me was quiet and docile—though I must admit it was not romantically handsome— and I rode back at the appointed time to meet the two fair singers. I soon saw their little carriage coming towards me. It had two seats: Lauretta and Teresina occupied the principal one, while on the other, with her back to the horses, sat their maid, the fat and brown-cheeked little Neapolitan Gianna. In addition, the carriage was packed with boxes, satchels, and baskets, of all shapes and sizes, such as always accompany ladies on their travels. And there were also two pug dogs, which Gianna was holding in her lap, and which began to bark when I gaily saluted the company.

"All had gone very well, and we were completing the last section of the journey, when my steed all at once conceived the idea that it was high time to be returning homeward. Being aware that stern measures were not always blessed with a high degree of success, in such cases, I felt advised to have recourse to milder means of persuasion; but the obstinate brute remained insensible to all my well-meant exhortations. I wanted to go forward. He wanted to go backward. And all the advantage that my efforts gave me was that, instead of taking to his heels for home, he ran around in circles. Teresina leaned out of the carriage and had a hearty laugh. Lauretta held her hands before her face and screamed as if my life were in danger.

"Together, these responses served to give me the courage of despair. I drove the spurs into the brute's ribs. But the result was not what I had hoped for. I was abruptly hurled from his back, and found myself sprawling on the ground. The horse, now, stood perfectly still; and, stretching out his long neck, he regarded me with what I could only take to be a look of derision. I, alas, was unable to rise to my feet: the driver of the carriage had to come and help me. Lauretta, meanwhile, had jumped out, and was weeping and lamenting. Teresina did nothing but laugh. As for me, I had sprained my ankle in my fall: it was impossible for me to mount the horse and ride again. What was I to do? Well, my erstwhile steed was tied to the carriage, while I, perforce, got into it. . . .

"So now, my friend, you can imagine us all—two rather robust young women, a fat servant girl, two pug dogs, a dozen boxes, satchels, and baskets, and myself as well, all packed into a small vehicle. Imagine Lauretta's complaints over her lack of comfort, crowded in as she was; the maid's witless Neapolitan chattering, the yapping of the dogs, Teresina's sulky silence, and the inexpressible pain I had now begun to feel in my foot, and you will have some idea of my enviable situation!

"Before long, Teresina declared that she could not stand it any longer. The driver stopped the carriage. In a trice she was out on the road, had untied my horse, and was up in the saddle, prancing and curvetting around us. I must indeed admit that she cut a fine figure. The dignity and carriage which marked her ordinary bearing were still more pronounced when she was on horseback. In a few moments she asked for her guitar, and, dropping the reins on her arm, she began to sing proud Spanish ballads with a full-toned accompaniment. Her thin silk dress fluttered in the wind, and light played in sparkling sheen upon its folds, while the white feathers of her hat waved and quivered as if in accompaniment to the air she sang. Altogether, she made such a romantic picture that I could not take my eyes off her, even though Lauretta was scolding her for making herself look like a fantastic simpleton, and was predicting that she would suffer for her senseless daring.

"But no accident occurred. Either the horse had lost his stubbornness, or else he preferred the fair singer to the would-be-paladin. Be that as it may, Teresina did not dismount from the horse and re-enter the carriage until we were almost at the city gates.

"If you had seen me then at concerts and operas, if you had observed my joyous concentration on music of all sorts, if you had heard me as a diligent accompanist at work at the piano on arias, duets, and I don't know what besides—if you had been a witness of all this, my friend, you would have realized, by the complete change in my behavior, that my being itself had been completely changed. Indeed, there was a new and rich spirit within me. I had conquered, cast off, forgotten, all my rustic shyness; and now I sat at the piano with my score before me like an experienced professional, directing my prima donna's performance. My mind was filled with happy melodies. And it was with a reckless disregard of all those laboriously studied rules of counterpoint that I composed for Lauretta a vast variety of canzonets and arias.

"She sang them all: but only in her own room. Why would she never sing any of my pieces at a concert? I could not understand it. And, while Lauretta continued to inspire me, the eyes of my imagination would suddenly be filled also with the sight of Teresina curvetting on her proud steed, with her lute in her hands, like the figure of Art itself in some romantic disguise. Without consciously thinking of Teresina, without having any aim in view, I wrote several songs of a high and serious nature. And something of the difference between the two sisters permeated my mind, although at the time I scarcely realized it. Lauretta played with her notes like some capricious fairy queen, forever regal and forever blessed: there was nothing upon which she ventured that was not crowned with success. But never did a roulade cross Teresina's lips. Nothing more than a simple interpolated note, at most a *mordent*, sounded from her throat when the sisters sang together. Yet her long-sustained notes gleamed like meteors through the darkness of night, and awakened strange spirits who came and gazed with earnest eyes into the very depths of my heart. I do not know, now as I look back upon it, how I remained in ignorance so long!

"The sisters were granted a benefit concert, and in it I joined with Lauretta in a long *scena* from *Anfossi*. As usual, I presided at the piano. We came to the last *fermata*, and Lauretta was exerting all her skill, demonstrating all her art; she warbled trill after trill, like a nightingale; she executed sustained notes, and then long elaborate roulades—a whole *solfeggio*. In fact, I thought that this time she was almost carrying the thing too far. As I was musing to this effect, I felt a soft breath on my cheek: Teresina stood behind me. And at this moment Lauretta took a good start with the intention of swelling up to a 'harmonic shake,' and so passing back into *a tempo*. The Devil entered into me: I jammed down the keys with both hands; the orchestra followed suit; and it was all over with Lauretta's trill, just at the supreme moment when she was to sweep her audience to the highest pitch of astonishment.

"She turned to me with such a look of fury that I felt almost annihilated, crushed her roll of music in her hand, and threw it at my head; then she rushed, as if smitten by madness, through the orchestra, and into the off-stage waiting room. As soon as we had played through the piece, I followed her.

"She wept and raved. 'Out of my sight, you blackguard!' she screamed, as soon as she saw me. 'You devil, you've completely ruined me! Ruined my reputation, my honor—and my trill. Out of my sight, you devil's brood!'

"She made a rush as if to attack me physically, but I escaped through the door. And while someone else was performing on the stage, Teresina and the music director succeeded in so far pacifying her as to win her consent to coming out again. But she made one condition: I was not to be allowed to touch the piano.

"Then, in the last duet that the sisters sang, Lauretta did contrive to introduce the swelling 'harmonic shake,' and was rewarded with a storm of applause. Whereupon she settled down into the best of humors.

"But I could not get over the outrageous treatment which I had received at her hands in the presence of a large audience; and I made up my mind that I would leave her the next morning, and return to my native town. I was actually engaged in packing my things when Teresina came into my room. Observing what I was about, she exclaimed in astonishment, 'What! Are you going to leave us?' And I gave her to understand that after the affront which Lauretta had put upon me I could not think of remaining any longer in her society.

" 'And so,' responded Teresina, 'you are going to let yourself be driven away by the preposterous conduct of a little fool, who is now heartily sorry for what she has done? I ask you, where else than with us can you better live in your art? And let me tell you, too, that it only depends on yourself and your behavior, to keep her from such pranks as this. You are too pliable, too soft, too gentle. What is more, you rate her powers too highly. It is true that her voice is not bad, and it has a wide range. But those fantastic warblings and flourishes, those extravagant runs, those never-ending shakes—what are they but delusive artifices of style, which people admire in the same way that they admire the fool-hardy agility of a tightrope walker? Do you really think that such things as that can make any deep impression, that they can stir the heart? The "harmonic shake" which you spoiled,' she continued with emphasis, 'is a thing I cannot tolerate. When she attempts it, I always feel anxious and pained. And then this scaling up into the region of the third line above the stave—what is that but a violent straining of the natural voice? And the natural voice, after all, dear friend, is the only thing that really moves the heart. . . . I like the middle notes and the low notes; a sound that goes through to the heart, a quiet and easy transition from note to note—those are the things I love above all. No useless ornamentation; a firm, clear, strong note; a definite expression, which reaches and transports the mind and the soul—that's real, true singing, and that's how I sing.

" 'If you can't be reconciled to Lauretta,' she added, a little wist-fully, 'then think of Teresina, who indeed likes you so much that you shall, in your own way, be her musical composer. Don't be cross—but all your elegant canzonets and arias cannot match this single piece. . . .

And in her lovely, resonant voice she sang a simple devotion canzona which I had written a few days before.

"I had never dreamed that it could sound like that. I felt the power of the music going through and through me. Tears of joy and rapture stood in my eyes. I grasped Teresina's hand, and as I pressed it to my lips I swore, over and over and over again, that I would never leave her.

"Lauretta showed a certain envious attitude towards my intimacy with her sister, but she suppressed any obvious sign of vexation; for the fact was, as I soon realized, that she could not do without me. In spite of her skill in singing, she read badly, and she was uncertain in time and beat. Teresina, on the contrary, sang everything at sight, and her ear for time was perfect in its accuracy. Never did Lauretta give such free rein to her capricious and violent temper as when her accompaniments were being practiced: they were never right; they were nothing but a necessary evil anyway; the piano ought not to be heard at all; it must always be *pianissimo*. So there was nothing to do but give way to her again and again, and alter the time just as the whim happened to strike her at the moment. Now, however, I took a firm stand against her. I combatted her impertinences. I taught her that an accompaniment devoid of energy was nothing short of inconceivable, and that there was a marked difference between supporting the song—carrying it along—and letting it run riot, without time and without form. Teresina faithfully lent her assistance in all this. And now I composed nothing but church pieces, and wrote all the solos for a voice of low register. It is true that Teresina also tyrannized over me not a little, but I submitted to her despotism with a good grace. She had, I assured myself, more knowledge of good German seriousness, and (so at least I thought) deeper appreciation of it, than her sister could possess.

"When we were touring in south Germany, some time after the incident I have just recalled, we met, in a little town, an Italian tenor who was making his way from Milan to Berlin. My fair companions were delighted with their fellow countryman. And he, for his part, attached himself closely to them, and cultivated Teresina's acquaintance, especially, with such eagerness and success that to my great vexation I soon came to feel that my rôle among them was only secondary. At last affairs came to a sudden climax. One day, as I was about to enter the sisters' sitting room with a roll of music under my arm, the voices of my companions and the tenor, engaged in an animated conversation, fell upon my ear. My name was mentioned. I pricked up my ears. Unashamed, I listened. Lauretta was telling the whole tragic story of the concert in which I had cut short her trill by prematurely striking the concluding notes of the bar. '*Assino tedesco!*' the tenor exclaimed.

"I felt as if I must rush into the room and throw the flighty hero out of the window; but I restrained myself. I continued to listen, however. And I heard Lauretta go on to say that she had been minded to send me about my business immediately, but had been so moved to compassion by my clamorous entreaties as to tolerate me for some time longer, since I was studying singing under her. This, to my utter amazement, Teresina confirmed.

" 'Yes, he's a good child,' I heard the latter add. 'He's in love with me now, and he sets everything for the alto. He is not without talent, but he must rub off that stiffness and awkwardness which are so characteristic of the Germans. I hope to make a capable composer out of him. Then he shall write me some good things—for as yet there is very little written for the alto voice—and after that I shall let him go his way. He's a terrible bore,' she went on, 'with his billing and cooing and lovesick sighing; and he bothers me much too much with his tedious compositions, which so far have been poor stuff.'

" 'I at least got rid of him,' Lauretta interrupted. 'And you know, Teresina, how the fellow pestered me with his arias and duets.'

"And now she began to sing a duet of my composing, which formerly she had praised very highly. The other sister took up the second voice; and both in tone and in execution they burlesqued me in the most shameful manner. The tenor laughed until the walls rang with the echo of his mirth. My limbs seemed frozen. But at once I came to an irrevocable decision. I quietly slipped away from the door and back to my own room, the windows of which looked out upon a side street. Opposite was the post office. The post-coach for Bamberg had just driven up to take on the mails and passengers. The latter were standing ready waiting in the gateway, but I still had an hour to spare. . . .

"Hastily packing my things, I generously paid the whole of the bill at the hotel, and hurried over to catch the post-chaise. As I crossed the broad street I saw the fair sisters and the Italian standing at the window, and leaning out to hear the sound of the post-horn. I leaned back in the corner of the chaise, and dwelt with a good deal of satisfaction upon the crushing effect of the bitter and scathing letter which I had left behind for Lauretta and Teresina at the hotel."

With evident gratification, Theodore tossed off the rest of the fiery Aleatico which Edward had poured into his glass. The latter, opening a new bottle and skilfully shaking off the drops of oil which floated on top of the wine, remarked, "I should not have dreamed Teresina capable of such artfulness and falsity. I cannot banish from my mind the recollection of the charming picture she made—on your mind and through you on mine—as she sat singing Spanish ballads on horseback, while the steed gracefully pranced and curvetted along the road."

"That was her climactic point," Theodore interrupted. "I still remember the strange impression which the scene made upon me. I forgot my pain. She seemed to me like a creature of some higher race. It is indeed true that such moments are turning points in one's life, and that in them images arise which time is powerless to dim. Whenever I have succeeded in any fine *romanza*, it has always been when Teresina's image has stepped forth from the treasure house of memory, in clear bright colors, at the moment of writing it."

"At the same time," said Edward, "let us not forget the artistic, and 'temperamental,' Lauretta. And, casting all rancor to the winds, let us drink to the health of the two sisters."

They did so. And as he raised his glass Theodore exclaimed, "Oh, how the fragrant breezes of Italy rise from this wine and fan my cheeks! My blood courses through my veins with quickened energy. Oh, why was I obliged so soon to leave that glorious land?"

"As yet," interrupted Edward, "as yet, in all that you have told me, there has been no connection, so far as I can see, with the delightful painting we were looking at. And so I believe that you still have something to tell me about these two sisters. Of course I perceive that the two ladies in the picture are none other than Lauretta and Teresina—but come, you must have something more to say."

"You are right," replied Theodore. "They are Lauretta and Teresina;

and I still have something more to say, to which my sighs and ejaculations, my longing for the lovely land of Italy, will form a fitting introduction. . . .

"A short time ago," he now plunged again into his narrative, "perhaps two years since, as I was about to leave Rome, I made a little excursion on horseback. Before a village inn, as I went riding along, I saw a charming young girl; and the thought came to me, how pleasant it would be to receive a glass of wine from the hands of that pretty child. I pulled up before the door, in an avenue so thickly planted with shrubs that only patches of sunlight could make their way through the leaves. In the distance I heard sounds of singing, and the tinkling of a guitar. And I pricked up my ears and listened, as I became conscious that the two female voices were affecting me in quite a singular way.

"Strange recollections were stirring dimly in my mind, but they refused to take definite shape. By this time, however, I was so interested that I got down from my horse, and slowly approached the vine-covered arbor from which the music seemed to proceed—eagerly listening, meanwhile, to catch every sound. The second voice had fallen silent. The first sang a canzonet alone. As I drew nearer, the sense of familiarity faded; the initial attraction ceased to beckon me; but I was still interested. The singer was now in the midst of an elaborate and florid *fermata*. Up and down she warbled, and down and up; at length, holding one note for a long time, she stopped. Then all at once a woman's voice broke out in a torrent of abuse, maledictions, vituperations, curses. A man protested. Another man laughed. The second female voice joined in the altercation. The quarrel waxed louder and more violent, with true Italian fury. At last I stood directly in front of the arbor, and an abbot rushed out and almost knocked me down. As he turned his head to look at me, I recognized my good friend Signor Lodovico, my musical newsmonger from Rome."

" 'What in the name of wonder—' I exclaimed. But he interrupted me, screaming.

" 'Oh, sir, sir!' he cried. 'Save me! Protect me from this mad fury, this crocodile, this hyena, this tiger, this devil of a woman! It is true that I did what I did: I was beating time for her to Anfossi's canzonet, and I brought down my baton too soon while she was in the midst of the *fermata*. I cut short her trill. I admit it. But why did I meet her eyes, the devil-goddess! Deuce take all *fermate*, I say!'

"In a most curious state of mind, I hastened into the arbor, taking the priest back with me. And at first glance I recognized the sisters Lauretta and Teresina. The former was still shrieking and raging. Her sister was still earnestly remonstrating with her. The host of the inn, his bare arms crossed over his chest, was looking on and laughing, while a serving-girl was placing fresh flasks of wine on the table. And now my entrance still more strangely complicated the scene.

"For both sisters knew me at once. No sooner had they caught sight of me than they literally threw themselves upon me, apparently in a transport of affection. 'Ah, Signor Teodoro!' they exclaimed, and both embraced me. The quarrel of a moment before was totally forgotten.

" 'Here you have a composer,' said Lauretta to the abbot, 'who is as charming as an Italian, and as strong as a German.' Then both sisters, continually interrupting each other, began to recount the happy days we had spent together, to tell how they had discovered my musical abilities while I was still a youth, to praise my compositions, to recall our hours of practice together; never did they enjoy singing anything, they said, but what I had arranged or composed.

"Teresina at length informed me that a manager had engaged her as his first singer in tragic parts for his next music festival; but now, she said, she would give him to understand that she would sing for him only on condition that the composition of at least one tragic opera was entrusted to me. The tragic was above all others my special field, she averred, and so on, and so on.

"But now Lauretta maintained that it would be a great pity if I did not follow my bent for the light and the graceful—in a word, for opera buffa. She had been engaged as prima donna for this type of composition; and it was simply a matter of course—it went without saying—that no one but I should write the piece in which she was to appear. . . .

"You may imagine what my feelings were, as I stood there between the two! In short, you perceive that the company which I had just joined was the one which Hummel painted, and that the painting shows the group at precisely the moment when the priest is about to cut short Lauretta's *fermata*."

"But," Edward broke in, "did they not make any allusion to your departure, or to the scathing letter you left behind?"

"Not with so much as a syllable," Theodore answered. "And you may be very sure that I said nothing about any of that. The fact is, I had long ago banished all animosity from my heart, and had come to look upon my adventure with the two sisters in the light of a merry prank. I did, however, make one oblique reference to the subject, not addressing them, but speaking to the priest. I told him that, several years before, the same mischance had befallen me, in one of Anfossi's arias, as had been his ill luck today; I painted the period of my association with the sisters in tragicomic colors, and, throwing off many a keen side-blow, I gave them an unmistakable understanding of the superiority which the ripe experience of the intervening years had given me, both in life and in art.

" 'And a good thing it was,' I concluded, 'that I cut that *fermata* short. For it was evidently meant to last through eternity. And I am firmly of the opinion that if I had left the singer alone I should be sitting at the piano now.'

" 'But, Signor,' said the priest, 'what director is there who would dare to lay down rules for the prima donna? Your offense was much more heinous than mine, for you were in the concert hall, and I was here in a leafy arbor. Besides, I was director in imagination only; what I did was of no importance whatever. And if the sweet fiery glance of those heavenly eyes had not fascinated me, moreover, I should not have made an ass of myself.'

"The abbot's last words had a calming effect; for although Lauretta's 'heavenly eyes' had begun to flash with anger as he was speaking, she was quite appeased by the time he had finished with his pretty compliment.

"We spent the evening together. It was fourteen years since I had left my fair friends, and many changes had taken place in that time. Lauretta, though she looked somewhat older, had by no means lost her charm. Teresina had worn somewhat better, and her figure was as graceful as before. Both were dressed in rather gay colors, and their manners were exactly as I remembered them—that is, they were, let us say, fourteen years younger than the ladies themselves. At my request, Teresina sang some of the serious songs which had once so deeply affected me, but I fancied that they did not sound quite the same as when I had first heard them. And Lauretta's singing, also, seemed to me to be quite different from my recollection of it, even though her voice had not appreciably lost anything in power or range.

"The sisters' behavior to me, their feigned ecstasies, their crude praise—even though this last took the form of gracious patronage—had done much to put me in a bad humor; and now my mood deteriorated still further in the obtrusiveness of this comparison between the romantic images in my mind and the not overly pleasing reality. I was restored to a more amiable temper at last by the drolleries of the priest—who in the most saccharine phrases imaginable was playing the *amoroso* to both sisters at once—as well as by numerous glasses of the good wine. And we ended by spending a very pleasant evening in perfect concord and companionable gaiety. The sisters were most pressing in urging me to accompany them to their home, so that we might at once discuss the parts which I was to write for them and begin to make our plans without delay. But, needless to say, I did not accept their invitation. And I left Rome without making any effort to find out where they lived."

"And yet, after all," Edward reflected, "it is to them that you owe the awakening of your musical genius. . . ."

"That I know well!" Theodore replied. "I admit that I owe this to them, and many good melodies besides. And that is just the reason why I did not want to see them again. Every composer, as I said a minute ago, has experienced certain impressions which time does not obliterate. The spirit of music spoke, and the artist heard the creative word which suddenly awoke the answering spirit within himself; and that inner spirit was never to sleep again. Thus it is unquestionably true that when a melody has been called in this way from the depths of the composer's being, it seems to belong to the singer who fanned the artist's first inner spark. It is as if one heard her voice, and merely recorded what she had sung.

"But it is in the human heritage of us weak mortals," Theodore continued, "that we are all too prone to drag what is super-earthly down within the narrow enclosure of this earthly life where we, poor clods, dwell. And so it comes to pass that the singer becomes the lover, or even the wife. The spell is broken. And all that melody of her nature, which was formerly the revelation of glorious things, is now voiced in complaints about broken soup plates or the ink-stains on fresh linen. Happy is the composer who never again, as long as he lives, sets eyes upon the woman who by some mysterious power kindled the flame of music within him! Even though the young artist's heart may be rent by anguish and despair when he must part from his lovely enchantress, nevertheless it is precisely so that she will continue to exist for him as a divinely beautiful strain of music itself: it is so that she will live on and on in his heart and mind, never losing her youth or her loveliness, and forever engendering harmonies in which he forever feels the presence of his love. For what is she, now, but the Highest Ideal which, working its way from within outward, is at last reflected in external form?"

"A strange theory, but not impossible," Edward commented. And the two friends, arm in arm, made their way from the Sala Tarone, and out into the street.

BERTHOLD THE MADMAN

HUDDLED INTO A WRETCHED POST-chaise, which the moths had left from instinct—as the rats desert a sinking ship—I stopped at last at the inn in the G— market place, feeling as if half my bones had been dislocated by my breakneck journey. Every possible misfortune that might have befallen me had, it seemed, lighted upon my carriage, which now stood virtually shattered before the post-station at the last stop. After a lapse of many hours, four jaded and emaciated horses, with the help of several peasants and my own servant, had succeeded in dragging the crazy vehicle as far as this. Knowledgeable folk came by, shook their heads, and averred that thorough repairs were called for—and that these might take two, or even three, days.

As I looked about me, the place appeared fairly agreeable, the country was pretty enough; and yet I felt nothing less than appalled by this threat of delay. If, gentle reader, you were ever obliged to spend three days in a little town where you did not know a soul, but were forced to remain a stranger to every inhabitant—and if some deep sorrow had not destroyed your need for society and companionship—you will be able to appreciate my annoyance. It is in words that the meaning, the spirit of all life, here below, manifests most directly; but the denizens of your small towns are like members of some isolated orchestra, which by dint of relentless and solitary practice has worked into its own way of playing and singing, so that the tone of the stranger is discordant to their ears and at once reduces them to silence.

Having taken, perforce, a room at the inn, I was striding up and down within its four close walls, in thorough ill-humor, when it suddenly occurred to me that a friend at home, who had once spent two years in G—, had mentioned one of the local residents, a scholarly and intelligent man, with whom he had passed considerable time. His name, I recalled, was Aloysius Walter, and he was a professor at the Jesuits' College. I now resolved to look him up and turn my friend's acquaintance to my own advantage.

At the College, I was informed that Professor Walter was that very moment delivering a lecture, which would soon, however, be over; and then I was left to decide for myself whether I would come back at some later time or wait in one of the outer rooms until he should be free. I chose the latter; and I interested myself, during the necessary interval, in examining the College building.

The cloisters, colleges, and churches of the Jesuits are everywhere constructed and decorated in that Italian style which, based upon the antique form and manner, prefers elegance, and even splendor, to pious solemnity and an austerely religious dignity. In this case, the halls—themselves lofty, airy, and light—were rich in architectural embellishment, and adorned with images of the saints. These last were set against the walls, between the Ionic pillars, and were in singular contrast to the carvings over the doorways, which invariably represented either a dance of genii or arrangements of fruit and other delicacies of the table.

Soon the professor came into the hall where I was waiting, and I introduced myself by reference to my friend and claimed the hospitality of his acquaintance for the period of my forced sojourn in the town. I found him just as my neighbor had described him: clear in his discourse, familiar with the ways of the world—in short, quite the superior sort of priest, whose education has been thorough and scientific, and who, peering over the edges of his breviary into mundane human life, has often sought to know what is going on there. When he took me to his room, and I saw that it was furnished with an elegance quite in the modern taste, my mind returned to the thoughts that had occurred to me while waiting in the hall outside, and I repeated them to the professor.

"You are quite right," he said. "We have banished from all our edifices that gloomy solemnity, that alien majesty as of some oppressive tyrant, which in Gothic architecture seems to bear down upon the human spirit and gives rise to a feeling of inner discomfort; and we have very properly endowed our buildings with the ancients' lively sense not only of beauty but also of cheer."

"But," I objected, "does not the sacred dignity, that lofty majesty, which in Gothic architecture seems, as one may say, to be striving after Heaven—does not that proceed from the true spirit of Christianity? Is it not true that the spirit of Christianity, itself supersensual, is in direct opposition to that sensuous spirit of the antique world which is content to remain within the limits of the merely earthly?"

The professor smiled. "The higher kingdom should be recognized in this world," he said, "but this recognition can be awakened by cheerful symbols, such as life—even the spirit which descends from that higher kingdom into our earthly existence—presents. Our home, of a surety, is above. But while we dwell here our kingdom is of this world also."

"Exactly," thought I to myself, somewhat wryly. "In everything you have done you have indeed shown that your kingdom is of this world—indeed, of this world only." But I did not communicate my thoughts to Professor Aloysius Walter, who continued, without interruption.

"What you say of the magnificence of our buildings here in G— can only refer properly to the attractive appearance of their architectural style. Here where we cannot afford to use marble, and where the great masters of the art of painting will not work for us, we are obliged—in conformity with the modern fashion—to put up with substitutes. If we get anything as good as polished plaster we have done a great deal! And what appears to be a choice combination of different kinds of marble is often nothing more than the painter's skilful artisanship. This is the case in our church, which, thanks to the liberality of our patrons, has been newly decorated."

I naturally expressed, at this point, a desire to see the church. The professor led me downstairs. And when I entered the Corinthian colonnade which formed the nave of this place of worship I felt the pleasing—too pleasing—effect of its graceful proportions. To the left of the high altar a lofty scaffolding had been erected, and on this a man was at work repainting the walls in antique style.

"Well, Berthold, how are you getting on?" the professor called out to him.

The painter turned his head and looked at us, but immediately resumed his work. And his only answer to the visitor's greeting was an indistinct, and indeed almost inaudible, muttering: "Great lot of trouble—crooked, confused stuff—no rule to make use of—beasts—apes—human faces—human faces—miserable fool that I am!"

But the last five words were not mumbled. The man cried them aloud in a lamentation which only the deepest agony of the soul could produce; and the effect upon my own spirit was profound. The words, the tones, the expression of the painter's face as he spoke—all this, coupled with the glance he had cast at the professor when the latter addressed him, seemed to bring to my realization, to my actual senses, the whole struggling life of an unfortunate artist. The man could scarcely have been more than forty years old; his appearance, disfigured as it was by the dirty and undignified costume of a house painter, yet had something about it that was indescribably noble; and the deep grief which discolored and distorted his face could not extinguish the fire that sparkled in his black eyes. I asked the professor for some particulars about the man, and was told, in reply, that he was a "foreign artist."

"He came here just at the time when the repairs to the church had been decided upon," my host went on, "and undertook the work which we were extremely glad to offer him. Indeed, his arrival was a stroke of sheer good fortune for us, since neither in the town itself, nor anywhere in the neighborhood for miles around, could we have found a painter who was so admirably equipped to do all that we require. Besides, he is the most good-natured soul in the world, and we all love him heartily; so for that reason, too, he has got on very well here in our College. In addition to paying him good wages for his work, we board him here with us—though that, I must admit, does not lay a very heavy burden of expenditure upon us, for he is abstemious almost to excess. Of course this," the professor added, "may be due to some weakness in his constitution."

"But," said I, "he seemed so peevish just now—so irritable."

"There is a special cause for that," my host replied, and changed the subject. "But let us look at some very fine pictures, on the side altars, which by a lucky chance we obtained some time ago. There is only one famous original—a Domenichino—among them," he continued. "The rest are by unknown masters of the Italian school. But if you are free from prejudice you will be forced to confess that every one of them might bear a very celebrated name."

I found myself, when I looked at the paintings, in full agreement with the professor. Strangely enough, the "famous original" was one of the weakest—if not the very weakest—in the collection, while the beauty of much of the anonymous work was striking. But one of the altarpieces was covered up, and I asked why this was.

"That picture is the work of a young artist of our own day—certainly his last, for his flight is checked," my informant replied, somewhat enigmatically. "Just now we are obliged, for certain reasons, to keep it covered; but tomorrow, or the day after, I shall perhaps be in a position to show it to you."

I should have liked to make further inquiries, but as the professor hurried away out of the church I understood readily enough that he was unwilling to tell me anything more. We went back to the College, and I was happy to accept my host's invitation to accompany him, that afternoon, to some public gardens in the neighborhood.

It was a pleasant excursion, from which we returned home late, and I had scarcely reached the inn when rain began to pour down in torrents. About midnight, however, the sky cleared, and the thunder died away to a murmur in the distance. Through the open windows the warm air brought into my room the witching odors of the rain-soaked earth and the fresh summer night; and, tired as I was, I was irresistibly tempted to go out again for a walk . . . I succeeded in waking the surly manservant, who had been snoring for at least two hours, and in convincing him that to take a stroll at midnight was not necessarily a sign of madness; and I soon found myself in the street.

As I came to the Jesuits' church, I was surprised to see light shining through the windows; and when I drew closer and found the little side-door ajar, I made bold to go in. Before a niche in the wall a wax taper was burning, and between the light and the niche itself a net had been hung; behind this, I could see a dark figure running up and down the ladder which stood against the wall, and making lines upon the niche. It was Berthold, who was accurately tracing, with black charcoal, the shadow of the net, while on a tall easel, beside the ladder, stood the drawing of an altar. If, gentle reader, you are at all acquainted with the art of painting, you will understand, without further explanation, the use of the net, the shadow of which Berthold was sketching; and you will understand, too, why I was struck by the ingenuity of his contrivance. He was about to paint a projecting altar in the niche; and in order to make a large copy, with due correctness, of the small drawing, he was obliged to put a net—like a graph—over both the sketch itself and the surface on which the sketch was to be copied. In this instance, he had to paint on a semicircular surface instead of one which was flat; and the correspondence of the squares formed by the lines of the net, as they curved on the concave wall, with the straight lines of the sketch—together with accuracy in the architectural proportions which were to be brought forward in perspective—could not have been obtained without that simple and ingenious contrivance.

I was cautious enough not to stop in front of the candle, lest my shadow should betray me, but even so I could stand near enough to the painter to observe him closely. He appeared to me to be quite another man . . . Perhaps it was the effect of the wax taper's light, but as I saw him now his face had a good color and his eyes sparkled with inner satisfaction; and when he had finished sketching in the lines, and stopped, with his hands on his hips, to look at his work, he whistled a merry tune.

Now he turned around, and pulled down the net. And as he did so he suddenly caught sight of my figure, there beside him in the shadow.

"Hullo, hullo! Is that you, Christian?" he called out.

I went up to him at once, explained how the light had attracted me to the church, praised the cleverness of his management of the net, and introduced myself to him as a devotee of the noble art of painting. To all this, however, Berthold offered no response at all. Instead, he remarked:

"Christian is nothing more nor less than a sluggard. He was to have stayed with me faithfully through the whole night, and now he is certainly sound asleep somewhere! I must get on with my work, for probably things won't be right for my painting here on the screen tomorrow—but I can't do it alone!"

I suggested that I would be glad to assist him. And he answered by laughing aloud, seizing me by the shoulders, and exclaiming, "Oh, that's a capital joke! Now what will Christian say, when he finds out tomorrow that I've been able to do without him, and that he is an ass? Come on, stranger, and help me a little with this building . . ."

He lighted several candles, and we scurried about through the church to collect a number of planks and blocks; soon he had erected a sufficiently high scaffolding inside the screen.

"Now hand me my things, quickly," said Berthold, as he climbed to his place.

I was astonished by the rapidity with which he made a large copy of the drawing. And he drew his lines not only boldly but always clearly and correctly as well, without a single error. Having been accustomed to such matters in my early youth, I was of good service to him. Standing now above and now below him, I fixed the long rulers at the places he indicated and held them there, pointed the charcoal and handed it to him, and so on.

"You are a capital assistant!" he cried, in appreciative delight.

"And you," I responded, "are one of the best architectural painters that could be imagined. But tell me—have you applied this bold and ready hand of yours to no other sort of painting? Excuse the question—"

"What do you mean?" Berthold asked.

"Why, what I mean is," I replied, "that you are fit for something better than painting marble pillars on church walls. Architectural painting is, after all, a subordinate art. The historical painter, the landscape painter, stands far higher in the scale of accomplishment—for with such an artist the mind and fancy, not confined to the narrow boundaries of geometric lines, are free for wider and more lofty flights. In such work as this which you are doing, on the contrary, even the only imaginative feature—as for instance this trick of perspective by which you deceive the senses—depends upon accurate calculation: the good result therefore is not the product of genius, but of mathematical speculation."

As I spoke, the painter laid aside his pencil, and rested his head on his hand.

"Friend stranger," he began, in a solemn but somewhat indistinct voice, "you speak profanely when you try to arrange the different branches of art by scale and rank, like the vassals of some proud earthly king. And still more profane is it to give your esteem only to those presumptuous fools who, deaf to the clang of the chains that enslave them, and incapable of feeling the pressure of earthly matters, desire to think themselves free, and to rule light and life after their own fashion—yes, even to be gods. Do you not know the fable of Prometheus, who wished to be a creator, and stole fire from Heaven to animate his lifeless figures? He succeeded: the forms he fashioned strode living among living men, and from their eyes shone forth the heavenly fire that burned within them. But the impious being who had dared to attempt the divine was condemned to frightful and unending torment, with no hope of redemption while time should endure. The heart which had felt divinity, in which the desire after the super-earthly had awakened to audacious activity, was torn by the vulture which was born of revenge and now fed upon the vitals of the presumptuous one. The man who has attempted the heavenly can never again be free from earthly pain."

The painter stood absorbed in his own meditations.

"Berthold," I exclaimed, "what has all this to do with your art? I do not think that anyone can deem it presumptuous to represent the human form, either in painting or sculpture."

But the painter laughed, in bitter derision. "Oh, ho! Child's play is no presumption! And with those folk it is all child's play. They dip their brushes comfortably into color, and they daub at a canvas with the honest desire of producing human beings there; but the thing always turns out as if some poor ineffective drudge of Nature had undertaken to make men, and had failed. Tragic as this may be, such folk as these are no presumptuous sinners, but only poor innocent fools.

"Yet if one strives to attain the highest—not the mere sensual, like Titian, but the highest in divine nature, the Promethean spark in man—then one stands upon a precipice, one trembles on a narrow edge above the yawning abyss. And such a one is caught in a devilish hoax: he sees nothing but the clouds soaring above him, and below him he sees that which he had imagined he would find above the stars."

The painter sighed deeply, passed his hand across his forehead, and gazed upward. "But why do I talk all this mad stuff to you, comrade, and leave off the painting I ought to be doing? Look here at my work, man. This is what I call well and honestly drawn. See the beauty of the concept! All the lines combine to achieve a given purpose—a predetermined and clearly conceived effect. Only that which is done by measure, so, is wholly human; what is beyond is of evil. Can we not conceive that the Deity has expressly created us to accomplish and arrange for His own good purpose that which is exhibited according to measured and comprehensible rules? In a word, can we not believe that He has made us just as we in our turn build sawmills and construct spinning machines to be the mechanical agents of our needs? Professor Walter was lately maintaining that certain beasts were created to be eaten by other beasts, and that this arrangement in the end contributed to our advantage and convenience. Thus cats, he said, for example, had an innate propensity to devour mice, so that they might not nibble at the sugar which was set ready for our breakfast. And the professor was right in the long run: animals, and we ourselves with them, are but well-ordered machines, made to find and work and knead certain materials for the table of the unknown King . . . Come, come, man, hand me up the pots!

"I mixed all the colors yesterday, by daylight," he went on, practically, "so that this candlelight might not deceive me. See, they are all numbered, standing there in the corner. Hand me up Number One, my young friend. Grey with grey . . . What would our dry and weary life be, if the Lord of Heaven had not put such motley playthings into our hands! The man of reasonable behavior does not, like a curious boy, try to break the box which gives out music when he turns the handle, to see where the sounds come from: it is just natural, says this reasonable man, that the music comes from inside the box, because I turn the handle . . . Now because I have drawn this architectural device, as I may call it, correctly according to perspective, I know that it will give the impression of actual sculpture to the spectator. Now, boy, reach me up Number Two. Now I paint in colors which are toned down according to rule, and the object here appears to recede five yards. I know all that well enough— Oh, we are amazingly clever! How is it that objects diminish in the distance? This one stupid question asked by a Chinese could put Professor Eytelwein himself to confusion—but he could get out of his trouble by remembering the music box, and saying that he had often turned the handle, and had always got the same result . . .

"Violet, Number Two, youngster!" he went back to his sharp directions. "Another rule, and a thick brush, well washed out! Ah, what is all our striving and struggling after what is higher, but the helpless, unconscious act of an infant who hurts the nurse that feeds him? . . . Violet, Number Two, I said! Quick, young man! The ideal is an evil, lying dream, produced by some fermentation in the blood . . . Take away the pot, young man: I am coming down. The Devil lures us with puppets, to which he glues angels' wings . . ."

I am unable to repeat literally all that Berthold said, as he went on with his rapid painting, and treated me as if I were merely his apprentice. He continued to speak in the same tone, and mood, in which he had begun, scoffing at the limited nature of all human endeavor. Ah, well I knew that I was looking into the depths of a mind that had received a mortal wound, and that uttered its complaints only in bitter irony! And so we worked on until morning dawned, and the light of the candle paled before the sun. Berthold painted zealously all through the night, but he became more and more silent: only single words—towards the end, only sighs—escaped from his burdened heart.

He had planned in the entire altar, with all its gradation of color; and already the picture stood out prominently.

'That is admirable! Admirable!" I cried in delight.

"Do you think," asked Berthold, faintly, "that I shall make something of it? I took great pains, at least, to make my drawing correct; but now I can do no more."

"Not a stroke more, dear Berthold!" I exclaimed. "It is almost incredible, how you have made so much progress, in such a work, in a few hours. But you work too hard. You exert yourself too much. You are too lavish with your power."

"Yet these are my happiest hours," said Berthold. "Perhaps I talked too much—but it is only in words that I find relief for the pain which consumes my heart."

"I know that you are very unhappy, my poor friend," I responded. "I can see that some dreadful tragedy has seared your life . . ."

The painter did not speak for a moment. He slowly took his materials into the chapel, extinguished the lights, and then came up to me and seized my hand.

"Could you be cheerful," he faltered, "nay, could you have one quiet moment, if you were conscious of a terrible, irreparable crime?"

I stood stock-still, and speechless, in amazement, as the bright sunbeams fell upon the painter's pallid and agitated countenance; but he gave me no time to frame a reply to his astounding words. Looking almost like a spectre, he staggered through the little door that led from the church into the College, and I felt that I must not follow him.

But I could scarcely wait for the hour of my morning appointment with Professor Walter. And when at last I met that learned man, I told him the whole story of what had happened, and had so much excited me, during the night just past. I described, with all the vividness at my command, the strange conduct of the painter, and I did not hold back a word that he had spoken, not even those which related most intimately to himself. But the more I hoped, as the moving story proceeded, for the professor's sympathy, the more indifferent he appeared to be. Indeed, he smiled upon me in a most unpleasant manner as I continued to talk about Berthold, and as I pressed him to tell me all he knew of this unfortunate man.

"He is a strange creature, that painter," said the professor. "As I told you before, he is gentle, good-tempered, sober, industrious; but he is weak in the intellect. Otherwise he would never have come down— even though he did commit a crime—from being a great historical painter to becoming a poor dauber of walls."

This expression, "dauber of walls," annoyed me as much as the professor's general attitude of indifference. I tried to convince him that Berthold was even now a most estimable artist, and deserving of the highest, the most active, sympathy.

"Well," said the professor at last, "since you take so much interest in the man you shall hear all that I know of him; and that is a great deal. By way of introduction we will go into the church at once. As Berthold has worked hard all night he will rest during the morning. If we found him in the church my plan would fail."

We went into the church forthwith. And, immediately, the professor had the cloth removed from the covered picture. To my astonishment and awe, I beheld a work of almost magical beauty, such as I had never seen before. The composition was in the style of Raphael, simple and of a heavenly sublimity: Mary and Elizabeth were sitting on the grass in a beautiful garden; the children, Jesus and John, were playing with flowers before them; and in the background, towards the side, a male figure was seen in prayer. Mary's lovely and divine face, the dignity and nobility of her entire figure, filled me with amazement and the deepest admiration. She was beautiful, more beautiful than any merely earthly woman, and her expression indicated the higher power of the Mother of God, like that of Raphael's Madonna in the Dresden Gallery. Ah, was not the most profound yearning for eternity perforce awakened in the human heart by those wonderful eyes with their deep encircling shadow? Did not those gentle, half-parted lips speak the language of consolation, sing, as in angels' sweetest melodies, of the infinite happiness of Heaven? An indescribable compulsion moved me with the desire to cast myself in the dust before her, the Queen of Heaven. I seemed to have lost the power of speech. I could not turn my eyes from that incomparable vision.

But when at last I came to myself, so to speak, and examined the picture more closely, I saw that Mary and the children were the only figures which were entirely finished. The last touches had evidently not been given to Elizabeth, and the man in prayer was not yet painted over. Approaching nearer, I perceived in this man the features of Berthold. And I knew already what I should hear when the professor presently spoke.

"This picture is Berthold's last work," he said. "We got it several years ago in N—, in Upper Silesia, where one of our colleagues bought it at an auction. Although it was unfinished, we had it fitted in here, in the place of a wretched altarpiece we had had formerly. When Berthold first came, and saw the picture, he screamed and fell unconscious to the floor. After that, he was careful to avoid looking at it; and he told me in confidence that it was the last work of its kind that he would ever do. I hoped to be able gradually to persuade him to finish the painting, but he rejected with the utmost abhorrence every suggestion of that sort. And to keep him in good spirits, and in full possession of his powers, I was forced to keep the picture covered for so long as he should remain in the church. If his eye fell upon it, only by accident, he ran as if driven by some irresistible power, and threw himself sobbing upon the ground; a kind of paroxysm seized him, and for days he would be totally unfit for work."

"Poor soul!" I said, and felt that I was speaking to Berthold himself. "How did the hand of the Devil take such a deadly hold upon your life?"

"Oh, the hand as well as the arm grew in his own body," the professor remarked. "He was his own demon, his own Lucifer, who flashed the infernal torch upon his own life. That is plain enough to anyone who knows his biography."

I entreated the professor at once to keep his promise of telling me all that he knew about the life of the unhappy painter; but he demurred.

"That would take much too long, and would cost too much breath," he answered. "Besides, let us not spoil the cheerful day by such gloomy stuff. We will have a good luncheon and then go to the mill, where an excellent dinner awaits us."

I did not, however, desist from my pleas. And after much talk on both sides I obtained some sort of satisfaction from the professor. I learned that one of the students at the College had become warmly attached to Berthold, immediately upon the painter's arrival; that little by little the man had communicated to this youth the detailed story of his life; that the student had carefully written it all down; and that the professor, in fine, now had the manuscript.

"The lad," said the professor to me, "was just such an enthusiast as—pardon me!—you are. But this work of writing down the strange events of the painter's life served him as a capital exercise in style."

With much trouble I now got the professor's promise that he would lend me the manuscript at the close of our pleasure-party. And for the rest of the day—whether because of my own violent curiosity or through the fault of my host's attitude—I was more uneasy than I had ever been in my life. The professor's icy coldness whenever he spoke of Berthold had already repelled me; but now, from his conversation with his colleagues who were the companions of our jaunt, I realized that in spite of all his learning, and all his knowledge of the world, he had no sense of the sublime—in fact, that he was as gross a materialist as a man could well be. He had completely adopted the system, or philosophy, of consuming and being consumed, which Berthold had mentioned to me in our night talk. All the endeavors of the mind, all the powers of invention and creation, he traced back to certain states of the stomach and entrails; and on this subject he gave voice to all sorts of monstrous conceits. Thus he very seriously averred, for instance, that man's every thought proceeded from the marriage of two fibres in the human brain. And I realized how the professor, with all this absurd folderol, must torture poor Berthold, who attacked the notion of any favorable influence, from a higher region, in the irony of his own despair. Professor Walter must again and again have plunged daggers into wounds still fresh and bleeding, I knew.

But at last the long and distressing day came to an end, and the professor put a few sheets of manuscript in my hand. "There, my dear enthusiast, is the student's handiwork," he said. "It is not badly written, but it is very odd. And the author, against every rule, insists on thrusting in the painter's discourses, word for word, without giving the reader any notice of what he is about. I will make you a present of the work—by virtue of my office I have a right to dispose of it—because I know perfectly well that you are no writer. The author of the *Fantasiestücke in Callot's Manier* would have cut it in his own mad fashion, and would have printed it at once. I need expect nothing of the sort from you!"

Professor Aloysius Walter was unaware that he actually stood in the presence of that "traveling enthusiast," although he might easily enough have found it out. And thus, gentle reader, I am enabled to give you the short history of the painter, Berthold, as written out by the student at the Jesuit College at G—. It fully explains the manner in which Berthold conducted himself in my presence; and you, reader, will be able to see how man may be plunged into destructive error by the spirit of destiny.

" 'Only let your son follow the bent of his mind, and go to Italy,' said the old painter, Stephen Birkner, to Berthold's parents. 'He is already a clever artist, and it is true that here at D— there is no lack of opportunity for studying and copying excellent originals of every school; but nevertheless he must not stay here. The free life of an artist must have its beginning for him in the happy land of art: for the first time, there, his studies will take living form, and will thus produce individual creative work, as it springs from his own thought. Mere copying is now of no further use to him. You know that the growing plant requires plenty of sun, if it is to thrive and bring forth its blossoms and fruit. Your son is endowed with the true artistic temperament and talent—so you may feel perfectly at ease about all the rest!'

"The boy's parents took the old painter's advice. They scraped together all the money that their means would permit, in order to fit out the youth for his long journey, and so he set off. His warmest wish—to travel in Italy—was thus accomplished.

" 'When Birkner told me the decision my father and mother had come to, I literally jumped for joy. Until the time came for my departure, I wandered about as in a dream. In the gallery where I was in the habit of copying great works of art, I could not make one single stroke with my pencil. Instead, I prevailed upon the Director, and all the artists who had been to Italy, to talk to me of that land where art flourished. Then at last the fateful day and hour arrived. The parting from my parents was painful, for they felt a gloomy presentiment that they would never see me again. Even my father, usually a firm and resolute man, had difficulty in restraining his emotion.

" 'My fellow artists cried: "Italy! You will see Italy!" And then my desire and ambition burned with a more powerful flame within me, and consumed, as it were, my deep melancholy. I stepped boldly forth. The path of an artist seemed to begin at my parents' door.'

"Berthold had studied every kind of painting, but he had devoted himself especially to landscapes, at which he worked with ardent love and zeal. He expected to find in Rome abundant nurture for his passion in, and talent for, this branch of art, but this was not the case. The circle of artists and dilettanti in which he moved assured him constantly that the work of the historical painter stood on the highest pinnacle of the painter's art, and that all the rest were but subordinate to it. He was advised—if he wished to become an eminent artist—to abandon at once the kind of work he had chosen, and to devote himself to this higher type. And this advice, coupled with the utterly new and overwhelming impression made upon him by Raphael's mighty frescoes in the Vatican, caused him to determine to give up landscape painting altogether. He made sketches after the manner of the Raphaels, and also copied small oil paintings by other celebrated masters. All these things were very cleverly done by his practiced hand, and the artists and dilettanti who were now his associates warmly praised his work. But he felt that such praise should afford him only temporary solace, and should especially spur him on to further efforts.

"For he himself saw quite clearly that his sketches and copies lacked all the fire of the originals. The divine thought in the mind of Raphael, of Correggio, must inspire him, he believed, to his own creation; but when he tried to catch such thought and fix it in his own inventive fancy it vanished from him as in a mist. All that he sketched was like any obscure and confused fumbling of the mediocre man's mind, lifeless and without meaning. While he was involved in these vain efforts, a profound melancholy took possession of his soul; and he would often escape from his friends and go out into the countryside around Rome, where, alone, he would sketch and paint groups of trees and isolated details of the landscape.

"Even these attempts, however, were not so successful as his earlier endeavors. And, for the first time in his life, he began to doubt the reality of his powers as an artist. His proudest hopes seemed to be on the point of vanishing.

" 'Ah, my revered friend and instructor,' Berthold wrote to Stephen Birkner, 'you expected great things of me. But here, at the very place and time when the light of inspiration should be glowing within me, I have discovered that what you took for artistic genius was nothing but the merest sort of gift—a kind of dexterity of the fingers. Tell my parents that I shall come home soon, and shall learn some trade by which I can make my living'—and so on and on.

"Birkner, however, wrote back: 'Oh, if I could only be with you, my dear pupil, to support you in your mood of depression! It is your very doubts that prove your calling as an artist. The man who believes, with steadfast unwavering confidence in his own powers, that he will always progress—that man is a blind fool. He merely deceives himself. He lacks the proper spur to effort, which is, necessarily, the thought of his own deficiency. As for yourself, on the contrary, you must persevere, and you will soon gain strength and new courage. When that time comes you will quietly pursue—no longer fettered by the opinions or advice of friends who are perhaps unable to apppreciate you—the path which your own nature has designated for you. It will then be left to your own judgment to decide whether you become a painter of landscapes or of historical pieces. And you will cease to think of any hostile separation of the branches of one trunk.'

"It happened that, about the time when Berthold received this letter of comfort and stimulus from his old friend and teacher, the fame of a painter called Philip Hackert was spreading widely throughout Rome. Some of the landscapes which he had exhibited, and which were distinguished by an extraordinary grace and clarity, showed real genius in the artist; and even the historical painters admitted that this pure imitation of Nature held excellence and true greatness. Listening to all this, Berthold breathed freely again. He no longer heard his favorite branch of art treated with contempt. He saw honors and high place given to a man who toiled over this kind of work. And, as if set alight by a sudden spark, his very soul burned with the conviction that he must study under Hackert, who was now in Naples. In high spirits, he wrote to tell Birkner, and also his parents, that he had now, after painful conflict, found the right way, and that he hoped to devote himself to work and become an accomplished artist in his own style. So to Naples, forthwith, he went.

"Hackert, an honest and good-hearted German, received his young German pupil with great kindness; and Berthold from the first made great efforts to follow his master. He quickly attained facility in making faithful representations of the different kinds of trees and shrubs; and he was not a little successful in achieving those misty effects that are to be found in Hackert's pictures. He thus received much praise. But it seemed to him nevertheless that something was lacking, not only in his own paintings, but in his master's also—something to which he could not give a name, yet which was plainly to be seen in the pictures by Claude Lorrain, and the wild landscapes of Salvatore Rosa. Before long he was conscious of a want of confidence in his instructor, and he felt particularly dissatisfied when Hackert, with unwearied zest, painted some dead game which the King had sent him.

"Berthold soon succeeded, however, in conquering such presumptuous thoughts—as he considered them—and, with virtuous resignation and true German industry, he went on following the pattern set by his master, until in a short time he could all but equal him. At Hackert's own suggestion he sent a large landscape, which he had faithfully copied from Nature, to an exhibition that was to consist chiefly of pastoral and still-life pieces in the Hackert style. All the artists and connoisseurs admired the young man's faithful and neatly executed works, and praised him loudly. There was only one exception to this chorus: one man, elderly and rather oddly attired, said never a word about Hackert's pictures, but smiled significantly whenever the multitude broke out into extravagant praise; and Berthold noticed that when this stranger stood before his landscape he shook his head with an unmistakable air of deep pity, and upon that was about to retire.

"Being somewhat set up by the general praise which had come to him, Berthold could not help feeling indignant with the stranger. He approached him, then, and, speaking somewhat more sharply than was necessary, he said: 'You do not seem to be satisfied with the picture, sir, although I must say there are excellent artists and connoisseurs who think it not so bad. Pray tell me where the fault lies, so that I may improve the picture according to your kind suggestions.'

"The stranger glanced keenly and appraisingly at Berthold, and said, very seriously: 'Young man, much good might have come out of you.' The not unnatural effect of this comment upon the aspiring painter was one of profound embarrassment. Indeed the speech, and the look, of this man filled the youth with repulsion. He had not the courage to say anything more, or to follow the stranger as he slowly stalked out of the salon. And when Hackert came in, a few moments later, he hastened to tell him of the curious encounter.

" 'Ha! Do not take that to heart,' smiled the master. 'I know this man: he is an old crab, who kicks at everything and is pleased by nothing. I met him in the anteroom, as I was coming in. He is a rich, and queer, old fellow, who was born of Greek parents in Malta, and he is not a bad painter. Everything he does has a fantastic look about it, but this is the result of his absurd notions about art, and of the utterly worthless system which he has constructed. I know well enough that he has no opinion of me, but I am quite ready to forgive him for that, since he cannot throw any doubt upon my honorably acquired success.'

"Berthold had felt as if the critical gentleman from Malta had touched a sore place in his soul, only for the purpose of probing and healing it. But now he speedily drove this notion from his mind, and worked on happily, as before.

"The success of this large painting, which was so universally admired, gave him courage to begin a companion piece to it. Hackert himself selected one of the loveliest spots in the beautiful and unique environs of Naples. And, as the first picture had represented sunset, this second landscape was to show the effect of dawn. Berthold had a number of strange trees to paint, a number of vineyards, and, above all, a good deal of mist.

"He was sitting one day on a large flat stone in the chosen spot, completing the sketch for the great picture, from Nature, when he heard a voice near him. 'Bravo! Well done!' the voice said. The critic from Malta was standing beside him, looking at his work.

" 'You have forgotten only one thing,' that gentleman now added, with a sarcastic smile. 'Only look yonder, my dear young friend, at the wall of the distant vineyard: the one covered with green tendrils. The door is half open, don't you see? You must show that with its proper shading. The half-open door creates a surprising effect!'

" 'You are joking, sir,' exclaimed Berthold, 'and without reason. Such accidental details are by no means as contemptible as you think; and my master loves to employ them just because he knows them to be not unimportant. Only think of the suspended white cloth in the landscape of one of the Dutch painters, and remember how that could not be omitted without marring the general effect. You, however, seem to be no friend of landscape painting in general. And as I have given myself up to it, heart and soul, I beg that you will allow me to go on working in tranquillity.'

" 'You are much mistaken, young man,' said the stranger. 'I tell you again, as I told you before, that a good deal might be made of you. For your works clearly show an unwearied striving towards some far from commonplace ideal. But that goal, unfortunately, you cannot attain, because the path you have taken does not lead to it. Only mark what I tell you. Perhaps I may succeed in keeping alive that spark of flame in your soul which you, witless as you are, are trying to smother, and perhaps I shall succeed in making it flare up brightly enough to enlighten you. Do you think I am so foolish as to rank landscape lower than historical painting, or to fail to recognize the common goal toward which the painters of both schools should strive? The apprehension of Nature, in the deepest sense of that higher import which can kindle all things to a higher life— that is the sacred purpose of all art. Can the mere dim copying of Nature lead to this holy end?

" 'How poor, how stiff and forced,' he continued, warmly, 'is the appearance of a manuscript which has merely been copied from some other manuscript in a foreign tongue which the copyist does not understand! He is unable to give the proper significance to the strokes which he so laboriously imitates. It is thus that your master's landscapes are merely correct copies of an original author who writes in a language which is strange to the conscientious copyist. The initiated artist hears the voice of Nature, which speaks to him in wondrous sounds out of trees, hedges, flowers, mountains, and waters, imparting to him its unfathomable mysteries which become transformed in his heart into a presentiment of the sublime. It is then, and thus, like the spirit of God, itself, that talent possesses him to communicate this presentiment to the visible work of his hands. Have you yourself, young man, not felt strangely affected as you looked at the landscape of the old masters? Assuredly you were not wondering whether the leaves of the lime trees, the pines, the plane trees, might or might not have been made more true to Nature, whether the background should have been more misty, or the water more clear! Instead of all this, the spirit which breathed from the whole masterpiece lifted your own soul to a higher region, the reflection of which you seemed to behold.

" 'Listen to me, young man! Study Nature in the mechanical details, sedulously and carefully, so that you may attain the practiced skill of representation; but do not take this practiced skill for the art itself. If you have penetrated into the significant heart of Nature, her pictures will arise within you in brightness and beauty!'

"The man from Malta was silent. But as Berthold, deeply moved by what he had heard, stood with downcast eyes before him, incapable of uttering a word, the stranger suddenly left him, saying, as he turned away, 'I had no intention of discouraging you from your work, but I know that a higher spirit is slumbering within you. I have cried out to it in strong words, that it might awake, and move its wings with freshness and vigor. Farewell!'

"Berthold felt as if the strange critic had only put into words that which had already been stirring in his soul. And now his own inner voice broke forth: 'No! All this striving, this constant effort, is but the uncertain and deceptive groping of the blind. Away with all that has hitherto dazzled me!'

"He was in no condition, now, to accomplish another stroke of work with his present master, or in his present vein of endeavor. He left Hackert, and wandered about filled with a wild unrest, loudly imploring the revelation of that higher power of which the stranger had spoken to him.

" 'Only in sweet dreams was I happy—yes, only so was I truly blessed. In such moments of imaginative rapture, everything that the critic from Malta had said became true. I would lie under the green hedges, while magical exhalations played around me, and the voice of Nature sounded audibly and melodiously among the dark trees. "Listen, listen, oh, initiated one!" I seemed to hear that voice say. "Hear the great primeval tones of creation, as they now fashion themselves into harmonies accessible to your human mind!"

" 'And as those chords came more and more clearly to my ears, I felt as if a new sense had come to life within me. I could apprehend, with a strange and convincing perspicuity, what had been unfathomable before. As if with curious hieroglyphics, I traced in the air the pattern of the secrets which had been revealed to me in characters of fire. And this hieroglyphic writing was an extraordinary landscape, in which trees, hedges, flowers and waters seemed to come to life, making, with each movement, the most exquisite music.'

"But, as poor Berthold said, it was only in dreams that he felt real happiness. For his strength was broken, and his mind was even more disturbed than it had been in Rome, when he had wished to be a historical painter. If he strode through a dark wood, a troubling sensation of awe came over him. If he went out and looked at the distant mountains, he felt as if ice-cold claws had gripped his heart; he could not breathe; he seemed to be dying from some merciless inner anguish. All Nature, which used to smile upon him so kindly, had now become a threatening monster; and her voice, which had greeted him sweetly in the murmur of the evening breeze, the rippling of the brook, the rustling of the leaves on the trees above him, now whispered to him harshly that he was doomed and lost. At last, however, the dreams themselves began to work their consolation. He became calmer. Nevertheless he avoided being alone in the open air; and so it was that he accompanied two cheerful German painters on various trips to outlying districts of Naples, famous for their scenic beauty.

"One of these young men, whose name was Florentin, was at this time more intent upon the enjoyment of life than upon the serious study of painting—a state to which his portfolio abundantly testified. Groups of dancing peasant girls, village processions, rural festivals—all such subjects as these, whenever he chanced to meet them, he could transfer to paper with a sure and ready hand. Every drawing, even though it were a mere sketch, had life and motion. In spite of these human preoccupations, however, this painter's mind was by no means closed to the higher aspects of art. On the contrary, he penetrated more deeply than any of his contemporaries into the unfamiliar meaning and importance of the old masters. In one of his sketch books, for example, he had copied in outline the frescoes of an old convent church, now pulled down, in Rome. The pictures represented the martyrdom of Saint Catherine, and the unique beauty, the extraordinarily happy conception, of these cartoons made a very peculiar impression upon Berthold.

"He could see flashes, now, of light and hope penetrating into the gloomy wasteland that had surrounded him, and in consequence he became capable of appreciating Florentin's cheerful mind and love of life. And since the latter, when representing in his work the charms of human living, especially stressed the very sense and principle of humanity, so now Berthold came to take this human principle as the ground upon which he must stand, instead of floating away into boundless space. While Florentin was making quick sketches in his book, Berthold tried to copy the lovely presentation of Saint Catherine, and was fairly successful; but, as in Rome, he failed to give his figures the animation which they had in the original.

"He complained of this to Florentin, whom he looked upon as greatly his superior in true artistic genius, and at the same time he told him all that the critic from Malta had said about art. 'The stranger is right, dear brother Berthold,' Florentin responded. 'And I rank the genuine landscape quite as high as those profoundly significant sacred histories, depicted by the old masters. More, I maintain that as painters we should first gain power and skill by the representation of that organic Nature which is nearest to us, so that we may be able to find light for her darker regions. As for yourself, Berthold, I advise you to practice sketching figures, and concentrating your thoughts upon them. Perhaps then you will find your way more clearly.'

"And as Berthold followed his friend's suggestion, it seemed to him as if the dark clouds, which had spread all over his life, were passing away.

" 'I tried to represent by hieroglyphic characters that which seemed to me no more than an obscure feeling in my innermost soul, as I had done in my dream. But the hieroglyphics became human figures, which moved, in strange configurations, about a focus of light. This focus was to be the noblest form that was ever evoked by a painter's fancy; but when this form appeared to me in a dream, encircled by the rays of Heaven, my effort to catch its features was in vain. Every attempt to represent it was an utter failure, and all my force and vision seemed to fade away in a state of futile though most ardent desire.' Florentin perceived the condition of his friend, who was excited to a morbid degree, and gave him all the comfort in his power. He often assured him that this was the very time when illumination was most likely to come to him. But Berthold merely slunk about as if he were dreaming, and all his efforts came to no more than the feeble exertions of a puling infant.

"In the vicinity of Naples there was one villa which offered the finest of all views of Vesuvius and the sea, and which, on this account, was hospitably kept open to foreign artists, especially landscape painters, by the Duke who was its proprietor. Berthold had often worked from this vantage point. But there was a grotto in the park where, still oftener, he had given himself up to the fantastic longings that tore his heart. Here, one day, he sat in deep depression, yearning for a star to shine upon his dark path, and lighten the obscurity in which he wandered, when he heard a rustling sound in the hedge near by. Raising his eyes, he saw an exquisitely beautiful woman standing before him.

" 'The sunbeams fell upon her angelic countenance. She cast upon me a glance which no words could describe. It was Saint Catherine. No, more than the Saint herself, it was my ideal. Transported with joy, I cast myself on the ground at her feet, and with a benign smile the figure vanished. My most fervent prayer had been fulfilled.'

"At this moment Florentin came into the grotto, and was astonished when Berthold, his face beaming with rapture, pressed him to his heart, while tears of happiness streamed from his eyes. 'My friend, my friend!' he stammered, 'I am happy—I am blessed—she is found! Found!'

"He hurried to his studio, stretched his canvas, and began to paint as if inspired by divine power. Now he called before him the superterrestrial woman—for so he thought her—with the full glow of life. From this moment his whole being was entirely changed. The melancholy which had preyed upon his heart gave way to serenity and cheerfulness. As he industriously studied the masterpieces of the old painters, many of his copies were now perfectly successful. And, for the first time, he began to produce paintings which really astonished the connoisseurs.

"As for landscapes, they were no more to be thought of. And Hackert himself admitted that the youth had not found his proper vocation until now. He had orders for many large works, such as altarpieces for churches, and he usually selected the more cheerful subjects of Christian tradition; but the noble form of his ideal shone forth from them all.

"And now someone discovered that this angelic figure was a perfect representation of the face and form of the Princess Angiola T—. Waggish folk insinuated that the young German painter was smitten by the brilliant eyes of that lovely lady. But Berthold himself was outraged when the resemblance of his ideal to the actual Princess was pointed out to him; absurd prattle, this, which tried to drag what was heavenly down to the earthly level . . .

" 'Do you believe,' he demanded, 'that such a being could actually roam this earth? No. The vision of highest beauty and goodness was revealed to me in a wondrous vision: it was the moment of the artist's consecration.'

"So he went on with his work, and paid no attention to gossip or surmise. And he lived very happily until, after Bonaparte's conquests in Italy, the French army bore down upon the Kingdom of Naples, and the fearful destructiveness of revolution was let loose upon the peaceful city. The King and Queen had left Naples, and the Republicans took over. The Vicar-General had concluded a disgraceful truce with the French commander, and the French envoys soon arrived to receive the tribute money that was to be paid them according to its terms. The Vicar-General fled, to escape the wrath of the city's inhabitants. And the people, feeling themselves deserted by him, by the state, in short, by all who could defend them against the oncoming enemy, broke out in a revolt that loosened all the bonds of society. They set all law and order at defiance; they plunged into a state of wild anarchy; their furious hordes rushed through the streets, and with the cry of 'Viva la Santa Fede!' they plundered and burned the houses of the nobles, who, they thought, had sold them to the enemy.

"Efforts to restore order were made by Moliterno and Rocca Romano, who were the favorites of the people, and had been elected as leaders; but all these attempts failed. The Dukes della Torre and Clement Filomarino were murdered, but the thirst for blood among the raging populace was not yet satisfied. Berthold, making his escape, half dressed, from a burning house, found himself straightway surrounded by a mob, that was rushing, with flaring torches and glittering unsheathed knives, towards the palace of the Duke of T—. And, taking him for one of themselves, the maddened men bore the painter along with them, shouting, 'Viva la Santa Fede!' as they went.

"What happened next happened very quickly. In a few minutes the Duke, his servants, everyone who resisted the rioters, had been killed, and the palace, into which Berthold had been forced by the pressure of the throng, was in flames. Thick clouds of smoke filled the long corridors; and Berthold, his life now endangered by the fire, darted blindly through one door after another, vainly seeking a way out of the house. Suddenly a piercing shriek of agony and terror fell upon his ear. He followed the sound into a hallway, and found a woman struggling with a *lazzarone*, who held her fast and was about to plunge a knife into her heart. The painter looked at them, and his very consciousness was frozen in horror:

it was the Princess!—it was Berthold's angelic ideal—who was struggling there . . .

"It was but the task of a moment for Berthold to seize the *lazzarone*, fling him to the ground, and plunge his own knife into the murderer's throat, then to catch the Princess in his arms and fly with her through the flaming ruins. He got down the steps and out of the palace. He dashed on, and on, through the dense throng of people in the street. No one tried to stop him. With the bloody knife in his hand, with his face begrimed with smoke and soot, with his clothes torn and dirty, it was small wonder that he was taken for a plunderer and murderer, and that the mob willingly conceded his right to carry off his prey! At last he fell exhausted, beneath an old wall in a deserted section of the city, to which, as if by instinct, he had run to escape his peril. For a little while, he lost consciousness; and when he came to himself, it was to find the Princess kneeling by his side and bathing his forehead in cold water.

" 'Oh, thanks be to Heaven!' she cried, in the softest and most lovely voice that Berthold had ever heard. 'Thanks be to all the saints that you have recovered, my rescuer, the preserver of my life! I owe everything to you—you are everything to me! The saints have saved you, my all!'

"Berthold raised himself from the ground. It seemed to him that he was dreaming—that he must be dreaming. But as he fixed his eyes upon the Princess, he saw that this was indeed no dream. Yes, it was she; it was that celestial vision that had kindled the divine spark within his breast. 'Is it possible? Can it be true? Am I actually living and breathing in this world?' he cried.

" 'Yes,' the Princess answered. 'You are living. You are living for me. What you did not venture even to hope has happened through a miracle. Oh, I know who you are—you are the German painter, Berthold, who loves me; you are the painter who has ennobled me and made me immortal in beautiful works of art. And you never thought to come to claim me, except in dreams? But now life itself has brought us together. You have saved my life, and I am yours forever. We must make our escape now!'

"As the Princess spoke, a strange sensation oppressed Berthold's heart—like the sudden pain that disturbs a sweet dream. But when the beautiful woman put her full white arms around him, as he pressed her passionately to his heart, a rapture he had never before known throbbed through his veins, and in the almost incoherent joy of possessing earth's greatest felicity, he cried, 'Ah, now I know that it was no delusion out of a dream! I am embracing my bride—my wife, from whom I shall never be parted!'

"Escape from the city was at first impossible: at the gate stood the French Army, whose entrance the people, though badly armed and without leaders, were able to dispute for two days. Berthold succeeded, however, in fleeing with Angiola from one hiding place to another, until at last they could make their way out of Naples. And now Angiola, deeply enamored of the painter, refused to think of remaining in Italy. She wished her family to believe her dead. She desired to belong wholly to Berthold, in secure and unchallenged possession. The jewels she had been wearing—a diamond necklace and some valuable rings—sufficed to provide them with all necessaries in Rome, whither they had proceeded by slow stages; and at last they arrived happily at M—, in southern Germany, where Berthold intended to settle, and to support himself by his art. Was this not a state of felicity beyond all possible dreams, that Angiola—that creature of celestial loveliness, that ideal of all his sublime visions—had now become his own, when every social law had seemed to raise an insurmountable barrier between him and his beloved?

"Berthold could scarcely comprehend his happiness. He abandoned himself to his inexpressible joy, until the voice within him became too loud to ignore, as it bade him think of his art. He determined now to establish his fame here at M—, by a large picture for the Church of the Virgin there. The entire design was to be the very simple one of Mary and Elizabeth sitting on the grass in a beautiful garden, with the infant Christ and the little Saint John playing before them; but all Berthold's efforts to obtain a pure spiritual visualization of his picture proved fruitless. As in that unhappy period of earlier crisis, the sacred figures eluded him; and it was not the heavenly Mary—no, it was an earthly woman, it was his Angiola, fearfully distorted—that stood before his mind's eye.

"He believed that he could defy the miserable power that seemed to have mastered him, and he prepared his colors and began to paint. But his force and talent were gone, and all his endeavors were—as they had been before—only the feeble exertions of an unthinking child. Everything he painted seemed stiff and lifeless; and even Angiola—Angiola, the living embodiment of his ideal—became, when she sat for him and he tried to paint her, a mere wax image on the canvas, staring at him with glassy eyes. More and more every day, his spirit fell prey to a despondency that consumed all the happiness of his life. He would not—nay rather, he could not—work any more. And thus he fell into a state of poverty which was the more crushing because Angiola never uttered a word of complaint.

" 'The grief that gnawed deeper and deeper into my soul—that grief which was the offspring of a hope inevitably betrayed, when I tried to summon powers that were no longer mine—soon reduced me to a condition which might be compared to madness. When my wife bore me a son, what should have been cause for great joy only served to increase my misery. My long-suppressed discontent broke out in open, burning hate. She—Angiola alone—had been the cause of my unhappiness; she was not the ideal which had appeared to me, but had only assumed the form and face of that heavenly visitant in order to destroy me. In wild fury of despair, I cursed her and her innocent child. I wished them both dead, that I might be freed from the insupportable anguish by which I was tortured, as by so many burning knives. I brooded on thoughts of Hell. In vain did I read, in Angiola's now dead-white face, and in her tears, the madness and impiety of my conduct. "You have cheated me out of my life, cursed woman!" I thundered at her. And when she fell fainting before me and clasped my knees, I pushed her away with my foot.'

"Berthold's insane and cruel behavior to his wife and child aroused the attention of the neighbors, who, in turn, passed the information on to the town magistrates. It was decided that he must be sent to prison. But when the police entered his dwelling, he had vanished, with his wife and child, without leaving so much as a trace behind.

"Soon afterward, however, the painter appeared at N—, in Upper Silesia. He had got rid of his wife and child. And now he cheerfully began to paint the picture which he had vainly attempted a short time before. He could finish only the Virgin Mary and the children, Jesus and John, however, for he fell desperately ill, and came close to the death he desired. Everything that belonged to him, including the unfinished picture, was sold to meet the expenses of his mere maintenance. And when he

had in some measure recovered, he departed, a sick and miserable beggar.
He afterward made a poor living by a few jobs of wall decoration."

"There is something terrible in this history of Berthold," I said to
the professor. "Although so much is not plainly expressed, I believe that
he actually, and recklessly, murdered his innocent wife and child."

"He is an insane fool," the professor replied. "I do not give him
credit for enough courage to perform such an act. On this point he never
speaks plainly. And the question is, whether it be not a mere fancy that
he had anything to do with their deaths. He has now gone back to painting the similitude of marble. This very night he will finish the altar. This
accomplishment will put him in a good humor; and perhaps you may
learn something about this critical aspect of the strange affair, from his
own lips."

I must confess that, now that I had read Berthold's story, the thought
of passing the midnight hours alone with him in the church was a thing
to make me shudder a little. I thought that there might be something of
the Devil in him, in spite of his good nature and genially candid air. And
I chose rather to seek his company at noon, that very day, in broad sunlight.

I found him on the scaffolding, painting the veins of marble on the
wall. But his mood was reserved and ill-tempered. Climbing up to him,
I reached him the pots, while he stared at me in amazement. "I am your
helper," said I, softly, and this drew a smile from him. Then I began to
talk of his life, so as to let him know that I was acquainted with his whole
story; and he seemed to think that he himself, as we worked together
through the night, must have communicated everything to me. Very, very
gently I came to the frightful catastrophe, and then I said, suddenly:

"Did you actually, in your unholy madness, murder your wife and
child?"

At this, he let the paint pot and the brush fall. And, staring at me
with a countenance so distorted as to be hideous, he raised both hands
above his head and cried out:

"No! These hands are unstained by the blood of my wife, of my
son! Another such word from you, and I will plunge myself and you down

from the scaffolding, so that both our heads shall be crushed on the stone floor!"

I felt, at this moment, that I had got myself into a rather odd situation, and I deemed it advisable to change the subject at once. "Look here, dear Berthold," I said, as quietly and coolly as possible, "see how that ugly dark yellow is running on the wall . . ."

He turned his eyes to the spot I indicated. And, as he was painting out the yellow, I slipped noiselessly down from the scaffolding, left the church, and went to the professor, to share his good-natured laughter over my prying curiosity and the thoroughly merited chastening it had brought me.

My carriage was by this time repaired, and I left G—; but not before Professor Aloysius Walter had solemnly promised that in case anything happened to Berthold he would write me at once.

About half a year had gone by, when I received a letter from the professor. He expressed himself in very prolix terms in regard to the pleasure of our meeting at G—; and then he came to the news of Berthold:

"Soon after your departure affairs took a singular turn with our whimsical painter. He suddenly became quite cheerful, and he finished the great altarpiece in the most splendid style; it is now the wonder of everybody. He then disappeared. And, since he took nothing with him, and a few days later we found a hat and stick lying on the bank of the near-by stream, we are all of the opinion that he met a voluntary death."

SALVATOR ROSA

*The celebrated painter Salvator Rosa comes to Rome, and
is attacked by a dangerous illness. What befalls him
during this illness.*

CELEBRATED PEOPLE COMMONLY HAVE MUCH
ill said of them, whether this abuse is based
on truth or not. And no exception is to be
found in the case of that admirable artist,
Salvator Rosa, whose paintings, instinct with
the breath of life itself, cannot fail to communicate their strange and sensitive mood to
even the most casual onlooker.

At the time that Salvator's fame was
ringing through Naples, Rome and Tuscany—
indeed through all Italy—and painters, anxious
to please the public, were striving to imitate
his uniquely individual style, his malicious and neglected rivals were making every effort to besmirch his glorious reputation with a variety of filthy
rumors. It was affirmed, for example, that during an earlier period of his
life, Rosa had belonged to a company of bandits and that it was from this
contact with lawlessness that he had drawn all the wild, defiant, fantastically attired figures which he later introduced into his work, just as the
gloomy and ominous wilderness of his landscapes—the *selve selvagge*, to
use Dante's phrase—were faithful reproductions of the secret haunts and
hiding places of the banditti. What was still worse, these same detractors
openly accused the painter of having been involved in the bloody and
unholy revolt launched against Spanish rule by the notorious Masaniello

in Naples. They even described the share he had taken in it, down to the most minute details.

According to this report, Aniello Falcone, the painter of battle scenes, and one of the most important influences of Salvator's student days, had been roused to a bloodthirsty fury of revenge because one of his kin had been struck down, in a hand-to-hand encounter, by the soldiers of the Spanish oppressors. He immediately collected together a band of daring spirits, chiefly young painters, put arms in their hands, and gave them the name of *"La Campagnia della Morte."* And in truth this "company of death" inspired all the fear and consternation its terrible name suggests. Throughout the day, they patrolled the streets of Naples in little groups, and mercilessly slaughtered every Spaniard unfortunate enough to cross their paths. They did more—they forced their way into holy sanctuaries and relentlessly murdered their helpless foes whom terror had driven to take refuge there. At night, they clustered round their chief, the obsessed and blood-lusting Masaniello, and painted portraits of him by flaring torchlight, so that soon there were hundreds of these little pictures circulating in Naples and its environs.

This was the murderous band to which Salvator Rosa is supposed to have belonged, working diligently at his butchering by day, and just as diligently at his painting by night. I believe, however, that the truth about him has been stated by the celebrated art critic, Taillasson. His works are characterized, says this writer, by defiant originality and by a forceful eccentricity of concept and expression. He delighted in studying Nature, not in the gentle allurement of green meadows, flourishing fields, sweet-smelling groves, murmuring springs, but in its awesome aspects, in towering masses of rock, in the wild seashore, in savage inhospitable forests; and the voices that he loved to hear were not the whisperings of the evening breeze or the musical rustle of leaves, but the soaring of the hurricane and the thunder of the cataract. Whoever examines Salvator's desolate landscapes, peopled with strange and savage figures, here standing apart, there moving stealthily about in groups, will find himself involuntarily taking up a disquieting train of thought: "This is where a frightful murder took place—there's where the bloody corpse was flung into the ravine," and so on . . .

Admitting all this, and even admitting that Taillasson is right when he maintains that Salvator's "Plato," no, that even his "St. John Proclaiming the Advent of the Saviour in the Wilderness," look just a little like highway robbers—admitting this, I say, it is nevertheless unjust to argue from the character of the works to the character of the artist himself, and to assume that he, who represents with lifelike fidelity that which is savage and terrible, must himself have been a savage and terrible man. He who prates most about the sword is often he who would wield it with least skill; he who feels in the depths of his soul all the horrors of a bloody deed, so that, taking the palette or the pencil or the pen in his hand, he is able to give living form to his feelings—this man is often the one least capable of practicing similar deeds.

Enough! I don't believe a single word of all those evil reports by which men sought to brand the excellent Salvator as a remorseless murderer and robber; and I hope that you, gentle reader, will share my opinion. Otherwise, I see grounds for fearing that you might perhaps entertain some doubts respecting what I am about to tell you of this artist. The Salvator I wish to put before you in this tale—that is, according to my conception of him—is a man emanating the fire and exuberance of life, but at the same time a man of the noblest and most loyal qualities, and capable, like all those who think and feel deeply, of controlling even that bitter irony which arises from a clear realization of the significance of life.

I scarcely need add that Salvator was no less renowned as a poet and musician than as a painter. His genius was revealed in magnificent refractions. I repeat again, I do not believe that Salvator had any share in Masaniello's bloody deeds. On the contrary, I think it was the horrors of that fearful time which drove him from Naples to Rome, where he arrived a helpless and poverty-stricken fugitive, just at the time when Masaniello fell.

Not over-well dressed, and with a scanty purse, containing not more than a few bright sequins, in his pocket, he crept through the city gate just after nightfall. Somehow or other, he didn't exactly know how, he wandered as far as the Piazza Navona. In better times he had once lived there, in a large house near the Pamfili Palace. Muttering moodily to himself, he gazed up at the large plate-glass windows, which shone as they caught light. "Oh, yes," he exclaimed peevishly, "it'll cost me dozens of yards of painted canvas to be able to open my studio up there again!"

Then all at once he began to feel as if he were paralyzed in every limb, and also more weak and feeble than he had ever been in his life before. "But shall I," he murmured between his teeth as he sank down upon the stone steps that led up to the house door, "shall I really be able to cover enough canvas in the way those fools want it done? Alas! I have a notion that that will be the end of it!"

A piercingly cold night wind blew through the street, and Salvator recognized the necessity for seeking some sort of shelter. Rising with difficulty, he staggered on into the Corso, and then turned into the Via Bergognona. At length he stopped before a little house, with only a couple of windows, where a poor widow lived with her two daughters. This woman had taken him in, for a very small sum, the first time he had come to Rome, an unknown and unnoticed stranger. And so he hoped again to find lodgings with her, of the sort best suited to the sad condition of his purse.

He knocked confidently at the door, and several times called out his name aloud. At last he heard the old woman slowly and reluctantly awakening out of her sleep. She shuffled to the window in her slippers, and began to rain down a shower of abuse upon the wretch who had come to annoy her like this in the middle of the night; her house was not a wineshop, and so on, and so on. Then there ensued a good deal of cross-questioning before she recognized her former lodger's voice.

But on Salvator's complaining that he had been obliged to flee from Naples and was unable to find a shelter in Rome, the old dame cried, "By all the blessed saints of Heaven! Is that you, Signor Salvator? Well, now, your little room upstairs, that looks out on the court, is still standing empty, and the old fig tree has pushed its branches right through the window and into the room, so that you can sit and work just as if you were in a beautiful cool arbor. Oh, and how pleased my girls will be that you have come back again, Signor Salvator! Do you know, my Margarita's grown a big girl and fine-looking? You won't give her any more rides on your knee now. And—and your little kitten, just think of it, three months ago she choked herself with a fish bone. Ah, well, we all shall come to the grave at last. But, d'you know, my fat neighbor, the one you laughed at, and painted in such funny ways—d'you know, she *did* marry that young fellow, Signor Luigi, after all! Ah, well! *Nozze e magistrati sono da dio destinati*, they say."

"But," cried Salvator, interrupting the old woman, "but, Signora Caterina, I entreat you by the blessed saints, do, please, let me in; and *then* tell me all about your fig tree and your daughters, your cat and your fat neighbor—I am perishing outside here, of weariness and cold."

"Bless me, how impatient we are!" rejoined the old dame; "*Chi va piano va sano, chi va presto more lesto*, I tell you. But you are tired; you are cold. Where are the keys? Quick, with the keys!"

But the old woman still had to wake up her daughters and kindle a fire—and oh! she was such a long time about it, such a long, long time. At last she opened the door and let poor Salvator in; but scarcely had he crossed the threshold than, overcome by fatigue and illness, he dropped on the floor as if dead. Happily the widow's son, who lived at Tivoli, chanced to be staying at his mother's that night. He was at once turned out of his bed to make room for the sick guest, an imposition to which he willingly submitted, while he helped his mother care for the stricken man.

The old woman was very fond of Salvator, whom she rated, so far as his artistic powers went, above all the other painters in the world. And in everything that he did she also took the greatest pleasure. She was therefore quite beside herself when she saw him in such a lamentable condition. She wanted to run to the near-by monastery and call in her father-confessor, so that he might fight against the adverse power of the disease with consecrated candles or some powerful amulet. On the other hand, her son thought it would be better to try to get hold of an experienced physician at once. So off he ran then and there to the Piazza di Spagna, where he knew that the distinguished Doctor Splendiano Accoramboni lived. And he met with the best success. No sooner did the Doctor learn that the painter Salvator Rosa lay ill in the Via Bergognona, than he promised to call and see the patient at an early hour in the morning.

Salvator now lay unconscious, struck down by a most severe attack of fever. The old dame had hung up two or three pictures of saints above his bed, and was praying fervently. The girls, though bathed in tears, exerted themselves from time to time to get the sick man to swallow a few drops of the cooling lemonade which they had made, while their brother, who had taken his place at the head of the bed, wiped the cold sweat from his brow. And so morning found them, when with a loud noise the door opened, and the distinguished Doctor Splendiano Accoramboni entered the room.

If Salvator had not been so seriously ill that the two girls' hearts were melted in grief, they would, I think—for they were in general frolicsome and saucy—have enjoyed a healthy laugh at the Doctor's extraordinary appearance, instead of retiring shyly, and greatly alarmed, into the corner, as they did. It may interest you, gentle reader, to learn of the outward look of the little man who presented himself at Dame Caterina's in the Via Bergognona in the grey of the morning. In spite of all his excellent capabilities for growth, Doctor Splendiano Accoramboni had not been able to advance beyond the respectable stature of four feet. In the days of his youth, however, he had been distinguished for his elegant figure: before his head—always indeed somewhat ill-shaped—and his big cheeks and his stately double chin had put on too much fat, before his nose had grown fleshy and spread out—owing to overmuch indulgence in Spanish snuff—and before his little belly had assumed the shape of a wine tub from too much fattening on macaroni, the priestly cut of garments, which at that time he had affected, had suited him down to the ground. He had then been in truth a pretty little man, and accordingly the Roman ladies had styled him their *caro puppazetto*.

All this, however, was long since a thing of the past. A German painter, seeing Doctor Splendiano walking across the Piazza di Spagna, said—and he was perhaps not far wrong—that it looked as if some strapping fellow of six feet or so had walked away from his own head, and that this had fallen on the shoulders of a little marionette clown, who now had to carry it about as his own. This curious little figure strutted about clad in many-colored patchwork—an immense number of pieces of Venetian damask of a large flowered pattern that had been cut up in making a dressing gown. High up round his waist he had buckled a broad leather belt, from which hung an excessively long rapier; while his snowwhite wig was surmounted by a high conical cap, not unlike the obelisk in St. Peter's Square. Since the said wig, like a skein of yarn all tumbled and tangled, was spread out thick and wide all over his back, it might very well have been taken for the cocoon out of which the fine silkworm had crept.

The worthy Splendiano Accoramboni stared through his big bright spectacles, with his eyes wide open, first at his patient, then at Dame Caterina. Calling her aside, he croaked with bated breath, "There lies our talented painter Salvator Rosa, and he's lost if my skill doesn't save him, Dame Caterina. Tell me, when did he come to lodge with you? Did he bring many of his large and beautiful pictures with him?"

"Ah, my dear Doctor," replied Dame Caterina, "the poor fellow only came last night. And as for pictures—why, I don't know nothing about them; but there's a big box below, and Salvator begged me to take very good care of it, before he became unconscious like what he now is. I dare say there's a fine picture packed in it, for he was painting in Naples."

This was, in fact, far from the truth; but we shall soon see that Dame Caterina had good reason for imposing upon the Doctor in this way.

"Good! Very good!" said the Doctor, simpering and stroking his beard. Then, with as much solemnity as his long rapier—which kept catching in all the chairs and tables he came near—would allow, he went up to the sick man and felt his pulse, snorting and wheezing the while, so that the sound had a most curious effect in the midst of the reverential silence which had fallen upon all the other people in the room.

Then he ran over in Greek and Latin the names of a hundred and twenty diseases that Salvator had not, then followed this by listing almost as many that he might have had, and concluded by saying that on the spur of the moment he didn't recollect the name of the disease which was actually afflicting the painter, but that he would within a short time find the right word for it, and, therewith, the proper remedies as well. Then he took his departure with the same solemnity with which he had entered, and left them all full of trouble and anxiety.

At the foot of the stairs the Doctor asked to see Salvator's box; Dame Caterina showed him one—which contained two or three of her deceased husband's cloaks now laid aside, and some old worn-out shoes, but which, naturally, she did not open. The Doctor smilingly tapped the box, on this side and on that, and remarked in a tone of satisfaction, "We shall see! We shall see!" Some hours later he returned with a very beautiful name for his patient's disease, and brought with him some big bottles of an evil-smelling potion, which he directed to be given to the painter in large and constantly repeated doses.

This was a task of no little difficulty, for Salvator showed the greatest aversion for—utter loathing of—the stuff, which looked, and smelled, and tasted, as if it had been concocted from the turbid waters of Acheron itself. Whether it was that the disease, since it had now received a name, and in consequence really signified something, had only just begun to put forth its virulence, or whether it was that Splendiano's potion created too much disturbance inside the patient, it is at any rate certain that the poor painter grew weaker and weaker from day to day, from hour to hour. And notwithstanding Doctor Splendiano Accoramboni's assurance that, after the vital process had reached a state of perfect equilibrium, he would give it a new start like the pendulum of a clock, they were all very doubtful as to Salvator's recovery, and thought that the Doctor had perhaps already given the pendulum such a violent start that the mechanism was irremediably impaired.

Now it happened one day, when Salvator seemed scarcely able to move a finger, that his fever suddenly reached the raging point, and in a momentary, delirious accession of strength, he leaped out of bed, seized the full medicine bottles, and hurled them fiercely out of the window. At just this instant Doctor Splendiano Accoramboni was coming into the house, and so it chanced that two or three bottles came bang upon his head, smashing all to pieces, while the brown liquid ran in streams all down his face and wig and ruff.

Hastily rushing into the hallway, he screamed like a madman, "Signor Salvator has gone out of his mind! He's become insane! No skill can save him now—he'll be dead in ten minutes. Give me the picture, Dame Caterina, give me the picture—it's mine, the scanty reward of all my trouble! Give me the picture, I say!"

But when Dame Caterina opened the box, and Doctor Splendiano saw nothing but the old clothes and worn-out shoes, his eyes spun round in his head like a pair of firewheels; he gnashed his teeth; he stamped; he consigned poor Salvator, the widow, and all the family to the Devil; and then he sped out of the house like an arrow from a bow, or as if he had been shot from a cannon.

After the violence of the paroxysm had spent itself, Salvator again relapsed into a deathlike coma. Dame Caterina was now fully persuaded that his end had really come, and away she hurried as fast as she could to the monastery, to call Father Boniface to come and administer the sacrament to the dying man. Father Boniface returned with her immediately, and looked at the patient. He said he was well acquainted with the peculiar signs which approaching death is wont to stamp upon the human countenance, but that for the present there were no such indications on the face of the comatose Salvator Rosa. Something might still be done, he felt sure, and he promised to procure help at once; only Doctor Splendiano Accoramboni with his Greek names and infernal medicines was not to be allowed to cross the threshold.again. The good Father set out at once, and the troubled household was soon to learn how well he had kept his word.

Salvator slowly returned to consciousness; at first he thought that he was lying in a beautiful flower-scented arbor, for green boughs and big leaves were interlaced above his head. He felt a salutary warmth glowing in his veins, but it seemed to him as if somehow his left arm was bound fast, so that he could not move it. "Where am I?" he asked.

Then a handsome young man, who had been standing at his bedside, but whom he had not noticed until just now, fell upon his knees before the painter, and, grasping Salvator's right hand, kissed it and bathed it with tears. Meanwhile he kept saying, again and again, "Oh, my dear sir! My noble master! Now all is right; you are saved; you shall get better."

"Do tell me what has happened?" began Salvator.

But the youth begged him not to exert himself. The painter, he said, was too weak to talk. "You see, my esteemed and excellent sir," began the young stranger, "you see, you were very ill when you came from Naples. But your condition was not, I warrant, by any means so dangerous but that a few simple remedies would soon have set you, with your strong constitution, on your feet again, if Carlos' well-intentioned blunder in running off for the nearest physician had not thrust you into the hands of the redoubtable Pyramid Doctor, who was making all preparations for bringing you to your grave."

"What do you say?" exclaimed Salvator, laughing heartily, notwithstanding his feeble state. "What do you say?—the Pyramid Doctor? Oh, yes, although I was very ill, I saw that the little knave in damask patchwork, who condemned me to drink his horrid, loathsome Devil's brew, wore on his head the obelisk from St. Peter's Square—and so that's why you call him the Pyramid Doctor?"

"Why, good Heavens!" said the young man, laughing in his turn. "Why, Doctor Splendiano Accoramboni must have come to see you in his ominous conical nightcap! Do you know, you may see it flashing every morning from his window in the Piazza di Spagna like a portentous meteor. But it's not by any means because of this cap that he's called the Pyramid Doctor; for that, there's quite another reason. First let me tell you that Doctor Splendiano is a great lover of painting, and possesses in truth quite a choice collection, which he has gained by a rather peculiar practice. With eager cunning he lies in wait for painters and their illnesses. More especially he loves to get foreign artists in his toils: let one of them but eat an ounce or two of macaroni too much, or drink a glass more of Syracuse wine than is altogether good for him, and the Doctor will afflict him with first one and then the other disease, designating it by a formidable name, and promising a cure at once. He generally bargains for a picture as the price of his attendance; and since only the most obstinate constitutions are able to withstand his powerful remedies, it generally happens that he gets his picture out of the chattels left by the poor foreigner, who meanwhile has been carried to the Pyramid of Cestius, and buried there.

"It need hardly be said that Signor Splendiano always picks out the painter's best work, and also does not forget to instruct his men to pick up along with it whatever other canvases are at hand. The cemetery near the Pyramid of Cestius is Doctor Splendiano Accoramboni's cornfield, which he diligently cultivates, and for that reason he is called the Pyramid Doctor. Dame Caterina had taken great pains, of course with the best intentions, to make the Doctor believe that you had brought a fine painting with you; you may imagine therefore with what eagerness he concocted his potions for you. It was a fortunate thing that in your delirium of fever you threw the gentleman's bottles at his head. It was also a fortunate thing that he left you in anger. And no less fortunate was it that Dame Caterina, who believed you were in the agonies of death, called on Father Boniface to come and administer the sacrament to you. Father

Boniface understands something of the art of healing; he formed a correct diagnosis of your condition and sent for me—"

"Then you also are a physician?" asked Salvator in a faintly quavering tone.

"No," replied the young man, turning crimson, "no, my estimable and worthy sir, I am by no means a physician, like Signor Splendiano Accoramboni; I am, however, a surgeon and blood-letter. And I felt as if I should sink into the earth with fear—with joy—when Father Boniface came and told me that Salvator Rosa lay critically ill in the Via Bergognona, and was in need of my help. I hurried here at once, opened a vein in your left arm, and you were saved. Then we brought you up into this cool airy room that you occupied when you were here before. Look, there's the easel which you left behind you; yonder are a few sketches, which Dame Caterina has treasured as if they were relics of the saints. The virulence of your disease is subdued. Simple remedies such as Father Boniface can prepare are all that you need, except good nursing, to bring back your strength again.

"And now," the youth broke off suddenly, "permit me once more to kiss this hand—this creative hand that charms from Nature her deepest secrets, and clothes them in living form. Permit poor Antonio Scacciati to pour out all the gratitude and immeasurable joy of his heart that Heaven has granted him the opportunity to save the life of our great and noble painter, Salvator Rosa."

Therewith the young surgeon threw himself on his knees again, and, seizing Salvator's hand, kissed it and bathed it in tears as before.

"I don't understand," said the artist, raising himself up a little, though with considerable difficulty, "I don't understand, my dear Antonio, what it is that moves you, so especially, to show me all this respect. You are, you say, a surgeon; and we don't in a general way find this trade going hand in hand with the love of art—"

"As soon," replied the young man, casting down his eyes, "as soon as you have picked up your strength again, my dear sir, I have a good deal to tell you that now lies heavy on my heart."

"Do so," said Salvator. "You may have every confidence in me, I assure you; for I don't know that any man's face has ever made a more direct appeal to my heart than yours. The more I look at you the more plainly I seem to trace in your features a resemblance to that incomparable young painter—I mean Sanzio."

When Antonio heard this, a proud and radiant light came into his eyes, and he vainly struggled for words with which to express his emotion.

At this moment Dame Caterina appeared, followed by Father Boniface, who brought Salvator a medicine which he had mixed scientifically according to prescription, and which the patient dutifully swallowed with more tolerance and assurance than he had ever felt in his heart for the Acheronian waters of that Doctor of the Pyramid, Splendiano Accoramboni.

II

By Salvator Rosa's intervention Antonio Scacciati attains to a high honor. Antonio discloses to Salvator the cause of his persistent trouble, and the painter consoles him and promises his aid.

And Antonio's words proved true. The simple but salutary remedies of Father Boniface, the careful nursing of good Dame Caterina and her daughters, the warmer weather which now came—all co-operated so effectively with Salvator's naturally robust constitution that he soon felt sufficiently well to think about work again, and even to make a few sketches for later reference.

Antonio scarcely ever left Salvator's room. He was all rapt attention when the painter worked on some drawing or cartoon, and his judgment on many points showed that he must have indeed probed some of the secrets of art.

"See here," said Salvator to him one day, "see here, Antonio, you understand these matters so well that I believe you have not merely cultivated your excellent judgment as a critic, but must, at one time or another, have wielded the brush, too."

"You will remember," rejoined Antonio, "how I told you, my dear sir—when you were just about coming to yourself again after that long period of unconsciousness—that I had several things to tell you which lay heavy on my mind. Perhaps this is the time for me to unburden myself to you.

"You must know then," he began, "that though I am by calling a surgeon, and blood-letter—the man who opened the vein in your arm for you—my soul belongs entirely to art: the art to which, after bidding eternal farewell to this trade which I loathe, I intend to devote myself forever."

"Ho! Ho!" exclaimed Salvator, "Ho! Ho! Antonio, weigh well what you are about to do. You are a clever surgeon, and perhaps will never be anything more than a bungling painter all your life. For, with your permission, I must tell you that, young as you are, you are decidedly too old to begin now to use the charcoal. Believe me, a man's whole lifetime is scarce long enough to acquire a knowledge of the True—still less the practical ability to represent it."

"Ah! But, my dear sir," replied Antonio, smiling blandly, "don't imagine that I should now have come to entertain the foolish idea of taking up the difficult art of painting, had I not practiced it already on every possible occasion, even from my early childhood. In spite of the fact that my father obstinately kept me away from everything connected with art, Heaven was yet graciously pleased to throw me in the way of some celebrated artists. I must tell you that the great Annibal interested himself in the lonely boy, and also that I may with justice call myself Guido Reni's pupil."

"Well, then," said Salvator with a sharpness to which those who knew him were not unaccustomed, "well, then, my good Antonio, you have indeed had great masters, and so it must follow that, without detriment to your surgical practice, you must have been a great pupil. Only I don't understand how you, a faithful disciple of the gentle and elegant Guido, whom you perhaps outdo in elegance in your own pictures—for pupils do practice that sort of thing in their enthusiasm—how you can find any pleasure in my work, or how you can really regard me as a master?"

At these words, which indeed sounded a good deal like mockery, the hot blood rushed into the young man's face.

"Oh, let me lay aside all the timidity which generally keeps my lips closed," he said, "and let me frankly lay bare the thoughts I have in my mind! I tell you, Salvator, I have never honored any master from the depths of my soul, as I do you. What overwhelms one in your work is the scope, the almost supernal sweep of the perception: you penetrate the deepest secrets of Nature; you have deciphered the mysterious hieroglyphics of her rocks, of her trees, and of her waterfalls; you hear her sacred voice, you understand her language, and you possess the power to write down what she has said to you. Yes, I prefer to describe your bold and free approach to painting as the act of *writing down*. Man apart, for all his strivings, does not suffice you. You behold him only in the midst of Nature, and in so far as his inner being is influenced and affected by her phenomena. And in these facts I see the reason why you are only truly great in landscapes, Salvator, in which you set your wonderful figures. Historical painting confines you within limits which check your imagination, to the detriment of your genius for communicating your higher intuitions of Nature."

"That's talk you've picked up from historical painters who envy me," Salvator interrupted. "Like them, Antonio, you throw me the choice bone of landscape painting so that I may gnaw away at that, and thus spare their own good flesh. Perhaps I do understand the human figure and all that is dependent upon it. But this senseless parroting of the words of others—"

"Don't be angry," continued Antonio, "don't be angry, my good sir. I am not blindly repeating anybody's remarks, and I should not for a moment think of trusting to the judgment of our painters, here in Rome at any rate. Who can help greatly admiring the bold draftsmanship, the powerful expression, but above all the living movement of your figures? It's plain to see that you don't work from a stiff, inflexible model, or even from a dead skeleton form; it is evident that you yourself are your own breathing, living model, and that, when you sketch or paint, you have the figure you want to put on your canvas reflected in a great mirror before your eyes."

"The Devil! Antonio," exclaimed Salvator, laughing, "I believe you must often have had a peep into my studio when I was not aware of it, since you have such an accurate knowledge of what goes on inside."

"Perhaps I may," replied Antonio. "But let me go on. I am not by a long way so anxious to classify the pictures which your genius suggests to you as are those pedantic critics who take such great pains in that direction. In fact, I think that the term 'landscape,' as generally employed, has very little application to your paintings. I should prefer to call them historical representations, in the highest sense of these words. As we look at your work we actually feel as if this or the other rock, or this or the other tree, were gazing at us like some gigantic but sentient being, with thoughtful, earnest eyes; and so again, on the other hand, this or the other group of fantastically attired men seems to resemble some remarkable stone which has been endowed with life. All Nature, breathing and moving in harmonious unity, lends her vital accents to the sublime thought which leaped into existence in your mind.

"This," the youth continued, "is the spirit in which I have studied your pictures. And so in this way it is, my noble master, that I owe to you my truer perceptions in matters of art. But please don't imagine that I have fallen into childish imitation of you. However much I should like to possess the free bold pencil that you wield, I do not attempt to conceal the fact that Nature's colors appear to me different from those I see in your pictures. Although it is useful, I think, in order to acquire technique, for the pupil to imitate the style of this or that master, yet, as soon as he comes to stand in any sense on his own feet, he ought to aim at representing Nature as he himself sees her. Nothing but this actuality of perception, this unity with oneself, can give character and truth to the artist's work. Guido shared these convictions; and that fiery man Preti who, as you are aware, is called *Il Calabrese*—a painter who certainly, more than any other, has pondered over the meaning of his art—also warned me against all imitation. Now you know, Salvator, why I so much respect you, and do not wish to imitate you at all."

Through the rather lengthy interval of the young man's speech, Salvator had kept his eyes fixed, immovable and unchanging, upon him; he now clasped him tumultuously to his heart.

"Antonio," he then said, "the words you have just now uttered are those of true wisdom. Young as you are, you are nevertheless, so far as the true perception of art is concerned, a long way ahead of many of our older and much-vaunted masters, who give forth a good deal of stupid and trivial twaddle about their painting, but never get at the root of the matter.

"Body alive, man!" he exclaimed. "When you were talking about my pictures, I do believe that I began to understand myself for the first time! And because you do not imitate my style—do not, like a good many others, take a tube of black paint in your hand, or dab on a few glaring colors, or even show two or three crippled figures with repulsive faces looking up from the midst of filth and dirt, and then say, 'There's a Salvator for you!' —just for that very reason I think a good deal of you. I tell you now, my lad, you'll not find a more faithful friend than I am—that I can promise you with all my heart and soul."

Antonio was beside himself with joy over the kind way in which the great painter thus testified to his interest in him. And as Salvator expressed an earnest desire to see his pictures, the young man took him then and there to his studio.

The famous painter had in truth expected to find some examples of fairly good work from the youth who had spoken so intelligently about art, and had created the impression of really having something to him; he was nevertheless greatly surprised by the quality of Antonio's pictures. Everywhere he found boldness in conception, and accuracy in drawing. And the freshness of the colors, the good taste in the arrangement of the drapery, the uncommon delicacy of the hands and feet, the exquisite grace of the heads—these were all so many evidences that Antonio was no unworthy pupil of the great Guido Reni. But the young novice had avoided his master's besetting sin of the willingness, only too conspicuous, to sacrifice expression to beauty. It was plain that Antonio was endeavoring to reach Annibal's strength, without having as yet arrived at that goal.

Salvator spent considerable time in the thoughtful, and silent, examination of each picture. Then he said: "Listen to me, Antonio: it is indeed undeniable that you were born to follow the noble art of painting. For not only has Nature endowed you with the creative spirit from which the finest thoughts pour forth in an inexhaustible stream, but she has also granted you the rare ability to surmount the difficulties of the painter's technique in a short space of time. It would only be false flattery if I were to tell you that you had yet advanced to the level of your masters, that you can yet achieve Guido's exquisite grace, or Annibal's strength; but certain I am that you far excel all the painters who hold up their heads so proudly in the Academy of St. Luke here—Tiarini, Gessi, Sementa, and all the rest of them, not even excepting Lanfranco himself, for he only understands fresco painting. And yet, Antonio, and yet, if I were in your place, I should deliberate awhile before throwing away the lancet altogether and confining myself entirely to the pencil. That sounds rather strange, but, again, listen to me. Art seems to be having a bad time of it just now, or rather the Devil seems to be very busy among our painters nowadays, bravely setting them all by the ears. If you cannot make up your mind to put up with every sort of annoyance, to endure more and more scorn and contumely in proportion to the extent your art advances and your fame spreads, to meet everywhere the malice and duplicity of those who force their friendship upon you in order to ruin you the more surely afterwards— if you cannot, I say, make up your mind to endure all this, then I advise you to let painting alone. Think of the fate of your teacher, the great Annibal, whom a rascally band of rivals so malignantly persecuted, in Naples, that he did not receive one single important commission, and was everywhere rejected with contempt—a circumstance which most assuredly contributed to his early death. Think of what happened to Domenichino when he was painting the dome of the chapel of St. Januarius. Didn't these villains of painters—I won't mention a single name, not even the rascals Belisario and Ribera—didn't they bribe Domenichino's servant to scatter ashes in the lime? Naturally, the plaster wouldn't hold fast on the walls, and the painting had no stability. Think of all this, and examine yourself well, to make sure whether or not your spirit is strong enough to endure such things. For if it is not, your artistic strength itself will be broken, and you will lose not only the resolute courage for work, but also your ability."

"But, Salvator," replied Antonio, "it would hardly be possible for me to have more scorn and contumely to endure, supposing I took up painting entirely and exclusively, than I have already experienced as a mere surgeon. You have been pleased with my pictures, you have indeed! And at the same time you have declared your inner conviction that I am capable of doing better things than several of our painters at the Academy. But these are just the men who turn up their noses at all that I have industriously produced, and say contemptuously, 'Do look, here's our surgeon and blood-letter wants to be a painter!'

"And for this very reason," he added, firmly, "my resolve is only the more indomitable; I will sever myself from a trade that grows with each passing day more hateful to me. Upon you, my honored master, I now stake all my hopes. Your word has power; if you would speak a good word for me, you might influence those narrow academicians who are suspicious of all youth and innovation."

"You have great confidence in me," rejoined Salvator. "But now that we thoroughly understand each other's views on painting, and I have seen your work, I don't really know that there is anybody for whom I would rather take up the cudgels."

After making this characteristically warmhearted assertion, Salvator once more inspected Antonio's pictures. This time he paused before a painting of "Magdalene at the Saviour's Feet," which he especially praised.

"In this Magdalene," he said, "you have deviated from the usual interpretation. Your Magdalene is not a thoughtful virgin, but rather a lovely, artless child; and yet she is such a marvelous child that hardly anybody but Guido could have painted her. There is a unique charm in her fragility; you must have been truly inspired when you set about this picture; and, if I mistake not, the original of this Magdalene is alive and to be found in Rome. Come, confess, Antonio, you are in love!"

Antonio's eyes sought the ground, and his voice was almost inaudible in his shyness. "Nothing escapes your penetration, my dear sir," he confessed. "Perhaps it is as you say, but do not blame me for it. That picture I set the highest store by, and hitherto I have guarded it as a holy secret from all men's eyes."

"What did you say?" interrupted Salvator. "None of the painters here has seen your picture?"

"No, not one," Antonio replied.

"Very well, then, Antonio," continued Salvator, his eyes sparkling with delight. "Very well, then, you may rely upon it, I will overwhelm your arrogant and envious judges, and will bring you the honor you deserve. Entrust your picture to me; bring it to my studio secretly, by night; and then leave all the rest to me. Will you do this?"

"With the greatest delight in the world," replied Antonio. "And now—since you have guessed that I am in love—I should very much like to talk to you about my troubles in that sphere, as well. But I feel that I ought not to do so today, after we have opened our minds to each other on the subject of art. May I entreat you to grant me your assistance, both in word and deed, later on, in this other matter that concerns my heart?"

"I am at your service," said Salvator, "for both. Only let me know when and where you require my aid."

Then, as he was going away, he once more turned round and said, smiling, "See here, Antonio, when you disclosed to me the fact that you were a painter, I was very sorry that I had spoken about your resemblance to Sanzio. I took it for granted that you were as foolish as most of our young folk, who, if they bear but the slightest facial resemblance to any great master, at once trim their beard or hair as he does, and then imagine it is their next concern to imitate his style in art as well, even though it is a manifest violation of their natural talents to do so. Neither of us has mentioned Raphael's name, but I assure you that I have discerned in your pictures clear indications that you have grasped the full significance of the inimitable spirit and thought which are reflected in the works of this greatest painter of the age. You understand Raphael, and would give me a different answer from that of Velasquez when I asked him not long ago what he thought of Sanzio. 'Titian,' he replied, 'is the greatest painter; Raphael knows nothing about flesh tones.' This Spaniard, I think, understands flesh, but not criticism; and yet these men in St. Luke elevate him to the clouds because he once painted cherries which the sparrows picked at."

It happened that not many days after this the Academicians of St. Luke met together in their church to pass judgment on the works to be shown at the forthcoming exhibition. And there Salvator had sent Scacciati's fine picture. In spite of themselves the painters were greatly struck with its grace and power. And from all lips nothing was heard but the most extravagant praise when Salvator informed them that he had brought the picture with him from Naples, as the legacy of a young painter who had been cut off in the prime of his days.

It was not long before all Rome was crowding to see and admire this picture by the unknown Neapolitan who had died so young. It was unanimously agreed that no such work had been done since Guido Reni had won his fame. Some even went so far in their just enthusiasm as to place this exquisitely lovely Magdalene above Guido's similar subjects.

Salvator watched the fate of his protégé's work closely; and, among the crowd of people who were always gathered round Scacciati's picture, he one day observed a man who, besides presenting a most extraordinary appearance, behaved as if he were insane. Well advanced in years, he was tall, thin as a spindle, with a pale face and gleaming grey eyes, a long sharp nose and a chin equally long and, in fact, elongated further by a little pointed beard. On the top of his light sand-colored wig he had set a high hat with a magnificent feather; he wore a short dark red mantle, or cape, with many bright buttons, a sky-blue doublet slashed in the Spanish style, immense leather gauntlets with silver fringes, a long rapier at his side, light grey stockings drawn up above his bony knees and gartered with yellow ribbons; and there were bows of the same sort of yellow on his shoes.

This remarkable figure was standing before the picture like one enraptured: he raised himself on tiptoe; he stooped down till he appeared shrunken; then he jumped up with both feet at once, heaved deep sighs, groaned, shut his eyes so forcefully that the tears began to trickle down his cheeks, opened them wide again, fixed his concentrated gaze upon the charming Magdalene, sighed again, murmured in a thin, querulous, falsetto of a voice, "Ah! *Carissima—benedettissima! Ah! Marianna—Mariannina—bellissima!*" and more to the same effect. Salvator, who had a whimsical fancy for such oddities, drew near to the old fellow, intending to engage him in conversation about Scacciati's work, which seemed to afford him so much exquisite delight.

But without paying any attention to the stranger who now stood beside him, the old gentleman now began volubly to curse his poverty, which made it impossible for him to pay a million sequins for the picture, and place it under lock and key where nobody could set his infernal eyes upon it. Then, hopping up and down again, he blessed the Virgin and all the holy saints for the death of the reprobate artist who had painted this heavenly picture which was driving him to despair and madness.

Salvator concluded that the man either was out of his mind, or was an Academician of St. Luke with whom he was unacquainted.

All Rome was agog over Scacciati's wonderful picture. People could scarcely talk about anything else—and this of course was convincing proof of the excellence of the work. So it followed that when the painters were again assembled in the church of St. Luke, to decide about the admission of certain other pictures which had been submitted for exhibition, Salvator Rosa suddenly asked whether the painter of the "Magdalene at the

Saviour's Feet" was not worthy of the honor of posthumous membership in the Academy. They all with one accord, including even that hair-splitter in criticism, Baron Josépin, declared that such a great artist, alive, would have been an ornament to the Academy, and expressed their sorrow at his death in the choicest phrases, although, like the crazy old man, they were praising Heaven in their hearts that he was in no position to offer them any future competition. And they were so far carried away by their enthusiasm that they not only unanimously passed a resolution to the effect that the admirable young painter whom death had snatched away so early, from the service of Art, should be nominated posthumously as a member of the Academy, but added that masses should be read, for the benefit of his soul, in the church of St. Luke. They therefore asked Salvator to tell them the full name of the deceased, the date of his birth, the place where he was born, and other such matters.

Then Salvator rose in his seat, and said in a loud voice, "Signors, the honor you are anxious to render to a dead man you can more easily bestow upon a living one who walks in your midst. I must tell you now that the 'Magdalene at the Saviour's Feet'—the picture which you so justly exalt above all other artistic productions that the last few years have given us— is not the work of a dead Neapolitan painter as I pretended (this I did simply to get an unbiased judgment from you). That painting, that masterpiece, which all Rome is admiring, is from the hand of Signor Antonio Scacciati, the surgeon and blood-letter."

The painters sat staring at Salvator as if they had been struck by lightning. They were all incapable of either moving or uttering a single sound. He, however, after enjoying a few moments of silent exultation over their embarrassment, continued, "Well, now, Signors, you would not tolerate the worthy Antonio among you because he is a surgeon; but I think that the illustrious Academy of St. Luke has great need of a surgeon to set aright the limbs of the many crippled figures which emerge from the studios of its members. But of course you will no longer scruple to do what you ought to have done long ago: namely, elect that excellent painter Antonio Scacciati to membership."

The Academicians, swallowing Salvator's bitter pill, pretended to be highly delighted that Antonio had in this way given such incontestable proof of his talent. And with all due ceremony they named him a member of the Academy.

As soon as it became known in Rome that Antonio was the painter of the remarkable picture, he was overwhelmed with congratulations, and even with commissions for important work, which poured in upon him from all sides. Thus by Salvator's shrewd and well-thought-out stratagem the young man emerged all at once from his obscurity; and the first real step that he took on his artistic career was one which carried him to great honor.

Antonio was wholly given over, like a child, to ecstasies of delight. So much the more therefore was Salvator amazed when, some days after his election to the Academy, he came to his friend's studio with his face pale and distorted, his whole appearance utterly miserable and woebegone.

"Ah! Salvator!" the youth broke out. "What advantage has it been to me that you have helped me to rise to a level far beyond my expectations, that praise and honor are now heaped upon me, that the prospect of a completely successful artistic career is opening out before my eyes? Oh, I am utterly miserable! For the picture to which, next to you, my dear sir, I owe my great triumph, has become the source of my enduring misfortune."

"Careful!" replied Salvator. "Don't sin against either your art or your picture. I don't believe a word about the terrible misfortune which, you say, has befallen you. You are in love, and I presume you can't get all your wishes gratified at once, on the spur of the moment; that's all it is. Lovers are like children; they scream and cry if anybody so much as threatens to take their toys from them. Now stop all this lamentation, I beg you; for I tell you I am not going to stand for it! Come now, sit down there quietly, and tell me all about your fair Magdalene, and give me the history of your love affair, and let me know what are the stones of offense that we have to remove; for I promise you my help beforehand. The more adventurous the schemes are which we shall have to undertake, the better I shall like them. In fact, my blood is coursing hotly in my veins again, and my general diet, so to speak, requires that I engage in a few wild pranks. But go on with your story, Antonio, and, as I said, let's have it quietly without any sighs and wails, without any Ohs! and Ahs!"

Antonio took his seat on the stool that Salvator had pushed up to the easel at which he was working, and began his tale.

"There is a high house," he said, "in the Via Ripetta, with a balcony which projects far over the street so as to strike the eye, immediately, of anyone who comes in through the Porta del Popolo. And there dwells perhaps the most bizarre creature in all Rome, an old bachelor with every fault that belongs to that type. In short, he is avaricious, vain, anxious to appear young, amorous, and foppish. He is tall, as thin as a switch; he wears a gay Spanish costume, a sandy wig, a conical hat, leather gauntlets, a rapier at his side—"

"Stop, stop!" Salvator interrupted the young man's recital. "Excuse me a minute or two, Antonio." Then, turning about the painting at which he was working, he seized his charcoal, and in a few free bold strokes sketched on the other side of the canvas the eccentric old gentleman whom he had seen behaving like a lunatic in front of Antonio's "Magdalene."

"By all the saints!" cried Antonio, as he sprang to his feet, and, forgetful of his unhappiness, burst out into a loud laugh. "By all the saints! That's he! That's Signor Pasquale Capuzzi, whom I was just describing; that's he to the life!"

"So you see," said Salvator calmly, "that I am already acquainted with the worthy gentleman, who, no doubt, will turn out to be your bitter enemy. But go on."

"Signor Pasquale Capuzzi," continued Antonio, "is as rich as Croesus, but at the same time, as I just told you, he is both a sordid miser and an incurable fool. The best thing about him is that he really loves the arts, particularly music and painting. But he mixes so much folly with all his devotion that even in these things there's no getting on with him. He considers himself the greatest composer in the world, and, as for performance, he thinks there's not a singer in the Papal choir who can even approach him. Accordingly he looks down upon our old Frescobaldi with contempt; and when the Romans talk about the wonderful charm of Ceccarelli's voice, he assures them that Ceccarelli knows as much about singing as a pair of top boots, and that he, Capuzzi, is quite sure of the right way to charm the public. But as the first singer of the Pope bears the proud name of Signor Odoardo Ceccarelli di Merania, so our Capuzzi is greatly delighted when anybody calls him Signor Pasquale Capuzzi di

Senigaglia; for it was in Senigaglia that he was born. And the popular rumor goes that his mother, being startled at sight of a seal (sea-dog) suddenly rising to the surface, gave birth to him in a fisherman's boat; that accounts, it is said, for a good deal of the cur in his nature.

"Well, be that as it may, the fact is that several years ago he brought out an opera on the stage, and that it was fearfully hissed. But that hasn't cured him of his mania for writing execrable music. Indeed, when he heard Francesco Cavalli's opera, *Le Nozze di Teti e Peleo*, he swore that the composer had filched his sublimest ideas from his own immortal works! And for that, indeed, Capuzzi came near being thrashed, and even stabbed. He still has a craze for singing arias, and accompanies his hideous squalling on a wretched, jarring, jangling guitar, all out of tune. His faithful Pylades is an ill-bred dwarf, whom the Romans call Pitichinaccio. There is a third member of the company—guess who it is?—Why, it is none other than the Pyramid Doctor, who kicks up a noise like a melancholy ass and yet fancies he's singing an excellent bass, quite as good as Martinelli of the Papal choir.

"Now these three estimable people are in the habit of meeting in the evening on the balcony of Capuzzi's house, where they sing Carissimi's motets, until all the dogs and cats in the vicinity break out into dirges of miaowing and howling, and all the neighbors heartily wish that the Devil would make off with the whole blessed trio.

"With this grotesque old fellow, Signor Pasquale Capuzzi, of whom my description will have enabled you to form a tolerably adequate idea, my father lived on terms of a certain intimacy, because he was the barber who trimmed his wig and beard. When my father died, I undertook his same responsibility, and Capuzzi was in the highest degree satisfied with me, for, as he once affirmed, I knew better than anybody else how to give his mustache a bold upward twirl. But the real reason was that I was satisfied with the few pence with which he rewarded me for my pains. He firmly believed, however, that he rewarded me more than richly, since, while I was trimming his beard, he always closed his eyes and croaked through an aria from one of his own compositions, which, as you may imagine, almost split my ears. Yet it is true that the old fellow's crazy gestures afforded me a good deal of amusement, and so I continued to attend him and expected only to continue to be thus mildly entertained.

"But one day, as I quietly ascended his stairs, knocked at his door, and opened it, instead of the prancing old fool, a young girl—an angel of light—came to meet me! You know my Magdalene; it was she.

"I stood stock-still, rooted to the spot. No, Salvator, you shall have no Ohs! and Ahs! Well, the first sight of this, the loveliest girl I had ever seen, threw me into transports of sudden and ardent love. The old man informed me with a smirk that the young lady was the daughter of his brother Pietro who had died at Senigaglia, that her name was Marianna, and that her mother was dead also. As her uncle and guardian, he had taken her into his house.

"You can easily imagine that henceforward Capuzzi's house was my Paradise. But no matter what devices I had recourse to, I could never succeed in getting Marianna tête-à-tête, even for a single moment. Yet at the same time her tender glances and many a stolen sigh, and many a soft pressure of the hand, resolved all doubts as to my good fortune. The old man divined what I was after—which was not a very difficult thing for him to do. He told me bluntly that my behavior towards his niece was not such as to please him altogether; and he asked me what was the real purport of my attentions.

"Then I frankly confessed that I loved Marianna with all my heart, and that the greatest earthly happiness I could conceive was to make her my wife. But, at that, Capuzzi, after measuring me from top to toe, burst out in a guffaw of contempt, and declared that he would never have believed that such ambitious ideas could haunt the brain of a paltry barber. I was almost boiling with rage; I said he knew very well that I was no paltry barber, but a good surgeon; and, moreover, in so far as concerned the noble art of painting, I was a faithful pupil of the great Annibal Caracci and of the unrivaled Guido Reni. But the contemptible Capuzzi only replied with a still louder guffaw; and in his horrible falsetto he squealed out, 'Well, now, my sweet Signor barber, my excellent Signor surgeon, my honored Annibal Caracci, my beloved Guido Reni, you be off to the Devil, and don't ever show yourself here again, if you don't want your legs broken.'

"Therewith the ill-tempered, knock-kneed old fool laid hold of me with no less an intention than to kick me out of the room, and throw me down the stairs. But that, you know, was past enduring. In my fury I seized the old fellow and turned him upside down, so that his legs stuck up, above his head, in the air. And there I left him screaming aloud, while I ran down the stairs and out of the house door—which, I need hardly say, has been closed to me ever since . . .

"And that's how matters stood when you came to Rome," Antonio continued, "and when Heaven inspired Father Boniface with the happy idea of calling me in to treat you. Then, when your clever trick had brought me the success for which I had so long been vainly striving—that is, when I was accepted by the Academy of St. Luke, and all Rome was heaping praise and honor upon me to a lavish extent—I went straightway to the old gentleman, and suddenly presented myself before him in his own library, as if I were some threatening apparition from the other world. Such at least he must have thought me, for he turned pale as a spectre, himself, and retreated behind a great table, trembling in every limb.

"Then in a firm and earnest way I represented to him that it was not now a paltry barber or a surgeon and blood-letter, but a celebrated painter, an Academician of St. Luke, Antonio Scacciati, to whom he would not, I hoped, refuse the hand of his niece Marianna. But you should have seen into what a passion the old fellow flew! He screamed; he flourished his arms about like one possessed of devils; he yelled that I, a ruffianly murderer, was seeking his life, that I had stolen his Marianna from him because I had portrayed her in my picture, and that this was driving him mad, driving him to despair, for all the world, all the world, were fixing their covetous, lustful eyes upon his Marianna, his life, his hope, his all. But I had better take care, he shrieked at me; he would burn my house down over my head, with me and my picture in it. And therewith he kicked up such a din, shouting, 'Fire! Murder! Thieves! Help!' that I was utterly confounded, and only thought of making my way out of his presence as best I could.

"The crackbrained old fool is over head and ears in love with his niece. He keeps her under lock and key. And as soon as he succeeds in getting a dispensation from the Pope, he will compel her to a shocking marriage with himself. There is no more hope for me!"

"I wouldn't quite say that," said Salvator, laughing. "I am of the opinion that things are in the best possible state for you, right now. Marianna loves you, of that you are convinced; and all we have to do is to get her out of the power of that fantastic old gentleman, Signor Pasquale Capuzzi. I should like to know what there is to hinder a couple of stout enterprising fellows like you and me from accomplishing it! Pluck up your courage, Antonio! Instead of wailing, and sighing, and swooning like a lovesick swain, it would be better to set to work to think out some plan for rescuing your Marianna. You just wait and see, Antonio, how brilliantly we'll circumvent the old dotard; in such an adventure, the wildest extravagance hardly seems to me wild enough! I'll get things started at once, and find out what I can about the old man, and about his ordinary habits of life. But you must not be seen in this affair, Antonio. Go quietly home now, and come back to me early tomorrow morning; then we'll consider our first plan of attack."

Herewith Salvator shook the paint out of his brush, put on his cloak, and hurried to the Corso, while Antonio betook himself home as Salvator had bidden him—his heart comforted and full of optimism again.

III

Signor Pasquale Capuzzi turns up at Salvator Rosa's studio.
What takes place there. The cunning scheme which Rosa and
Scacciati carry out, and its consequences.

Next morning Salvator, having in the meantime inquired into Capuzzi's habits of life, very greatly surprised Antonio by a description of them, even down to the most minute details.

"Poor Marianna," said Salvator, "leads a tormented existence with the crazy old fool. There he sits sighing at her and ogling her, the whole day long, and, what is worse still, in order to soften her heart, he sings her the entire catalogue of love songs that he has ever composed or intends to compose. At the same time he is so monstrously jealous that he will not even permit the poor young girl to have the usual female attendance, for fear of intrigues and amours which the maid might be induced to engage in. Instead, a hideous little monster, with hollow eyes and pale flabby cheeks, appears every morning and evening to perform for sweet Marianna the services of a lady's maid. And this little monster is nobody else but that distorted Tom Thumb, that dwarfed henchman, Pitichinaccio, who must don female attire, and attend to these duties. Whenever Capuzzi leaves home, moreover, he carefully locks and bolts every door; and in addition to that there is always a confounded fellow keeping watch below—a man who was once a *bravo*, but later became a gendarme, and now lives on the ground floor of Capuzzi's house. It seems, therefore, that it would be almost impossible to effect an entrance into Marianna's prison. But nevertheless I promise you, Antonio, that this very night you shall be in Capuzzi's own apartment; and you shall see your Marianna, though this time it will only be in Capuzzi's presence."

"What do you say?" cried Antonio, with considerable excitement. "What do you say? We shall manage it tonight? I thought you said it was impossible."

"There, there," Salvator went on soothingly, "keep calm, Antonio, and let us consider quietly how we may safely carry out the plan I have conceived. But, before we go on, I must tell you that I have already scraped up an acquaintance with Signor Pasquale Capuzzi, without knowing it. That wretched spinet, which stands in the corner there, belongs to the old fellow, and he wants me to pay him the preposterous sum of ten ducats for it. When I was convalescent I longed for music, which always comforts me and does me considerable good; so I begged my landlady to get me some such instrument as that. Dame Caterina soon found out that there was an old gentleman, living in the Via Ripetta, who had a fine spinet to sell. And I had the instrument brought here. I did not trouble myself about either the price or the owner. It was only yesterday evening that I learned quite by chance that the gentleman who had planned to cheat me, with this rickety old thing, was Signor Pasquale Capuzzi. Dame Caterina had enlisted the services of an acquaintance living in the same house, and indeed on the same floor, as Capuzzi—and now you can easily guess where I collected my parcel of news."

"Yes," replied Antonio, "then the way to get into the house is discovered also; your landlady—"

"I know very well, Antonio," said Salvator, cutting him short, "I know what you're going to say. You think you can find a way to your Marianna through Dame Caterina. But you'll find that we can't do anything like that. The good dame is far too talkative. She can't keep the smallest secret. And so we can't for a single moment think of employing her in this business. Now just listen quietly to me . . . Every evening when it's dark, Signor Capuzzi—although it's very hard work for him, knock-kneed as he is—carries his little friend the miniature eunuch home in his arms, as soon as the latter has finished his duties as maid. Nothing in the world could induce the timid Pitichinaccio to set foot on the streets at that time of night. So that when—"

At this moment there was a knock at Salvator's door, and, to the consternation of both men, Signor Pasquale Capuzzi entered the room in all the splendor of his gala attire. On catching sight of Scacciati he stood stock-still, and then, opening his eyes wide, gasped for air as though he had some difficulty in breathing. But Salvator hastily ran to meet him, and took him by both hands, saying, "My dear Signor Pasquale, your presence in my humble dwelling is a very great honor. May I presume that it is your love for art which brings you to me? You wish to see the newest things I have done, perhaps to give me a commission for some work? Please tell me, my dear Signor Pasquale, how can I serve you?"

"I have a word or two to say to you, my dear Signor Salvator," stammered Capuzzi painfully, "but—alone—when you are alone. With your leave I will withdraw and come back again at a more convenient time."

"By no means," said Salvator, holding the old gentleman fast, "by no means, my dear sir. You need not stir a step; you could not have come at a more convenient time. For, since you are a great admirer of the noble art of painting, and since you are, indeed, the patron of all good painters, I am sure you will be greatly pleased when I introduce to you Antonio Scacciati, here, the leading painter of our time, whose glorious work—the wonderful 'Magdalene at the Saviour's Feet'—has excited the most enthusiastic admiration throughout all Rome. You too, I need hardly say, have also formed a high opinion of the work, and you must be very anxious to know the great artist himself."

The old man was seized with a violent trembling; and while he shivered away as if he had been suddenly attacked by a fit of the ague, he shot fiery wrathful looks at poor Antonio. The young painter approached the old gentleman, however, and, bowing with courtly courtesy, assured him that he esteemed himself happy at meeting in such an unexpected way with Signor Pasquale Capuzzi, whose great learning in music as well as in painting was a theme for wonder not only in Rome but throughout all Italy; and he concluded by requesting the honor of his patronage.

This behavior of Antonio's, in pretending to meet the old gentleman for the first time in his life, and in addressing him in such flattering phrases, soon appeased and calmed the eccentric visitor. He forced his features into a simpering smile, and, as Salvator now let go of his hands, he gave his mustache an elegant upward curl, at the same time stammering out a few unintelligible words. Then, turning to Salvator, he requested payment of the ten ducats for the spinet he had sold him.

"Oh, that trifling little matter can be settled later on, my dear sir," was Salvator's answer. "First have the goodness to look at this sketch of a picture which I have drawn, and drink a glass of good Syracuse wine while you do so." Salvator meanwhile placed his sketch on the easel and moved up a chair for the old gentleman. And then, when he had taken his seat, the artist presented him with a large and brimming goblet.

Signor Pasquale was very fond of a glass of good wine—when he was not obliged to pay anything for it. And now he ought to have been in an especially happy frame of mind. For, besides nourishing his heart with the hope of getting ten ducats for a toneless and wornout spinet, he was sitting before a splendid, boldly designed picture, the rare beauty of which he was quite capable of estimating at its full worth. And he indicated his good humor in divers ways: he simpered most charmingly; he half closed his eyes; he assiduously stroked his chin and mustache; and he lisped time after time, "Splendid! Delicious!" But his companions did not know to which he was referring, the picture or the wine.

When Capuzzi had thus worked himself round into a thoroughly happy state, Salvator suddenly began: "They tell me, my dear sir, that you have a most beautiful and amiable niece, named Marianna—is it so? All the young men of the city are so smitten with love that they can do nothing but run stupidly up and down the Via Ripetta, almost dislocating their necks in their efforts to look up at your balcony for a sight of your sweet Marianna, to snatch a single glance from her heavenly eyes."

And as Capuzzi heard these words, all the charming simpers, all the good humor which had been called up into the old gentleman's face by the good wine, were suddenly gone. Staring gloomily before him, he said sharply, "Ah, that's an instance of the corruption of our abandoned young men! They fix their infernal eyes, these notorious seducers, upon mere children! For I tell you, my good sir, that my niece Marianna is nothing but a child, nothing but a child, who has only just outgrown her nurse's care."

Salvator turned the conversation upon something else. The old gentleman recovered himself. But just as he, his face again radiant with sunshine, was on the point of putting another full goblet to his lips, Salvator returned to the attack. "But do tell me, my dear sir," he said, "if it is indeed true that your niece, with her sixteen summers, really has such beautiful auburn hair, and eyes so full of Heaven's own loveliness and joy, as has Antonio's 'Magdalene'? It is generally maintained that she has."

"I don't know," replied the old gentleman, still more sharply than before, "I don't know. But let us leave my niece in peace; rather let us exchange a few instructive words on the noble subject of art, as your fine picture here of itself invites me to do."

But whenever Capuzzi raised the goblet to his lips to take a good draught of the excellent vintage, Salvator began anew to talk about the beautiful Marianna; so that at last the old gentleman jumped up from his chair in a perfect passion, banged the cup down upon the table and almost broke it, and screamed in a high shrill voice, "By the infernal pit of Pluto! By all the Furies! You will turn my wine into poison—into poison, I tell you! But I see through you—you and your fine friend Signor Antonio, you think to make sport of me. You'll find yourselves deceived, all the same. Pay me the ten ducats you owe me, immediately; and then I will leave you and your associate, that barber fellow Antonio, to make your way to the Devil."

In answer to this, Salvator shouted, as if mastered by the most violent rage, "What! You have the audacity to speak to me like this, in my own house? Do you think I'm going to pay you ten ducats for that worthless box? The wood-worms have long ago eaten all the goodness and all the music out of it! Not ten—not five—not three—not one ducat shall you have for it. It's scarcely worth a farthing! Away with the broken-down thing!" And he kicked the little instrument again and again, till the strings were all jarring and jangling together.

"Oh!" screeched Capuzzi. "But justice is still to be had in Rome! I will have you arrested, sir—arrested and cast into the deepest dungeon in the city!" And he started to rush out of the room, blustering like a hailstorm.

But Salvator took fast hold of him with both hands, and pushed him down into the chair again, while he softly murmured in his ear, "My dear Signor Pasquale, don't you understand that I was only teasing you? You shall have, for your spinet, not ten, but *thirty* ducats, cash down." And he went on repeating, "Thirty bright ducats in ready money," until Capuzzi said in a faint and feeble voice, "What are you saying, my dear sir? Thirty ducats for the spinet without its being repaired?"

Then Salvator released his hold of the old gentleman, and asserted on his honor that within an hour the instrument should be worth thirty —nay, forty—ducats, and that Signor Pasquale should receive as much for it.

Taking in a fresh supply of breath, and sighing deeply, the old gentleman murmured, "Thirty—forty ducats!" Then he began, "But you have grossly wounded my feelings, Signor Salvator."

"Thirty ducats," exclaimed Salvator, cutting him short. And he continued to repeat, "Thirty ducats! Thirty ducats!" as long as the old gentleman continued to sulk, till at length Capuzzi said, radiant with delight, "If you will give me thirty—I mean forty—ducats for the spinet, all shall be forgiven and forgotten, my dear sir."

"But," rejoined Salvator, "before I can fulfill my promise, I still have one little condition to make, which you, my honored Signor Pasquale Capuzzi di Senigaglia, can easily grant. You are the first musical composer in all Italy, besides being the foremost singer of the day. When I heard in the opera *Le Nozze di Teti e Peleo* the great scene which that shameless Francesco Cavalli has thievishly taken from your works, I was enraptured. If you would only sing me that aria while I put the spinet to rights, you would confer upon me a pleasure than which I can conceive of none more enjoyable."

Puckering up his mouth into the most winning of smiles, and blinking his little grey eyes, the old gentleman replied, "I perceive, my good sir, that you are yourself a clever musician, for you possess taste, and you know how to respect merit more than these ungrateful Romans. Listen—just hear this aria of all arias."

Therewith he rose to his feet, and, stretching himself up to his full height, spread out his arms and closed both eyes, so that he looked like a cock preparing to crow. And he at once began to screech in such a way that the walls rang again, and Dame Caterina and her two daughters straightway came running in, under the impression that such lamentable sounds must betoken some accident or other. At sight of the crowing old gentleman they stopped on the threshold, utterly astonished; and thus they formed the audience of the incomparable musician Capuzzi.

Meanwhile Salvator, having picked up the spinet and thrown back the lid, had taken his palette in hand, and in bold firm strokes had begun on the cover of the instrument the most remarkable piece of painting that any of his companions had ever seen. The central idea was a scene from Cavalli's opera *Le Nozze di Teti*, but there were a great many other personages mixed up with it in the most fantastic way. Among them could easily be recognized Capuzzi, Antonio, Marianna (faithfully reproduced from Antonio's picture), Salvator himself, Dame Caterina and her two daughters; and even the Pyramid Doctor was not wanting. And all were grouped so intelligently, judicially, and ingeniously, that Antonio could not conceal his astonishment over the artist's intellectual power as well as his technique.

Meanwhile old Capuzzi had not been content with the aria which Salvator had requested him to render. Carried away by his musical madness, he went on singing—or rather screeching—without intermission, working his way through the most awful recitatives from one execrable scene to another. He must have been going on for nearly two hours when he sank back in his chair, breathless, and with his face as red as a cherry. And by this same time Salvator had so far worked out his sketch that the figures began to wear a look of vitality, and the whole, viewed at a little distance, had the appearance of a finished work.

"I have kept my word with respect to the spinet, my dear Signor Pasquale," breathed Salvator in the old man's ear. Capuzzi started up, at this, as if he were awakened out of a deep sleep. Immediately his glance fell upon the painted instrument, which stood directly opposite him. Then, opening his eyes wide as if he saw a miracle, and sticking his conical hat jauntily on the top of his wig, he took his walking stick under his arm, made one bound to the spinet, tore the lid off the hinges, and holding it above his head, ran like a madman out of the room, down the stairs, and away, away out of the house altogether, followed by the hearty laughter of Dame Caterina and both her daughters.

"The old miser," said Salvator, "knows very well that he has only to take that painted lid to Count Colonna or to my friend Rossi, and he will at once get forty ducats for it, or even more."

Salvator and Antonio then deliberated how they should carry out their plan of attack which was to be set in motion when night came. And before long they had worked out their scheme to the most minute detail.

As soon as it was dark, Signor Capuzzi, after locking and bolting the door of his house, carried the little monster of a eunuch home as usual. The whole way the little wretch kept whining and growling, complaining that not only did he sing Capuzzi's arias till he got catarrh in the throat (and that he had burned his fingers cooking the macaroni), but now he had to lend himself to duties which brought him nothing but sharp boxes on the ear and rough kicks, which Marianna lavishly distributed to him whenever he came near her. Old Capuzzi consoled the dwarf as well as he could, and promised to provide him an ampler supply of sweetmeats than he had enjoyed hitherto. Indeed, as the little creature would not cease his growling and querulous complaining, Pasquale even went so far as to say he would have an elegant abbot's coat made for the little torment, out of an old black plush waistcoat upon which the dwarf had often set covetous eyes. The pampered creature demanded a wig and a sword as well. And so, arguing on these points, they arrived in the Via Bergognona, for that was where Pitichinaccio lived, only four doors from Salvator's boarding place.

The old man set the dwarf cautiously on the pavement, and opened the street door; and then, with Pitichinaccio in the lead, the two men began to climb up the narrow stairs, which were more like a rickety ladder for hens and chickens than steps for respectable people.

But they had scarcely ascended halfway when a terrible racket broke out above them, and the coarse voice of some wild drunken fellow was heard cursing and swearing, and demanding to be shown the way out of this damned house. Pitichinaccio squeezed himself close to the wall, and entreated his employer, in the name of all the saints, to go on ahead. But before Capuzzi had mounted two steps, the fellow who was above came tumbling headlong downstairs, caught hold of the·old man, and dragged him along with the force of a whirlwind out through the open door below and into the middle of the street. There they both lay, Capuzzi underneath and the drunken brute like a heavy sack on top of him. The old gentleman screamed piteously for help; two men ran up at once and with considerable difficulty freed him from the heavy weight lying upon him; the drunken fellow, as soon as he was lifted up, reeled away, cursing.

"Good God! What's happened to you, Signor Pasquale? What are you doing here at this time of night? What lusty quarrel have you been getting mixed up in, in that house there?" demanded Salvator and Antonio—for it was they who had come to Capuzzi's rescue.

"Oh, I shall die!" groaned the old gentleman. "That son of the Devil has crushed all my limbs; I can't move."

"Let me look," said Antonio, feeling all over the victim's body; and suddenly he pinched his right leg so sharply that Capuzzi screamed aloud.

"By all the saints!" cried Antonio, in consternation. "By all the saints! My dear Signor Pasquale, you've broken your right leg in the most dangerous place. If you don't get speedy help you will within a short time be a dead man, or at any rate be lame for the rest of your life."

A scream of terror escaped the old man's breast. "Calm yourself, my dear sir," continued Antonio. "Although I'm now a painter, I haven't altogether forgotten my surgical practice. We will carry you to Salvator's house and I will at once bind up—"

"My dear Signor Antonio," whined Capuzzi, "you nourish hostile feelings towards me, I know."

"But," broke in Salvator, "this is no longer the time to talk about enmity. You are in danger, and that is enough for honest Antonio to exert all his skill on your behalf. Lay hold, friend Antonio."

Gently and cautiously they lifted up the old man between them. And while he went on screaming with the unspeakable pain caused by his broken leg, they carried him to Salvator's lodging house.

Dame Caterina came out of her rooms at once: she said that she had had a foreboding that something was going to happen, and so she had not gone to bed. But as soon as she caught sight of the old gentleman, and heard what had befallen him, she began to heap reproaches upon him for his bad conduct.

"I know," she said, "I know very well, Signor Pasquale, who you've been taking home again. Now that you've got your beautiful niece Marianna in the house with you, you think you've no further call to have womenfolk about you, and you treat that poor Pitichinaccio most shameful and infamous, putting him in petticoats. But look to it. *Ogni carne ha il suo osso.* Why, if you have a girl about you, don't you need womenfolk? *Fate il passo secondo la gamba,* and don't you require anything either more or less from your Marianna than what is right. Don't lock her up as if she were a prisoner, nor make your house a dungeon. *Asino punto convien che trotti.* You have a beautiful niece, and you must alter your ways to suit her, that is, you must only do what she wants you to do. But you are an ungallant and hardhearted man, yes, and even in love, and jealous as well, they say, which I hope at your years is not true. Your pardon for telling it all to you straight out, but *chi ha nel petto fiele non puo sputar miele.* So now, if you don't die of your broken leg, which at your great age is not at all unlikely, let this be a warning to you; and leave your niece free to do what she likes, and let her marry the fine young gentleman as I know very well."

And so the stream of words flowed on uninterruptedly, while Salvator and Antonio cautiously undressed the old gentleman and put him to bed. Dame Caterina's reproaches stabbed him like darts; but whenever he attempted to say anything in his own defense, Antonio signed to him that all speaking was dangerous, and so he had to swallow his bitter gall. At length Salvator sent Dame Caterina away, to bring some ice-cold water that Antonio wanted.

The two friends had by now satisfied themselves that the fellow they had sent to Pitichinaccio's house had done his duty well. Notwithstanding his apparently terrible fall, Capuzzi had not received the slightest injury beyond a slight bruise or two. Antonio put the old gentleman's right foot in splints, and bandaged it up so tightly that he could not move. Then he and Salvator wrapped him up in cloths that had been soaked in ice-cold water—as a precaution, they alleged, against inflammation—so that the old gentleman shook as if with the ague.

"My good Signor Antonio," he groaned feebly, "tell me if it is all over with me. Am I going to die?"

"Compose yourself," replied Antonio. "If you will only compose yourself, Signor Pasquale! As you have come through the first dressing with so much endurance, and without fainting, I think we may say that the danger is past; but you will require the most attentive nursing. At present we mustn't let you out of the doctor's sight."

"Oh, Antonio," whined the old gentleman, "you know how much I like you, how highly I esteem your talents. Don't leave me. Give me your dear hand—so! You won't leave me, will you, my dear, good Antonio?"

"Although I am now no longer a surgeon," said Antonio, "although I've quite given up that uncongenial trade, yet I will in your case, Signor Pasquale, make an exception, and will undertake to attend you. For this I shall ask nothing except that you give me your friendship, your confidence, again. You were a little hard upon me—"

"Say no more," lisped the old gentleman, "not another word, my dear Antonio—"

"Your niece will be half dead with anxiety," said Antonio again, "at your not returning home. You are, considering your condition, brisk and strong enough, and so as soon as day dawns we'll carry you home to your own house. There I will again look at your bandage, and arrange your bed as it ought to be, and give your niece instructions for your care, so that you may soon be well again."

The old gentleman heaved a deep sigh, closed his eyes, and remained silent for some minutes. Then, stretching out his hand toward Antonio, he drew the young man down close beside him, and whispered, "It was only a jest that you had with Marianna, was it not, my dear sir?—one of those innocent merry notions that young folks have—"

"Think no more about that, Signor Pasquale," replied Antonio. "Your niece did, it is true, strike my fancy. But I have now quite different things in my head, and—to confess it honestly—I am very pleased that you did return a sharp answer to my foolish proposal. I thought I was in love with your Marianna, but what I really saw in her was only a fine model for my 'Magdalene.' And this probably explains how it is that, now that my picture is finished, I feel quite indifferent to her."

"Antonio," cried the old man, in a strong voice, "Antonio, what a splendid fellow you are! What comfort you give me—what help—what consolation! Now I know that you don't love my Marianna, I feel as if all my pain were gone."

"Why, I declare, Signor Pasquale," said Salvator, "if we didn't know you to be a grave and sensible man, with a true perception of what is becoming to your years, we might easily believe that you were yourself, by some infatuation, in love with that sixteen-year-old child!"

Again the old gentleman closed his eyes, and groaned and moaned at the horrible pain which now returned with redoubled violence.

When the first warm rays of morning came shining through the window, Antonio announced to the old gentleman that it was now time to take him to his own house in the Via Ripetta. Signor Pasquale's reply was a deep and piteous sigh. Salvator and Antonio lifted him out of bed and wrapped him in a wide mantle which had belonged to Dame Caterina's husband, and which she lent them for this purpose. The old gentleman implored them by all the saints to take off the villainous cold bandages in which his bald head was swathed, and to give him his wig and plumed hat. And also, if it were possible, Antonio was to put his mustache a little in order, so that Marianna might not be too much frightened at the sight of him.

Two porters with a litter were standing all ready before the door. Dame Caterina, still storming at the old man, and mixing a great many proverbs in with her abuse, carried down the bed, in which they then carefully packed him; and so, accompanied by Salvator and Antonio, he was taken to his own house.

When Marianna first caught sight of her uncle in this wretched plight, she screamed, and began to weep. Without noticing her lover, who had come along into the house, she grasped the old man's hands and pressed them to her lips, bewailing the terrible accident that had befallen him; so much pity did the gentle child show for the old man who plagued and tormented her with his amorous folly. Yet at this same moment a woman's quick intuition asserted itself in her; for it only needed a few significant glances from Salvator to put her in full possession of all the facts of the case. Now, for the first time, she stole a glance at the happy Antonio, blushing hotly as she did so; and a pretty sight it was to see how a roguish smile gradually broke through, and quickly routed, her tears.

Salvator, for his part, had not expected, despite the "Magdalene," to find the little maiden half so charming, or so adorably pretty, as he now discovered her to be; and, while almost inclined to envy Antonio his good fortune, he felt that it was all the more necessary to get poor Marianna away from her objectionable uncle, let the cost be what it might.

Signor Pasquale Capuzzi forgot his trouble when his lovely niece received him so affectionately, which was indeed more than he deserved. He simpered and pursed up his lips so that his mustache was all askew, and groaned and whimpered, not with pain, but simply and solely with senile infatuation.

Antonio arranged his bed in the most professional manner, and, after Capuzzi had been laid on it, tightened the bandage still further, at the same time so muffling up his left leg, as well, that his victim had to lie there motionless like a log of wood. Meanwhile, Salvator withdrew and left the lovers alone with their happiness.

The old gentleman lay buried in cushions; moreover, as an extra precaution, Antonio had bound a thick piece of cloth, well steeped in water, round his head and over his ears, so that he might not hear the lovers whispering together. This was the first time they fully unburdened their hearts to each other, and now they vowed eternal fidelity, in the midst of tears and rapturous kisses. Old Capuzzi could have no idea of what was going on, for Marianna was careful, at frequent intervals, to ask him how he felt, and even permitted him to press her little white hand to his lips.

In the middle of the morning, Antonio left the house—to procure, as he said, all the things that the old gentleman required for his best care, but in reality to invent some means for putting him, at any rate for some hours, in a still more helpless condition, as well as to consult with Salvator about the next steps in their campaign.

IV

Of the new attack made by Salvator Rosa and Antonio Scacciati upon Signor Pasquale Capuzzi and upon his company, and of what happens in consequence.

Next morning Antonio arrived at Salvator's lodging in a state of melancholy dejection.

"Well, what's the matter?" cried Salvator when he saw him come in, "what are you hanging your head about? What's happened to you now, you lucky dog? Can you not see your sweetheart every day, and kiss her and press her to your heart?"

"Oh! Salvator, my happiness is all over; it's gone forever," cried Antonio. "The Devil is making sport of me. Our stratagem has failed, and we now stand on a footing of open enmity with that cursed Capuzzi."

"So much the better," said Salvator, "so much the better. But come, Antonio, tell me what's happened."

"Just imagine, Salvator," began Antonio, "yesterday when I went back to the Via Ripetta after an absence of at the most two hours, with all sorts of medicines, whom should I see but the old gentleman standing in his own doorway, fully dressed! Behind him was the Pyramid Doctor and the deuced ex-gendarme, while a confused something was bobbing in and out between their legs. It was, I believe, that little monster Pitichinaccio. No sooner did the old man catch sight of me than he shook his fist at me, and began to heap the most fearful curses and imprecations upon me, swearing that if I did but approach his door he would have all my bones broken.

" 'Be off to the Devil, you blackguard of a barber,' he shrieked. 'You think you can outwit me with your lying knavery. Like the very Devil himself, you lie in wait for my poor innocent Marianna, and you imagine that you are going to get her into your toils—but just you wait! I will spend my last ducat to have your last breath stamped out of you, and before you know it, too! And your fine patron, Signor Salvator, the murderer—bandit —who's cheated the gallows—he shall be sent to join his captain Masaniello, in Hell! Anyhow, I'll have him out of Rome in short order; that won't be any trouble at all.'

"The old fellow raged on and on; and as the damned ex-gendarme, incited by the Pyramid Doctor, was making preparations to bear down upon me, and a crowd of curious onlookers began to collect, what could I do but quit the field with all speed? I didn't like to come to you in my great trouble, for I know you would only have laughed at me and my inconsolable complaints. Why, you can hardly keep back your laughter now!"

As Antonio ceased speaking, Salvator did indeed burst out laughing heartily.

"At last," he cried, "at last the thing is beginning to be really interesting! And now, my worthy Antonio, I will tell you in detail all that happened at Capuzzi's after you had gone. You had hardly left the house when Signor Splendiano Accoramboni, who had learned—God knows in what way—that his bosom friend, Capuzzi, had broken his right leg during the night, came in with a most solemn air, accompanied by a surgeon. Your bandage, and the entire method of treatment you have adopted with Signor Pasquale, could not fail to excite suspicion. The surgeon removed the splints and bandages, and they discovered, what we both very well know, that there was not even so much as an ossicle of the worthy Capuzzi's right foot dislocated, much less broken. It didn't require any uncommon sagacity to understand all the rest."

"But," said Antonio, utterly astonished, "but my dear, good sir, do tell me how you have learned all that! How do you get into Capuzzi's house and find out everything that happens there?"

"I have already told you," replied Salvator, "that an acquaintance of Dame Caterina lives in the same house, and, moreover, on the same floor, as Capuzzi. This acquaintance, the widow of a wine dealer, has a daughter whom my little friend Margaret often goes to see. Now girls have a special instinct for ferreting out other girls' affairs; and so it came about that Rose—that's the name of the wine dealer's daughter—and Margaret soon discovered in the living room a small vent-hole, leading into a dark closet that adjoins Marianna's apartment. Marianna had been by no means inattentive to the whispering and murmuring of the two girls, nor had she failed to notice the vent-hole either. And so the way to a mutual exchange of communications was soon opened and made use of.

"Whenever old Capuzzi takes his afternoon nap the girls gossip away to their hearts' content. You will have observed that little Margaret, Dame Caterina's and my favorite, is not so serious and reserved as her elder sister, Anna; in fact she is an arch, frolicsome, droll little thing. Without expressly making mention of your love affair I have asked her to get Marianna to tell her everything that takes place in Capuzzi's house. She has proved a very apt pupil in the matter; and if I laughed at your pain and despondency just now it was because I knew what would comfort you, knew I could prove to you that the situation had now taken a most favorable turn. I have quite a few bits of excellent news for you."

"Oh, Salvator!" cried Antonio, his eyes sparkling with joy. "How you have suddenly raised my hopes! Heaven be praised for the vent-hole! I will write to Marianna; Margaret shall take the letter with her—"

"No, no, we can have none of that, Antonio," replied Salvator. "Margaret can be useful to us without exactly becoming your love messenger! Besides, accident, which often plays many fine tricks, might carry your amorous confessions into old Capuzzi's hands, and so bring an endless amount of fresh trouble upon Marianna, just at the very moment when she is on the point of getting the lovesick old fool under her thumb. For listen to what happened next . . . The way in which Marianna received the old fellow when we took him home has quite made him over. He is now fully convinced that she no longer loves you. He is sure that she has given him at least one-half of her heart, and that all he has to do is to win the other half. And Marianna, since she tasted the sweet poison of your kisses, has advanced three years in shrewdness, artfulness, and experience.

"She has succeeded in making the old man believe, not only that she had no share in the trick we played him, but that she hates our goings-on, and will meet with scorn every device on your part to so much as approach her. In his excessive delight old Capuzzi was too hasty for his own good: he swore that if he could do anything to please his adored Marianna he would do it immediately; she had only to give utterance to her wish. Whereupon Marianna modestly asked for nothing except that her *zio carissimo* would take her to see Signor Formica in the theatre outside the Porta del Popolo. This request rather stumped Capuzzi. There were consultations with the Pyramid Doctor and with Pitichinaccio. But at last Signor Pasquale and Signor Splendiano decided that they would take Marianna to this theatre tomorrow. Pitichinaccio, it was determined, should accompany them in the disguise of a handmaiden—a plan to which he gave his consent only on condition that Signor Pasquale would make him a present, not only of the plush waistcoat, but also of a wig, and, as well, that every night either he or the Pyramid Doctor would be sure to carry him home. That bargain they finally made; and so the curious leash will certainly go dragging after pretty Marianna to see Signor Formica tomorrow, in the theatre outside the Porta del Popolo."

But who, my readers may be asking, was Signor Formica? And what had he to do with the theatre outside the Porta del Popolo?

At the time of the Carnival in Rome, it is a frightful calamity if the theatre managers have been unlucky in their choice of a composer, or if the first tenor at the Argentina Theatre has lost his voice on his way from South America, or if the male prima donna of the Valle Theatre is laid up with a cold—in brief, if the chief springs of recreation which the Romans were hoping to find dry up at their source; and then comes Holy Thursday and at once cuts off all the hopes which might perhaps have been realized. It was just after one of these unlucky Carnivals—almost before the strict fast days were past—that a certain Nicolo Musso opened a theatre outside the Porta del Popolo, where he stated his intention of putting nothing but light impromptu comic sketches on the boards.

The advertisement was drawn up in an ingenious and witty style, and consequently the Romans formed a favorable preconception of Musso's enterprise. But in any case their hunger for dramatic entertainment was so great that they would have snatched greedily at even the poorest pabulum of this description. The interior arrangements of the theatre, or rather of the small booth, did not say much for the pecuniary resources of the zealous manager. There was no orchestra, nor were there boxes. Instead, a gallery was put up at the back, where the arms of the house of Colonna were conspicuous—a sign that Count Colonna had taken Musso and his theatre under his especial protection. The stage was merely a platform of slight elevation, covered with carpets and hung round with curtains, which, according to the requirements of the piece, had to represent a wood or a room or a street. Add to this that the spectators had to content themselves with sitting on hard uncomfortable wooden benches, and it was no wonder that Signor Musso's patrons on first entering his house were pretty loud in their grumblings at him, for calling a paltry wooden booth a theatre! But no sooner had the first two actors appeared on the stage and exchanged a few words than the attention of the audience was arrested. As the piece proceeded their interest soon reached the point of applause; their applause grew to admiration; their admiration to the wildest pitch of enthusiastic excitement, which found vent in loud and continuous laughter, clapping of hands, and screams of "Bravo! Bravo!"

And indeed it would not have been very easy to find anything more perfect than these extemporized representations of Nicolo Musso's; they overflowed with wit, humor, and talent, and they lashed the follies of the day with an unsparing scourge. The audience was entirely carried away by the incomparable characterization which all the actors achieved, but particularly by the inimitable mimicry of Pasquarello, by his marvelously natural imitations of the voice, gait, and postures of well-known personages. People could never get enough of his inexhaustible humor, and the tang and appositeness of his improvisations. The man who played the rôle of Pasquarello in this theatre, and who called himself Signor Formica, seemed to be animated by a spirit of singular originality: often there would be something so strange in his tone, or his gesture, that the folk on the benches, even in the midst of the most unrestrained outbursts of laughter, would suddenly feel a cold shiver down the spine. He was excellently supported by Dr. Gratiano, who in pantomimic action, in voice, and in his talent for saying the most delightful things mixed up with apparently the most extravagant nonsense, had possibly no equal in all the world. This part was taken by an old Bolognese named Maria Agli.

Thus in a short time all literate Rome was to be seen hastening in a continuous procession to Nicolo Musso's little theatre outside the Porta del Popolo, while Formica's name was on everybody's lips, and people shouted with wild enthusiasm, "*Oh! Formica! Formica benedetto! Oh! Formicissimo!*"—not only in the theatre but also in the streets. They looked upon him, indeed, as a supernatural visitant, and many an old lady who split her sides with laughter in the theatre, would suddenly look grave and say solemnly, "*Scherza coi fanti e lascia star santi,*" if anybody ventured to speak the least word in disparagement of Formica's acting.

This odd situation arose from the fact that outside the theatre Signor Formica was an inscrutable mystery. Never was he seen anywhere, and all efforts to trace him to his lodging were vain, while Nicolo Musso on his part maintained an inexorable silence in regard to the comedian's retreat.

And this was the theatre which Marianna was so anxious to attend.

"Let us make a decisive onslaught upon our foes," said Salvator. "We couldn't have a finer opportunity than when they're returning home from the Teatro Musso."

Then he imparted to Antonio the details of a plan, which, though it appeared adventurous and daring, that young man embraced with joy. For it held out to him no less a hope than that he should be able to carry off his Marianna from the loathsome old Capuzzi. He also heard with approval that Salvator himself was especially concerned with the prospect of chastising the Pyramid Doctor.

So it happened that, when night came, Salvator and Antonio each took a guitar and went to the Via Ripetta, where, with the express intention of plaguing old Capuzzi, they honored the lovely Marianna with as fine a serenade as ever was heard! For Salvator played and sang in masterly style, while Antonio, as far as the range of his excellent tenor would allow him, almost rivaled Odoardo Ceccarelli. Although Signor Pasquale appeared on the balcony and tried to silence the singers by hurling abuse upon them, his neighbors, attracted to their windows by the good singing, shouted to him to be still: he and his companions howled and screamed like so many cats and dogs, they said, and yet he wouldn't listen to real music when it did come into the street; he might just go inside and stop up his ears, they added, if he didn't want to listen to this admirable performance. And so Signor Pasquale had to bear, almost all night long, the torture of hearing Salvator and Antonio sing songs which at one time were the sweetest of love songs and at another mocked at the folly of amorous old fools. From the street, the serenaders plainly saw Marianna standing at the window, though they also heard Signor Pasquale beseeching her in the most honeyed phrases and admonitions not to expose her lovely throat to the noxious night air.

Next evening the most remarkable company that the neighborhood had ever seen proceeded down the Via Ripetta towards the Porta del Popolo. All eyes were turned upon them, and people asked each other if these were maskers left from the Carnival. Signor Pasquale Capuzzi, spruce and smug, all elegance and politeness, wearing his gay Spanish suit well brushed, parading a new yellow feather in his conical hat, and stepping along in shoes too small for him, as if he were walking among eggs, was leading pretty Marianna on his arm; her slender figure could not be seen, still less her face, so completely was she smothered—even to an unusual extent—in her veil and wraps. On the other side of the young girl marched Doctor Splendiano Accoramboni in his great wig, whose locks fell more than halfway down his back, so that to anyone looking at him from behind there appeared to be a huge head walking along on two little legs. Close behind Marianna, and almost clinging to her, waddled the little monster

Pitichinaccio, wearing a fiery red skirt, and with a hideous covering of bright-colored flowers on his head.

This evening Signor Formica outdid even his own past performances; and—something he had never done before—he introduced short songs into his improvised program, which burlesqued the style of certain well-known singers. Old Capuzzi's fondness for the stage, which in his youth had almost amounted to infatuation, was now stirred up in him anew. In a rapture of delight he kissed Marianna's hand time after time, and protested that after this he would visit Nicolo Musso's theatre with her every single evening. Signor Formica he extolled to the very skies; and he joined, hand and foot, in the boisterous applause of the rest of the spectators. Signor Splendiano was less satisfied, and kept continually admonishing Signor Capuzzi and lovely Marianna not to laugh so immoderately. In a single breath he ran over the names of twenty or more diseases which might arise from over-indulgence in this sort of response. But neither Marianna nor Capuzzi heeded him in the least. As for Pitichinaccio, he was very uncomfortable. He had been obliged to sit behind the Pyramid Doctor, whose great wig completely blocked his vision. Not a single thing could he see on the stage, nor catch a glimpse of any of the actors; and he was, moreover, repeatedly bothered and annoyed by two officious and impertinent women who had placed themselves near him. They called him a sweet and comely little lady, and asked him if he were married— though to be sure, they interpolated he was very young—and whether he had any children, who, they'd take their oath, were dear little creatures, and so forth. The cold sweat stood in beads on poor Pitichinaccio's brow; he muttered and whimpered, and cursed the day he was born.

After the conclusion of the performance, Signor Pasquale waited until the rest of the audience had withdrawn from the theatre. The last lamp was extinguished just as Signor Splendiano had made use of it to light a small piece of wax torch. And then Capuzzi, with his worthy friends and Marianna, slowly and circumspectly set out on the return journey.

Pitichinaccio wept and screamed; Capuzzi, greatly to his vexation, had to take him on his left arm, while with the right hand he led Marianna. Doctor Splendiano showed the way with his miserable little bit of torch, which burned with difficulty, and then only in a feeble sort of way;

the wretched light it cast merely served, indeed, to reveal to them the thick darkness of the night.

While they were still a good distance from the Porta del Popolo they suddenly realized that they were surrounded by several tall figures closely enveloped in wide cloaks. As suddenly, the torch was knocked from the Doctor's hand, and sputtered out on the ground. Both Capuzzi and the Doctor stood as if thunderstruck, without uttering a sound. Then, without their knowing where it came from, a pale reddish light fell upon the muffled figures, and four grisly skulls riveted their hollow ghastly eyes upon the Pyramid Doctor.

"Woe—woe—woe betide you, Splendiano Accoramboni!" the terrible spectres chanted in deep sepulchral tones. Then one of them wailed, "Do you know me? Do you know me, Splendiano? I am Cordier, the French painter, who was buried last week, and whom your medicines brought to his grave."

Then the second joined in: "Do you know me, Splendiano? I am Küfner, the German painter, whom you poisoned with your infernal syrups."

Then the third echoed: "Do you know me, Splendiano? I am Liers, the Fleming, whom you killed with your pills, and whose brother you defrauded of a picture."

Then the fourth took up the refrain: "Do you know me, Splendiano? I am Ghigi, the Neapolitan painter, whom you dispatched with your powders."

And lastly, all four together intoned, "Woe—woe—woe upon you, Splendiano Accoramboni, cursed Pyramid Doctor! We bid you come— come down to us beneath the earth. Away—away—away with you!" And so saying they threw themselves upon the unfortunate Doctor, and, lifting him up in their arms, whisked him away like a whirlwind.

Now, although Signor Pasquale Capuzzi was at first almost overcome by terror, he recovered his courage with remarkable, and amazing, promptitude as soon as he saw that it was only his friend Accoramboni with whom the dreadful phantoms were concerned. Pitichinaccio, meanwhile, had stuck his head, with the flower bed that was on it, under his master's mantle, and clung so fast round his neck that the old gentleman was utterly unable to shake him off.

"Pluck up your spirit," Capuzzi exhorted Marianna, when nothing more was to be seen of the spectres or of the Pyramid Doctor. "Pluck up your spirits, and come to me, my sweet little ducky bird! As for my worthy friend Splendiano, it's all over with him. May Saint Bernard—who also was an able physician and gave many a man a lift on the road to happiness—may he, I say, help him, if the vengeful painters whom he hastened to get to his Pyramid break his neck! But who'll sing the bass of my canzonas now? And this booby, Pitichinaccio, is squeezing my throat so that, adding in the fright caused by Splendiano's abduction, I fear I shall not be able to produce a pure note for perhaps six weeks to come. But don't you be alarmed, my Marianna, my darling! It's all over now."

The young girl assured him that she had quite recovered from her fright, and begged him to let her walk alone without support, so that he could use both arms to free himself from his troublesome pet. Signor Pasquale, however, only took firmer hold of her, saying that he wouldn't suffer her to go one foot from his side, in that pitch darkness, for anything in the world.

But at the very moment when the old gentleman, now at his ease again, was about to proceed on his road, four horrific figures of fiendish mien rose up just in front of him as if they had sprung out of the earth; they wore short flaring red mantles, and fixed their keen glittering eyes upon him, while at the same time they made frightful noises—yelling and whistling.

"Ugh! Ugh! Pasquale Capuzzi! You cursed fool! You amorous old devil! We belong to your fraternity. We are the evil spirits of love; and we have come to carry you off to Hell—right into the fires of Hell—you and your little Pitichinaccio." Thus screaming, the Satanic pack descended upon the old man. Capuzzi fell heavily to the ground, and Pitichinaccio along with him, each giving vent to his distress and fear in loud piercing cries, like the protests of a whole troop of donkeys being beaten.

Marianna, in the meantime, had torn herself away from the old man's grasp and jumped to one side. And now one of the devils clasped her softly in his arms, and whispered the glad words, "O Marianna! My Marianna! At last we've managed it! My friends will take the old man a long, long way from here, while we find some safe place to hide."

"O my Antonio!" whispered Marianna softly.

But suddenly the scene was illuminated by the light of several torches, and Antonio felt a stab in his shoulder. Quick as lightning he turned round, drew his sword, and struck at his attacker, who, with his stiletto upraised, was just preparing to aim a second blow. The young man now saw that his three companions were defending themselves against a superior number of gendarmes. He succeeded in beating off the man who had first assaulted him, and speedily joined his friends. Although they were maintaining their ground bravely, the contest was too unequal; the gendarmes would infallibly have been victorious had not two other men suddenly ranged themselves with a shout on the side of Antonio's party, one of them immediately cutting down the attacker who was pressing that youth the hardest.

In a few minutes more the contest was decided against the police. Several of their number lay stretched on the ground, seriously wounded; the rest fled with loud shouts toward the Porta del Popolo.

Salvator Rosa (for he it was who had hastened to Antonio's assistance and cut down his opponent) wanted to take Antonio, and the young painters who were disguised in the devil's masks, and then and there pursue the gendarmes into the city.

Maria Agli, however, who had come along with Salvator, and, notwithstanding his advanced age, had tackled the police as stoutly as any of the rest, urged that this would be imprudent; for the guard at the Porta del Popolo would be certain to have word of the affair and would arrest them. So they all betook themselves to Nicolo Musso, who gladly received them in the shelter of his narrow little house not far from the theatre. The artists took off their devil's masks and laid aside their mantles—which had been rubbed over with phosphorus—while Antonio, who, beyond the insignificant scratch on his shoulder, was not wounded at all, exercised his surgical skill in binding up the wounds of the others: Salvator, Agli, and his young comrades. For they had none of them got off without being wounded, though none of their injuries was in the slightest degree dangerous.

The adventure, notwithstanding its wildness and audacity, would undoubtedly have been successful, had not Salvator and Antonio overlooked one person, who managed to upset everything. The *ci-devant bravo* and gendarme, Michele, who lived on the ground floor of Capuzzi's house, and was, after a fashion, his general servant, had, in accordance with his master's instructions, followed the party to the theatre—but at some distance, for the old gentleman was ashamed of the tattered reprobate. In the same way the gendarme was following them homeward. When the spectres appeared, Michele, who, be it remarked, feared neither death nor Devil, was sure that something strange was afoot, and hurried back as fast as he could run in the darkness to the Porta del Popolo, where he raised an alarm. He then returned straightway with all the gendarmes he could find, just at the moment when, as we know, the devils fell upon Signor Pasquale, and were about to carry him off as the "dead" artists had the Pyramid Doctor.

In the very hottest moment of the fight, one of the young painters distinctly noticed that one of the masks took Marianna in his arms (for she had fainted), and made off to the city gate, while Signor Capuzzi ran after him with incredible swiftness, as if he had quicksilver in his legs. At the same time, by the light of the torches, the painter also caught a glimpse of a queer little creature clinging to Capuzzi's mantle and whimpering; this, no doubt, was Pitichinaccio.

Next morning Doctor Splendiano was found, unhurt, near the Pyramid of Cestius; he was fast asleep, doubled up like a ball and squeezed into his wig, as if into a warm soft nest. When he was awakened, he rambled in his talk, and there was some difficulty in convincing him that he was still on the surface of the earth, and in Rome to boot. And when at length he reached his own house, he returned thanks to the Virgin and all the saints for his rescue, threw all his tinctures, essences, medicated syrups, and powders out of the window, burned his prescriptions, and vowed to heal his patients in the future through no other means than by anointment and the laying on of hands, as some celebrated physician of former ages, who was at the same time a saint (Splendiano was not able to recall his name just at the moment), had with great success done before him. For that renowned physician's patients had died, just like anyone else's; but at any rate before they drew their last breath, they already saw the gates of Heaven open before them, and everything else, in fact, that the saint wanted them to see.

"I can't tell you," said Antonio next day to Salvator, "how my heart boils with rage every time I think of my wound! Death and destruction take that repulsive Capuzzi! I tell you, Salvator, that I am determined to force my way into his house. I will cut him down if he opposes me; and I will carry Marianna off under his very eyes."

"An excellent plan!" replied Salvator, laughing. "An excellent plan! Splendidly contrived! Of course I presume you have also found some means for transporting Marianna through the air to the Piazza di Spagna, so that the police shall not seize you and hang you before you can even reach that place of refuge. No, my dear Antonio, violence can do nothing for you this time. You may lay your life on it, too, that Signor Pasquale will now take steps to guard against any open attack. Moreover, our adventure has made a good deal of noise! And the gossip and the public amusement, at the absurd way in which we have read a lesson to Splendiano and Capuzzi, has roused the police out of their slight slumber. You may be sure that they will now exert all their feeble efforts to trap us. No, Antonio, let us have recourse to craft. *Con arte e con inganno si vive mezzo l'anno, con inganno e con arte si vive l'altra parte*, says Dame Caterina; nor is she far wrong.

"Besides," the painter added, with wry candor, "I can't help laughing to see how we've gone and acted for all the world like thoughtless boys. And I shall have to bear most of the blame, for I am a good deal older than you. Tell me now, Antonio, supposing our scheme had been successful, and you had actually carried off Marianna, where would you have fled to, where would you have hidden her, and how would you have managed to get the priest to marry you before the old man could interfere and prevent it?

"But you shall, in a few days," he continued, reassuringly, "really and truly run away with your Marianna. I have let Nicolo Musso, and also Signor Formica, into the whole secret; and we three together have devised a plan which can hardly fail. So cheer up, Antonio; Signor Formica will help you."

"Signor Formica?" repeated Antonio in a tone of indifference which almost amounted to contempt. "Signor Formica! How can that buffoon be of any help to me?"

"Ho! Ho!" laughed Salvator. "Please bear in mind, I beg you, that Signor Formica is worthy of your respect. Don't you know that he is a sort of magician, who is secretly master of the most mysterious arts? I tell you,

Signor Formica will help you. Old Maria Agli, the clever Bolognese Doctor Gratiano, is also in on the plot, and will, moreover, have an important part to play in the way things work out. You shall abduct your Marianna, Antonio, straight from Musso's theatre."

"You are cheering me with false hopes, Salvator," said Antonio. "You have just now said yourself that Signor Pasquale will take precautions to avoid any public attack. How can you suppose, then, after his recent unpleasant experience, that he can possibly make up his mind to visit Musso's theatre again?"

"It will not be such a difficult thing as you imagine, to entice the old man there," Salvator replied. "What will be more difficult to effect, however, will be to get him into the theatre without his satellites. But, be that as it may, what you have now got to do, Antonio, is to have everything prepared and arranged with Marianna, so as to be entirely ready to flee from Rome the moment the favorable opportunity arises. You must go to Florence; your skill as a painter will in itself quickly recommend you there; and you shall have no lack of acquaintances, nor of honorable patronage and assistance—that you may leave to me to provide for. After we have had a few days' rest, we will see what is to be done further. Once more, Antonio—live in hope; Formica will help you."

V

Of the new mishap that befalls Signor Pasquale Capuzzi. Antonio Scacciati successfully carries out his plan in Nicolo Musso's theatre, and flees to Florence.

Signor Pasquale was only too well aware who had been at the bottom of the mischief that had descended upon him and the poor Pyramid Doctor near the Porta del Popolo, and so it is easy to imagine his fury against Antonio, and against Salvator Rosa, whom he rightly judged to have been the ringleader in the whole business. He was untiring in his efforts to comfort poor Marianna, who was quite ill from fright—or so she said. In reality she was mortified by the success of the scoundrel Michele and his gendarmes, in tearing her from her Antonio's arms. Meanwhile little Margaret was assiduous in bringing her tidings of her lover; and

Marianna now based all her hopes upon Salvator's ingenuity and enterprise. With impatience she waited from day to day for something new to happen, and by a thousand petty tormenting ways she let the old gentleman feel the effects of this impatience; but though she thus tamed his amorous folly and made him humble enough, she failed to exorcise the evil spirit of love that haunted his heart. After she had made him experience to the full all a willful girl's most capricious humors, and had then suffered him just once to press his withered lips upon her tiny hand, he would swear in his excessive delight that he would never cease fervently kissing the Pope's toe until he had obtained a dispensation to wed his niece, the paragon of beauty and amiability. Marianna was particularly careful not to interrupt him in these outbursts of passion, for by encouraging the gleams of hope in the old man's breast she fanned the flame of hope in her own: the more he could be lulled into the belief that he held her fast in the chains of devotion, the more easy it would be for her to escape him.

Some time had already passed, when one day at noon Michele came pounding up the stairs, and—after he had had to knock a good many times to induce Signor Pasquale to open the door—announced with considerable garrulousness that there was a gentleman below who urgently begged to see Signor Pasquale Capuzzi, who he knew lived there.

"By all the blessed saints of Heaven!" cried the old patron of the arts, exasperated. "Doesn't the scoundrel know that in no circumstances do I receive strangers in my house?"

But the caller was of very respectable appearance, reported Michele. He was rather oldish, the gendarme added, talked well, and called himself Nicolo Musso.

"Nicolo Musso," murmured Capuzzi, thoughtfully, "Nicolo Musso, who owns the theatre beyond the Porta del Popolo—what can he want with me?" Whereupon, carefully locking and bolting the door, he went downstairs with Michele, to converse with Nicolo in the street before the house, instead of permitting him to come inside.

"My dear Signor Pasquale," began Nicolo, coming to meet him, as he came out of the door, and bowing with polished ease, "it gives me great pleasure that you deign to honor me with your acquaintance. You place me under a very great obligation. Since the people of Rome saw you in my theatre—you, a man of the most approved taste, of the soundest knowledge, and a master in various arts—since then, I tell you, not only has my fame increased, but my receipts have doubled. I am therefore all the more deeply pained to learn that certain wicked and wanton youngsters made a murderous attack upon you and your friends as you were returning from my theatre at night. But I pray you, Signor Pasquale, by all the saints, don't harbor any resentment against me, or my theatre, on account of this outrage, which shall be severely punished. Don't deprive me of the honor of your company at my performances!"

"My dear Signor Nicolo," replied the old man, simpering "be assured that I never enjoyed myself more than I did when I visited your theatre. Your Formica and your Agli—why, they are actors who cannot be matched anywhere. But the shock of that treacherous assault almost killed my friend Signor Splendiano Accoramboni; it even came near to proving the death of me. No, it was too much, and though it has not prejudiced me against your theatre, it certainly has turned me against the road that leads there. If you will put up your theatre in the Piazza del Popolo, or in the Via Babuina, or in the Via Ripetta, I certainly will not fail to visit you every single evening. But there's no power on earth shall ever get me outside the Porta del Popolo again after nightfall!"

Nicolo sighed deeply, as if greatly troubled. "That makes things very hard for me," said he then, "harder perhaps than you will believe, Signor Pasquale. For unfortunately—I had based all my hopes upon you. I came to solicit your assistance."

"My assistance?" asked the old gentleman in astonishment. "My assistance, Signor Nicolo? In what way could my assistance profit you?"

"My dear Signor Pasquale," replied Nicolo, drawing his handkerchief across his eyes, as if brushing away the tears that were about to fall, "my most excellent Signor Pasquale, you will remember that my actors are in the habit of interspersing their performances with song. I was thinking of imperceptibly extending this practice more and more; then my idea was to get together an orchestra, and, in a word, at last, evading all prohibitions to the contrary, to establish an opera house. You, Signor Capuzzi, are the first composer in all Italy; and we can attribute it to nothing but the inconceivable frivolity of the Romans and the malicious envy of your rivals that we do not hear your pieces exclusively at all the theatres. Signor Pasquale, I came to request you on my bended knees to allow me to give your immortal works, as far as circumstances will permit, on my humble stage."

"My dear Signor Nicolo," said the old gentleman, his face all sunshine, "what can we possibly be up to, standing here talking in the public thoroughfare? Pray deign to have the goodness to climb up one or two rather steep flights; pray accompany me up to my poor dwelling."

Almost before Nicolo had got into the room, the old gentleman produced a great pile of dusty music manuscripts, flipped open a page, and, taking his guitar in hand, began to deliver himself of a series of the frightful high-pitched shrieks which were his peculiar version of singing.

Nicolo behaved like a man in rapture. He sighed; he uttered extravagant expressions of approval; he exclaimed at intervals, "*Bravo! Bravissimo! Benedettissimo Capuzzi!*" until at last he threw himself at the old man's feet, as if utterly beside himself with ecstatic delight, and grasped his knees. But he clutched them with such force that the old gentleman jumped off his seat, crying out with pain, and exclaimed, "By the saints! Let me go, Signor Nicolo; you'll kill me."

"No," replied Nicolo, "no, Signor Pasquale, I will not get up until you have promised that Formica may sing in my theatre, the day after tomorrow, the divine arias which you have just executed."

"You are a man of taste," groaned Pasquale, "a man of deep insight. To whom could I better entrust my compositions than to you? You shall take all my arias with you. Only let me go. But, good God! I shall not hear them—my divine masterpieces! Oh, do let go of me, Signor Nicolo."

"No," cried Nicolo, still on his knees, and tightly pressing the old gentleman's thin spindle-shanks together, "no, Signor Pasquale, I will not let you go until you have given me your word that you—the composer—will be present in my theatre the night after tomorrow. You need not fear any new attack! Why, don't you suppose that the Romans, once they have heard your work, will escort you home in triumph by the light of hundreds of torches? But even if that should not happen, I myself and my faithful comrades will arm ourselves and accompany you to your home."

"You yourself will accompany me home, with your comrades?" asked Pasquale. "And how many may that be?"

"Eight or ten persons will be at your command, Signor Pasquale. Now do yield to my pleadings, and make up your mind to come."

"Formica has a fine voice," murmured Pasquale. "How nobly he will perform my arias!"

"Do come! Oh, do come!" exhorted Nicolo again, clutching the old gentleman's knees with renewed pressure.

"You will pledge yourself that I shall reach my own house without being molested?" asked the old gentleman.

"I pledge my honor and my life," was Nicolo's solemn reply, as he still tightened his grip.

"Agreed!" cried the old gentleman. "I will be in your theatre on the evening of the day after tomorrow."

At that good word, Nicolo leaped to his feet and pressed Capuzzi in so close an embrace that the poor man, quite breathless, gasped and panted.

Just then, Marianna came into the room. Signor Pasquale tried to warn her away with a look of harsh reproach; but she took not the slightest notice of this. Going straight up to Musso, she addressed him as if in anger: "It is no use for you, Signor Nicolo, to attempt to entice my dear uncle to go to your theatre. You are forgetting that the infamous trick lately played on him by the lecherous marauders, who were lying in wait for me, almost cost him the life I love so dearly, and endangered his worthy friend Splendiano as well—indeed, that it almost cost my life too. Never will I give my consent to my uncle's exposing himself again to such risk. You might as well cease your entreaties, Nicolo. And you, my dearest uncle, you will stay quietly at home, will you not, and not venture out beyond the Porta del Popolo again after dark?"

Signor Capuzzi was thunderstruck. He opened his eyes wide and stared at his niece. Then he rewarded her with the most saccharine words of endearment, and proceeded to explain at considerable length how Signor Nicolo had pledged himself so to arrange matters as to avoid every danger on the return home.

"None the less," said Marianna, "I stick to my word; and I beg you most earnestly, my dearest uncle, not to go to the theatre outside the Porta del Popolo. I ask your pardon, Signor Nicolo, for speaking out frankly, in your presence, but certain unpleasant suspicions cannot be avoided. You are, I know, acquainted with Salvator Rosa and also with Antonio Scacciati. What if you are acting in league with our enemies? What if you are only trying to entice my dear uncle into your theatre, in order that they may the more safely carry out some new scheme of villainy against me? For I know that my uncle will not go without me," she added.

"What a suspicion!" cried Nicolo, in evident alarm. "What a terrible suspicion, Signorina! How can you entertain such a bad opinion of me? Have I such an evil reputation that you imagine I could be guilty of this basest treachery? But if you think so unfavorably of me, if you mistrust the assistance I have promised you, why then let Michele, who, I know, was responsible for your rescue—let Michele accompany you, and let him take a large body of gendarmes with him, who can wait for you outside the theatre. For of course you cannot expect me," he added, "to fill my auditorium with police."

Marianna fixed her eyes steadily upon Nicolo's, and then said, earnestly and gravely, "What did you say? That Michele and gendarmes should accompany us? Now I see plainly, Signor Nicolo, that you mean honestly by us, and that my ugly suspicion was unfounded. Please forgive me for my unkind thoughts. And yet I cannot banish my nervousness and anxiety about my dear uncle; I must still beg him not to venture on this dangerous expedition."

Signor Capuzzi had listened to all this conversation with a variety of strange and shifting expressions that unmistakably announced the nature of the struggle going on within him. But now he could no longer contain himself; he threw himself on his knees before his beautiful niece, seized her hands, kissed them, bathed them with the tears which ran down his cheeks, and exclaimed as if beside himself, "My adored, my angelic Marianna! Fierce and devouring are the flames of the passion which burns my heart. Oh! This alarm, this anxiety—it is the sweetest manner of confessing that you do indeed love me!"

And then he besought her not to give way to fear, but to attend the theatre and hear the finest arias which had ever been written by the most divine of composers.

Nicolo, too, did not diminish, much less cease, his entreaties. He plainly showed his disappointment, until Marianna at last permitted her scruples to be overcome. Now she promised to lay all fear aside, and to accompany the best and dearest of uncles to the theatre outside the Porta del Popolo. Signor Capuzzi was in ecstasies: he was convinced that Marianna loved him; and now he could actually hope to hear his music on the stage, and win the laurel wreath which had so long been the vain object of his desires. He was on the point of seeing all his dearest dreams fulfilled. Now he would let his light shine in perfect glory before his true and faithful friends; for he never thought for a moment that Signor Splendiano and little Pitichinaccio would fail to accompany him, as they had on the first occasion . . .

The night that Signor Splendiano had slept in his wig near the Pyramid of Cestius, he had encountered, besides the spectres who had carried him away, various other sinister apparitions. The whole cemetery was alive, and hundreds of corpses had stretched out their skeleton arms towards him, moaning and wailing that even in their graves they could not get over the torture caused by his wretched drugs and poisoned syrups. And after that the Pyramid Doctor, although he could not contradict Signor Pasquale's assurance that the whole thing had been only a wild freakish trick placed upon him by a parcel of godless boys, grew melancholy. Though he was not ordinarily inclined to superstition, yet he now saw spectres everywhere, and was tormented by forebodings and bad dreams.

As for Pitichinaccio, he could not be convinced that those were not real devils, come straight from the flames of Hell, who had fallen upon Signor Pasquale and himself; and the bare mention of that dreadful night was enough to make him scream in renewed terror. All the asseverations of Signor Pasquale that there had been nobody behind the masks but Antonio Scacciati and Salvator Rosa, and some of their madcap friends, were of no effect, for Pitichinaccio wept the more loudly, and swore that, in spite of his terror and apprehension, he had clearly recognized both the voice and the behavior of the devil Fanfarelli, in the one who had pinched his belly black and blue.

It may therefore be imagined what an almost endless amount ·of trouble it cost Signor Pasquale to persuade the two to go with him once more to Nicolo Musso's theatre. Splendiano was the first to decide that he would go—after he had procured from a monk of St. Bernard's Order a small consecrated bag of musk, the perfume of which neither dead man nor Devil could endure. With this he intended to arm himself against all assaults from the nether world! Pitichinaccio could not resist the temptation of a promised box of candied grapes; but Signor Pasquale was required besides expressly to consent to his wearing his new abbot's coat, instead of the petticoats which he affirmed had proved an immediate source of attraction to the Devil.

What Salvator feared seemed therefore to be actually about to take place; and yet his plan depended entirely, he continued to repeat, upon Signor Capuzzi's being in Nicolo's theatre alone with Marianna, without his faithful satellites. Both Antonio and Salvator were now racking their brains to find a way to keep both Splendiano and Pitichinaccio from going along with Signor Pasquale. Every scheme that occurred to them for the accomplishment of this desideratum had to be given up because of the lack of time, for the principal feat, in Nicolo's theatre, had to be carried out on the evening of the following day.

But Providence, which often employs the most unlikely instruments for the chastisement of fools, interposed on behalf of the distressed lovers, and put it into Michele's head to perpetrate a series of blunders, thus accomplishing by hazard what Salvator and Antonio had failed to achieve by craft.

That same night there was heard in the Via Ripetta, in front of Signor Pasquale Capuzzi's house, such a chorus of fearful screams, of cursing and raving and abuse, that all the neighbors were aroused from even the soundest sleep; and a body of gendarmes, who had been pursuing a murderer as far as the Piazza di Spagna, hastened up with torches, supposing that some fresh deed of violence was being committed. But when they, and a crowd of other people whom the noise had attracted, came upon the scene of what they thought would be murder, they found poor little Pitichinaccio lying as if dead on the pavement, while Michele was thrashing the Pyramid Doctor with a formidable bludgeon. And they saw the Doctor reel to the ground just at the moment when Signor Pasquale painfully scrambled to his feet, drew his rapier, and furiously attacked Michele. Round about were lying pieces of broken guitars. Had not several people grasped the old man's arm, he would assuredly have run Michele right through the heart. The ex-bravo, now becoming aware, by the light of the torches, whom he had been assaulting, stood as if petrified, his eyes almost starting out of his head. Then, with a terror-stricken scream, he tore his hair and begged for mercy and pardon. Neither the

Pyramid Doctor nor Pitichinaccio was seriously injured, but they had been so soundly cudgeled that they could neither get up nor even stir, and had to be carried home.

Signor Pasquale Capuzzi had actually brought this mishap upon himself.

We know that Salvator and Antonio had complimented Marianna with the finest serenade that could be heard; but I have forgotten to say that, to the old gentleman's exceeding indignation, they repeated this performance on several successive nights. At length Signor Pasquale, whose rage was kept in check only by his neighbors, was foolish enough to have recourse to the authorities of the city, and to urge them to forbid the two painters to sing in the Via Ripetta. The authorities, however, replied that it would be a procedure unheard of in Rome to prohibit anybody's singing and playing the guitar where he pleased, and added that it was irrational to ask such a thing.

So Signor Pasquale determined to put an end to the nuisance himself, and promised Michele a large reward if he seized the first opportunity to fall upon the singers and give them a good sound drubbing.

Michele at once procured a stout bludgeon, and lay in wait every night behind the house door. But it happened that Salvator and Antonio judged it prudent to omit their serenading in the Via Ripetta for some nights preceding the execution of their plan, so as not to remind the old gentleman of the existence of his adversaries. Marianna remarked, quite innocently, to her uncle, however, that, though she hated Antonio and Salvator, yet she liked their singing, for nothing was so pleasant as to hear music floating upward in the night air.

Signor Pasquale made a mental note of this comment, and, as the essence of gallantry, purposed to surprise his love with a serenade on his own part; a serenade, needless to say, which he had himself composed, and had carefully practiced with his faithful friends. On the night just before the one in which he was hoping to celebrate his greatest triumph in Nicolo Musso's theatre, he stealthily slipped out of the house, and went to call his associates, with whom he had previously arranged the little musical offering. But no sooner had they struck the first few notes on their guitars than Michele, whom Signor Pasquale had thoughtlessly forgotten to apprise of his design, rushed out from behind the door—enthusiastic at the opportunity to earn, at last, his promised reward—and began to beat the musicians most unmercifully, with results which we have already witnessed. Of course no further mention was made of either Splendiano or Pitichinaccio accompanying Signor Pasquale to Nicolo's theatre; for they were both beplastered all over and confined to their beds. Signor Pasquale, however, was unable to stay away, although his back and shoulders were smarting not a little from the drubbing he had himself received; every note in his arias was a blandishment which drew him to the performance with irresistible fascination.

"Well now," said Salvator to Antonio, "since the obstacle which we took to be insurmountable has moved out of our way of its own accord, everything will depend entirely upon your own skill on finding the favorable moment for making off with your Marianna. But I needn't advise you any further; you'll not fail. In fact, permit me to greet you now as the betrothed of Capuzzi's lovely niece, who in a few days will be your wife. I wish you happiness, Antonio; and yet I feel a shiver run through me when I think of your marriage."

"What do you mean, Salvator?" asked Antonio, utterly astounded.

"Call it a crotchet, call it a foolish fancy, or what you will, Antonio," rejoined Salvator. "At any rate I love the fair sex; yet there is not a woman —not even the one on whom I foolishly dote and for whom I would gladly die—who does not excite in my heart, as soon as I think of a close union with her, such as marriage is, a distrust that makes me tremble with the most unpleasant forebodings. That which is inscrutable in the nature of woman mocks all the weapons of man. She whom we believe to have surrendered herself to us entirely, heart and soul, whom we believe to have unfolded all her being to us, is the first to deceive us, and along with the sweetest of her kisses offers us the most pernicious of poisons."

"And my Marianna?" asked Antonio, amazed.

"Pardon me, Antonio," continued Salvator, "even your Marianna, who is the spirit of loveliness and grace, has given me a fresh proof of how dangerous the mysterious nature of woman is to us. Just call to mind what was the behavior of that innocent, inexperienced child when we carried her uncle home, how at a single glance from me, she divined everything —everything, I tell you—and, as you yourself admitted, proceeded to play her part with the utmost sagacity and finesse. But that is not to be compared with what took place on the occasion of Musso's visit to the old gentleman! The most studied poise, the most inscrutable cunning—in short, all the skill and resourcefulness of the most experienced woman of the world—could not have carried it off with more assurance. She could not have prepared the way for us any better. Our feud with the irascible old fool—well, I know that any sort of cunning scheme seems justified, but—come, my dear Antonio, never mind my fanciful crotchets, but be happy with your Marianna; as happy as you can."

If a monk had taken his place beside Signor Pasquale Capuzzi when he set out with his niece for Nicolo Musso's theatre, everybody would have thought that the strange pair were being led to execution. Ahead of the pair stalked the valiant Michele, repulsive in appearance, and armed to the teeth; and behind Signor Pasquale and Marianna followed at least twenty gendarmes.

Nicolo received the old gentleman and his young lady, with every mark of respect, at the entrance to the theatre, and conducted them to the seats which had been reserved for them, immediately in front of the stage. Signor Pasquale felt highly flattered by this mark of honor, and gazed about him with proud and sparkling eyes, while his pleasure, his joy, were greatly enhanced by the discovery that all the seats near and behind Marianna were occupied only by women. A couple of violins and a bass fiddle were being tuned behind the curtains of the stage; the old gentleman's heart beat with expectation; and when all at once the orchestra struck up the *ritornello* of his work, he felt an electric thrill of delight.

Formica came forward in the character of Pasquarello, and sang— sang in Capuzzi's own voice, and with all his characteristic gestures—the most completely impossible aria that had ever been heard in Rome. The theatre shook with the audience's loud and boisterous laughter. They shouted; they screamed wildly, "O Pasquale Capuzzi! Our most illustrious composer and artist! *Bravo! Bravissimo!*" The old gentleman, not perceiving the ridicule and irony of the laughter, was in raptures of delight. The aria came to an end. And now the people cried, "Sh! Sh!" as Doctor Gratiano, played on this occasion by Nicolo Musso himself, appeared on the stage, holding his hands over his ears and shouting to Pasquarello for goodness' sake to stop his ridiculous screeching.

Then the Doctor asked Pasquarello how long he had taken to the confounded habit of singing, and where he had got that execrable piece of music.

Whereupon Pasquarello replied that he didn't know what the Doctor would like to hear; the Doctor was like the Romans, Formica added, and had no taste for real music, since he failed to appreciate the most talented of all musicians. The aria had been written by the greatest of living composers, in whose service he had the good fortune to be, receiving instruction in both music and singing from the master himself.

Gratiano then began guessing who this might be, and mentioned the names of a great number of well-known composers and musicians. But at every distinguished name Pasquarello only shook his head contemptuously.

At length Pasquarello said that the Doctor was only exposing his gross ignorance, since it was plain that he did not know the name of the greatest composer of the time. This supreme musician was none other than Signor Pasquale Capuzzi, he explained, who had done him the honor of taking him into his service. Could he not see that he, Pasquarello, was the friend and servant of Signor Pasquale?

Then the Doctor broke out into a loud long roar of laughter and cried, What! Had Pasquarello, after running away from his good patron, the Doctor—in whose service, besides getting his wages and food, he had had his palm tickled with many a copper—had he gone and become the henchmen of the biggest and most inveterate old coxcomb who ever stuffed himself with macaroni, of the patched Carnival fool who strutted about like a satisfied old hen after a shower of rain, of the snarling skinflint, the lovesick old poltroon, who infected the air of the Via Ripetta with the disgusting bleating which he called singing? And so on, and so on . . .

To this, Pasquarello, exceedingly incensed, made reply that it was nothing but envy which betrayed itself in the Doctor's words; he, Pasquarello, was of course speaking with his heart in his mouth (*parla col cuore in mano*) ; the Doctor was by no means the man to pass judgment upon Signor Pasquale Capuzzi di Senigaglia; he was speaking with his heart in his mouth. The Doctor himself was strongly tainted with all the faults which he claimed to discern in the excellent Signor Pasquale; but he, Pasquarello, was speaking with his heart in his mouth. He had often heard no less than six hundred people at once laugh most heartily at Doctor Gratiano. And so on and so forth . . .

Then Pasquarello spoke a long panegyric upon his new master, Signor Pasquale, attributing to him all the virtues under the sun; and he concluded with a description of his character, which he portrayed as being the very essence of amiability and grace.

"Heaven bless you, Formica!" muttered Signor Capuzzi to himself. "Heaven bless you, Formica! I perceive that you have planned to make my triumph perfect, since you are upbraiding the Romans for all their envious and ungrateful persecution of me, and are letting them know *who* and *what* I really am."

"Ha! Here comes my master!" cried Pasquarello at this moment. And there entered on the stage forthwith—none other than Signor Pasquale Capuzzi himself, just as he breathed and walked! Here were his very clothes, face, gestures, gait, postures; in fact so perfectly did this new arrival counterfeit the Signor Capuzzi in the audience that the latter, quite aghast, let go Marianna's hand, which hitherto he had held fast in his own, and tapped himself, his nose, his wig, in order to discover whether he was not dreaming, or seeing double, whether he was really sitting in Nicolo Musso's theatre and dare credit what he saw as a miracle.

Capuzzi on the stage embraced Doctor Gratiano with great kindness, and asked how he was. The Doctor replied that he had a good appetite, and slept soundly, at his service (*per servirlo*) ; but as for his purse—well, it was suffering from a galloping consumption. Only yesterday he had spent his last ducat for a pair of rosemary-colored stockings for his sweetheart, and now he was just going to walk round to one or two bankers to see if he could borrow thirty ducats—

"But how can you pass by your best friends?" asked the stage Capuzzi. "Here, my dear fellow, here are fifty ducats. Come, take them."

"Pasquale, what are you about?" demanded the real Capuzzi, in an undertone.

Doctor Gratiano began to talk punctiliously about a note, and interest; but Signor Capuzzi declared that he could not think of asking for either from such a friend as the Doctor was.

"Pasquale, have you gone out of your senses?" exclaimed the real Capuzzi, in a slightly louder voice.

After many grateful embraces Doctor Gratiano took his leave. And now Pasquarello drew near with a good many bows, and extolled Signor Capuzzi to the skies, adding, however, that his purse was suffering from the same complaint as Gratiano's; and he begged for some of the same excellent medicine that had cured his. Capuzzi on the stage laughed, remarked that he was pleased to find that Pasquarello knew how to turn his good humor to advantage, and threw the comedian several bright gold ducats.

"Pasquale, you must be mad! You are possessed of the Devil!" cried the real Capuzzi, aloud. And the audience called to him to be still.

Pasquarello now soared to even higher flights in his eulogy of Capuzzi, and came at last to speak of the aria which the lover of the arts had composed, and with which the comedian-singer hoped to enchant everybody in Rome. The fictitious Capuzzi clapped Pasquarello heartily on the back, and went on to say that he might venture to tell him, Pasquarello, his faithful servant, in confidence, that in reality he knew nothing whatever of the science of music; as to the aria of which he had just spoken, he continued, as well as all pieces that he had ever supposedly composed, why, he had stolen them out of Frescobaldi's canzonas and Carissimi's motets.

"I tell you you're lying in your throat, you knave!" shouted the Capuzzi in the audience, jumping up from his seat. Again he was told to keep still; and the woman who sat next to him pulled him back to the bench.

"It's now time to think about other and more important matters," continued the Capuzzi on the stage. He was going to give a grand banquet the next day, he explained, and Pasquarello must bestir himself and see to all the preparations. Then he produced and read over a list of all the rarest and most expensive dishes, making Pasquarello tell him how much each would cost, and at the same time giving him the money for them.

"Pasquale! You're insane! You've gone mad! You good-for-nothing ne'er-do-well! You spendthrift!" shouted the real Capuzzi, at intervals, becoming more and more enraged as the cost of this most nonsensical of dinners rose higher and higher.

At length, when the list was finished, Pasquarello asked why his patron wanted to give such a splendid banquet.

"Tomorrow will be the happiest and most joyous day of my life," replied the fictitious Capuzzi. "For know, my good Pasquarello, that I am going to celebrate tomorrow the auspicious marriage of my dear niece Marianna. I am going to give her hand to that brave and honest young man, the best of all artists, Antonio Scacciati."

Hardly had the words fallen from his double's lips when the real Capuzzi leaped to his feet, utterly beside himself, quite out of his mind, his face all aflame with the most fiendish rage, and clenching his fists and shaking them at his counterpart on the stage, he yelled at the top of his voice, "No, you won't, no, you won't, you rascal! You scoundrel, you— Pasquale! Do you mean to cheat yourself out of your Marianna, you hound? Are you going to throw her in the arms of that blackguard—sweet Marianna, your life, your hope, your all? Ah! take care! Take care, you crazy fool! Just remember what sort of a reception you will get from yourself! You will beat yourself black and blue with your own hands, so that you will have no zest left for thinking about banquets and weddings!"

But the Capuzzi on the stage clenched his fists like the Capuzzi in the audience, and shouted, in exactly the same furious way, and in the same high-pitched voice, "May all the spirits of Hell sit at your heart, you abominable and absurd Pasquale, you atrocious skinflint, you lovesick old fool, you gaudy tricked-out ass with the cap and bells dangling about your ears! Take care lest I snuff out the candle of your life, and so at length put an end to the infamous tricks which you try to foist upon myself, the good, honest, modest Pasquale Capuzzi!"

And to the accompaniment of the most fearful cursing and swearing from the real Capuzzi, the double on the stage dished up one fine anecdote after the other about him.

"You'd better not try," shouted the fictitious Capuzzi at last, "you'd better not dare, Pasquale, you amorous old ape, to interfere with the happiness of these two young people! I tell you, Heaven has destined them for each other!"

At this moment, like a tableau, at the back of the stage appeared Antonio Scacciati and Marianna locked in each other's arms. Although the old gentleman was ordinarily somewhat feeble on his legs, fury now gave him strength and agility. With a single bound he was on the platform, had drawn his sword, and was charging upon the counterfeit Antonio. He found, however, that he was held fast from the back. An officer of the Papal Guard had stopped him, and said in a serious voice, "Recollect where you are, Signor Pasquale; you are in Nicolo Musso's theatre. Without intending it, you have today played a most ridiculous rôle. You will not find either Antonio or Marianna here."

Then the two persons whom Capuzzi had taken for his niece and her lover approached, along with the rest of the actors. The faces were all completely strange to him. His rapier dropped from his trembling hand; he took a deep breath as if awakening out of a bad dream; he clutched his brow with both hands; he opened his eyes wide. A presentiment of what had happened suddenly dawned upon him, and he shouted, "Marianna!" in such a stentorian voice that the walls rang with the echo.

But his niece was beyond reach of his cries. Antonio had taken advantage of his opportunity while Pasquale, oblivious to all about him and even to himself, was quarreling with his double. He had made his way to Marianna, and had run back with her through the audience, and out at a side door, where a carriage stood ready. And away they went as fast as their horses could gallop, towards Florence.

"Marianna!" screamed the old man again. "Marianna! Oh, she is gone! She has fled! That wretch Antonio has stolen her from me! Hurry! Go after them! Have pity on me, good people, and take torches, and help me to look for my little darling. Oh! You serpent!"

And he tried to make for the door. But the officer held him fast, saying, "Do you mean that pretty young lady who sat beside you? I believe I saw her slip out with a young man—I think it was Antonio Scacciati —a long time ago, when you had just begun your idle quarrel with one of the actors who wore a mask like your face. You needn't get upset about it. Every inquiry shall be instigated at once, and Marianna shall be brought back to you as soon as she is found. But as for yourself, Signor Pasquale, your preposterous behavior here, and your murderous attempt upon the life of that actor, compel me to arrest you."

Signor Pasquale, his face as pale as death, was incapable of uttering a single word or even a sound. And so he was led away by the very same gendarmes who were to have protected him against masked devils and phantoms. Thus it came to pass that on the self-same night on which he had hoped to celebrate his triumph, he was plunged into the midst of trouble, and all the frantic despondency which amorous old fools feel when they are deceived.

VI

Salvator Rosa leaves Rome and goes to Florence. The
story's conclusion.

Everything here beneath the sun is subject to continual change; and perhaps there is nothing which can be called more inconstant than human opinion, which turns round in an everlasting circle like the wheel of fortune. He who reaps great praise today is overwhelmed with bitter censure tomorrow, while today we trample under foot the man who tomorrow will be raised far above us.

Among all those who, in Rome, had disdained and mocked old Pasquale Capuzzi, for his sordid avarice, his senile lechery, his insane jealousy, there was none who had not wished poor tormented Marianna her liberty. But now that Antonio had successfully carried off his sweetheart, all the ridicule and mockery was suddenly changed into pity for the old dunder-pate, whom they saw wandering about the city streets with his chin sunk on his breast, utterly disconsolate. Misfortunes seldom come singly; and so it happened that Signor Pasquale, soon after Marianna had been taken from him, also lost his boon companions. Little Pitichinaccio choked himself in foolishly trying to swallow an almond kernel in the middle of a cadenza. And the life of the illustrious Pyramid Doctor Signor Splendiano Accoramboni was brought to a sudden end by a slip of the pen, for which he had only himself to blame. Michele's drubbing had done such thorough work with him that he fell into a fever. He decided to make use of a remedy which he claimed to have discovered; so, calling for quill and ink, he wrote out a prescription in which, by employing a wrong sign, he increased the quantity of a powerful substance to a dangerous extent. Scarcely had he swallowed the medicine than he sank back on the pillows and died, establishing, however, by his own death, in the most splendid and satisfactory manner, the efficacy of the last tincture which he ever prescribed.

As already remarked, all those whose laughter had been the loudest, and who had repeatedly wished Antonio success in his schemes, had now nothing but pity for the old gentleman; and the bitterest blame was heaped, not so much upon Antonio, as upon Salvator Rosa, whom, not incorrectly, they regarded as the instigator of the whole plan.

Salvator's enemies, of whom he had a goodly number, exerted all their efforts to fan the new flame of public disapproval. "You see!" they said. "He was a member of Masaniello's ruffian band; and he is ready to turn his hand to any mischief, to any disreputable enterprise. We shall be the next to suffer from his presence in the city. This wild-natured painter is a dangerous man."

And the jealous faction that had leagued together against Salvator did actually succeed in stemming the tide of his prosperous career. He sent out from his studio one picture after the other, all bold in conception, and splendidly executed; but the so-called critics shrugged their shoulders, now pointing out that the hills were too blue or the trees too green, now saying that the figures were too tall or too broad, always finding fault where there was no fault to be found, and seeking to detract from the artist's hard-earned reputation in every conceivable way. Especially bitter in their persecution of him were the Academicians of St. Luke, who could not forget how he had taken them in with the surgeon. They even went beyond the limits of their own profession, and recited the clever stanzas which Salvator at that time wrote, hinting very plainly that he did not cultivate his fruit on his own garden soil, but plundered his neighbors' arbors. For these reasons, therefore, Salvator could not manage to provide himself with the luxuries he required. Instead of being visited by the most eminent of the Romans in a large studio, he had to remain with Dame Caterina and his green fig tree; but even in these poor surroundings he had for a time enjoyed comfort and tranquillity of mind.

Salvator took the malicious machinations of his enemies to heart more than he should have done. He even began to fear that some insidious disease, the result of chagrin and dejection, might be gnawing at his vitals.

In this unhappy frame of mind he designed and executed two large pictures which aroused a veritable uproar in Rome. Of these, one represented the transitoriness of all earthly things; and in the principal figure, that of a wanton female bearing in her person all the indications of her corrupt vocation, everyone could recognize the mistress of one of the cardinals. The other painting portrayed the Goddess of Fortune dispensing her rich gifts: but cardinals' hats, bishops' mitres, gold medals, decorations of orders, were falling upon bleating sheep, braying asses, and other witless and contemptible animals, while well-formed men in ragged clothes were straining their eyes upward in the vain hope of catching even the smallest bounty. Salvator had given free rein to his embittered mood, and the animals' heads bore close resemblances to the features of various eminent persons. It is easy to imagine, therefore, that the tide of hatred rose against him, and that he was more harshly persecuted than ever.

Dame Caterina warned him, with tears in her eyes, that for the last several days, as soon as it began to be dark, she had observed, lurking about the house, suspicious characters who apparently dogged his every footstep. Salvator saw that it was time to quit Rome; and Dame Caterina and her beloved daughters were the only people whom it caused him pain to leave. In response to the repeated invitations of the Duke of Tuscany, he went to Florence. Here he was at last richly indemnified for all the mortification and anxiety which he had had to struggle against in Rome, and here all the honor and all the fame which he so truly deserved were freely conferred upon him. The Duke's gifts and the high fees which he received for his pictures soon enabled him to move into a large house and to furnish it in the most magnificent style. There he was wont to gather round him the most illustrious authors and scholars of the day, among whom it will be sufficient to mention Evangelista Toricelli, Valerio Chimentelli, Battista Ricciardi, Andrea Cavalcanti, Pietro Salvati, Filippo Apolloni, Volumnio Bandelli, Francesco Rovai. They formed an association for the prosecution of artistic and scientific pursuits, and Salvator was able to contribute an element of the fantastic to the meetings, which stimulated and enlivened their tone, and counteracted their academic monotony. The banqueting hall was like a beautiful grove set with fragrant bushes and flowers and splashing fountains; and even the dishes, which were served up by pages in eccentric costumes, had an exotic and fabulous look, as if they had come from some distant enchanted land. These meetings of writers and savants in Salvator Rosa's house were called at that time the Accademia de' Percossi.

Though Salvator's mind was in this way devoted to science and art, yet his real and true nature came to life most vividly when he was with his friend Antonio Scacciati, who, along with his lovely Marianna, led the pleasant carefree life of an artist. They often recalled the poor old Signor Pasquale whom they had deceived, and talked over all that had happened in Nicolo Musso's theatre. And one day Antonio asked Salvator how he had contrived to enlist, in his cause, the active interest not only of Musso but of the peerless comedian Formica, and of Agli too. Salvator replied that it had been very easy, for Formica was his most intimate friend in Rome. It had been a work of both pleasure and love for the actor, Salvator explained, to arrange everything on the stage in accordance with the instructions the painter gave him. Antonio protested that, though still he could not help laughing over the scene which had paved the way to his happiness, he yet wished with all his heart that he might be reconciled to the old gentleman, even if he should never touch a penny of Marianna's fortune, which Capuzzi had confiscated; his work as an artist brought him in a sufficient income. Marianna, too, was often unable to restrain her tears when she thought that her father's brother might go down to his grave without having forgiven her the trick which she had played upon him. And so Pasquale's hatred overshadowed like a dark cloud the brightness of their happiness. Salvator comforted them both—Antonio and Marianna—by saying that time had adjusted still worse difficulties, and that chance would perhaps bring the old gentleman into friendly reach of them again, in some less dangerous way than if they had remained in Rome or were to return there now.

And indeed a prophetic spirit spoke through Salvator.

A considerable time had elapsed since Salvator's arrival in Florence, when one day Antonio burst into his friend's studio, breathless and pale as death. "Salvator!" he cried. "Salvator, my friend, my protector! I am lost if you do not help me! Pasquale Capuzzi is here! He has procured a warrant for my arrest, for the seduction of his niece."

"But what can Signor Pasquale do against you now?" asked Salvator. "Has the Church not joined your life and Marianna's?"

"Oh!" replied Antonio, giving way completely to despair. "The blessing of the Church itself cannot save me from ruin. Heaven knows by what means the old man has been able to approach the Pope's nephew. But at any rate it is the Pope's nephew who has taken the old man under his protection, and has infused into him the hope that the Holy Father will declare my marriage with Marianna null and void; and even worse, that he will grant old Signor Capuzzi a dispensation to marry Marianna."

"Wait!" cried Salvator. "Now I see it all; now I see it all! What threatens to be your ruin, Antonio, is that man's hatred towards me. For I must tell you that this nephew of the Pope's, a proud, coarse, boorish clown, was among the animals in my picture to whom the Goddess of Fortune was dispensing her favors. That it was I who helped you to win your Marianna, though indirectly, is well known, not only to this man, but to all Rome—which is quite reason enough for them to persecute you, since they cannot do anything to me, and you are my friend. And so, Antonio, having brought this misfortune upon you, I must make every effort to assist you, and all the more that you are indeed my dearest and most intimate friend, as you and all the world know well. But, by the saints! I don't see how I am going to frustrate your enemies' little game—"

With these words Salvator, who had continued to work at his painting all during this talk, now laid aside brush, palette, and maulstick, and got up from his easel. Crossing his arms over his breast, he began to pace up and down the room, while poor Antonio remained entirely wrapped up in his own thoughts, and kept his eyes fixed despondently upon the floor.

At length Salvator paused in his walk and said with a smile, "See here, Antonio, I cannot do anything myself to defeat your powerful enemies, but I know one person who can help you and who will help you, and that is—Signor Formica."

"Oh!" said Antonio. "Don't jest with an unhappy man, whom nothing can save!"

"What! You are despairing again?" exclaimed Salvator, who was now all of a sudden in the merriest humor; and he laughed aloud. "I tell you, Antonio, my friend Formica shall help you in Florence as he helped you in Rome. Now just go quietly home and comfort your Marianna, and then calmly wait and see how things turn out. I trust you will be ready at the shortest notice to do whatever Signor Formica, who is fortunately here in Florence at the present time, may ask of you."

And as Antonio promised this most faithfully, hope and confidence revived in him again.

Immediately after this conversation between the two friends, Signor Pasquale Capuzzi was not a little astonished to receive a formal invitation from the Accademia de' Percossi, to be present at their next meeting. "Ah!" he exclaimed, "Florence is the place, I see, where a man's merits are recognized, where Pasquale Capuzzi di Senigaglia, a man gifted with outstanding talents, is known and valued."

And the thought of his own knowledge and his own art, and the tribute that was now paid him on their account, overcame the repugnance which he would otherwise have felt toward a society of which Salvator Rosa was the leading spirit! So Capuzzi's Spanish gala dress was more carefully brushed than ever; his conical hat was furbished with a new feather; his shoes were provided with new ribbons; and thus Signor Pasquale appeared at Salvator's looking as brilliant as a rose-chafer, his face all sunshine. The magnificence which he saw on all sides of him, even the splendor of Salvator himself—who had received him dressed in the richest apparel—inspired the old gentleman with deep respect; and, after the manner of little souls, who, though at first proud and puffed up, at once grovel in the dust whenever they come into contact with that which they consider a superior version of what they themselves base their pride upon, Pasquale's attitude towards Salvator, to whom he would gladly have done harm in Rome, was now marked by nothing but humility and obsequiousness.

And the happiness of his first moments continued. So much attention was paid to Signor Pasquale, indeed, from all sides, his judgment was appealed to so unconditionally, so much was said about his services to art, that he felt as if new life had been infused into his veins; and an unusual spirit was awakened within him, so that his utterances on many points were more sensible than might have been expected. If it be added that never in his life before had he been so splendidly entertained, and never had he drunk such deliciously stimulating wine, it will readily be conceived that his pleasure was intensified from moment to moment, and that he forgot all the wrong which had been done him at Rome, as well as the unpleasant business which had brought him to Florence. Often after their banquets the Academicians were wont to amuse themselves with short impromptu dramatic representations; and so this evening the distinguished playwright and poet Filippo Apolloni called upon those who generally took part in them, to bring the festivities to a fitting conclusion with one of their customary performances. As host, Salvator then immediately withdrew to make all the necessary preparations.

A few minutes later, the bushes at the farther end of the banqueting hall began to move, the branches with their foliage were parted, and a little theatre, provided with benches for the spectators, was seen.

"By the saints!" exclaimed Pasquale Capuzzi, terrified. "Where am I? Surely that's Nicolo Musso's theatre!"

Without heeding his exclamation, Evangelista Toricelli and Andrea Cavalcanti—both of them grave, respected, indeed venerable men—took him by the arm and led him to a seat directly in front of the stage. Then they took their own places, one on each side of their honored guest.

This was no sooner done than there appeared on the boards—Formica in the character of Pasquarello . . .

"You blackguard, Formica!" shouted Pasquale, leaping to his feet and shaking his clenched fist at the stage. But Toricelli and Cavalcanti's stern, reproving glances compelled him to sit still and keep quiet.

Pasquarello, on the stage, now wept and sobbed and cursed his destiny. He averred that fate brought him nothing but grief and disappointment, declared that he didn't know how he should ever set about it if he wanted to laugh again, and concluded by saying that if he could look upon blood without fainting, he should certainly cut his throat, or should throw himself in the Tiber if he could only forget to keep swimming once he hit the water.

Doctor Gratiano now joined him, and inquired what was the cause of his trouble.

Whereupon, Pasquarello asked him whether he did not know about what had taken place in the house of his master, Signor Pasquale Capuzzi di Senigaglia, whether he did not know that an infamous scoundrel had carried off pretty Marianna, his master's niece?

"Ah!" murmured Capuzzi, "I see you want to make your apologies to me, Formica; you wish for my pardon—well, we shall see."

Doctor Gratiano expressed his sympathy, and observed that the scoundrel must have gone to work very cunningly to have eluded all the inquiries which had been instituted by Capuzzi.

"Ho! Ho!" rejoined Pasquarello. And he went on to say that the Doctor need not imagine that the scoundrel, Antonio Scacciati, had succeeded in escaping the sharpness of Signor Pasquale Capuzzi, supported as he was, moreover, by powerful friends. On the contrary, Antonio had been arrested, his marriage with Marianna had been annulled, and Marianna herself had been restored to Capuzzi's guardianship.

"Has he got her again?" shouted Capuzzi, beside himself. "Has he got her again, good Pasquarello? Has he got his little darling, his Marianna? Has that knave, Antonio, been arrested? Heaven bless you, Formica!"

"You take too keen an interest in the play, Signor Pasquale," said Cavalcanti, quite seriously. "Please do allow the actors to proceed with their parts, without interrupting them in this disturbing fashion."

Ashamed of himself, Signor Pasquale sat down again, for he had once more jumped to his feet.

Doctor Gratiano, on the stage, now asked Pasquarello what had taken place next.

A wedding, replied Pasquarello; a wedding had taken place. Marianna had repented of what she had done; Signor Pasquale had obtained the desired dispensation from the Holy Father, and had married his niece.

"Yes, yes," murmured Pasquale Capuzzi to himself, while his eyes sparkled with delight, "yes, yes, my dear, good Formica; he will marry his sweet Marianna, the happy Pasquale. He knows that the little darling has always loved him, and that it was only Satan who led her astray."

"Why, then, everything is all right," said Doctor Gratiano, "and there's no cause for all this lamentation."

Pasquarello began, however, to weep and sob more violently than before, until finally, as if overcome by terrible, and wholly insupportable, pain, he fainted away. Doctor Gratiano, at this, began to run up and down the stage in great distress. He was so sorrry he had no smelling salts with him; he felt in all his pockets; and at last, he produced a roasted chestnut, which he held under the unconscious Pasquarello's nose. The clown at once recovered, sneezing violently, and begging his companion to attribute his faintness to his weak nerves. And now he told how Marianna, immediately after the marriage, had been afflicted with the saddest melancholy, and, continually calling for Antonio, had treated the old gentleman with contempt and aversion. But the old fellow, in the infatuation of his passion and his jealousy, had not ceased to torment the poor girl in the most absurd, and also most abominable, way. And here Pasquarello mentioned a host of mad tricks which Pasquale had played, according to stories which were really current in Rome about him.

Signor Capuzzi sat now upon thorns. He murmured at intervals, "Curse you, Formica! You are lying! What evil spirit possesses you?" And he was only prevented from bursting into a violent passion by the watchfulness of Toricelli and Cavalcanti, who never let him escape their earnest gaze.

Pasquarello concluded his narrative with the information that Marianna had at length succumbed to her unsatisfied longing for her lover, her great distress of mind, and the innumerable tortures which were inflicted upon her by her execrable old guardian, and had died in the flower of her youth.

At this moment the room was filled with the sound of a mournful *De profundis*, sung by hollow, husky voices; and men clad in long black robes appeared on the stage, bearing an open coffin, within which was seen the corpse of lovely Marianna wrapped in a white shroud. Behind it came Signor Pasquale Capuzzi in the deepest mourning, staggering along feebly and blubbering aloud, beating his breast, and crying in tones of utter despair, "O Marianna! Marianna!"

As soon as the real Capuzzi caught sight of his niece's corpse he broke out into loud lamentations, and both Capuzzis, the one on the stage and the one in the audience, gave vent to their grief in the most heart-rending wails and groans, "O Marianna! O Marianna! O unhappy me! Alas! Alas for me!"

Let the reader picture to himself the open coffin with the corpse of the lovely child, surrounded by the hired mourners singing their dismal *De profundis* in hoarse voices, and then the comical masks of Pasquarello and Dr. Gratiano, who were expressing their grief in the most ridiculous gestures, and lastly the two Capuzzis, wailing and screeching in despair. Indeed none of the witnesses of this extraordinary spectacle could help feeling—even in the midst of the unrestrained laughter to which the sight of the wonderful counterfeit had moved them—a sensation of eerie discomfort.

Now the stage was suddenly darkened, and, to the accompaniment of lightning and thunder, a pale ghostly figure rose from some nether depths. And this apparition bore most unmistakably the features of Capuzzi's dead brother, Pietro of Senigaglia, Marianna's father.

"O you infamous brother, Pasquale! What have you done to my daughter?" wailed the spectre, in a dreadful hollow voice. "Despair, you atrocious murderer of my child! You shall find your reward in Hell!"

Capuzzi on the stage dropped to the floor as if struck by lightning, and at the same moment the real Capuzzi tumbled unconscious from his seat. The bushes rustled together again; the stage was gone; and with it the dead Marianna and the living Capuzzi and the ghastly apparition, Pietro. Signor Pasquale Capuzzi lay in such a dead faint that it took some time, and a good deal of effort, to revive him.

At last he came to himself with a deep sigh, and, stretching out both hands before him as if to ward off the horror that threatened him, he called out in a husky voice, "Leave me alone, Pietro." Then a torrent of tears ran down his cheeks, as he cried, "Oh! Marianna, my darling child —my—my Marianna."

"But recollect yourself," said Cavalcanti. "Recollect yourself, Signor Pasquale. It was only on the stage that you saw your niece dead. She is alive. She is here, to beg your forgiveness for the thoughtless step to which she was driven by love, and also by your inconsiderate conduct."

And now the real Marianna, and behind her Antonio Scacciati, ran forward from the rear of the hall and threw themselves at the old gentleman's feet—for he had meanwhile been placed in an easy-chair. Marianna, looking most charming and beautiful, kissed his hands and besought him to pardon her and Antonio, to whom she had been united with the blessing of the Church.

But suddenly the hot blood surged into the old man's pallid face and fury flashed from his eyes. Far from offering forgiveness, he cried to his niece in a voice half choked with wrath, "Oh! You wretched ingrate! You poisonous serpent that I nourished in my bosom!" Then the venerable Toricelli, with grave and thoughtful dignity, stood before Capuzzi, and informed the raging dotard that he had been shown a representation of the fate that would inevitably and irremediably overtake him if he had the persistence to carry out his wicked purpose against Marianna's and Antonio's peace and happiness. Signor Toricelli depicted in awesome colors the folly and madness of amorous old men, who call down upon their own heads the most ruinous mischief which Heaven can inflict, since all the love which might have fallen to their share is lost, and instead hatred and contempt shoot their fatal darts at them from every side.

At intervals, the lovely Marianna cried out, "O my uncle, I will love and honor you as my own father. But you will sentence me to a cruel death if you rob me of my Antonio!" And all the eminent scholars by whom the old gentleman was surrounded averred solemnly, with one accord, that it would not be possible that a man like Signor Pasquale Capuzzi di Senigaglia, a patron of art and himself an artist, should not forgive the young people, and assume the rôle of father to the most lovely of ladies. It was not possible, they asserted further, that he could refuse to accept with joy, as his son-in-law, such an artist as Antonio Scacciati, who was highly esteemed throughout all Italy and richly crowned with all the laurels of fame.

Everyone could see, at this point, that a violent struggle was going on within the old gentleman's spirit. He sighed, moaned, clasped his hands before his face; and, while Toricelli was continuing to speak in a most impressive manner, and Marianna was appealing to him in the most touching accents, and the rest were extolling Antonio as best they knew how, he kept looking down—now upon his niece, now upon Antonio, whose splendid clothes and rich gold chains of honor bore testimony to the truth of what was said about his renown as an artist.

And at last the fury disappeared from Capuzzi's countenance. He sprang to his feet with radiant eyes, and pressed Marianna to his heart. "Yes, I forgive you, my dear child," he said. "I forgive you, Antonio. Far be it from me to disturb your happiness. You are right, my worthy Signor Toricelli; Formica has shown me, in the tableau on the stage, all the mischief and ruin that would have befallen me had I carried out my insane scheme. I am cured, quite cured of my folly. But where is Signor Formica, where is my good physician? Let me thank him a thousand times for my cure; it is he alone who has accomplished it. The terror that he has made me feel has brought about a complete revolution within me."

Pasquarello stepped forward. Antonio threw himself upon his neck, crying, "O Signor Formica, you to whom I owe my life, my all— Oh! Take off that disfiguring mask, and let me see your face! For Formica must no longer be a mystery to me!"

So Pasquarello took off his cap and his mask, which looked just like a real face, since it offered not the slightest hindrance to the play of human expression. And with those few motions this Formica, this Pasquarello, was transformed into—Salvator Rosa!

"Salvator!" exclaimed Marianna, Antonio, and Capuzzi, all of them utterly astounded.

"Yes," said that extraordinary man, "it is Salvator Rosa, whom the Romans would not recognize as painter and poet, but who in the character of Formica drew from them, without their being aware of it, almost every evening for more than a year, in Nicolo Musso's wretched little theatre, the most noisy and most demonstrative storms of applause. It is he from whose mouth they willingly took all the scorn, and all the satire and derision of evil, which they would on no account perceive in Salvator's poems and pictures. It is Salvator Formica who has helped you, dear Antonio."

"Salvator," began old Capuzzi, "Salvator Rosa, although I have always looked upon you as my worst enemy, yet I have always prized your artistic skill. And now I esteem you as the worthiest friend I have. I beg you to accept my friendship in return."

"Tell me," replied Salvator, "tell me, my worthy Signor Pasquale, what service I can render you. And accept my assurance beforehand, that I will leave no stone unturned to accomplish whatever you may ask of me."

And now the genial smile which had not been seen upon Capuzzi's face since Marianna had been carried off, began to steal back again. Taking Salvator's hand, he murmured in the painter's ear, "My dear Signor Salvator, you possess an unlimited influence over good Antonio; beseech him in my name to permit me to spend the short remainder of my life with him, and my dear daughter Marianna, and to accept at my hands the inheritance left her by her mother, as well as the good dowry which I was thinking of adding to it. And he must not look jealous if I occasionally kiss the sweet child's little white hand. And please ask him, too, every Sunday at least, when I go to mass, if he will be so kind as to trim my rough mustache; for there's nobody in all the wide world understands that art so well as he does."

It cost Salvator an effort to repress his laughter over this last grotesque yet characteristic plea. But before he could make any reply, Antonio and Marianna, embracing the old gentleman, assured him that they should not believe he was fully reconciled to them, and should not be really happy, until he came to live with them as their dear father, never to leave them again. Antonio added that not only on Sunday, but every other day as well, he would trim Capuzzi's mustache as elegantly as he knew how. And accordingly the old gentleman was perfectly radiant with delight. Meanwhile, a splendid supper had been prepared, and the entire company now turned in the best of spirits to its enjoyment.

As I take my leave of you, beloved reader, I hope with all my heart that, in following the story of the remarkable Signor Formica, you have derived as much pure pleasure from it as Salvator and all his friends experienced on sitting down to their supper.

THE LEGACY

Not far from the shores of the Baltic Sea is situated the ancestral castle of the noble family Von R—, called R—sitten. It is a wild and desolate district, where hardly anything more than a single blade of grass shoots up here and there from the bottomless drift-sand; and instead of the garden that generally embellishes a baronial residence, the bare walls are approached on the landward side by a scant forest of firs. With their never-changing vesture of gloom, the trees disdain the bright garniture of spring; and in the forest, instead of the chirping of birds awakened to fresh gladness, nothing is heard but the ominous croak of the raven and the whirring scream of the storm-boding sea gull.

A quarter of a mile from the ancestral residence, Nature suddenly changes. As if by the wave of a magician's wand, one is transported into the midst of thriving fields, fertile arable land, pleasant meadows. The traveler sees, too, the large and prosperous village, with the land steward's spacious quarters; and at the angle of a pleasant thicket of alders he may observe the foundations of a large, but never-completed, castle, which one of the former proprietors had intended to erect. This lord's successors, however, living on their property in Courland, were content to leave the building in its unfinished state; nor would Freiherr Roderick von R—proceed with the structure when he again took up his residence on the estate of his forefathers; for the lonely old castle was better suited to his temperament, which was morose and averse to human society. He had its ruined walls repaired as well as circumstances would permit; and then he shut himself up within them along with a sullen house steward and a small domestic staff.

Freiherr Roderick was seldom seen in the village, but on the other hand he often walked and rode along the sea strand. And there were people who declared that from a distance he could be heard talking to the waves, and that he was known to listen to the rolling and hissing of the surf as though he could hear the answering voice of the spirit of the sea. Upon the topmost summit of the castle's watchtower he had a sort of study fitted up and supplied with telescopes—with a complete set of astronomical instruments, in fact. There during the daytime he frequently watched the ships sailing past on the distant horizon like white-winged sea gulls; and there he spent the starlight nights engaged in astronomical, or, as some professed to know, with astrological labors, in which the old house steward assisted him. At any rate, the rumor was current during his own lifetime that he was devoted to the occult sciences, or the so-called Black Art, and that he had been driven out of Courland in consequence of the failure of an experiment by which an august princely house had been most seriously offended. The slightest allusion to his residence in Courland moved him to obvious disquiet; but for all the troubles which had there disturbed the tenor of his life he frankly held his predecessors entirely to blame. All the evil, he said, had followed upon their wicked desertion of the home of their ancestors. In order to bind, for the future, at least the head of the family to the ancestral castle, he succeeded in putting the property under entail. The sovereign was the more willing to ratify this arrangement because by its means he would secure for the service of his country a family which was distinguished for all chivalrous virtues, and which had already begun to spread its ramifications abroad as well.

Neither Roderick's son, Hubert, nor the next Roderick, who was named for his grandfather, would live in their ancestral castle; both preferred Courland. It is conceivable, too, that, being gayer and more fond of social life than the gloomy astrologer, they were repelled by the grim loneliness of the ancient estate. Freiherr Roderick had granted shelter and subsistence on the property to two old spinster aunts, his father's sisters, whom he had found living in indigence, having been but niggardly provided for. They, together with an aged serving-woman, occupied the small, but well-heated, rooms of one of the wings. Except for them, and the cook, who had a large apartment on the ground floor adjoining the kitchen, the only other person in the house was a worn-out *chasseur*, who tottered about through the lofty rooms and halls of the main building, and discharged the duties of concierge. The rest of the servants lived in the village with the land steward.

The only time when the desolated and deserted castle took on any semblance of life and activity was late in autumn, when the snow first began to fall and the season for wolf hunting and boar hunting arrived. Then arrived Freiherr Roderick with his wife, attended by relatives and friends and a numerous retinue, from Courland. The neighboring nobility, and even amateur lovers of the chase who lived in the town hard by, came down in such numbers that the main building, together with the wings, barely sufficed to hold the crowd of guests. Well-kept fires roared in all the stoves and fireplaces, while the spits were roasting food from early dawn until late at night, and hundreds of lighthearted people, both masters and servants, were constantly running up and down the stairs. Here was heard the clinking and rattling of drinking glasses and the roar of jovial hunting choruses, there one might listen to the footsteps of the pleasure seekers who were dancing to the sound of shrill music: the echoes of mirth and celebration reverberated everywhere, so that for four or five weeks together the castle was more like a first-rate hostelry situated on a main highroad than the abode of a country gentleman.

Precisely this period of time Freiherr Roderick devoted, as well as he was able, to serious business; for, withdrawing from the revelry of his guests, he discharged the duties attached to his position as lord of the entailed estate. He not only had a complete statement of the revenues laid before him, but he listened to every proposal for improvement and to every least complaint of his tenants, endeavoring to establish order in every detail, and to check all wrongdoing and injustice, just as far as lay in his power.

In these matters of business he was conscientiously assisted by the old advocate V—, whose family, from father to son, had been legal agents of the R— family, and administrators of their estates in P— for many, many years. According to his routine, old V— was wont to set out for the castle at least a week before the day fixed for the arrival of the Freiherr. So in the year 179– the time came round again when old V— was to start on his journey to R—sitten. However healthy and alert the old man, now seventy years of age, might feel, he nevertheless was quite sure that a helping hand would do him no harm in dispatching his business.

So he said to me one day, as if in jest, "Cousin!" (I was his great-nephew, but he called me "cousin," because his own Christian name and mine happened to be the same) —"Cousin, I was thinking it would not be amiss if you went along with me to R—sitten, and felt the sea breezes blow about your ears a bit. Besides being of some use to me in my often laborious work, you may, for once, see how you like the rollicking life of a hunter, and how, after drawing up a neatly written protocol one morning, you may frame the next when you come face to face with the glaring eyes of a grim shaggy wolf or a wild boar gnashing his teeth, and you have to be sure whether you know how to bring him down with a well-aimed shot."

Of course I could not have heard such extraordinary accounts of the merry hunting parties at R—sitten, or entertain such a truly heartfelt affection for my excellent old great-uncle as I did, without being highly delighted that he wanted to take me with him this time. As I was already pretty well skilled in the sort of business he had to transact, I promised to work with unwearied industry, so as to relieve him of all possible care and trouble.

Next day we set out in the carriage on our way to the castle, well wrapped up in good fur coats, and drove through a thick snowstorm, the first harbinger of the coming winter. On the journey the old gentleman told me many remarkable stories about Freiheer Roderick, who had established the entail on the estate, and appointed my uncle, young as he was at that time, to be his executor. He spoke of the old nobleman's harsh and violent character, which seemed to be a general family inheritance; even the present master of the estate, he added, whom he had known as a mild-tempered and almost effeminate young man, had acquired more and more of the same disposition as the years went by. He therefore strongly advised me to behave with as much resolute self-reliance and as little embarrassment as possible, if I desired to receive any consideration from the Freiherr. Then he went on to describe the rooms in the castle which he had selected to be permanently his own; for, he explained, they were warm and comfortable, and so conveniently remote from the main rooms that we could withdraw from the noisy convivialities of the hilarious company whenever we pleased. The apartment which was thus on every visit reserved for him, consisted of two rooms, their walls warmly hung with tapestry, close beside the large hall of justice, in the wing opposite that in which the two old ladies lived.

At last, after a rapid but fatiguing journey, we arrived at R—sitten, late at night, and passed through the village on our way to the castle. It was Sunday, and from the tavern came the sounds of music, and dancing, and merrymaking; the steward's house was lighted up from basement to garret, and music and song were going on there too. All the more striking, therefore, was the inhospitable desolation into which we now drove. The sea wind howled as if chanting dirges as it beat sharply about us, while the sombre firs, as though they had been roused by the wind from a deep trance, groaned hoarsely in a responding chorus. The bare black walls of the castle towered above the snow-covered ground. We drew up at the gates, and found them locked.

No shouting or cracking of whips, no knocking or hammering, was of any avail; the whole castle seemed to be dead. Not a single light was visible at any of the windows. The old gentleman called out in his strong stentorian voice, "Francis, Francis, where the deuce are you? In the Devil's name, rouse yourself; we are freezing here outside the gates. The snow is cutting our faces till they bleed. Why the Devil don't you stir yourself?" Then the castle watchdog began to growl, and a wandering light showed itself flickering from one window to another on the ground floor. There was a rattling of keys, and soon the ponderous wings of the gate creaked back on their hinges.

"Ha! A hearty welcome, a hearty welcome, your worship. Ugh! It's rough weather!" cried old Francis, holding the lantern above his head, so that the light fell full upon his withered face, which was drawn up into a curious grimace that was meant for a friendly smile. The carriage drove into the court, and we got out; then I obtained a full view of the old servant's extraordinary figure, almost hidden in his wide old-fashioned *chasseur's* livery, with its many extraordinary lace decorations. Although only a few grey locks remained above his broad white forehead, the lower part of his face bore the ruddy hue of health; and, notwithstanding that the cramped muscles of his visage gave it something of the appearance of a whimsical mask, yet the rather stupid good nature which beamed from his eyes and played about his mouth compensated for all the rest, and gave him a merry air.

"Now, old Francis," began my great-uncle, knocking the snow from his fur coat in the entrance hall, "now, old man, is everything prepared? Have you had the hangings in my rooms well dusted, and the beds carried in? And have you had a big roaring fire both yesterday and today?"

"No," replied Francis, quite calmly. "No, your worship, we've got none of that done."

"Good Heavens!" burst out my great-uncle, "I wrote to you in plenty of time. You know that I always come exactly when I say I will. Here's a fine piece of stupid carelessness! I shall have to sleep in rooms as cold as ice."

"But you see, your worship," continued Francis, most carefully clipping with his snuffers a burning thread from the wick of the candle, and stamping it out with his foot, "but, you see, sir, none of that would have done much good, especially the fires, for too much wind and snow have taken up their quarters in the rooms, driving in through the broken windows, and then—"

"What!" my uncle interrupted, spreading out his fur coat and placing his arms akimbo. "Do you mean to tell me that the windows are broken, and you, the caretaker of the house, have done nothing to get them mended?"

"But, your worship," resumed the old servant calmly and composedly, "but we can't very well get at them through the great masses of stones and rubbish that are lying all over the floor."

"Damn it all, how have stones and rubbish come to be in my room?" cried my uncle.

"Your lasting health and good luck, young gentleman!" said the old man, bowing politely to me, as I happened to sneeze. But he immediately added, "They are the stones and plaster of the partition wall which fell in at the great shock."

"Have you had an earthquake?" blazed up my uncle, now fairly in a rage.

"No, not an earthquake, your worship," replied the old man, grinning all over his face, "but three days ago the heavy wainscot ceiling of the great hall of justice fell in with a tremendous crash."

"Then may the—" My uncle was about to rip out a terrific oath in his violently passionate manner, but jerking up his right arm above his head and taking off his foxskin cap with his left, he suddenly checked himself. And turning to me, he said with a hearty laugh, "On my word, cousin, we must hold our tongues; we mustn't ask any more questions, or else we shall hear of some still worse misfortune, or have the whole castle tumbling to pieces about our ears. But," he continued, wheeling around again to the old servant, "but, bless me, Francis, could you not have had the common sense to get me another room cleaned and warmed? Could you not have quickly fitted up a room in the main building to hold our hearings in?"

"All that has been already done," answered the old man, pointing to the stairs with a gesture that invited us to follow him, and at once beginning to ascend them.

"Now there's a most curious noodle for you!" exclaimed my uncle, and turned to follow old Francis.

Our way now led through long and lofty vaulted corridors, in the dense darkness of which Francis' flickering light threw a strange reflection. The pillars, capitals, and varicolored arches appeared to be floating before us in gigantic shapes, and the grotesque paintings on the walls, over which the lights and shadows glided, seemed all of a tremble, while we could imagine that the portraits' voices were whispering, to the sound of our echoing footsteps, "Wake us not. Oh! Wake us not—do not disturb the capricious spirits who sleep here in these old stones."

At last, after we had traversed not only these halls but also a long series of cold and gloomy apartments, Francis opened the door of a salon in which a fire blazing brightly in the grate seemed to offer us a homelike welcome with its pleasant crackling. I felt quite comfortable the moment

I entered; but my uncle, standing still in the middle of the room, looked round him and said in a tone which was so very grave as to be almost solemn, "And so *this* is to be the hall of justice!"

Francis held his candle above his head, so that my eye fell upon a light area about the size of a door, in the wide dark wall. Then he said, in a pained and muffled voice, "Justice has been already dealt out here."

"What possesses you, old man?" asked my uncle, as he quickly threw aside his fur coat and drew near the fire.

"It slipped through my lips. I couldn't help it," replied the old caretaker. In silence, then, he lit the great candles, and opened the door of the adjoining room, which was very snugly fitted up for our reception.

In a short time a table was spread for us before the fire, and the old man at once served us with several well-prepared dishes, followed in turn by a brimming bowl of punch, concocted in true Northern style—a very acceptable sight to two weary travelers like my uncle and myself. My uncle, tired from his journey, went to bed as soon as he had finished supper; but my mind was much too stimulated by the novelty and strangeness of the place, as well as by the punch, to allow me to think of sleep. Meanwhile, Francis cleared the table, stirred up the fire, and bowing and scraping politely, left me to myself.

Now I sat alone in the lofty spacious *Rittersaal* or Knight's Hall. The snowflakes had ceased to beat against the lattice, and the storm had ceased to whistle; the sky was clear, and the bright full moon shone in through the wide oriel windows, illuminating with magical effect all the curious room's dark corners, into which the dim light of my candles and the fire could not penetrate. As is often to be found in old castles, the walls and ceiling of the hall were ornamented in a peculiar antique fashion, the former with fantastic paintings and carvings, gilded and colored in gorgeous tints, the latter with heavy wainscoting. Standing out conspicuously from the great pictures, which represented for the most part wild bloody scenes in bear hunts and wolf hunts, were the heads of men and animals carved in wood and joined on to the painted bodies, so that the whole, especially in the flickering gleam of the fire and the soft moonlight, had an effect as if all were alive and instinct with terrible reality. Between these pictures, reliefs of knights had been inserted, of life size, walking along in hunting costume; probably they were the ancestors of the family, who had delighted in the chase. Everything, both in the paintings and in the carved work, bore the dingy hue of extreme old age; so much the more conspicuous therefore was the bright bare patch on that one of the walls through which two doors led into adjoining apartments. I soon concluded that there, too, there must have been a door, which had been bricked up later; and that, I figured, was why this new part of the wall—which had neither been painted like the rest, nor yet ornamented with carvings— formed such a striking contrast with the others.

Who does not know with what mysterious power the mind is enthralled in the midst of unusual and singularly strange circumstances? Even the dullest imagination is aroused when a man suddenly comes into a valley surrounded by fantastic rocks, or within the gloomy walls of a church or an abbey, and the fancy begins to have glimpses of things it has never yet experienced. When I add that I was twenty years of age, and had drunk several glasses of strong punch, it will easily be conceived that as I sat thus in the *Rittersaal* I was in a more peculiar frame of mind than I had ever been in before.

Let the reader picture to himself the stillness of the night within, and the rumbling roar of the sea without—the peculiar piping of the wind, which rang upon my ears like the tones of a mighty organ played upon by spectral hands—the scudding clouds which, shining bright and white, often seemed to peep in through the rattling oriel windows like monsters sailing past: in truth, I felt, as a slight shudder shook me, that possibly a new sphere of existence might now be visibly and perceptibly revealed to me. But this feeling was like the shivery sensations one has on hearing a vividly told ghost story, such as we all actually enjoy. And at this moment it occurred to me that I should never be in a more suitable mood for reading the book which, in common with everyone who had the least leaning towards the romantic, I at that time carried about in my pocket—I mean Schiller's *Ghost-seer*.

So I took up the book; I read and read; and my imagination became ever more and more excited. I came to the marvelously enthralling description of the wedding feast at Count von V—'s; and just as I was reading of the entrance of Jeronimo's bloody figure, the door leading from the gallery into the antechamber flew open with a tremendous bang.

I started to my feet in terror; the book fell from my hands. Within the very same moment, however, all was still again; and I began to be ashamed of my childish fright. The door must have been pushed open by a strong gust of wind, or in some other natural manner, I said to myself. "It is nothing; my overstrained imagination transforms every ordinary occurrence into something supernatural." Having thus calmed my fears, I picked up my book from the floor, and again threw myself into the armchair. But now I heard a sound of soft, slow, measured footsteps moving diagonally across the hall, accompanied at intervals by a sighing and moaning; and in this sighing and moaning there was expressed the deepest trouble, the most hopeless grief, that a human being can know.

"Ah! It must be some sick animal locked up somewhere in the basement," I told myself. "Such delusions at nighttime, when distant sounds appear close at hand, are well known to everybody. Who will permit himself to be terrified by such a thing as that?"

Thus I calmed my fears again. But now there was a scratching at the new portion of the wall, while louder and deeper sighs were unescapably audible, as if they were being gasped out by someone in the last throes of mortal anguish. "Yes, yes; it is some poor animal locked up somewhere. I will shout as loudly as I can; I will stamp violently on the floor; then all will be still, or else the animal imprisoned below will make itself heard more distinctly, and in its more natural voice," I thought. Yet the blood ran cold in my veins; the cold sweat, too, stood upon my forehead; and I remained sitting in my chair as if transfixed, quite unable to rise, still less to cry out.

At last the abominable scratching ceased, and I again heard the footsteps. Life and motion seemed once more to be awakened in me; I leaped to my feet, and went two or three steps forward. But just then an ice-cold draft of wind swept through the hall, while at the same moment the moon cast its now bright light upon the statue of an austere if not almost terrible-looking man; and then, as though his warning voice rang through the louder thunder of the waves and the shriller piping of the wind, I distinctly heard the words: "No further, no further! Or you will sink beneath all the fearful horrors of the world of spectres!"

Again the door was slammed shut, with the same violent bang as before, and I plainly heard the footsteps passing through the anteroom, then going down the stairs. The main door of the castle was opened with a creaking noise, and quickly closed again. There were sounds as if a horse were being brought out of the stable, and after a while taken back again. And finally all was still.

As silence fell, my attention was attracted to my old uncle in the adjoining room; he was groaning and moaning painfully. This realization brought me fully to consciousness again; I seized the candles and hurried to his bedside, where I saw that he appeared to be struggling with an ugly, unpleasant dream.

"Wake up, wake up!" I cried loudly, taking him gently by the hand, and letting the full glare of the light fall upon his face.

He started up with a stifled shout, and then, looking kindly at me, said, "Yes, you have done quite right—you have certainly done right, cousin, to wake me. I have had a very disagreeable dream, and it's all solely because of this room and that hall. For they made me think of the past, and of the many strange things that have happened here. But now let us turn to and have a good sound sleep." Therewith the old gentleman rolled himself in the bedclothes and appeared to fall asleep at once. But when I had extinguished the candles and had likewise crept into bed, I heard him praying in a low undertone.

Next morning we began work in earnest; the land steward brought his account books, and various other people came, some to get a dispute settled, some to have arrangements made about other matters. At noon my uncle took me with him to the wings where the two old Baronesses lived, so that we might pay our respects to them with all due form. After Francis announced us, we had to wait some time before a little old dame, bent with the weight of sixty years, and attired in gay-colored silks, who styled herself the noble ladies' lady-in-waiting, appeared, and led us into the sanctuary. There we were received with comical ceremony by the old ladies, whose curious style of dress had gone out of fashion years and years before. I, especially, was an object of astonishment to them when my uncle, with considerable humor, introduced me as a young lawyer who had come to assist him in his business. Their countenances plainly indicated their belief that, because of my youth, the welfare of the tenants of R—sitten was being placed in jeopardy.

Although there was a good deal that was truly ridiculous in the whole of this interview with the old ladies, I was nevertheless still shivering from the terror of the preceding night; I felt as if I had come in contact with an unknown power, or rather as if I had grazed the outer edge of a circle, one step across which would be enough to plunge me irretrievably into destruction; it seemed as though it were only by the exertion of all the power of my will that I should be able to guard myself against *that* awful dread which never slackens its hold until it ends in incurable insanity. Hence it was that the old Baronesses, with their remarkable towering headdresses, and their peculiar woolen gowns, tricked off with gay flowers and ribbons, instead of striking me as merely ludicrous, had an appearance that was both spectral and awe-inspiring. From their yellow withered faces and blinking eyes, my fancy seemed to glean ocular proof of the fact that they had succeeded in establishing themselves on at least a good footing with the ghosts who haunted the castle, as it derived oral confirmation of the same fact from the wretched French which they croaked, partly between their tightly closed blue lips and partly through their long thin noses; and I felt also that they themselves possessed the power of setting trouble and dire mischief at work.

My uncle, who always had a keen eye for a bit of fun, entangled the old dames in his ironical way in such a skein of nonsensical twaddle that, had I been in any other mood, I should not have been able to choke down my immoderate laughter; but, as I have just said, the Baronesses and their prattle were, and continued to be, in my regard, spectral, so that my old uncle, who was seeking to afford me a special diversion, glanced across at me time after time, utterly astonished.

After dinner, then, when we were alone together in our rooms, he burst out, "In Heaven's name, boy, tell me what is the matter with you. You don't laugh; you don't talk; you don't eat; and you don't drink. Are you ill, or is anything else wrong with you?"

I now hesitated not a moment in telling him in detail all my terrifying and truly awful experiences of the previous night. I did not conceal anything; and above all I did not conceal the fact that I had drunk a good deal of punch and that I had been reading Schiller's *Ghost-seer*. "This I must confess to," I added, "for only so can I credibly explain how it was that my overstrained and active imagination could create all those ghostly phantoms, which exist only within the sphere of my own brain."

I fully expected that my uncle would now pepper me well with the stinging shots of his wit for this fanciful ghost-seeing of mine; but, on the contrary, he grew very grave, and his eyes became riveted in a set stare upon the floor, until he jerked up his head and said, fixing me with his keen fiery eyes, "Your book I am not acquainted with, cousin; but your ghostly visitants were due neither to it nor to the fumes of the punch. I must tell you that I dreamed exactly the same things that you saw and heard. Like you, I sat in the easy-chair beside the fire (at least I dreamed I did); but what was only revealed to you in vague noises I beheld and distinctly comprehended with the eye of my mind. Yes, I saw that foul fiend come in; I saw him step across, stealthily and feebly, to the bricked-up door, and scratch at the wall in hopeless despair until the blood gushed out from beneath his torn fingernails. Then he went downstairs, took a horse out of the stable, and after a time put him back in again. Did you also hear the cock crowing in a distant farmyard up at the village? You came and woke me, and I soon got the best of the baneful ghost of that terrible man, who is still able to disturb in this fearful way the quiet existence of the living."

The old gentleman stopped; and I did not like to question him further, being well aware that he would explain everything to me at what he considered the proper time. But after sitting silent for a while, deeply absorbed in his own thoughts, he spoke again: "Cousin, do you think you have courage enough to encounter the ghost once more now that you know all that happens—that is to say, to encounter him along with me?"

Of course I assured him that I now felt quite strong enough, and ready to do anything he wished.

"Then let us watch together during the coming night," my uncle went on to say. "There is a voice within me which tells me that this evil spirit must flee, not so much before the power of my will as before my courage, which rests upon a basis of firm conviction. I feel that it will be not at all an act of presumption on my part, but rather a good and pious deed, if I venture life and limb to exorcise this foul fiend that is keeping the sons in banishment from the old castle of their ancestors. But what am I thinking about? There can be no risk in the case at all; for with such a firm, honest mind and pious trust as I feel myself to possess, I and everybody with me cannot fail to be, now and always, victorious over such ghostly antagonists. And yet, if, after all, it should be God's will that this evil power be enabled to work me mischief, then you must bear witness, cousin, that I fell in honest Christian fight against the spirit of Hell, which was here busy with its fiendish work. As for yourself, keep at a distance; no harm will come to you then."

Our attention was busily engaged with divers kinds of business until evening came. Then, as on the day before, Francis cleared away the remains of the supper, and brought us our punch. The full moon shone brightly between the flying clouds, the sea waves roared, and the night wind howled and shook the oriel window till the panes rattled. Although inwardly excited, we forced ourselves to converse on indifferent topics. The old gentleman had placed his striking watch on the table. As it struck twelve, the door flew open with a terrific bang, and, just as on the preceding night, soft slow footsteps moved stealthily across the hall in a diagonal direction, to the same accompaniment of the sounds of sighing and moaning. My uncle turned pale, but his eyes shone with unusual brilliance. He rose from his armchair, and stretched his tall figure up to its full height, so that as he stood there with his left arm propped against his side and with his right pointing out towards the middle of the hall, he had the appearance of a hero issuing his commands. But the sighing and moaning were growing louder and more perceptible every moment, and then the scratching at the wall began—more horribly, even, than on the previous night.

My uncle strode forward, straight towards the walled-up door, and his steps were so firm that they echoed as he passed along the floor. He stopped immediately in front of the place, where the scratching noise continued to grow worse and worse, and said in a strong solemn voice, such as I had never before heard from his lips, "Daniel, Daniel! What are you doing here at this hour?"

What followed was a horrible unearthly scream, and then a dull thud as if a heavy weight had fallen to the floor. "Seek for pardon and mercy at the throne of the Almighty; that is the place where you should be. Depart from the scenes of this life, in which you can nevermore have part!"

And as the old gentleman uttered these words in a tone still stronger than before, a feeble wail seemed to pass through the air and die away in the blustering of the storm, which was just beginning to rage anew. Crossing over to the door, my uncle slammed it to, with such force, here also, that the echo rang loudly through the empty anteroom.

There was something close to the supernatural in both his language and his gestures, and when he resumed his seat in his armchair his face seemed transfigured. He folded his hands and prayed without speaking any words aloud. In this way several minutes passed; and then he said simply, in the gentle tone which always went right to my heart, and which he always had so completely at his command, "Well, my boy?"

Agitated and shaken by awe, terror, fear, and also by pious respect and love, I threw myself upon my knees before him and my warm tears fell upon the hand he offered me. He clasped me in his arms, and, pressing me to his heart, he said very tenderly, "Now we will go and have a good quiet sleep, good cousin." And so we did.

As nothing of an unusual nature occurred on the following night, we soon recovered our former cheerfulness, a matter which changed my attitude toward the old Baronesses. For though there still continued indeed to be something ghostly about them and their odd manners, yet their fantastic quality seemed now to emanate from a diverting ghost, which the old gentleman knew how to call up in a droll fashion.

At length, after the lapse of several days, the Baron himself put in his appearance, with his wife and a large staff of servants, for the hunting; the invited guests also arrived; and the castle, now suddenly awakened to animation, became the scene of the noisy life and revelry which I had been prepared to find there. When the Baron came into our hall soon after his arrival, however, he seemed to be disagreeably surprised by the change in our quarters. Casting an ill-tempered glance towards the bricked-up door, he turned abruptly around and passed his hand across his forehead, as if he were trying to get rid of some disagreeable recollection. My great-uncle mentioned the damage done to the hall of justice and the adjoining apartment. But the Baron found fault with Francis for not accommodating us better, and then, becoming suddenly good-natured, he told the old gentleman to order anything he might want to make his new rooms comfortable; for the apartment was much less satisfactorily furnished than the one he had usually occupied.

On the whole, the Baron's bearing toward my old uncle was not merely cordial, but also richly colored by a certain deferential respect, as if the relation in which he stood towards him was that of a younger relative. But this was the sole trait that could in any way reconcile me to his harsh, imperious character, which now became more and more apparent every day. As for me, he seemed to notice me very little; if he did notice me at all, he saw in me nothing more than the usual secretary or clerk. On the occasion of the very first important memorandum that I drew up, he began to point out mistakes, as he conceived them to be, in the wording. My blood boiled, and I was about to make a caustic reply, when my uncle interposed, informing him briefly that I did my work exactly as he wished me to, and that in legal matters of this kind he alone was responsible. When we were left alone, I complained bitterly of the Baron, for whom, I said, I should never feel anything but aversion.

"I assure you, my boy," replied the old gentleman, "that the Baron, notwithstanding his unpleasant manner, is really one of the most admirable and kindhearted men alive. As I have already told you, he did not take on this manner until he became lord of the entailed estate; before that he was a modest and gentle young man. Besides, he is not, after all, so bad as you make him out to be; and further, I should like to know why you have taken such a dislike to him."

As my uncle said these words he smiled mockingly, and the blood rushed hotly and furiously into my face. I could not pretend to hide from myself—I saw it only too clearly, and felt it too unmistakably—that my peculiar antipathy to the Baron arose from the fact that I had fallen in love, to the point of madness, with a lady who seemed to me to be the loveliest and most fascinating being who had ever trod the earth—and who was none other than the Baroness herself!

Her appearance had cast a powerful and irresistible spell upon me at the very moment of her arrival, when I first saw her walking along the corridors, clad in her Russian sable cloak—which fitted so closely as to emphasize the exquisite symmetry of her form—and with a rich veil wrapped about her head. The two old aunts, decked out in more extraordinary gowns, and more lavishly beribboned headdresses than I had yet seen them wear, were sweeping along one on each side of her, and cackling their welcomes in French, while the Baroness was looking about her in a manner so gentle as to baffle all description, nodding graciously first to one and then to the other, and then adding in her flutelike voice a few German words in the pure sonorous dialect of Courland. All this had made a truly remarkable and most unusual picture, and my imagination involuntarily connected it with the ghostly midnight visitant—the Baroness being the angel of light who was to break the ban of the spectral powers of evil.

This wondrously lovely lady stood forth in startling reality before my mind's eye. At that time she could hardly have been as much as nineteen years old; and her face, as delicately beautiful as her figure, seemed to be the very expression of the most angelic nature. But what I felt most poignantly was the indescribable fascination of her dark eyes; for a soft and dreamy gleam of aspiration shone in them like moonshine over dewy meadows, while, as it seemed to me, a perfect Elysium of rapture and delight was revealed in her sweet and beautiful smile. She often seemed to be completely lost in her own quite private thoughts, and at such moments her lovely face would be swept by dark and fleeting shadows. Many observers would have concluded that she was wracked by present trouble of some sort, or even by physical pain; but it seemed to me rather that she was struggling with forebodings of a future that might be fraught with dark misfortunes; and with these, strangely enough, I connected the apparition of the castle, though I could not give the least explanation of why I did so.

On the morning following the Baron's arrival, when the company assembled at breakfast, my old uncle had introduced me to the Baroness; and, as usually happens with people in the frame of mind in which I then was, I behaved with indescribable—even ludicrous—gaucherie. In answer to the beautiful lady's simple inquiries as to how I liked the castle, and so forth, I entangled myself in the most extraordinary and nonsensical phrases. Whereupon the old aunts, not unnaturally, ascribed my embarrassment simply and solely to my profound and humble respect for the noble lady, and thought they were called upon condescendingly to take my part, which they did by praising me in French as a very nice and clever young man, as a *garcon très joli*. This vexed me; so suddenly recovering my self-possession, I threw out a *bon mot* in better French than the old dames were mistresses of. And at this they opened their eyes wide in astonishment, and pampered their long thin noses with a liberal supply of snuff. The Baroness turned from me to talk with a more serious air to some other lady, and I realized that my *bon mot* had bordered closely upon mere foolishness; this vexed me still more, and I mentally consigned the two old ladies to the Devil.

My old uncle's irony had long since brought me through the stage of the languishing lovesick swain, who in childish infatuation coddles his love troubles; but I knew very well that the Baroness had made a deeper and more powerful impression upon my heart than any other woman hitherto. I saw and heard, and thought of, nothing but her. Nevertheless I had a most explicit and unequivocal consciousness that it would be not only absurd, but even utter madness, to dream of an *amour*, while I perceived no less clearly the impossibility of gazing and adoring at a distance, like a lovelorn boy. Of such conduct I should have been perfectly ashamed. But what I could do, and what I resolved to do, was to reach the status of friendship with this beautiful girl, without allowing her to obtain any glimpse of my real feelings: in more romantic terms, to drink the sweet poison of her looks and words, and then, when far away from her, to bear her image in my heart for many, many days, perhaps forever.

I was excited by this romantic and chivalric attachment to such a degree that, as I pondered over it during sleepless nights, I was childish enough to pour out my heart in pathetic monologues, and even to sigh lugubriously, "Seraphina! O Seraphina!" till at last my old uncle woke up and cried, "Cousin, cousin! I believe you are dreaming aloud. Do it by daytime, if you possibly can contrive it, but at night have the goodness to let me sleep!"

I was very much afraid that the old gentleman, who had not failed to remark my excitement on the Baroness' arrival, had heard the name, and would overwhelm me with his sarcastic wit. But next morning all he said, as we went into the hall of justice, was, "God grant every man the proper amount of common sense, and sufficient caution to keep his emotions well in hand! It's a bad lookout when a man becomes transformed into a fantastic coxcomb without so much as a word of warning." Then he took his seat at the great table and added, "Write neatly and distinctly, my boy, so that I may be able to read your script without any trouble."

The respect, indeed the almost filial veneration, which the Baron felt toward my uncle, was manifest on all occasions. Thus, at the dinner table, the venerable gentleman had to occupy the seat—which many envied him —beside the Baroness. As for me, chance threw me first in one place and then in another; but for the most part, two or three officers from the neighboring capital would attach me to their company, in order that they might empty to their own satisfaction their budget of news and amusing anecdotes, while diligently passing the wine back and forth. So it came about that for several days in succession I sat at the lower end of the table, at a great distance from the Baroness.

At length, however, chance brought me nearer to her. Just as the doors of the dining hall were thrown open to the assembled company, I happened to be in the midst of a conversation with the Baroness' companion and confidante—a lady no longer in the bloom of youth, but by no means ill-looking, and not without intelligence—and she seemed to take some interest in my remarks. According to etiquette, it was my duty to offer her my arm, and I was not a little pleased when she took her place quite close to the Baroness, who gave her a friendly nod. It may be readily imagined that all that I now said was intended not only for my fair neighbor, but also, and mainly, for the Baroness. Perhaps the inward tension of my feelings imparted an especial animation to my remarks; at any rate my companion's attention became more riveted with every succeeding moment; in fact, she was at last entirely absorbed in the visions of the kaleidoscopic world which I unfolded to her gaze. As I have remarked, she was not without intelligence; and it soon came to pass that our conversation, completely independent of the multitude of words spoken by the other guests (words which jumped first to this subject and then to that), maintained its own free course, as I would drop an effective phrase now and again, shifting the talk where I wanted it to go. For I did not fail to observe that my companion shot a significant glance or two across to the Baroness, and that the latter took pains to listen to us. And this was particularly the case when the conversation turned upon music, and I began to speak with enthusiasm of this glorious and sacred art. Nor was I reticent in disclosing that, despite the fact of my having devoted myself to the dry and tedious study of the law, I possessed tolerable skill on the harpsichord, could sing, and had even set several songs to music.

The majority of the company had gone into another room to take coffee and liqueurs; but, unawares, without knowing how it came about, I found myself near the Baroness, who was talking with her confidante. She at once addressed me, repeating in a still more cordial manner, and in the tone in which one talks to a personal acquaintance, her inquiries as to how I liked living in the castle, and so on. I confessed to her that, for the first few days, not only the desolation of its situation, but also the ancient castle itself, had affected me strangely, but I added quickly that even in this mood I had found much to interest me. And I concluded by saying that now my only wish was to be excused from the excitement of the hunt, for I had not been accustomed to such sporting adventures.

The Baroness smiled, and said, "I can readily believe that this wild life in our fir forests cannot be very congenial to you. You are a musician, and, unless I am utterly mistaken, a poet as well. I am passionately fond of both arts. I can also play the harp a little, but I have to do without it here in R—sitten, for my husband does not like me to bring my instrument with me. Its soft strains would scarcely harmonize with the wild shouts of the hunters and the ringing blare of their bugles, which are the only sounds that ought to be heard here at such a time as this. And oh, how I should like to hear a little music!"

I protested that I would exert all the skill I had at my command to fulfill her wish, for there must surely be an instrument of some kind in the castle, even though it were only an old harpsichord. Then the Lady Adelheid (the Baroness' confidante) burst out into a silvery laugh and asked, did I not know that within the memory of man no instrument had ever been heard in the castle except cracked trumpets, and hunting horns which in the midst of joy would only sound lugubrious notes, and the twanging fiddles, untuned violoncellos, and braying oboes of itinerant musicians? The Baroness repeated that she should like to have some music, and especially should like to hear me play. And both she and Adelheid racked their brains, all to no purpose, to devise some scheme by which they could arrange to have a decent pianoforte brought to the castle.

At this moment old Francis crossed the room. "Here's the man who always can give the best advice, and can get hold of everything, even things before unheard of and unseen," said Lady Adelheid; and forthwith she called him to her. As the lady-in-waiting endeavored to make the old servitor understand what it was that was wanted, the Baroness listened with her hands clasped and her head bent forward, a gentle smile turned towards the old man's face. She made a most attractive picture, like some lovely and winsome child that is all eagerness to have a long-wished-for toy at last in its hands . . .

Francis, after having declared in his long-winded manner why it would be downright impossible, for several reasons, to procure so wonderful an instrument in such a great hurry, finally stroked his beard with an air of self-flattery and said, "But the land steward's lady up at the village performs on the clavichord, or whatever is the outlandish name they now call it, with uncommon skill, and sings to it so fine and mournful-like that it makes your eyes red, just like onions do, and makes you feel as if you would like to dance with both legs at once."

"And you say she has a pianoforte?" interposed Lady Adelheid.

"Aye, to be sure," continued the old man; "it comes straight from Dresden, a—" ("Oh, that's fine!" interrupted the Baroness)—"a beautiful instrument," went on the old man, "but a little weakly; for not long ago, when the organist began to play on it the hymn, 'In all Thy works,' he broke it all to pieces, so that—" ("Good gracious!" exclaimed both the Baroness and Lady Adelheid) "so that," went on the old man again, "it had to be taken to R— to be mended, and cost a lot of money."

"But has it come back again?" asked Lady Adelheid impatiently.

"Aye, to be sure, my Lady, and the steward's wife will reckon it a high honor—"

At this moment the Baron chanced to pass. He looked across at our group with some appearance of astonishment, and murmured, with a sarcastic smile, to the Baroness, "So you have to take counsel of Francis again, I see?" The Baroness cast down her eyes, blushing, while old Francis, breaking off, terrified, suddenly threw himself into military posture, his head erect, and his arms close and straight down his side.

The old aunts came sailing down upon us in their woolen gowns, and carried the Baroness off with them. Lady Adelheid followed her. And I was left alone as if spellbound. A struggle began to rage within me, between my rapturous anticipation of now being able to be near the lovely creature whom I adored, who completely swayed all my thoughts and feelings, and my sulky ill-humor and annoyance at the Baron, whom I regarded as a barbarous tyrant. If he were not a cruel despot, I asked myself, would the grey-haired old servant have assumed such a slavish attitude toward him?

"Do you hear? Can you see? I say," cried my great-uncle, tapping me on the shoulder later, as we were going upstairs to our own apartment. "Don't force yourself so on the Baroness' attention," he continued, as we reached our rooms. "What good can come of it? Leave such behavior to the young fops who like to pay court to ladies; there are plenty of them to do it." I told him how all this exchange of talk had come about, and challenged him to say if I had deserved his reproof. His only reply to this, however, was, "Humph! Humph!" as he drew on his dressing gown. Then, having lit his pipe, he took his seat in his easy-chair and began to talk about the adventures of the hunt on the preceding day, bantering me on my bad shots.

All was quiet in the castle now; all the visitors, both gentlemen and ladies, were busy in their own rooms dressing for the evening. For the musicians with the twanging fiddles, untuned violoncellos, and braying oboes, of whom Lady Adelheid had spoken, had now arrived, and a merry-making of no less importance than a ball, to be given in the best possible style, was in immediate preparation. My old uncle, preferring a quiet sleep to such foolish pastimes, stayed in his chamber. I, however, was determined to join the guests, and I had just finished dressing when there came a light tap at our door, and Francis entered. Smiling in his self-satisfied way, he announced to me that the clavichord had just arrived from the land steward's wife, in a sledge, and had been carried into the Baroness' apartments. Lady Adelheid sent her compliments, and asked that I go over at once.

It may be conceived how my pulse beat, and also with what a delicious tremor of the heart I opened the door of the room in which I was to find her. Lady Adelheid came to meet me with a happy smile. The Baroness, already in full dress for the ball, was sitting in a meditative attitude beside the mysterious case, or box, in which slumbered the music that I was now called upon to awaken. When she rose, her beauty shone upon me with such splendor that I stood staring at her like a bumpkin, unable to utter a word.

"Come, Theodore"—(for, according to the kind custom of the North, which is found again farther south, she addressed everybody by his or her Christian name)—"Come, Theodore," she said pleasantly, "here's the instrument; it has just come. Heaven grant it be not altogether unworthy of your skill!"

As I opened the lid I was greeted, however, by the rattling of a score of broken strings; and when I attempted to strike a chord, the effect was hideous and abominable, for all the strings which were not broken were completely out of tune. "No doubt our friend the organist has been putting his delicate little hands upon it again," said Lady Adelheid, laughing; but the Baroness was very much annoyed and said, "Oh, it really is a piece of bad luck! I am doomed, I see, never to have any pleasure here."

I searched in the case of the instrument, and fortunately found some coils of strings, but no tuning key anywhere. Whereupon, there arose fresh laments. "Any key will do if the ward will fit on the pegs," I explained. And then, both Lady Adelheid and the Baroness ran back and forth in gay spirits, with the result that before long a whole magazine of bright keys lay before me on the sounding board.

Thus aided, I set to work diligently, and both the ladies continued to assist me as much as they could, trying first one peg and then another. At length one of the tiresome keys fitted, and together they exclaimed joyfully, "This will do! It will do!"

But when I had drawn the first creaking string up to just the proper pitch, it suddenly snapped, and the ladies recoiled in alarm. The Baroness, handling the brittle wires with her delicate little fingers, gave me the numbers as I wanted them, and carefully held the coil while I unrolled it. Suddenly one of them coiled itself up again with a whir, wringing an impatient "Oh!" from the Baroness. Lady Adelheid enjoyed a hearty laugh meanwhile; and I pursued the tangled coil to the corner of the room. After we had all united our efforts to extract a perfectly straight string from it, and had tried it again, to our mortification it once more broke. But at last —at last—we found some good coils; the strings began to hold; and gradually the discordant jangling gave place to pure melodious chords.

"Oh! It will play! The instrument is getting into tune!" exclaimed the Baroness, looking at me with her lovely smile. And quickly did this common interest banish all the strangeness and shyness which the artificial manners of social intercourse impose! A kind of confidential familiarity arose between us, which, burning through me like an electric current, consumed the nervous timidity and constraint which had lain like ice upon my heart. That peculiar mood of diffused melting sadness, which is engendered by such love as mine, had quite left me. And so it happened that—when the pianoforte was brought into something like tune—instead of interpreting my deeper feelings in dreamy improvisation, as I had intended, I began with those sweet and charming canzonets which have reached us from the South.

During this or the other *Senza di te* (Without thee), or *Sentimi idol mio* (Hear me, my darling), or *Almen se non poss'io* (At least if I cannot), with numberless *Morir mi sentos* (I feel I am dying), and *Addios* (Farewell), and *O dios!* (O Heaven), a brighter and brighter brilliancy shone in Seraphina's eyes. She had seated herself close beside me at the instrument; I felt her breath fanning my cheek; and as she placed her arm behind me on the chair back, a white ribbon, suddenly disengaged from her beautiful ball dress, fell across my shoulder, where by my singing and Seraphina's soft sighs it was kept in a continual flutter backwards and forwards, like a true love messenger. It is a wonder how I kept from losing my head . . .

As I was running my fingers aimlessly over the keys, thinking of a new song, Lady Adelheid, who had been sitting in one of the corners of the room, crossed quickly to us, and, kneeling down before the Baroness, begged her, as she took both her hands and clasped them to her bosom, "Oh, dear Baroness! Darling Seraphina! Now you must sing too."

To this the lady of the castle replied, "Whatever are you thinking about, Adelheid? How could I dream of letting our virtuoso friend hear such poor singing as mine?" And she looked inexpressibly lovely, as, like a shy good child, she cast down her eyes and blushed, her modesty timidly contending with the natural desire to sing.

That I too added my entreaties can easily be imagined; nor, upon her making mention of some little Courland *Volkslieder*, or popular songs, did I desist from my entreaties until she stretched out her left hand towards the instrument and tried a few notes by way of introduction. I rose to make way for her at the piano, but she would not permit me to do so, asserting that she could not play a single chord, and for that reason, since she would thus have to sing without accompaniment, her performance would be poor and uncertain.

She began in a sweet voice, pure as a bell, that came straight from her heart, and sang a song whose simple melody bore all the characteristics of those *Volkslieder* which proceed from the lips with such a lustrous brightness, so to speak, that we cannot help perceiving, in the glad light which surrounds us, our own higher poetic nature. A mysterious charm lies in the insignificant words of the text, which converts them into a hieroglyphic scroll representative of the unutterable emotions which crowd our hearts. And the Baroness' little song said, in words, only, "Lately I was dancing with my sweetheart at a wedding; a flower fell out of my hair; he picked it up and gave it me, and said, 'When, sweetheart mine, shall we go to a wedding again?' " It, too, was utterly simple. When, on her beginning the second verse of the song, I played an *arpeggio* accompaniment, and further when, in the inspiration which now took possession of me, I at once stole from the Baroness' own lips the melodies of the other songs she sang, I must have appeared in her eyes, and in those of the Lady Adelheid, to be one of the greatest of masters in the art of music; for they overwhelmed me with enthusiastic praise.

The lights from the ballroom, which was situated in one of the other wings of the castle, now shone across into the Baroness' chamber, whilst a discordant bleating of trumpets and French horns announced that it was time for all the company to gather for the ball. "Oh, now I must go," said the Baroness. And as I started up from the pianoforte, she added, "You have afforded me a delightful hour; these have been the pleasantest moments I have ever spent in R—sitten." With these words, she offered me her hand; and as in the extreme intoxication of delight I pressed it to my lips, I felt her fingers close upon my fingers with a sudden convulsive tremor. I do not know how I managed to reach my uncle's chamber, and still less do I know how I got into the ballroom. There was a certain Gascon who was afraid to go into battle because he was all heart, and every wound would be fatal to him. I might be compared to him; and so might everybody else who is in the same mood that I was in; every touch was then fatal. The Baroness' hand—her tremulous fingers—had affected me like a poisoned arrow; my blood was burning in my veins.

On the following morning my old uncle, without asking any direct questions, was soon able to draw out of me a full account of the hour I had spent in the Baroness' society, and I was not a little abashed when the smile vanished from his lips and the jocular note from his words, and he grew serious all at once. "My dear young kinsman," he said, "I beg you will resist this folly which is taking such a powerful hold upon you. Let me tell you that your present conduct, harmless as it now appears, may have the most terrible consequences. In your thoughtless fatuity you are standing on a thin crust of ice, which may break under you before you know it, and submerge you with a dreadful shock. I shall take good care not to hold you fast by the coattails, for I know you will scramble out again in short order; and then, when you are lying sick unto death, I am sure you will say, 'I caught this little bit of a cold in a dream.' But I warn you that a malignant fever will gnaw at your vitals, and years will pass before you recover yourself, and become a man again. The deuce take your music if you can put it to no better use than to cozen sentimental young women out of their quiet peace of mind."

"But," I began, interrupting the old gentleman, "but have I ever had the audacity to think of myself as the Baroness' lover?"

"You puppy!" cried my indignant relative. "If I thought that, I would pitch you out of this window." At this juncture the Baron came in, and put an end, naturally, to our painful conversation. And the business to which I now had to turn my attention brought me back from those lovesick reveries in which I saw and thought of nothing but Seraphina. . . .

In general society, the Baroness only occasionally interchanged a few friendly words with me, but hardly an evening passed in which a secret message was not brought to me from Lady Adelheid, summoning me to Seraphina's side. It soon came to pass that our music alternated with conversations on various topics. Whenever Seraphina and I began to become too absorbed in sentimental dreams and vague aspirations, the Lady Adelheid, though now hardly young enough to be so naïve and droll as she once had been, was yet quite able to intervene with all sorts of merry, even if somewhat chaotic, nonsense. From several hints she let fall, I soon discovered that the Baroness really had something preying upon her mind, just as I had surmised from the look in her eyes, the very first moment I saw her; and I clearly discerned the hostile influence of the apparition of the castle. Something terrible had happened, or was to happen. Although I was often strongly impelled to tell Seraphina in what way I had come in contact with the invisible enemy, and how my old uncle had exorcised this unquiet spirit, undoubtedly forever, I yet felt my tongue tied by a hesitation, which was inexplicable even to myself, whenever I opened my mouth to speak of these matters.

One day the Baroness failed to appear at the dinner table. It was said that she was a little unwell, and could not leave her room. Sympathetic inquiries were addressed to the Baron, as to whether her illness was of a grave nature. He smiled in a very disagreeable way—in fact, his manner was almost one of bitter irony—and said, "Nothing more than a slight catarrh, which she has got from our blustering sea breezes. These winds of ours, here, can't tolerate any sweet voices; the only sounds they will endure are the hoarse 'Halloos' of the chase." At these words the Baron hurled a keen searching look at me across the table—for I sat diagonally opposite him. He had not spoken to his neighbor, but to me. Lady Adelheid, who was seated beside me, blushed a scarlet red. Fixing her eyes upon the plate in front of her, and fidgeting about on it with her fork, she whispered, "And yet you must see Seraphina today; your sweet songs, today also, shall bring soothing and comfort to her poor heart."

Adelheid addressed these words to me; and at this moment it struck me that I was, apparently, almost entangled in a base and forbidden intrigue with the Baroness, which could only end in some terrible crime. My old uncle's warning fell heavily upon my heart. What should I do? Not see her again? That was impossible so long as I remained in the castle; and even if it were possible for me to leave the castle and return to K—, I had not the will to do any such thing. Oh! I felt only too deeply that I was not strong enough to shake myself out of this dream, which had been mocking me with delusive hopes of happiness. Adelheid I almost regarded in the light of a common go-between. I could despise her; and yet, upon second thought, I could not help being ashamed of my own folly. Had anything ever happened during those blissful evening hours which could, in the least degree, lead to any nearer relation with Seraphina than was allowed by propriety and morality? How dare I let the thought enter my mind that the Baroness would ever entertain any tenderness for me? And yet I was convinced of the danger of my situation.

We left the dinner table earlier than usual, in order to set out again after some wolves which had been seen in the forest close to the castle. A little hunting was just the thing I wanted in my present excited frame of mind. I expressed to my uncle my intention to accompany the party. He gave me an approving smile and said, "That's right; I am glad you are going out with them for once. I shall stay at home, so you can take my firelock with you, and buckle my whinger round your waist. In case of need, it is a good and trusty weapon, if only you keep your presence of mind."

That part of the wood in which the wolves were supposed to lurk was surrounded by the huntsmen. The winter day was bitter cold; the wind howled through the firs, and drove the light snowflakes straight into my face, so that when it came on to be dusk I could scarcely see six paces before me. Quite numbed by the frost, I left the place that had been assigned to me, and sought shelter deeper in the wood. There, leaning against a tree, with my firelock under my arm, I forgot the wolf hunt entirely; my thoughts had traveled back to Seraphina's warm room. After a time, shots were heard in the far distance, but at the same moment there was a rustling in the bank of reeds near by, and I saw, not ten paces from me, a huge wolf about to run past. I took aim, and fired, but missed. The brute, with glaring eyes, sprang towards me; I should have been lost had I not had sufficient presence of mind to draw my hunting knife, and, just as the beast was flying at me, to drive it deep into his throat, so that the blood spurted out over my hand and arm.

One of the Baron's keepers, who had been stationed not far from me, came running up with a loud shout, and at his repeated "Halloo!" all the rest soon gathered round us. The Baron hastened up to me, saying, "For God's sake, you are bleeding—you are bleeding. Are you wounded?" I assured him that I was not. Then he turned to the keeper who had stood nearest me, and overwhelmed him with reproaches for not having shot after me when I missed. And notwithstanding that the man maintained this to have been perfectly impossible, since the wolf had rushed upon me in the very same moment, and any shot would have risked hitting me, the Baron persisted in saying that he ought to have taken special care of me as a less experienced hunter.

Meanwhile the keepers had lifted up the dead animal; it was one of the largest they had seen in a long time; and everybody admired my courage and presence of mind, although to myself what I had done appeared quite natural. I had not for a moment thought of the danger I had run. The Baron in particular seemed to take very great interest in the matter;

I thought he would never be done asking me whether, though I was not wounded by the brute, I did not fear the ill effects that would follow from the fright. As we went back to the castle, the Baron took me by the arm like a friend, and I had to give my firelock to a keeper to carry. He still continued to talk about my heroic deed, so that eventually I came to believe in my own heroism, and, losing all my constraint and embarrassment, felt that I had established myself in the Baron's eyes as a man of courage and uncommon resolution.

The schoolboy had passed his examination successfully, was now no longer a schoolboy, and all the submissive nervousness of the schoolboy had left him. I now conceived that I had earned a right to try to gain Seraphina's favor. Everybody knows, of course, what ridiculous performances the fancy of a lovesick youth is capable of. In the castle, over the smoking punch bowl, by the fireside, I was the hero of the hour. Besides myself the Baron was the only one of the party who had killed a wolf—and mine was a very formidable one. The rest of the hunters had to be content with ascribing their bad shots to the weather and the darkness, and with relating thrilling stories of their former exploits and the dangers they had escaped. As for me, I thought, while adulation was thus being heaped upon me, that I might reap an especial share of praise and admiration from my old uncle as well; and so, with a view to this end, I related to him my adventure at considerable length. Nor did I forget to paint the savage brute's wild and bloodthirsty appearance in very startling colors. The old gentleman, however, only laughed in my face and said, "God is powerful even in the weak."

I had tired of drinking, and of the company, and I was going quietly along the corridor towards the hall of justice, when I saw a figure with a taper slip before me. On entering the hall I could see that it was Lady Adelheid. "This is the way we have to wander about like ghosts or sleepwalkers in order to catch you, my brave hunter," she whispered, taking my arm.

The words "ghosts" and "sleepwalkers," spoken in that hall, fell like lead upon my heart; they immediately brought to my recollection the spectral apparitions of those first two awful nights. As then, so now, the wind came howling in from the sea in deep organ-like cadences, rattling the oriel windows again and again and whistling fearfully through them, while the moon cast its pale gleams directly upon the mysterious place in the wall where the scratching had been heard. I fancied I discerned stains of blood upon it. And doubtless Lady Adelheid, who still had hold of my hand, must have felt the cold—not to say icy—shiver which ran through me.

"What's the matter with you?" she whispered softly. "What's the matter with you? You are as cold as marble. Come, I will call you back to life. Do you know how very impatient the Baroness is to see you? And until she does see you she will not believe that the wolf did not get his teeth into you. She is in a terrible state of anxiety about you. Why, my friend— Oh! How have you awakened this interest in the little Seraphina? I have never seen her like this before. Ah! So now the pulse is beginning to tingle? See how quickly the dead man comes to life! Well, come along —but softly, still! Come, we must go to the little Baroness."

I suffered myself to be led away in silence. The way in which Adelheid spoke of the Baroness seemed to me undignified, and the innuendo of an understanding between us positively shameful. When I entered the room along with Adelheid, Seraphina, with a low-breathed "Oh!" advanced three or four paces quickly to meet me; but then, as if recollecting herself, she stood still in the middle of the room. I ventured to take her hand and press it to my lips. Allowing it to rest in mine, she asked, "But, for Heaven's sake! Is it your business to sport after wolves? Don't you know that the fabulous days of Orpheus and Amphion are long past, and that wild beasts have quite lost all respect for even the most admirable singers?"

By this graceful turn, in which the Baroness at once effectually guarded against all misinterpretation of her warm interest in me, I was put immediately into the proper key and the proper mood. So why I did not take my usual place at the pianoforte I cannot explain, even to myself, nor why I sat down beside the Baroness on the sofa. Her next question, "And how did you happen to walk into such danger?" was an indication of a tacit agreement that conversation, not music, was to engage our attention for that evening.

After I had narrated my adventure in the woods, and mentioned the warm interest which the Baron had taken in it, delicately hinting that I had not thought him capable of so much feeling, the Baroness began in a tender and almost melancholy tone, "Oh, how violent and rude you must think the Baron! But I assure you it is only while we are living within these gloomy, ghostly walls, and during the time there is hunting going on in the dismal fir forests, that his character completely changes, at least his outward behavior does. What principally disturbs him in this unpleasant fashion is the thought, which constantly haunts him, that something terrible will happen here. And that undoubtedly accounts for his being so greatly agitated by your adventure, which fortunately has had no ill consequences. He won't have the meanest of his servants exposed to danger, if he knows it, still less a new-won friend whom he has come to like; and I am perfectly certain that Gottlieb, whom he blames for having left you in the lurch, will be punished. Even if he escapes being locked up in a dungeon, he will yet have to suffer the punishment, so mortifying to a hunter, of going out, the next time there is a hunt, with only a club in his hand instead of a rifle.

"The circumstance that hunts like those which are held here are always attended with danger," she continued, "and the fact that the Baron, though always fearing some sad accident, is yet so fond of hunting that he cannot desist from provoking the demon of mischief, make his existence here a kind of conflict, the ill effects of which I also have to feel. Many queer stories are current about his ancestor who established the entail; and I know myself that there is some dark family secret locked within these walls like a horrible spectre which drives away the owners, and makes it impossible for them to bear with the place for more than a few weeks at a time, and that only amid a tumult of jovial guests. But I— Oh, how lonely I am in the midst of this noisy, merry company! And how the ghostly influences which breathe upon me from the walls stir and excite my very heart! You, my dear friend, have given me, through your music, the first cheerful moments I have spent here. How can I thank you sufficiently for your kindness!"

I kissed the hand she extended to me, as I told her that even on the very first day, or rather the very first night, I had experienced the ghostliness of the place in all its horrors. And as the Baroness stared fixedly into my face, I went on to describe my impression of the ghostly character of the building, discernible everywhere throughout the castle, particularly in the decorations of the present hall of justice. I also spoke of the strange effect of the roaring of the wind from the sea, and other odd influences of Nature. Possibly my voice and my expression indicated that I had something more on my mind than what I said. At any rate, when I concluded, the Baroness cried vehemently, "No, no; something dreadful happened to you in that hall, which I never enter without shuddering. I beg you— pray, pray, tell me everything."

Seraphina's face had grown deadly pale; and I saw plainly that it would be more advisable to give her a faithful account of all that I had experienced than to leave her excited imagination to conjure up some apparition that might perhaps, in a way I could not foresee, be far more horrible than the truth. As she listened to me her fear and strained anxiety increased from moment to moment; and when I mentioned the scratching on the wall she cried, "It's horrible! Yes, yes, it's in that wall that the awful secret is concealed!" But as I went on to describe with what spiritual power and superiority of will my old uncle had banished the ghost, she sighed deeply, as though she had shaken off a heavy burden that had weighed oppressively upon her. She leaned back in the sofa and held her hands before her face.

Now I first noticed that Adelheid had left us. A considerable pause ensued, and as Seraphina still continued silent, I rose softly, and, going to the pianoforte, endeavored in swelling chords to invoke the bright spirits of consolation to come and deliver Seraphina from the dark influence to which my narrative had subjected her. Soon I began to sing, as softly as I was able, one of the Abbé Steffani's canzonas. The melancholy strains of the *Ochi, perchè piangete* (O eyes, why weep you?) roused the young Baroness out of her revery, and she listened to me with a gentle smile upon her face, and bright pearl-like tears in her eyes. How am I to account for my sudden action in kneeling down before her, how say why she bent over towards me? How, above all, explain that I threw my arms about her, and that her long and ardent kiss was imprinted on my lips? How am I to account for it that I did not lose my senses when she drew me softly towards her, how can I say what moved me to tear myself from her arms, and, quickly rising to my feet, to hurry across to the pianoforte?

Turning from me, the Baroness took a few steps towards the window, then she turned round again and approached me with an air of almost proud dignity, which was not at all usual with her. Looking me straight in the face, she said, "Your uncle is the most worthy old gentleman I know; he is the guardian angel of our family. May he include me in his pious prayers!"

I was unable to utter a word; the subtle poison that I had imbibed with her kiss burned and boiled in every pulse and nerve. And, at this moment, Lady Adelheid came in. The violence of my inward conflict burst out at length in a passionate flood of tears, which I was unable to repress. Adelheid looked at me with wonder, and smiled dubiously; I could have murdered her. The Baroness gave me her hand, and said with inexpressible gentleness, "Farewell, my dear friend. Fare you right well; and remember that nobody, perhaps, has ever understood your music better than I have. Oh, those notes will echo long, long in my heart!"

I forced myself to utter a few stupid, disconnected words, and hurried up to my uncle's rooms. The old gentleman had already gone to bed. I remained outside in the hall, and, falling upon my knees, I wept aloud; I called upon my beloved by name; I gave myself up completely and with utter heedlessness to all the absurd folly of a lovesick lunatic, until at last the extravagant noise I made awoke my uncle. But his loud call, "My boy, I believe you must have gone mad; or else you're having another tussle with a wolf. Be off to bed with you, if you will be so very kind"—these words compelled me to enter his room, where I got into bed with the fixed resolve to dream only of Seraphina.

It must have been some time past midnight when I thought I heard distant voices, a running back and forth, and an opening and banging of doors—for I had not yet actually gone to sleep. I listened attentively and soon I heard footsteps approaching the corridor. The hall door was opened, and immediately after that came a knock on our door.

"Who is there?" I cried.

A voice from without answered, "Your worship, wake up, your worship, wake up!"

I recognized Francis' voice, and as I asked, "Is the castle on fire?" the old gentleman awoke in his turn and asked:

"Where—where is there a fire? Is it that cursed apparition again? Where is it?"

"Oh, please get up, your worship!" begged Francis. "Please get up; the Baron wants you."

"What does the Baron want me for?" inquired my uncle further. "What does he want me for at this time of night? Does he not know that all legal business goes to bed along with the lawyer, and sleeps as soundly as he does?"

"Oh!" cried Francis, now anxiously. "Please, good sir, please come quickly. My lady the Baroness is dying."

With a cry of dismay, I started up. "Open the door for Francis," said the old gentleman to me. But as I tumbled about the room almost distracted, and could find neither door nor lock, my uncle had to come and help me.

Francis came in, his face pale and troubled, and lit the candles. We had scarcely thrown on our clothes when we heard the Baron calling in the hall, "Can I speak to you, good V—?"

"But what have you dressed for, cousin? The Baron only wanted me," the old gentleman asked me, as he was on the point of going out.

"I must go down—I must see her and then die," I replied tragically, and as if my heart were rent by hopeless grief.

"Yes, just so; you are right, cousin," my uncle said, and he banged the door to in my face, so that the hinges creaked, and then I could hear him locking it on the outside.

At the first moment, deeply incensed by this restraint, I thought of breaking the door down; but quickly reflecting that this would be an act of unmitigated folly, provoking the most disagreeable consequences, I made up my mind calmly to await the old gentleman's return. Then, however, let the cost be what it might, I resolved that I would escape his watchfulness. I heard him talking vehemently with the Baron, and several times I distinguished my own name, but could not make out anything further. Every moment my position grew more intolerable. At length I understood that someone brought a message to the Baron, who immediately hurried off. And then my old uncle came back into our room.

"She is dead!" I cried, running towards him.

"And you are a stupid fool," he interrupted coolly; then he laid hold upon me and forced me into a chair.

"I must go down," I cried, "I must go down and see her, even though it cost me my life."

"Do so, my good child," said he, locking the door, removing the key, and putting it in his pocket.

I now flew into a perfectly frantic rage. Stretching out my hand towards the rifle, I screamed, "If you don't instantly open the door I will send this bullet through my brains."

But at this the old gentleman planted himself immediately in front of me, fixed his keen piercing eyes upon me, and said: "Boy, do you think you can frighten me with your idle threats? Do you think I should set much value on your life if you could go and throw it away in childish folly like a broken plaything? What have you to do with the Baron's wife? Who has given you the right to insinuate yourself, like a tiresome puppy, where you have no claim to be, and where you are not wanted? Do you wish to go and act the lovesick swain at the solemn hour of death?"

I sank back in my chair utterly confounded.

After a while the old gentleman went on more gently, "And now let me tell you that this supposed illness of the Baroness is in all probability nothing at all. Lady Adelheid always loses her head at the least little thing. If a raindrop falls upon her nose, she screams, 'What fearful weather it is!' Unfortunately the noise she made reached the old aunts, and they, in the midst of unreasonable floods of tears, put in an appearance armed with an entire arsenal of restoratives, aromatic drops, elixirs of life, and the deuce knows what. A fainting spell—" The old gentleman checked himself; doubtless he observed the struggle that was going on within me. He took a few turns through the room; then again planting himself in front of me, he had a good hearty laugh and said, "Cousin, cousin, what non-sensical folly have you now got in your head? Ah, well! I suppose it can't be helped; the Devil will play his pretty games here in a variety of ways. You have tumbled very nicely into his clutches, and now he's making you dance to a sweet tune."

He again took a few turns up and down the room, and again went on speaking: "It's no use to think of sleep now; and it occurred to me that we might have a pipe, and so spend the few hours that are left of the dark-ness and the night." With these words he took a clay pipe from the cup-board, and proceeded to fill it slowly and carefully, humming a song to himself; then he rummaged about among a heap of papers, until he found an unused sheet, which he picked out and rolled into a spill and lighted.

Blowing the tobacco smoke from his mouth in thick clouds, he said, speaking between his teeth, "Well, my heroic young kinsman, what was that story about the wolf?"

I do not know why, but this calm, quiet behavior of my wise old uncle had a strange effect upon me. I seemed to be no longer in R—sitten; and the Baroness was so far, far distant from me that I could only reach her on the wings of thought. The old gentleman's last question, however, annoyed me. "But do you find my hunting exploit so amusing," I broke in, "so well suited to banter?"

"By no means," he rejoined, "by no means, cousin. But you've no idea what a comical figure such a whippersnapper as you cuts, and how ludicrously he acts as well, when Providence for once honors him by putting him in the way to meet with something out of the usual run of things. I once had a college friend who was a quiet, sober fellow, and always on good terms with himself. By accident he became entangled in an affair of honor—I say by accident, because he himself was never in any way aggressive—and although most of the fellows looked upon him as a poor thing, as a poltroon, he yet showed so much firm and resolute courage in this affair as to excite everybody's admiration. But from that time onward he was also completely changed. The sober and industrious youth became a bragging, insufferable bully. He was always drinking, and rioting, and fighting about all sorts of childish trifles, until he was run through in a duel by the Senior of an exclusive corps. I merely tell you the story, cousin; you are at liberty to think what you please about it. But to return to the Baroness and her illness—"

At this moment, however, he was interrupted, as light footsteps were heard in the hall. I fancied, too, that there was the sound of an unearthly moaning in the air. "She is dead!" The thought shot through me like a fatal flash of lightning.

The old gentleman quickly rose to his feet and called out, "Francis, Francis!"

"Yes, my good sir," the old servitor replied from without.

"Francis," went on my uncle, "rake the fire together a bit in the grate, and if you can manage it, you had better make us a good cup or two of tea. It is devilish cold," he added, turning to me, "and I think we had better go and sit before the fire and talk a little."

He opened the door, and I followed him mechanically. "How are things going on below?" he asked Francis. "Oh," replied the faithful old man, "there was not much the matter. The Lady Baroness is all right again, and ascribes her little fainting fit to a bad dream."

I was going to break out into an extravagant manifestation of joy and gladness, but a stern glance from my uncle kept me quiet. "And yet, after all, I think it would be better if we lay down for an hour or two," he said. "You need not mind about the tea, Francis."

"As you wish, your worship," replied Francis, and he left the room with the wish that we might have a good night's rest, although in fact the cocks were already crowing.

"See here, my boy," said the old gentleman to me, knocking the ashes out of his pipe on the grate, as we were left alone again, "I think, cousin, that it's a very good thing no harm has come to you either from wolves or from loaded rifles." And I can say for myself that I now saw things in the right light, and was ashamed to have given the old gentleman good grounds for treating me like a spoiled child . . .

Next morning he said to me, "Be so good as to step down, my good lad, and inquire how the Baroness is. You need only ask for Lady Adelheid; she will supply you with a full budget, I have no doubt."

You may imagine how eagerly I hastened downstairs. But just as I was about to knock gently at the door of the Baroness' anteroom, the Baron came hurriedly out.

He stood still in astonishment, and scrutinized me with a gloomy and searching look. "What do you want here?" burst from his lips.

Notwithstanding the tumultuous beating of my heart, I controlled myself sufficiently to reply, in a firm tone, "To inquire on my uncle's behalf after the health of my Lady, the Baroness."

"Oh! it was nothing—one of her ordinary nervous attacks. She is now having a quiet sleep, and will, I am sure, make her appearance at the dinner table quite well and cheerful. Tell him that—tell him that." The Baron said this with a certain emphatic assurance, which seemed to me to imply that he was more concerned about the Baroness than he was willing to admit. I turned to go back to my uncle, when the Baron suddenly seized my arm and said, while his eyes seemed to flash fire upon me, "I have a word or two to say to you, young man."

Here I saw the deeply injured husband before me, and I feared there would be a scene which would perhaps end ignominiously for me. I was unarmed; but at that moment I remembered I had in my pocket the ingeniously fashioned hunting knife which my uncle had given me after we first came to R—sitten. I now followed my host, who rapidly led the way, with my heart firm in determination not even to spare his life if I ran any risk of being treated dishonorably.

The Baron took me into his own private room, the door of which he locked behind him. Now he began to pace restlessly back and forth, with his arms folded one over the other; then he stopped in front of me and repeated: "I have a word or two to say to you, young man."

By this time I had wound myself up to an audacious pitch of courage, and I replied, raising my voice, "I hope they will be words which I may hear without resentment."

He stared hard at me in astonishment, as though he had failed to understand me. Then, fixing his eyes gloomily upon the floor, he folded his arms behind his back, and again began to stride up and down the room. He took down a rifle and put the ramrod down the barrel to see whether it were loaded or not. My blood boiled in my veins; grasping my knife, I stepped close up to him, so as to make it impossible for him to take aim at me. "That's a handsome weapon," he said, replacing the rifle in the corner. I retired a few paces, the Baron following me. Slapping me on the shoulder, perhaps a little more violently than was necessary, he said, "I dare say I seem to you, Theodore, to be excited and irritable; and I really am so, owing to the anxieties of a sleepless night. My wife's nervous attack was not in the least dangerous; that I now see plainly. But here—here in this castle, which is haunted by an evil spirit, I always dread something terrible happening; and then it's the first time she has been ill here. And you—you alone were to blame for it."

"How that can possibly be, I have not the slightest conception," I replied calmly.

"I wish," continued the Baron, "I wish that damned piece of mischief, my steward's wife's musical instrument, were chopped up into a thousand pieces, and that you—but no, no; it was to be so, it was inevitably to be so, and I alone am to blame for all. I ought to have told you, the moment you began to play music in my wife's room, the whole state of the case, and to have informed you of my wife's temperament and condition of mind."

I was about to speak, but my host stopped me. "Let me go on," said he. "I must prevent your forming any rash judgment. You probably regard me as an uncultivated country squire, deaf and blind to the arts; but that is not true by any means. There is a particular consideration, however, based upon deep conviction, which causes me to forbid the introduction here, as far as possible, of such music as can powerfully affect any person's mind, and to this I myself am of course no exception. Now you must know that my wife suffers from a morbid excitability, which will finally destroy all the happiness of her life. Within these strange walls she is never free from that strained overexcited condition, which at other times occurs but temporarily, and then generally as the forerunner of a serious illness. You will ask me, and quite reasonably too, why I do not spare my delicate wife the necessity of coming to live in this weird castle, and mix in the wild confusion of a hunting party. Well, call it weakness—be it so; in a word, I cannot bring myself to leave her behind. I should be tortured by a thousand fears, and quite incapable of any serious business, for I am perfectly sure that I should be haunted everywhere, in the hall of justice as well as in the forest, by the most appalling ideas of all kinds of fatal mischief happening to her. And, on the other hand, I believe that the sort of life which we lead here cannot fail to benefit her delicate health. Indeed, the tang of the sea breezes, sweeping in that peculiar fashion through the fir trees, and the deep baying of the hounds, and the merry ringing notes of our hunting horns *must* get the better of all your sickly languishing sentimentalizings at the piano, which no man ought play in *that* way. I tell you, you are deliberately and systematically torturing my wife to death."

These words he uttered with great emphasis, while his eyes flashed with a feverish fire. The blood mounted to my head; I made a violent gesture against the Baron with my hand; I was about to speak, but he cut me short. "I know what you are going to say," he began, "I know what you are going to say, and I repeat that you are taking the right road to kill my wife. That you intended this I cannot of course for a moment maintain; and yet you will understand that I must put a stop to the thing. In short, by your playing and singing you work her up to a high pitch of excitement, and then, when she drifts without anchor and rudder on the boundless sea of dreams and visions and vague aspirations which your music, like some vile charm, has summoned into existence, you plunge her down into the depths of horror with a tale about a fearful apparition which you say came and played pranks with you up in the hall of justice. Your great-uncle has told me everything. But will you please now repeat to me all you saw, or did not see, all you heard, felt, divined by instinct?"

I braced myself and embarked calmly upon the story of how everything had happened from beginning to end, the Baron merely interposing, at intervals, a few words expressive of his astonishment. When I came to the part where my old uncle had confronted the ghost and exorcised him with a few mighty words, the Baron clasped his hands, raised his eyes toward Heaven, and said with deep emotion, "Yes, he is the guardian angel of the family. His mortal remains shall rest in the vault of my ancestors."

When I finished my narrative, the Baron murmured to himself, "Daniel, Daniel, what are you doing here at this hour?" as he folded his arms and strode up and down the room.

"And was that all, Herr Baron?" I asked, making a movement as though I would retire.

Starting up as if out of a dream, the Baron took me kindly by the hand and said, "Yes, my good friend, but now you must set about curing my wife—whom you have harmed so unintentionally. You alone can do so."

I felt that I was blushing, and had I stood opposite a mirror I should undoubtedly have seen in it a very blank and ridiculous reflection. The Baron seemed to exult in my embarrassment; he kept his eyes fixed intently upon my face, smiling with perfectly galling irony. "How in the world can I cure her?" I managed, with an effort, to stammer out at length.

"Well," he said, cutting me short, "you have no dangerous patient to deal with, at any rate. I now shall make my own demands upon your talent. Since the Baroness has been drawn into the enchanted circle of your music, it would be both foolish and cruel to tear her away from it all of a sudden. Go on with your music, therefore. You will always be welcome during the evening hours in my wife's apartments. But gradually select a more energetic, less brooding kind of music, and effect a clever alternation of the cheerful sort with the serious. And above all things, repeat your story of the frightful ghost very, very often. The Baroness will grow familiar with it; she will forget that a ghost haunts this castle; and the story will have no stronger effect upon her than any other tale of enchantment which is put before her in a romance or a book of ghost stories. That is all I want you to do, my good friend."

With these words the Baron left me. I went away. I felt as if I were annihilated, to be thus humiliated to the level of a foolish and insignificant child. Fool that I was to have supposed that jealousy was stirring his heart! He himself sends me to Seraphina; he sees in me only the blind instrument which he may use or dispose of as the moment dictates. A few minutes before, I had really feared the Baron; deep down within my heart lurked the consciousness of guilt; but it was a consciousness which allowed me to feel distinctly the beauty of the higher life for which I was ripe. Now all these feelings had been engulfed in the blackness of night; and I saw only the stupid boy who in childish obstinacy persists in mistaking the paper crown which he has put on his hot temples for a real diadem of gold . . .

I hurried away to my uncle, who was waiting for me. "Well, my boy, why have you been so long? Where have you been keeping yourself?" he cried, as soon as he saw me.

"I have been having some words with the Baron!" I quickly replied, carelessly and in a low voice, without being able to look at the old gentleman.

"Well, I'll be damned!" he said, with mock astonishment. "But my boy, that's just what I thought. I suppose the Baron has challenged you, cousin?" The ringing peal of laughter into which the old gentleman immediately afterwards broke out taught me that this time too—as always—he had been able to read me through and through. I bit my lip, and dared not speak a word, for I knew very well that it would only be the signal for the old gentleman, who was bursting with humor, to overwhelm me beneath the torrent of his raillery.

The Baroness appeared at the dinner table in an elegant morning robe, the dazzling whiteness of which rivaled that of the fresh-fallen snow beyond the windows. She looked worn and low-spirited; but she began to speak in her soft and melodious accents, and as she raised her dark eyes a sweet and yearning look seemed to shine from them, and a fugitive

blush came into her cheeks. She was more beautiful than ever. But who
can fathom the follies of a young man whose blood is too hot in his head
and heart? The bitter pique which the Baron had stirred up within me I
now transferred to the Baroness. The entire business seemed to me a lurid
mystification; and I was now determined to show that I was possessed of
alarmingly good common sense, to say nothing of remarkable sagacity.

Like a petulant child, I shunned the Baroness and escaped Adelheid
when she pursued me, and found a place where I wished to sit, away at
the lower end of the table between the two officers, with whom I began
to carouse right merrily. We kept our glasses going gaily during dessert,
and I was, as so frequently is the case in moods like mine, extremely noisy
and loud in my joviality. A servant brought me a plate with some cakes
on it, and informed me they were "From Lady Adelheid." I took them;
and as I looked closer I observed that on one of them the words "and
Seraphina" had been scratched. My blood coursed tumultuously in my
veins. I sent a glance in Adelheid's direction, which she met with a most
sly and archly cunning look; and taking her glass in her hand, she gave
me a slight nod. Almost mechanically I murmured to myself, "Seraphina!"
then taking up my glass in my turn, I drained it at a single draught.

My glance darted quickly in her direction; I perceived that she also
had drunk at the very same moment, and was now setting down her glass.
Our eyes met, and a malignant demon whispered in my ear, "Unhappy
wretch, she does love you!" One of the guests now rose, and, in conformity
with the custom of the North, proposed the health of the lady of the
house. Our glasses rang in the midst of a tumult of joy. My heart was
torn with rapture and despair; the wine burned like fire within me; everything was spinning round in circles; I felt as if I must hasten and throw
myself at her feet and there sigh out my life. "What's the matter with
you, my friend?" asked my neighbor, thus recalling me to myself; but
Seraphina had left the hall.

We rose from the table. I was making for the door, but Adelheid
held me back, and began to talk about various matters. I neither heard
nor understood a single word. She grasped both my hands and, laughing,
shouted something almost into my ear. I remained dumb and motionless,
as though affected by catalepsy. All I remember is that I finally took a
glass of liqueur out of Adelheid's hand in a mechanical way and drank it

off. And then I recollect being alone at a window. And after that I rushed out of the hall, down the stairs, and out into the wood.

The snow was falling in thick flakes; the fir trees were moaning as they waved to and fro in the wind. Like a maniac I ran round and round in wide circles, laughing and screaming loudly, "Look, look and see! Aha! Aha! The Devil is having a fine dance with the boy who thought he would taste forbidden fruit!" Who can tell what would have been the end of my mad prank, if I had not heard my name called loudly from outside the wood? The storm had abated; the moon shone out brightly through the broken clouds; I heard dogs barking, and perceived a dark figure approaching me. It was the old man Francis.

"Why, why, my good master Theodore," he began, "you have quite lost your way in this heavy snowstorm. His worship is awaiting you with much impatience."

I followed the old man without speaking, and found my great-uncle working in the hall of justice.

"You have done well," he cried, on seeing me. "You have done a very wise thing to go out in the open air a little and cool off. But don't drink quite so much wine the next time; you are far too young, and it's not good for you."

I did not utter a word in reply, and it was also in silence that I took my place at the table.

"But now tell me, my boy," he went on, "what it was the Baron really wanted you for?"

I told him everything, and concluded by stating that I would not lend myself to the doubtful cure which the Baron had proposed.

"And it would not be practicable," the old gentleman interrupted, "for tomorrow morning early we set off home, cousin."

And so it was that I never saw Seraphina again.

As soon as we arrived in K— my old uncle began to complain that this time he felt the effects of the fatiguing journey more than he ever had before. His moody silence, broken only by violent outbursts of the worst possible ill-humor, announced the return of his gout. But when one day I was suddenly called in, I found the old gentleman confined to his bed and unable to speak: he had suffered a paralytic stroke. He held a letter in his hand, which he had crumpled up tightly in a spasmodic seizure. I recognized the handwriting of the land steward of R—sitten; but, completely upset by my grief, I did not venture to remove the letter from the sick man's grip. I felt sure that his end was near. But his pulse began to beat regularly again, even before the physician arrived; and, in short, the old gentleman's remarkably tough constitution resisted the mortal attack, although he was in his seventieth year. That selfsame day the Doctor pronounced him out of danger.

We had a more severe winter than usual; this was followed by a rough and stormy spring; and hence it was more the gout—an attack brought on by the inclemency of the season—than the effects of the shock of apoplexy which kept him for a long time confined to his bed. During this period he made up his mind to retire altogether from every sort of business activity. He transferred his office of administrator to others; and so I was cut off from all hope of ever going to R—sitten again. The old gentleman would allow no one to wait on him but me; and it was to me alone that he looked for all amusement and diversion. And though, in the hours when he was free from pain, his good spirits returned and he showed no lack of ready wit, even making mention of various hunting exploits—so that I fully expected any moment to hear him banter about my own heroic encounter at the castle—he never once made any allusion to our visit to R—sitten. As may well be imagined, I was very careful myself, perhaps simply out of shyness, not to touch upon the subject.

My harassing anxiety and continual attendance upon the old kinsman, whom I deeply loved, had thrust Seraphina's image into the background of my mind. But as soon as his illness abated somewhat, my thoughts returned all the more vividly to that moment in the Baroness' room, a moment which I now looked upon as a star—a bright star—that had set, for me at least, forever. And a small thing that now happened, and that made me shudder with an icy thrill that was like a communication from another world, revived all the anguish I had formerly felt.

One evening, as I was opening the wallet I had carried while I was at R—sitten, there fell out of the papers I was unfolding a dark curl, wrapped about with a white ribbon. I immediately recognized it as Seraphina's hair. But, on examining the ribbon more closely, I distinctly noted upon it the stain of a spot of blood! Perhaps Adelheid had skilfully contrived to secrete the little token about my person during the moments of the insane vagueness in which I had spent the last days of our visit; but why was the blood spot there? It excited ominous forebodings, and almost converted this too pastoral love token into an awful admonition, pointing to a passion which might end in bloodshed. I was sure, too, that this was the same white ribbon that had fluttered about me in light and wanton play, as it were, the first time I sat near Seraphina; now mysterious night had stamped it, I felt, as an emblem of mortal injury. Boys ought not to play with dangerous and unfamiliar weapons: I was beginning to realize that . . .

At last the storms of spring ceased to bluster, and summer asserted her rights; and if the cold had formerly been almost unbearable, so now too was the heat when July came in. My old uncle visibly gathered strength, however, and followed his usual custom of frequent visits to a pleasant public park in the suburbs. One still, warm evening, as we sat in the sweet-smelling jasmine arbor there, he was in unusually good spirits: not, as was generally the case, overflowing with sarcasm and irony, but in a gentle, almost soft and melting, mood. "Cousin," he began, "I don't know why it is, but I feel so good and warm, and comfortable all over, today, better than I have felt in many years. I believe it means that I am going to die soon."

I naturally made an effort to drive these gloomy thoughts from his mind.

"Never mind, my boy," he responded. "In any case I'm not long for this world; and so I will now discharge a debt I owe you. Do you still remember our autumn in R—sitten?"

This question thrilled and struck me to silence; before I was able to bring myself to reply he continued: "It was Heaven's will that your entrance into that castle should be signalized by memorable circumstances, and that you should become involved, against your own wish, in the darkest secrets of the house. The time has now come when you must learn all that happened, and all its meaning. We have often enough talked about things which you, cousin, rather dimly guessed at than really understood. In the alternation of the seasons Nature symbolically represents the cycle of human life. That is a trite remark; but I interpret it differently from everybody else. The showers of spring fall upon the earth, summer's mists fade away, and it is the pure atmosphere of autumn which clearly reveals the distant landscape; then at last earthly existence is swallowed up in the night of winter. I mean that the government of the Power Inscrutable is more plainly revealed in the clear-sightedness of old age.

"To old age," he continued, "glimpses are granted of the Promised Land, the pilgrimage to which begins with the death of the earthly body. How clearly do I see at this moment the dark destiny of that house, to which I am knit by closer ties than blood relationship can weave! Everything lies disclosed to the eyes of my spirit. And yet the things which I now see, in the form in which I see them—the essence of them, that is— that I cannot tell you in words; for no human speech is capable of encompassing it. But listen, my son, I will tell you as well as I am able. You must think of it as some remarkable story that might really happen; and lay up carefully in your soul the knowledge that the mysterious relations into which you ventured to enter, not perhaps without being summoned, might have ended in your destruction . . . But—that's all over now."

The history of the R— legacy, which my old uncle told me, I retain so faithfully in my memory even now that I can almost repeat it in his own words (he spoke of himself in the third person). So then, as he told it, I tell it now . . .

One stormy night in the autumn of 1760 the servants of R—sitten were wakened out of their heaviest midnight sleep by a terrific crash, as if the whole of the spacious castle had been knocked into a thousand pieces. In a moment everybody was on his feet; lights were lit; the house steward, his face deadly pale with alarm and bewildered terror, came up, panting, with his keys. But as they all proceeded through the passages and halls and rooms, suite after suite, and found everything safe—as they heard in the appalling silence nothing but the creaking rattle of the locks, which occasioned some difficulty in opening, and the ghostlike echo of their own footsteps—they began one and all to be utterly astounded. Nowhere was there the least trace of damage.

The old house steward was oppressed by an especially ominous sense of apprehension. And, thus moved, he went up into the great Knight's Hall, which had a small room adjoining, where Freiherr Roderick von R— used to sleep when engaged in making his astronomical observations.

Between the door of this little room and that of a second chamber was a postern, leading through a narrow passage immediately into the astronomical tower. But as soon as Daniel (that was the house steward's name) opened this postern, the storm, blustering and howling terrifically, showered him with rubbish and broken pieces of stones, so that he jumped back in terror. Then suddenly, dropping the candles, which went out with a hiss on the floor, he screamed, "O God! O God! The Baron! He's dashed to pieces!"

At the same moment he heard sounds of lamentation proceeding from the Freiherr's little bedroom, and as he ran in he saw the servants gathered around their master's corpse.

They had found him fully dressed—indeed more magnificently dressed than they had ever seen him—and with a calm and serious look upon his unchanged countenance, sitting in his large and richly decorated armchair as though resting after earnest study. But his rest was the rest of death. When day dawned it was seen that the turret which crowned the tower had fallen in. The huge square stones had broken through the ceiling and floor of the observatory, and then, bearing down in front of them a powerful beam that ran across the tower, they had dashed in, with redoubled impetus, the lower vaulted roof, and dragged down a portion of the castle walls and of the narrow connecting passage. Not a single step could be taken beyond the postern threshold without risk of falling at least eighty feet into a deep chasm.

The old Freiherr had foreseen the very hour of his death, and had sent word of it to his sons. So it happened that the very next day saw the arrival of Wolfgang, Freiherr von R—, eldest son of the deceased, and now lord of the estate. Relying upon the probable truth of the old man's foreboding, he had left Vienna, which city he chanced to have reached in his travels, as soon as he received the ominous letter, and had hastened to R—sitten as speedily as possible. The house steward had draped the great hall in black, and had had the old Freiherr laid out in the clothes in which he had been found, on a magnificent state bed; and this bed he had surrounded with tall silver candlesticks in which wax candles were kept burning. Wolfgang ascended the stairs, entered the hall, and drew close to his father's corpse, without speaking a word. There he stood with his arms folded on his chest, gazing with a fixed and gloomy look, and with knitted brows, into his father's pale countenance. He was like a statue. Not a tear came from his eyes. At last, with an almost convulsive movement of his arm towards the dead man, he murmured hoarsely, "Did the stars compel you to bring misery upon the son whom you loved?"

Clasping his hands behind him and stepping a short pace backwards, the Baron raised his eyes towards Heaven and said in a low and well-nigh broken voice, "Poor, obsessed old man! Your carnival farce with its shallow delusions is now over. Now you must surely see that the possessions which are so niggardly dealt out to us here on earth have nothing in common with the Hereafter beyond the stars. What will—what power— can reach beyond the grave?"

The Baron was silent again for some seconds, then he cried passionately: "No, your perversity shall not rob me of a grain of my earthly happiness, which you strove so hard to destroy!" And therewith he took a folded paper out of his pocket and held it up between two fingers to one of the burning candles that stood close beside the bier.

The flame licked out at it and blazed high; and as the reflected light flickered and played upon the face of the corpse, its muscles seemed to move and the lips to twitch as if the dead man were uttering soundless words, so that the servants who stood some distance off were overcome with awe. The Baron calmly finished what he was doing by carefully stamping out with his foot the last fragment of paper that fell blazing to the floor. Then, casting a parting moody glance at his father, he hurriedly left the hall.

On the following day Daniel reported to the Freiherr the damage that had been done to the tower, and described at great length all that had taken place on the night when their dear master had died; and he concluded by saying that it would be a very wise thing to have the tower repaired at once, for, if it were to collapse any further, there would be some danger of the whole castle—well, if not tumbling down, at any rate suffering serious damage.

"Repair the tower?" the Freiherr interrupted the old servant curtly, his eyes suddenly flashing with anger. "Repair the tower? Never, never! Don't you see, old man," he went on more calmly, "don't you see that the tower could not have fallen in this way without some special cause? Suppose it was my father's own wish that the place where he carried on his unhallowed astrological labors should be destroyed? Suppose ne himself had made certain preparations which enabled him to bring down the turret whenever he pleased, and so destroy the interior of the tower? But be that as it may . . . And if the whole castle tumbles down, I shan't care: I shall be glad. Do you fancy for one moment that I am going to live in this weird owl's nest? No. My wise ancestor who had the foundations of a new castle laid in the beautiful valley yonder—he has begun a work which I intend to finish."

"Then will all your faithful old servants have to take up their bundles and go?" asked Daniel, crestfallen.

"That I am not going to be waited upon by helpless, weak-kneed old fellows like you is quite certain," the Baron answered, harshly. "But for all that I shall turn none of you out. You may all enjoy the bread of charity without working for it."

"And am I," cried the old man, greatly hurt, "am I, the house steward, to be forced to lead a life of someone who is utterly useless?"

Then the Freiherr, who had turned his back upon the steward, and was about to leave the room, wheeled suddenly around, his face absolutely ablaze with fury, strode up to the old man, and, stretching out his clenched fist towards him, shouted in a thundering voice: "You, you hypocritical old villain! It's you who helped my father in his unearthly practices up in the tower! You hovered over his heart like a vampire. Nor is it unlikely that it was you who took advantage of your poor lord's mad folly to plant in his mind those diabolical ideas which have brought me to the brink of ruin. I ought to kick you out like a mangy flea-bitten dog!"

The old retainer was so terrified by these harsh and terrible words that he threw himself upon his knees before the Freiherr; but the Baron, as he spoke the last sentence, thrust forward his right foot, perhaps quite unintentionally (as is frequently the case in anger, when the body mechanically obeys the mind, and what is in the thought is imitatively realized in action), and hit the old man on the chest with such force that he rolled over with a stifled scream. Rising painfully to his feet, and uttering a most singular sound, like the howling whimper of an animal wounded to death, he looked the Freiherr through and through with a gaze that glared with mingled rage and despair. The purse of money which the

Freiherr threw down, as he went out of the room, was left lying on the floor where it fell.

Meanwhile all the nearest relatives of the family who lived in the neighborhood had arrived, and the old Freiherr was interred with much pomp in the family vault in the church at R—sitten. And now, after the invited guests had departed, the new lord of the estate seemed to shake off his gloomy mood, and to be prepared to enjoy, as he should, the property that as eldest son he had inherited. Along with V—, the old Freiherr's executor, who won the new Baron's full confidence in the very first interview they had, and who was at once confirmed in his office, Baron Wolfgang made an exact calculation of his sources of income, and considered how large a part he could devote to making improvements and how large a part to building a new castle. V— was of the opinion that the old Freiherr could not possibly have spent all his income every year, and that there must certainly be money concealed somewhere. For he had found nothing among the dead man's papers except one or two bank notes for insignificant sums, and the ready money in the iron safe was but very little more than a thousand thalers. And who would be so likely to know the answer to this riddle as Daniel, who in his obstinate self-willed way was perhaps only waiting to be asked about it?

The Baron was now not a little concerned over the thought that Daniel, whom he had so grossly insulted, might let large sums of money molder in some hiding place sooner than disclose their whereabouts to him; not so much, of course, from any motives of self-interest—for of what use could even the largest sum of money be to him, a childless old man, whose only wish was to end his days working in the castle?—as from a desire to take vengeance for the affront put upon him. He now gave V— a detailed circumstantial account of the entire scene with Daniel, and concluded by saying that, from several bits of information he had received, he had learned that it was Daniel alone who had contrived to nourish in the old Freiherr's mind the inexplicable aversion to ever seeing his sons in R—sitten.

V— declared that this information was entirely false, since there was not a human creature on the face of the earth, he added, who would have been able to guide the Freiherr's thoughts in any way, far less determine them for him. And he undertook finally to draw from Daniel the secret, if he had one, of the place in which they would be likely to find money concealed.

His task proved far easier than he had expected. No sooner had he begun, "But how comes it, Daniel, that your old master has left so little ready money?" than the steward replied, with a most unpleasant smile, "Do you mean the few trifling thalers, your worship, which you found in the little strongbox? Oh, the rest is lying in the vault in the wall of our gracious master's little bedroom. But the best," he went on to say, while his smile became an abominable grin, and his eyes flashed with malicious fire, "but the best of all—several thousand gold pieces—lies buried at the bottom of the chasm beneath the ruins."

V— at once summoned the Freiherr. They proceeded to the tower, and then into the bedroom. There Daniel pushed aside the wainscot in one of the corners, and a small lock became visible. While the Freiherr was staring at the polished lock with covetous eyes, and making preparations to unlock it with the keys of the great bunch which he dragged with some difficulty out of his pocket, Daniel drew himself up to his full height, and looked down with almost malignant pride upon his master, who had now stooped low in order to see the lock better.

Daniel's face was deadly pale, and his voice trembled as he said, "If I am a dog, my lord Freiherr, I have also at least a dog's fidelity." Therewith he held out a bright steel key to his master, who greedily snatched it out of his hand, and with it easily succeeded in opening the door.

They stepped into a small and low-vaulted chamber, where they at once saw an open coffer. In it were many moneybags, and upon them lay a strip of parchment, written over in the old Freiherr's familiar hand, large and old-fashioned.

"One hundred and fifty thousand Imperial thalers in old Fredericks d'or, money saved from the revenues of the entailed estate of R—sitten; this sum had been set aside for the building of the castle. Further, the lord of the entail who succeeds me in the possession of this money shall, upon the highest hill situated eastward from the old tower of the castle (which he will find in ruins), erect a high beacon tower for the benefit of mariners, and cause a fire to be kindled on it every night. R—sitten, on Michaelmas Eve of the year 1760.　　　　　　　"Roderick, Freiherr von R."

The Freiherr lifted up the bags one after the other and let them fall again into the coffer, delighted at the ringing clink of so much gold coin. Then he turned round abruptly to the old house steward, thanked him for the fidelity he had shown, and assured him that they were only vile tattling calumnies which had induced him to treat him so harshly in the first instance. He should not only remain in the castle, but should also continue to discharge his duties, uncurtailed in any way, as house steward, and at double the wages he was then having.

"I owe you a large compensation; if you will take money, help yourself to one of these bags." As he concluded with these words, the Baron stood before the old man, with his eyes bent upon the ground, and pointed to the coffer; then, approaching it again, he once more ran his eyes over the bags.

A burning flush mounted into the old house steward's cheeks, and he gave voice to that awful howling whimper—a noise as of an animal wounded to death, according to the Freiherr's previous description of it to V—. The latter shuddered, for the words which the old man murmured between his teeth sounded like, "Blood for gold."

Of all this the Freiherr, absorbed in the contemplation of the treasure before him, had heard nothing at all. Daniel was trembling in every limb, as if shaken by the ague. Approaching the Freiherr with bowed head, in a humble attitude, he kissed his hand, and drawing his handkerchief across his eyes under the pretext of wiping away his tears, he said in a plaintive voice, "Alas, my good and gracious master, what am I, a poor childless old man, to do with money? But the doubled wages I gladly accept, and will continue to do my duty faithfully and zealously."

The Freiherr, who had paid no particular heed to the old retainer's words, now let the heavy lid of the coffer fall shut with such a bang that the whole room shook and vibrated. Then, locking the chest and carefully withdrawing the key, he said carelessly, "Very well, very well, old man." After they entered the hall, however, he went on talking to Daniel. "But you said something about a quantity of gold pieces buried underneath the ruins of the tower?" he reminded him.

Silently the steward stepped towards the postern, and after some difficulty unlocked it. But as soon as he threw the little door open the storm drove a thick mass of snowflakes indoors, and a raven, disturbed out of some dark corner, flew, croaking and screaming, into the hall, where it dashed with its black wings against the windows, until it regained the open postern and disappeared into the chasm. The Freiherr stepped out into the corridor; but he glanced downwards only once, and started back trembling.

"A frightening sight! I'm quite dizzy!" he stammered, as he sank almost fainting into V—'s arms. Then recovering himself, with an effort, he glared at the steward and asked, "Down there, you say?"

Meanwhile the old man had been locking the postern, and was now leaning against it with all his bodily strength, while he gasped and grunted in his exertions to get the great key out of the rusty lock. Having at last accomplished this, he turned his attention to the Baron, and, changing the huge key about back and forth from one hand to the other, he replied, with a peculiar smile, "Yes, there are thousands and thousands down there—all my dear dead master's beautiful instruments—telescopes, quadrants, globes, shadow boxes, they all lie smashed to atoms underneath the ruins between the stones and the big tie-beam."

"But money—the actual money," interrupted the Baron. "You spoke of gold pieces, old man?"

"I only meant things upon which thousands of gold pieces had been spent," the old retainer answered. And not another word could be got out of him.

The Baron appeared highly delighted to have all at once come into possession of the means requisite for carrying out his favorite plan, namely, that of building a new and magnificent castle. The old Freiherr's executor indeed stated it as his opinion that, according to the will of the deceased, the money could be applied only to the repair and complete finishing of the interior of the old castle; and he added that no new erection would be likely to succeed in equaling the commanding size and the severe and simple character of the old ancestral residence. The Freiherr, however, persisted in his intention, and maintained that in the disposal of property respecting which nothing was stated in the deeds of the entail the irregular will of the deceased could have no validity. He at the same time led V— to understand that he should conceive it to be his duty to improve and ornament R—sitten as much as the climate, soil, and surroundings would permit. For, he explained, it was his intention to bring home shortly, as his dearly loved wife, a lady who was in every respect worthy of the greatest sacrifices.

The air of mystery with which the Freiherr spoke of this alliance, which possibly had been already consummated in secret, cut short all further questions on the part of the family advocate. Nevertheless he found in it to some extent a redeeming feature, for the Freiherr's eager grasping after riches now appeared to be due not so much to avarice, strictly speaking, as to the desire to make one dear to him forget the more beautiful country she was relinquishing for his sake. Otherwise he could not avoid considering the Baron avaricious, or at any rate insufferably close-fisted, seeing that, even though rolling in money, and even when gloating over the new-found Fredericks d'or, he could not resist resentfully observing: "I know the old rascal has concealed the greatest part of his wealth from us, but next spring I will have the ruins of the tower raked over, under my own eyes."

The Freiherr now summoned architects to R—sitten and discussed with them at great length the question of the most convenient way to proceed with his castle building. He rejected one drawing after another; in none of them was the style of architecture sufficiently rich and grandiose. So he began to draw plans himself; and the stimulus of this employment, which constantly placed before his eyes a sunny picture of the happiest future, put him into such a genial humor that it often bordered on wild exuberance, and even communicated itself to those around him. His generosity and profuse hospitality now belied all imputations of avarice, at any rate.

Daniel also seemed to have forgotten the insulting treatment to which he had been subjected. Towards the Freiherr, although often followed by him with mistrustful eyes on account of the treasure buried in the chasm, his bearing was both quiet and humble. But what struck everybody as extraordinary was that the old man appeared to grow younger from day to day. Possibly this might be because he had begun to forget his grief for his former master. Possibly it was also, in part, because he was not now obliged, as he once had been, to spend the cold nights in the tower without sleep, and because he got better food and good wine, such as he liked. But whatever the cause might be, the old greybeard seemed to be growing into a vigorous man with red cheeks and a well-nourished body, who could walk firmly and laugh loudly—whenever he had anything to laugh at.

This pleasant tenor of life at R—sitten was disturbed, before long, by the arrival of a man whom one would have judged to be quite in his element there. This was Wolfgang's younger brother, Hubert. And at the sight of him Wolfgang cried out, with his face as pale as death: "You miserable blackguard, what do you want here?"

Hubert threw himself into his brother's arms, but Wolfgang drew back and led his brother away, up to a remote room, where he locked the door upon the two of them. They remained closeted for several hours, and at the end of that time Hubert ran down in a state of great agitation, and called for his horses. V— intercepted him, inspired by the hope that he might perhaps stifle in the bud what might else end in a bitter lifelong quarrel between the brothers and besought him to stay, at least for a few hours more. At the same time the Freiherr came downstairs and called out, "Stay here, Hubert! You will think better of it."

Hubert's countenance cleared. He assumed an air of composure, and, quickly pulling off his fur coat, and throwing it to a servant behind him, he grasped V—'s hand and went with him into the large salon, saying with a scornful smile, "So the lord of the estate will tolerate my presence here, it seems." But V— thought that the unfortunate misunderstanding would assuredly be smoothed away now, for only separation, and continued existence apart from each other, he imagined, could have fostered their mutual antagonism.

In the salon Hubert took up the steel tongs which stood near the fireplace, and as he proceeded to break up a knotty piece of wood that would only smoke, not burn, and to rake the fire together better, he said to V—, "You see what a good-natured fellow I am, and how skilful I am in all domestic matters! But Wolfgang is full of the most extraordinary prejudices, and—he is a bit of a miser too." V— did not deem it advisable to attempt to fathom further the relations between the brothers, particularly since Wolfgang's face and conduct and voice plainly showed that he was struggling to control violent emotions.

Late that evening, V— had occasion to go up to the Freiherr's room. He required his decision on some matter or other connected with the entail on estate. He found the lord of the castle, in a state of nerves, pacing up and down the room with long strides, his arms folded behind his back. When he saw V—, he stopped his pacing, and, taking him by both hands and looking him gloomily in the face, he said in a broken voice, "My brother has come back."

"I can guess what you are going to say," he continued almost before his visitor had opened his mouth to put a question. "Unfortunately you know nothing. You don't know that my unfortunate brother—yes, I will not call him anything worse than unfortunate—that, like a spirit of evil, he crosses my path everywhere, shattering my peace of mind. It is not his fault that I have not been made unspeakably miserable; he has tried his best, but Heaven willed it otherwise. Ever since he learned that an entail had been placed on the property, he has persecuted me with deadly hatred. He envies me this inheritance, which in his hands would only be scattered like chaff. He is the wildest spendthrift I ever heard of. His load of debt enormously exceeds his share of the unentailed property in Courland. And now, pursued by his creditors, who never stop dunning him, he has hurried here to me to beg for money."

"And you, his brother, refuse to give him any?" V— was about to interrupt him. But the Freiherr, letting go of V—'s hands and taking a long step backwards, went on in a loud and vehement tone.

"Yes; I refuse," he said. "I neither can nor will give away a single thaler of the revenues of the entail. But listen, let me tell you the proposal I made the insane fellow a few hours ago, and made in vain; and then pass judgment upon the sense of duty by which I am actuated. Our unentailed possessions in Courland are, as you are aware, considerable; the half that falls to me I am willing to renounce, but in favor of his family, not himself. For Hubert has married, in Courland, a lady who is beautiful, but poor. She and the children she has borne him are starving. The estates should be put in trust; enough should be set aside out of the revenues to support him, and his creditors should be paid by arrangement. But what does he care for a quiet life—a life free of anxiety? What does he care for wife and children? Money, ready money, and large quantities, is what he will have, to squander in disgraceful folly. Some demon has acquainted him with the secret of the hundred and fifty thousand thalers, half of which he in his mad fashion demands, maintaining that this money is movable property and quite apart from the entailed portion. This I must and will refuse him; but the feeling haunts me that he is plotting my destruction in his heart."

No matter how great the effort which V— made to win the Freiherr away from this suspicion against his brother—in which, of course, since he was unfamiliar with all the circumstances of the disagreement, he could only appeal to broad and somewhat superficial moral principles—he could not boast of the smallest success. Baron Wolfgang commissioned him to carry on negotiations, so to speak, with his hostile and avaricious brother Hubert. V— proceeded to do so with all the circumspection of which he was master; and he was not a little gratified when Hubert at last announced, "Be it so then; I will accept my brother's proposals, but upon condition that he will now, since I am on the point of losing my honor and my good name forever through the severity of my creditors, make me an advance of a thousand Fredericks d'or in hard cash, and will further grant that in time to come I may take up my residence, at least for a short time occasionally, in our beautiful R—sitten, along with my good brother."

"Never, never!" exclaimed the Freiherr violently, when V— laid his brother's amended counter-proposals before him. "I will never consent to have Hubert staying in my house, for even a single minute after I have brought home my wife. Go, my good friend, assure this incubus that he shall have two thousand Fredericks d'or, not as an advance, but as a gift —only, tell him to go, tell him to go."

V— now learned for the first time that the basis of the quarrel between the two brothers must be sought for in this mysterious marriage of Wolfgang's.

Hubert listened to V— proudly and calmly, and when he finished speaking replied in a hoarse and curiously resonant tone, "I will think it over. But at present I shall stay on for a few days in the castle." V— exerted himself to convince the discontented younger brother that the Freiherr, by making over his share of their unentailed property, was really doing all he possibly could do to indemnify him, and that on the whole Hubert had no cause for complaint against the arrangement. But at the same time the legal expert admitted that all institutions of the nature of primogeniture, which vested such preponderant advantages in the eldest born to the prejudice of the remaining children, were in many respects obnoxious, unjust, and, in a word, hateful.

Hubert, when the conversation reached this point, tore his waistcoat open from top to bottom like a man whose breast was cramped and who wanted to relieve his lungs by fresh air. Thrusting one hand into his open shirt-frill and planting the other against his hip, he spun round on one foot in a quick pirouette and cried in a sharp voice, "Pshaw! What is hateful is born of hatred." Then bursting into shrill laughter, he said, "What condescension my lord of the entail shows in being thus willing to throw his gold pieces to the poor beggar!" And V— saw plainly that all idea of a complete reconciliation between the brothers was quite out of the question . . .

To the Freiherr's annoyance, Hubert established himself in the rooms that had been allotted to him in one of the castle's wings, as if he were settling down for a very long stay. He was observed to hold frequent and long conversations with the house steward. What was more, the latter was sometimes even seen to accompany him when he went out wolf hunting. Otherwise he was very little in evidence, and studiously avoided meeting his brother alone—a precaution by which the Freiherr was much relieved. V— felt how strained and unpleasant this state of things was, and was obliged to confess to himself that the peculiar uneasiness which marked all that Hubert said and did was such as to destroy, intentionally and effectually, all the pleasure of the place. He now understood perfectly why the Freiherr had manifested so much alarm on his brother's arrival.

One day as V— was sitting by himself in the hall of justice among his law papers, Hubert came in with a grave and more composed manner than usual, and said in a voice that bordered upon melancholy, "I will accept my brother's last proposals. If you will contrive that I have the two thousand Fredericks d'or today, I will leave the castle this very night: on horseback and alone."

"With the money?" asked V—.

"You are right," replied Hubert; "I know what you would say—the weight of the gold! Give it me in bills on Isaac Lazarus of K—. For to K— I am going this very night. Something is driving me away from this place. The old fellow has bewitched it with evil spirits."

"Do you mean your father, Herr Baron?" asked V— sternly.

Hubert's lips trembled; he clung to the chair as though to keep from falling, then, controlling himself, he cried, "Today then, please," and staggered to the door, not, however, without some exertion.

"He now sees that no deceptions are any longer of avail, that he can do nothing against my firm will," said the Freiherr, as he drew up the bills on Isaac Lazarus of K—. It was plain that a burden was lifted off his heart by the departure of the brother whom he regarded as his enemy; and for a long time he had not been in such cheerful spirits as he was at supper that evening. Hubert had sent his excuses; and there was no one who regretted his absence.

The room which V— occupied was somewhat remote from the rest of the house, and its windows looked upon the castle yard. In the night he was suddenly aroused from his sleep, and he had a strange impression that what had awakened him was a distant and pitiable moan. But listen as he would, all continued to be as still as the grave, and so he was obliged to conclude that the sound which had fallen upon his ears was the delusion of a dream. At the same time, however, he was seized with such a peculiar feeling of breathless anxiety and terror that he could not remain in bed. He got up and went over to the window. And he had not been standing there long when the outer door was opened, and a man, carrying a blazing torch, came out of the castle and crossed the courtyard. V— recognized the figure as that of old Daniel, and saw him open the stable door and go in, and soon afterwards bring out a saddle horse. Now a second shape came into view out of the darkness, a man well wrapped in furs, and wearing a foxskin cap on his head. V— saw that this was Hubert; but after the young man had spoken excitedly with Daniel for some minutes, he went back into the castle. Daniel then led the horse into the stable again, and locked the door, and also that of the castle, after he had returned across the courtyard in the same way in which he traversed it before.

It was evident that Hubert had intended to go away on horseback, but had suddenly changed his mind. And it was no less evident that there was a dangerous understanding of some sort between Hubert and the old house steward. V— looked forward to the morning with burning impatience; he would then, he had at once decided, acquaint the Freiherr with what he had witnessed in the night. Really it was now time to take precautionary measures against the attacks of Hubert's malice, which, V— was now convinced, had been betrayed in his agitated behavior of the day before.

But next morning, at the hour when the Freiherr was in the habit of rising, V— heard people running back and forth, doors opened and slammed shut, and a tumultuous confusion of voices talking and shouting. When he went out of his room into the corridor he met servants everywhere; but they all, without heeding him, ran past with ghastly pale faces, upstairs, downstairs, in and out of the rooms. At length he ascertained that the Freiherr had disappeared, and that they had been looking for him for hours in vain. As he had gone to bed in the presence of his personal attendant, he must have got up later, and gone away somewhere, in his dressing gown and slippers; and he must have taken the large candlestick with him, for this, strangely, was also missing.

V—, his heart agitated with dark forebodings, ran up to the ill-fated hall, the little room adjoining which Wolfgang had chosen, like his father, for his own bedchamber. As he feared, the postern leading to the tower stood wide open. With a cry of horror V— shouted, "There—he lies dashed to pieces at the bottom of the ravine." And it was so.

There had been a fall of snow, so that all they could distinctly make out from above was the rigid arm of the unfortunate man protruding from between the stones. Many hours passed before the workmen succeeded, at great risk, in descending into the chasm by means of ladders bound together, and drawing up the Freiherr's body by the aid of ropes. In the last agonies of death the Baron had kept a tight hold upon the silver candlestick; the hand in which it was clenched was the only uninjured part of his whole body, which had been crushed and broken in the most hideous way as it rebounded on the sharp-edged stones.

Just as the body had been recovered and carried into the hall, and as it was placed upon the very same spot on the large table where a few weeks before old Roderick had lain dead, Hubert burst in, his face distorted by the frenzy of despair. Utterly overpowered by the fearful sight he moaned, "Brother! O my poor brother! No! This is something I never prayed for, from even the worst demons who had entered into me!" This suspicious self-exculpation made V— tremble. He felt that he must take

action against Hubert as the Freiherr's murderer. The young man, however, had fallen unconscious to the floor. The servants carried him to his
bed where strong restoratives brought him to himself again.

Soon he made his appearance in V—'s room, pale and sorrow-stricken,
and with his eyes half clouded with grief. And, too weak to stand, he sank
down into an easy-chair, as he said, "I have wished for my brother's death,
because my father had made over to him the best part of the property
through the foolish conversion of it into an entail. He has now found
a death that was frightful. I am now lord of the entailed estate, but my
heart is filled with pain: I cannot—I shall never be happy . . . I confirm
you in your office. You shall be invested with the most extensive powers
in respect to the management of the estate. But here in this place I cannot bear to live." With that he left the room, and in two or three hours
he was on his way to K—.

It appeared that the unfortunate Wolfgang had got up in the night,
probably with the intention of going into the other little room where
there were a number of books. In the stupor of sleep he had mistaken the
door, and had opened the postern, taken a step out, and plunged headlong down. All this was publicly stated. But after everything had been
said, there was nevertheless a good deal that was strained and unlikely
in this explanation. If the Baron was unable to sleep and wanted to get
a book out of the library, this of itself excluded all idea of a sleep stupor;
but only such a dazed condition could account for any mistaking of the
postern for the door of the other room. Then again, the postern was
locked, and a good deal of exertion had been required to unlock it.

These improbabilities V— accordingly put before the domestics, who
had gathered round him; and at last the Freiherr's body-servant, Francis
by name, said, "Nay, nay, your worship; it couldn't have happened in
that way."

"Well, how then?" asked V— abruptly and sharply.

But Francis, a faithful, honest fellow, who would have followed his
master into his grave, was unwilling to speak out before the rest; he stipu-
lated that what he had to say about the event should be confided to V—
alone, in private. V— thus learned that the Freiherr used often to talk
to Francis about the vast treasure which, he believed, lay buried beneath
the ruins of the tower, and also that frequently at night, as if goaded by

some malicious fiend, he would open the postern, the key of which Daniel had been obliged to give him, and would gaze with longing eyes down into the chasm where the supposed riches lay.

There was now no doubt about it; on that ill-omened night the Freiherr, after his servant had left him, must have taken one of his usual walks to the postern, where he had been, most likely, suddenly seized with dizziness, and so had fallen over the edge. Daniel, who also seemed much upset by the Freiherr's terrible end, thought it would be a good thing to have the dangerous postern walled up. And this was at once done.

Freiherr Hubert von R—, who had then succeeded to the domain under the entail, went back to Courland without once showing himself at R—sitten again. V— was invested with full powers for the absolute management of the property. The building of the new castle was not proceeded with; but on the other hand the old structure was put in as good a state of repair as possible. After several years had passed, Hubert came back to R—sitten, one day late in the autumn, but after he had remained shut up in his room with V— for several days, he returned to Courland. Stopping on his way through K—, he deposited his will with the government authorities there.

The Freiherr, whose character appeared to have undergone a complete metamorphosis, spoke more than once, during his short stay at R—sitten, of presentiments of approaching death. And these apprehensions were really not unfounded, for he died the very next year. His son, named, like the deceased Baron, Hubert, soon came over from Courland to take possession of the rich inheritance, and was followed by his mother and his sister.

This youth seemed to unite in his own person all the bad qualities of his ancestors: he showed himself to be proud, arrogant, impetuous, avaricious, in the very first moments after his arrival at R—sitten. He wanted to have several things, which did not suit his notions of what was right and proper, altered then and there: the cook he kicked out of doors; and he attempted to thrash the coachman, in which effort, however, he did not succeed, for the big brawny fellow had the impudence not to submit to it. In fact, the second Hubert was on the high road to assuming the rôle of a harsh and severe lord of the estate, when V— interposed in his firm earnest manner, declaring most explicitly that not a single chair should be moved, that not even a cat should leave the house if she liked to stay in it, until after the will had been opened.

"You have the presumption to tell me, the master of the estate," began the Baron.

V—, however, abruptly broke in on the young man, who was foaming with rage, and said, as he measured him with a keen searching glance, "Don't be in too great a hurry, Herr Baron. At all events, you have no right to exercise authority here until after the opening of your father's will. It is I—I alone—who am now master here; and I shall know how to meet violence with violent measures. Please recollect that by virtue of my powers as executor of your father's will, as well as by virtue of the arrangements which have been made by the court, I am empowered to forbid your remaining in R—sitten if I think fit to do so; and so, if you wish to spare me this disagreeable step, I would advise you to go away quietly to K—."

The lawyer's earnestness, and the resolute tone in which he spoke, lent the proper emphasis to his words. Hence the young Baron, who was charging with far too sharp-pointed horns, felt the weakness of his weapons against the firm bulwark of the other's character and position, and found it convenient to cover the shame of his retreat with a burst of scornful laughter.

Three months passed, and the day arrived on which, in accordance with the expressed wish of the deceased, his will was to be opened at K—, where it had been deposited. To the court chambers in addition to the officers of the law, the Baron, and V—, came an unknown young man of noble appearance, whom V— had brought with him, and who was taken to be V—'s clerk, since he had a parchment deed sticking out from the breast of his buttoned-up coat. The young Baron treated this stranger as he did almost all the others, with scornful contempt; and he went on to demand, with noisy impetuosity, that they should make haste and get done with all their tiresome unnecessary ceremonies as quickly as possible and without so many words and so much scribbling. He couldn't for the life of him make out, he added, why any will should be needed at all in the matter of the inheritance, and especially in the case of entailed property; and no matter what provisions were made in the will, he averred, it would depend entirely upon his decision, whether or not they should be observed. After casting a hasty and surly glance at the handwriting and the seal, the Baron acknowledged them to be those of his dead father. Then when the clerk of the court prepared to read the will aloud, the young Baron, throwing his right arm carelessly over the back of his chair and leaning his left on the table—while he drummed with his fingers on its green cover—sat staring with an air of indifference out of the window. So the reading was begun.

After a short preamble, the deceased Freiherr Hubert von R— declared that he had never possessed the entailed estate as its lawful owner, but that he had only managed it in the name of the deceased Freiherr Wolfgang von R—'s only son, called Roderick after his grandfather. He it was to whom, according to the rights of family priority, the estate had fallen on his father's death. Among Hubert's papers would be found an exact account of all revenues and expenditure, as well as of existing movable property, and all other details.

The will went on to relate that Wolfgang von R— had, during his travels, made the acquaintance in Geneva of Mademoiselle Julia de St. Val, and had fallen so deeply in love with her that he resolved never to leave her side again. She was very poor, and her family, although noble and of good repute, did not rank among the most illustrious. For these reasons Wolfgang dared not expect to receive the consent of old Roderick to a union with her, for the old Freiherr's aim and ambition was to promote by all possible means the establishment of a powerful family. Nevertheless he ventured to write, from Paris, to his father, acquainting him with the fact that his affections were engaged. But what he had foreseen was precisely realized: the old Baron declared categorically that he had himself chosen the future mistress of the domain, and therefore no mention could be made of any other.

Upon receiving this word, Wolfgang, instead of crossing the Channel to England, as he was to have done, returned to Geneva, under the assumed name of Born, and married Julia. After the lapse of a year his wife bore him a son, and this son became on Wolfgang's death the lawful lord of the entailed property. In explanation of the fact that Hubert, though acquainted with all this, had kept silent so long and had represented himself as lord of the entail, various reasons were assigned. These were based upon agreements formerly made with Wolfgang, but they seemed for the most part insufficient and devoid of real foundation.

The young Baron sat staring at the clerk of the court as if thunder-struck, while the latter went on proclaiming all this bad news in an exasperatingly monotonous and jarring tone. When he finished, V— rose. He took by the hand the young man whom he had brought with him, and said, as he bowed to the assembled company, "Here I have the honor to present to you, gentlemen, Freiherr Roderick von R—, lord of the entailed estate of R—sitten."

Baron Hubert looked at the youth, who had, as it were, fallen from the clouds to deprive him of the rich inheritance together with half the unentailed Courland estates, with suppressed fury in his gleaming eyes. Then, threateningly shaking his clenched fist at the hated stranger, he ran out of the court without uttering a word.

Baron Roderick, now challenged by the court officers, produced the documents which he had brought to establish his identity as the person whom he represented himself to be. He handed in an attested extract from the register of the church where his father had been married, which certified that on such-and-such a day Wolfgang Born, merchant, born in K—, had been united in marriage with the blessing of the Church to Mademoiselle Julia de St. Val, in the presence of certain witnesses, who were named. Further, he produced his own baptismal certificate (he had been baptized in Geneva as the son of the merchant Born and his wife, Julia, née de St. Val, begotten in lawful wedlock), and various letters from his father to his mother, who was long since dead, but none of these letters had any other signature than W.

V— looked through all these papers with a cloud upon his face; and as he put them together again, he said, somewhat troubled, "Ah, well! God will help us!"

The very next morning Freiherr Hubert von R— presented, through an advocate whose services he had succeeded in enlisting in his cause, a statement of protest to the government authorities in K—, actually calling upon them to effectuate the immediate surrender to him of the entail of R—sitten. It was incontestable, maintained the advocate, that the deceased Freiherr Hubert von R— had not had the power to dispose of entailed property either by testament or in any other way. The testament in question, therefore, was nothing more than an evidential statement, written down and deposited with the court, to the effect that Freiherr Wolfgang von R— had bequeathed the entailed estate to a son who was at that time still living; and accordingly it had as evidence no greater weight than that of any other witness, and so could not by any possibility legitimately establish the claims of the person who had announced himself to be Freiherr Roderick von R—. Hence it was rather the duty of this new claimant to prove by action at law his alleged rights of inheritance, which were hereby expressly disputed and denied, and so also to take proper steps to maintain his claim to the estate, which now, according to the laws of succession, fell to Baron Hubert von R—. By the father's death the property came immediately into the hands of the son. There was no need for any formal declaration to be made of his entering into possession of the inheritance, since the succession could not be alienated; at any rate, the present owner of the estate did not propose to be disturbed in his possession by claims which were perfectly groundless. Whatever reasons the deceased might have had for bringing forward another heir of entail were quite irrelevant. Incidentally, it might be remarked that he had himself had an intrigue in Switzerland, as could be proved, if necessary, from the papers he had left behind him; and it was quite possible that the person whom he alleged to be his brother's son was his own child, the fruit of an unlawful love, for whom in a momentary fit of remorse he had wished to secure the entail.

However great was the balance of probability in favor of the truth of the circumstances as stated in the will, and however revolted the judges were, particularly by the last clauses of the protest, in which the son felt no compunction at accusing his dead father of a crime, yet the views of the case there stated were after all the right ones. And it was only due to V—'s tireless exertions, and his explicit and solemn assurance that the proofs which were necessary to establish legitimately the identity of Freiherr Roderick von R— should be produced in a very short time, that the surrender of the estate to the young Baron was deferred. Thanks to V— the contrivance of the administration of the entire property in trust was, moreover, agreed to, until after the case should be settled.

V— was only too well aware of the difficulties in the way of his keeping his promise. He had gone through all old Roderick's papers without finding the slightest trace of a letter, or any kind of a statement, bearing upon Wolfgang's relation to Mademoiselle de St. Val. He was sitting absorbed in thought in old Roderick's little bedroom—every hole and corner of which he had searched—and was working at a long statement of the case that he intended dispatching to a certain notary in Geneva; this man, who had been recommended to him as shrewd and energetic, he was about to request to procure and forward certain documents, which would establish the young Freiherr's cause on firm ground. It was midnight; the full moon shone in through the windows of the adjoining hall, the door of which stood open. And as he sat there, V— fancied he heard a noise as of someone coming slowly and heavily up the stairs, and also at the same time a jingling and rattling of keys.

His attention was arrested; he rose to his feet and went into the hall, where he plainly made out that there was someone crossing the anteroom, and approaching the door of the hall where he now was. In a moment the door was opened and a man came slowly into the room. He was dressed in night clothes. His face was ghastly pale and distorted. In one hand he carried a candlestick with the candles burning, and in the other a huge bunch of keys. V— at once recognized the house steward, and was on the point of addressing him and asking what he wanted so late at night, when an icy shiver gripped him and held him silent. There was something so unearthly and ghostlike in the old man's manner and bearing as well as in his set, pallid face, that V— realized almost immediately that he was in the presence of a somnambulist.

Crossing the hall diagonally, with measured strides, the old man went straight to the walled-up postern which had formerly led to the tower. He came to a halt directly in front of it, and uttered a deep, shuddering moan that seemed to come from the bottom of his heart, and was so awful and so loud that the whole apartment echoed with the sound, making V— tremble with dread. Then, setting the candlestick down on the floor and hanging the keys on his belt, Daniel began to scratch at the wall with both hands, until the blood began to stream from beneath his fingernails, the while he kept on moaning and groaning as if tortured by nameless agony. Then he placed his ear against the wall in a listening attitude, and after that he waved his hand in a gesture as if hushing someone.

Next he stooped down and picked up the candlestick; and finally he stole with the same soft measured footsteps back to the door.

V— took his own candle in his hand and cautiously followed the sleepwalker. They both went downstairs. The old steward unlocked the great main door of the castle, and, after him, V— slipped cleverly through. They went to the stable, where old Daniel, to V—'s complete astonishment, placed his candlestick so skilfully that the entire interior of the building was sufficiently lighted without the least danger of fire. Having fetched a saddle and bridle, he put them on one of the horses, which he had loosed from the manger, carefully tightening the girth and taking up the stirrup straps. Pulling the tuft of hair on the horse's forehead outside the front strap, he took him by the bridle and led him out of the stable, clicking with his tongue and patting his neck with one hand. On getting outside in the courtyard he stood several seconds in the attitude of one receiving commands, which he promised by sundry nods to carry out. Then he led the horse back into the stable, unsaddled him, and tied him to the manger again. This done, he took his candlestick, locked the stable, and returned to the castle, finally disappearing into his own room, the door of which he carefully bolted. V— was deeply agitated by this scene; the presentiment of some fearful deed rose up before him like a black and fiendish spectre, and refused to leave him. Being so keenly alive as he was to the precarious position of his protégé, he felt that it would at least be his duty to turn what he had seen to the young man's account.

Next day, just as dusk was beginning to fall, Daniel came into V—'s room to receive some instructions relating to his department of the household. V— took him by the arms, and, forcing him into a chair, in a confidential way began to speak to him: "See here, my old friend Daniel, I have long been wishing to ask you what you think of all this confused mess into which Hubert's peculiar will has tumbled us," he said. "Do you really think that the young stranger is Wolfgang's son, begotten in lawful marriage?"

The old man, leaning over the arm of his chair, and avoiding V—'s eyes—for V— was watching him most intently—replied, doggedly, "Bah! Maybe he is; maybe he is not. What does it matter to me? It's all the same to me who's master here now."

"But I believe," went on V—, moving nearer to the old retainer, and placing his hand on his shoulder, "but I believe you possessed the old Freiherr's full confidence; and in that case he assuredly would not conceal from you the real state of affairs with regard to his sons. He told you, I dare say, about the marriage which Wolfgang had made against his will. Did he not?"

"I don't remember having ever heard him say anything of that sort," replied the steward, yawning noisily in the most ill-mannered way.

"You are sleepy, old man," said V—. "Perhaps you have had a restless night?"

"Not that I am aware," the other rejoined coldly. "But I must go and order supper." Whereupon he rose heavily from his chair and rubbed his bent back, yawning again, and that still more loudly than before.

"Stay a little while, old fellow," cried V—, taking hold of his hand and endeavoring to force him to resume his seat.

But Daniel preferred to stand in front of the study table. Propping himself against it with both hands, and leaning across towards V—, he asked sullenly, "Well, what do you want? What have I to do with the will? What do I care about the quarrel over the estate?"

"Well, well," interposed V—, "we'll say no more about that now. Let us turn to some other topic, Daniel. You are in a bad humor, and yawning, and all that is a sign of great weariness. I am almost inclined to believe that it really was you last night, who—"

"Well, what did I do last night?" asked the old man without changing his position. Nor did he move, at first, as V— went on: "Last night, when I was sitting upstairs in your old master's little bedroom next to the great hall, you came in at the door, your face pale and rigid; and you went across to the bricked-up postern and scratched at the wall with both your hands, groaning as if in very great pain. Do you walk in your sleep, Daniel?"

The old man dropped back into the chair which V— quickly managed to place for him, but not a sound escaped his lips. His face could not be seen, in the gathering dusk of the evening; V— only noticed that he was breathing in short gasps, and that his teeth were chattering.

"Yes," continued V— after a short pause, "there is one thing that is very strange about sleepwalkers. On the day after they have been in this peculiar state, in which they have acted as if they were perfectly wide awake, they don't remember the least thing that they did."

Daniel did not stir.

"I have come across a condition very like what yours was yesterday, once before in the course of my experience," proceeded V—. "I had a friend who regularly began to wander about at night, as you do, whenever it was full moon—more, he often sat down and wrote letters. But the most extraordinary thing was that if I began to whisper softly in his ear I could soon manage to make him speak; and he would answer correctly all the questions I put to him. Even things that he would most jealously have concealed when awake now fell from his lips unbidden, as though he were unable to offer any resistance to the power that was exerting its influence over him. Deuce take it! I really believe that if a man who's given to walking in his sleep had ever committed any crime, and had hoarded it up as a secret for no matter how long, it could be extracted from him by questioning when he was in this peculiar state. Happy are they who have clear consciences, like you and me, Daniel! We may walk in our sleep as much as we like. There's no fear of anybody extorting the confession of a crime from us! But come now, Daniel! When you scratch so horribly at the bricked-up postern, you want to go up to the astronomical tower, don't you? I suppose you want to go and experiment like old Roderick—eh? Well, next time you come, I shall ask you what you want to do."

While V— was speaking, the old man had been shaken with continually increasing agitation. But now, as the other fell silent, Daniel's whole frame seemed to heave and rock convulsively past all hope of calming; and in a shrill voice he broke out into a string of meaningless gibberish. V— rang for the servants. They brought lights. And as the old man's fit did not abate, they lifted him up as if he had been a mere automaton, not possessed of the power of voluntary movement, and carried him to his bed. After continuing in this frightful state for about an hour, he fell into a sleep so profound that it was like a dead faint. When he awoke he asked for wine. And, after he had got what he wanted, he sent away the man who was going to sit with him, and locked himself as usual in his room.

V— had indeed really resolved to make the attempt he spoke of to Daniel, although at the same time he could not forget two facts. In the first place, the old retainer, having now been made aware of his propensity to walk in his sleep, would probably adopt every measure of precaution to avoid him; and on the other hand, confessions made while a man was in this condition would not be exactly fitted to serve as a basis for further proceedings. In spite of all this, however, V— repaired to the hall on the approach of midnight, hoping that Daniel, as frequently happens to those afflicted in this way, would be constrained to act involuntarily.

About midnight a great noise sounded from the courtyard. V— plainly heard a window being broken. Then he went downstairs, and as he traversed the passages he was met by rolling clouds of suffocating smoke, which, he soon saw, were pouring out of the open door of the house steward's room. The steward himself was just being carried out, to all appearance dead, to be put to bed somewhere else. The servants now told how, about midnight, one of the undergrooms had been awakened by a strange hollow knocking from his room; he thought something must have happened to the old man, and was preparing to get up, and go and see if he could help him, when the night watchman in the court shouted, "Fire! Something's ablaze!"

At this outcry several servants at once appeared on the scene; but all their efforts to burst open the steward's bedroom were unavailing. Then they hurried out into the court, but the resolute watchman had already broken in the window—for the room was in the basement story—had torn down the burning curtains, and by pouring a few buckets of water on them had at once extinguished the fire. The house steward they found lying on the floor, in the middle of the room, unconscious. In his hand he still held the candlestick tightly clenched, and it was the burning candles which had caught the curtains, and so caused the fire. Some of the blazing rags had fallen upon the old man, burning his eyebrows and a great deal of the hair on the top of his head. If the watchman had not seen the fire, Daniel must have been helplessly burned to death.

The servants, moreover, to their no little astonishment, found the room door secured on the inside by two quite new bolts, which had not been there the previous evening. And V— realized that the old man had wished to make it impossible for himself to get out of his room; for the blind impulse which urged him to wander in his sleep he could not resist.

The old man now fell seriously ill; he did not speak; he took but little nourishment; and he lay staring before him with the reflection of death in his set eyes, as if he were clasped in the unescapable grip of some hideous thought. V— believed he would never rise from his bed again.

V— had done all that could be done for his client, and he could now only wait the result in patience. So he soon resolved to return to K—. When his departure was fixed for the following morning, and as he was packing his papers together late at night, he happened to lay his hand upon a little sealed packet which Freiherr Hubert von R— had given him. It bore the inscription, "To be read after my will has been opened," but for some unaccountable reason it had hitherto escaped his notice. He was on the point of breaking the seal when the door opened and, to his amazement, Daniel came in with a still, ghostlike step. Placing upon the table a black portfolio which he carried under his arm, he sank upon his knees with a deep groan, and grasping V—'s hands with a convulsive clutch he said, in a voice so hollow and hoarse that it seemed to come from the bottom of a grave, "I should not like to die on the scaffold! There is One above who judges!" Then, rising with some trouble and with many painful gasps, he left the room as he had come.

V— spent the whole of the night in reading what the black portfolio and Hubert's packet contained. The two agreed in all circumstantial particulars, and suggested naturally what further steps were to be taken. As soon as he reached the near-by city, V— immediately hurried to Freiherr Hubert von R—, who received him with rude arrogance. But the remarkable result of the interview, which began at noon and continued without interruption until late at night, was that the next day the Freiherr made a declaration before the court to the effect that he acknowledged the claimant to be, in accordance with his father's will, the son of Wolfgang von R—, eldest son of Freiherr Roderick von R—, and begotten in lawful wedlock with Mademoiselle Julia de St. Val; and furthermore he acknowledged him as rightful and legitimate heir to the entail. As he left the court he found his carriage, with post-horses, standing before the door; he stepped in and was driven off at a rapid rate, leaving his mother and his sister behind him. They would perhaps never see him again, he wrote, along with other perplexing statements.

The young Roderick's astonishment at this unexpected turn which the case had taken was very great. He pressed V— to explain to him how this wonder had been brought about, what mysterious power had been at work in the matter. V—, however, evaded his present questions by giving him the hope of learning everything at some future time, when he should have come into possession of the estate. For the surrender of the entail to him could not be effected immediately, since the court, not content merely with Hubert's declaration, also required Roderick to prove his own identity to their satisfaction. V— proposed to the Baron that he should go and live at R—sitten; Hubert's mother and sister, embarrassed for the moment by his sudden departure, would prefer, he added, to go and live quietly on the ancestral property rather than stay in the expensive and noisy town. The joyous delight with which Roderick welcomed the prospect of living, at least for a time, under the same roof with the Baroness and her daughter, betrayed the deep impression which his lovely and graceful cousin Seraphina had made upon him. In fact, the Freiherr made such good use of his time in R—sitten that, at the end of a few weeks, he had won Seraphina's love as well as her mother's cordial approval of her marriage with him. All this was for V— rather too quick work, since Roderick's claims to be lord of the entailed property still continued to be rather doubtful . . .

The life of idyllic happiness at the castle was interrupted by letters from Courland. Hubert had not shown himself at all at the family domain there, but had traveled direct to St. Petersburg, where he had entered the military service; he was now in the field against the Persians, with whom Russia happened to be just then waging war. This news made it necessary for the Baroness and her daughter to set off immediately for their Courland estates, where everything was in confusion and disorder. Roderick, who now regarded himself in the light of an accepted son-in-law, insisted upon accompanying his beloved. And so, since V— likewise returned to K—, the castle was left again to its former loneliness. The house steward's malignant disease grew worse and worse, so that he gave up all hope of ever getting about again; and his office was conferred upon the old *chasseur*, Francis, who had been Wolfgang's faithful servant.

At last, after long waiting, V— received, from Switzerland, the favorable information he had been waiting for. The priest who had married Roderick was long since dead; but there had been found in the church register a memorandum in his handwriting, to the effect that the man of the name of Born, whom he had joined in the bonds of wedlock with

Mademoiselle Julia de St. Val, had established completely to his satisfaction his identity as Freiherr Wolfgang von R—, eldest son of Freiherr Roderick von R— of R—sitten. Besides this, two witnesses of the marriage had been discovered, a merchant of Geneva and an old French captain who had since moved to Lyon. To them also Wolfgang had in confidence stated his real name; and their affidavits confirmed the priest's note in the church register. With these memoranda in his hands, drawn up with proper legal formalities, V— now succeeded in securing his client in the complete possession of his rights; and as there was now no longer any hindrance to the surrender of the entail to him, it was to be put into his hands in the ensuing autumn. Hubert had fallen in his first engagement, thus sharing the fate of his younger brother, who had likewise been slain in battle a year before his father's death. In this way the Courland estates fell to Baroness Seraphina von R—, and made a handsome dowry for her to take to the happy Roderick.

November had already set in when the older Baroness, together with Roderick and his betrothed, arrived at R—sitten. The formal surrender of the entailed estate to the young Baron took place at once, and his marriage with Seraphina was solemnized immediately thereafter. Many weeks passed amid a continual whirl of pleasure; but at last the more or less exhausted guests began gradually to quit the castle—to V—'s great satisfaction, for he had made up his mind not to take his leave of R—sitten until he had initiated the young lord of the manor into all the relations and duties connected with his new position, down to the minutest particulars. Roderick's uncle had kept account of all revenues and disbursements with the most detailed accuracy; hence, since this older Hubert had retained only a small sum annually for his own support, the surplus revenues had all gone to swell the capital left by the old Freiherr, till the total now amounted to a considerable sum. Hubert had used the income of the entail for his own purposes during the first three years, but to cover this he had given a mortgage on the security of his share of the Courland property.

From the time when old Daniel had revealed himself to V— as a somnambulist, V— had chosen old Roderick's bedroom for his own study, in order that he might the more securely gather from the old man what he afterwards voluntarily disclosed. So it was in this room and in the adjoining great hall that the new Freiherr transacted business with V—. Late one night they were both still sitting at the great table by the bright blazing fire; V— had his pen in his hand, and was noting down various totals, and calculating the riches of the lord of the estate, while the latter, leaning his head on his hand, was blinking at the open account books and formidable-looking documents. Neither of them had paid any attention to the hollow roar of the sea, nor the anxious cries of the sea gulls as they dashed against the windowpanes, flapping their wings and flying back and forth, announcing the oncoming storm. Neither of them heeded the storm, which arose about midnight, and was now roaring and raging with wild fury round the castle walls, so that all the sounds of ill omen awoke in the fireplace and narrow corridors, and began to whistle and shriek in a weird, unearthly fashion. At last, after a terrific blast, which made the whole castle shake, the hall was completely lit up by the murky glare of the full moon, and V— exclaimed, "Awful weather!" The Freiherr, entirely absorbed in the consideration of the wealth which had fallen to him, replied indifferently, as he turned over a page of the receipt book with a satisfied smile, "It is indeed; very stormy!"

But, as if clutched by the icy hand of Dread, he started to his feet as the door of the hall flew open, and a pale spectral figure became visible, striding in with the stamp of death upon its face. It was Daniel, who, lying helpless in the power of disease, was deemed, in the opinion of V— as of everybody else, incapable of moving a single limb! But, coming again under the influence of his propensity to wander in his sleep at full moon, he had, it appeared, been unable to resist that superhuman urgency.

The Freiherr stared at the old man without uttering a sound; and when Daniel began to scratch at the wall, and moan as though in the painful agonies of death, Roderick's heart was filled with horrible dread. With his face ashy pale and his hair standing on end, he leaped to his feet, strode towards the old man, and stood over him in a threatening attitude. "Daniel, Daniel, what are you doing here at this hour?" he cried in a loud firm voice, so that the hall rang again.

Then the old man gave voice to that same unearthly howling whimper, like the death cry of a wounded animal, which had been wrung from him when Wolfgang had offered to reward his fidelity with gold; and he fell to the floor. V— summoned the servants; they lifted the old steward up; but all attempts to restore animation proved fruitless. Daniel was dead.

When he saw this, the Freiherr cried, almost beside himself, "Good God! Good God! Now I remember having heard that a sleepwalker may die on the spot if anybody calls him by his name. Oh! Oh! Unfortunate wretch that I am! I have killed the poor old man! I shall never have another peaceful moment as long as I live."

After the servants had carried the body away and the hall had been emptied, V— took the Freiherr, who was still continuing his self-reproaches, by the hand, and led him in impressive silence to the walled-up postern. "The man who fell down dead at your feet, Freiherr Roderick," he said, "was the murderer of your father."

The Freiherr fixed his eyes in a stare upon V— and beyond him, as though he saw the foul fiends of Hell. But V— went on, "The time has come now for me to reveal to you the hideous secret which, weighing upon the conscience of this monster, and keeping him accursed, compelled him to roam abroad in his sleep. The Eternal Power has seen fit to make the son the unconscious instrument of vengeance upon the murderer of his father. The words which you thundered in the ears of that fearful sleepwalker were the last words which your unhappy father spoke."

V— sat down in front of the fire, and the young Freiherr, trembling and unable to speak a word, took his seat beside him. Then V— began to tell him the contents of the document which Hubert had left behind him, the seal of which was not to be broken until after the opening of the will. In it Hubert lamented, in expressions testifying to the deepest remorse, the implacable hatred against his elder brother which had taken root in him from the moment that old Roderick established the entail. He was deprived of all weapons for a fight. Even if he succeeded in maliciously setting the son at variance against the father, it would serve no purpose, since even Roderick himself now lacked the power to deprive his eldest son of his birthright; nor would he on principle have ever done so, no matter how his affection might have been alienated from him. It was only when Wolfgang formed his connection with Julia de St. Val, in Geneva, that Hubert saw his way to effecting his brother's ruin. And that was the time when he came to an understanding with Daniel, to provoke the old man by villainous devices into taking measures which should drive his first-born son to despair.

He was well aware of old Roderick's opinion that the only way to assure an illustrious future for his family, through the generations to come, was by means of an alliance with one of the foremost families of the country. The old man had read this alliance in the stars; and he was convinced that any pernicious derangement of the constellation would only bring destruction upon the dynasty he had founded. So it was that Wolfgang's union with Julia seemed to the old man to be nothing short of a sinful crime, committed against the ordinances of the Power which had stood by him in all his worldly undertakings; and any means that might be employed for Julia's ruin he would have regarded as justified for the same reason. For Julia had, as he saw it, ranged herself against him like some demoniacal principle.

Hubert knew that his brother loved Julia passionately, almost to madness, in fact, and that the loss of her would infallibly destroy all his happiness, would even perhaps kill him. And Hubert was all the more ready to assist the old man in his plans because he had himself conceived an illicit affection for Julia, and hoped to win her for himself. It was, however, determined by a special dispensation of Providence that all attacks, even the most virulent, were to be thwarted by Wolfgang's resoluteness; more, that he should contrive to deceive his brother. The fact that his marriage had actually been solemnized, and later, the fact that a son had been born, were kept secret from Hubert. To old Roderick's mind, however, there occurred, along with the presentiment of his approaching death, the idea that Wolfgang had really married this Julia whom he considered as his family's enemy. In the letter which commanded his son to appear at R—sitten on a given day to take possession of the estate under the rights of the entail, he cursed him if he did not sever his connection with her. This was the letter that Wolfgang had burned beside his father's corpse.

To Hubert the old man wrote his conviction that Wolfgang had married Julia, but that he would certainly leave her. This, however, Hubert took to be a fancy of his visionary father's; so it turned out that he was not a little dismayed when, in his first talk with his brother at R—sitten, Wolfgang with perfect frankness not only confirmed the old man's supposition, but also went on to add that Julia had borne him a son, and that he hoped in a short time to surprise her with the pleasant intelligence of his high rank and great wealth. For she had hitherto taken him for merely what he called himself—Born, a merchant from K—. He intended to go to Geneva himself to fetch his beloved wife. But before he could carry out this plan he was mysteriously overtaken by death.

Hubert now carefully concealed what he knew about the existence of a son born to Wolfgang in lawful wedlock with Julia, and so usurped the property that really belonged to his nephew. But before more than a few years had passed, he became a prey to bitter remorse. Destiny reminded him of his guilt, indeed, in a terrible fashion, through the hatred which grew up, and developed more and more bitterly, between his own two sons.

"You are a poor starving beggar!" said the elder, a boy of twelve, to the younger. "But I shall be lord of R—sitten when our father dies, and then you will have to be humble and kiss my hand when you want me to give you money to buy a new coat."

The younger, goaded to ungovernable fury by his brother's proud and scornful words, threw at him the knife which he happened to be holding in his hand, and almost killed him. Their father, in constant fear of some dire catastrophe, sent the younger boy away to St. Petersburg; and he served afterwards as an officer in the armies under Suwaroff, and fell fighting against the French.

The remorseful Hubert held back from revealing to the world the dishonest and deceitful way in which he had acquired possession of the entailed estate, because of the shame and disgrace which the disclosure would have brought upon him; but he would not rob the rightful owner of a single penny more. He had inquiries set on foot in Geneva, and learned that Madame Born had died of grief at the incomprehensible disappearance of her husband, but that young Roderick Born was being brought up by a worthy man who had adopted him. Hubert then caused himself to be introduced to his nephew under an assumed name as a relative of Born the merchant, who, he said, had perished at sea, and he forwarded at given times sufficient sums of money to give the young heir-of-entail a good and suitable education. How he carefully treasured up the surplus revenues from the estate, and how he drew up the terms of his will, we already know. Regarding his brother's death, Hubert wrote in strangely obscure terms, but they allowed this much to be inferred, that there must be some mystery about it, and that he had taken part, indirectly at least, in some heinous crime.

The contents of the steward's black portfolio made even this last riddle clear. Along with Hubert's traitorous correspondence with Daniel was a sheet of paper written and signed by Daniel himself. V— read a confession at which his very soul trembled, appalled. It was at Daniel's instigation that Hubert had come to R—sitten; and it was Daniel again who had written and told him about the one hundred and fifty thousand thalers that had been found. It has been already described how Hubert was received by his brother, and how, deceived in all his hopes and wishes, he was about to leave immediately when he was prevented by V—. But Daniel's heart was tortured by an insatiable thirst for the vengeance which he was determined to take on the young man who had proposed to kick him out like a mangy cur. He it was who relentlessly and incessantly fanned the flame of passion by which Hubert's desperate heart was consumed. While in the fir forests hunting wolves, out in the midst of a blinding snowstorm, they reached an agreement to bring about his destruction.

"Make away with him!" murmured Hubert, looking askance and taking aim with his rifle. "Yes, make away with him," snarled Daniel, "but not in *that* way, not in *that way!*" And he made the most solemn asseverations that he would murder the Freiherr, and not a soul in the world should be the wiser.

When Hubert had got his money, however, he repented bitterly of the plot. He determined to leave the place at once, in order to shun all further temptation to violence and disaster. Daniel himself saddled his horse and brought it out of the stable. But as the Baron was about to mount, the other said to him in a sharp, strained voice, "I thought you would stay on the estate, Freiherr Hubert, now that it has just fallen to you. The proud lord of the entail lies dashed to pieces at the bottom of the ravine, below the tower."

The steward had observed that Wolfgang, tormented by his lust for gold, often used to rise in the night, go to the postern which formerly led to the tower, and stand gazing with longing eyes down into the chasm, where, according to the old retainer's testimony, vast treasures lay buried. Relying upon this habit, Daniel waited near the hall door on that ill-omened night; and as soon as he heard the Freiherr open the postern leading to the tower, he entered the hall and walked over to where the Freiherr was standing, close by the brink of the chasm. Suddenly aware of the presence of his revenge-maddened servant, in whose eyes he caught the dreadful gleam of murder, the Freiherr turned round and said, with a cry of terror, "Daniel, Daniel, what are you doing here at this hour?"

But Daniel shrieked wildly, "Down with you, you mangy cur!" and with a powerful push of his foot he hurled the unhappy man over the broken threshold into the deep chasm.

Terribly agitated by the revelation of this awful deed, Freiherr Roderick found no peace in the castle where his father had been murdered. He went to his Courland estates, and only visited R—sitten once a year, in autumn. Francis—old Francis—who had strong suspicions as to Daniel's guilt, maintained that the guilty steward often haunted the place at full moon; and he described the nature of the apparition much as V— afterwards experienced it for himself when he exorcised the evil spirit. It was the disclosure of these circumstances, also, which stamped his father's memory with dishonor, that had driven young Freiherr Hubert out into self-imposed and fatal exile.

This was my old great-uncle's story. Now he took my hand, and, while his eyes filled with tears, he said, in a broken voice, "My boy, my boy! Now *she* too—the beautiful lady—has fallen a victim to the dark destiny, the grim, mysterious power, which has established itself in that ancient ancestral castle. Two days after we left R—sitten the Freiherr arranged an excursion on sledges as the concluding event of the hunt season. He drove his wife himself; but as they were going down the valley the horses, for some unexplained reason, suddenly took fright, and began to snort and kick and plunge most savagely. 'The old man! The old man is after us!' screamed the Baroness in a shrill, terrified voice. At this same moment the sledge was overturned with a violent crash, and the Baroness was hurled to a considerable distance. They picked her up lifeless—she was quite dead. The Freiherr is utterly inconsolable, and has settled down into a state of passivity and negation that will kill him. We shall never go to R—sitten again, cousin!"

Here my uncle paused. As I left him my heart was torn by emotion; and nothing but the all-soothing hand of Time could assuage the deep pain which I feared would cost me my life . . .

Years passed. V— was resting in his grave, and I had left my native country. Then I was driven northwards, as far as St. Petersburg, by the devastating war which was sweeping over all Germany. On my return journey, as I was not far from K—, I was driving, one dark summer night, along the shore of the Baltic, when I perceived in the sky before me a remarkably large bright star. On coming nearer I saw by the red flickering flame that what I had taken for a star must be a large fire, but could not understand how it could be so high up in the air.

"Postilion, what fire is that before us yonder?" I asked the man who was driving me.

"Oh! Why, that's not a fire," he replied. "It's the beacon tower of R—sitten."

"R—sitten!" As soon as the postilion mentioned the name all the experiences of the eventful autumn days which I had spent there recurred to my mind with lifelike reality. I saw the Baron, Seraphina, and also the remarkably eccentric old aunts—myself as well, with my boyish milk-white face, my hair elegantly curled and powdered, and my delicate sky-blue coat—yes, I saw myself in my lovesick folly, sighing like a furnace, and making lugubrious odes on my mistress' eyebrows. The sombre, melancholy mood into which these memories plunged me was relieved by the bright recollection of V—'s genial jokes, shooting up like flashes of colored light, and I found them now still more entertaining than they had been so long ago. Thus agitated by pain mingled with much peculiar pleasure, I reached R—sitten early in the morning and got out of the coach in front of the post-house, where it had stopped. I recognized the house as that of the land steward; I inquired after him. "Begging your pardon," said the clerk of the post-house, taking his pipe from his mouth and giving his nightcap a tilt, "begging your pardon; there is no land steward here; this is a Royal Government office, and the Herr Administrator is still asleep."

On making further inquiries I learned that Freiherr Roderick von R—, the last lord of the entail, had died sixteen years before without descendants, and that the entail in accordance with the terms of the original deeds had now escheated to the state. I went up to the castle; it was a mere heap of ruins. I was informed by an old peasant, who came out of the fir forest, and with whom I entered into conversation, that a great many of the stones had been employed in the construction of the beacon tower. He also could tell the story of the ghost which was said to have haunted the castle, and he affirmed that people often heard unearthly cries and lamentations among the ruins, especially at full moon.

Poor shortsighted old Roderick! What a malignant destiny did you conjure up to destroy with the breath of poison, in the first moments of its growth, that race which you intended to plant with firm roots to last on till eternity!